WIND FROM T P9-AFL-349

Set against the exotic background of the Bahama Islands, WIND FROM THE CAROLINAS is the saga of wealthy, aristocratic families from the Carolinas, Georgia and Virginia who fled the South after the American Revolution for the exotic Bahama Islands, remaining loyal to England. Abandoning their plantations for the islands, they established new dynasties in the Bahamas, where the Crown rewarded their loyalty with huge grants of land.

"WILL HOLD THE READER SPELLBOUND."
--Chattanooga Times

"Robert Wilder does for the lush Bahamas what James Michener did for Hawaii."
--Houston Chronicle

"Wilder's characters are created with skill and conviction. They will not soon be forgotten . . ."
--Los Angeles Herald-Examiner

"A superb story of a never-to-be-forgotten dynasty."
--Pittsburgh Press

"Generation follows generation in a tempestuous flow of happenings, in a narrative that ranges from human nobility to willful emotionalism . . . The book is a story of living, fighting, peacemaking, designed to hold attention from the first page to the last."
--Chicago Tribune

WIND FROM THE CAROLINAS

Robert Wilder

Bluewater Books & Charts
Landfall Enterprises, Inc.
Fort Lauderdale, FLorida
1995

To a lovely young lady of my acquaintance

Rebecca Jane Thomson

With affection

Bluewater Books & Charts
Landfall Enterprises, Inc.
1481 SE 17th Street Causeway
Fort Lauderdale, FL 33316
Tel. 954-763-6533 ☎ Fax. 954-522-2278

ISBN 1-877838-09-8

WIND FROM THE CAROLINAS is fiction and as such certain liberties have been taken but not with the basic facts. Certainly, the settlement of the Bahama Islands was the result of one of the most dramatic of migrations. From the plantation aristocracy of Carolina, Virginia and Georgia came families who were passionately sincere in their loyalty to the British Crown and wanted nothing to do with the American Revolution and its theory of democracy. At the close of the War for Independence they found life all but unendurable. They were hated and reviled as Tories by what they considered to be a disorganized rabble. They were subjected to taunts and violence. At their request transports of the Royal Navy took entire families, their slaves, livestock, furnishings, and, in some cases, even the bricks of their manors to the Bahamas. There they attempted to recreate the Colonial magnificence they had known with mansions, slave quarters and vast cotton fields. The failure was tragic and the history of the Out Islands has been one of wealth and poverty in cycles brought about by influences far beyond their shores. I am indebted to Michael Finn and the Development Board, in Nassau, for assistance and to the publications of the Deans Peggs Research Fund for some little-known material.

–R.W.

Wind from the Carolinas

❧ I ❧

THE STORM, which for three days had spun in great, looping gusts from the Hatteras Cape, had worn itself out in the Carolina Low Country. Now, there were only occasional drizzles and a heavy mist steaming through the scrub oak and palmetto. It curled upward to darkly glistening pine tops and lay there, floating as a wavering scarf.

Strung for almost a mile back through the shadows, thrown in slanting lines by the tall, bronze-scaled trees, a train of carts and wagons was at a halt. Save for a slight movement now and then as men, women and animals shifted position, the procession seemed an enormous carving in relief against the wooded setting. The iron rims of the wheels on tarpaulin-rigged vehicles were deep in bare, sandy ruts. Unaware that they neared the journey's end, grateful for this respite, the heads of oxen and horses sagged in their weariness.

An overseer and three of his assistants rode down the line inspecting the cargo. Canvas, tightly lashed, was sheeted over an almost incredible assortment of household goods. Fragile porcelain and glassware had been carefully packed in sawdust-filled hogsheads. There were huge copper and iron pots, kettles and pans, heavy spits and other utensils for the kitchen. Beneath the protective coverings there was furniture for fifteen or more rooms. In crates were family portraits, chests of silver, curtains of lace and draperies of luminous brocade. Enormous chandeliers with their tinkling pendants were tightly padded. Exquisitely carved mantelpieces and parquet flooring had been taken apart, crated and braced. Doors, with graceful fanlights, had been removed from their frames and stacked between layers of cotton quilting. There were bales of clothing and box upon box of miscellaneous items. Cameron Hall, on the Ashley River some fifty miles away, had been stripped of everything which could be transported. Only the great, empty shell remained. The bricks, brought from England almost a century ago, had mellowed with the suns, the rains and the winds until they were now a soft, dusty pink. These, also, would later be razed and brought to the coastal city. When this had been done, nothing would remain of Cameron Hall but the foundation, the wasting fields, the long, canted lines of the slave quarters and the plantation buildings of wood which would stand, gaunt and stark, in their fading whitewash.

Trailing the wagons and drays came the livestock: cattle, swine and a few sheep. With them were the saddle and carriage horses, too finely bred to be harnessed to the cargo wagons. In the van of the animals came the black men and women and children. These were the field hands whose caste kept them apart from the house servants, some of whom rode on the carts or ambled unhurriedly beside them talking with subdued animation.

Heading the file was a splendid coach of crimson with a trim of gold leaf. A uniformed driver and footman sat immobile on the high box, paying a deliberately scornful inattention to the activity below them. Both would have liked to get down, walk around a bit and stamp their cramped legs, but a pride in their positions kept them stolidly uncomfortable and they stared ahead with frowning impatience.

A wheel was being changed. Its spokes were splayed from the hub as splintered kindling. A dozen Negro men strained to hold the axle and coachbed at a level while smith and wheelwright struggled with a heavy replacement.

Ronald Cameron, booted and in breeches with a greatcoat of dove-gray, stood a little to one side watching the work. Beside him, unconsciously imitating the feet-apart, hands-on-hip posture, Robert Bruce Cameron glanced up now and then at the towering figure of his father. When the man absently pulled a bay leaf from a nearby shrub and chewed meditatively upon it, the boy did the same. When Ronald Cameron studied the crimsoning sky to the west, Robert Bruce crinkled his eyes speculatively in the same direction. They were much alike, these two, despite the fact that Robert Bruce was sixteen and Ronald Cameron nearing forty. The man was not unaware of his son's reflection of his own actions and the faintest of smiles touched his mouth as he laid a hand on the shoulder at his side. In time, he thought, the lad's frame would be as heavy and powerful as his own.

"Order." Ronald Cameron spoke the word as though to himself. "Without order there is nothing. Man struggles through a swamp, clawing desperately to find a place on which to stand."

Robert Bruce nodded gravely although he had no real understanding of the words or why his father had so abruptly voiced them. Throughout the journey and long before, he had fought against betraying the inner excitement which filled him. This unbelievable thing which was happening—the dismantlement of Cameron Hall, the uprooting of the family and a manner of life he had known from infancy—were things he still could not quite comprehend. He understood that his father had not embarked on this venture without a silent anguish. Many times he had found him standing by a window, staring with brooding eyes into the distance. Or, as sometimes happened, sitting alone, hands locked beneath his chin in silent meditation. But it had never occurred to Robert Bruce to ask why this must be done.

"Will we get to Charlestown tonight, Father?"

"When the wheel is on I am sending the coach ahead with your aunt and sister. Grayson and a couple of men will go with them. I will feel better when they are safely housed with Mr. Renevant and his family in the city."

"May I stay with you?"

Ronald Cameron glanced at his son with quiet affection. "Naturally." He nodded. "Otherwise how will you learn how things should be done?" His gaze traveled down the long line which now seemed interminable. "God knows what disposition I will be able to make with everyone and everything. Somewhere on the outskirts; quarters, a stockade, something. I can't have a hundred blacks running around loose, to say nothing of the livestock. Also, the wagons must be guarded. Yes, you will stay with me." He smiled again. "You are a good lad for company; never talking too much when it isn't necessary."

Within the coach, sitting on the edge of the richly upholstered seat, a girl of fourteen swung her feet restlessly. She pulled aside the window curtain and looked out. Her hands held a small, beaded purse. She began to toss it from palm to palm with a determined gesture of impatience. The woman beside her tapped the moving fingers with an admonitory fan. The tossing action halted with a stubborn reluctance. Young eyes, beneath heavy lashes, regarded the woman with faint hostility.

"Why can't I get out and stand with Father and Robert Bruce?"

"Because young ladies do not loiter beside the road. It would be unseemly."

"Pish! And tish!" The slender figure flounced back against the seat. "If I am a lady then I should be able to stand anywhere at any time without it making the slightest difference. I wish I were a boy."

The woman's mouth softened with a tender, understanding and almost imperceptible smile as she studied the rebellious figure beside her. The beauty, she thought, was emerging slowly from an adolescent frame but it was there for all to see as it ripened.

[3]

"Did you ever wish you were a boy, Aunt Martha?" The query came abruptly.

"I suppose so," Martha Cameron reflected. "Although I really don't remember. There must have been times when I envied your father's freedom and wanted to share it. But," the smile was slightly wistful, "that was such a long time ago. One learns to accept things as they are."

"I won't." The statement was defiant but not impudent. "I mean, I won't if I don't like them. When I am grown I will do exactly as I please." It was a promise made with honest conviction.

"Even a man finds that difficult, Caroline; difficult if not impossible."

"And that is another thing. I hate the name of Caroline." There was a quiet vehemence in the tone. "Virginia Stapleton hates her name, also. I should think parents would have more imagination than to name a girl after a colony. We talked about it, Virginia and I." She laughed softly. "Just suppose I had been born in New Hampshire instead of Carolina? That would be a fine name, wouldn't it? New Hampshire Cameron. Mistress New Hampshire Cameron." The tip of her tongue curled out over the upper lip. "Mistress Pennsylvania Cameron." The laughter came with a sudden restoration of good humor over the fancy.

"I never particularly cared for Martha. It always sounded so dowdy, plain, simple. I wasn't at all that way." The aunt picked up a small embroidery hoop and pulled at a thread. "I always wished I had been named Jean Louise. Caroline is really very pretty."

There was a moment of silence and then a slight jolt as the coach was settled on the new wheel.

"If we are really going to those Bahama islands, as Father says . . ." the girl speculated. "And I suppose we are, from the way everything has been torn apart . . . I am going to change my name. I'm going to call myself Bahama. Bahama Cameron. That sounds like something, doesn't it? No more wishy-washy Caroline." She turned to face the woman with undisguised curiosity. "What do you suppose it will really be like, Aunt Martha; living on a little island somewhere in the middle of the ocean?"

"I wish I knew, child." Martha Cameron sighed.

"Please don't call me child. I'm not, you know."

"Very well—Bahama." Martha bent her head to hide the bright humor in her eyes. "I will try to remember."

"Do you suppose there will be monkeys in coconut trees and savages with spears; castaways from wrecked ships and romantic things like that; cannibals and native drums?" The imagination betrayed itself in the excited questioning.

"Not after your father gets there." Martha Cameron spoke with a dry amusement. "You can be quite certain Ronald would not tolerate such confusion. No—" she was quietly meditative for a moment—"I imagine, in time, it will be something like Cameron Hall as it was. There are quite a few English families there now. Something called the Elutherian Adventurers. I think that is the phrase. I read a pamphlet on the islands. It was quite informative but, I must admit, a little vague as to just what they were doing. Colonizing, I assume, although 'adventurers' has a frivolous sound."

"But it won't really be the same, will it?" A shadow of doubt crept into the words. "We won't know anyone. I mean the way it was at Cameron Hall where friends came to visit and there were parties with dancing—even if I wasn't allowed to do more than peek down from the gallery while everyone was having a good time."

"I'm afraid nothing will ever be the same."

Martha Cameron closed her eyes and leaned her head back against the seat. In this softly gentle and fragrant land, she and Ronald had been born. The third generation of Camerons in the new world. She could imagine no other home than the graceful manor on the Ashley; no manner of life beyond its boundaries. Years of memories now crowded each other in her mind. She was no maiden aunt by choice. Her first and only sweetheart had broken his neck as he took a hunter over a high fence on a dare. She had never found another man to take his place although there had been suitors from neighboring plantations. Always she had told herself, someday I'll marry. But the time passed. The years accelerated. She was twenty and then, incredibly, twenty-five and -seven, an accepted spinster. If she cried silently sometimes into her pillow with a sense of lonely frustration, there had been no one to see or know.

Ronald had married at twenty-four, in the full vigor of his manhood. It had been a splendid wedding; Cameron Hall ablaze with lights, guests from as far away as Charlestown. The bride had been a dazzling, beautiful, planter's daughter of Virginia birth. The children had come two years apart. Robert Bruce and Caroline. The succession had been established. Behind her closed eyelids Martha Cameron relived the days and nights of her brother's inconsolable grief when his young wife died of a strange fever and left him a widower with two children to rear. He did not remarry and Martha, without conscious effort, had taken over as mother and aunt, mistress of the Hall. Ronald had not seemed to want it any other way. Now, she felt a tight constriction of her heart. Everything familiar was being left behind. All of it now only something to be recalled wistfully and in time, she supposed, dimly remembered or forgotten entirely. From this familiar scene they were moving into a world

[5]

which must be completely strange; a place of furious hurricanes, surrounded by an alien sea; of small, desolate islands on which they would be without friend or neighbor. She sighed again. Her brother was a stubborn, resentful man. He had determined upon this course and nothing would swerve him. If he had any doubts as to the wisdom of the decision made, nothing in his manner betrayed them. He strode out upon this adventure as confidently as he would upon the familiar fields of Cameron Hall.

The War for Independence had been won and ended almost ten years ago but the old angers, the hatreds and suspicions, remained. There had been many families in the Low Country, such as the Camerons, who had been and were honest in their convictions and loyalty to the Crown. They wanted no part of the rude and democratic tide which swept over the colonies. Throughout the struggle they had remained steadfast to their English ties. The King, stupid and gross as he was, maintained the symbol of permanence. The order of things was fixed and immutable, where each man knew his place and accepted it without question from birth. There was the master and it followed there must be the servant. In this revolution they could see nothing but chaos. It was inconceivable to them that a system of government which had endured for centuries should be rudely torn apart. What could replace it; this federation which, even during the war, had been wracked with petty jealousies and self-interest? Throughout the conflict they had remained steadfast to the old ties, contemptuous of the rabble following Washington and his tatterdemalion army.

On the great plantations the English pattern of aristocracy had been preserved. Their owners grew wealthy through the accumulation of land and the flourishing crops of cotton, rice and indigo. Their children were privately tutored or, in many instances, sent to the motherland for an education. The social pattern was rigidly controlled. As the conflict between Crown and insubordinate colonies widened, so did the resentment of those who fought for liberty take fire. The artisan and tinker, the smith and settler on his small farm, drew together in a common anger. In towns and villages a militia was recruited and much of its fury was spent in looting and vandalism. Tory and Rebel were words spoken in hot fury; Traitor and Royalist expressions of contempt and hatred. Slaves were induced to flee. Plantations were fired, the manors gutted. In an effort to protect themselves such families as the Camerons, the Stapletons, Whitneys, Austins and Duveens had armed a corps of resistance. So it happened that frequently neighbor fought neighbor, friend fired upon friend, in the fierce, local skirmishes. Feuds were born to last for generations.

Now the fighting was over. A ragged band of colonists had defeated the King and his forces. The power of England had been pushed from the shores and across the sea. But those who had triumphed against seemingly insuperable odds were in no humor to forgive or forget those who had remained loyal to King and Crown. There had been battles between the revolutionary militia and the Loyalists in Greenville County, and in Charlestown itself there was a section contemptuously spoken of as "Tory Row." For three years Charlestown had been under British control. Clinton's troops were wantonly brutal in their treatment of the patriots and the policy was later carried on by Tarleton and Cornwallis. These things were not readily forgotten. The hatred festered and spread its poison.

For those families who now found life unendurable under the victorious rebels, a way out was opened. Some returned to England but others looked in the direction of the island possessions, the Bahamas off the coast of Florida. Lord Dunmore, who had been the last Royal Governor of Virginia, gathered about him members of the plantation aristocracy. Emigration to the Bahama Islands was proposed. There the old order could be reestablished, the familiar way of life recreated. The movement meant tremendous sacrifices. The plan was argued, debated, discarded and revitalized.

The Crown supported the idea. Vast tracts of land were offered to men of substance. In some cases entire islands were deeded to those with influence in high places. For others the Bahama Governor was empowered to grant every head of a family forty acres and "to every white, black man, woman or child in a family, twenty acres at a quit rent of two shillings a hundred acres." More than six thousand Loyalists had quit their homes and land and were ready to embark on this strange new venture. To them the Crown promised protection, transportation and the security of established order. Old peers and former squires had allied themselves with Dunmore. Unconsciously, or perhaps inevitably, the pattern which had gone down to defeat in the colonies was being redrawn. In long sessions Dunmore and his friends talked learnedly of the islands and the wealth to be garnered there. The Island of Jamaica was cited as an example. Enormous fortunes in sugar and rum had been made in Jamaica. Why, they told each other, could not the same thing be done in these Bahamas? When doubting questions were raised the more enthusiastic pointed out that one need not necessarily live out his life on an island. Once the plantations had been cleared and planted the owners could retire to the familiar comforts of England, leaving their island baronies to the work of black slaves and white overseers. Now and then they could make the sea journey to their properties to see that they were being run efficiently. These excursions would be little more than a pleasant holiday from the winter rigors of England's climate.

After long and careful deliberation Ronald Cameron had decided to make the move. He was a landholder of substance with a moderate fortune on deposit in London. Also, he was not without friends and relatives in England who held close ties with the Crown. After a study of maps and charts, long correspondence with the Governor of the Bahamas, he had decided upon the island of Exuma which lay southeast of New Providence in the long, broken chain. There had followed more correspondence and the use of influence in England. Finally all arrangements were completed. A British transport would call at Charlestown. All Ronald Cameron owned—slaves, cattle, seed cotton, overseers and even the bricks of his manor would be carried to this new home by a ship of the British flag. There he would do what had been done before by the first Cameron who had come to the Low Country of Carolina. A cotton plantation would be laid out, the manor rebuilt, the slaves put to work in the new fields. Cane could be grown, rum distilled and sold to English merchants. In the Bahamas he would no longer be forced to endure the hostility and contempt of a victorious mob which had become increasingly belligerent and insolent beneath its sleazy and, he was honestly convinced, spurious cloak of democracy. In time these colonies would discover there was no such thing as a classless society and revert to the natural divisions. For this, though, he would not wait.

Because he was a man long accustomed to making his own decisions, Ronald Cameron had not thought it necessary to explain or elaborate on his plans to his sister. This and that were to be done. That was all Martha and the children needed to know. So, as Martha Cameron sat patiently in the coach with Caroline beside her, she was possessed by doubts, small fears and uncertainties. All of her life she had known nothing but security. Into what outlandish world were they moving? She was comforted, in a measure, by the knowledge of her brother's resoluteness and self-confidence. He had grown to man's estate on the land. His father and grandfather—the latter a bearded patriarch who wore the kilt and had been buried in it—had been exacting teachers. To Ronald they had passed on a great respect for the soil and what it could yield if properly treated. The Camerons had never left the plantation in the hands of their overseers as so many did. They watched over what they owned and added to it with judgment and canny wisdom. Ronald had been put on a pony almost from the time he could walk. In the company of father and grandfather he had ridden and inspected every acre, each mile. The workings of the factories for the processing of cane and cotton, the problems of slaves and marketing, were familiar and understood. Ronald had grown from a serious youth to an equally serious man. Yet, Martha understood, he was not without humor or love. He had a gift for sudden laughter, a pleasure in good companions, fine horses, food and drink. He should, she thought, have married again for he was a man of robust appetite and a need for a woman. There were mulatto children among the slave girls which attested to this and Martha doubted they were all the seed of the white overseer Grayson, or his assistants. Her slightly embarrassed thoughts about this were interrupted as the coach door was opened and Ronald stood in the frame.

"I'm going to send the coach with you and Caroline on ahead. Grayson and a couple of the men will ride with you. That way you can make Charlestown before dark. Robert Bruce and I will spend the night with the train."

"Whatever you think best, Ronald." Martha was relieved. She had hoped they wouldn't have to rest over even in the elaborate, tented pavilion which the slaves erected each evening. There had been long stretches when they had not been near anyone's plantation nor the home of a friend. "I will be happy to be in the city."

Caroline leaned forward, stretching a pleading hand toward her father. "May I stay with you and Robert Bruce? I won't be any trouble."

Ronald Cameron studied his young daughter with grave pleasure. There were times when the resemblance to her mother filled him with an almost uncontrollable anguish and he disguised this with a gruffness he never really felt. Now, however, he took her hand and smiled his refusal.

"No." He spoke the word kindly. "I will be easier in my mind if I know you are safely at the Renevants."

"I'm safe enough with you." She didn't pout or beg. It was a simple statement of fact.

How unlike she and Robert Bruce were, Ronald thought. The boy was methodical, slow of decision, inclined to weigh everything. Caroline was impetuous and impatient with convention. At heart she was a rebel. In time she could become a problem.

Cameron merely shook his head and then turned to his sister.

"Extend my compliments to George and Madame Renevant. Tell him I will be grateful if he would have his factor ride out to meet us tomorrow. Perhaps he will have some solution for the disposition of the blacks and the wagons until the ship is ready to receive them."

He closed the door and gave an order to the coachman. The heavy vehicle lumbered forward, gathered speed under the urging of a whip and began to run silently through the yielding ruts. Cameron watched it draw away with Grayson and two armed men riding before and beside it. The miles they must travel were without danger. There were a few half-starved Cherokee Indians roaming the outskirts of Charlestown but they were without any aggressive spirit; cringing and cowardly as mongrel dogs who would steal only when no one was in sight. He turned away and called to one of the remaining white men.

"We'll camp here for the night. Arrange a corral as best you can for the stock." He had no real concern for the disposition of the blacks. He had always treated his slaves well and never had one beaten, preferring to trade or sell the recalcitrant ones. Those he kept were submissive. "Alternate the drovers throughout the night in a series of watches."

"Yes, sir, Mr. Cameron." The assistant overseer was a towheaded young man with the curious name of Spithead. Ronald had often wondered about its origin. "Will you have the big tent erected for yourself?"

Cameron studied the sky for a moment. "No. Stretch a tarpaulin. It will be a clear night, I believe. The storm is over. We'll bed down comfortably enough. Take what supplies we will all need from the commissary wagon. You know the order of things." He turned to Robert Bruce. "I think we might get a few doves or kick out some quail before darkness or the twilight nesting. We'll spit them for our supper. Would you like that?"

The eager light in the boy's eyes was answer enough. Catching it, Cameron thought they must spend more time together. Communication between them was sometimes difficult. He was not quite sure why. Perhaps they were too much alike; given to introspection and both with small talent for light and inconsequential conversation. This was a matter of regret, for he had a pride and genuine love for his son. Already Robert Bruce was a good horseman, a fair shot with the heavy pistol and better than average with the fowling pieces they used for sport.

"I'll get the gun," Robert Bruce nodded, "and the charges for it."

"Have King bring us two," Cameron called after the retreating figure. "You're man enough to carry your own."

Robert Bruce turned and flashed his father a grateful smile.

They took half a dozen fine, plump doves and three quail before the light began to fail them. Walking back through the rapidly falling darkness they both felt a sense of silent communion.

"How long will the sailing be to the Bahamas, Father?" Robert Bruce asked the question abruptly but in the tone of one who had been giving the matter long and serious thought.

"I'm not certain. A week, perhaps longer if the wind does not hold steady. The ship will be large and probably cumbersome. It is a transport of the King's Navy and not built for speed."

"There will be things to learn, won't there, Father? I mean, living among the islands we will have to know how to sail small boats; even large ones, if we are to get about from one place to the other."

"Aye! There will be things to learn," Cameron agreed. "But that would be true of any new place."

They strode through the knee-high grass, neither feeling an urge to talk or make conversation. Oddly assorted questions ran through Cameron's mind. What would he really find on this island with the curious name of Great Exuma? How was the quality of the soil? Would it grow cotton as everyone expected? How, in the beginning, was he to feed and house his family, to say nothing of almost a hundred slaves? He thought now how much more prudent it would have been if he had made a preliminary inspection for himself instead of taking the word of Dunmore. For a moment he was appalled at the magnitude of the task he had undertaken and then his confidence returned. What the first Cameron had done in the Low Country of Carolina he could do on this island in the Bahamas. There would be problems and even hardships. These must be expected, met and overcome with fortitude and determination.

"Are there still pirates there?" Robert Bruce, also, had been thinking of the island waters. "Men like Blackbeard and the others?"

"There are pirates everywhere, lad." Cameron permitted himself a wintery smile. "Some walk upon the land. Others sail the seas. It should not surprise you to find them anyplace."

"At least I won't have Mr. Price, will I?" The boy laughed quietly.

Harold Price had been an exacting and exasperating tutor at Cameron Hall. He had flatly refused to accompany the family on this expedition to the Bahamas, preferring to seek a position in Charlestown.

"You find a comparison between Mr. Price and Blackbeard?" Cameron glanced at Robert Bruce from the corner of his eye.

"I know Mr. Price is real. Blackbeard I have only read about." He laughed openly now. "It would please him to hear me talking this way for he was always at me to be what he called logical." He looked up at the man and his expression changed to one of mild surprise. "We have never talked this way before, Father, have we? I mean, just because we like talking with each other?"

"No, I don't suppose we have. You grow older and that brings us closer together. We can talk man to man, which wasn't possible before." He slowed his stride. "What we build in the islands now, Robert Bruce, you will someday inherit and have to manage. There will be many going to the Bahamas who will try and fail just as they did here in Carolina. When they discovered there was a deal more to it than simply sitting before a fire, they left their estates in the hands of overseers or factors and went back to England. That will not be my way nor yours. What we make we will keep and see it prosper beneath our own eyes." He paused and then continued. "As to Mr. Price. I expect we can find a schoolmaster to take his place. I should like to have you know of things beyond the doing of sums, reading and writing. The mind is fertile. You must learn to cultivate it. The harvest is rewarding."

There was a small cloud of doubt in the boy's eyes. He understood his father put great store in the idea of knowledge for the sake of knowledge. They walked the remaining distance in silence, each occupied with his own thoughts.

The camp showed through the distance in the small fires which dotted it, and the odor of burning pine richly scented the air. The flames bent when the light wind brushed against them intermittently or flared straight at the sky during a lull. It did not surprise Cameron that order had been so quickly established. He would have been astonished if this had not been so, for once he had given instructions he expected them to be carried out. This bivouac had the disciplined formation of a military encampment. It progressed from the black field hands, who had grouped themselves at a distance and at their own fires, to the house servants, easier in their manner and more sure of their position, to the white employees—Spithead, King, Carson and the others—and finally, to the slanting overhang of a canvas lean-to which had been erected for the master. This was the natural progression, the chain of authority and situation.

Cameron's personal servant, Gabriel, stood waiting before their shelter. He took the fowling pieces and the birds, put them aside and brought basins of warm water and towels for both Camerons. He did this without speaking.

"We will do for ourselves this night, Gabriel." Cameron thrust his hands into the water. "Have the birds cleaned and spitted. We will tend them. I will have some brandy and a bottle of sack."

"Yes, mastah." The slave moved backward and into the shadows.

"Do you know"— Cameron spoke half to himself and partly to Robert Bruce—"over a hundred blacks, and I can't call by name more than a couple of dozen." He mused on this for a moment and then chuckled quietly. "I don't know what we would do without the Bible. Gabriel. Moses. Peter. Paul. Ezekiel. Even Jonah. I have no idea how the field hands call themselves. I must ask Grayson sometime. To me they are as nameless as cattle."

"How do you suppose they feel, Father—to be nothing but animals of labor?"

Cameron turned with a small expression of surprise. "I'm not sure I know the answer. I've never thought about it. For as long as I can remember the blacks have always been at Cameron Hall and on the plantations of our friends. They were as much a part of the scene as the fields, the streams, the woods." He finished washing and dried his hands slowly, thoughtfully. "It makes for an interesting speculation, lad. For when you come to consider it, they must feel all things in a greater or lesser degree: anger, pain, resentment or a dull acceptance of things as they are. Yet until you asked the question it never occurred to me to wonder." He paused, watching as Gabriel returned, followed by two of the house girls and another male house slave. A tiny light of humor illuminated his expression and he all but whispered to Robert Bruce, "I suspect Gabriel is a little outraged by this informality."

He studied the Negroes as they went about their work. The man drove two forked sticks into the ground on both sides of the small fire. The girls stood at one side, watching and waiting for instructions. He wondered how, during this trip, they managed to appear in stiffly starched aprons and caps.

On their overnight halts during the journey the tented pavilion had been set up each evening. The flooring was in sections and quickly put together. Silver, crystal, china and the serving dishes together with a table and chairs had been unpacked from one of the wagons. The meal had been served as it would have been at the Hall with Gabriel standing motionless behind his master's chair. Now, this continued effort at ceremony seemed a little ridiculous.

"Tell the girls we won't need them, Gabe."

The big black nodded in their direction and they disappeared. In his hands he held a decanter of brandy, two glasses hung by their stems from his fingers. There was a moment of indecision in his eyes and then he gravely placed bottle and glasses on a fallen pine nearby. Cameron watched with quizzical interest as the slave disappeared again and returned a moment later with an opened bottle of Rhenish wine. Gravely he held the cork for his master's inspection. When Cameron indicated his satisfaction he placed the bottle alongside the brandy.

Cameron tilted the decanter over a glass, hesitated and then, pouring a small amount, handed it to Robert Bruce.

"A touch of good brandy will do you no harm. You are man enough now to taste it if you wish. There is satisfaction in a small amount of spirits at the end of the day. A drink between father and son makes for understanding."

Gabriel brought a long-stemmed pipe of clay, held it for Cameron's hand. Then he went to the fire and carried back a flaming sliver of pine. When the tobacco was glowing he stepped away and merged himself with the shadows.

Robert Bruce tested the brandy on his tongue and found it a thing of unpleasant taste but he would not admit his disappointment. Cameron drew contentedly upon his pipe, sipping his brandy and casting a sidelong glance now and then at his son. The fire sent out little waves of heat and the two settled themselves on the fallen log and inclined their bodies toward the warmth. The slave who had placed the notched sticks into the ground came back now with the birds they had shot. They were spitted on an iron rod and he placed it above the fire in the triangular slots. Then he squatted and, indifferent to the heat, began to turn the birds slowly so they would roast evenly.

Cameron emitted a gusty sigh of satisfaction. His expression was contemplative. Now and then he took a little swallow of the brandy, appearing not to notice that his son had put his glass on the ground.

"Stubbornness is an unfortunate quality of the Scot, Robert Bruce." Cameron made the statement abruptly as was his habit.

It had taken the boy some time to adjust himself to this curious practice; for thoughts, without relation to each other, seemed to spring from his father's mind. He said nothing and waited for the explanation which was certain to follow.

"Now the sensible thing," Cameron blew upon the ember in the pipe's bowl, "would have been for the family to make the journey to Charlestown in the coach. That way we would have covered the distance in a few days. Grayson could have followed with the train. He is a good man and long in service. I know I can trust him. But, I had it in my mind I was the only one who could superintend this move properly. I must be on hand to see everything done in the correct order. As a result we have all suffered unnecessary inconveniences to accomplish what was not really necessary. Aye! The Scots are a stubborn lot, never bending to the wind of expediency. However," he turned and smiled at the boy, "had we done it that way, then you and I should not be sitting here this night as we are. I am beginning to find a deal of companionship in you, Robert Bruce."

The boy flushed beneath this compliment and the rare demonstration of affection. Until recently his father had always seemed a remote, unapproachable figure. From him stern commands were issued and they were to be obeyed without question. True, they had ridden together over the fields at Cameron Hall. They had hunted together. But these adventures had seemed impersonal things and more as a teacher might take a pupil to learn certain things by doing them. Now, for the first time, he felt a kinship, a sense of companionship which was new and heart-warming.

"How do you find me, lad?" The question came hesitantly. "Am I fierce and a man to be obeyed rather than understood?"

"I don't know, Father. We have spent little time together. I know Mr. Price better." It was an honest reply but one made with difficulty.

The man was not offended. He drew meditatively on his pipe. "That is natural; unfortunate but natural. As you grow older we shall remedy it. As a puling babe we had nothing in common. I was proud and happy in having a son but that was all. What do you share with a wee one? Now, though, you are coming to an age when we can talk as man to man. I would ask that if you find me unreasonable at times, speak out. I will make an honest consideration of what you have to say and in the end we will shake hands on what has been decided, whether for or against your beliefs."

They made a fine meal on the roasted birds and the sweet yams which had been buried in coals until they broke apart in a steaming richness. At Cameron's offer Robert Bruce had tried the wine and found it sour to his taste. A little boldly he said as much.

"It is what is known as a dry wine," Cameron agreed, "and takes a little getting used to." Gabriel brought his master a fresh pipe and the man drew upon it with slow pleasure. He was in the mood for talk in this newly discovered intimacy with his son. "I remarked before that the Scots are a stubborn lot, but they hold no candle to the Englishman. Take this wine, for example. It is called 'sack.' In truth it is a French word, *sec*. But the Englishman will not tolerate the foreign pronunciation. He twists it to suit himself as he does with sherry, which comes from a district in Spain called Jerez. Now there is a word which sits uneasily on an Englishman's tongue. He calls it 'sherry' and the Spaniards be damned." There was silent laughter in his expression. He arose and stretched his big frame. "Let us have a look around before we take to our beds for the night."

Under a star-shot sky and in the silence of a clear night they walked the length of the encampment, past the groups at their fires where the men and women stood up respectfully as they passed. In the darkness the train of men and animals, the heavily loaded wagons, seemed far more vast than during the daylight when it was stretched out in a long file.

"Will we be able to get all of this and the people on the ship, Father?"

"Down to the last brick from the Hall if I have my way." There was a half grin on his face. "And that is a thing I usually do. There may be

[15]

some argument but I will not budge. When we land in the Bahamas it will be with all we own. There will be no looking back."

"Do you think we will ever return to the mainland?" To Robert Bruce the islands seemed incredibly remote and a little frightening in their isolation.

"If there is an occasion for it." Cameron's reply was bitterly short. He knocked out his pipe and ground the scattered coals into the dirt before continuing. "For my part I find nothing here any longer which binds me to the land. An insolent rabble has seized the King's property. Let them brawl now among themselves. In time they will sicken of this democratic idea, for it is against the nature of all things and founded on a false premise. Man is not born free and equal. It is nonsense to say so. Is a drayman's spavined mare as fine an animal as a blooded hunter? Do you match a mongrel in beauty and intelligence against a noble setter? These Colonials think so but they will find they are wrong and the bloodshed and senseless revolt will have been for nothing."

They returned to their shelter, where pallets and blankets had been laid. A second fire was kindled near the opening where its heat would seep into the lean-to. Nightshirts had been put out for them and they undressed quickly, covering themselves with the enveloping garments. Robert Bruce shivered and thought it would have been better to have slept in their clothing.

"Good night, lad. This has been a fine day and evening. From it I have learned more of you than I expected, though to tell the truth not much has really been said between us." Cameron's big hand lay for a moment on his son's shoulder.

"Good night, Father." Robert Bruce burrowed quickly beneath the covers and drew his knees up toward his chin. For what seemed a long time he lay there awake, listening to his father's even breathing. Once he saw the shadow of Gabriel as the Negro came quietly to heap the fire and lay upon it an oak log which would burn throughout the night. Sleep was long in coming, for his mind was crowded with old memories and new fancies. Awake, he listened and catalogued the sounds: the persistent hooting of an owl; the almost inaudible threnody of the muted chanting of the blacks as they sang quietly; the snapping of a branch as it broke in the fire. He thought of the islands to which they were going. Scallops of green and gold they must be with an ocean he had never seen, breaking constantly upon them. From the deck of a ship he would see them as had Columbus and feel the great throbbing of excitement. He would be awakening to a completely new world and this, in itself, was a thing of wonder for a boy. It was upon this that he finally went to sleep.

᷒ II ᷒

*"Day-O! Fishman comin'.
Swimp from d' ocean
Crab from d' sea.
Wan' fresh fish
You gotter see me."*

THE SOFT call of the fish peddler echoed with a haunting, plaintive
melody of his own fashioning down King Street as he trundled a dripping cart along the cobbles. It was an hour when few persons but the
servants were awake and about. From the delicately wrought gates of
lacy iron the cooks came, and with them small house boys to carry the
purchases back to the kitchen. The black women, their voluminous
skirts so stiffly starched they could almost stand alone, frowned and
made disparaging comment as they took their selections of the big gray
shrimp, blue crabs, crimson snapper, pompano and silver mullet covered with wet sacks. They argued over price and quality only for the
sake of conversation, and the peddler nodded an amiable agreement.
This was part of the ritual and a delaying action which, in a subtle
fashion, turned into easy banter and an exchange of gossip and news.
The fish man brought with him bulletins of interest from the waterfront and morsels of information gathered on his early rounds. So, they
stood in the warming street once the purchases had been made and their
laughter and words were rich with the humor of their people as they
made sly and whispered comment on the eccentricities of their white
masters.

Behind the gates the sun had barely touched the gardens. It glistened
on the still-damp leaves of magnolia trees and crept toward the vines of
wisteria and jessamine which were laced in a subdued riot of color. Later
in the day the carefully tended, shadowed plots would offer a cool retreat for those who still slept behind the jalousied windows.

Only on the lower floors of the gracious homes along King Street was there any activity and this was muted and keyed to the hour.

In his room, the floor-to-ceiling windows of which opened upon a second-story piazza, Ronald Cameron leaned back in a chair. A towel was fastened about his neck, extending down to cover a shirt of fine, ruffled linen. The slave, Gabriel, carefully worked the lather on his master's face with a brush of beaver hair and then with rhythmic strokes sharpened a razor's blade on a strop. Cameron submitted to this daily trial with impatience. He had been awake for hours, making a breakfast on coffee and fresh rolls as was the French custom of his hosts, the Renevants. Later they would sit down to a heartier meal but at the moment, Cameron's stomach grumbled over the meager fare. He was an early riser by long habit and found the morning indolence of the household an irritation. He needed to be up and about, doing something although there was nothing really pressing him at the moment. His slaves were secure in a stockade the British had used to imprison their captives during the time of occupation. After the King's forces quit the town the enclosure on the outskirts had been left standing. As the razor's edge ran crisply through the stubble on his cheeks he half smiled as he thought of what Renevant had told him over their pipes last night. After the fire which had practically destroyed Charlestown in 1740 the men of the city had banded together to form an insurance company. The insignia was a small leaden disk showing, in relief, the Royal Exchange of London. These markers were placed on the gates of the homes insured by the company. During the occupation the British troops took them to mean a mark of Royal ownership and so made no attempt to occupy, loot or destroy them. The Renevant mansion had been one of these.

Renevant, of French Huguenot descent, had mildly attempted to dissuade his guest from what he considered the sheer folly of moving to the Bahamas. In time the animosities would die out, restitution for confiscated properties made, the order of things would be reestablished. It was madness to abandon the great and productive plantation on the Ashley River for this adventure into the unknown. Cameron had small patience with the arguments. No one could say how long this outrageous experiment in democracy would last. It was possible, in time, there would even be agitation for the freeing of the black slaves. There was no telling to what extravagance this Colonial insanity would extend once it began to run unchecked. Renevant had merely shrugged at his friend's vehemence. If Cameron had decided upon this course, only experience and not words would change his opinion and determination. Smilingly

[18]

he had refilled their small glasses of brandy and offered the hospitality of his home for as long as Cameron wanted to stay.

Now, on his fourth morning as a guest in this home of quiet charm and friendliness, Cameron was filled with a consuming sense of urgency. He was bored by inactivity and found little of interest in the city's social life and the apparently endless calls and intimate receptions with which his host had attempted to entertain him. With Renevant he had visited the Commercial Exchange, the warehouses and taverns. He had talked with ships' captains whose voyages had taken them to the islands and with merchants and planters from the Low Country. Most of those who had their businesses in the city were of the same mind. Conditions would stabilize, old angers die and be forgotten; a fine and spirited trade would open up between such a port as Charlestown and Europe. The Bahamas, he heard, were barren of food, and the only intercourse between New Providence and the Out Islands was in small boats. There was a general opinion that a venture into the Bahamas on a large scale at this time was nothing short of foolhardy. Cameron listened with polite attention but nothing which had been said served to change his mind. If he entertained any doubts he kept them to himself. Besides, he had already made an all but irreparable move. Cameron Hall lay behind him. There could be no return.

George Renevant had many commercial interests. One of them was in a barkentine which made regular sailings between Charlestown and New York. Two days ago the master of the vessel had reported sighting a British transport slowly beating its way southward along the coast. He had spoken the ship and learned she was out of Plymouth, and Charlestown bound. This, Cameron felt sure, was the vessel for which he waited. If it was, then she might make port on this day and they could start loading before the week's end. An almost uncontrollable excitement gripped him at the idea and he all but threw off the towel before Gabriel had finished, so great was his desire for activity.

When the slave had at last finished, wiping away the final traces of lather with a cloth dipped in a basin of warm water, Cameron leaped up and strode out upon the piazza. A gentle wind had sprung up, sweeping landward from the bay and bringing with it a heady perfume of the sea, the marsh and mud flats. Cameron drew in a deep breath of satisfaction. The bay was a sheet of rippled copper beneath an orange-colored sun. All along the waterfront there was activity as the wind filled the sails of weathered sloops and ketches as they moved in from the fishing banks. Larger vessels lay at anchor and small boats plied between them and the docks and warehouses. What delighted Cameron's eye, however, was the sight of a large ship moving slowly in from the sea. She was still far out, looming darkly upon the horizon. Cameron felt certain she was the transport. By God, things would begin to move now! He had heard enough of the carping skepticism, the dark predictions. He turned about and strode inside to finish dressing.

In a spacious cabin aboard the transport *Ranger,* Sir Henry Wentfield, special agent for the Crown, breakfasted with the ship's captain. The latter attacked his food almost angrily, as though it were somehow responsible for the irritation he felt. There was no denying his orders. They were explicit. He was to transport the family, household goods and slaves of one Ronald Cameron, from the port of Charlestown to the Bahamas. He pushed his plate away and signaled the mess boy to take it from the table.

"They'll stink up my ship until she'll smell like some bloody slaver. She'll not be fit for a white man after this. Damn it, man! This is no river scow to be transporting cattle. What in hell is this Cameron thinking of?" He pushed away from his seat and with hands locked behind his back paced up and down the cabin.

Sir Henry finished his coffee, into which a small amount of brandy had been laced, and touched a napkin to his mouth. He was in full sympathy with the captain's anger. The *Ranger* was an old ship of the line whose armament had been removed and the conversion made from a fighting vessel to a transport. However, she had a fine history, and Sir Henry could understand her master's fury over the ignoble service to which she had been turned.

"Perhaps," he made a small attempt at mollifying the captain, "these domesticated blacks do not smell as they do when fresh from Africa."

"They all smell." The captain would not be denied his indignation. "I have passed a slaver at a league's distance and the stench will turn your stomach. There'll be no cleansing of the *Ranger* once we've had them aboard. A ton of burning sulphur will not purify the space belowdecks. And more than that"—he whirled and leveled a finger at Sir Henry—"I have orders that on my next trip I am to carry the bricks of his manor back to the Bahamas in ballast. What in God's name is the man thinking of? There are forests in plenty on the islands. Must this Cameron have a house of bricks and make of my ship a damned hod carrier?"

Sir Henry nodded appreciatively. "Mr. Cameron has influence at the Court and with the Admiralty. Apparently he intends to use it."

"Bloody Colonials." The captain drove a fist into the palm of one hand. "Why can't they be satisfied to stay where they are? God knows they fought hard enough against the King's forces."

"Mr. Cameron was one of the exceptions. He made no secret of his loyalty to the King. I suspect this has made his position here untenable. One can't really blame him for wanting to escape the animosity which must persist." Sir Henry was mildly sympathetic.

The captain was not to be dissuaded from his resentment. "Then let him sell off his damned slaves, cows and pigs, and return with his family to England which, after all, is the only fit place for a gentleman." The officer stared moodily through a port. "I'll never understand how we failed to put down this rebellion, Sir Henry." He shook his head, perplexity creasing his brow. "The King's troops against farmers, tradesmen, tinkers and stable boys. It was those damn Hessian swine who did us in. If we had fought the Colonials with proper regiments, things would have been different." He glared at Sir Henry as though the defeat was, somehow, his fault.

"I'm afraid not, Captain." Wentfield swiveled his chair about from the table and arose. "What we had to contend with was an idea, man's liberty. That is a formidable adversary. You cannot always strike it down with bayonet and sword." He dropped his napkin beside his plate. "I'm going on deck to have a look at this Charlestown. It is my first visit here, you know."

"It is a pleasant enough city, if it can be called that." The captain made the admission grudgingly. "Although hell's own heat lies upon it during the summer months. I was here during our occupation. There are homes of stately beauty—built by Englishmen, of course—and as fine a waterfront as you could find." He whistled tunelessly. "It is a damned shame we have lost it." He moved toward the companionway. "The passage in is a tricky one. I had better see about the working of my ship before we run aground on one of the damned sandbars." He stamped out of the cabin, leaving Sir Henry to follow.

On deck, Sir Henry leaned upon the rail and watched with interest as the town began to take shape in the distance. The vessel moved slowly, carrying only enough sail now to give her steerage way. The water had turned from the blue-green of the open sea to an ocher color as the Cooper and Ashley rivers fed their silt from the back country into the tide. His handsome face broke into a half smile as he thought of what the choleric captain had said last night: "These damned Colonials of Charlestown have a saying: 'The Ashley and Cooper rivers meet here to form the Atlantic Ocean.' They mean it, too."

The silhouette of the city was softly sketched against the morning's curtain. From his place on deck Sir Henry could see the slender spires of churches, the gleaming white of the balconied homes and the bulking warehouses and docks. The broad harbor swarmed with the activity of small boats, their patched sails taut in a freshening breeze. Gazing shoreward, he thought what a pleasant place this must be in which to live as contrasted to the foggy gloom of London with its dirt and noise, the wretched streets and bone-chilling climate, endured with a stoic pride by its citizens. Sir Henry's mind was one which roved freely and without prejudice. He caught himself wondering as to the manner of men these colonies had bred, and envied them their will to resist against the seemingly insuperable odds of England's power. He could not share the captain's angry contempt for what the officer had termed "tinkers and stable boys." The men who had guided the Revolution were possessed of courage and determination. He was surprised to find himself wishing he had a part in this tremendous venture. Freedom of this sort was a new concept. He wondered if it could endure.

As the *Ranger* slid through the yellowed waters Sir Henry studied the long island, covered with a scrubby growth from which slender, crested trees of palmetto rose. It lay on the starboard side of the vessel and in its shallows men worked from stubby, flat-bottomed craft with nets such as Wentfield had never seen before. They cast them in a great, flashing circle and then tugged them boatward with drawstrings, presumably making a pouch. He made a mental note to inquire what catch they made in this strange fashion. On the channel markers and over the water, large birds with jowl-like beaks cruised effortlessly or simply sat with drooping heads in solemn meditation. Everything he looked upon was new, strange and fascinating.

As the transport eased her way shoreward small boats raced out to meet her. They were laden with fruits, vegetables and live fowl. From them the vendors shouted their wares. To Sir Henry's precise mind this seemed a ridiculous procedure. Why didn't they wait until the ship was at anchor and then bargain for their wares? Certainly they didn't really expect the vessel would heave to here in mid-channel. After watching their antics for a while and listening to the completely unintelligible cries, he decided the display was a form of diversion; a break in the day's routine. He was puzzled, also, by the fact that the small craft were usually manned by a white and a black man. Was it possible a lowly fisherman could own a Negro slave? He jotted this down in his memory for future explanation.

Walking forward along the deck, Sir Henry found himself thinking of this man Ronald Cameron. Although his mission aboard the *Ranger* was only incidentally concerned with Cameron, having more to do with the entire problem of those individuals and families who wished to emigrate to the Bahamas, Ronald Cameron was by far the most important and influential on his list. Again his imagination was plucked by the adventuresome spirit which had been nurtured in the hearts of these

Colonials. It must be endemic to this new country. He looked forward to a meeting with Cameron and to his subsequent tenure of service in the Bahamas, where he would serve as a special aide to the Governor in the settlement of the immigrant families.

Before leaving England he had briefed himself as thoroughly as possible on the islands, but there was surprisingly little information available. There were the stiffly formal reports of the various governors, the logs of ships which had put in at Nassau, the sketchy comments of the vessels' masters—but they all added up to little more than the fact that the islands did exist. Pirates and adventurers had found the island maze a haven from which they could sweep out in their craft and prey upon the West Indian commerce. Even the Colonial Rebels had sent a small sea force which had temporarily forced the capitulation of the Governor and the forts of Nassau and Montague. To a certain extent now, the lawlessness had disappeared and the Crown was achieving an order of sorts. The big question remained whether the Bahamas could ever become self-sufficient. Could the vigor and determination of such men as Dunmore, Cameron and the others transform these scattered islands into a productive colony of thriving plantations? The answer would only come with the years. Regretfully he considered his small part in what might be an exciting adventure. Meditatively his gaze roved over the bright sparkle of the Carolina morning, so different from the dank confusion of London's docks. Then, surprisingly enough, he asked himself why he must ever return to England. He was without wife or indissoluble family ties. True, he was forty and hardly the age at which to go adventuring. But then, why not? It was a bold concept and contrary to his nature, but there was something in the air here which seemed to make all things possible. I will wait, he told himself. Once in the Bahamas I will have sufficient time in which to make up my mind. Then he smiled at this unconscious expression of a latent conservatism. Why must he always weigh things in this fashion? Adventure should be met head on, with enthusiasm and spirit for the unpredictable. If a man stopped to consider the pros and cons, then he drank a flat beer. He turned away from the rail and crossed the deck. He had letters to write and there might be a ship sailing from Charlestown on which they could be posted for England.

In the candlelit dining room with the French doors opening upon the garden the four men, George Renevant, Ronald Cameron, Sir Henry and Captain Sharpe, of the *Ranger*, sat at the long table which had been cleared of everything save a large silver punch bowl. A slave touched a taper to the dark mixture of rum, brandy and coffee with slices of orange and lemon peel afloat. The punch flamed with a silky blue color as it was ladled into the mugs and ceremoniously placed before the host and his guests.

"To the success of your venture, Ronald." Renevant offered the toast with a smile. "And a fair wind from the Carolinas to speed you on your way."

Even Captain Sharpe drank to the toast in a mellow humor. A fine meal and the easy companionship of the company had soothed, in part, his brooding indignation. These damned Colonials did themselves well, he admitted to himself. He had accepted this invitation to dine at the Renevant home with grudging reservations. He was fully prepared to dislike both Mr. Renevant and Ronald Cameron, particularly the latter even though he was an outspoken Loyalist. Now, the wine and the fine meal of game and fish with a great variety of vegetable courses had erased most of his resentment. He turned the slender cigar of Havana tobacco between his fingers and savored its fragrance. He took a swallow of the spiced punch and belched with soft appreciation. He had all but forgotten the sense of indignity in having his ship turned into a ferryboat.

"You haven't given us your opinion on what lies ahead for the colonists of the islands, Captain Sharpe," Renevant suggested. He was aware of the captain's diminishing hostility.

"They'll last a year, maybe." The reply was blunt. "Mind you," he added quickly, "I take no pleasure in the prediction. It is a judgment based on some experience."

"But why, Captain Sharpe?" Cameron was mildly curious. "The plantations in Jamaica have flourished."

"The Bahamas are not Jamaica. That is damned well why, Mr. Cameron. In Jamaica they have been able to grow the sugar cane on a large scale. This they have turned into rum and sugar for export. Mining has been done in the mountains. You will not find these things in the Bahamas. You'll starve to death, Mr. Cameron." He made the statement without rancor. "You'll do that or spend a fortune importing food from the mainland or learn to eat coconuts, bananas and fish."

"I've heard no reports of starvation in the Bahamas, Captain." There was an edge to Cameron's words now.

"Aye! Perhaps that is because the people are too weak from hunger to complain." Sharpe chuckled complacently at his obvious jest. "I do not mean that literally, sir, but you will find conditions far different from those you expect. Oh"—he made a concession—"there is a rare beauty in the islands; days and colors to take away your breath. There is a soft and easy way of life there. Your niggers will like it. But for such a man as yourself, accustomed as you are to such comforts as these"—he indicated the handsomely paneled room with a wave of one hand—"and the rich soil of your Low Country, things will not be as you imagine. There will be much to contend with, situations with which you are unfamiliar, and during the season of the hurricanes you'll expect the damned islands to go flying off through the sky." He finished his rum punch and waited while the slave came forward quickly to replenish the cup. "It would be my advice, if you are determined upon this course, to leave your family here. Go and see for yourself. Have a look around first."

"Those who have already settled there seem well satisfied." Renevant made the suggestion deftly in an attempt to ward off the explosion he could see gathering on Cameron's face. "How do you account for that, Captain?"

"Those are little people, Mr. Renevant." Sharpe lifted his shoulders, dismissing them. "They went to the islands because they were given land. On it they raise their produce. They trade with it in Nassau or barter between each other on the different islands. There is an abundance of fish in the water. The life is easy if a man's ambition does not carry him too far. But," he frowned, "nothing of the reckless size which Mr. Cameron, Lord Dunmore, the families from Georgia and Virginia, contemplate has ever been attempted before. I am not unfamiliar with conditions here and how the great plantations have been managed. I do not think you can recreate them on these islands. I don't even know whether you can grow cotton. There is no water for your rice fields, no climate for the indigo, no natural resources. You will not subsist for long on a beautiful sunrise and the pleasant climate of the trade winds."

"You paint a gloomy picture, Captain Sharpe." Sir Henry had been listening with intense interest.

"I was asked for my opinion and I gave it, Sir Henry." Captain Sharpe was almost indifferent to the obvious impact of his words.

"Nevertheless," Cameron scowled and there was a stubborn, tight line about his jaw, "I will go as I have planned and will take all I own here with me."

"Aye." Captain Sharpe nodded tolerantly. "There is no dissuading a Scot once he has made up his mind. I'll wish you well, Mr. Cameron. My orders are to transport you to the Bahamas. This I will do." He took a heavy watch from a weskit pocket and consulted it with a ponderous gravity. "It grows late and time I returned to my ship. One more suggestion, however. Sell off most of your livestock here in Charlestown." A wry smile touched his lips. "There will be little time or opportunity for riding to the hounds on the islands although your hunters may come in handy for meat once you have tired of fish."

"Damn you for your insolence, Sharpe." Cameron pushed away from the table and stood, his big hands clenched.

Sharpe was not intimidated. He surveyed the figure in its attitude of towering rage. "If I am insolent then you, sir, are a damned fool." He knocked the ash from his cigar and stared up into Cameron's face.

"Gentlemen. Gentlemen." Renevant arose quickly and interposed himself between Cameron and the.still-seated captain. "Nothing can be resolved or changed through a display of temper." He divided a quick smile between the men. "That is a strong punch." His gesture toward the bowl was a conciliatory explanation. "It sometimes leads to strong words. It has been a most pleasant and informative evening. Let us not have it spoiled."

"I have no wish to offend against your hospitality, Mr. Renevant." The captain, also, left his chair and stood surveying Cameron coolly. "If my words were ill-considered I apologize for them." He extended his hand toward the Scot.

Cameron hesitated for only the shade of a second and then he shrugged. "My apologies to you, Captain Sharpe. I suspect this isn't the only difference of opinion we shall have before the trip to the islands has been made. Let us avoid what we can now." He took the officer's hand in a firm grip.

They strolled from the room, down a spacious hall and out upon a narrow porch which extended about three sides of the house. The night was of a velvet fragrance from the jessamine which bloomed only in the darkness. Below, on a graveled driveway, a coach stood waiting. The groom leaped from the box and quickly held the door open.

"At any hour you care to name tomorrow, Mr. Cameron," Captain Sharpe suggested, "I'll have a cutter sent for you. It will not be a bad idea for us to go over everything together and make the best possible disposition of your family, your slaves and"—a tiny smile was barely visible—"what stock you finally decide to take with you."

"I am an early riser, Captain."

"Then let us say nine o'clock. It will be a pleasure to see you aboard the *Ranger*."

After the coach had spun out of the driveway and its yellow, candle-lit side lamps vanished beyond view from the porch, Renevant placed a hand upon his friend's broad shoulder.

"You are quick to temper, my friend." He spoke softly.

"I am sorry, George." Cameron acknowledged the charge. "It was unforgivable."

"Not between old friends." Renevant glanced up at the sky where stars showed between the leaves of a towering magnolia tree. "I have a suggestion. There is a discreet establishment on Legare Street where you may have a turn at the cards or dice. There are also some extremely attractive young ladies of amiable disposition. It seems to me you are in need of a diversion."

Cameron's laugh was quick. "You do not change over the years, George. All vexation may be solved with a wench and a bed. Perhaps you are right. They may relieve my choler." He clapped a hand against his friend's back. "By all means then let us try your specific on Legare Street. I am not too preoccupied for a little gaming and wenching. God knows I have been too long away from both, and who can say how long it will be before I see a white girl again. I hear they are scarce in the islands." He laughed again, a booming sound of good humor. "I should have thought to ask Captain Sharpe about that. He seems so well informed on everything else."

⋞ III ⋟

IN THE gossamer haze of early morning the island of New Providence seemed to float just above the harbor's surface. There was as yet no wind. That would come later when the trade freshened to bend the feathered tops of the tall palms and kick small waves into a choppy sea.

In the bay the sloops and small ketches lay at anchor or nudged at the straggling docks running out from a shelving beach. Aboard them, hunched figures leaned over iron braziers and fanned the smoldering charcoal into glowing life. The warehouses and shops along the sandy road, which was Nassau's principal artery of commerce, were still shuttered and the open marketplace deserted. The town awoke slowly and to an unhurried tempo. Time here was without any real meaning and one day was much the same as another. In the little frame houses the inhabitants had not yet begun to stir and in the Governor's Mansion the colony's chief official snored deeply into his pillow, his mind still clouded by the fumes of too much rum punch taken the night before. He would have slept less soundly had he been aware of the trials before him with the arrival of the *Ranger* and Ronald Cameron. In this daybreak silence Nassau seemed to be an abandoned place. A skeletal dog ambled along the shore without destination. He halted to sniff at a decaying fish head at the water's edge and then passed on to relieve himself against one of the mountings of the ancient cannon pointing seaward.

All of Nassau was keyed to this sea. The forts of Montague and Nassau had their guns fixed upon the harbor's entrance, for it was through here the marauding French and Spanish pirates had swept to seek a temporary haven or loot the community after exacting tribute from its citizens. This sea was a broad highway. It carried the ships from England with their much needed supplies. On it the Bahamians traveled from island to island and brought their scanty produce to Nassau's market for sale or barter. From it the islanders drew much of their sustenance. It provided the fish and crabs which were the principal items of diet along with the yams, grown on small plots, the wild and slightly sour bananas, fruits and berries. It yielded the sponges which were put out to dry in stinking messes and when cleaned brought a good price in England. The rolling, bucking motion of their boats was a more familiar footing to the men, women and children than the land. It also offered a beauty of which most of the people were unaware. There were great splotches of purple, blue, green and yellow, the water taking its color from the bottom. In the clear depths multihued fish swarmed with incredible brilliance and variety. Now it was picking up the early sun's light.

Seaward, leagues out beyond the long, narrow island which protected Nassau from the sea's buffeting, the *Ranger* lay becalmed. She drifted aimlessly with the current, turning all but imperceptibly in the slow measure of a sedate, cumbersome dance or as some huge, blinded monster might grope its way.

Captain Sharpe, with his first officer, stood on the quarterdeck and scanned a cloudless sky. Now and then one of them would hold up a wetted finger to feel upon its damp surface the faint indication of a wind. The vessel's canvas lay in slack folds and the crew idled until the first of the morning's breeze would bring them into action. Now there was nothing to do but wait.

Sharpe measured the lengthening arc of the sun through squinted eyes. "We should be getting it soon, Mister Morrison," he spoke to the mate, "if it is to come at all."

"Aye, sir." There was no real concern in the first officer's reply. The *Ranger* was far enough at sea and they were in no danger of piling up on a reef with this slow drifting. It was simply a matter of containing their impatience until the sails should fill. "In half an hour, I would say." He bit from a small plug of chewing tobacco. "I, for one, will be glad to have this voyage over." He offered the unasked-for opinion with unusual boldness.

Captain Sharpe snorted his impatience. He glanced to the deck below where the figures of Ronald Cameron, his son and daughter, together with Sir Henry, stood in a group at the rail and peered over the side at the indigo-colored water or gazed toward where the island of New Providence should lie.

"Take no comfort in the thought, Mister Morrison." Sharpe was bitter in his reply. "You may be sure we will be set upon another when this is done. We are in the ferrying business, a passenger and cattle scow. We'll ply back and forth, having no more to do with real sailing than a bargeman on the Thames. We'll bring out these damned Colonials until the islands can hold no more. Then," he checked an impulse to spit out his disgust, "they'll sicken of the whole business and we'll have to bring them back again."

Mister Morrison made no reply. None was expected. The abuse Captain Sharpe felt was the honest emotion of a man much put upon.

There was, for a moment, almost complete silence throughout the ship. Then, as though from some deep and unfathomable pit, there sounded the rising notes of an ageless lament from Cameron's slaves in the dark hold. It slid up on a minor key, rising in a haunting, spine-tingling melody. The chorus was untrained, the chant seeming to take form as it progressed. In its sobbing rhythm there was fear and loneliness, anxiety and anguish. It was as primitive as the cry of a trapped animal and seemed not to issue from human throats but from lost and wandering souls in a netherworld who cried out, knowing they would not be heard. It was a song without understandable words; a thing of mourning which had drifted up in spasmodic bursts of terror from the time the *Ranger* had weighed anchor and set her course from Charlestown harbor.

"If we had the wind those damn niggers put into their singing we could have made a record passage." The mate attempted a light pleasantry. The brief smile accompanying the words was quickly erased by Captain Sharpe's ferocious expression. "I'm sorry, sir. I meant it only as a joke of sorts."

"I find nothing humorous in it, Mister Morrison." Sharpe pinched his nose between thumb and forefinger. "The sound runs me out of my mind and the stink would drive the devil out of hell."

There was no denying the sweetish, musky odor pervading the ship. It seemed to seep through the calking of the decks and no amount of wind during the trip had been able to blow it entirely away.

In the darkness of the hold, which was illuminated only by a single lamp, the slaves were huddled fearfully together; formless shadows within shadows and when one moved it seemed as though a segment of an amorphous mass had broken away momentarily, only to be absorbed again. They moaned in unison, not against the confinement but out of fear of the unknown. To what were they being taken?

Ronald Cameron was not a man devoid of feeling. His blacks had each been given a pallet of straw ticking and a blanket. They had been fed regularly and well. He cared for them as he would valuable animals. During the run down from Charlestown they had been taken on deck in groups of fifteen or so for an hour's airing. These excursions, though, had only increased their lamentation. The spectacle of the boundless, lonely sea had thrown most of them into an almost uncontrollable terror. Two of them, a young buck and a girl, had leaped up from a huddled band

and hurled themselves overboard while the others had screamed in their fearful misery. Thereafter, as much as he disliked it, Cameron had them shackled together before they were herded topside.

At Charlestown, where the loading had been done from flat-bottomed barges, the house slaves had been docile enough. Long association with their master and the family had given them a sophistication the field hands did not have. The latter, in some cases, had to be driven aboard at the end of a lash by the white overseers. Now, though, the terror had become contagious, clutching at them all, and their behavior was unpredictable.

"Mark my words, Mister Morrison," Sharpe spoke gravely, "in time these blacks will be the curse of all white men. They multiply like animals and their owners encourage the breeding for it is to their profit. In time, on these islands, they will far outnumber their masters and overrun the land. The whites will contest with each other for the black bodies in a bloody business. Slavery is an unnatural state and it will not endure. You will see." He made the prophecy with dark satisfaction and turned away. "I'm going to my cabin. Call me at the first sign of the wind."

"Aye, sir." Morrison touched at his forehead with a token gesture of salute. He began to pace back and forth, conning the sea and sky.

With his children and Sir Henry at the rail on the main deck, Ronald Cameron stared eastward to where faint, blue smudges of the islands lay upon the horizon. He railed silently against the calm which held the ship motionless. It had been a trying voyage during which he and Captain Sharpe had continually been on the point of explosion. Before sailing he had been forced to yield on several matters. It was obviously impossible to take all the livestock. He had agreed to a compromise: a half-dozen horses, one bull and three cows, a sow and her litter. There was simply no room for more and the feed alone was an almost insoluble problem. He had grown incoherently furious over the superstitious idiocy of his slaves, the panic of the animals, and the outspoken skepticism of Captain Sharpe had been a constant goad.

"I'll tell you what the Bahamas need," Sharpe had once exploded. "It is not the plantation aristocracy such as yourself and the others but a few good smiths, carpenters and artisans. Do you know there is not so much as a tuppenny nail in the whole damn stretch of the islands which doesn't have to be imported. You'll find no market for your cotton even if you succeed in growing it, for the Lancashire mills can have it bought and picked up easier and cheaper in the ports of Charlestown and Savannah."

The two had been on the point of actual physical combat several times, and only the calming intervention of Sir Henry had maintained

[31]

an uneasy truce. Sharpe and Cameron spoke to each other only when it was necessary.

Straining to the tips of their toes, Caroline and Robert Bruce leaned far over the railing and watched the play of bright-hued fish as they swam leisurely in the clear depths or streaked as rainbow lights within the shadow of the ship's beam. Sir Henry glanced at them with a smile. He had found much pleasure in their company during the long hours of the day when there was little to do but walk the deck, count the waves or mark the distant passing of a schooner or barkentine in the West Indian trade. He had the rare quality of being completely natural with children and they recognized it, with the result that they could talk as adults and without constraint. The contrast in the personalities of the brother and sister interested Wentfield. The girl was all airy, dancing fancy of subdued excitement. There was, also, a curious quality of stubborn determination which was not willful but rather an expression of complete self-confidence. Matured, Sir Henry thought, she would be a remarkable young woman, possessed of great beauty and a mind of lance-point sharpness. Robert Bruce, on the other hand, was almost solemn, inclined to weigh each question and answer. They had plied him with a thousand queries about the England they had never seen; the cities of London and Liverpool; the manners and habits of the people. These he could and did reply to, but their eager minds roved the Bahamas, to which they sailed. What would they be like? Sir Henry had to confess his ignorance. The islands would be as new to him as they were to the Camerons.

"Will we go ashore today, do you think?" Caroline turned and addressed the question both to her father and Sir Henry.

"Let us hope so." Cameron was blunt. "Although Captain Sharpe has not seen fit to advise me of his intentions."

"Sharpe is not really a difficult man, Mr. Cameron." Sir Henry was faintly amused by the obvious suspicion of the *Ranger*'s captain. "He is unhappy with the job he has been given."

"He is a stubborn ass and I shall say so in a letter to his superiors."

Sir Henry thought with amusement that the quality of obstinacy was not confined to the vessel's master. He spoke to Caroline in reply to her question.

"We are making for Nassau. Captain Sharpe showed me the chart last night. There is a passage called the Northwest Providence Channel. It is through this we will have to pass, skirting many small islands or cays, as they are known. From Nassau it is some distance to Great Exuma Island but I assume we will lay over in the Nassau harbor while the captain and I both report to His Excellency, the Governor." He paused and then addressed a comment and a suggestion to Cameron. "I am as ignorant of the situation as you are, Mr. Cameron, but it is my recommendation you accompany us when we call upon the Governor. It is inconceivable to me you can simply put your family, slaves and overseers on Great Exuma without having made arrangements for provisioning and maintaining them."

"That was my intention, Sir Henry." An all but inaudible sigh escaped him. During the voyage he'd had time to think of many things, and the magnitude of the task ahead had assumed frightening but unconfessed proportions. "I must," he continued heavily, "find temporary and suitable accommodations for the children and their aunt in Nassau and engage someone familiar with the island waters to go with us to Exuma. I can't," he concluded with a wry smile, "toss a hundred slaves and all of my household goods into a bush." He turned to Sir Henry with an attitude all but apologetic. "I am not the opinionated fool my intolerant exchanges with Captain Sharpe might indicate. Believe me, I have weighed the many consequences of this move but I have not permitted my doubts to collect, for fear they would overwhelm me. What has been done can be done again. At least," his eyes crinkled with a sudden humor, "that is what I keep telling myself."

"It is my mission to assist you and the other colonists in every way." Sir Henry tried to be reassuring but he, also, for reasons he could not name exactly, was beginning to entertain some doubts as to the wisdom of the venture on Cameron's scale. "From what I know and what the captain has told me there are already some families of substance on Exuma. You will not, I believe, find it a deserted island. After all, there have been settlers here for over one hundred years. It is no savage land."

There was a faint creaking of a yard, and high on the towering mast one of the royals ballooned a little. On deck they all felt the first, cooling brush of a breeze on their faces. There was a shouted command from Mister Morrison and the crew sprang into action. Slowly the great, square sails filled and the helmsman spun hard upon his wheel. A tremor of life crept through the ship and as she moved, a small wave began to cream about her bows.

"At least," Sir Henry expressed the thoughts of them all, "the wind comes and that is something for which to be grateful.

Small fingers of light pushed through the shuttered blinds of the room and touched the face of the Governor's wife. Sabrina Heath stirred and lifted a hand to shield her eyes. She awoke reluctantly and with an obsessive feeling of desperation. Her eyelids lifted reluctantly

[33]

and she stared, for a while, at the sagging canopy overhead. It bore ugly speckles of mildew which all the washing seemed unable to remove. She hated the canopy for it seemed to confine her more completely to this bed. She hated the canopy, the room, the bed, and awoke each morning with this coal of fury hot within her.

Lying motionless now, she listened to her husband's wheezing snores and a feeling of helpless nausea engulfed her. His Excellency, Sir Gerald Heath, in the opinion of his young wife was a pig. He grunted and snorted in his sleep like some winded animal. Half turning, she stared at the heaving mound of his belly with disgust and wondered for the thousandth time why she had married him, this gross man who was twenty years her senior and an unbelievable bore.

She sighed and pulled the covers down from her slim body. The shift she wore was of sheer Irish linen and as revealing as a cobweb. On the wall at the side of the bed there was a brocaded bell pull. She jerked at it angrily to summon the slave who would bring the morning's tea. She put her feet into sandals and reached for a robe lying across a chair.

Sir Gerald's breathing made a high, whistling sound and then he belched in his sleep.

"You are a swine." She spoke aloud, knowing he would not hear and not caring if he did. "A pig." Somehow this made her feel better. She smiled with quiet satisfaction.

Waiting for the slave she wandered aimlessly about the big room, her glance falling now and then upon the shapeless huddle which was Sir Gerald Heath. In England it had seemed a desirable match. Sir Gerald had appeared to be a hearty man of booming good humor. She the daughter of a well-to-do squire. It was not until after the ceremony that she discovered Sir Gerald's estates were heavily mortgaged and he was inextricably in debt, seeking frantically and with little success to assuage his creditors and keep his impoverished estates from confiscation. As a husband he was demanding, throwing himself upon her to glut himself with her youth. As the first year of their marriage lengthened she discovered he was a man of peevish disposition, of sullen manner when crossed, and with a boorish attitude toward everyone. He was though, by incredible good fortune, possessed of influential relatives who were well received at Court. Through them, or because of them, his appointment as Governor of the Bahamas had been managed. Sabrina suspected it was because they were so eager to have him out of England and be rid of him. Sir Gerald, however, had accepted the post as an honor well deserved and swanked about his club, boastfully telling everyone how he intended to manage this part of the Empire.

To Sabrina the appointment had, at first, seemed to be an all but inconceivable miracle. Sir Gerald had pictured to her an island paradise. The Bahamas were to be their remote kingdom over which they would rule unhampered. He would be the sole authority, His Excellency, the Governor.

In her mind, and she had been only eighteen at the time, she saw herself as the First Lady of this new world of jewel-like islands. There would be, of course, an island aristocracy of ladies and gentlemen. Created on a smaller scale, also, would be the brilliance of London and the Court itself. There would be uncountable black slaves to do her bidding; handsome officers of the Governor's Guard would pay homage to her acknowledged beauty. There would be ships of the Royal Navy putting into Nassau's port and with them more handsome young officers with whom to flirt and coquette. The Governor's Palace would be richly furnished, set in tropical splendor, blooming with exotic flowers, alive with the flashing colors of parrots and other strange and wonderfully exciting birds. Her fancy knew no limits and for a while it even made Sir Gerald passably endurable.

She was quickly disillusioned. The tropical paradise had turned out to be only this miserable island with its shiftless inhabitants. Her slaves were without grace or training; little more than ignorant savages who must be continually retrained to do even the simplest of tasks. They could not even remember from one day to the next how to set a table. Sir Gerald, instead of a Governor of absolute authority, was at perpetual odds with his Assembly. Oh, she conceded, there was a certain wild beauty about the islands. But God in heaven, one could not exist upon that. They were dependent almost entirely on food supplies from the mainland. Each bolt of cloth and pin must be carried on a ship from England. There had even been times when the Governor's House had had to make its bread from a coarse root peculiar to the islands.

Sabrina's existence was one of perpetual boredom. She awoke each morning knowing exactly what the day would be like and what it would bring. The petty annoyances of the household. The insufferable pomposity of her husband, who seemed not to realize he had been banished to this ignominious post. There was no place to go, nothing to do but find some shade within the garden or sit and work at a useless piece of embroidery out of sheer desperation. The nights, unless he was completely stupefied with drink, brought Sir Gerald and his rutting. There were times when she all but screamed her protest at this callous violation. She had argued hopefully for a suite of rooms of her own, some measure of privacy, a door she could bolt. Sir Gerald would not hear of it. He was no man to trot barefooted from bed to bed, and a wife's place was beside her husband. She suffered him now in icy silence.

[35]

Her bitter ruminations were interrupted by a light tapping on the door as the slave girl brought her usual breakfast: tea, a slice of papaya with lime, biscuits and preserves. Without speaking or being spoken to, the girl placed the tray on a table and opened the slitted blinds to the morning's breeze and sparkling sunlight. Then, with an awkward curtsy, she all but tiptoed on her bare feet as she left the room but her solemn eyes cut a quick glance at the lumpy mound of Sir Gerald, who was stirring uneasily as the bright day slanted across his bed. Watching, Sabrina took a malicious pleasure in the thought she was responsible for his unhappy awakening. Deliberately she clattered the china and pot, scraped a chair on a bare section of the floor near the window. She pushed the shutters open and allowed them to slam shut beneath a gust of wind.

"In God's name, woman!" Sir Gerald bounced up with a roar. "Must you make all that noise over a simple cup of tea?" During his turnings in the night his tasseled cap had worked itself off. His sandy and unruly hair stood on end. Later, dressing, he would cover it with a proper wig but at the moment he looked like a spiked and startled porcupine. "Now that you have awakened me with this uproar fetch me a tot of rum. There is a foul taste in my mouth."

"Get it yourself." She was airily indifferent to his wrath. Breaking a biscuit in half she spread it with the jam, a compound of lemons, limes, oranges and sugar. "I doubt there is any left from the way you were swilling it last night. Must you be such a beast over everything?"

Sir Gerald heaved himself ponderously over the bed's side and planted bare feet on the floor. Standing up he balanced himself unsteadily, his small eyes staring with red hatred at the slim, cool figure of the girl who was his wife.

"A beating is what you need, madam." He all but bellowed his wrath. "And you may be certain that one of these days I will give it to you."

Sabrina eyed him sardonically. "Then," she spoke without a rising inflection, "you had better never go to sleep again for I will stick a knife in that hillock you call a belly." Her tone was pleasantly modulated, almost friendly, as though they were discussing an event of small social importance.

Sir Gerald stumbled across the room to where a bottle, a ewer of water and a glass were upon a knee-high taboret. He mixed himself a tepid drink and gulped the mixture, sloshing it around in his mouth before swallowing. Then he walked to the windows and flung the shutters wide open. He stood, breathing deeply of the fresh air.

"What a rare bitch you are." He spoke without turning to face her and in his tone there was a touch of wonder and curiosity. "All cooing and submissive coquettishness, a trembling maid of downcast eyes before marriage, and now this—a hostler's slut."

"The Governor's Lady." She made the correction sweetly. "Although," she added as a mild afterthought, "this room does have the smell of a stable when you are in it." She put her fingers to her mouth and smothered a yawn with an exaggerated delicacy.

He wheeled upon her. "Must I endure your insolence every morning?"

"It is my only diversion, Gerald. Would you deny me that?"

He grunted, hiked his night shift up and scratched at a bare rump. "You are easily entertained. Would to God it were so with me. Daily I must contend with the indolence of the people, the indifference of the Crown, the cupidity of the damned English tradesmen who charge twice what everything is worth, the poverty of these godforsaken islands."

"I thought you enjoyed being His Excellency, the Governor of the Bahamas." She eyed him with elevated brows.

He spat deliberately, knowing how offensive it would be to her and taking a small pleasure in her shudder of revulsion. Then he turned again and stared moodily out of the window, across the tops of the tall, slender, gray-trunked palms. He was unaware of the garden's beauty with its riotous color of climbing vines, the great spreading of the banyan tree, the blossoming shrubs which seemed to grow without care and in tropical confusion. He saw only what he wanted to see, heard only those sounds against which his ears revolted. He gazed upon a ramshackle settlement strung along the shore. Heard the soft, indifferent laughter of the natives as they lazed in the sun or lay sprawled in the shade. The whites were no better than the freed Negroes of the colony. They worked only when they were forced to it by the necessity of buying a little food or a jug of rum. They spent their days coasting along in their small boats, visiting back and forth in the Out Islands. They were satisfied with a diet of yams, fish and the big conchs. When disaster struck, as it did sometimes in the form of a hurricane or a blight which destroyed the crops, they expected things to be set right by the Governor. They were without spirit or pride. There were those among them who formed a villainous crew who worked in the dark, changing the lights to bring an unwary ship upon a reef and then salvaging the cargo which washed ashore. This they sold openly to the merchants and spent their loot in wenching and carousing. In a smaller way they were little different from the pirates who once ravaged the islands and sacked Nassau itself. Where, he asked himself wearily, was the bright, energetic colony he had hoped to find and encourage? Not here, certainly.

He continued to stare at the scene below and beyond his window. The marketplace was slowly filling. Straggling toward it along the sandy road a few men and women, some white, some black, and others with a peculiar bleached color which made them seem almost albinos. They carried their stalks of bananas, small baskets of produce, on their heads. They dragged a squealing pig with a tether on a hind leg or clutched a scrawny chicken in each hand. A few were bringing fresh fish from their boats while others simply lay upon the scabrous decks without movement or purpose. There was no novelty in the scene. It was repeated daily. If Nassau itself was wretched, then the Out Islands were the poor relatives of wretchedness. From Iguana and the more distant Turks Island a few of the more industrious brought cargoes of salt from the evaporating pans. Others came with their cargoes of sponges. A few of the more recent arrivals were growing pineapples and working with cane and cotton, but all of this was done at a maddeningly slow tempo. No one really seemed to care for anything beyond his own needs.

Sir Gerald sucked at a tooth and thought bitterly of the Crown's indifference. These islands had a geographical importance, standing as they did between the encroachment of the Spaniards in Florida and Cuba and the Dutch incursions into the West Indies. They had a strategic importance and should have had a large place in the commerce between England and the now free colonies on the mainland. Instead of encouraging their development the Crown appeared to be satisfied to have them lying here, useless and impoverished in the sun. To make things worse, and Sir Gerald was inclined to take a dim view of everything this morning, the Crown was encouraging the immigration of Loyalist families from the American colonies. They were an arrogant lot, for the most part. Accustomed to a far greater measure of local autonomy than was enjoyed in the Bahamas they were openly critical of the antiquated system of governmental control encountered in the islands. They were, in general, well-to-do and came, not as poverty-ridden refugees, but as men of substance. A few barely made an effort to hide their contempt for His Excellency and what they considered to be his inept and indecisive efforts. It was true they brought with them badly needed English pounds and this had a stimulating effect on a laggard economy. But also, there was an unbearable snobbishness which Sir Gerald found maddeningly offensive. They were clannish and the Governor's effort to meet and deal with them on a plane of equality was quietly rebuffed. They had been the plantation aristocracy of the mainland and expected to be treated with every deference here. They spoke in a lordly fashion of the great plantations to be and their revitalizing effect on the islands. The Governor was only supposed to expedite their plans.

Sir Gerald was certainly not opposed to a general improvement in the Bahamian economy. God knew he had tried to infuse some spirit into the islanders but they were a shiftless and indifferent lot. However, he did not propose to be treated as a mere lackey, the Crown's warden whose only purpose was to lend assistance. He should be consulted and deferred to by these colonists who were settling on Eluthera, Andros, Cat Cay, Harbor Island and Exuma. By God, they would learn soon enough that the Governor was an office of importance! Here it was the Crown. His stomach growled uncomfortably. And, he reflected, if his troubles were not enough, he was cursed with a wife who was as beautiful as she was shrewish.

He recrossed the room and poured himself another drink. It was sour in his mouth and he all but retched as it coursed its way to his stomach.

"I suppose getting drunk in the morning does help." Sabrina made the comment with a clinical interest. "In time I may cultivate a taste for it myself." She lifted her clear eyes to meet his and for the first time there was a hint of pleading in her expression. "Why don't you let me go back to England, Gerald? There is no need for both of us to be so completely miserable. There are girls enough among the slaves to sate you. My position here seems little different."

"Keeping you miserable is one of the few small pleasures left to me." His Excellency all but leered but the early liquor was making his features flaccid and the result was more of an idiotic smirk. "I like to see you writhe a little upon the spit as it turns. I do indeed."

She shrugged and pushed away the cup of cooling tea. She thought a little helplessly of the interminable months and years she must spend here before relief of some sort came. Perhaps, and this was always in her mind, Gerald would prove himself to be so inept he would be recalled. Then a weariness engulfed her. What did England hold for them? She could think of no satisfactory answer.

Sir Gerald was wandering about the room with a ponderous lack of direction or purpose. Watching him, she caught herself thinking, I am not really an unpleasant person. I have made myself so because what I have is not what I expected. I have kicked out and screamed like some disappointed child.

"We could get on a little better, Gerald"—she was surprised to hear herself uttering the words—"if there was some give and take between us. I am not talking about love or, perhaps, even affection. But we could be pleasant with each other."

Sir Gerald halted abruptly and regarded her with suspicion. "Whenever you extend the olive branch to me, Sabrina, I look for the asp concealed within its leaves." He was so pleased with the analogy of his reply that he broke into heavy laughter. "By gad, that is good! I must remember it."

[39]

"I am certain you will." She lifted her shoulders with a shrug and then stood up. "If you would only make some effort at social contacts. There are a few families here in Nassau not entirely without grace but you ignore them. Why?"

"Because they only want to use my office for their own ends. Anyhow, with what will we entertain? My miserable stipend from the Crown? I assume you mean that the Government House should be a perpetual scene of gaiety, of levees and fetes and some regal splendor. No, my girl. You will have to make up your mind as I have mine. This is a form of exile."

"I am not content to leave it so." She was momentarily defiant.

"When you find a solution let me know." He strode to the bell pull and jerked it. "We are too late here, my girl. Too late or too early, I am not certain which. Too late because fifty or seventy-five years ago this was a place of pirate richness and the administrators made themselves wealthy by sharing the spoils. Too early because it will take some great Continental upheaval to put these islands on their feet. A war between the colonies on the mainland or an attempt by England to recapture them. Then you would see these islands blossom into affluence as a mid-point in the conflict. I have no faith in the great dreams these Loyalist refugees are bringing to the islands."

There was a timid knock upon the door and at Sir Gerald's call it was opened. A girl and a black manservant, the latter in a faded livery of sorts, stood in the opening. The male slave carried a basin of steaming water, towels and razor for his master. The girl bore over her arms fresh garments for her mistress. So unvarying were the mornings that the Governor's household no longer needed to be told or instructed in the routine. First, the raised voices of the master and mistress. Then, a period of comparative silence. Finally, the abrupt jangling of the bell which would summon them to dress and bathe the Governor and his Lady.

The day had begun.

✌ IV ✌

Within the lee of Hogg Island the *Ranger* lay at anchor, the great hook visible in a full ten fathoms of water as it held on the sand and coral bottom. Overhead the gulls screamed and wheeled, and around the vessel the small, sweep-propelled craft of Nassau swarmed. The boatmen, black, white and *mestizo,* lifted their faces toward the high deck and languidly called their wares of fresh fruit, fowl and vegetables. They didn't really seem to care whether they found any purchasers among the crew who stared down at them with indifferent curiosity.

At the vessel's side the captain's gig had been lowered. Seated, Captain Sharpe was in full dress uniform: blue coat with polished buttons of brass; white breeches fastened below the knee to stockings of sheer cotton, his feet in buckled slippers of black. He held himself stiffly erect, every inch the master of a ship of the line although he was aware the *Ranger* had been reduced to this lowly duty. With him in the craft, dressed in conservative gray and brown, were Ronald Cameron and Sir Henry Wentfield. They were on their way for a meeting with His Excellency, the Governor.

At a command the gig's crew bent to their oars with sharp precision and picked up the rhythm of the coxswain's chant. The bow lifted slightly above the small waves as it drove toward the shore. They ignored the bumboats which scattered at their approach, sculling frantically to avoid a collision. Then they fell in behind the gig, following it in a weaving, nautical procession. The islanders shouted good-natured and ribald comments on the seamanship of the visitors and offered to lead them to fine girls and places of drink in the town.

From his place in the gig Cameron's gaze took in each detail of the harbor and the settlement, strung without seeming order along the beach. A fort of gray stone with its crenellated wall rose above the collection of shacks. Even from this distance it seemed badly in need of repair. There were wide cracks in the sides in which the green of weeds and vines showed, and one corner of the structure had broken away entirely.

The land sloped upward from the shore in a matted tangle of palms, scrubby trees which looked as though they were a species of oak and huge, umbrellalike trees with enormous roots. Cameron had no idea what these were called for he had never before seen their kind. On the elevation, just above treetop level, he could see the outlines of a building. From a staff on the peaked roof the English flag stood out brightly in the morning's wind. He had not seen it so displayed since the surrender of the King's forces in the colonies. Now, the sight of it here in these remote islands filled him with a tremendous sense of pride. Where the flag was shown, there he would find order and stability. It represented everything in which he believed: the King, the Crown, the ancient verities. This was English soil and he an Englishman. He was a stranger but no alien.

Turning for a moment, he looked back to where the *Ranger* lay. He fancied he could see the figures of Robert Bruce and Caroline still at the ship's rail where he had left them. They had been reproachfully silent when he had said they would have to wait until later in the day before he could take them ashore. He knew they followed the gig's progress with unhappy and disappointed eyes. There, he thought, are my seed. Here they will be planted to grow and proliferate. They will mature and the time will come when my grandchildren and great-grandchildren will hold to a part of these islands which seem so new and strange to us today. Difficulties were meant to be overcome. He expected to meet them and would not be overwhelmed by the unfamiliar nature of these seas and their islands. Everything he owned had been staked upon this venture. He would hold to his course no matter how insurmountable the problems seemed at first.

The gig grounded on the sand of the landing stage and the crew went over to pull it high upon the shore. Earlier in the morning Captain Sharpe had sent one of his junior officers to Government House, delivering a letter to His Excellency asking for an appointment. The word had been returned for a meeting at this hour.

As they stepped upon the land they were all but surrounded by an idling and curious throng of natives. Most of them were black but there was a color range of many variations. In this year, Sir Henry had told Cameron, there were roughly three thousand whites scattered throughout the islands and almost twice that number of blacks. The slave trade was still brisk here although some of the Africans had been given their freedom by masters who had given up their attempts at colonizing the islands and returned to the mainland or England. As he glanced over

[42]

the small crowd Cameron noted there were among it men and boys with a plaster-white skin and straw-colored hair. The sun seemed to have had no effect upon their pigmentation and this gave them a startling individuality. Gazing at them Cameron wondered if this was some curious genetic result of interbreeding. Sharpe had told him of an island, St. George's Cay, where there were no blacks at all and that the fifty or so families there all bore the same name.

Awaiting them on the sandy road fronting the shore was an open carriage. On a panel there was a faded design in gold and red, the Royal insignia. The coachman and groom were in spotless livery but the clothing had long ago lost its original elegance and there were visible patches of mending on sleeve and coat. The groom held the door of the landaulette open and a young, uniformed officer advanced to meet them.

"I am Captain Birch," he introduced himself. "Military aide to His Excellency who presents his compliments and welcomes you to Nassau. I am to accompany you to Government House." He made the formal declaration with a slightly bemused air as though he found it just a little comical, and there was an undeniable hint of laughter in his eyes.

The *Ranger*'s master took command of the situation and made reply for them all. "I am Captain Sharpe, of His Majesty's ship the *Ranger*. This is Sir Henry Wentfield, on a special mission, and this is Mr. Ronald Cameron." He seemed to accent Cameron's lack of title or rank.

"Gentlemen." Captain Birch bowed in acknowledgment. There was an unmistakable grin on his face now as he indicated the carriage. "We do our best to be impressive under strained circumstances. But," the smile broadened, "we are a long way from the mother country. The Government there sometimes seems unaware of our existence. A little varnish, for instance, would make that vehicle almost impressive in the islands. Unfortunately, our requests and requisitions have been ignored."

Cameron took an immediate fancy to young Birch. He seemed utterly without affectation and with a highly developed sense of the ridiculous. An effort at ceremony under the circumstances would have been ludicrous. He only hoped the officer had patterned himself from the Governor. He offered his hand with a cordial spontaneity.

"The wheels and cushions seem sturdy enough, Captain. In the end I suppose those are the only important considerations."

Birch shook hands with a shaded twinkle. "As you say, Mr. Cameron, those and the horse are our first concern. If you will please." He indicated they should precede him into the carriage.

When they were seated and the vehicle had made a tight turn before starting up the narrow inclined road, Birch pointed out a few places of interest: the market; Vendue House where slaves were auctioned publicly; the beam-to-beam clutter of Out Island boats as they rocked gently just offshore.

"A schooner out of New York by way of Liverpool brought us word of your coming, Sir Henry." He made easy conversation. "And of you, also, Mr. Cameron. The office of the Foreign Secretary is extremely industrious in the matter of correspondence." Cameron could have sworn Birch's tongue had thrust at his cheek. "The Governor is looking forward to this meeting." He eyed Cameron with a bland pleasure.

As the carriage climbed the hill Cameron noted an abrupt change from the careless atmosphere on the waterfront. Here and there, among the slender and graceful palms which whispered with soft rustling, there were homes of some distinction whose size and carefully maintained gardens and walls gave unmistakable indication of wealth, background and position. Apparently, all of Nassau did not depend upon the small fishing craft filling its harbor. This section was in sharp contrast to the casual atmosphere of the beach where the dwellings were little more than shacks. As though sensing what was in Cameron's mind, Captain Birch made an inclusive gesture with one hand.

"There is a core of aristocracy here, Mr. Cameron. It is tightly entrenched behind those bougainvillea-covered walls. It is inclined to regard the Bahamas as a special preserve. I suspect you will find the people congenial, coming as you do from the Carolina plantation country."

From anyone else, spoken in a less casual tone, Cameron thought the statement would have carried with it impertinence. He was made curious but not angry.

"That is a curious inference, Captain Birch." He turned to eye the officer.

"I meant no offense." Captain Birch was undisturbed. "But I have had an occasion to visit the plantations of Georgia and recognized the feudal system. It is duplicated here. Whether that is good or bad I would not care to suggest. There is, however, a sturdy independence among the Out Islanders. They have had to become self-sufficient and that makes them a little impatient with special privileges. You will find here, I think, much which is familiar and much completely new."

"I will adapt myself to what I will find." Cameron spoke thoughtfully.

The Government House was an impressive building set upon the incline's brow and overlooking the harbor and the town below. The grounds were meticulously cultivated and Negroes worked among the garden plots, weeding flower beds, trimming shrubs and vines. Uniformed sentries flanked the entrance at the top of a wide, short flight of steps. They came to smart attention as Captain Birch led the party to the open doors. They passed along a narrow central corridor where the

[44]

once bright red carpeting had faded to a soft rose and halted before closed double doors of impressive height. Here, also, there were uniformed sentries. These seemed an unnecessary precaution and Cameron began to suspect His Excellency indulged himself slightly in ridiculous pomp. Then he shrugged mentally. It was really no concern of his. If Sir Gerald Heath had a fancy for surrounding himself with a uniformed display it was a personal matter.

The sentries swung the doors open and Captain Birch guided them into an enormous room. Heavy drapes were drawn over the tall windows but sufficient light filtered through to illuminate the chamber. At the far end His Excellency sat in a heavy chair behind a table of polished mahogany. For a moment it seemed as though he intended to remain seated in the presence of his visitors. Then, after a deliberate and unmistakable pause, he heaved himself up and stood impassively while Captain Birch made the presentations.

Cameron was surprised at his reaction, which was one of immediate dislike. He could not say why and it disturbed him, for he was unaccustomed to snap judgments. This is a pompous fool, he thought to himself; a man of great vanity. The Governor was formally dressed for the occasion. His clothing fitted well. The wig was faultlessly brushed and powdered. There was an expression of strained politeness in his manner as he invited them to chairs and then resumed his place. His hands wandered aimlessly through a few scattered papers. Then he glanced quickly and directly at Sir Henry and his manner was almost accusing.

"Our instructions," the use of the plural was obviously intended to convey a remote and unapproachable majesty, "are to assist you in every way, Sir Henry, and to provide you with accommodations at the Governor's Mansion for the duration of your visit and official duties." What might have been spoken graciously was peevish.

"I have no wish to intrude upon your privacy, Your Excellency." Sir Henry ignored the pettishness. He smiled engagingly. "My duties are vaguely defined; merely to aid in every possible way the settlement here of those who are migrating from our former colonies on the mainland. Actually, I have no idea what this entails."

Sir Gerald nodded indifferently. "God knows what the Government is thinking of." He picked up a sheet of paper and scanned it as though for the first time, although its contents were thoroughly familiar to him. He glanced from it to Ronald Cameron. "You have influential friends in England it seems, Mr. Cameron." This was an annoyed accusation as if Cameron had already demanded special consideration which had upset the entire system of government in the Bahamas. He sighed resignedly. "What can we do for you?"

"Nothing." Cameron was blunt to the point of insult. He could meet this petty arrogance with a temper of his own. "As to my connections in England"—he shrugged them off indifferently—"I am indebted for them to the charm of the Cameron ladies who made fortunate marriages. A cousin or two at Court are handy contrivances." He deliberately understated the situation, understanding well that Sir Gerald was aware of how high the influence reached.

"I may say your grant on Exuma exceeds anything I have known in the islands before." Again the annoyance was unconcealed. It was obvious His Excellency was willing to consider the immigration of Ronald Cameron and his family as a personal affront and burden. "Do you propose to take advantage of it all?"

"Why not?" Cameron was short. "I am accustomed to a large holding of land."

The antagonism between Cameron and the Governor was apparent to everyone in the room. It had appeared to spring from no single source. They simply had disliked each other on sight. Sir Henry seemed to be on the point of interposing a comment. Then he reconsidered and remained silent.

"You will find the Bahamas a damned sight different from the Carolinas." Sir Gerald appeared to take some satisfaction in the notion.

"I would consider it most remarkable if they were not."

There was a moment of strained silence. Then His Excellency relaxed. It was as though he realized the futility of attempting to overawe Cameron.

"We will do what we can for you." The words were almost pleasant.

"Thank you." Cameron, also, unbent slightly.

"Lady Heath and I will expect you for dinner at seven o'clock. You, also, Sir Henry and Captain Sharpe." The Governor was terminating the interview.

"I should like to get my ship unloaded, Your Excellency." Captain Sharpe was in no mood for social amenities. "I have a hundred blacks belowdecks. To say nothing of the cattle and horses. If I may say so they make a damnable stink and I will be relieved to have done with them."

In a remarkable demonstration Sir Gerald Heath's belly heaved with silent laughter. "To paraphrase Mr. Cameron, Captain Sharpe—I would consider it most remarkable if you did not." He laughed openly now, a curious grunting sound in his throat. He turned to Captain Birch. His manner now was friendly. "Roger, have you any knowledge of Great Exuma?"

"There is a fair harbor there, Your Excellency. That is the extent of my information."

"Then," Sir Gerald rose, "we had better make further inquiries. It is possible Captain Sharpe will need the services of a pilot. Anyhow, we can discuss the matter more easily over a glass of port this evening. Is that satisfactory, Captain Sharpe?"

"I have little choice." Sharpe was stiffly impatient. "My orders are to land Mr. Cameron and his family on Great Exuma. I am accustomed to carrying out my orders. Mr. Cameron will be landed if I have to run the *Ranger* aground to do it."

Oddly enough, Sharpe's annoyance only seemed to increase the Governor's amiability. He walked with the company to the doors, the gracious host. He even smiled cordially at Cameron.

"We will put a carriage at your disposal, Mr. Cameron, if you would care to look over the island of New Providence. Although, there are few passable roads outside of Nassau itself. Captain Birch here will be your escort."

Cameron did not refuse the courtesy. He was accustomed to getting along well with all manner of men. It would be nonsense to protract this antagonism he felt.

"Thank you. My sister and children will be happy for a little time away from the ship. I am indebted to you for the courtesy."

"And I am in need of fresh water and some provisioning," Captain Sharpe intruded impatiently. "Is there a Harbormaster?"

"To be sure. To be sure." Sir Gerald loftily dismissed the officer's problems. "You just discuss it with Captain Birch. Roger seems to know a little of something about everything. It is an invaluable talent. Until seven o'clock then." He bowed them out with surprising graciousness. The doors were closed by the sentries.

Retracing their steps down the corridor Cameron was puzzled by the contradictory character of the Governor, for he was a man, apparently, who could slide from arrogance to a certain heavy charm without effort. He would take some knowing and, in the end, some handling.

Outside again they all squinted their eyes against the hard sunlight.

"Damn!" Captain Sharpe's annoyance erupted in the single word.

Birch was quietly amused. "We take a more leisurely view of things here in the islands, Captain. However, they do get done. We shall see to everything in good time." He turned to Cameron with a smile. "Now let us see about getting your family ashore. I am looking forward to showing you the island of New Providence."

All throughout the long dinner, during which a series of completely unfamiliar dishes had been served, Cameron was acutely aware of Sabrina Heath. There was about her a curious, porcelain quality which was almost startlingly contradicted by a subtle, animal-like vitality and deliberate sensuality. Beauty she had in great measure, he thought. But beyond that, and without seeming effort, she managed to give the impression of a sleek cat turning with quiet ecstasy in the sun. She was slender to the point of delicacy and yet voluptuous. A strange and disturbing combination. Cameron had watched her from his place across the table. Once she had looked up suddenly to catch his glance upon her and she smiled with an ancient wisdom. Her eyes dropped with unmistakable provocation.

"It is unfortunate you must leave us so soon, Mr. Cameron." She seemed to be making idle conversation.

"I had no reason to regret my decision until this evening, Lady Heath."

"I only hope you will find reasons to bring you back to Nassau frequently."

The others at the table—Martha Cameron, Captain Birch, Sir Henry, Captain Sharpe and Sir Gerald—appeared unaware of the small byplay between Cameron and Sabrina. She, however, knew well enough what she was doing. This man Cameron had attracted her from the moment of their meeting. He was of the same age or thereabouts as her husband but there the similarity ended. Where Gerald was all soft and paunchy, Cameron was lean and hard. He appeared as a man who had spent long hours in the saddle or at vigorous outdoor exercise. His physical appeal stirred latent passions within her. She found herself wanting to reach over and link her fingers in the strong, weathered hand. Aware of a gaze upon her, she lifted her eyes and caught the quizzical glance of Roger Birch. The captain knew what was going on but she was unembarrassed although, for a while, she had engaged in a passing affair with the Governor's aide. But this, she told herself, had sprung from boredom rather than any real emotion. She found herself thinking of Ronald Cameron in quite a different way. He was a man to possess a woman against her will and the thought stirred her with a disquieting eroticism.

The dinner had proceeded without seeming constraint. From his place at the head of the table the Governor had been ponderously jovial as the wine and earlier rounds of punch went to his head. Martha Cameron, seated on his right, had displayed the proper interest in everything he said and His Excellency, flattered by this undivided attention, had once reached over and patted her hand with a porcine playfulness. Even Captain Sharpe had unbent a little and dropped his quarrelsome attitude. He was willing to concede His Majesty's Government the right to order its ships in any manner it saw fit. This was something in the nature of a real concession. Now the meal was all but finished. They waited only for the dessert, and Sabrina was inwardly rebelling against the custom of withdrawing and leaving the men to their port and discussion. It was a ridiculous ceremony, she thought. She wondered a little helplessly what in the world she and Martha Cameron would find to talk about during the dreary time they must spend together.

In an effort to delay the moment she bent slightly over the table toward Cameron, well aware of the fact that the pressure thrust her firm breasts slightly upward.

"Tell me, Mr. Cameron. Is it true, as Roger told us earlier, you are having your manor, the bricks themselves, sent to the islands from Carolina?"

"I am a Scot and chary of leaving things of value behind me. Besides," he was thoughtful for a moment and his strong, handsome features clouded, "it is the only home I have ever known. I gave it up with regret and hope to recreate it here."

Sir Gerald paused in the spooning of a soft banana custard into his mouth. "I should have thought a man of your station would have preferred to return to England." He washed down the dessert with a mouthful of sweet wine.

"I don't think England would have satisfied me," Cameron answered slowly. "As much as I dislike everything the Rebels stand for, I must confess that the measure of independence we enjoyed in the colonies— a thing of self-determination—is not easily relinquished. I do not subscribe to the theory of democracy but neither do I think I would be quite happy under the strict conventions of the homeland. There is a contradiction there. I admit it."

"You will find rebels enough here in the islands." Sir Gerald growled angrily at the thought. "They flaunt authority. We have the devil of a time collecting the taxes from the Out Islanders. Some of them are little better than pirates. They change the lights to bring ships up on the reefs and then blandly tell the Crown nothing was salvaged. We are due our tithe, you know, in such cases, but unless a representative of the Crown is on hand at the moment of the vessel's striking, not so much as a cask of pickled beef seems to be recovered. They are thieves and liars, all of them."

"I suppose Out Islander is a designation into which I will fit." Cameron mused on the novelty of this for a moment. "In time I may, also, become something of a problem to you and your tax assessors. There is a communicable virus in the idea of independence. I have watched it spread."

"Sir, you are a problem already!" Surprisingly enough Sir Gerald's laughter boomed. His face was flushed from the wine, and small pearls of perspiration were upon his brow. He was, though, in a remarkably good humor. He turned to his wife and made an effort to rise. "My dear, we will excuse you now."

"No." Sabrina made the declaration with a mild firmness. "We have so few visitors, I do not intend to be shunted off like some naughty child. There is no reason in the world why Mistress Cameron and I should not enjoy the company of you gentlemen."

"Well! 'Pon my word. Well!" Sir Gerald was uncertain how to cope with this defiance. Then he laughed again and wiped his mouth with the back of his hand. "You see," he addressed the surprised Cameron, "what a whiff of independence in the air does? The ladies refuse to withdraw. 'Pon my word!"

"I have often wondered why they should." Cameron smiled at Sabrina. "I am not too satisfied with the custom. A strictly masculine company can become damnably tiresome, if you want my opinion."

"I thank you, sir." From her place Sabrina managed to suggest a mocking curtsy.

"I suppose you would like to share the pipes and port?" His Excellency was determined to retain his mood of good-natured humor.

"Why not? I have tried both in secret."

"The de'l you have?" Sir Gerald was honestly surprised. "The de'l you have." He repeated the words.

"Now that we have solved that," Sabrina addressed her husband, "suppose you tell us why Mr. Cameron is already a problem."

"Ha!" The question delighted His Excellency. "Ask Captain Sharpe here. He has the answer."

Captain Sharpe shook his head. He, also, was mellowed by the food and wine. He had already endured all that could be expected of a fine vessel's master and was resigned to the situation.

"I'll not be drawn into further discussion." The statement was not unpleasantly made. "In Mr. Cameron I have found a match for my own stubbornness. We shall call the game a draw."

A slave brought the port and long-stemmed clay pipes with a silver jar of tobacco. After a moment's hesitation, surprised that the ladies remained at the table, he placed small glasses before them all. Martha turned hers down but Sabrina left the one at her place up. There was a moment of awkward pause and then Sir Gerald pushed the tobacco container toward Cameron.

When the pipes were alight and the port was making its rounds, Sabrina watched Cameron as he drew contentedly upon the strong tobacco.

[50]

"I wonder how it started?" She fingered a few shreds of the brown leaf from the jar. "I mean, what made the first man or Indian or whoever it was take some of this leaf, crumble it in his hand and say, 'This ought to taste good if I put some fire to it'? Chew it. Season food with it. Those things I could understand. But what made him set fire to it?"

"I have wondered myself, Lady Heath." Sir Henry gazed down the length of his pipe. "It would seem to be a completely unnatural thing to do. However, I salute that first, venturesome unknown and give him my gratitude."

"Lady Heath, gentlemen," Sir Gerald leaned back comfortably in his chair, "is given to strange fancies. Even as her husband I must confess she frequently surprises me. We may have set a new fashion this evening."

"And one I would enjoy." Martha Cameron glanced about the table. "Women don't really like each other. It is barbaric to throw them together; Christians to the Christians instead of the lions. We deserve better treatment."

"I shall issue a decree, madam." Sir Gerald actually beamed. "Henceforth, in Nassau at least, there shall be no withdrawing. Ha!" He seemed delighted with the idea of such an edict.

"You will, of course, be coming to Nassau frequently?" Sabrina addressed the question to Cameron. "We do have a society of sorts here, provincial though it may be."

"I'm afraid, at first, I must contend with laying out a plantation and the erection of temporary quarters. Those are not things which I can turn over to my overseers. However," he nodded in Martha's direction, "I leave hostages behind me in the persons of my sister and daughter. Captain Birch showed me a house here today which is for lease. It will do until we have our own again. My son, Robert Bruce, will come with me to Great Exuma."

"Young Caroline," Birch commented with a reminiscent grin, "seemed to have decided opinions on that this afternoon. I found her a most charming guest and remarkably poised for one so young. I am afraid, Mr. Cameron, you have bred a rebel within your own household."

"Aye!" he admitted. "Caroline has a will of her own. It is a facet of character I would prefer to see in a man."

"She confided in me today," Birch continued. "I suggest you search the *Ranger* thoroughly for a stowaway before you sail!" He was amused by the recollection of the girl's stubborn anger at being left behind.

"I loathe children," Sabrina was wide-eyed innocence, "but you must

[51]

bring her to see us." She spoke to Martha but her glance was upon Cameron. "We may have things in common. I, also, rebel at times."

The port was finished, the pipes dying. Sabrina allowed her eyes to rove about the table and then arose. The company followed her move. Sir Gerald was yawning openly.

"Would you care to see the gardens by moonlight?" Sabrina fell in quite naturally at Cameron's side and took his arm without affectation. Sir Henry escorted Martha while His Excellency, stumbling a little sleepily, was flanked by Captains Birch and Sharpe. "They are supposed to be quite beautiful." She looked up into his face, oblivious of the others.

Cameron was momentarily confused. He was unaccustomed to such forthrightness in a woman of quality. Her manner was direct, completely without the artificiality, the clinging helplessness, with which he was familiar. Her fingers were unnecessarily firm on his arm.

"I am sometimes suffocated by all of this tropical beauty," she continued lightly as they strolled toward the open, glassed doors. "There seems something almost a little indecent in the cloying lushness with which everything grows. I often feel the need for a harsher landscape and its vitality. A barren moor, the Scottish highlands, Ireland's mountains. Oh, how I miss England! I sometimes wonder if I will ever see it again."

Moonlight fell as a shower of bright silver on the garden and the air was heavy with the perfume of the magnolia and jessamine. There was no wind to move through the palms and they rose motionless against the sky, like crested plumage. A broad terrace extended the width of the residence. They walked to its far end and stood for a moment in silence.

"I am so lonely in this place." She sighed quietly.

Cameron was disturbed by her presence. It had been a long time since he had known the inviting touch of a woman's hand or heard the appealing note in a voice. She was aware of this.

"I embarrass you, do I not?" There was a discernible mockery in the question. "I am thinking that perhaps you are a part of the rugged landscape which I so need. Men grow strangely soft in these islands. It is a way of life against which I rebel. There is granite in you. It appeals to me. Do I make an awkward situation for you, Ronald Cameron?"

"Under the circumstances, yes." His voice had an unnaturally harsh sound. "For what you do so openly is usually done in secret. I am long out of practice in the matter of flirtation and since my wife's death I, also, have been much alone."

"At least you confess to no scruples." Her hand moved down until her fingers linked with his. "I do not coquette lightly. Neither do I hesitate

[52]

when I want something. I should like to go to Exuma with you. It is as uncomplicated, in statement, as that. I am a woman in need of a man. At the moment it seems you are he." She turned him deliberately and began retracing their steps along the flagged walk to where the others stood in a patch of light as it came through the doors. "Does that shock and discomfit you?"

"You employ unfamiliar tactics for a lady."

"Then perhaps I am a tavern wench at heart and not at all the Governor's Lady. The line of demarcation is an invisible one." She matched her step to his. "But, again, what I feel tonight I may not feel tomorrow. I wear my heart on my sleeve, a little to one side as I do my bonnet."

"Then it is well I leave soon for Exuma, for you are a damned attractive woman. Although, I am not sure you are what you so earnestly pretend to be."

"Accuse me of anything but pretense. There will be other times and other nights, for you will be coming to Nassau."

"An intrigue with the Governor's wife would not be the best possible way for me to start a new life in these islands."

"Are you always so practical?"

He laughed. "I confess only that I am out of my depth and floundering a little."

As they rejoined the group His Excellency was yawning openly. His eyes were heavy, his features slack. He regarded his wife and Cameron with sullen suspicion and then grunted indifferently. She ignored him and spoke to Martha.

"If you would care to stay ashore instead of returning to the ship I will have rooms prepared for you."

"Thank you, no." Martha smiled a brief appreciation. "The children are aboard and will be expecting us."

"Honored," the Governor mumbled sleepily. "Honored. Any time." He swayed a little. "Strenuous day. Things to cope with." He seemed on the point of going to sleep standing up and his speech was thick. "Anything we can do ask Roger here." He took his aide's arm. "Good man, Roger."

They bade their good nights and went to the waiting carriage which carried them down the gently sloping hill to the dock where the captain's gig waited.

"She has a gleam in her eye, that one." Sharpe spoke abruptly and with complete irrelevancy. He glanced at Cameron. Bright moonlight illuminated their faces. "I suspect it was a thing you noticed, Mr. Cameron."

"Should I have?" Cameron asked mildly.

There was a crinkle of laughter about the captain's eyes and then it vanished. "No," he replied slowly, "perhaps you are right. It is safer not to. I should not like to have His Excellency as an enemy in these waters."

Undressing in his cabin Cameron thought back over the evening. I should not, he told himself, like to be in the Governor's slippers this night for he must know he is a cuckold for any man who strikes her fancy.

He turned out the cabin light and lay upon the berth, wide awake. His mind began sorting the things to be done. First, tomorrow he would settle Martha and the children in Nassau. Then he must go over in detail what could be stored here in a warehouse and what should be taken. It would be good to put his feet upon his own land again even though that land was an unfamiliar island awash in this moonlit sea. Then he remembered he was not leaving Robert Bruce, only Martha and Caroline. Robert Bruce was the future and he must be prepared for it. In his son lay the family name and the generations to come. It was good to know he had such a sturdy sapling for the transplanting. It was upon this he finally went to sleep.

❦ V ❧

GREAT EXUMA lay as a brilliant ornament of dark, green jade flecked with gold and its white beaches were washed by the colored seas surrounding it. Within the crooked arm of a land spit the harbor offered shelter to the *Ranger* as she swung at anchor.

Cameron, the head overseer Grayson, and Robert Bruce stood upon the shore and watched as the last of the supplies were being brought over. They were ferried on a flat, shallow draft barge, one of several which Cameron had ordered built to specifications in Nassau. There was no way of unloading direct from the transport for there were no docking facilities and the water shallowed abruptly, making it impossible for the ship to move in closer.

The construction of the barges was only one of the many things which had mounted in a maddening confusion during the seemingly interminable time they were held over in Nassau. Cameron had cursed and stormed against the delays keeping them in the port there. The natives drove him to towering rages with their indolence, for the general attitude seemed to be that if something wasn't done today then tomorrow would serve just as well. Captain Sharpe, pushed to desperation, threatened to turn his ship about and sail away. Cameron alternately cajoled, argued and entreated the master. The two had reached a point where they spoke to each other only when it became absolutely necessary.

The stock had become restive and near panic. The mood of the slaves was unpredictable. Sanitation, a problem from the time the *Ranger* had stood out from Charlestown, was now well nigh past solving. The animal dung and human excrement moved in buckets on a human chain from the hold to top deck where it was dumped into the harbor. The stalls had to be washed down daily and the slave quarters fumigated as best they could. There were many times during the endless days when Cameron wished he had never heard of the Bahamas.

[55]

The slaves were an increasing vexation. They were frightened and even the most docile near open rebellion against this all but unbearable confinement. There had been no place to keep them save belowdecks on the *Ranger*. Bringing them up for an airing only increased their uneasiness and suspicion. From the ship they could see other black men sculling their boats around the harbor in apparent freedom. This they could not understand and it only served to increase a growing resentment and nurture the seeds of revolt. They became blankly sullen and openly defiant by turns. For the first time in his life Cameron had ordered a flogging. Two Angola bucks had refused to take their places in the line which passed the buckets from hold to deck. Their insubordination excited the others. Cameron had them taken, bound to the mast and flayed while frenzied wails of terror and anger arose from those who were forced to watch.

Lying as she did in the open sea with the sun beating down upon her, the *Ranger* threatened to become a pest-ridden vessel. Strange fevers broke out among the slaves; their bodies erupted in pus-filled sores. The heat boiled the tar out of the deck's seams and the air below was unbelievably fetid. In desperation Captain Sharpe had taken her out to cruise about aimlessly, allowing the wind to blow as best it could through her open hatches. Some measure of relief had been achieved with this, but when the ship was again at anchor the same, unbearable conditions reasserted themselves. The vessel was as explosive with tempers and hatreds as a fused powder keg. Its stench was a solid thing to turn men's stomachs. The crew was on the verge of mutiny and the keening moans of the blacks made the days and nights hideous. When the wind came from the proper quarter the sound and smell of the *Ranger* drifted over the island of New Providence. A delegation of the community's inhabitants formally called upon His Excellency and demanded the ship be forced to quit the harbor before it brought the plague to everyone. Cameron, despising himself and the Governor, had been forced to beg the man for more time and a measure of understanding. It was simply impossible to leave until certain, inescapable arrangements had been completed. Reluctantly and with bad temper, the Governor had consented to a brief span of time.

Cameron had worked with his overseers from the first splitting of daylight in the east until the sun dipped beneath the horizon at eveningtime. Martha and Caroline, together with most of the house slaves, had been settled in the residence he had leased. Cameron, with Robert Bruce, remained aboard the ship, for the man was unwilling not to share that which Sharpe, his officers and crew must endure.

All of the household goods had to be shuttled from the transport to shore and stored in a waterfront warehouse. Daily, Cameron and his white overseers were forced to recruit native boatmen and laborers for the task. The Bahamians were not inclined to work and he had to offer exorbitant wages. A steady flow of gold drained from his purse and he would lie awake at night wondering if it would ever end and whether his once seemingly plentiful resources would last. He became drawn and tight, quick of temper and terrible in his wrath at the slightest mishap.

Captain Sharpe, in one of his rare moments of assistance, had pointed out that once they had landed at Exuma and the *Ranger* sailed, leaving them there, they would be without any means of transport or communication. He advised Cameron to purchase a boat and even volunteered to pick one out. A stout, well-built ketch-rigged craft was finally selected. The owner promptly asked three times what it was worth. Grimly, Cameron had paid. Then he engaged a captain and an unenthusiastic crew of two, for he knew nothing of handling a boat. At least they would not be marooned. As some order began to emerge from the endless confusion Cameron had sent the ketch ahead with Grayson, who would look over the island and await the *Ranger*'s arrival.

Captain Birch had proved to be an invaluable and unexpected ally. The young officer seemed to delight in solving or circumventing the innumerable problems which confronted them each day. He began to look upon the adventure as a personal affair and he was as tireless and merry as though the entire thing was some sort of holiday excursion. He placated the now almost inarticulate Governor. He soothed Sharpe, rounded up a labor gang, found Out Islanders who were informed and willing to give advice and share their knowledge of conditions on Exuma. He arrived each morning on the beach, smartly uniformed, smiling and cheerful. A couple of times he had brought young Caroline with him in the carriage. The two seemed to share some secret confidences and, sitting in the coach, the girl would watch with an alert interest as Birch persuaded the unwilling Bahamians to work for her father.

It was obvious to everyone concerned that once on Great Exuma they would have to live, for a while at least, under the most primitive conditions. Shelters must be created from the brush. Pens and corrals would have to be erected for the livestock; a barracoon established for the slaves until they had adjusted themselves to the completely unfamiliar conditions. Water must be found or wells dug. The supplies would have to be hoarded and they must learn to live partly on what the land and the sea provided. Finally, the day came when the barges had been hoisted to the *Ranger*'s deck; the last piece of furniture stored under lock in the warehouse; the final instructions given to Martha for the maintenance of the household in Nassau; a drink taken with Captain Birch and a stiffly polite and formal call paid upon the Governor. The *Ranger* sailed.

Now, from what seemed a wild and fantastic nightmare, a semblance of form was emerging. The slaves were landed. The livestock had been driven down ramps and into the water. They swam to shore with angry snorts and excited bellows and were promptly rounded up and herded into the corrals. Curiously enough, the mood of the slaves changed with the familiar feel of land beneath their feet. Their sullen and resentful attitude disappeared. The more intelligent among them voluntarily and without any instruction drove the cattle into the pens. Others began examining the brush for materials with which they could construct simple huts or shelters. There was even the sound of husky laughter and they chattered excitedly among themselves, digging hands experimentally into the soil to feel its texture; they exclaimed over the few wild orange trees they found growing, the caressing warmth of the sun, the lush undergrowth and the stands of lignum vitae, coconut palms and wild bananas. They responded automatically to the novelty and primitive call of this island. Listening to them, watching their antics, Cameron felt an overwhelming sense of relief. He would not have known how to contend with rebellious slaves in this situation.

Grayson, sensitive to the mood of the blacks, glanced at his employer and smiled briefly.

"They'll do well enough I think now, sir."

"God knows I hope so." The response was a prayer.

The barge they were watching grounded on the beach and was quickly unloaded. As the bales, casks and boxes were carried up far out of reach of any tide their supplies made an imposing pile. With a little ingenuity they would all make out well enough.

"This is the last of it, sir." Grayson surveyed the mound with satisfaction. "I'll say now I never thought we'd make it."

"We had to make it. There was no place else for us to go." Cameron sighed gratefully.

"I thought it best to wait until your mind was more at ease." Grayson watched as a couple of dozen slaves carried the barge up the beach. "Miller and Whitehead want to quit and return to Charlestown with the *Ranger*." He nodded to where the two assistant overseers stood a little apart. "There is no way to keep them, sir, short of force."

"I want no man against his will." Cameron regretted the loss of the two subordinates. "I will give them a draft on the bank in Charlestown for their wages. Can you get along without them?"

Grayson half smiled, thinking of what they all had been through during the past weeks. "In your own words, sir—we will have to get along without them." He took a twist of black, molasses-flavored tobacco from his pocket and bit off a piece. He chewed upon it meditatively before continuing. "With respect, sir, but, do you know exactly where we are? I mean, where does our land begin and end?"

The land in Cameron's grant from the Crown was clearly defined but until he had a starting point Cameron could not say exacty where it lay. In his papers there was a map, but until a Royal Surveyor came from Nassau to mark the boundaries for them they would simply have to appropriate what they needed. Sir Henry had promised to expedite this phase of the colonization.

"We are upon Great Exuma." Cameron chuckled. "I consider that to be a major triumph. As to our bounds? I am not certain." His gaze roved over the wooded island. There was timber for the cutting, land for the clearing and planting. Some sort of crop—beans, cowpeas, yams and cane—must be put into the ground as quickly as possible unless they were to depend upon Nassau or the other Out Islands for everything they needed to sustain themselves. "For the moment, Grayson, we'll simply say what we stand upon is ours. It will do until someone comes along to dispute it."

From the *Ranger* now the captain's gig was being rowed swiftly toward shore. In its stern, Captain Sharpe in full dress uniform sat and gazed imperturbably at the piled confusion high on the beach. He was determined to make this leave-taking as formal as possible and had clothed himself for the occasion. When the gig grounded he stepped ashore and advanced unhurriedly to where Cameron, Grayson and Robert Bruce waited. He bowed briefly.

"I have carried out my orders, Mr. Cameron. Now, with your permission, I am making sail." He stared about and seemed to unbend a little. "I bear you no ill will, sir. Although I cannot say this time hasn't frequently driven me to the point of breaking. As for my ship, God knows how I will ever cleanse her, but that is neither here nor there. My orders are to return to Savannah, pick up some Loyalist families with more modest aspirations than your own. After this is done I'll call at Charlestown. If your bricks are on the docks as promised, I'll load them in ballast. Though," he shook his head with honest bewilderment, "how you expect to recreate a plantation manor from the Ashley River here is beyond me."

"The first Cameron faced much the same problem in Carolina, Captain Sharpe. The thought does not dismay me."

"Well, sir," Sharpe was grimly amused, "it damn well should!"

Cameron ignored the jibe. "A couple of my assistant overseers want to return to the mainland with you, Captain. Will you take them?"

"If they can bear the stink they are welcome to come along."

Cameron called to the two white men and they came over slowly, their eyes darting in every direction in an effort to avoid their employer's accusing gaze.

"Grayson tells me you want to leave my service." He measured his words to conceal their anger.

"Yes, sir." The man named Whitehead spoke for them both. "It is nothing personal, sir. You have always treated us well. But this isn't exactly what we expected."

"What in hell did you expect?" The rage exploded. "Flower-covered native girls rowing out in canoes to meet you; a hammock beneath a palm tree?"

Whitehead couldn't hide a grin. "I'll have to admit, sir, something like that would have helped. Anyhow, we decided we'd like to go home." He stooped suddenly, picked up a handful of the grainy soil and allowed it to sift through his fingers. "I'm damned if I believe you can grow cotton in this, sir. And I've been a cotton man all of my life."

"I'll make it grow." The reply was emphatic.

Whitehead regarded Cameron for a moment and a slow, agreeing wonder crept into his expression. "Yes, sir." He spoke with awed respect. "Yes, sir, I expect you will."

Cameron strode over to where a chest with some of his personal effects stood. From a portfolio he took quill and ink together with a pad of blank bank drafts. Seating himself on an upturned cask he wrote out an order for their wages. Returning to the little group he handed the paper to Whitehead.

"I have made it out for the full month although the date is short of that. You are good men. I am sorry to lose you." He offered them his hand in turn.

Cameron stood with his son and Grayson as the captain's gig was rowed back to the ship. It was with a disturbing sense of sudden loneliness that they watched the transport make sail and move slowly out of the harbor. They kept her in view until she had rounded the island's tip. Now, for a moment, there was complete silence. Even the slaves had stopped talking among themselves. They had no idea where they were, these black men and women, but nothing which lay ahead could be worse than what the vanishing ship represented. At least, their bare feet could dig into this warm earth. There was a bright sky above them. These were well-remembered things. They were content to have them so.

In the light swell of the harbor the small ketch rocked. A couple of gulls on graceful wings circled her, hoping for some refuse to be thrown overboard. The Bahamian crew was fishing with hand lines from her side.

"Well, sir." It was Grayson who spoke first. "Here we are." He pulled at one ear with an expression of wry amusement. "I'm damned if I don't feel like some castaway on a desert island."

"It's not that bad, Mr. Grayson. There are families on Eluthera, Andros and even here, I understand. Once we are settled we'll take the ketch and spend a little time getting acquainted. One thing, we will not have to worry about runaway slaves, for they can't get off the island. I suggest you try to bring some sort of order out of all of this. I want to walk and think for a while." He lifted his face to the sun. "At least we are blessed with an agreeable climate. Sleeping in the open for a while will be no hardship. The blacks will shift for themselves quickly enough."

Grayson stood looking after the pair, father and son, as they walked down the curving beach together. He had known no other employer. His father and grandfather had worked for the Camerons. In him there was a deep respect for this man, although he had to admit to himself, given a choice he would not have traded the Ashley plantation for all the islands in the Bahamas. Well, they were here and he would do his best. He looked around and spotted the three white assistants who were left. Wells, Thompson and Spithead. He shouted for them to join him while the slaves watched and waited with dumb curiosity.

Ronald Cameron walked with head bent. He was neither weary nor dejected but only thinking soberly of what lay ahead. Beside him Robert Bruce kept silent until his father was ready to speak. To him this was a magnificent adventure. A thing to be read about in books. Aboard the *Ranger* Captain Sharpe, in a rare moment of unbending, had given him some charts of the islands. They were filled with such exciting names as Deadman's Cay, Soldier Cay, Pudding Cut, Man-of-War Cay, Spanish Wells, Six Shilling Cay. He could barely suppress his inner excitement over the idea of what lay ahead; how it would be to grow to manhood here. There was so much to learn, to do, to explore and understand. He would learn to sail and handle the ketch. With his father he would ride, walk and be taught the things he should know. Unlike Cameron Hall this was not something which he would inherit someday as having been built by others. Here, on this raw ground, he would be able to see it develop from nothing. That Cameron Hall could be duplicated on the island was something he took for granted. His father had said it would be done. Having made this statement he could not understand now why the man seemed to look upon everything this day in such a somber mood.

"What do you think of things as they have gone, Robert Bruce?" The question came suddenly, as was the man's habit.

"That you have done what you said you would, Father." The boy's eyes were shining.

"Aye, we have done that." A touch of humor softened the lines about the mouth. "We are here, but I'll confess now there were times when I doubted how this venture would go. Even now we are only at the beginning of things. As Grayson put it, we could be well-provisioned castaways at the moment." He halted and looked about. "There is a rare beauty here."

The beach swung in a long, lazy crescent. It was heavily fringed by massed palms which were bent toward the water, for this was the lee side of the island. The sand was soft and glistening beneath their feet. Small waves raced upon the shore with a foaming curl and a hissing sound. It seemed as though no man had ever before put his feet here.

Cameron bent and picked up a small, trumpet-shaped shell, softly pink in color. He turned it in his fingers thoughtfully.

"Life here will be what we make it, no better and no worse. That may sound to you as a commonplace remark but it isn't. In a more settled place a man is often influenced by the presence of others. He must accommodate himself to them. Here we will be all but alone. The soil we turn will be virgin. The seeds we plant will be the first this land has known. In a way we are like God's first man, able to walk with great strides upon the earth or creep humbly. It is for us to choose." His hand reached out to rumple the boy's hair with a strong gesture of companionship. "I suspect by now you have learned I am not a humble man by nature. We shall shape this island to our needs and liking."

"Do you think Captain Sharpe will really come back with the bricks as he said and we can build Cameron Hall as it was?"

"Sharpe will come back for he said he would. I'll give the man his due. This was not an easy voyage for him. As for Cameron Hall—I shall have to find masons and builders in Nassau when the time comes. It will be no simple thing to do, for these Bahamians seem disinclined to work. But in time we will rebuild it as it was." He paused and then turned to regard his son with an expression of troubled seriousness. "I would not have you think, Robert Bruce, that even with all the confusion in Nassau I overlooked the matter of a tutor for you. It was in my mind but I did not see how a classroom could be set up on the beach. I know you will understand."

"Aye, Father." The mimicry was exact. "I'll do my best to put up with things as they are. It will not be easy, as you say."

When they at last retraced their steps to the landing site a semblance of form was shaping itself out of the confusion. At a quarter of a mile's distance Grayson had marked off the boundaries for the slaves. He issued the heavy cane knives to each and left Spithead to watch over the blacks.

"There is no need to erect a barracoon," Grayson explained to his employer. "For as you say, there is no place for them to go."

In a remarkably short space of time and without direction the slaves had cut huge piles of wattles and branches from the dense undergrowth. Now they were busily and happily lacing this material into conical huts of primitive design, not unlike those to be found in their native Africa.

Watching them, Cameron wondered. From what knowledge did they build these things? Save for a few of the older men and women his slaves were of a second generation, born in the Southern colonies and in slavery. They knew nothing firsthand of Africa. How was it they now instinctively plaited and bound together these moundlike dwellings? He walked over and examined one. They were tight, not really waterproof but secure enough unless they were beaten upon by a heavy storm. As he passed among them they paused in their labors and stood back with shy smiles of pride. Contentment was in their manner now. They were building their own village and it was a good feeling, reaching far back into time. They were accustomed to the feel of the earth and did not look beyond this day. That they would be fed, cared for and worked they took for granted, for such things had always been so. What they did now was intuitive and they never thought to question the wisdom of their hands.

"This is a rare thing, Robert Bruce." He spoke softly. "Put it away in your mind as an example of how an animal will adapt itself to its environment."

They strolled back toward the slight rise above the beach where Wells was directing other blacks in erecting lean-to shelters for the small mountain of supplies and staking out tents for sleeping quarters.

"We'll be secure enough come sundown, sir." Wells spoke with pride. "Short of a hurricane everything will stand. It's not Cameron Hall by a long shot but it will do." The man seemed to be sharing a sense of achievement with Cameron.

"I can see we are not needed here." With a hand he turned his son's shoulder.

They walked to the water's edge where Cameron hailed the ketch. The crew could be seen aboard her but the men either didn't hear or chose to ignore the shout. It was not until Cameron loosed a shattering bellow that one arose leisurely, walked to the stern and dropped into a dinghy. He rowed slowly toward shore, stopping once to peer down at the water at something which caught his attention. The little craft grounded and the rower, a towheaded youth, leaped out and pulled his boat onto the sand. Since Cameron had left the hiring of the crew to Grayson, they were strangers to him.

"I'm Cameron." He was a little angry over the indifferent manner in which his call had been answered. "This is my son Robert Bruce. What is your name and why didn't you answer my first shout?"

"I'm Gurney. Tom Gurney." There was a faint, indefinable accent to the speech. "We thought you were just yellin' for the hell of it."

"Why should I stand on the beach and call at nothing?"

"I'm damned if I know." Gurney was cheerfully unimpressed by his employer's anger. He whistled softly and his eyes glanced unconcernedly over the treetops.

Cameron controlled an impulse to grab the youth by the neck and shake him. Then he thought better of it. From what he had seen of these Bahamians they were an independent lot. They might well sail the ketch off and back to Nassau, leaving them all stranded here.

"Row us out to the boat, Gurney. I would like to examine her and get to know the captain."

"That'd be Pinder." Gurney nodded agreeably. There was no deference in his manner; no appending of the word "sir" when he spoke to his employer. Neither was it deliberately insolent.

"Is that how you address the captain? Pinder? Nothing more?"

"Well, I've knowed him all my life. That's his name, ain't it. Oh!" A broad grin of understanding broke upon his face. "You mean like Captain Pinder. He'd bust out laughin' if I did that."

When they were seated, Gurney shoved the dinghy away, followed it into knee-deep water and then jumped in. He took up the oars and pulled through the small waves. Halfway out he halted, allowed the sweeps to trail and picked up a wooden pail with a glass bottom. He passed it to Robert Bruce.

"You want to see somethin', boy? Hold it to the water and look down."

Robert Bruce did as directed and immediately the entire sea bottom was revealed. There were hunks of coral, great patches of weed which swayed back and forth in the current. There were an unbelievable number and variety of fish in the most brilliant colors imaginable. He was looking at a new and incredible world. A huge ray raised a cloud of sand as it streaked away with an undulating motion of its body.

"Father?" Eagerly Robert Bruce handed the bucket to his father.

"I'll look another time." Even as he refused, Cameron wondered why. He was curious and yet, a reserve he had not yet mastered held him in check. He would feel foolish in front of this Gurney, who was already regarding him with delighted wonder as having come across a completely unfamiliar species of man. "Just now I am anxious to talk with Captain Pinder."

On the ketch one of the men was bending over a charcoal brazier, feeding black chips to the already glowing mound. The other had four or five of the enormous clams called conchs at his side. He held a heavy knife and watched with curiosity as Cameron and Robert Bruce came up and to the boat's deck. Neither man made an effort to rise.

"That there's Pinder." Gurney pointed to the captain at the brazier. "The other's Greenleaf. This," he addressed his companions, "is Mr. Cameron and his son. He wanted to talk with the captain." A droll expression of detached amusement crossed his features.

Pinder made a gesture with one finger, sweeping it down from his forehead in an arc of casual recognition. Then he puffed out his cheeks and blew upon the embers. Greenleaf merely nodded and hefted one of the conchs.

Cameron regarded the trio with a tight anger. He was far from being adjusted to such casual familiarity from those he employed. There was a deference due to the man who paid the wages. It should spring automatically from those who accepted them. Then, his sense of humor asserted itself. Under these conditions what he was demanding was ridiculous. He would not be a strutting fool. I will, he told himself, adjust myself as my blacks have to the unfamiliar. If this is the way of the Bahamas I'll have to get used to it.

In an iron pot half filled with water, Pinder cut up a couple of onions, a few potatoes, added some crumpled bay leaves and peppers. He put the kettle on the brazier and then squatted back on his haunches, eying Cameron and Robert Bruce with a friendly interest.

"Set, why don't you? We're stirrin' up some chowder. I was figurin' on comin' ashore later to say how-do. You got your hands full, ain't you?" He indicated the shore. "I hear how you plan to build a real stone house here. That'll be somethin' to see." He swirled the vegetables in the water with a wooden spoon.

Cameron picked up one of the trumpet-shaped clams. The shell was turned in a great, wrapping fold. It was partly open at one side and seemed impenetrable.

"Most people, when they see a conch for the first time, wonder at the same thing." Greenleaf seemed to know what was going through Cameron's mind. "They say, how the hell do you get to it? I'll show you, for you may want to do it for yourself."

At the broad top of the shell there was a knoblike protuberance. Greenleaf took his knife and chipped expertly away at the base. Small pieces of shell flew as the blade followed its circular course. After a moment the man took the knob in his fingers and pulled. It came out as a bung from a cask and with it the long, pinkish hunk of dripping meat which was the clam.

"Trouble with a conch is it don't keep. You gotta use it quick before it spoils." The blade chopped up and down, slicing the clam into chunks which were tossed into the pot. "It makes a real good chowder an' a salad, though. I was a hand once on a schooner that sailed to the Massachusetts colony. They make a chowder there in Boston but it don't compare much to what a conch'll do."

Cameron picked up a piece of the clam meat and put it tentatively in his mouth. The meat was slightly rubbery but with the fresh, salt taste of the sea. He chewed upon it reflectively and looked up to find Pinder's glance bent upon him.

"You think you're goin' to like it here?"

"I have left myself little choice, Captain Pinder. I shall have to like it."

Pinder poked at the charcoal bed with a stick, breaking the red heap apart. "There is them that tried an' give up." He whistled softly. "They wanted everythin' too fast an' when it didn't come that way they quit an' let go."

Cameron tried to define the accent of these Bahamians and then gave up. It was a soft combination of several tongues—black, white, Indian.

"I'm not in the habit of abandoning a venture once I have embarked upon it."

"Well, I hope you stick to it. I think, maybe, these islands must be among the most pleasant in the world. Take my family, now." He paused to dump a tin plate of minced clams into the pot. "They come to the Bahama with what was called the Elutherian Adventurers along with a William Sayle, who had been the Royal Governor of Bermuda. That would be around 1650. They settled at Spanish Wells. I guess there are more Pinders in these islands than any other name. They got along and multiplied because they were willin' to give a little here an' there; stretch themselves, you might say, like a good line will before it breaks. I guess that's the real secret of any place. One year the crops will be good. The next a blight'll hit 'em. One year the sponges come up as you grain 'em fine an' healthy. The next year some buggers git into 'em an' they lay in the crawls an' just stink an' fall away in slime instead of cleansin' out the way they should. One November you got a fine, tight house an' the next day a hurricane comes up an' blows it to hell away. So, like I say, you got to stretch some or you'll snap like a fiddle string that's tuned sharp. Right now you got the look of a man who's been wound up too tight. If I was you I'd just go off fishin' someplace."

Cameron's smile was one of brief acknowledgment. He had allowed himself to be drawn too fine with the worry and uncertainty. The problems he had encountered had been completely unfamiliar and he was not accustomed to having to wait upon the decisions of others as had been the case in Nassau.

"You may be right." He nodded. "This has been the devil's own voyage, Captain. But, I'll take your advice and roll a little with the waves. Next week I'd like to cruise some of the nearby islands. Also," he put a hand on Robert Bruce's arm, "I'll be grateful if you will take my son on as an apprentice hand and teach him the way of a ketch and what he will need to know of sailing and navigation."

Pinder winked at Robert Bruce. "We'll make a real conch out of you, lad. An islander. The boys here learn those things about the time they are ready to walk. I'd say you look as smart as any of them."

"I'll do my best to learn." Robert Bruce was eagerly grateful.

"Then we'll prepare the articles of apprentice seaman." Pinder said this gravely although his eyes were bright with amusement. "We'll sign you on the *Skipjack* here as an extra hand; without wages, of course."

Cameron leaned back on a thwart, lifted his face and allowed the sun to fall upon it. In this relaxed attitude he felt the accumulated tensions of the past weeks drain from him. Curiously enough, Pinder, Greenleaf and young Gurney no longer seemed as strangers but as agreeable companions. There was a time, he thought, for the exercising of authority and a time just to be a man among other men. He was by nature of an agreeable disposition and yet, a moment ago he had been made angry by the easy informality when anything more would have been pretentious nonsense.

The chowder was bubbling softly. The only motion a slight rocking of the ketch. He turned to look over the side and into the clear water. As Greenleaf tossed small pieces of unwanted conch overboard there was a swarming of large and small fish from the bottom. The gulls screamed their frenzied hunger, diving and contesting with the fish and among themselves for the morsels.

From his inside coat pocket Cameron took a case of fine Russian leather. In it were half a dozen of the Havana cigars which had been a present from George Renevant. He offered them now to Pinder and the crew. Gurney picked up a piece of burning charcoal with tongs and passed it around until the tobacco was alight.

Pinder drew upon the cigar, tasting the richness of it. He studied Cameron through the light haze of smoke.

"You're some different than I expected." The admission came casually. "I heard back there in Nassau you were an all-time hell raiser for sure."

"I can be difficult, Captain Pinder," Cameron admitted. "But, it is not my nature. I was embarked upon a sea of unfamiliar troubles. I was taught a great respect for order. I did not find it in Nassau. Disorder disturbs me. You'll have to admit you islanders take a little knowing. I am accustomed to meeting each day with a plan and carrying it out. In Nassau the fashion seems to be to let things go and see what happens." He sniffed appreciatively. "Your chowder smells good."

"When it's ready you can sample it an' if you'd like to stay aboard we can cook up some fish and corn mush. In the meantime"—he rose and then stopped to enter the small cabin, returning with a gallon, wicker-covered demijohn—"this is the last of the rum out of a Spanisher that piled on a reef off Booby Rocks. We salvaged most of the cargo before the Crown's man heard about it an' came a-runnin'. It's good rum. Help yourself."

As though it were the most natural thing in the world for him to be doing, Ronald Cameron, Esq., swung the jug across his arm and allowed the rich, brown liquid to trickle down his throat. Then he wiped the back of his hand across his mouth and handed the jug to Greenleaf. For the first time since he had left Cameron Hall he felt completely at ease. There was a warm, natural friendliness about these men. They were independent, self-sufficient. They were here, working for him, because the sea was their life, but he understood they would quit if they found employment too arduous or his manner overbearing. As Pinder had said, to survive you must be able to run a little before the wind. This, he knew, would not be easy, for he was accustomed to complete authority and unquestioning obedience. In these matters, he told himself, I will have to yield in a measure. But I will try.

ᴇᵍ VI ᵍᵉ

THE DAYS were woven into weeks and the weeks into months while the plantation on Great Exuma began to take a shape and substance beneath the many hands of the men, women and children who worked long hours upon the land.

From the time of first being put ashore they had not been entirely without communication with Nassau. A small, interisland schooner, the *Traveler,* put in at Exuma harbor about every six weeks and brought with it the mail, some periodicals and newspapers from England and the mainland, together with such supplies as had been ordered on its previous trip. Also, the ketch made it possible to visit the adjacent islands so there had been some small contact with the world beyond these shores.

As a result of Cameron's early and urgent request and Sir Henry's intervention with His Excellency, a Royal Surveyor and his party had come down and marked off the boundaries of the Cameron grant. It stretched along the lee shore and then inland in a great rectangle of acres which, when cleared and planted, would not compare unfavorably with the plantation on the Ashley. When the survey had been completed and trails cut, Cameron could take one of the saddle horses and ride his land. No matter that it was wild, overgrown and densely forested now. Out of it he would bring what he wanted and when the *Ranger* returned with the manor bricks he would start building.

First, though, there had been the felling of the land; the cutting, piling and burning of the brush and the defining of the fields. When this had been done, certain sections were immediately planted in the prolific Guinea corn, cowpeas, yams, tomatoes, beans and Indian corn. For these things were the staples of the slaves' diet as well as their own. Here and there, as a test, Cameron had put out one-two cotton; small, isolated patches. He was anxious to test the yielding qualities of the soil. When

[69]

he rode, as he often did, through the mother-of-pearl sunsets upon his land he could look upon it and say this is good. It is a good thing which I have done and am doing.

On a small bluff overlooking the sea the site for the manor had been laid out. Trees had been cut, the timber sawed by gangs into acceptable lumber which was stacked for drying. There was little more that could be accomplished here now until the actual construction was ready to start. For that, Cameron knew he would need carpenters, masons and artisans. Such craftsmen would have to be recruited in Nassau or among some of the settlers on the Out Islands who possessed such skills.

The slaves, with the few supervising whites, had been welded into a tight, self-sufficient community. According to their natures the sows had farrowed, a brood mare was with colt, the chickens, purchased on Eluthera, laid their fertile eggs with the resulting chicks. Life was reaching out from a dozen sources. From Pinder and Greenleaf some of the more intelligent slaves had been taught the art of knitting the heavy twine nets, the seines in which quantities of fish could be taken at one time when dragged through the shallow waters off the beach. There were almost a hundred persons to feed three times a day and their principal diet came from the sea. This was a never-ending task at which everyone worked.

Robert Bruce and Tom Gurney had struck up what to Cameron seemed an almost wordless companionship. Watching them together sometimes he wondered how they managed to communicate, for they rarely spoke. It was a silent communion but friendship they certainly had, inarticulate though it might be. Robert Bruce all but lived aboard the ketch now. He slept with the others on the deck or within the small cabin. He took his meals with them save at eveningtime, when he came ashore to have dinner with his father. At such times he was bursting with small bits of information as to the ways of the sea and the islands surrounding them. He was eager to learn about everything which touched their lives and absorbed information as a sponge soaks up water.

From Pinder and Greenleaf the boy had drawn much lore and knowledge of the Bahamas. He had proved himself a willing, if sometimes clumsy, hand on the ketch. True to his word Pinder had taken the job of instructing him seriously and they began with the rigging of all small sailing vessels, the rudiments of sailing and navigation. Actually, when at sea, the captain rarely had need to consult his compass. He took his bearings from the color of the water around him and never missed the landfall he wanted. From the long, shirtless days in the sun Robert Bruce had been tanned to the color of fine Cordovan leather. There was a new maturity in his body, manner and speech. He was filling out with the promise of becoming a man as powerful in frame as his father. Watching, listening and talking with his son, Cameron was filled with a rare pride. When the time came, Robert Bruce would be man enough to take charge of this island plantation. Cameron did not think it at all strange that his son now frequently used the plural *we* in talking about their land. He would say, "When we build the house, Father." There was still a quiet deference in his manner toward the man but it sprang from respect rather than from an awareness of authority.

They had visitors, for word of their settlement had been passed through the other inhabited Out Islands. There were two families, the Drakes and the Fergusons, on the far tip of Great Exuma. They made the trip down by boat because there were no roads to follow. They came out of curiosity and stayed to wonder at the size and ambition of the Cameron project, for they held only modest grants and were content to work them to their immediate needs. Ferguson grew some cotton and castor bean plants. He pressed the oil from the latter and sold it in Nassau along with the few bales his land yielded. He also was breeding horses; tough, small animals for plowing and heavy work. Cameron arranged with him to purchase three teams, for he could not put his own fine-blooded animals to the plow without breaking them entirely.

They also had visits from families on Eleuthera and St. George's Cay, who brought with them, as gifts, stems of the sweet, cultivated bananas, oranges and lemons and promised to send or bring seedlings for Cameron's planting. They were quiet, soft-spoken people for they lived much alone and within themselves. Their excursions to Great Exuma were in the nature of holidays. For these occasions Cameron always killed a sheep and it was set to roasting over an open pit fire for a midday picnic. Drake grew a small amount of cane which he converted into a rough brown sugar and a heavy rum. Now and then he would bring down with him a jug and this was added to the party. It was a curiously peaceful world in which these people lived and their only contact with the outside came through the few English missionaries who traveled a regular circuit through the Out Islands and set up small and rival churches where they could. Cameron was always the gracious host and he regretted only that he as yet had no place for entertaining such visitors, as had been the custom in Carolina where the manor was frequently filled with guests who came to stay for weeks at a time. However, he did the best he could under the circumstances and the visitors always left happy and with invitations to the Camerons to make the trip to their own islands. These were pleasant interludes in the unvarying routine of all their lives and served to fill man's need for contact with his fellow beings, for these could indeed be strands of loneliness.

The animals Cameron had brought with him thrived on the forage which was so abundant. There was a plentiful and natural supply of what the islanders called Guinea grass. The cattle and sheep were allowed to range freely, for there was no real way they could be lost through straying too far. There was no reason to build fences although the saddle horses were kept in a corral and their exercising was part of Robert Bruce's duty. In exchange for what he had learned from Gurney, Robert Bruce taught young Tom to ride and they raced the animals along the long, smooth stretch of beach daily.

The stock was healthy and contented. In time there would be a fine herd of cattle, sufficient for export to Nassau. The flock of sheep would expand and the wool could be taken for carding and spinning by the slave women. In his mind he could see the plantation as a completely self-sufficient fief. He waited impatiently now for the *Ranger* and the masonry. Not until his house stood upon the knoll as he visualized it would he have the feeling of permanency, of having thrust his roots deeply into this soil.

Because time was a burden on his hands and there was really nothing which could not be taken care of by Grayson, Wells and Spithead, Cameron cruised in the ketch, exploring the entire length of the Exuma cays which stretched for almost ninety miles from Bacon Cay in the north to Great and Little Exuma. He marked with surprise how varied was the topography of the islands. Some were low and barren, offering no possible subsistence for settling. Others had rolling hills and were densely covered with vegetation. Most of them had fine, sheltered anchorages. As he became more familiar with the islands Cameron unconsciously fell beneath their spell. It was a world of silent beauty. The sea was incredibly varied in its coloring and at sunrise and sunset the sky became one enormous, flaming opal beneath which a man could only stand in quiet, breathless wonder. There was such a great and peaceful enchantment about the islands that he no longer wondered at the manner of the natives. It was impossible to be in a hurry over anything here, for one day was so much like another. Time ceased to have any real significance.

Lying on his cot at night Cameron frequently caught his thoughts straying back to the Hall on the Ashley River. That, also, had been the good life. He had never expected to know another. Now that it was behind him, though, he did not regret his decision. This was his own, limited kingdom. Thinking of the years which were ahead he could see only contentment and prosperity for him and those who would come after. He needed only his home, finished and ready, furnished as it had been in Carolina, to make this dream complete. In time Robert Bruce would marry; a girl of good family from Nassau, or perhaps even England. He was not sure about this. England seemed so remote but it would do the boy no harm to make a visit when he was older. Perhaps there would be a daughter of some squire from Virginia, Georgia or Carolina. There was no haste. In time a suitable young lady would be found and the succession completed through many children. Caroline, of course, would also marry but this would not be the same as Robert Bruce's wedding. Caroline's children would bear a different name. Here there must always be a Cameron and that could come only through Robert Bruce. In the boy all of his ambitions lay.

In the garden of the house in Nassau, Caroline idly tossed a ball for the puppy which had been a present from young Captain Birch. In the scattered shade of a banyan tree Martha worked at the useless embroidery continually occupying her time. She found the waiting here almost unendurably dull. They had practically no social life. A few formal calls had been made. They attended church regularly and twice had been invited to the Governor's residence for tea. But Martha felt alien. She could not adjust herself to this insular way of living. She longed for the comfortable home she had known in Carolina. The friends she had made from childhood; the visits back and forth between the scattered plantations which took weeks of planning. Here there was nothing. Captain Birch called frequently. He seemed fascinated by Caroline's precocity, her exuberance and adaptability. He accorded Martha the respect which was due age and since Martha didn't feel at all aged this annoyed her and she was sometimes short of temper with him when he was overly solicitous as to her health and well-being.

Caroline sat cross-legged on a grass mat, leaned back on her arms and spoke to the sky.

"I am going to marry Captain Birch."

Martha drew a thread. "Today?"

"Of course not today." She jumped up and threw out her arms in a world-embracing gesture. "I think it will be when I am seventeen. He will be twenty-eight then, which is a good age for a husband, don't you think?"

"I'm sure I don't know." Martha half smiled. "Have you asked for his hand yet?"

"Of course not." Caroline studied her aunt. "You don't take me very seriously, do you?"

"I'm not quite certain how to take you, Mistress Bahama." This was the truth. Caroline frequently astonished her. "But I suspect if you have determined to marry Captain Birch, you will. In many ways you are as stubborn as your father. You are becoming something quite outside my experience."

Martha Cameron was willing to admit Caroline was a problem. The girl seemed completely without a maidenly reserve or any sense of the proprieties. She was as natural and unaffected as the puppy at her feet. In some mysterious manner she had collected a large and varied acquaintance in Nassau, and particularly, along the waterfont and in the market. The people there seemed to delight her unconventional nature. Despite Martha's remonstrances, she would call from their carriage during an afternoon drive. She hailed black and white alike by their first names and in return was flashed bright smiles of greeting or the lifting of a battered palm hat in salutation.

"How in the world do you know all of these people?" Martha asked the question one day in honest and confused bewilderment.

"Oh, I usually walk down here in the afternoons when you are taking a nap." Caroline was unperturbed. "The people talk with me and I talk with them. It isn't difficult. They're very friendly and curious. I even watched a slave auction at Vendue House. The men were bidding for a mulatto wench. It was a spirited thing and they grew quite angry with each other. I don't know why. She looked shiftless and not a very good worker."

Listening, Martha was startled to recognize the unmistakably mocking note of wisdom in her niece's voice. How in the world, she wondered, could the child know about such things? But then, as she frequently was reminded, a girl of fourteen is no longer a child.

"I can see I'll have to give up my afternoon nap. A slave market is hardly the place for you to be loitering."

"I don't loiter. That word has an odd sound, hasn't it? Loiter." She tested it on her tongue. "It sounds like thick syrup pouring."

"Your father would be outraged if he knew what you had been doing." Martha didn't really believe this but she had to say something.

"No he wouldn't." Caroline was emphatic. "He might be angry but he wouldn't be outraged. Father is afraid of me. I don't mean afraid afraid. I guess puzzled is a better word. Am I very much like my mother, Aunt Martha? I think he thinks so. That is what disturbs him."

"In many ways you are like her." Martha's thoughts went back to the bright, laughing, flashing girl who had married Ronald Cameron. "You have her beauty and her independence. She was thought to be extremely unconventional. I don't think Ronald ever became reconciled to this."

"Did she make Father unhappy?" The question was asked with a slight frown.

"I think they were the happiest couple I have ever known. Ronald was different then, also. With her he was always laughing and joking. It was as though he had a secret star in his pocket. When she died, much of his laughter died with her."

"I wish I had known her."

"When you are a little older look in the mirror. You will see her reflection."

There was a distant tinkling of a bell at the walled gate and a few moments later one of the house girls came to announce Captain Birch.

The young officer strode across the lawn to where they sat, with the jaunty air of a man who knows an entertaining secret. Watching him Martha thought he must be continually amused by the official antics in this small world of his on the island of New Providence. His tongue seemed always in his cheek and he regarded everything with a quizzical air of interest.

"Your servant, ma'am and Mistress Cameron." He made a correctly formal bow but his eyes were bright. "I deliver a message from Sir Gerald and Lady Heath. It is a matter which could have been intrusted to a servant but I preferred to do it in person since such social activity is rare. The Governor is planning a beach picnic and requests your presence."

"Sit down, Captain." Martha indicated a chair and considered Captain Birch in a new light, reflecting upon Caroline's declaration of intentions. "Will you have some tea or rum punch?"

"Neither, thank you." He spread the tails of his uniform coat and took the indicated place.

"Did you know, Captain Birch," Martha spoke slowly, "my niece plans to marry you?"

"You think that embarrasses me but it doesn't." Caroline was undisturbed. "When the time came I would have told him myself."

"This comes as something of a surprise, Mistress Bahama. I am, of course, honored."

"I wouldn't take Caroline's decisions lightly, Captain." Martha enjoyed watching him.

"Oh, I don't!" He dismissed the idea at once. "Over these months I have come to know Mistress Cameron very well. I would never take her lightly."

"My name is Bahama. Bahama Cameron." She was completely unruffled by the exchange. "You know it quite well and, besides, you are not so old or handsome you can afford to be patronizing."

"That is what I like about her," Birch mused aloud as though Caroline wasn't there. "She is direct. I live in a world of official circumlocution where one never says what one means. This is a breath of fresh

[75]

wind. Also, she is a remarkably well-informed young lady with a wit and ready tongue I find completely surprising."

"You make me tired." Caroline feathered a yawn with her fingertips. "If you aren't more careful I may not marry you at all."

"The prospect leaves me desolate." He winked broadly at her and then turned inquiringly to Martha. "May I tell His Excellency you will honor us at the fete next Saturday?"

"I don't know what to say." Martha was doubtful. Actually, she had retired within herself so much these past few years that the prospect of meeting and having to talk for an entire afternoon with strangers was frightening. "Must we decide today?"

"Of course we'll go, Aunt Martha. You are always saying how little there is to do here in Nassau with Father and Robert Bruce away."

Martha sighed. "I do wish," there was a slightly complaining note in her voice, "Ronald hadn't been so impetuous; bundling us all here to these islands while he decides where and when to build a house. We would have been ever so much more comfortable in Charlestown until everything was ready."

"Please say you'll come." Birch dropped his manner of inconsequential chatter. "You will enjoy it, I think. There will be a small band of native musicians. Everything will be informal, alfresco. The beach is pleasant and there will be shelters to shield you from the sun. I would consider it an honor to serve as your escort."

"Very well." Martha smiled. She disliked having to make decisions. Ronald had always done that for her. "Thank His Excellency and say we will be delighted."

Captain Birch arose and bowed again with stiff formality although there was a pleased sparkle in his glance.

"I will take my leave then." He picked up his four-cornered hat.

"I'll walk with you to the gate." Caroline fell in at his side. She did this as though it was the most natural thing in the world for her to be doing. "Excuse me, Aunt Martha."

Martha Cameron, looking after the pair, was bewildered by Caroline's straightforward yielding to her impulses. She had an idea this wasn't at all the proper conduct for a young lady of breeding. Yet, she had always been that way. There was about her a maturity which went beyond her years. I do wish, she thought unhappily, Ronald would come back and take charge of things again. In another year the child will be more than I can cope with.

At the gate Birch halted and turned to look down into her brightly impudent face.

"You are quite a remarkable young lady, Bahama."

"I think so."

"In many ways you astonish me."

"I know. I astonish Aunt Martha, also. She keeps calling me 'child.' I am not at all a child. Fourteen, going on fifteen, is grown up even if some persons don't think so. Anyhow, I shall be ever so much wiser at seventeen."

"I await the day with impatience." He laughed softly. "Now that I have been spoken for."

"You may joke about it if you wish. It won't do you any good. I have made up my mind."

Birch did a surprising thing. With his fingertips he gently lifted her chin and gazed down into her clear eyes. The mood of easy banter had left him. He considered her seriously. This young girl had a self-possession which went far beyond anything he had ever encountered before. In many ways it was disturbing. It was impossible to think of her as being only fourteen or so, and yet, this was an indisputable fact. He shook his head, puzzled.

"You are a very lovely girl, Mistress Bahama. Don't let anything or anyone change you. However," he shook his head wonderingly, "that isn't likely. I look forward to your advancing years."

From the beach Ronald Cameron and Robert Bruce, together with the overseers and some of the slaves, had watched as the *Ranger* stood in from the open water and came to anchor within the sheltering arm of the harbor. Now Cameron was in the master's cabin. In one hand he held a softly pink brick. Then, between both hands he broke it in two easily and there was an expression of quiet misery on his face.

"This was something on which I had not counted." He seemed to be speaking to himself.

Captain Sharpe was moved by the man's obvious unhappiness. He cleared his throat.

"We have had our differences, Mr. Cameron, but do not think I am so mean of spirit as to take pleasure in this. You can see for yourself what happens. There was nought but a pile of rubble delivered to the docks in Charlestown. There were no more than a couple of hundred whole bricks and those, as you see, fall apart when pressured. It is a miracle your manor stood as long as it did."

"There are a hundred years of family history in these few bricks." Cameron replaced the pieces on the sacking in which Captain Sharpe had brought them. "I suppose it was too much to expect them to last a hundred more."

"Left standing, perhaps." Sharpe was made uncomfortable by his visitor's unhappiness. "But when prized apart and razed, they lost their collective strength."

"Having weathered so much I suppose I expected them to be indestructible."

"Sit down." Sharpe offered a chair. "Have a drink and a pipe with me." He rang a small bell to summon the cabin boy.

Cameron slumped in the seat. Unconsciously his hand strayed to the pieces of brick. With thumb and forefinger he ground a fragment to powder.

When they had a drink and the pipes alight, Sharpe took a chair opposite his guest.

"This will change your plans some, will it not?"

"Aye." Cameron nodded. "I had thought to reproduce Cameron Hall here. I will not be able to build as well as I expected."

"A house of good lumber will last a hundred years also." Sharpe drew upon his pipe. "There is no real reason for such despair, man."

"In the eye of my mind," Cameron sipped the rum, "I could see the manor rising here as it had stood on the Ashley. Everything was to be as it once was. Now," he stared blankly out of an open port, "I find only confusion."

"Come, man." Sharpe was uncomfortable in the face of such melancholy. "A house is only what you make it. Build well here with what is at hand."

"I suppose so." Cameron nodded. "It will have to be from the beginning. I cannot stick to the original plans now. Perhaps it is better than what I had in mind; a great house of brick is not really suited to these islands. I will make something more in the character of the place. That means an architect, new plans. I am not certain I can find such a man in Nassau. I may even have to send to Charlestown for him." He finished the rum and stood up, offering his hand. "Thank you for your trouble, Captain."

Together they walked to the deck and stood in quiet contemplation of the sparkling morning.

"This will be my last voyage here, Mr. Cameron." Sharpe offered his hand. "My orders now are to return to England. Perhaps," he hid a smile, "I shall get a new ship. Who knows? But I wish you well."

As he was sculled back to shore in the ketch's dinghy by Tom Gurney, Cameron tried to readjust himself to this new development. First he would have to return to Nassau. It was possible the town held a firm of architects or an individual who could draw the plans. He knew what he wanted now. No severe Georgian façade of brick but a wide, sweeping, winged and balconied house which would be open to the beauty of this place.

"How long will the trip in the ketch be to Nassau, young Tom?"

"With a fair wind we should make it well within a few days, Mr. Cameron."

"Then blow us up a wind for Nassau, Tom. I'll speak to Captain Pinder. Perhaps we can set out in the morning."

"Aye, sir. We've been a long time out of Nassau. It will be good to see the town and some people again."

The dinghy danced along the tops of the ripples. Cameron leaned back in the stern and felt the warmth creep up on his body. What a place, he thought. It inspires a man to do nothing. Life could be made too easy.

"When do the storms come to these islands, Tom?" He was thinking ahead of the building which must be done; the lumber to be cut or purchased; the manor and then the permanent slave quarters; the workmen to be engaged. What would have been simple in Carolina here assumed the proportions of Creation itself. "For how long do they last?"

"They begin in September, usually, and last through November. Sometimes we don't get them at all; they sweep around us or run out to sea before reaching the Bahamas. Other years they'll fair lift the islands from the water. A man never knows what to expect."

"The worst, Tom Gurney. Always expect the worst. You'll rarely be disappointed."

✦ VII ✦

IT HAD BEEN a year of endless delays; of frustrations and uncertainties; of labor which could not be depended upon and material late in delivery or twice lost in a wreck upon the dangerous shoals and reefs scattered the length of the cays.

Now, though, the house rose as some poised bird upon the bluff overlooking the sea. The balconied galleries extended from the central portion and seemed like outspread wings in flight. It shone in the fresh white of its paint, and the afternoon's sun fired the glass in its windows until the structure seemed to blaze with light.

Many times during the interminable months Cameron had occasion to reflect upon the warning Captain Sharpe had uttered so prophetically that night in Charlestown. Every nail, each gallon of paint, pipe, locks, hinges for doors and cabinets had to be imported, for these things were stocked only in limited quantities in Nassau. They came from the States, from the mainland, or direct from England in slow merchant ships. The drain upon his financial resources had been appalling and there had been many times when he bleakly wondered if there were sufficient pounds in his London accounts to see the end of this project. Throughout all the harassments of building, the productive work of the plantation had to go on without interruption, for there were mouths to feed and cash to be made through the sale of cotton and the hardwood shipped to Nassau.

Unless they were kept at work the slaves were inclined to grow restive. They sulked or complained of imaginary illnesses. Also, they had seen black men who now walked in freedom. On Watlings Island and at the far tip of Great Exuma there were properties which had been abandoned by their owners. The families had returned to England and such of their slaves who could not be sold were freed. These blacks, so abruptly emancipated, moved into the houses of their former masters but they were too indolent to keep them in repair. And so, the plantation homes decayed. The wind whimpered through broken windows, rain spilled upon the floors, porches and doorframes sagged, roofs decayed in a spectacle of disintegration. The former slaves grew only enough to sustain themselves, but they walked with a proud dignity now and this was not lost upon the Cameron Negroes with whom contact was sometimes made. There were small cells of rebellion and Cameron had reluctantly consented to the lash, for fear was the only thing which could preserve order. Fear and work. The combination quieted the rebellious spirits and the huge fields were now white with the first cotton crop and from sunup to sundown the slaves moved down the long rows dragging tubular sacks behind them. These were fastened at the waist and the hands moved back and forth, plucking the bolls, thrusting them into bags which fattened and trailed like gorged gray serpents as the pickers moved. At least there would be a crop for baling and shipping.

Ronald Cameron had driven himself and everyone about him, for as the delays and obstacles mounted he began to regard the plantation as a personal adversary intent upon destroying him. He referred to the grant now as "It" and gave his acres a malignant personality to be subdued through the sheer force of his will and drive. He became a man short of temper, given to sudden rages. The labor he had been able to hire for the construction of the manor had been of the most uncertain quality. A few were skilled carpenters and masons from Nassau who had been induced to work only upon the promise of exorbitant wages. Others of small ability had to be recruited from the settlers on adjacent Out Islands. All took the most leisurely attitude toward their labors. They frequently left for days at a time to go back to their homes. Others grew discontented and without a word of explanation or regret packed up their tools and returned to Nassau, from which place they had to be rehired at higher wages and the promise of a shorter workweek. There was a small but constant traffic between the islands in the little sloops. Men came, worked for a few days and then disappeared. If they returned at all it was with the casual explanation they had gone fishing or home for a rest. Against this indifferent attitude Cameron had railed, stormed and cursed until even Grayson, the most loyal and sympathetic of his overseers, had threatened to quit and go back to Charlestown. Once the man had even been bold enough to suggest his employer abandon the entire venture.

"You'll bankrupt yourself, Mr. Cameron." They had been sitting at dusk upon a pile of stacked lumber with, as yet, only the skeleton of the manor rising behind them. "If that doesn't happen you'll grow so weary of this place you'll curse the day you put your feet upon the island. This is a fair lonely place."

"You may draw your wages and leave whenever you like." Cameron's face had darkened with anger.

"Come, man." Grayson adopted what, for him, was an unusual attitude of familiarity. "I would not leave you now but we both know what you are in for. I have been too long in your employ not to speak honestly."

"Aye," Cameron agreed dourly. "So, don't talk to me of failure. Can't you see there is no turning back now? Every pound I have is being staked on this plantation. I must succeed in it for there is no alternative. I can see what you will not look for—a prosperous operation, a fine trade with England through Nassau. I'll grow cotton here in such quantities and of such quality as these islands have never seen. I will have my family gathered under our own roof again with my son growing up to take his place and, eventually, mine."

Cameron sucked upon a dry pipe. As an experiment he had set out some tobacco in a small patch but it did not grow well. He thought it must be because they were too near the sea and the salt air had an unhealthy effect upon the plants.

"I know." Cameron seemed to be talking to himself. "This has been a bad year or more for us all; a time to try our patience. It is, as you said, a fair lonely place where a man is without friends or companionship. Do you not believe I have thought many times of how it would be to stretch my legs beneath a tavern table and enjoy a pipe and a bowl, with later a wench to tumble in a featherbed? Good God, man! Do you suppose I have enjoyed this exile? I have endured it because I must and because once I have set my mind to a thing it is not in my nature to give up easily." He made an effort to control himself. "Things have not gone too badly considering what we have had to surmount."

Grayson thought they could have hardly gone worse without driving them all mad. He held his tongue.

"We will ship near a hundred bales of cotton this year. The stock flourishes. The slaves have been difficult at times but not unmanageable. All of this is more than we had a right to expect in the beginning. A man must have his dream, Grayson. This is mine."

"I know, sir. But it is not reasonable to expect other men to share it. I, for one, miss the Carolina. I cannot fill my days with nothing but work and my nights with a nigrah girl. I should like to have a wife and start raising a family, but how do I ask a woman to share this isolation? I will stay with you for another planting and then I will go home. Wells feels the same way. These islands are not for us. Only Spithead," he smiled, "is satisfied and that is because he has been sparking Ferguson's daughter at the other end of the island. He seems content enough. In time, as he grows a little older, he will prove a good man for you."

Cameron made no effort to hide his disappointment. "If you must go, then that is the way it will have to be. I am not unmindful of your long and faithful service. But a Cameron plantation without a Grayson on it will not be the same."

The conversation had taken place months ago and was never referred to again. Now, what many times had seemed impossible had become a reality. The main house was finished. Behind it, half a mile away, the slave quarters had been set up; long rows of boxlike cabins, whitewashed inside and out. They had replaced the primitive thatched huts. The first of the household furnishings had been brought from Nassau in a specially chartered schooner. The rest would follow and with it Martha, Caroline and the household servants. It was a time of tremendous satisfaction.

On the ketch Cameron stood with Robert Bruce and watched the shoreline recede. They were Nassau bound. There rose the manor. Behind it, stretching for acres, the cotton was full white.

"Look at it well, lad." Cameron spoke softly. "In the years to come you will remember how it looked this day."

Robert Bruce stood almost as tall as his father as they balanced themselves, shoulder to shoulder, against the rolling of the boat.

"I was thinking, Father," he spoke thoughtfully, "once in Nassau we can let Captain Pinder and Mr. Greenleaf go. I can handle the ketch now with the help of Tom Gurney. Once Aunt Martha and Caroline are with us we will not use it much save for trips between the islands here. We are going to be much alone, are we not?"

"Aye," Cameron agreed. He turned to regard his son for a moment. "Would you think it strange if I married again, Robert Bruce? I suspect you are too young to have a knowledge of such things but a man is not really complete without a woman. Although the memory of your mother makes me hard to satisfy. It is a pity she could not have lived to see you and your sister. There is a pride in me for you, lad. Tell me. How would you feel about a stepmother?"

"If she would make you happy, Father, then I would feel as you would want me to feel." He grinned. "Maybe I should also be thinking of a wife. I shall be twenty in a year. Is that too young, do you think?"

"The years have gone so quickly, I forget sometimes you are almost a man. I suppose when you feel the need of a wife, then you are old enough to have one." He chuckled. "But where do we look for wives, you and I, Robert Bruce? Here among the islands there are families of quality or," he laughed again, "should we go to Charlestown and insert an advertisement in the newspaper? 'Wanted. Two wives for a couple of Out Islanders. Father and son.'"

"I think I'll wait awhile." Robert Bruce smiled at his father's fanciful turn of mind. "I have barely learned to handle this boat in heavy weather. I suspect a wife would offer more difficulties than I have knowledge for."

The wind was freshening now and the ketch heeled jauntily under filled sails and the bow thrust against the water with a hissing sound. Looking aft at the island as it receded—the fringe of palms like a green necklace along the stark, white beach, the frothy creaming of the waves as they broke upon a reef—Cameron was again struck by the soft, compelling beauty of these seas. They induced a man to complacency for it seemed incredible that here nature could prove to be an adversary of strength. From what quarter could misfortune come when this small portion of the world was so blessed by such an agreeable climate and situation?

He took a deep breath of satisfaction and steadied himself against the craft's rolling motion. What he had accomplished so far was only the beginning but he was undismayed by what the future might hold. Here, on Great Exuma, he would build as well as any Cameron before him. There was a market for his cotton and cane. It was up to him to see that the land produced it in quantities. He would diversify his crops. On a section of the acres he was already experimenting with sisal, from whose tough fibers cordage could be spun. He would send to the island of Cuba for the pineapple plants. The fruit would be an expensive novelty in England if he could ship it there. Also, the fruits of lime, lemons, oranges and banana could be raised in quantities. Everything lay at hand. The Camerons needed only to grasp it firmly.

Nassau drowsed peacefully in the warm sun. Nothing disturbed the unhurried tempo of life which had adjusted itself to a tropical languor. It was true there had been a marked increase in trade during the past year but even this was carried on in a most leisurely manner. The island of New Providence was becoming an important way stop in the West Indian trade. British, French, Dutch, Spanish and American merchantmen frequently lay at anchor at the same time within the harbor.

The merchant trade of Nassau expanded as the maritime traffic increased. Along the waterfront there were new buildings; commission houses, shops, taverns, drinking and eating places. Warehouses went up on sturdy docks. Commission merchants did a brisk business in sponges, brasiletto wood, cotton and cane. To supply the ships, the sloops of the Out Islanders brought a steady flow of fresh vegetables and fowl to the market. During the day the waterfront was given over to business. At night it was a noisy sector of roistering sailors. There were large establishments and small cribs where patient girls waited. Musicians, with their gourds and stringed instruments, traveled from tavern to tavern. There were bloody fights, the quick flashing of knives, arguments which were settled with fists, brass knuckles or cudgels. No respectable person ventured into the district after sundown.

Up from the shoreline new homes were being built on spacious grounds. There was a small but steady increase in the population. Loyalist families, whose fortunes were safely invested in England, found Nassau a pleasant haven. These were the landed gentry from the American colonies. They brought with them an expansive way of life. Because of well-paying investments in the mother country they had no need to work the land here. The isolation of the Out Islands offered no attraction. They wanted only the security and climatic comfort which the island afforded. The pattern of life was congenial and familiar. Here there was no rude talk of democracy; no nonsense of one man being the equal of another. The distinctions of class were rigid and they kept them so. The society they formed was closely knit and into it no tradesman or outsider could hope to intrude. Under their direction a race track was laid out and here they ran their horses for high stakes, watching the contests from their carriages and later taking their refreshments from well-filled hampers stocked with food and wine.

Many of the families had secretly interested themselves in the flourishing slave trade. They supplied the money for the crews and ships which brought the miserable cargoes from the Guinea Coast. It was the fashion to pretend a fastidious horror over the trade of selling the black men and women. From the security of their homes they complained of the stench whenever a slaver was anchored offshore. But they smugly banked their profits and urged the captains to faster runs. Auctions at Vendue House were turned into a social event. Well-dressed ladies and gentlemen sat in their open rigs to watch and listen to the bidding, and occasionally bought a likely-looking buck or wench.

Coming, as they did, from the plantation country of Virginia, Georgia and Carolina, most of the families were linked by marriage or claimed a distant kinship. They associated only with each other and made no effort at contact beyond their own tight circle. There was a constant visiting back and forth with balls and outdoor fetes beneath the palms to provide amusement. Among them Cameron had friends and even a few relatives, but during this visit to Nassau he made no effort to renew old ties.

He stood at the door of a warehouse now and watched as the last few loads of his household furnishings were stacked onto carts, barrows and wagons for loading. A schooner, the *Lark,* had been chartered to take everything to Great Exuma.

As a concession to the stinging rays of the sun he wore a broad-brimmed hat of plaited palm leaf. In his conservative dress this gave him an oddly rakish appearance of which he was not unaware. It pleased him a little to realize this was so. Feet apart, hands thrust into breeches pockets, he followed the procession of drays with his eyes. Behind him the warehouse owner was locking the doors.

"You'll be taking your family with you this time, will you not, Mr. Cameron?" The man pocketed the key and joined him. "How do you find Great Exuma?"

"In the words of my overseer 'a fair lonely place,' but it will not be that way any longer. I am glad to have everything settled and I thank you for the good care which you have taken of my effects."

"It has been a pleasure to be of service, sir." The warehouse factor lifted his cap.

Walking from the building, across the road of rutted sand, Cameron thought of the multitude of small things demanding his attention before he could leave Nassau. His musings were interrupted by a voice.

"Mr. Cameron."

He glanced up quickly. An open carriage had halted a few paces away. In it, shading herself with a small parasol, Lady Heath bent slightly forward. A gloved hand was partly lifted in greeting.

"Lady Heath." He swept the palm hat from his head and bowed. His glance took in each detail of her slender beauty. "You surprise me. I did not know it was the custom for ladies to be abroad in the day's heat."

"I do not follow custom." She extended her hand to him with a spontaneous gesture. "I make it." The laughter in her eyes faded. "That is not true," she amended unhappily, "for I lead a most miserably conventional life. Come," she made a motion to a place beside her, "drive with me for a little while. I am trying to escape from boredom."

Cameron hesitated. This was a deliberate breach of custom and it would not go unnoticed. A lady, more, a married woman and the Governor's wife, did not ride unaccompanied with a gentleman.

"You hesitate," she chided gently.

"Only for your sake, madame."

"I have no interest in what people may say or think."

"Very well." He stepped into the carriage and seated himself. "Since you feel that way I see no reason to deny myself the pleasure of your company."

She gave an order to the coachman and the light rig moved along the road. As they traveled he was aware of the curious stares directed at them.

"Are you uncomfortable, Mr. Cameron?"

"Not past the point of endurance, Lady Heath."

"I am weary of being Lady Heath. You must have guessed it. Call me Sabrina." She tilted the parasol at an angle to provide a little shade for them both. "Tell me. How is your island paradise?"

"Far from a paradise as yet although, given time, it may turn into just that."

"But you are still without an Eve?"

"I said it was far from perfect, ma'am."

The carriage rolled silently along the bay-front street. There were few persons abroad at this time of day. A knot of lounging seamen rocked unsteadily at a tavern door and they followed the vehicle's progress and its feminine occupant with hungry eyes. She made a demurely compelling picture beneath the sunshade of colored silk. Where the buildings thinned out to an occasional shack the road took a winding turn. Here it was little more than lightly defined wheel tracks, splattered with coins of shade from the overhanging trees. A cooling breeze on the ridge touched their faces. Sabrina Heath made no effort at conversation. Her face in profile was one of classical delicacy.

"How is His Excellency?" Cameron asked the question, not out of any genuine concern for Sir Gerald's health, but only because he was uncomfortable in the silence. "I had intended to call and pay my respects. On my last visit to Nassau I was so occupied with my personal affairs I neglected to perform the courtesy."

"Gerald is on one of his tiresome inspection trips to one of the Out Islands. They inflate his ego so he endures the discomfort." She tapped the driver's shoulder with the parasol's tip. "Take the road which leads along the beach, Joshua." She turned to Cameron. "It is a pleasant drive. I am kidnapping you, sir."

"You find me a willing captive, ma'am. Although, I am afraid it may be your reputation rather than my freedom which is at stake."

A husky laughter burbled in her throat and she eyed him with mischievous humor.

"For a Scot you turn a pretty phrase, Mr. Cameron. I have always believed the Scots to be men of dour disposition and without humor. A fig for my reputation. You forget I am Caesar's wife and can do no wrong."

"I have always doubted that was Caesar's opinion." He was stimulated by her piquancy and the novelty of this light exchange with a gentlewoman.

She leaned her head back against the cushion, turning her face a little to study his features. "I have thought of you often, Ronald Cameron. I have wondered a little about it, for you are not, you must admit, the dashing gallant who sweeps a woman off her feet. I doubt you have ever done an impetuous thing in your life and yet, there is an attraction. I will not deny it. Perhaps it is the sheer vigor and strength of a stallion. I cannot imagine you importuning a woman for her favor. I think that is what appeals to me."

"You play a little dangerously with words, Lady Heath."

"Please." She touched his hand lightly. "No more Lady Heath. Let it be Sabrina. You disrobe me with your glance yet call me Lady Heath. The combination is a little preposterous. Let it be one thing or another."

"Very well. No man could be insensible to your beauty so let us be honest with each other. How and why this is happening between us I cannot say. But I find you a damned provocative woman. You are a lady with the instincts of a wench. It is an irresistible combination. I have been long without that which your manner and words suggest. That you are the Governor's wife is of no importance, for I hold him in no high regard and my conscience would not bother me."

"La!" She laughed softly and her eyes were bright with amusement. "You are an outspoken man. That, also, I believe is in the nature of a Highlander." Her hand slid beneath his arm and he felt the pressure of her fingers on his wrist. "Let me say I, also, am without scruples. I despise my husband and endure him because I have no choice."

"You do not cast me in an attractive role; as an instrument of your spleen."

"I did not mean that." She was surprisingly contrite. She sighed gently. "We could make a pair, you and I, Ronald Cameron. I would complement your natural conservatism. Given the chance we might be as free and wild as the wind which blows over your island of Exuma at the time of the equinox."

"I have heard it leaves destruction in its path." He smiled down at the petal-like face as it rested, cheek upon the cushion.

"But that is no concern of the wind. Is it?"

The road they traveled, having wound along the slight ridge, began a gradual descent toward the ocean. The beach there lay clean and deserted. The palms were heavily massed like a huge screen at the high-water mark. Pieces of bleached driftwood lay, half-buried bones in the sand. Sabrina again touched the coachman's shoulder.

"We will walk for a while. Wait for us here."

Cameron felt no surprise. What was happening was astonishing, yet by her very casualness she seemed to make it nothing more than a conventional stroll along the strand. This woman, this girl—for she was little more than that—was as direct as a man in her desires. There was no false coquetting, no pretense, no modest reluctance. He thought, God in Heaven. Am I to tumble the Governor's wife on the beach like some servant girl? He stepped from the carriage and extended a hand to assist her in alighting. She took his fingertips with a quick smile.

"It does not bother you that the slave may talk?"

The coachman's features were as impassive as a carved mask. He stared straight ahead, oblivious of their presence and actions.

She dropped lightly to the ground and stood beside Cameron. For a moment their bodies touched. He could feel the warmth of her thigh against his leg. Neither moved to break the spell but her breath came in a short gasp. Finally, and with seeming difficulty, she spoke.

"The slaves talk only among themselves and that has no more meaning than the chattering of monkeys."

She gathered the folds of her skirt in one hand and they picked their way over the scattered fronds which crackled and broke beneath their weight. With her arm linked with his she seemed to lead him and he could not help but wonder with what man or men she had walked this way before. Yards down the beach a palm tree lay uprooted, torn from the earth by a storm. Within its shelter there was a little clearing in the dense vegetation. It was secluded from all curious eyes.

"This will not be easily undone, Sabrina." He fought to keep his voice steady.

"I have no intention it should be."

She dropped her parasol and turned suddenly, beseechingly. Then, with a whimpering cry, she was in his arms. The strength of passion in one who appeared so delicately formed astonished him.

"Take me," she whispered fiercely and her fingers dug at his neck. "This could have happened the first night we met. I felt it between us. It is something I can't explain."

There, in the sand and warm shade with only the wheeling seabirds to look on, they made love. It was savage, primitive and abandoned. All of the loneliness which had been locked within Cameron for years welled and overflowed into this woman. He possessed her with a violent hunger he had not believed possible, and she was, by turns, wildly incoherent and murmuringly tender.

Later, she lay with her body half curled and her head in his lap. Her hair had become loosened and fell in a shimmering cascade which half shielded her face. He brushed it back and his fingertips tenderly caressed her cheek. Her breath came softly, evenly, and her lips were parted in a smile of contentment. The only sound was that of the small waves breaking upon the beach and the light wind as it rustled through the high palms.

"Ronald."

"Yes."

She shook her head. "I only wanted to speak your name, my lover." She sighed deeply, gratefully. "You are the man I knew you would be."

"And you are a woman such as I have never known."

"Aye!" She mimicked the exclamation he so often used. "We are a pair. I had not believed such madness possible. There was a fury. It was a thing to be done to the wild skirling of pipes. There is an unsuspected violence in you, Cameron. It strikes a responsive chord."

"What happened will not easily be forgotten."

"I do not intend it should be." She sat up and pushed back her hair, binding it into a knot at the nape of her neck. "Unless," the words were barely audible, "you think me a complete wanton and not to be trusted with any man, take me with you when you go back to your island. I could make you happy. It is my chance, my only chance for happiness and it may not come again."

"I would take you if I could." His hands rested on her shoulders. "You know it is impossible. You are married; the wife of the Governor. Even on the Out Islands the scandal would reach and touch you."

"Am I to be left here, then?" She pleaded with her eyes. "To see you only on those rare occasions when you come to Nassau? Whatever you may believe, I have not given myself to you lightly. There have been other times, other men. I will not cheapen what I now feel by denying this. But what happened was of no consequence beyond the moment. This has not been true with you."

"I believe you but it does not change the situation."

"Do not decide now, here. Think upon it. Tonight. There is a side gate at the south end of the garden. It will be unlocked. Come to me. I will be waiting."

"I will try." Even as he spoke the words Cameron knew they were false. This was a hopeless affair. "I will come if I can."

She was not misled. "That means you will not. No," she shook her head quickly, "don't protest. Let there be honesty between us."

Sunlight flooded the dining room. It poured in broad shafts through the windows. Martha Cameron toyed with her breakfast. Now and then she glanced down the length of the table to where her brother ate with a robust appetite. She envied him. He was bedeviled by no fears, no uncertainties plagued him. Despite the many difficulties he had encountered, his enthusiasm for this new life he had undertaken had not flagged.

"I have arranged passage back to Great Exuma for us on the *Traveler*." He put down his coffee cup and his glance traveled with warm affection between Martha and Caroline. "The three of us will make the trip aboard her. Robert Bruce will return with the ketch."

Martha took a deep breath of resolution. This was the moment she had been dreading. But, it must be met now with firmness.

"I am not going with you, Ronald." She forced herself to keep her tone casual.

Cameron stared at her incredulously. "Not going?" He touched his lips with a napkin. "Of course you will go, Martha. What will there be for you here after we have left?"

"I am not staying in Nassau." Never before had Martha Cameron so openly defied her brother. "I will go home; to Charlestown, at least. This island life may suit you but I am lonely. I find the days intolerable. I miss the things I have always known." She smiled a little weakly. "I suspect I am without your pioneering spirit, Ronald. I long for familiar things; my friends, an hour of trivial gossip, someone in for lunch or tea. The days here are never-ending, the monotony unendurable. I shall take a small house in Charlestown."   ·

"But that is ridiculous, Martha." He was gentle, trying to be reasonably patient in the face of this outrageous pronouncement. "What will we do without you, the children and I?"

"You will survive very well, I suspect." She was almost amused by this pretense of dependency. "As for Caroline and Robert Bruce, they are no longer children. You have only to look at them to see that." There was a trace of humor in her eyes as she glanced at Caroline. "Your daughter is already talking of marriage. Not in the immediate future, of course."

"This is preposterous." He did not even hear what she had said about Caroline. "Who will manage the house?" He was bewildered.

"I would like to think I had some other purpose in life, Ronald." She rebuked him with a touch of regret.

"Damn it, Martha, you simply cannot pack up and leave me. We need you."

"Need is not exactly the word I would like to hear. Want me would sound better."

"All right." He was angry. "We want and need you."

She shook her head. "You will have to get along without me. The house servants are well trained. Your man Gabriel is perfectly capable of running the household if you give him the chance. I am not complaining," she added. "What I have done these years has been by choice. I have been housekeeper and foster mother. At Cameron Hall this was the natural order of things. But I am not happy in this alien world nor will I be contented on your island, shut off from everyone and everything I have known. If I am to be an aging spinster then it shall be among familiar surroundings."

"I won't hear of it." He lowered his head and shook it vigorously.

"I am afraid you will. If you refuse to allow me to go freely and with your blessing then I have a little money of my own. I shall use it. I will not, though, grow old and eventually go to my grave in these godforsaken islands."

He stared at her as though confronted by a complete stranger. Then his expression softened.

"Have I really used you so badly, Martha?"

"No. Of course not." She was quietly emphatic. "I remained unmarried by choice. You know that. The children I have loved. They took the places of those I might have had myself. But Robert Bruce is a young man; Caroline a young lady. They, you, have no real need for me in this new life other than to see that your house is well managed. In your heart you know this is true. Let me go, Ronald, with your love and blessing or I shall go without them."

"I did not know you felt this way, Martha." There was a touch of sincere regret in his tone.

She smiled again and shook her head. "You never bothered to ask. No one troubled to inquire. I was told we were going to the Bahamas. Now, I am weary of the responsibility. I miss the people and the scenes I have always known. You have the work, the excitement, of building a new life. I have nothing but fading memories."

"Very well, Martha." He did a surprising thing. Rising from his chair he walked the length of the table and kissed her tenderly on the cheek. "You go with my heartfelt wishes. I will make inquiries and arrange passage on the first ship with passenger accommodations. There may be times when business will bring me to Charlestown. In time you may want to visit us here. We will not say good-bye, any of us."

⤦ VIII ⤧

THE GOVERNOR poured himself a second drink from the brandy decanter and then stared moodily at the amber-colored liquor without making a move to touch it. He lifted his eyes to glance across the room to where his wife sat within a ring of soft light cast by the candles in their wall brackets.

Sabrina Heath was well aware of the appraising study. She also had full knowledge of the reason for it. Now, though, she elected to adopt an attitude of complete unawareness. With an unconcerned innocence she pretended an absorption in the small piece of sewing with which she had occupied the evening. Sooner or later, she knew, Gerald would lose control of himself and the thing between them would be out and in the open. She had known for three months that which Gerald so broodingly suspected. Now and then she had wondered idly, and without any real concern, how the situation would be met. It provided a certain amount of diversion to speculate on the measure of his temper. She heard now, rather than saw, her husband as he heaved himself from his chair. He walked heavily across the room, turned, retraced his steps and then started on the third trip. Abruptly he halted, planted his feet wide apart and with lowered head glared at her.

"Well?" The word rumbled in his throat. "Whose is it?"

"Whose is what?" She looked up with simulated surprise.

"Don't attempt to cozen me, madame." His voice shook with emotion and he managed to make the form of address a sarcasm. "For months you have kept me away from you with one female excuse after another. I have lived a monk's life, as you well know, by yielding to your protestations. There has been one pretext after another. Against my command you even moved into rooms of your own and each night I have heard the key turn in its lock."

"It is a small privacy for which I have asked. What you would not grant, I took." She bit at a thread, her fine, even teeth cutting through it with a tiny click. "It could have been done gracefully."

"Damn it, madame!" He shouted now and the fury purpled his face. "Do you think you talk with some fuzzy-cheeked schoolboy? You grow heavy with child and it cannot be mine. Even the stays into which you lace yourself so tightly cannot disguise what is happening."

"It will be a relief, then, not to have to corselet myself so uncomfortably since it hides nothing."

Sir Gerald snatched up his brandy and gulped it down in a single swallow. He was experiencing a feeling of helpless rage, confronted by this bland admission of guilt. What did one do with a woman who refused to deny, to grow tearful with protestation, to plead for understanding and forgiveness? Such things he could have dealt with but this left him baffled. Should he drag her from the seat by her hair and hurl her to the floor, demanding an expression of repentance? Was he to beat her until the outcries brought the house slaves running and later to spread the scandal through the town? He had no answer for any of these questions.

"I demand the name of your lover." Even to his own ears this sounded ridiculously inadequate, almost defensive. "Who is he? Birch? Someone in the guard? An officer in the regiment? An Out Island sponger? A tradesman? Some young fisherman?"

"What possible difference can it make?" She asked the question with an infuriating calmness. "If I gave you his name would you call him out? Is this something to be settled at pistol's point so everyone would know the Governor had been made a cuckold? I think not, and so the name is of no importance. Besides," she shrugged prettily, knowing well how far she was driving him and taking a malicious pleasure in the goad, "I am not at all certain I know."

He moved with a swiftness remarkable in so paunchy a man. One hand was lifted to strike her; to wipe from her mouth in a bloody smear the smile of complacent satisfaction. Then, the uplifted arm dropped lifelessly to his side. He sank into a chair, staring blankly at the floor.

"I did not honestly think you would do this to me." He mumbled the words with a pathetic absence of force and his fingers locked and unlocked themselves.

"Then you are a far more stupid man than I had imagined."

"There is a position, a *noblesse oblige,* involved."

"A sour fig for position and obligation." She stared at the bent figure with genuine anger. "What really wounds you is that I admit it openly. Why should I deny the obvious? You have kept me on this wretched island against my will. I have begged you to permit me to return to England. It could have been easily explained. My health demanded a change, the climate of this place is unsuitable. Any number of reasons would have spared your pride. Even when you refused me this I offered you terms. I said: Let us, at least, be pleasant with each other without talk of love or affection. But you would not have it that way. I must be, for you, a vessel; an instrument for your convenience, your satisfaction. If I am a wanton it is you who made me feel that way from the beginning; a sow for the boar. Well, I chose not to have it that way. A man attracted me. Now, I am to have a child. You may even have an occasion to strut a little in public over this proof of your virility. We'll have a cannon fired as a salute to the birthing."

His head lifted and there was the faintest gleam of satisfaction in his eyes. "So! Your lover doesn't want you?" He made an attempt at laughter. "Ha! Suppose I denounce you, throw you and your bastard upon the street? What will you do then?"

"You are being ridiculously melodramatic, Gerald. You will, of course, do nothing of the sort. Your vanity would not permit it. Now," she was being reasonably patient, "have your brandy and we will say nothing more about the situation."

Somehow she managed to convey the impression that it had been she who had suffered his dereliction.

The *Traveler* stood out from Great Exuma harbor, her canvas taut under the wind which had been freshening all day, and she heeled rakishly beneath its thrust.

The arrival and departure of the interisland schooner, traveling on a more or less regular schedule between the settlements and Nassau, was always an occasion of some small excitement and interest. She was a link with the world outside; a bearer of news, a carrier of acquaintances, and sometimes, friends. Even Ronald Cameron, who rarely permitted his emotions to display themselves, could not resist the temptation to stroll down to the beach and watch as the vessel put in. The captain was invariably invited to the manor for a rum drink and, if the hour was right, whatever meal the time called for. Since there was a constant traffic between the Out Islands and New Providence, Cameron had come to know many of the neighboring plantation owners, their wives, daughters and sons. When, as it frequently happened, some of these were passengers aboard the *Traveler,* their temporary stopover became a social occasion. There was talk of crops and prices; of the weather, the state of the former colonies on the mainland, a denunciation of the Home Government for its indifference to the welfare of the islands. Papers and periodicals, most of them months old, and an occasional letter from

England were brought by this marine post. If the vessel lay over the night, her passengers were always put up at the great house and there was much drinking among the men and discreet gossip among the ladies. Now and then a group of the Cameron slaves were gathered on the grounds where they sang in an untrained but haunting chorus the songs which had been handed down to them from Africa itself. The departure of the schooner always left a small sense of desolation in her wake.

Now, Cameron with Robert Bruce and Caroline watched the schooner as she sailed away. She made a trim sight, a soaring gull skimming the water. All three experienced a pang of loneliness but it was not a thing to be openly confessed.

"She makes a pretty sight." Cameron held a small packet of mail in his hand.

Their eyes followed the ship's course as she began to round the elbow of land. It would be six weeks, at least, until she called again and broke the unvarying pattern of their days and nights.

For Cameron and Robert Bruce the routine had been rigidly established. Of their white overseers only Spithead now remained. Grayson and the others upon whom Cameron had depended for so long had been unwilling to endure the monotony. They had found the life too lonely and left the employment of years with honest regret but unshakable determination. It had been Grayson who had expressed the sentiments of the others.

"It's the weird feeling the place gives you after a while, Mr. Cameron, sir. Nothing but the sound of the wind and the sea; no change to the days except at the time of the storms in the fall. 'Tis like being marooned on a different planet. I guess that is what the men can't stand. I also, for that matter. We miss the Carolina and that is the truth. There, at least, a man could mount a horse on a Saturday night and ride into a village or even a crossroads settlement. He could take a drink with a friend and maybe even ruffle the skirt of a girl. It's not," he smiled, "that we always did those things. There were months at a time when none of us left Cameron Hall, the difference being we knew we could. Here we know we can't. I think that is what gets to the heart of most of us. We are sorry to leave you but there it is."

Now, the three of them—the Camerons, father and son, and Spithead —carried on the work of half a dozen. They were mostly in the saddle from morning to night. The labor and detail seemed never-ending. At daybreak there was the sending of the slaves into the fields; the division of the gangs to certain sections; the acres for cotton, cane or new land to be cleared for future planting. The supervision did not end there for, left to themselves, the slaves would make only desultory motions toward the work assigned or neglect it altogether, squatting on their haunches in small groups, talking aimlessly, wasting the hours. As a result, the Camerons and Spithead were in constant movement from one end of the plantation to the other.

All of the things Cameron had formerly taken for granted he must now see to himself. There was the Saturday allowance ceremony at which time the slaves lined up to receive their week's rationing of the beans, corn and yams. These were the staples of their diet and supplemented the fish which were seined daily, to be eaten fresh or salted and dried in the sun. Even this matter of fishing could not be left to the blacks unattended. Without someone to direct the work they were inclined to lie about the beach in the warm day or frolic heedlessly in the water while the nets were heaped in untidy tangles.

There were, Cameron also discovered, innumerable disputes to be arbitrated or adjudicated. As time went on his appreciation for Grayson increased, for the man had somehow enforced a discipline without seeming effort. Now Cameron found himself involved in such petty annoyances as a dispute between a man and his woman or a girl who had left one buck for another. There were real and imaginary illnesses to be investigated, injuries to be treated. Frequently an unidentifiable malady would seem to strike fifteen or twenty of the slaves at the same time. They would remain on their pallets, insisting they were unable to work, but at the day's end their recovery was miraculous and health seemed to sustain them until the following morning. There were times when Cameron felt he carried the entire weight of this small universe upon his shoulders. Robert Bruce, he admitted, had matured beyond his years. He had accepted his share of the responsibility as best he could but he was still young and the blacks, while respectful, were inclined to view him with a certain tolerance as the Young Marstah who bore no real authority or position beyond that of being the Ol' Marstah's son. So Cameron himself must hold to the ultimate command and meet each crisis as it occurred. They hadn't, he mused, done too badly this year. One hundred bales of cotton had been shipped to Nassau. This was short of the yield he would have expected in the Low Country but still, everything considered, it was no small accomplishment. Next year, with new fields in production, they would do better, and if the market in Nassau held steady there would be a fine profit.

When he had time to think about it he was amazed at how well the house itself was run without the steadying hand of Martha. His man, Gabriel, had quietly assumed the command once it had been handed him. With a silent majesty he had imposed his will upon the house slaves. If there had been any dissension Cameron had not heard of it. Gabriel moved with a quiet dignity from kitchen to the second-story rooms, inspecting, correcting, instructing and, apparently, punishing when necessary. As a result the woodwork gleamed, the silver bore a bright polish, the meals were well cooked and served. Everyone fitted into his or her place without confusion or conflict. Only in the house did there seem to be complete order and Cameron sometimes wished he had half a dozen Gabriels to supervise the outside work as well.

After the first few months on the island, Cameron had taken to keeping a journal. One evening, for something to do, he read through part of it and was astonished at the unvarying quality of repetition.

> *Tuesday. 18. Employed ten hands in stripping fodder in Hercules field while others chopped cotton in the forepart of the day and burning weeds in the orange grove in the afternoon. Weather dry. Wind about west with a strong breeze.*
>
> *Wednesday. 19. Employed sixteen hands getting thatch for pea house. The rest of the hands weeding in the corn patches and cotton fields. A large quantity of fine yams dug. Weather and wind about the same as yesterday.*

Page after page. He leafed through them and could find little break in their uniformity. Day followed day without change. Reading the entries it would seem that the plantation, once having been set in motion, would continue on its course without interruption, and yet, this was not true. A thousand small harassments must be met daily. At nightfall he was bone tired, happy to slouch in a chair with a strong drink and pipe until it was time for the evening meal. He knew he was sometimes unreasonably irritable from the constant pressure which should not be upon him but somehow was. Why was it so different here from what it had been in Carolina? He searched his mind for the answer. At Cameron Hall he had needed only to make a pretense at supervision. The real, day-to-day work had been assumed by Grayson and his assistants. Here, he thought wryly, he was Grayson and the others.

Staring at the journal's pages he was confronted by the terrible monotony. It deadened a man's mind. Save for an occasional excursion picnic or a visit to a plantation on a neighboring island they awoke, worked and went to sleep with a stultifying regularity. He wondered unhappily if this was the proper heritage for Robert Bruce and the grandchildren he hoped to have someday. Could he, in all conscience, leave them to a life so tightly bounded? He caught himself thinking of Cameron Hall, on the Ashley. By comparison their lives there had been a riot of excitement and pleasure with the autumn hunts, the parties which took long planning, the arrival of a distant relative or friend for a visit. Time and distance gave these things a dazzling quality when, in truth, they had been but the simplest of diversions. He sighed a little with the memory but was unwilling to admit a mistake in judgment. The course he had taken was the right one. He would build well here. Over the years the Out Islands would become populated and their isolation ended. Until then? He had closed the journal with a slap of finality and walked outside into the star-powdered night.

Standing alone with only the soft brushing of the wind in the palms to make a sound, his mind had returned again and again to what lay ahead. More than anything else the future of Caroline troubled him. She was growing up without any contact with the small graces he associated with a young lady. If he had given proper thought to the matter he would have sent her back to Charlestown with Martha. There, at least, she could have been privately tutored and instructed in the proper demeanor or sent to one of the academies where association with girls of her own age would have been possible. In Charlestown she would have had the companionship of young ladies of her station. There would be the correct social contacts made and she would have had the benefit of association with gentlefolk. When the time came a suitable marriage would have been arranged. Here she was growing as wild and untended as the brush which must be cleared before a planting could be made. For companionship she had no one but a slave girl. For amusement only what the island offered and that was limited to a rare visit from the Fergusons, who sometimes brought their daughters. It was a barren life for so young a girl and yet he had never heard her voice a complaint. He ruminated on this, thinking how curious it was. She had never expressed any restlessness or dissatisfaction. From what surprising source did she draw this serenity? Sometimes she rode to the fields in the cool of the morning with him and Robert Bruce, but how she occupied the long hours of the days he had little idea. She had learned to sail a small sloop he had bought to supplement the ketch and he knew, from her casual mention, she sometimes took along young Tom Gurney. Together they roved and explored the many small cays or fished with hand lines from the boat. He was secretly unhappy over this association, feeling it was somehow improper conduct for a young lady. But, and he asked himself the question honestly, what was the alternative? Was she to sit idly in the house, awaiting the return of her father and brother? He could not bring himself to demand that.

Once, in one of their rare intervals alone, he had asked her if she would not like to go back to Charlestown and live with Martha. Or, and he had hoped this might prove more attractive, sail to England for a visit with relatives there.

"No." The reply had been prompt and emphatic. "I like it here."

"But," he persisted, "aren't you lonely? Don't you miss the friends you might have, girls of your own age—even young men to call? By the way, how old are you now?" It didn't occur to him that this was a strange question.

"Almost seventeen. I will be next month. I think that probably girls my age in Charlestown are silly with their giggling and nonsense. Why should I want to leave here?"

"Because," he was momentarily made uncertain by the direct question, "well, simply because this doesn't seem the proper setting for a young lady."

"Then why did you bring me, Father?" There was no impertinence in the question, only an honest curiosity. "Why did we leave Cameron Hall?"

He had no ready answer for this. It involved so many factors, real and intangible.

"Do you know something, Father?" There was a trace of humor in her eyes. "I think you are the dissatisfied one. I believe you miss Cameron Hall more than Robert Bruce and I do."

"Aye! There are times." He made the confession unwillingly.

"Would you like to know what I really think, Father?"

"Yes." He studied the poised figure before him and thought how little he really knew of this girl. "Yes, I would like to know."

"Then," she was direct, "I think you ought to marry again. Maybe you should have done it a long time ago. I think you are the lonely one with too much of your mind on the past. You should have a wife to help fill this empty house; a wife and maybe children, real Bahamians."

There was so much truth in what she said that he was startled by her perception. He had thought of marriage many times during the two years or so since coming to the island. But, for a wife he must have a lady of station. Where, in the Out Islands or even Nassau, was he to find such a person, one of the proper age and disposition? Who, on the mainland even, would willingly share this exile? He shook his head and took refuge in a generality.

"You," he groped for the correct words, "you are growing up. It will not be too many years before you will be thinking of marriage yourself. Your mother was married to me at seventeen. There is your future to think of. That is why I suggest Charlestown or even England."

She laughed openly now. "You are being evasive, Father. Anyhow, I am quite content for the time being here with you and Robert Bruce."

He shook his head stubbornly. "These are not the proper surroundings for you. If you want me to confess to a mistake, I will." He realized he was speaking to her as he might an adult. "I should have left you and Martha in Charlestown while Robert Bruce and I put this place in order.

[100]

It isn't," he hesitated, "it isn't fitting you should spend your days, un-chaperoned, aboard a small boat with someone like Tom Gurney, good lad that he is."

Her laughter was a rippling sound. "La! Tom Gurney is ascared to death of me. He still calls me Mistress Cameron even when there is no one around to hear."

"I still think it is improper conduct. Yet," he admitted, "I cannot deny you freedom when I have nothing else to offer."

She had taken his arm then and pressed it with tight affection to her side.

"You don't have to worry about me, Father. I know a great deal more than you suspect. And, in those things upon which you put such value, I am a lady as you would wish."

"I am certain of that." He was grave.

"Then stop worrying about me. I am not unhappy here. If I ever become really discontented I promise to come to you and say so."

He had left the matter there, for there seemed nothing more to say.

Now, as the topmasts of the little schooner vanished where the island curved in a sweeping arm, Cameron noticed it was Robert Bruce rather than Caroline who strained to toetips for a last sight of the vessel. Then, with unspoken accord, they all turned away from the sea and began to retrace their steps toward the house. Cameron glanced at his son. It had not occurred to him until now that the boy, also, might have his unconfessed spells of loneliness.

"When the seeding is done," he spoke casually, "we might take the ketch for a visit to Nassau. A change would do us all good. It will be well to get the trip in before the equinox and its unpredictable weather."

Robert Bruce nodded a quick agreement. Caroline appeared indifferent to the voyage. He had expected it would be she who would display some excitement at the prospect. As he had many times before, Cameron wondered about these two. How had the same seed produced such different results, this completely dissimilar flowering? What was really in their minds? What secret adjustments had they made to this new life? He would have liked to ask: Tell me what you really think. How you feel. For I have no way of knowing. I can only speculate. Of Robert Bruce he was more certain. The lad was more serious than he should have been but he was doing a man's work which occupied his mind and body. Caroline was the enigma. He had the uneasy feeling she merely bided her time and when the day of decision arrived she would make it without consulting him and, if need be, with a complete disregard for his wishes or counsel. He sensed this independence and it disturbed him.

[101]

At the house he went to the room which served as a library and an office for the transaction of the plantation's business. He dropped the packet of mail on the table he used as a desk. He took a pipe from a rack and settled himself in the chair. Idly he sorted through the mail. There were newspapers from England, long out of date although the reports they contained were fresh and interesting to him here. There were also journals from Charlestown and he noticed the spelling of the city's name had been changed. The "w" had been dropped and it was written Charleston now.

With the periodicals there was a single letter, the paper carefully folded and sealed. The handwriting of the address was large, bold and decisive, and also, unfamiliar. He turned it over and broke the wax.

The letter was in two sheets and he looked first at the second one for a signature. It was signed merely with an *S*. He went back to the first page and began to read.

RONALD, MY DEAR.

What I have to write is difficult, not so much because of the subject matter (although that is embarrassing enough) but only because I hope you will understand my reason for writing at all.

I am going to have a baby. Yours or, perhaps I should say, ours.

Please don't misunderstand me. This is not a plea for you to come to my assistance. I am asking nothing of you. I have admitted my condition quite frankly to Gerald (although it is becoming obvious enough) and he, of course, is in a fury, demanding the name of my seducer (which wasn't at all the way it happened, was it?) but I have told him nothing nor will I. He is a vengeful man and could possibly make things extremely difficult for you here. As it is, his position of Governor leaves him no choice but to proclaim the child (when it comes) as his own. My reason, then, for writing you is not too clear even to me but I think I just wanted you to know that the baby is yours.

I cry a little in secret for you sometimes and would that there was real love between us. But, I know in my heart this is not so. There is an attraction. I cannot honestly call it anything else. If it were more I would come to you and be indifferent to the scandal. But, even if you wanted me there are insurmountable difficulties for I do not see how you could explain a pregnant woman to your son and daughter.

So, as I said in the beginning, I am making no demands, asking nothing. It is possible that in this uncertain world this yet to be born child may someday need you. How or why I cannot say. But, if the time should ever come I would like to believe you felt some measure of obligation to it as your own.

I cannot say I am overjoyed at the prospect of bearing a child. No tender emotions fill me but neither, surprisingly enough, am I resentful. God willed that on a certain day at a certain time this should happen between us. Had I full knowledge of your virility I might have been more cautious. Now I am filled with an odd patience and seem to live in a world not quite real. Even you are, sometimes, difficult to recapture in my memory.

He finished the letter and stared at the heavily penned *S,* wondering at his absence of emotion. He should feel something: guilt, remorse, concern for the beautiful woman to whom he had so casually made love. He experienced none of these things. Not for a moment did he doubt or question what she had written. It would not be in her nature to lie and there was no reason for it. If she said the child was his then this was so. But, and this puzzled him, what had prompted her to write the letter? Was she unconsciously reaching for his hand and saying: Take me from this place which I find unendurable? Let me have the child in your home? He didn't think so. There was no suggestion of self-pity, of a woman having been wronged; no attempt to burden him with a confession of parenthood. Some curious, mystical premonition had made her want to let him know his relationship to this baby yet to be born. He smiled a little to himself. I should be a strutting cock to have fathered a child at my age. Then he thought, I am not old, only a few months short of fifty. Why then did he feel the years sometimes as though they were twice that many?

He arose and walked to an open window which looked out over the grounds and down to the water's edge. It was Sunday and there was no need for him to go to the fields. That, he thought, is why I feel old. I have given of my body and mind to this plantation. It occupies all my waking thoughts. Even when we have guests, as today, I catch myself thinking of what must be done tomorrow and not of what is being said. I am too much alone and it is making me dull and burdens me with years I have not yet accumulated.

He went back to the table and took up the letter again. This time he refolded it and then, on an impulse he couldn't explain, carefully locked it away in a cabinet drawer.

The small boat, with its crimson-dyed sail, seemed to skip lightly just above the surface of the water. The bow touched flirtatiously now and then with a wave and sent a shower of pearled spray into the air.

With one arm hooked negligently about the tiller, Juan Cadiz leaned back and smiled at the sky. Juan was in his early twenties and all of life was a juicy piece of fruit for his tasting. He wore nothing but a pair of white duck trousers which fell loosely just below the knee. His skin, played constantly upon by the sun and wind, was the sleek, dark color of oiled mahogany. A golden loop gleamed in one ear as it caught the afternoon's light. At his bare feet there was a small sack containing the

[103]

last of the provisions he had started with from Nassau four days ago. In it were dried beef, salty and tough, a few ship's biscuits, some bananas in danger of rotting and a coconut. Nearby were two water gourds, all but empty now, and a guitar inlaid with bits of mother-of-pearl. By stretching a little he could brush the strings with his toes. He did this caressingly and laughed with sudden good humor at the sound.

Juan had never done a hard day's work in his life. He had learned early, easily and quickly, almost from infancy, that he needed only to gaze with a handsome, brooding melancholy at a woman or a girl to have all things done for him. He could barely remember his mother and had no recollection at all of his father. He sometimes wondered if his mother could name her mate in the union which had resulted in Juan Cadiz. He was probably some wandering fisherman, sponger or sailor who had come upon this dark-eyed girl, made love and promptly forgotten her. Juan had no illusions and it bothered him not at all he was someone's bastard. No one ever called him anything but Juan and he had taken the name of Cadiz from a ship which, in his teens, had put in at Nassau. He liked the sound of the word.

When he was ten years old his mother had deserted him and he was left like a stray mongrel to forage for himself. Now he lived with a rare collection of villainy at the tip of the Long Island. Here there was a scattered collection of shacks inhabited by men, women and ever-present children who were drawn together by a common aversion to more labor than the day's needs called for. They brawled, fought, got drunk when they could and made love when the mood was upon them. This was often, for babies were born with a calendarlike regularity and were absorbed into the community without much thought or effort. If the mother went off with another man, someone simply added the new infant to his or her own brood and they grew up like puppies from different litters.

There had been a time when the settlement had made a profitable living from the wrecking of ships, either through the changing of lights or connivance with an unscrupulous captain. Misdirected, the vessels would tear their bottoms out on the sharp reefs and the cargo salvaged was sold for a fraction of its value to shady merchants in Nassau. Then there would be a time of riotous living with most of the community drunk and wandering about in an aimless daze until the purchased rum was gone. After that the residents sat moodily in the sun and waited for something to happen. Wrecking, though, had of late become a hazardous occupation. His Majesty's Lighthouse Service patrolled the waters in fast, armed sloops. Three men had been hanged in Nassau for tampering with the lights and others were in prison on Watlings Island. This had a sobering effect upon Juan's friends and companions. Much of the excitement of their lives had gone and they were reduced to fishing, tending some scraggly patches of yams and beans or fighting with each other out of boredom. Now and then, of course, there was an honest wreck and they scrambled among themselves for the prizes and were not at all concerned with the sailors who drowned and were later washed ashore. Sometimes there were survivors who, weary of the sea, joined the colony. It numbered some two hundred persons now and they lived together in a state of wary harmony with no one really trusting his neighbor where a chicken, pig or girl was concerned.

Rarely did Juan wonder about his mother. He could remember, though, with a startling clarity the day of her leave-taking. She had become enamored of a sponger who did not want to be bothered with a child. She tied a few belongings into a cloth and patted him casually on the head.

"I'm goin' away now, boy. With that face an' those eyes you get along fine. Women an' girls see to that. You don' never need to worry."

He hadn't.

The girls and women along Nassau's waterfront adopted him in turn. He was cooed over, fed and clothed. Never did he really want for anything and he roamed through the town like a sleek cat, luxuriating in the sun and the knowledge someone would always come along to supply his needs. He grew tall, finely muscled and darkly handsome with crisp, black hair and an engaging smile and easy manner. At an early age he was completely familiar with the cribs and brothels and his guitar had been a present from a girl in whose room a sailor had left it as he staggered out into the night and back to his ship.

Now, Juan shared a wattled shack on Long Island with a toothless old man by the name of Plymouth. They rarely spoke to each other and had nothing in common, neither respect nor affection. Juan stayed with the man only because it was too much trouble to move and find a place of his own. He had his boat and his guitar. The former he had found beached on a remote section of the island with two dead seamen sprawled in its bottom. One had a knife in his back and the other lay, parched and blackened, where he had died of thirst.

Whenever he felt like a little diversion he took his boat and went to Nassau. He had taught himself to play the guitar and there were always a few coins to be picked up in the taverns and grogshops by a man with a song and a ready smile. Coins and girls. They and a bed came easily to a man with a guitar, a bright insolence and a song when he felt like singing. He had a charm, this Juan, but behind it was a cold, reptilian calculation. He touched the guitar strings with his toes again and wondered contemptuously at the stupidity of the Nassau girls. The more indifferent you were the more eager they became. They would cook a meal, go for a bottle of rum, empty their thin purses and forsake a well-paying sailor for a word. All this he accepted without an expression of gratitude and when he had wearied of their fawning he sailed back to Long Island as he was doing now.

He coasted down the long stretch of cays dotting Exuma Sound under a light, quartering wind. With his eyes he measured the arc of the sun and estimated the time before darkness. He could easily make Long Island before nightfall but he was in no real hurry. There was enough food in the sack. He could catch a few fish and make a camp somewhere on Great Exuma beach.

For a couple of years now he had been curious about the plantation and the fine house on the island. He had sailed in and out of the harbor without stopping one day while the mansion was building. From the boat he had seen the skeleton of its structure. He wondered about the people who lived there. On an impulse he leaned against the tiller lightly and ducked his head as the boom came over. If, he thought, a man wanted to know something, then the best way was to see for himself. The worst that could happen would be that the plantation owner would order him from the land. But, and his eyes grew bright with amusement, if a man came in need no one on these Out Islands would refuse help. He reached for the water gourds and emptied their contents over the side. This was the excuse, if he needed one. He was out of water and perishing of thirst. He tossed the empty gourds back to the bottom and laid a course for the harbor.

Caroline, walking along a stretch of the beach where she gathered an occasional shell whose color struck her fancy, saw the boat as it came in. She thought how beautiful was the crimson of its sail against the clear afternoon sky. It was like some bright bird's wing. When it was apparent the craft was headed toward a spot upshore, she turned about and walked in that direction, wondering who the unexpected visitor might be.

Juan studied the sheltered harbor, saw the ketch at anchor in the deep water and a sloop moored to a short length of pier which had been built out at an angle. He glanced at the bottom. It was sandy and without coral snags. He could ride it right into shore if he wanted. Instead he made for the pier. From the distance he could see a Negro boy or man washing down the sloop. He also saw the figure of a woman or girl as she strolled up the beach. He smiled to himself. Another song, some quick easy laughter, a few words, and he might even be invited up to the plantation house. This would be the natural progression.

Caroline hesitated for a moment and then picked her way over the loose boards of the dock. The strange boat was only a few yards away now and the sail dropped while the craft drifted easily toward the pier. The slave in the Cameron sloop straightened up from his work and then moved silently to catch a line Juan was preparing to throw him.

The two small boats rocked gently side by side and Juan Cadiz stared up at Caroline with a sharp catching of his breath. He had never seen a girl of such crystal, unflawed beauty before. Her gaze was direct, curious but controlled. He stooped and picked up the two gourds.

"I am out of water. Could I get some?"

Her eyes did not leave his. She merely nodded in the direction of the slave. "Cass will fill them for you."

Juan handed the Negro the gourds and then crossed lightly from his boat to the sloop and then up on the pier.

Caroline could feel the sudden leaping of her heart. She had difficulty in breathing, as though she had been running. Never before had she seen a man as nearly naked as this one was and the sight filled her with a strange excitement. She had never known this sensation, it seemed to envelop her body, creeping upward from her legs grown suddenly weak. She made an effort to break the spell by turning away and could feel a hot flush mounting to her cheeks.

"Cass, get some water for the gentleman." She spoke with difficulty and gave the unnecessary order only because she was abruptly embarrassed and didn't know what to do or say. "Fill the gourds for him."

No one had ever referred to Juan as a gentleman before. He felt laughter welling within him. He waited for the slave to leave.

"My name is Juan. Juan Cadiz." He spoke slowly, noting with satisfaction her blush and the uncertain lowering of her eyes. "The water ran out early today. I live on the Long Island."

Caroline didn't really hear the words or if she did they had no real meaning. Never had it occurred to her a man could be beautiful. This one was. There was no other word for his appearance as he stood so easily before her. Unwillingly but with a compelling fascination she lifted her eyes to look at him again. She was acutely, agonizingly aware of the bare chest and legs, the bright impudence on his face, the white gleam of teeth against dark skin. She felt herself trembling.

Because where women were concerned Juan had developed a predatory instinct, a feral cunning which sensed a weakness, her confusion and indecision communicated itself. He began to feel easier in her presence; easier, relaxed and sure of himself. This could be no different from any of the others despite her beauty and the background of the imposing house upon the hill. He thought, If I reached out and touched her hand

[107]

now she would only stand there, quivering like a nervous horse. His gaze roved past her to the manor and he grew momentarily cautious. Just the same, this was no Nassau waterfront girl even though, at this moment, she unmistakably waited for him to make the first move. He was so certain of this that he took a couple of catlike steps toward her, careful not to approach her too quickly in either manner or speech.

"You live here?" It was a question without point.

"Yes." The reply was barely raised above a whisper. "My name is Caroline Cameron."

"I have sailed past here before when the house was building. Then there were only white men and slaves around."

"I—I lived in Nassau with my aunt."

Nothing of what was being said had any real meaning at the moment. Despite her inexperience Caroline understood this. Juan, also, knew they were merely juggling with time. He was stalking carefully, making no overt move which might startle her. As he studied her face, the eyes filled with question and betraying her inexperience, he played with the idea of possessing this girl and what she represented. How would it be to have this one, fresh and filled with a timorous longing she didn't understand? To take her and maybe someday live in that big house with nothing to do but have slaves run and fetch? She is scared, he told himself, because what she feels at this moment is new and she had no idea it could be this way. It would take all of the knowledge he had of girls; a sly cunning of their weaknesses. He would have to be assured but not too bold. The idea excited him and he balanced himself on the balls of his feet with an unconscious grace as though he walked a narrow beam.

Somehow, intuitively, Caroline knew what he was doing but nothing in her sixteen years had prepared her for such an encounter. She was vulnerable; repelled and attracted, unable to tear herself away but wanting to flee from the dock and close a door behind her.

Juan was aware of her uncertainty. "I could come again." He made the suggestion with a soft persuasiveness. "It is not much of a sail from Long Island. If you walk alone on the beach."

"I—I don't know." She was miserably aware of her stammer.

Juan indicated the house with a nod of his head. "Who lives here with you?" The words were soothing, reassuring.

"My father, my brother." She finished with a rush because every word was an effort. "My aunt went back to the mainland."

Juan Cadiz could neither read nor write, beyond the signing of his name, but he was infinitely wise in a matter of this sort. His senses were acutely tuned. She was young but not too young. That was apparent from the swift rise and fall of her breasts. She was in an unfamiliar torment and he hadn't even touched her. She was confused by what was happening, ready to bolt; gather her skirts and run. She was aware of the danger he represented but unable to resist it completely. He had seen this look on a girl's face before.

"My boat has the only red sail in the Out Islands. If you should see it would you come to the beach?"

"I—I might. I don't know. What are you saying to me?" A small spirit of outraged anger flared and then subsided weakly. "My father would be furious."

"Then we don't let him know, eh?" The smile was there. "Why should we make him angry at me?"

"I—I walk often alone on the beach." The statement was all but inaudible and in it there was submission. "Usually in the afternoons when my father and brother are in the fields. There is no one around but the slaves."

Juan laughed softly, with confidence. "Then, if I sail this way again it will be in the afternoon." He added with a disarming candor, "It is better your father doesn't know Juan Cadiz comes calling."

Of this Caroline was certain. From some secret well she drew a small measure of self-confidence in the face of this insolent assurance.

"I think my father would shoot you."

"I am sure of that." Juan shrugged. "I do not like to be shot at."

"Then you'd better not come again."

"You don't want me to?"

"I didn't say that." Without realizing it she sounded a tiny note of pleading. "I said, maybe it would be better if you didn't."

Juan glanced down the short length of the dock and saw the slave, Cass, returning with the water gourds dangling from his fingers.

"Just the same," he spoke quickly, "I will take the chance and come again. You will look, sometimes, in the afternoons for my sail?"

"Yes." She turned away and walked from him.

Juan watched her go, his eyes speculative. Then he laughed to himself. She would be waiting. He took the gourds from the slave and returned to his boat, dropping the unneeded water in the bottom and pushing away from the Cameron sloop's side. He hauled the triangular sail. After a moment it filled and he let his craft get underway before heading into the breeze and then taking it on a long, starboard tack. The boat's bows lifted daintily and she heeled a little. He did not glance back toward shore. He was sure of himself. She would be walking on the beach when he came again. Of this he was certain. He would make her wait a little first, though. Let her wonder and watch for Juan Cadiz.

Tom Gurney, coming out of the ketch's cabin where he had been taking a nap, stretched and yawned. His arms remained uplifted in surprise as he saw the red-sailed sloop as it passed some hundred yards away. He knew that sail, that boat. What the hell was someone like Juan Cadiz doing here? He glanced shoreward and saw only the slave on the dock. Maybe Cadiz had only sailed in and out of the harbor from curiosity. He yawned again and scratched at his rumpled hair. It was no business of his.

In her room Caroline lay upon the bed, staring at the ceiling; a strange, tingling excitement possessed her. It took her breath. Never had a man looked at her the way this Juan Cadiz had. It was almost as though he had touched and fondled her and she pressed clenched hands against the hard swell of her breasts. They hurt but with an unfamiliar pain. She had known few boys and no men at all save her father's friends who had come to Cameron Hall. There was something wild and frightening about this one. She wasn't sure why. Once, back in Carolina, she had been driving with Aunt Martha. They had passed a field as a stallion reared upon a mare. She had pretended to turn away quickly but her loins had suddenly been filled with the same exquisite agony she now felt. She thought about Captain Birch, in Nassau. He had been amusing, gay and filled with laughter. But this Juan Cadiz. He was the stallion. She rolled over and pressed her face into the bolster, stretching her legs because they hurt. What if he came again? What if he didn't come? Then she smiled contentedly to herself out of a knowledge beyond her years and experience. He would come and she would be waiting.

⇜ IX ⇝

WITH HEAD bent, Cameron walked slowly, wearily, between the rows of hip-high cotton or, he thought grimly, what would have been cotton if this damnable thing had not happened. Now the stalks were stripped of every leaf; nothing but the stems remained and the still nut-hard buds were deprived of the shade they must have for flowering.

In other rows Robert Bruce and Spithead also trudged. Field after field had been devastated by swarms of chanille worms and red bugs. The blight had come with a frightening mysteriousness. One day, or so it seemed, the plants had been hardy and full-leafed. The next they were covered with this swarming plague which had left them skeletal and drying beneath the merciless sun. Here and there were a few tattered leaves with ragged holes cut into them where the insects had fed so voraciously. Not until later would they learn that plantations on Eluthera and Watlings islands had been similarly afflicted. Now they could only survey their own ruin.

With a savage gesture Cameron tore whole plants out by their roots, beating them to the ground. The vermin scattered, crawling over the soil in an ugly swarm. He stamped upon them with a gesture of futile rage as though by destroying these few he could end the curse forever. Spithead and Robert Bruce crossed over to where he stood. There was an expression of bleak helplessness on their faces.

"It is all gone." Cameron's voice was harsh. "The entire crop. We won't pick a single boll. What isn't destroyed now will be by tomorrow, for there is no way of getting rid of them."

"I've never seen anything like this, Mr. Cameron." Spithead was filled with an incredulous wonder. "The weevil, yes, but not these things. Where did they come from all of a sudden?"

"How do I know, man?" Cameron's tone was impatient but not unkind. "The rain and then the sun brought them up out of the earth.

There's nothing to do but fire all the fields." He stood, shading his eyes and staring over the vast plantation. "Get the hands to making some torches and let's put it to the fire."

Spithead nodded and left them. Cameron watched him go with an unhappy expression. There was nothing to do but burn off the fields which would have to be replowed and then laboriously planted again. There would be no cotton, no money crop, this year.

"What a puny thing man is." He spoke half to himself, partly to Robert Bruce. "He thinks he has tamed the land, bent it to his will. But this is not so. The forces of nature are always waiting to destroy him at their pleasure. Now and then he is given a respite but that is all. The plague descends upon him without warning. I needn't tell you what a blow this is, for you know how I have depended on a cotton yield this year. It was cash I sorely need."

Cameron stared unseeingly over the acres. He was miserably aware of how thin he had stretched his resources. What with the labor and the material he had imported, the house represented a small fortune and he had been forced to draw heavily upon his accounts in England. A good crop would have replenished them.

"Let's go back to the house." He put his hand on his son's shoulder. "There is nothing for us to do here but watch the flames."

Together they walked across the field and to its edge where a slave held their horses.

"I haven't told you." Cameron mounted and waited until Robert Bruce was also in the saddle. "Some of my investments in England have gone bad this year. The shares I held have dropped far below the figure at which I bought them." There was a compulsion in him to pile calamity upon this adversity.

"We'll plant again, Father." Robert Bruce tried to sound cheerful and reassuring. "After all, there were bad times in Carolina and the Camerons survived them."

"Aye! We'll plant again for there is nought for us to do, but I am sick at heart over what has happened. I say to myself: Suppose we plant again and the pests come next year and the year after? I fear the legacy I hoped to leave you is not as fine as I imagined it would be."

"I'll make my own heritage, Father." Robert Bruce smiled at the man. It was an expression of warm understanding. They had come to know each other well during these past years and a companionship had built itself between them. "I am not waiting to be left a fortune. Anyhow, it is not like you to talk this way. We will get through this, together."

"Aye, lad." Cameron's expression softened. "I suppose so."

Despite the ill-fortune which had struck so unexpectedly there was no real, immediate crisis. The plantation was self-supporting. They need go outside for little and that little, he thought, they could do without if necessary. Unless a blight struck down every growing thing on the island they would do well enough. The cattle, fowl and swine were healthy. There was plenty of corn in storage. The bean and yam patches flourished. There were no wages to pay save those of Spithead and Tom Gurney. Robert Bruce now handled the ketch as though he had been born to the water and he had been able to dispense with the services of Captain Pinder and Greenleaf. He tried to assure himself there was no real need for worry.

"Have you read any of the London papers which come to me?" He asked the question of Robert Bruce as their horses walked slowly, side by side.

"I am not much for reading, Father." The answer came with a smile. "Since we rid ourselves of my tutor back in Carolina I haven't looked at a book."

"Aye! That tutor. We were going to replace him, weren't we?" Cameron grunted. "Just the same it would do you no harm to keep abreast of things, and the reading of a newspaper should put no great tax on your mind. Then you don't know there is considerable agitation in England to bring a halt to the slave trade. It may someday be something with which you will have to contend, for it would be a catastrophe both here in the islands and on the mainland. For how do you work a plantation without slaves and what would the blacks do if put upon their own? They are without land or the means of sustaining themselves. It is nonsense. They cry against it in London where they have no conception of our plantation system. Always you will find those who seek to overthrow an established order and create dissent. England has her share of these wide-eyed visionaries."

He halted his mount and looked back at the fields. Bright tongues of flame licked greedily at the dried and drying plants and a pall of black smoke rose in the air.

"I suppose," Robert Bruce was thinking of what his father had said, "if they ended slavery, then you would have to pay the blacks wages and they would work as other men."

Cameron snorted his impatience. "What need has a black for money? On what would he spend it? The same food and clothing he now gets for nothing. They are better off as they are with someone to look after them. Those fools in London don't understand this. It is a way of life and shouldn't be tampered with."

A groom took their horses as they dismounted at the house. Cameron turned for one last, backward glance at the burning fields and he sighed at the spectacle even though he knew what was going up in smoke was useless. It was true they had experienced some bad years in Carolina. But somehow, Cameron Hall had the feeling of permanency. There had always been the sense of security; of something well established. There had been friends of long standing, neighboring planters, who could gather and discuss a common adversity. Here, for the first time, he felt alien and alone.

They mounted the steps, standing for a moment on the porch, looking at the sky which was partly obscured by the smoke.

"I'm going over some accounts in the office." Cameron spoke heavily. "I'll look for those old newspapers. It will do you no harm to read a word or two now and then."

Juan Cadiz came out of the canted shack he shared with the old man, Plymouth, and stretched himself lazily in the warm sun. The community was about its usual, unhurried tasks. Here a man mended a fish net. A woman washed some clothing in a wooden tub, and a blackened kettle of water boiled over a fire. Two boats were careened on the beach and men and boys worked over their hulls, scraping them clean of barnacles and sea growth. Children frolicked in the clear water. An old man tended the racks of fish smoking between screens of palm fans. Some girls were sanding the conch shells which, when polished and of a deep color, could sometimes be sold in Nassau as souvenirs to sailors from the ships.

Most of the men and women had only a casual relationship with each other. A few were actually married, the ceremony being performed by the missionaries sent out from England's churches to bring a godliness to the island's inhabitants. When a man or a woman tired of the relationship they merely moved out of the house and set up a separate establishment, usually with another man or woman. They were all a mixed breed, some were felons who had been banished from the island of Bermuda. Others were the progeny of Spanish sailors and whatever girl happened to be handy. Some had Negro blood in them. All lived together on Long Island with a certain tolerance for each other.

Juan walked down the sandy path which divided the rows of shanties. He would take a swim and then shave. He fingered the gold loop in his ear. It had been a week since he had seen Caroline Cameron and he thought that today he might take his boat and sail over to Great Exuma.

He whistled to himself as he walked, thinking with what skill he had brought this girl from timidity, and sometimes rebellious defiance, to eager supplication. He had had to teach her every step in lovemaking from the first tight-lipped, frightened kiss to the touch of his hand upon

[114]

her breast. Now, she came running into his arms after he had beached his boat in the sheltered cove they had agreed upon as a meeting place. There they would spend an hour or more until he wearied slightly or she, fearing questions from old Cameron himself, would have to return to the house. It hadn't been easy for she had an independent will of her own, but she was attracted despite herself. There had been a challenge here which Juan found exciting. She was reluctant to become submissive and had drawn away in outraged anger at his first, familiar fondling. It was as though she recognized a danger in him. He had made no move to pull her back, letting her stand with blazing eyes and panting breath until she, dimly understanding the futility of resistance, had come, almost fearfully, into his arms. Now, and his self-satisfaction flowered at the thought, it was she who pressed against him with soft whimperings; she who waited anxiously on the beach for the first glimpse of his dyed sail; she who had discarded all pretense of modesty and took a delight in his strong, tanned body. It was Caroline who had hesitantly first spoken the words: "I love you, Juan." It was she who had pleaded with him to repeat the phrase for her. Over the past few months Juan had discovered what he vaguely suspected. Mistress Cameron was no different from the Nassau girls. They wanted possession and to be possessed. The conquest, he thought, was complete. When he treated her with an assumed indifference she became the trembling supplicant. When he took her, she responded with all the ardor of her youth.

Of late, though, an idea had been slowly forming in the mind of Juan Cadiz. Why be satisfied with a slice when he might have the whole loaf? Why not marry this one and put himself up there in the big house and be damned to her father and brother? They would have to accept what had been done.

"You have the look of a cat who has stolen a fish," a girl called to him from a doorway where she leaned against the jamb with only a short petticoat and camisole on. She had a vivid, dusky beauty and in her veins flowed the blood of a Spanish sailor and an Arawak Indian girl some generations back. "Where," she continued with an indolent interest, "is it you go so often in that boat of yours?"

Juan had been the girl's lover for a few months and she still yearned a little for him even though she now lived with another man, by the name of Basset and of more stable disposition.

"I'm trying to catch the fish, Maria." He grinned at her.

"I think you have a girl someplace. Who is she? What's her name? Is she pretty?"

"She is not so pretty or as wild as you."

[115]

"Basset has gone to Turtle Cove today." She made the statement an invitation.

"Some other time, maybe."

She shrugged indifferently and scratched at one bare ankle with her toes. Pity the girl who really falls in love with that Juanio, she thought. She will have to work for him from morning to night and when he has tired he will leave her. Without any real interest she wondered who the new girl was. Someone on Eluthera or Watlings. It couldn't be a Nassau girl for he wasn't often that long away from home. She was someone closer at hand.

Tom Gurney stood in the Cameron library. His plain, honest features were twisted with embarrassed indecision. He ran the brim of a plaited palm hat nervously through his fingers.

"Speak up, man, what is it?" Cameron was not impatient. He only wondered what had brought Gurney to the house. "There is something you want to say?"

"I don't know how to begin, sir, or whether to begin at all." Gurney was in a torment.

"You have been with me long enough to know I am not an unreasonable man." Cameron leaned back in his chair. "Out with whatever is on your mind. Is it more money you want or to leave my service entirely?"

"Oh no, sir! It is none of those things." Gurney's eyes raced around the room as though he sought an escape from it. He was wishing he had let things alone and never come to the house. "I am well contented with the little I have to do. It—it is about Mistress Caroline, sir."

"What about my daughter?" Cameron was tolerant. Some highhanded action on Caroline's part had evidently upset young Gurney. "What has she done now? Stolen the ketch?"

Gurney took a deep breath of resolution. "No, sir. It is nothing like that. I have not wanted to say anything, thinking it was not my place. I take your shilling, sir, and perhaps should let it go at that." He paused. "For the past few months Mistress Caroline has been meeting a man on the beach. I—I thought you ought to know about it."

"Caroline and a man." Cameron was incredulous. "Who? From where? One of the Ferguson boys, perhaps?"

"Not a boy, sir. A man. I know him. I have seen him many times in Nassau. His name is Cadiz. Juan Cadiz. There are things they say about him along the waterfront in Nassau. How he has had girls there and sometimes acts as a procurer, a pimp, for them and the sailors. How he has lived off of women. He is not fit to speak to Mistress Caroline, Mr. Cameron, sir."

Cameron's anger flared suddenly. What romantic nonsense had Caroline involved herself in now? For the hundredth time he wished he had sent her back to Carolina with Martha.

"How do you know this, Tom?"

"I have seen the boat, Cadiz's boat. She has a red sail. There isn't another like it in the islands. I have watched him come and they meet down the beach near that small cove where the bonefish are."

"You should have told me about this before."

"I was not sure it was my place to speak, sir." Gurney stood with his eyes on the carpet.

"All right, Tom." Cameron nodded. His head was sunk upon his breast. "You have done right to come to me. I thank you."

He sat for a few minutes, deep in thought, after Gurney had left. Then he rose heavily and rang for a house girl. When she came to the library he told her to fetch Mistress Caroline.

While he waited he paced up and down the room, wondering what he would say. For if anything had happened, he must share the blame.

Caroline came to the door. Seeing the expression on her father's face, she closed it behind her and stood waiting.

"You wanted to see me, Father?" She broke the silence between them.

"What is this damnable thing I hear about you meeting someone on the beach?"

"I thought Tom Gurney had a sneaky expression on his face. So. He has been talking."

"Answer my question, girl. Who have you been going to see in the afternoons and why haven't you told me about it?"

"Because I knew you would forbid me and I didn't want to disobey you." She was completely self-possessed beneath his glare.

"Do you know who this man is? What he is?"

"I know I am in love with him."

"God in heaven, girl! You are but out of swaddling clothes and have the impudence to talk about love as though it were some sweetmeat to be tasted and enjoyed. Love, indeed, and with this—this panderer, this nobody. I won't have it. Do you understand?" His voice rose despite the effort to keep it level. "I forbid you to see this man again."

"What will you do, Father, lock me in my room?"

He strode up and down, unwilling to face her cool, clear-eyed confidence and he felt a sudden helplessness.

"If I have to do that I will. Now." He wheeled to confront her. "I will tell you something more. I am going to send you back to the mainland where you belong with your Aunt Martha. We will go to Nassau and await a ship there which will take you to Charleston."

[117]

"I won't go, Father." She was unperturbed, defying him quietly. "It is no use in your saying I will."

"You will do as I say." He shouted now, aware of his inadequacy in dealing with this girl. "Do you think me so little a master of my own household that I will be defied by a slip of a child barely out of her teens?"

"I am not barely out of my teens and you know it. I haven't been for some time. The years pass and you refuse to admit it. I love Juan Cadiz and," she hesitated for a second, "and Juan loves me. If you are to send me to Charleston you will have to truss me up and carry me aboard the ship for I will not go willingly."

"You will do as I say."

"Not in this matter, Father."

"Child." He reached for her hand. Shouting was no good. Anger would not resolve this problem. There was in her a wild and stubborn streak. Inadvertently, he caught himself wishing Robert Bruce had some of it; this independence of thought. "You are my daughter. I love you. Is it unreasonable I should be concerned when I hear that you meet clandestinely with a man on a lonely beach? That you have been doing this without a word to me? Do you believe I can be indifferent to this Nassau waterfront vagabond who comes like some thief to pilfer your immature emotions? If he were any man at all he would have asked to see and speak with me. Certainly you know that."

"I told Juan you would probably shoot him on sight." Her eyes were suddenly bright with suppressed laughter. "But," she became grave, "Juan has not come because he was afraid to face you. I wouldn't let him. I knew what you would say because you wouldn't understand such a man as Juan Cadiz. He is a pirate at heart. I know that."

"You recognize this and yet continue to see him?" He stared unbelievingly at her, trying to probe this rebellious mind. "Do you think of me as someone with no judgment at all?"

"I think you are my father and that warps your judgment where I am concerned."

"Will you reflect for a moment?" He was defenseless against this logic. "I am a man of some experience. You are my only daughter. I want your happiness. But, with such a man as Gurney says this one is . . ." He was unable to finish with words suitable to her ears.

"Tom Gurney is an idiot. He has mooned after me for a year or more."

"Young Tom is an honest youth with a feeling for his responsibilities."

"I am not one of them, Father." She remained in complete possession of herself.

"Just how far has this thing gone?" He hesitated to ask the question. "Have you lost all sense of shame?"

For the first time, she evaded a direct reply to his question. The intimacy with Juan Cadiz had gone far beyond what she intended. He possessed her mind as he had her body and she found herself powerless to resist. It was an attraction of bright danger. She was aware of this. Yet, all of her resolution dissolved at his touch. Inexperienced as she was she was unhappily aware of the fascination. It was hypnotic. In his company she moved without a will of her own. Many times, lying in her bed at night, she had determined to free herself. In her heart she knew she would not. Emotions crowded upon each other until she grew dizzy with the thought of Juan. Here, now, with her father, she could be confident, even defiant. With Cadiz she was some helpless waif, eager for his rare moods of gentleness. She was well aware of the situation in which she had placed herself. He outraged all of her instincts, her upbringing, her background, her own innate sense of decency. He had taken her casually and with no tenderness. He had violated her innermost soul and yet, at the thought of him she grew weak and defenseless. There was no truth, no constancy in Juan. She had, at times, beat her fists against his chest in a fury of exasperation. He had only laughed and imprisoned her arms. The bright ring in his ear twinkled as did his eyes. She had no illusions about him. He would come to her only so long as he was entertained and interested. He would leave without a word of explanation or regret when he wearied of her. Of these things she was sure. What a damnable thing it was to be a woman, a girl. She had cried these words in silence to herself. What a weakling love made of you when it was centered upon such an unlikely person as Juan Cadiz. He was crude of manner and speech, a swashbuckling adventurer. What in God's name was the attraction? She could not answer.

"I asked you a question." Cameron startled her.

"I know." She lifted her gaze to meet his eyes. "It has gone no farther than I wanted it to." This was not the truth.

Cameron was deeply shocked by the implication of her words. He realized, for the first time, he no longer dealt with a child. He could not bring himself to pursue the question. He turned away, walked across the room and back again.

"We will not continue this conversation. I am the master in my household. I say you are going back to Charleston and that is an end to it."

"Very well, Father, if that is your decision."

He stared at her suspiciously. This docility disturbed him more than her defiance.

"The *Traveler* is due in a week. We will board her for Nassau and remain there until suitable accommodations on a vessel can be found. You will take your girl, Susan, to attend you." He relented a little. "In time you will thank me for what I do. You suffer from a malady common to girls and women of all ages. It is the attraction of the rake. They gladly throw themselves away on the least worthy of men. Why this is so I have no idea." He paused. "I do not want to confine you to the house. Promise me only that you will not see this man again."

"I cannot do that, Father."

"Then, by heaven," his voice shook with anger, "I shall set a watch over you. I will lock you in your room."

"That is your final word, Father? That and the fact you will send me to Charleston?"

"Yes!" He thundered the reply.

"Then," she made a brief curtsy in which there was respect and no suggestion of mockery, "I will go to my room. Lock me there if you wish."

He stared at the blank door after she had left and closed it behind her. Then he dropped dejectedly into a chair. His fingers strayed aimlessly over the objects on the table: the quill, a small knife to sharpen it; the ink container, the sanding box; a half-finished letter to a commission merchant in Nassau. He understood that nothing of what he said had made the slightest impression on this stranger who was his daughter. He wondered vaguely at the emotional suicide which so many of her sex seemed eager to commit. Always they were ready to throw themselves away on the most worthless of characters. What was the attraction? Why should the wencher, the profligate, prove so irresistible? He arose, unable to sit still. What damnable impulse had brought him to this island? Arrogance. He knew the answer. He had been a vain and arrogant man, unwilling to try to adapt himself to changing times. A little compromise here and there. That was all he had needed to make, and life in Carolina would have adjusted itself. He and he alone had placed his daughter in this jeopardy. At Cameron Hall, on the Ashley, their lives had been ordered and secure. Left there, Caroline would have grown to this young womanhood, eventually married suitably and not have thrown herself at the first vagabond who came along. The fault was his. He could not escape the blame.

Nothing which he told himself as he stood, staring out of the window, was reassuring.

He was deep in troubled thought. His daughter throwing herself away on a worthless Nassau panderer. Robert Bruce growing to manhood without the iron in his spirit which would be needed. The boy was too eager to accept a father's authority; too willing to say yes instead of no.

The plantation's soil was not proving out as he had hoped it would. Into what labyrinth had he led himself with this headstrong venture?

The little settlement on Eluthera boasted a small, whitewashed frame church. To it, at more or less regular intervals, came serious young ministers fresh from the theological seminaries of England. They traveled in a circuit among the Out Islands, bringing the Gospel where they could. They were eagerly fervent and were usually accompanied by their equally dedicated wives who shared the hardships, the disappointments and the pittance doled out by the Church of England.

It was a strange world in which they lived. They moved from island community to island community. Many of the whites came to the services as a diversion from the dull routine of their lives. The blacks, a few slaves and freedmen, came with a superstitious fervor, melding their own dark and fearful gods with this God of the white man. The youthful ministers were never certain to what the black men prayed and those with wisdom did not inquire.

Caroline and Juan Cadiz stood in the small chapel. The young minister and his wife waited a little uncomfortably. Juan finally drew four shillings from his pocket and put them in the man's hand.

"I'm afraid I have no regular certificate of marriage." The minister made the admission with a troubled air. "I could write on a plain piece of paper a testimony to the services." He was vaguely disturbed by the ceremony he had performed. The girl was obviously of gentle birth and rearing. The man—he could not define him. He had actually seemed to swagger as the wedding of the two was made. "Would that," he glanced at her, "be satisfactory?"

"What good is a piece of paper?" Juan was impatient. "I'm her husband. She's my wife. Nothing is going to change that."

"I want it." Caroline was emphatic.

The minister drew foolscap, quill and ink from a small traveling box behind the altar. He wrote a certificate of marriage. *Caroline Cameron to Juan Cadiz.* When it was sanded and dry, he put it in Caroline's hand.

"If I could draw," he smiled sheepishly, "I would embellish it with some doves and wedding bells. But I can't and so this will have to do. I hope you have done the right thing and will be very happy."

Juan laughed to himself and fingered the gold earring. Let old Cameron fume and rage now. It would do him no good. He had Juan Cadiz for a son-in-law and Juan Cadiz knew how to take care of himself. Maybe, not right away but one of these days, he would sit upon the porch of the plantation manor on Exuma. He would sit there and take his ease while a slave brought him rum drinks and fresh pipes when he called.

Cameron could rant about the place as much as he wanted. It wouldn't dissolve the marriage. This young one was insurance against the future. No more hand-to-mouth along Nassau's waterfront. He'd have gold to jingle in his pocket, fine clothes to wear.

They walked together from the chapel, down the sandy road which divided two rows of frame houses, toward the cove where his boat was anchored.

She took his hand with an almost shy gesture of possessiveness.

"Juan. Do you really love me? You've never said so. Doesn't it make a difference in how you feel now that we are married?"

"I don't feel any different." His bright eyes took in the figure of a girl who stood on a low stoop and gazed at them with curiosity as they passed. "Why should I feel different?"

"Well . . . because we're married. You are my husband. I'm your wife. Just saying that makes me feel different."

The gravity of the step she had taken began to impress itself upon her. For two days, after the meeting with her father in the library, she had remained in her room although the door was not locked. Never before had she defied Ronald Cameron, although in small matters rebellion had many times been near the surface. On the third day she had seen the crimson sail. Her father and Robert Bruce were inspecting the slave quarters. She had run down the stairs and to the beach in a state of breathless excitement.

Juan was surprisingly gentle that day. He had held her trembling body with quiet, soothing assurance.

"He has forbidden me to see you again. He is going to send me back to Charleston when the *Traveler* comes. I can't leave you, Juan. I'm a woman now. You have made me one. Tell me what we can do. I will die if I have to go back to Charleston and never see you again."

"We could get married." He brushed at her hair with one hand, smoothing it back from her troubled brow. "There's nothing to stop us from getting married if you want to. He'll come around once that is done. You wouldn't be the first girl to run away from home. We could find a minister on Eluthera."

"Do you really want to marry me, Juan?" She was secretly and honestly surprised.

"I just said so, didn't I?" The words had a rough edge of impatience.

"I know." She was doubtful. "It was the way you said it. As though it were something of no great importance."

Understanding what a reckless thing it was she did, the anxiety and pain it would bring to her father, Caroline sailed with him up the long

[122]

string of cays and then across to the island of Eluthera. They found the minister preparing to leave on his circuit tour of the settlements.

Now it had been done. For better or worse she was married to Juan Cadiz. Along the pathway there grew pink and white phlox. She stooped and picked a few, a small knot of blossoms, and with a smile tied their stems with a tough strand of the long, wiry grass.

"My bridal bouquet." She held it to her bosóm almost shyly. "I will try and make you a good wife. It all happened so quickly. I am a little scared now by the responsibility."

"What responsibility?" He was amused. "You didn't marry into a fine family with relatives. Cook a meal, after you learn how. Wash a shirt or a pair of pants for me at a tub. Make love on the beach when we feel like it. It isn't going to be much different from what we've been doing. Sooner or later your father will have to give in; especially if we bring along a grandson. Then we'll all settle down on Exuma. I'll get along with your father all right." There was an indifferent confidence in the statement.

"I don't think you'll get along with him at all." Her eyes brightened at the thought. "He isn't your kind of a man. He wouldn't understand you; a man who does nothing but sail about, playing a guitar and making love to a girl on a beach. Oh, no! Ronald Cameron isn't going to understand Juan Cadiz." She paused for a moment. "Juan, where are we going to live?"

"I'll throw the old man, Plymouth, out of the place on Long Island. Maybe," he grinned, "we'll even clean it up a little. The old man stinks. Then, one of these days, we'll sail over to Exuma and see your father." He glanced at her and the simple dress she wore. "You ought to have brought some clothes."

"I didn't know this was going to happen."

"Well," he was unconcerned, "one dress is about all any of the women on Long Island have. Most of them go about in their petticoats."

"We'll fix up your house. We'll clean and scrub until it is bright and shining. What is it like, Juan?"

"Well," he winked at her as though they shared a humorous secret, "one thing, it isn't like your house on Exuma. It has a roof, four walls and a couple of windows without shutters. When it rains and the wind blows you might as well be out in the storm. It doesn't have a floor, only some mats."

Her face clouded for a moment and then an inherently bold nature asserted itself. She laughed. After all, in her heart she knew this Juan was a rogue who took life as he found it and adjusted himself to the winds of chance the way he trimmed the sail of his boat.

[123]

"We'll fix it up. I won't complain. Just be good to me, Juan." She wanted reassurance but despised herself for the question. "You will be, won't you?"

"I may beat you once in a while." He halted and with his fingertips tilted her chin, meeting her clear eyes with his. "But I'll only use a light stick and not more than once a week. Remember, I've never been married before, either. It is as new to me as it is to you."

"But you've had so many girls."

"How would you know?"

She laughed with a sudden happiness. "I knew that the first day you came. When you looked at me on the dock. It felt, almost, as though you reached out and touched me. My heart said: This one has had many girls. You are only another. But my heart also said: I don't care."

"Whatever it was we did was because you wanted it that way. I didn't force you."

"I know." She dropped her gaze. "I was ashamed and frightened at first. You seemed like some pirate out of a book. I guess that was it." Her confidence was returning. She was his. Married. "You were exciting. I could hardly breathe. I couldn't have kept your hands off me if I had tried. I wanted to be touched even though it shocked me. I guess that is the way love is. I don't know."

He left her side, crossed the sandy path and pulled two oranges from a tree in a cabin's yard. He did this as though the property was his own. It was the way he did everything. He came back and handed her one of the fragrant globes. With his fine, white teeth he stripped the skin from his orange.

"That's your wedding breakfast." He watched her ineffectual efforts to peel the fruit. "That's all you'll get until we are home. Then it will be some cowpeas boiled with a piece of salt pork, and some fish if I feel like fishing. Maybe we can steal a chicken." His eyes brightened and he chuckled deep in his throat. "That's the good part of having nothing. No one can take it from you." He took her orange, peeled it and handed it back in halves.

The day was warm and fragrant and the sky without a cloud. A couple of children stood beside the path and watched them with solemn curiosity as they passed. Caroline took Juan's arm, pressing it close to her side. All of a sudden everything was all right. She was married to this wild creature, so different from anyone she had ever known. He was primitively exciting and beautiful. No matter that he was uneducated and scrawled his name with laborious difficulty in the little register which the minister kept. He would learn, in time, the small social graces which she took for granted. Juan would be quick to learn what was necessary for his survival. It was the animal in him.

"Is there any way I could let my father and Robert Bruce know I am all right?"

He shrugged. "We can go and tell them ourselves. What's done is done and your father can't change that. If you think I am afraid of him, I'm not. I'm your husband. You're my wife." He' whistled softly. "Your father must be very rich. How many slaves do you have on the plantation? How many rooms in the house? I'd like a rich father-in-law because I don't much care about working."

This should have disturbed her but it didn't. Already, she knew her Juan. Such a statement was as natural and unaffected as breathing.

"We ought to have a baby." He looked at her with sudden curiosity. "I'm surprised you're not heavy with one right now. Without a baby we won't bring the old man to us. Your father will say: All right. Go on and live with this Juan Cadiz on Long Island. You married him. But if he has a grandchild it'll be different. He'll have to say: Come back to the plantation. Raise your child here. That will suit me. I'll go to Nassau and have a tailor make me some fine clothes and have a nigger to fan me when I sit on the porch."

Despite Juan's bland confidence Caroline giggled inwardly. She didn't think this young husband of hers would do much sitting-around on Ronald Cameron's porch. She didn't say anything. Some of Juan's free soul would need a little taming. Time would take care of that. But, she wasn't at all sure she wanted him tamed. She was breathtakingly in love with the freebooter in him. Somehow, he didn't belong on a plantation with its daily round of never-ending tasks. She loved him for the way he was with all the laughter and mocking impudence in his eyes and manner. Please, she prayed softly to herself, don't let anything change him.

X

Although, from what Tom Gurney had told him, Cameron was certain Caroline had run away with Juan Cadiz and was probably living with him somewhere on the Long Island, it had taken him more than a week before he could bring himself to search his daughter out.

For the first time he felt old; a sudden aging of the spirit which had nothing to do with his body or the years. It was as though much of his will had been drained away as an unstopped bottle spills its contents. He found himself unable to cope with this crisis. Nothing had prepared him for it. The wall which he had hoped to build around him and his on this island was being breached in too many places and he sought desperately for some way of shoring it up again.

He sat alone in his library much of the time, leaving the plantation work to Robert Bruce and Spithead. He was without the determination to resolve the problem; unwilling to face up to it. He hoped, against the certain knowledge of Caroline's independence, she would return voluntarily. All the love and affection between them could not have been dissipated in so short a time.

He spent long hours staring unseeingly out of the window at the ocean's great splotches of color. How, the question hammered at his brain, how had he failed as a father? By not marrying again, perhaps, and giving Caroline the softening influence of even a stepmother. What had he done or not done to have brought this shining and bright girl to what he was certain was a tragic mistake? He was bewildered by her action. What in her nature had made her run off with this man, a waterfront procurer without background or future? He dug strong fingers at his hair with a gesture of desperation. The ways of a maid, enraptured by her first love, were inexplicable. How could he have handled this situation with more wisdom and tact? He didn't know and was unhappily aware of his incompetence.

Finally, he had roused himself from these moody reflections and sent for Tom Gurney.

"Do you know where this fellow, this Cadiz, lives?"

"When he's not in Nassau, sir, he has a shack on Long Island. There is a little settlement there; thieves, wreckers and just plain no-accounts who will work no more than they have to. It would be as good a place as any to start looking for him."

"We'll take the ketch, then. You and Robert Bruce can man her. I must find and talk with my daughter. We'll leave in the morning."

After talking with Gurney he had carefully loaded a heavy pistol and weighed it in his hand. Then, with a weary reluctance, he had replaced it in the fine, ebony case with its mate. Shooting this Cadiz would resolve nothing. The answer to Caroline's waywardness did not lie in such an act. It was in sympathy and reason. She had been swept off her feet by this adventurer; entangled in this web of deceit and rebellion by young emotions she did not understand. Telling himself this did nothing to assuage the cold fury which possessed him. He wanted to explode in physical violence; to beat this man into insensibility, smash his face or lay the lash upon his back.

Now he stood in the cockpit while Gurney and Robert Bruce worked the ketch into the small anchorage where a spindly dock straggled out from shore.

When the boat was fast, Robert Bruce spoke to him.

"Do you want me to go with you, Father?"

Cameron shook his head. He had not discussed Caroline with his son beyond telling him what had happened. He didn't even know how Robert Bruce felt about the situation.

"This is best done by myself."

As he walked to the shore a collection of mongrel dogs set up a fearful yapping, racing around before and behind him but never approaching within the length of a kick. A couple of men, scraping the bottom of a careened boat, looked up but made no comment. A few children gathered in a knot to watch in silence as he strode toward the miserable collection of small frame buildings and wattled huts. Here nets dried in the sun, chickens scratched aimlessly in the sand, women came to their stoops and stared at him with dull-eyed curiosity.

He had no difficulty in finding Caroline. The community was not that large. He had only to walk from one end to the other. She stood over a soot-blackened kettle hung on a tripod above a fire. With a long stick she poked at the clothing which steamed in the water. Her dress was gathered between her legs and fastened just above the knees. The effect was that of voluminous pantaloons. A strand of hair hung down limply over her forehead. She pushed it with the back of one hand as she looked up. In a hammock, stretched between two stunted trees, a dark-skinned man, bare of chest and wearing only seaman's ducks, idly fingered the frets on a guitar. He watched Cameron's determined approach with faint amusement.

"Hello, Father." Caroline was not disturbed by his sudden appearance. For all her manner they could be meeting on the manor's porch. "How are you?"

He could only stare at her. Was this girl with a dark smudge on one cheek, barefooted in the hot sand, tending a kettle of washing, his daughter? He looked from her to the man in the hammock. Cadiz was watching him with alert interest.

"I have come to talk with you, Caroline." He could barely force the words into a normal tone. "Unless you have lost all sense of reason."

"Of course, Father. I mean, of course we can talk. I can't offer you a chair. We don't have one."

"God in heaven, girl, what has brought you to this?" He all but strangled upon the question. "Is this the man?" He leveled an accusing finger at Cadiz.

"That is Juan, Father. My husband."

Juan laughed suddenly from his place in the hammock. Infuriated by the mocking sound, Cameron wheeled and started for him. Cadiz swung out of the canvas sling with an easy grace and waited, half-crouched, for the attack.

"Father!" The single word was as sharp as a pistol's report. It halted Cameron in his tracks. "There is no good of your fighting with Juan. He didn't drag me here. I came." She moved to place a restraining hand on his arm.

Cameron was shaking with impotent rage. He stood, spraddle-legged, his big hands clasping and unclasping in a spasm of anger.

"You are married—to this?" He was incredulous.

"Twelve days ago, Father. On Eluthera." She glanced with a warm affection at Juan. "I am your daughter but I am also Juan's wife. I told you I would not be sent back to Aunt Martha and Charleston. You forced me, Father."

He could not believe what he had heard. To have run away with this fellow would have been bad enough. That damage might have been repaired. But to have married him. He stared at her.

"You—you left home for this—this hovel? For this man who has transformed you from a dainty and fastidious girl into a fishwife; to wash his clothing and keep him comfortable?"

"If that is the way you want to put it, Father." She was not defiant. Neither was she cowed.

"Why? In the name of God tell me why?" All the pent-up anguish was in the words.

"Because I love him and he loves me."

Tears, excuses, protestations; those things Cameron could have understood. This simple statement of a fact left him all but speechless. The girl, this stranger who was his daughter, actually seemed radiantly happy in these squalid surroundings. His slaves were better housed. He looked from her to Cadiz with uncomprehending wonder. What was he to do? Grab her hand and drag her, fighting, to the ketch? Throw himself upon this Cadiz and beat him into a screaming madman? His body and spirit sagged. He was defeated and he knew it.

"I want you back home, Caroline."

"I would like to be home, Father, but not without Juan. You will have to make the choice or the decision."

Cameron turned to face Cadiz. He was leaning with a negligent and supple grace against a tree, listening and watching. He spoke now with that faint, difficult-to-define accent of the Bahamian.

"You see how it is. You have daughter an' a son-in-law or you have nothing, old man."

Again the rage leaped like a flame within Cameron. This whelp was so confident, so sure of his hold on Caroline. He kept his temper under rigid control. This was the moment of decision. He could turn about, walk back to the ketch and sail to Exuma. In doing this he would put his daughter out of his life for all time. Or, he could accept things as they were. He could not state the terms but only accept those which were offered. He walked to Caroline and took her shoulders in his hands.

"I want you home." He felt her tremble just a little and her eyes misted for a moment. "Nothing is more important to me than that. I want you home if you want to come."

"I have said how it would have to be, Father."

He nodded his head and folded her into his arms. She came willingly but not as one humbled. Her head rested on his chest and he could feel her quick breathing. In command of himself now he spoke past her to Cadiz.

"I do not like you. It is doubtful I ever shall."

"I can live." Juan lifted his shoulders indifferently.

"I could," Cameron continued, "possibly have the Church or the Governor put aside the marriage but I am afraid it is too late for that. I will not offer you my hand. I want my daughter home where she belongs.

[129]

If you are the price I must pay for that, then I will pay it but with reluctance."

Caroline drew away from him and shook her head determinedly.

"I will not have it that way, Father. You and Juan at each other's throats for the rest of our lives. If you want me home you will have to live with each other."

"Am I supposed to clap him on the back in friendship?" Cameron shouted his exasperation.

"I don't know how you will handle it but arranged between you it must be. Juan is my husband."

"All right," he assented drearily. "Come home where you belong. Bring your," the word stuck in his throat, "your husband with you. He can take his place on the plantation with the rest of us—Robert Bruce, Spithead and me."

"I don' muches workin' en no pea patch, pa-pa." Juan deliberately mimicked and broadened the Bahamian accent and dialect.

"And you stop that, Juan." Caroline turned upon him with tight anger. Her eyes were fired until they seemed green and yellow agates. "Don't make a joke of it. You will both have to give a little. Don't go out of your way to make things harder than they are."

Juan emitted a short, shrill whistle, part derision and part admiration for her temper. But he didn't pursue the subject. He picked up his guitar and brushed a few soft chords from its strings. Caroline watched him for a moment and then her manner softened. Was there ever such a complete rascal as this Juan of hers?

She forked out the shirts and the trousers and tossed them on a nearby bush to cool and drip. Then she wiped her hands on the side of her dress with the gesture of a sturdy peasant woman.

"How did you come, Father? In the ketch?"

Cameron nodded. He could not believe this self-reliant, completely unaffected girl was his daughter. How could she have changed so in less than two weeks? There was a new quality of maturity about her; a confidence which was adult and had nothing to do with the Caroline he had known.

"Go on back to the ketch, Father. Juan and I will be over in a day or so." She smiled happily. "He is teaching me how to handle the sloop. She has a red sail and is as graceful as a wild deer." She went to him, raised herself on the tips of her toes and kissed his cheek. "You'll see. Everything is going to be all right. Better than you think."

Cameron nodded an assent he didn't feel. How could things turn out all right with such a marriage? He turned away and walked toward the boat landing with a feeling of complete inadequacy. But, and he was forced to ask himself the question, what more could he have done? He smiled unconsciously. This new Caroline wasn't afraid of anything. When it was necessary she even spoke up to her new husband with authority.

Caroline stood watching until her father turned a corner at the end of the shacks. Then, she picked up one of the sodden garments and gestured to Juan.

"Help me wring these out. They'll dry quickly enough."

With twinkling eyes Juan took hold of one end and they twisted together while the water ran with spurts upon the ground.

"You don't wash my clothes anymore, hey? We have slaves to do it for us. I think I am going to like it on the plantation."

"You're going to work on the plantation." She grimaced as she tugged at the pants. "You're going to work with father and Robert Bruce, learn how it is managed. Someday we will own it and you will have to know how to run it with Robert Bruce."

Juan was skeptical. "I'd rather play the guitar and make love to you on the beach. Maybe sometimes I'll go to Nassau like I used to. I think, maybe, the girls there miss Juan Cadiz and his songs."

She was undisturbed. "You'll stay on Exuma with me. I'm all the girl you need. In time we'll raise a family." She frowned. "Do you suppose I can't have children, Juan? Why hasn't it happened already? I have heard of women who couldn't have babies."

"I'll make them for you now we are married. You wait and see. For a while, though, you don't be a mama. Just my girl like always before. Plenty of time for babies."

"I suppose so." She was doubtful. "My mother had Robert Bruce when she was eighteen."

"There's no hurry. They'll come when they come." He regarded her with a quizzical smile, thinking of what marriage did to a girl. It made her a woman, sure of her man, sure of herself. She even stood up against her father. He laughed suddenly. If that old man thought he was going to be a farmer he'd learn something different. Nothing, big house or the plantation, was going to change Juan Cadiz. When he got tired of things he'd sail off to Nassau and get drunk with the girls again.

"What are you laughing at?" She watched him with curiosity.

"At you. Me. Your papa. The whole damn world, maybe. Juan Cadiz in a big house with slaves to wait on him." He dropped back into the hammock, crossed his ankles, put his arms behind his head and stared up at the sky with humorous satisfaction. "It's pretty funny when you think about it."

Gurney and Robert Bruce watched Cameron as he came down the

dock and aboard the ketch. His face was a dark study and from it they could read nothing.

"We goin' back now, Mr. Cameron?" Gurney waited before casting off. "Without Mistress Caroline?"

"Yes."

Cameron said nothing more until they were underway and clearing the small cove.

"They're married." He spoke abruptly. "She married that fellow. My daughter Caroline. She was washing his clothing." He made the comment as though he could not believe what he was saying. "My daughter standing over a kettle of dirty clothing."

Neither Gurney nor Robert Bruce replied. The enormity of what Cameron had said left them without speech. Dumbly Robert Bruce wondered at his sister's temerity. Where had she found the courage, the strength of purpose, to defy her father? It was incredible. He experienced a small twinge of admiration for her daring, reckless though it was.

"They are coming to Exuma," Cameron continued, almost as though he were talking to himself. "I don't like it but what can I do? He's her husband. She won't come home without him." He locked hands beneath his chin and stared at the planking. "We'll have to make the best of it although God knows it turns my stomach."

In the cool and shaded bedroom of the Governor's Mansion, Sabrina Heath gave birth to a seven-pound baby boy. She was in a fresh bed, made while she lay upon it. The doctor and midwife stood by.

"He's a fine, strapping child, Lady Heath." Dr. Harrington washed his hands in a basin of water which a slave girl, standing just within the door, quickly took away. "A fine boy," he repeated.

"I suppose so." Sabrina regarded the infant with slightly puzzled curiosity. Out of an hour's dalliance with Ronald Cameron this had come. She didn't know what she felt. Certainly no great surge of mother love. "He yelled loud enough. I guess I did, also." She smiled. "I had no idea pain could be so terrible."

"It was a surprisingly easy birth, Lady Heath." The doctor was rolling down his sleeves and putting on his coat. He picked up his case. "Now," he patted her hand, "I think I will go down and have a drink of congratulations with Sir Gerald."

"By all means do that." She nodded. "I fancy Gerald is making quite a thing of it; becoming a father at his age and after all these years."

She watched him go. The midwife took a chair by the window and rocked placidly back and forth. The slave girl slipped quietly from the room. She closed her eyes with a sudden weariness.

In the dining hall Sir Gerald with Captain Birch and two other officers from his staff was at a table with a decanter of brandy between them. As the doctor entered they all looked up and swung about inquiringly.

"A son, Sir Gerald. As fine a boy as I have ever delivered."

"Well! That *is* good news." Captain Birch rose, followed by his brother officers. They raised their glasses in Sir Gerald's direction. "Congratulations and good health to the lady upstairs." Birch drained his glass. "What will you name him?"

"I fancy Lady Heath has already decided that for me. She seems to have handled everything else." It was with the greatest difficulty that Sir Gerald managed a wry smile, doing his best to look pleased; the proud father of a son and heir.

The officers refilled their glasses and Sir Gerald watched with a speculative moroseness. It could be any one of them he thought. Birch, Rodney, Kent. What a fine comedy this was. He sat and accepted congratulations from the trio when any one of them might well be the one who had made him a cuckold. If it was one of the three, was he secretly laughing to himself? Had Sabrina told her unidentified lover the child she carried was his? The thought was unbearable. He drank his brandy and quickly refilled the glass. Damn such thoughts. He was being made a fool. Damn and double damn.

As Sabrina had so confidently predicted he had done nothing to expose her and himself. To throw her out, to divorce her, to send her packing back to England, to rid himself of her insolent behavior, would have made him the laughingstock of Nassau. It might even cost him his appointment as Governor. He could not afford to admit the child she carried was not his. So, he had and continued to put on the best possible face. He had played the part of an expectant father so well he sometimes half believed it himself.

The physician accepted the offer of a tot of brandy and drank it with relish. It was a fine French liquor and came to the Governor's Mansion duty free.

"Your wife is resting easily, Sir Gerald. You may see her and your son now if you wish. The infant is in her arms this very moment and a midwife is standing by. There will be no complications. You gentlemen," he spoke to Birch and the others, "may also make a short visit. I am sure she would be delighted to see you."

"By all means." Sir Gerald heaved himself from the chair. "If you gentlemen would care to pay your respects."

They filed up the staircase and down the long gallery to Sabrina's room. Sir Gerald studied the faces of his officers keenly, trying to detect an eagerness which might reveal some clue as to the child's parentage.

[133]

There was nothing in their manner to indicate more than a courteous interest in the child and mother. Sir Gerald chewed upon his lip. Captain Birch? The fellow was too light of manner, too sure of himself. Sabrina had flirted outrageously with him for a month or more. It could be Birch, the damned whelp. Birch's manner, though, was anything but that of an eager father. If he could only be sure. Then he thought, What good would that do? Even if Sabrina told him the sire's name he could do nothing about it. No. The secret must be locked within him for all time.

Sabrina glanced up from the massed pillows as they filed respectfully into the room, led by Sir Gerald. She knew she looked pretty. Her hair had been arranged and there was a touch of French coloring on her cheeks. She seemed radiantly alive and smiled at their awkward grouping.

"Gentlemen." She inclined her head. "Come in, by all means." She pulled back a corner of the light blanket and exposed the peaceful, sleeping face of the infant. "Sir Gerald, I give you your son. We shall call him David. David Heath."

The Governor searched his mind for the first names of all those who might be the father. There wasn't a David among them so this was no good. He bent and looked at the child.

"Wrinkled little beggar, isn't he?"

"He probably worries." Sabrina's eyes were filled with mocking laughter. "Takes after his father."

The other officers dutifully inspected the small bundle and made what they imagined to be the appropriate gurgling noises which the baby was supposed to understand. Sabrina thought they were all acting pretty silly.

"If," Captain Birch spoke to her, "we can be considered as the child's godparents, I shall take it upon myself to teach him to ride. Rodney and Kent can instruct him in such manly sports as they are proficient."

"You'll wait a couple of days, won't you, Captain?" She regarded him humorously. Men took these things so seriously. "I don't think he is ready to sit a horse just yet."

"I must say you take this all very calmly, Sabrina." Sir Gerald cleared his throat. "After all, it isn't every day a child is born in the Governor's Mansion."

"Then I say, thank God for that." Sabrina sighed. "It could become something of a strain after a while. Now," she half closed her eyes, "I think I would like to sleep if you will excuse me."

Murmuring the proper apologies, Birch, Kent and Rodney tiptoed

[134]

from the room. Sir Gerald remained behind. He was plainly on the point of a momentous decision. Finally he cleared his throat.

"I can't pretend I like the situation." He spoke regretfully and without rancor. "I would that the babe was really mine. I suppose in time he will seem this way and I shall come to like, maybe even love him. As the years pass the knowledge of your infidelity will become less painful than it is at the moment. I may even be able to forget it entirely."

"That is generous of you, Gerald."

"I would like your reassurance that the father is not someone I see every day, sit at the table with sometimes, or share a pipe. I do not like the idea of being a complete fool."

"He is not one of your intimates, Gerald."

"At least that is something. By the way," the thought struck him suddenly, "who is David?"

She yawned delicately. "It is a name I read in a book. He did something about slaying a giant. I really forget the details."

"Humph!" Sir Gerald bent a little to look at the baby's face. "Funny-looking little beggar, isn't he?" He took a handkerchief from his sleeve and blew his nose with the sound of a trumpet. "Damn it, Sabrina. Why couldn't it have really been mine?"

Juan awoke as he did each morning with a shout of laughter on his lips. He had not yet accustomed himself to this big house; the bedroom which was larger than the hut he had once shared with Plymouth; the immaculate and starched curtains with their full-length draperies; the slaves who brought breakfast when he rang; the windows looking out upon the rolling slope down to the sea; the slender beauty of the girl beside him in the wide bed.

He swung out from beneath the coverings and went to the windows. He threw open the shutters and stood, marveling at the quiet beauty of the morning. He breathed deeply of the fresh, salt air and then began prowling about with the restless energy of a fine animal.

From her place on the down pillows Caroline watched him through half-open eyes. What a man she had married. He would wear no night clothing but insisted upon sleeping as naked as he had been born. The spectacle of him walking about without a thread on no longer startled her as it once had. She took a secret delight in his lithe movements. The rippling of muscle, the easy grace with which he poised himself. The insolent, devil-may-care attitude with which he treated everyone and everything. He was not at all impressed by the size of the plantation, the number of slaves, the manor. What a strange one he was, for he seemed to care for nothing but her, his guitar and boat. She giggled soundlessly thinking of her father. Cameron ignored his son-in-law insofar as it was possible. When he did address him, it was as Cadiz.

"I do not like the way you sound that." Juan had eyed the man coldly. "The way you say Cadiz. Call me Juan, if you like, or Mister Cadiz. It makes no difference but it is one or the other."

He outraged her father, she thought, dumfounded Robert Bruce and startled the house slaves, who were accustomed to the ways of the gentry.

He wore what he had always worn since she first knew him; a pair of white duck sailor's pants which were wide of cut and fell just below the knees. These and a shirt, frequently unfastened to the navel. He walked about in bare feet although he did, sometimes, put on a pair of sandals he had fashioned himself. Cameron had been aghast when he appeared for the first time at the dining table costumed in this fashion.

"Good God, man, don't you have any proper clothing?"

"What's wrong with this?" Juan had tasted the soup as it was put before him. "I would not like to be stuffed into those breeches and tight coat the way you are. But," he was innocence itself, "if you do not like them, then write an order on a tailor in Nassau. I'll go there someday and have him make me some clothes."

"Is there no gentleman's pride in you?" Cameron had thundered the question.

"What has pride to do with it?" He felt for Caroline's leg beneath the table and squeezed it. "You have money and I have none."

"Then earn your keep." Cameron restrained himself as best he could. "Ride to the fields with Robert Bruce and me in the morning. There is plenty to do, overseeing the work of the hands."

"I do not like work, I cannot ride a horse, and dislike telling other people what to do."

Cameron had difficulty in swallowing. "Do you intend to go through life doing nothing but sailing around in a boat with a red sail? Is there no manhood in you?"

Juan ate calmly. "There is man enough in me for your daughter. If you do not like the way I am, then we can always go back to my place on Long Island. What is so fine about working?"

Cameron finished the meal in silence. He had no answer for this airy indifference to responsibility. So, Juan continued to live as he had ever since coming to Exuma. He arose when it pleased him, ate when he felt like it, slept when sleepiness was upon him. He took Caroline in the sloop and they sailed the cays. They fished and broiled what they caught on sticks over a fire on the beach. In a sheltered cove they swam naked with much laughter.

Watching him now Caroline thought, I would not have him changed. I want him with laughter and not the seriousness of Robert Bruce and my father. If in time responsibility is thrust upon him, he will learn to accept it. Until then I want him as he is.

"Juan." She spoke softly and he turned from the window. "Do you love me?"

"Always that is the first question you ask in the morning. Is there nothing else on your mind?"

"Not when I see you that way."

He made no attempt to cover himself and she felt a shiver run through her body.

"Let's sail over to Long Island today and see my friends." He stood before her. "We will take some of your papa's rum and get everyone drunk."

"Maybe." She stretched with a delicious feeling of languor. "Maybe. Later."

He eyed her with a bright amusement and then came to sit on the side of the bed, stripping the covers down. In her shift of linen she seemed so small, so young.

"What is it you want?" He grinned.

Her arms went up to encircle his neck. "You know." The reply was half whispered. "Come back to bed. Come back to bed and make me a baby, Juanio."

~§ XI §~

AMONG THOSE who held large land grants in the Out Islands and had staked everything on the venture, one inescapable fact confronted them with a frightening certainty. The Bahama soil was not suited for the growing of cotton on a large scale.

Cameron knew this long before he was ready to admit the truth. The Exuma plantation covered two thousand acres and most of it had been put to cotton. The yield was pitifully small. Where, in the rich bottom land of the Carolina Low Country, he could estimate a bale to the acre, here he was fortunate to grow half that amount. And the decline was constant as the land exhausted itself. In an effort to revitalize it he had diversified the planting, growing beans, cane and fodder until the storehouses were glutted with the stuff. Save for the cane there was no market in Nassau for what he was growing. In the past two years he had shipped no more than five hundred bales of cotton to the commission merchants.

In an effort to learn whether the conditions on Exuma were unique, he and Robert Bruce had taken the ketch and visited plantations on Watlings Island and Eleuthera. The story in those places was the same. The land simply would not produce enough cotton to provide the income needed. The small landowners, those with a couple of slaves or none at all, were faring better. They grew what they needed, sold some of their fresh produce in the Nassau markets, took their living from the sea and earth.

Cameron had a hundred slaves, more if he counted the innumerable children which had been born during their years on Exuma. These must be clothed and fed, ministered to when ill, quartered and watched over. Also, and this had disturbed him more and more of late, there were unmistakable signs of truculence among the field hands. There were many black freedmen in the Out Islands and in some mysterious manner the Cameron slaves had made contact with them. The idea of freedom permeated slowly but it was taking root. There was a sullenness among them, a blank, passive defiance sometimes and a constant malingering at their work. The house slaves seemed well content but Cameron had begun to wonder how he, Robert Bruce and Spithead would cope with an open rebellion if it ever came. It was a thing which kept him awake many nights.

On Watlings Island they spent three days at the plantation of John Ormond. Ormond had been a neighboring planter on the Ashley and there had been many visits back and forth between the families. Here, as on the other island plantations, a determined effort had been made to preserve the gracious living of the Low Country. The ladies, Ormond's wife and his two daughters, ages sixteen and eighteen, brought out their prettiest gowns for the visitors. The evening meal, the only one which they were all able to have together, was taken in candlelit sumptuousness. The food was served on the finest linen with the best of china and silver. Every effort was made to recreate life as they had once known it. But, and Cameron sensed this, behind a brave front, the gentle courtesy and the easy informality of their talk, there was a gnawing feeling of desperation. For if the plantation failed here, to what were they to return?

Now, over their pipes and a bottle of fine Oporto, Cameron and John Ormond discussed the situation with measured gravity.

"I tell you, Ronald," Ormond half sighed, "I am about ready to give up and return to Carolina while I still have some funds left. Each year it grows a little leaner here. The Home Government can do nothing about it. My wife is discontented with the narrow strictures of her life. My daughters have little opportunity for a marriage which would be suitable to their breeding and background. I work hard and the ground is producing less and less of commercial value. I would to God I had never heard of these islands. Better to endure the democracy on the mainland than to sink each year into a form of genteel poverty."

"I'll rot here first." Cameron refilled his glass with the rich, ruby-colored wine. "I'll grow weeds before I return to the insolence of the rabble which has taken over Carolina. Besides, where would I settle? Cameron Hall was confiscated. I am too old to start over again. I will not allow these islands to defeat me."

Ormond smoked meditatively. His plantation, also, had been pre-empted by the victorious rebels. How could he return to Carolina? This time the Crown would offer no assistance. He would have to dig into his own, lean pocket for the cost of transporting everything back to the mainland.

"I hear," Ormond broke the unhappy silence, "that Amos Sitwell, on

Eluthera, gave his slaves their freedom, left them on the plantation to do with it what they will. He has gone or is going back to England. And there are others who no longer believe these islands offer the opportunity for which they hoped."

"Sitwell is a wealthy man. Many of the shares which I held in England have dropped so far as to be all but valueless." Cameron's jaw tightened. "I must make out here or fail entirely."

They smoked for a moment or two in silence, each occupied with his thoughts.

"How old is your son Robert Bruce?" Ormond spoke first. He, nor had any of the Ormonds, made any reference to Caroline although they must know of her marriage. News was somehow passed from island to island. "He is a likely-appearing lad."

"Robert Bruce will be twenty-one on his next birthday. A solemn man he has become, one with little humor in him," Cameron reflected. "It is partly my fault, I suspect, for I have given him responsibilities beyond his years. He is much with me and I have had little time for laughter."

"I was thinking of my eldest daughter, Constance," Ormond mused. "They have known each other since childhood. I noticed tonight, over the dining table, the glances passing between them. I would welcome a marriage between our families, Ronald."

"I suspect the young people will settle that between themselves." Cameron was thinking of Caroline and Juan Cadiz. "But," he smiled a little, "it would do no harm to give the situation a nudge where we can. Why don't you arrange to have your wife and daughters visit us for a while on Exuma? It would be a welcome diversion for us all. Who knows what may happen? Propinquity is a great matchmaker."

Seated between the two Ormond sisters, Robert Bruce was miserably aware of his inability to engage in small talk. Also, there was the rather formidable figure of Mrs. Ormond as she sat across the room with her knitting. Unwittingly she made a free exchange among the young people difficult. How, he wondered, if that was his purpose, did a man pay court to a girl in the presence of her mother? Constance had surprised him. From the gawky, shrilling child he remembered in Carolina she had matured into a lovely, poised young lady. He was old enough now to begin to think about marriage. Enviously he had watched Caroline and Juan. How complete they seemed, how they complemented each other, how full and rich their lives even under the disapproving eyes of his father.

Deborah, the younger sister, had brought out her collection of shells for his inspection and admiration but this subject had been quickly exhausted. A couple of times Constance's hand had touched his by seeming accident when she handed him a shell. It was, he thought, a most pleasant sensation and one he would have liked to pursue, but this couldn't be done under the watchful eyes of her mother. He wondered if it would be a breach of the proprieties to suggest a walk outside. But, he realized, this would accomplish nothing for Deborah would most certainly come along.

He only half listened as Deborah maintained a constant chatter about the most trivial of things. Now and then he caught Constance's eyes. Upon such occasions she quickly lowered them with an exaggerated modesty but there was a bright interest in her expression. They had exhausted most of the conversational subjects. The weather. A new colt foaled. The last visit of the *Traveler* and the news from Nassau. In none of these things did they have any real interest. He caught himself thinking of Caroline and Juan Cadiz. From what mysterious source did they draw their apparently inexhaustible zest for life? What sent their spirits soaring and made each new day an adventure? By comparison he felt an earthbound clod, tongue-tied and awkward.

"La! But it is warm in here tonight." Constance made a delicate, fanning motion with one hand.

"Why don't you go to the porch?" Mrs. Ormond didn't look up. "Or take Mr. Cameron for a walk through the gardens. There is a full moon."

"It would be a relief, Mama." Constance was properly reserved. "Would you like that, Robert Bruce?"

He arose almost too hastily. Anything, he thought, to escape from the suffocation of this room and the task of making conversation about nothing.

"I'll go with you." Deborah spoke hopefully.

"I need you here to help me ball a skein of yarn." Mrs. Ormond was quietly emphatic. "Constance is perfectly capable of showing Robert Bruce the gardens."

Deborah flounced back in her seat with a pout. "Why do I always have to hold the skein?" She was resentful.

"Because no one does it quite as well." Mrs. Ormond smiled with understanding at her daughter.

Outside, on the porch, Robert Bruce drew a deep breath of relief. He was aware of Constance as she shyly inserted her hand beneath his arm.

"It is terrible, isn't it? I mean, no one really has anything to say. I felt sorry for you in there. Sorry for all of us. We live on this island, seeing only an occasional visitor. A trip to Nassau becomes something to talk about for weeks. I sometimes feel as though I were in prison. Don't you often wish you were back in Carolina?"

"No-o." He didn't agree with her. "I like it well enough here."

"Well, I don't!" She was emphatic. "Maybe it is all right for a man. But I'm old enough now for the balls, the parties, the hunts." She eyed him mischievously. "For beaux. I would just like crowds of people around me and not wake up every morning to the same thing."

They strolled the length of the broad porch. A light wind from the sea hunted through the trees and vines. The air was heavy with the perfume of oleander which grew in profusion. She held possessively to his arm. In the soft moon's light there was a dusky beauty about her.

"It is strange." She spoke wonderingly. "We have known each other since we were children and my parents used to bring me to Cameron Hall for a visit or you all came to our plantation. But, I think this is the first time we have ever been alone together. I don't really know you at all, Robert Bruce. You are so—so reserved. I can't imagine you doing anything without thinking it over carefully first."

He wheeled her about almost roughly and planted an inexperienced kiss full on her half-parted lips. She gasped in the clumsy embrace and then clung to him for a fraction of a second.

"There." He was triumphant. "I didn't think about that first, did I?" He laughed self-consciously. "Maybe," he confessed, "maybe, though, I did. I guess I thought about it all evening and for the past two days we have been here."

"Well! I never." She pretended exasperated surprise. "What you must think of me."

He had regained some of his composure. "I think you're a pretty girl. Maybe the prettiest I have ever known."

"You're not sure?" She coquetted deliberately.

"Yes. I'm sure." He hesitated. "Exuma isn't so far away. I could sail over and call. I'll speak to your father and ask his permission."

"You'll get that fast enough." She was certain. "Papa is worried about having two girls on his hands. He is afraid Deborah and I will grow up to be old maids. There aren't many eligible young men in the Out Islands to come calling. I'm sure Papa would be relieved to have you call."

"What about you?"

She was properly reserved. "I like you, Robert Bruce. I always have. You're really very handsome when you're not being an old sobersides." She hesitated and then lowered her voice to a whisper. "Tell me about Caroline. I heard Mama and Papa talking about her, being married so suddenly and without any of the family. They acted as though it was some sort of a disgrace. What is he, her husband, like? Are they happy?"

"As far as I know they are. Juan? Well, I guess Juan isn't like anyone else." He laughed quietly. "Father doesn't know what to do about Juan.

You see, he just isn't like anyone we have ever known. He is something new and strange. Father sets a great store by hard work. Juan laughs at it. This upsets Father. He doesn't know how to cope with it."

"You mean this Juan doesn't do anything?" She was incredulous.

"Well"—there was a touch of dry humor in the reply—"he plays the guitar mighty well. He and Caroline go sailing in his boat." There was an unconscious touch of envy in the words. "I think Father would throw him off the plantation except he knows Caroline would go with him. He doesn't want that."

"It sounds so wildly romantic." She sighed wistfully. "Exciting. How did she meet him? Where?"

"Caroline has never said. No one knows. They just ran off, without saying a word, and were married by a missionary on Eluthera. He—Juan —looks like a pirate with a gold ring in his ear. He and my father don't speak to each other unless they have to."

"I wish something like that would happen to me." She spoke without thinking and then caught herself. "I don't suppose I really mean that."

"I guess you do." Robert Bruce made the statement reluctantly. "I suppose every girl would like to be swept off her feet and carried away by someone like Juan." In the pale moonlight Constance saw the fleeting smile. "I'm not very different or exciting. You'll have to take me as I am."

Her fingers locked in his with a reassuring pressure.

"I guess I'm not much like Caroline, either." She sighed again. "I'd like to be but I'm not." She turned to face him. "Are you really going to speak to Papa?"

"You ought to decide. I will if you want me to."

She glanced down the length of the porch and then lifted her face.

"You may kiss me, Robert Bruce."

He held her in a clumsy embrace and felt the pounding of his heart. He had never held a girl in his arms before; never kissed one save in the half-furtive games of childhood. He was surprised, even a little startled by her ardor, unaware of how unsophisticated it was.

She clung to him for a moment and then withdrew reluctantly. "Now." She spoke almost primly. "I suppose we had better go in. Mama must be certain I have shown you all of our gardens twice over. Although," she laughed with an amused wisdom, "I don't really believe that is the reason she suggested we go for a walk in the moonlight." Her fingers entwined with his and in their touch there was a warm possessiveness.

They walked slowly. "Do you love me, Robert Bruce?" She asked the question so softly it was barely audible. "Kissing doesn't mean love. I wouldn't like to think this was happening only because we have known each other for a long time and," she hurried the words, "it is convenient."

He had no ready answer. Words did not come easily, particularly the words which one should say to a girl.

"Well?" She was mocking him a little now.

"It—it is hard to say," he confessed honestly. "The word itself, 'love,' doesn't seem quite enough. More would make me sound silly. Somehow," he couldn't hold back a note of amusement, "when you read them in a book they seem natural enough." He halted and turned her gently toward him. " 'By the moon and stars I love you, Constance Ormond. Your eyes are pools of mystery.' " He injected a theatrical quality into his voice and struck a pose. " 'Your teeth are pearls from an azure sea. Your cheeks the petals from the fairest rose.' "

Her eyes were bright with laughter and she pressed fingertips against her lips to hold it back.

"Do you suppose," he asked, "anyone ever said anything like that to a girl and kept his face straight?"

She was laughing openly now, her face upturned to his. "I like you when you are being a little foolish. But, you forgot something."

"What?"

" 'I plight thee my troth.' They always say that in books, also, but I haven't the slightest idea what it means. Will you plight me your troth, Robert Bruce?"

"By my rood." He took her in his arms and she came with a fresh eagerness.

"It is better this way, isn't it?" She pulled his mouth against hers. "I mean, when we can laugh together. What is a rood?"

He kissed her with a new awakening of passion. One hand lingered for a moment on her breast and she did not resist. They both experimented a little timidly with a new sensation.

"I'll speak to your father in the morning." They drew apart and began walking to where the light spilled from an open doorway across the porch. "But," the tone was concerned, "if you really hate it in the islands . . ." He paused. "This would be our life here. You would have to make do with it."

"Would we never, never go back to Carolina?"

He shook his head. "I don't know. I haven't thought about it. Everything we have now is here. Anyhow, I think life must be a great deal different than the one we knew. The Rebels may have broken all the big plantations into small farms. I have been brought up on the land. It is all I know. I have not been trained for anything else. What would I do in Carolina; work some small tract? Take a clerkship? Hire for someone else as an overseer?"

"I suppose not." She was unhappily doubtful, then her features lightened. "But, it would be different. I mean," she glanced up at him, "to be married, have a home and servants of your own. In time, I suppose, it will not seem as strange and foreign as it does now. And later—in a few years—we could make a trip to Charleston just for a visit, couldn't we?"

"If it means so much to you, I suppose so." He took her hand, a little disturbed by her obvious discontent. "But this would be our life; that to which we always must return."

The pressure of her hand in his increased. "I don't think I will be unhappy with you, Robert Bruce."

Mrs. Ormond looked up from her knitting as they entered. She noted the subdued radiance in the eyes of her daughter and smiled to herself. Her thoughts flashed back over the years and she could remember them both as children. It all seemed so long ago. How different would their lives have been save for the war which had destroyed all they had taken for granted. But this, if it happened, would be a good marriage. Good for them all. It would yield some substance to this way of life, so new, unsettled and beset with unexpected difficulties and problems. When John Ormond had told her of his decision to migrate to the Bahamas she had voiced no word of protest. It was not in her nature to question her husband's judgment in such matters. She had left Carolina with a wrenching pang for everything familiar and which, she knew in her heart, she would never see again. But a marriage between Constance and Robert Bruce would settle once and for all the insecurity, the feeling of impermanence haunting her. It would be a new foundation on which to build. The stock on both sides was sturdy. It had conquered in the tangled wilderness of Carolina and would not fail here. The seed of such a mating must flourish. She regarded them with affectionate approval. They made a handsome young couple standing there in the pale, golden light of bracketed candles. She caught herself almost envying them their youth and the adventurous years which must lie ahead.

"Was it pleasant in the garden?" She put aside her knitting.

"Yes, Mama." Constance's reply was properly demure but there was a sparkle of suppressed excitement in her eyes. "The moon was lovely." She moved to seat herself on the arm of her mother's chair.

Deborah, who was laying out some picture cards at a table in a game of her own, looked up with amused wisdom over her parent's innocence.

"Everything grows in such profusion here." Mrs. Ormond sighed half-regretfully. "No matter how many yardmen we put to work it seems impossible to achieve the order we knew back home. There is, though," she confessed, "a certain wild beauty in these islands." She smiled at Robert Bruce. "You must visit us more often. Our social life is so restricted. I sometimes think we all, the old families who were close in Carolina, should make more of an effort to get together; to hold on to something we once knew and loved. But," she could not disguise a fleeting expression of distaste, "I must confess I do not care for travel on the water. It is always a disturbing experience. There seems to be so much of it. The water, I mean."

"Yes, ma'am." Robert Bruce felt compelled to say something. "There is a lot of water around and that is a fact."

Voices in the hallway caused them all to turn their heads toward the open double doors which closed off the withdrawing room. Ormond and Cameron crossed the threshold.

"We did not mean to talk for so long a time," John Ormond apologized. He opened the heavy case of a watch and consulted the hands. "I had no idea it was so late."

"Time passes quickly when you find a willing listener to your troubles." Cameron smiled ruefully.

"Would you care for some chocolate and biscuits?" Mrs. Ormond glanced at her husband and Cameron.

"No, thank you." Cameron placed his hands defensively across his stomach. "John's Oporto has left little room for anything more." He bowed to her. "If you will forgive us, we will to bed. I would like to be away early in the morning, probably before the household is awake. Accept our gratitude for your hospitality."

"I was saying to Robert Bruce"—Mrs. Ormond arose—"we old families, those of us who were friends and neighbors in Carolina, should make an attempt to get together oftener." She offered her hand to him. "Please come again." She looked from Constance to Robert Bruce. "I have an idea we shall be seeing more of your son. He seemed to find our garden most attractive." Her smile was warm and embracing.

"Mama!" Constance lowered her eyes in confusion.

"With your permission, sir," Robert Bruce said to Ormond.

"Well! What is this?" He looked fondly from his daughter to Robert Bruce. "Ronald and I were discussing just such a thing during our talks. There seems no need for matchmaking." He placed his hand on Robert Bruce's shoulder. "There is no one I would welcome more."

"Thank you, sir."

Ormond studied Deborah. "It is too bad you do not have a brother, Robert Bruce."

"Papa!" The younger girl swept her cards into an untidy heap with an impatient gesture. "I think you would throw me at the first young man who came along just to be rid of me." She looked at Robert Bruce and grinned wickedly. "Just the same, if you have any trouble with Constance . . ." She ran in laughing confusion from the room.

Later, as he stood in the doorway connecting the room occupied by his father with his own, Robert Bruce spoke of what had been said.

"What do you think of my calling upon Mistress Constance?"

Cameron was unfastening the pearled buttons of his ruffled shirt. He looked up and across the room at his son.

"If," he spoke slowly, "she pleases you, I think it would be a fine thing. There are not many young ladies of her station in the islands to choose from. You are both at a good age for marriage. Start early for it takes some time to get used to each other. These islands can be a lonely place. A comely wife can do much to make them more bearable." He stripped himself of his shirt and stood in singlet and short drawers. "I must confess to a great loneliness at times." He finished undressing and drew a shapeless nightshirt over his head. "Yes," he continued regretfully, "I am afraid I am too old, too set in my ways for such a thing."

There was a crystal decanter of brandy on a night table beside the bed. Cameron filled a small glass and was on the point of replacing the stopper when he halted the action.

"Would you join me? I too often forget you are no longer a boy."

Robert Bruce shook his head. "No thanks. I really don't like the taste of brandy." He made the confession with a trace of embarrassment. "I suppose I should get used to it. It seems to be the stripe of a man."

"That depends on how he uses it." He sipped at the liquor and then drained the glass. "Its misuse comes when a man attempts to hide behind it. He finds, then, that the bottle only serves to magnify his weakness." From a box on the bureau he selected a long, slender cigar. They were Havana made and its fragrance filled the room. Cameron sat on the edge of the bed, his legs spraddled, his heavy shoulders drooping with a weariness he did not attempt to hide. "I am bothered by many things, Robert Bruce."

Studying his father, Robert Bruce suddenly realized how much he had aged during these past few years.

"There is your sister, for one thing," Cameron continued, staring at the floor and speaking as though to himself. "I would get rid of the blackguard save for the fact that in some inexplicable way she seems to be happy with him. That passes all of my understanding. How a girl, gently reared, could become infatuated with this rover, unprincipled and of dubious background, is something I cannot understand. What strange chemistry is there between them?" He shook his head in bewilderment.

[147]

"I would leave it alone, Father." Robert Bruce made the statement emphatic. "You cannot rid yourself of Juan without driving Caroline away." He hesitated as though reluctant to continue and then a tiny smile broke across his face. "You will not like my saying this but the fellow has a way about him. I don't know what to call it; charm, I guess."

"Be damned to his charm." Cameron all but bellowed the words. "I am not some simpering girl to be captivated by a quick and easy smile and a gold ring in a scoundrel's ear. What sort of grandchildren am I to expect from such a union?" In agitation he stood up, stamped over to the table and poured himself a second glass of brandy.

"That is important to you, isn't it?" Robert Bruce watched his father.

"Important? Of course it is important. Everything we have has been staked on this venture in the Bahamas. I will not live forever and can only see the beginning. I want to leave behind me something of substance." He peered gloomily into his empty glass. "I am haunted by the specter of failure. It is an uneasiness I have never known before. I feel the foundations already crumbling beneath me. You are my only hope."

"You mustn't lay it upon my shoulders, Father, for this was not my choice." The tone was firm. "I will work at your side. We will do what we can together. What we cannot do—what cannot be done—we will have to accept."

"I have never been satisfied with half measures," Cameron grumbled. "Would you believe, Robert Bruce, I have walked our fields alone many a night? Alone, in the darkness, I have trod them. I have thrust my hand into the soil and cursed it for not producing more. It was," he shrugged with an unhappy smile, "a foolish and useless thing to do and yet, I have done it." He strode across the room and back. "If we cannot grow cotton in sufficient quantity what is there left?"

"We can always make a living here. Not as we knew it, perhaps. But this is a fair part of the world in which to live. I do not regret that we came."

"Aye!" Cameron agreed. "We can eke out a living but I had hoped to build better than that. It is a matter of pride, I suppose." He made the confession thoughtfully. "A man wants to leave an inheritance behind him." A small, grudging smile softened his expression. "He wants to be able to say: Look what I have done. But it also goes beyond that. For me it is not enough simply to exist. To sit down to my plate of fish and beans. There is, also, in me some small hope the colonies will fall into such disunion that the more sensible will demand their return to the mother country; to reunite with England."

Robert Bruce shook his head. "I doubt that, Father. Freedom seems to be a strong drink. Men having tasted it will not be content with a milder brew. No. Our future lies here and we will have to make what we can of it."

Cameron stood in moody thought for a moment. He seemed a formidable figure enveloped in the loose folds of the nightdress. Finally he nodded.

"I suppose you are right. We can only work, wait and see how the years balance themselves." He offered his hand, which was a surprising thing to do. "Good night, my son. We have an early start to make in the morning."

Caroline rested her back against one of the slender pillars of the porch. Juan lay sprawled on the boards with his head in her lap. The only sound was the muted washing of the sea. He twisted a little until his ear rested against her swollen abdomen.

"I do not hear him," he said skeptically. "I do not feel him move."

"He moves all right." She twisted her fingers gently through his hair. "Sometimes he kicks like a little mule. It is five months now and he wants to get out. Soon you will be Papa Juan. How does that sound?"

"I am not sure." His face was in the shadow and she could not see the expression on his face. "To have a girl to make love to on the beach is one thing. To be a papa is another."

"You should have thought about that on the beach."

"At such times," he whistled tunelessly, "one does not think. Now, this papa business is something new. So is having a wife. Suppose I take it in my mind someday to get into the boat and sail away? What do I do with a wife and child to take care of? It makes a man think."

"I'll tell you what you do." She was undisturbed. "You don't get in your boat and sail away. You stay here."

He turned to look up in her face with a lazy grin. "I don't think your papa likes me here." He managed a slightly injured tone. "I don't think he likes me at all for a son-in-law."

"He despises you." Silent laughter shook her. "You are like some bad dream. Each morning he wakes up and hopes you are gone. But," she was meditative, "I think, in a way, you are good for him. You take his mind off the fact the cotton won't grow as he wants it."

Juan was silent for a moment. "I thought," he mused, "I was marrying a very rich girl." He made the complaint sound mildly entertaining. "I said: Juan, now you will have two gold rings for your ears, maybe even a watch with a fob of seals so you will know what time it is even if it doesn't make any difference. There will be this big house on the Exuma plantation with many slaves to light your cigar and bring you a drink. There will be another house in Nassau and when we are tired of the

[149]

plantation we will go there for fun. A carriage will always wait for me and in the afternoons I will drive along the bay front, stopping at the taverns for a drink and pinching the round behinds of the girls who bring it to me." He stretched back his arms and pulled her face down to his, kissing her with a warm tenderness. "But," he continued solemnly, "what do I get? A papa-in-law who wants me to work doing something. He is not sure what; digging a hole and filling it up again, maybe. He does not like it because I sleep until noon sometimes. How does he know it is his beautiful daughter who will not let me sleep at night? I can't tell him that. Anyhow, I make a grandson for him and instead of being happy and offering me his brandy and cigars he pretends I am not in the same room. He doesn't even like it that I play my guitar. So, anyhow, I smoke his cigars, drink his brandy, sing my songs without a polite invitation. It is too much for one man to bear." He pretended a yawn of boredom. "I think I'll take the boat and go to Nassau for a while. I have some fine friends there. They must be missing me."

"I'll bet they do." She gave his hair a sharp tug and he yelped in simulated pain. "I saw some of your friends on Long Island. They seemed mostly girls. You are stuck, my Juanio. The guitar no longer makes music for the wenches in Nassau."

He sighed with pretended resignation. "Maybe just a little visit, a few days to see how everyone is?"

She shook her head. "You will stay here and wait with me for your son."

"You are sure?" He half sat up. "You promise me a boy? I do not like girls until they are about seventeen and have long legs like yours."

"You will have your son, Juanio. I promise you."

He grunted contentedly. "Then you will all see what a fine father I can be. I'll teach him to sail a boat, to play the guitar, to fish, to lie in the sun and do nothing." He laughed with sudden good humor. "That will make your papa madder than hell. He will be a wild man."

She said nothing for a moment. When she did speak it was a question. "Are you really happy here, Juan, with me?"

He did not answer immediately. She waited, holding his head against her breast.

"From the first day I saw you," he spoke quietly, "I said: That is my girl. Of all those I have known this shining one with the pride in her eyes, the beauty in the way she stands and walks, she is for me. After seeing her, no other will do. Mind you," his hand touched her cheek, "to make a marriage was not really in my mind but I am not sorry. It is good to be with you; to wake up sometimes at night and look at your face with

[150]

the fine honesty and contentment on it. It is good to be your husband. I am happy with you. But," he sat up, "don't think I will change much. To the end I will remain Juan as you first knew him."

"I wouldn't have you any other way."

"That is good then and we will have a fine life here together."

Faintly, on the clear, still night, there came the sound of voices mutedly raised in the strange music of the blacks. It was distant, far back in the slave quarters where, before some of the cabins, small fires winked and fluttered in the darkness and the huddled shapes about them seemed without form. What the slaves sang at night after the labors of the day were not the rhythmic chants of the fields. Those had a cadence, a beat to which they set the tempo of their work. This was a melody which flowed as naturally and effortlessly as water from a spring. They would sit or hunker down just outside the ring of light and then abruptly a voice would lift itself on a single note in a minor key. Then, without direction, others would slide into the chorus, improvising both the words and song as they progressed from phrase to phrase. The words had to do with the happy land, of the God Jesus who would one day gather them in a fine palace of marble walls and golden streets. They had heartbreak, loneliness, misery, and sometimes an ecstatic jubilance of deliverance from a world of toil. There were songs of the good boss and the bad boss, the white master and the fields to be worked until the day of kingdom come. The melody was their own, fashioned as they keyed their voices. It was primitive, linked to their bondage and the dark mystery of their native land from which they had been so brutally torn.

Listening, caught in the spell, Caroline shivered a little and pressed closer to Juan.

"All my life I have heard them sing that way," she whispered. "It still scares me a little and sometimes I want to cry."

Juan tightened his arm about her. "I have known many black men. It should scare you only when they don't sing. I am not of much education, as you know, but I sometimes wonder about them as I sometimes wonder about the horses which you, your brother, father and the overseers ride. Why do not those animals rear and say: I will not have you on my back any longer? I will run free and as I please. What stops the blacks from saying: I will not seed your fields any longer; haul your bales, chop your wood, cut your cane? If you beat me I will strike back. Think of that, white master, as you lie in your fine, soft bed. There are more of us than there are of you." He paused for a moment. "If I were a black man I would say those things. I would escape my slavery."

"Many of them were slaves in their own Africa, Juan. They have only

[151]

traded masters. But if they were free, they would still have to work to live. This way they are taken care of when they are sick, fed, clothed. They could hope for no more if free."

He shook his head. "I have heard that before but I do not believe it." He stood up and took her hand. "Also, I would not like to own another man. Now," he picked up the guitar, "I will have a little of your papa's rum and we will go to bed together. I will take some of the perfumed oil you have and rub that mound of a belly under which my son lies. Tomorrow, maybe, your papa and Robert Bruce will come home. It has been good to be alone together this way."

In their room he watched her as she undressed and slipped a sheer shift over her head. He had carried a glass of rum from downstairs and drank a little of it now. His expression was serious and thoughtful.

"Do you think," he spoke suddenly, "you could teach me to read and write?"

She turned in quick surprise, and with a small puzzled expression which vanished when she saw he had asked the question in honesty.

"You think that is a strange question?" he asked. "That Juan Cadiz should want to know those things?"

"No." She came to him quickly and stood looking up into his face. "No. I don't think it is strange."

"I am not too old to learn?"

"Of course not."

"We could do it here, alone in our room, with no one to look on or listen?"

"Yes. But," she touched his face, "I did not think it was in my Juanio to care what anyone else thought or said."

"In this I do. For you only do I give a damn about most things but this learning I would like to do in secret." He put aside the glass and then pressed the palms of both hands on her abdomen, holding them there with a light pressure. "I hold my son a little. When he comes and grows older I would not want him to be ashamed because his father is ignorant of what he will learn so easily."

"I am not ashamed." She covered his hands with hers. "Your son would not be either if he is the man of his father."

"Just the same," he made it sound casual, "I think tomorrow would be a good time to start. Instead of playing my guitar I will begin to learn how it is to write and to read from the books."

They lay together in the bed, her head just below his shoulder. For a while nothing was said.

"What will we name this son of ours?" he asked.

[152]

"John Cameron Cadiz. I have thought about it."

"That has a good sound," he agreed pensively. "So, tomorrow that is the first thing you will teach me. I will write it. John Cameron Cadiz. I would like to see the name come from my fingers."

✒ XII ✑

WHERE THE crude road along Nassau's waterfront ended against the scrub a miserable collection of shacks pressed upon each other in a tangled slum. Filth and garbage littered the narrow, open spaces. Flies swarmed and crawled over the refuse, roaches and vermin shared the mean dwellings with their slovenly tenants. It was a settlement avoided by all save those who were so indolent and half savage they were indifferent to their surroundings.

Now and then the authorities made a spiritless attempt to clean it up, to enforce even the most elementary principles of sanitation, but nothing of any lasting improvement was achieved. Those who lived in the spacious, breeze-swept houses on the hill made frequent appeals to the Government, demanding the entire area be put to the torch and the men, women and children with their packs of vicious, snarling dogs driven to some remote corner of New Providence. Once the military had gone into the district. The huts were burned to the ground, dogs were slaughtered by volleys of musket fire, the residents scattered. But no provision for the resettlement of the people had been made. So, in less than a year they had all drifted back, bringing with them increased litters of children and animals. The crazily built shanties, constructed of any material available, arose again in a fetid patchwork. The first few were added to over the months until the area was indistinguishable from its original condition of teeming poverty and putrid decay. The stench hung over it like an invisible cloud. With so much unoccupied land available on the island no one could say why these people chose to live as they did. A primitive, herding instinct drew them together. They created their own cesspool of humanity, resisting all attempts to dislodge and colonize them beyond the town's limits. The Government found it easier to ignore the existence of this civic cancer. It simply pretended it wasn't there.

[154]

In the semidarkness of one of the shacks a man lay upon a straw pallet. There was the waxy pallor of death upon his face. The woman who kneeled beside him wet a rag with water from a gourd and wiped his mouth and forehead with a weary helpless gesture. She knew he was dying as others had and this was only a small, futile effort to ease his final minutes. A mysterious sickness prowled through the squalor. It struck at a man here, a child or woman there, and they died in the misery of stinking sweat and their own excrement.

At first no one had paid much attention to the deaths. There was always a sickness of some sort. Fevers, dysentery and malnutrition were endemic. The strongest or those who developed an immunity survived. The others died. The victims were carried away by their relatives or friends and buried with little ceremony. Life here was the cheapest of all commodities. Now, though, there was the beginning of a panic. Never before had death swept with so broad a scythe in the quarter.

Because the authorities no longer even made a pretense at enforcing law and sanitation here the Government was, at first, unaware of what was happening. Such things as death certificates and medical reports from and of the area were never made, and so the way was open for a frightening epidemic. The plague began to creep out of its temporary confinement. It crawled forward slowly as a brush fire extends its periphery, unnoticed and seemingly innocent at first. It moved from the slum and began to strike haphazardly. A clerk in a store was stricken with the flux, a girl in a tavern took to her bed and died beneath the soiled covers. A woman who complained of retching, fever and uncontrollable bowels went to her place in the market as usual. She handled the fruit and vegetables which she sold and these were carried by the cooks to the homes in Nassau proper and served to the family. The sickness leaped without pattern from a mansion on the hill to a guard at the prison, a seaman from a ship in the harbor, a merchant and his family of three. No longer could it be ignored.

The Resident Medical Officer of the Crown was closeted with His Excellency, the Governor. They were alone, for what was being said between them could not yet be permitted to be heard beyond the closed doors.

"It is cholera and there is no use in our pretending it is anything else." The Medical Officer took a pinch of snuff and sneezed gustily. "I have warned you time and time again about that collection of hovels and their inhabitants. That is where it has come from and now it is in the town itself."

"You are certain?" Sir Gerald did not want to believe what he had been told. "There couldn't be a mistake?"

The Medical Officer was offended, his professional knowledge and competence questioned. "I have," he spoke coldly, "been a physician for thirty years. I know cholera when I see it. It will, if not contained, sweep through Nassau and over the entire island of New Providence. When the word of the plague gets out, and it will, there will be complete panic in Nassau. You will have a population in a wild frenzy, trying to escape by any means. I have seen it happen before and it is not something I want to see again."

Sir Gerald arose and walked up and down the room, hands clasped behind his back, his sagging belly quivering with each movement.

"What do we do?" He stared appealingly at the Medical Officer. "I know nothing of this sort of thing. Haven't you doctors found a specific for the disease? Burn sulphur candles or something?" His voice shook with an almost pleading note.

"There is no remedy for cholera. Some live. Others die. It is like a fire which must exhaust itself. You can burn sulphur candles or wave a witch's wand. Both are equally effective."

"My God, man!" The Governor was incredulous. "Do you mean to say we just do nothing?"

"We isolate the plague if we can." The doctor spoke matter-of-factly. "Fortunately," he steepled his fingers and blew across their tips, "we know its source. It has come from that collection of rabble and their hovels. It is spreading from there like an evil wind."

"One hundred, two hundred persons." The Governor was appalled. "What in the name of God will we do with them?"

"Isolation of the district will do no good. They will not obey a quarantine." The Medical Officer shook his head. "You would have to ring the area with troops and hold them in there at bayonet point. It is that or drive them from the island. That is impossible. Where would we settle them?"

"Don't ask me questions." Sir Gerald was filled with the anger of desperation. "Give me some answers. This is a medical problem. You give me the solution. I will supply the authority and force."

"All right," the Medical Officer assented. "It will take force. At the farthermost point on the island we will set up an encampment of tents. Then, you will have to send troops into the slum and drive every man, woman and child out. We will lodge those already sick in one area of the encampment, the well ones in another. As they become ill or recover we will shift them back and forth. Every sanitation precaution will be taken and no one will be permitted to leave the quarantine station."

"If that is what is necessary then that is what we shall do." The Governor, surprisingly enough, had a ring of authority in his voice. "I will put the power of my office behind the measure."

The physician nodded. "Now," he continued slowly, "we come to a difficult part. The plague has already spread. There are a dozen cases in Nassau proper right now. Most of them we can take care of for they are persons of no particular standing and we will move them out with the rest. But, it has reached into two homes on the hill, Sir Arthur Sommerville and Augustus Pope. These, I need not point out, are wealthy and influential families. The Popes, I believe, are close personal friends of yours. They, also, will have to be quarantined with the others. Are you willing to do that?"

The Governor's mouth dropped slightly open and he stared incredulously at the officer.

"Augustus Pope," he spoke with dismay, "has a cousin in the House of Lords. Pope himself is one of our most important residents. He has a wife, two daughters and a son. Are you telling me I must put bayonets to the backs of such personages and drive them like cattle to be housed in tents with that scum from the infected area? My God, man!" His anguish was apparent. "It could end my career. I would have the Home Government on my neck the minute the news reached London."

The Medical Officer nodded with understanding sympathy. "I am aware of your delicate situation. I do not like to compromise in this emergency but," he smiled thinly, "we must proceed with a certain regard for property. If Sir Arthur and Mr. Pope, and any other of our first families who contract the malady, will submit to the strictest, supervised quarantine in their homes—and this would include their slaves, who could be isolated—then, perhaps, we can make some exceptions. There is a risk, of course, but we are contending with persons of privilege. I recognize that as well as you do. It is one thing to quarantine a tavern wench and quite another to do the same with Lady Sommerville."

The Governor's face had lost all color. It was a sickly gray. His hands trembled as he went to a cabinet, took a bottle of brandy and drank from it without using a glass. After a moment he took a deep, sighing breath.

"Furthermore," the Medical Officer continued calmly, "the port will have to be closed." A faint, acid smile touched his lips. "In this we will have little trouble. Once the news of the epidemic is out, a ship won't set its course within miles of Nassau."

"This damnable thing will ruin us," the Governor moaned. "Our trade and commerce will come to a standstill. Nassau will become a pest-ridden island, cut off from all contact and aid. We depend almost entirely on supplies from abroad."

"We will survive." The officer spoke calmly. "Many will die but we will survive. The world always has. I have one more suggestion."

"Yes?" The Governor was both hopeful and fearful. "What is it?"

"You should make an official, public proclamation of the emergency. Explain it fully, so people will understand the danger, and tell them what we intend to do to meet it. I am not unaware of your problem with those long accustomed to being a class apart and treated with special deference. As always authority must bend to expediency. Many of these families have friends and relatives on plantations in the Out Islands. It should be suggested to them they find shelter beyond Nassau and New Providence until the plague has run its course. Allow them to leave for the Out Islands immediately. My suggestion," he added, "includes you, Lady Heath and your child."

"No." Sir Gerald drew himself up. "Lady Heath and the boy, yes. I will remain here where," he gestured helplessly, "I may not be of much real assistance but at my post where I belong."

"Very well." The Medical Officer stood up. "I imagine you will want a consultation with your military aide and such other officials of the Assembly as are necessary. The slum area and its inhabitants must be taken by complete surprise; the district ringed so tightly by soldiers not even a cat could slip through the cordon. There are two physicians in private practice here. I will enlist their assistance."

"Thank you for your advice." The Governor was honestly grateful. He walked to the door with the officer. As it was opened the two sentries were at stiff attention. His Excellency spoke to one of them. "I would like to see Captain Birch immediately." The soldier wheeled smartly and marched down the corridor.

For a man long accustomed to a pompous indolence the Governor moved with surprising firmness and determination. A special meeting was called at Government House. Through Captain Birch the ranking officers of the military were summoned and the small garrison alerted. A proclamation was drafted and copies made to be posted for all to read or have read to them. The members of the Assembly were at first stunned and then thrown into a noisy confusion when Sir Gerald told them what must be done. There were arguments and loud objections which the Governor put down with a new voice of complete authority. A site for the quarantine station was decided upon and wagons, loaded with tents and such provisions as could be gathered through undisguised confiscation, were sent to be set up in the restricted area. Not until this was ready could any move be made against the core of infection and its inhabitants.

When the overall plans had been drafted and accepted by the Assembly and detailed to the military, Sir Gerald took upon himself the distasteful task of personally calling upon the Sommervilles, the Popes. Bitter and angry words were exchanged, for neither Sir Arthur nor Augustus Pope was accustomed to being told what he was or was not to do. Curiously enough, Sir Gerald took on a new stature in these engagements. He was sympathetic but firm. The two families must yield. They could accept a strict quarantine here in their homes or become part of the mass isolation planned. Sir Arthur pounded with his cane upon a table until it was scarred beyond repair. He refused to submit to this ridiculous and, in his opinion, completely unnecessary indignity. Sir Gerald heard him through without a comment and then spoke with an unnerving bluntness which he had never displayed before.

"I have given you a choice, Sir Arthur. Give me now your answer for I will not tolerate further discussion."

Short of breath from his tirade Sir Arthur stared at the Governor for a moment. He had always considered His Excellency a stupid, gross man of little merit or character. This cold, decisive authority was something new and bewildering. When he finally did speak it was with a grudging respect.

"What in hell has come over you, Gerald? I never suspected you of such firmness."

Sir Gerald knew he had won his point. There was no further resistance in Sommerville. Unconsciously he tried to draw in his stomach and his back straightened. Actually, he was a little surprised himself at his uncompromising stand. Sommerville was a testy old aristocrat, long accustomed to having his own way. Frequently he had displayed an open contempt for the office of Governor. His Excellency was determined not to yield now on a single point.

"A guard will have to be placed over your household, Sir Arthur. I do not question your honor and your word that you will respect the quarantine. Your slaves are different. They must not be permitted to leave the grounds. Only your physician will be allowed to come and go."

Sir Arthur shrugged his compliance. "As you say. Damn it, man," there was a shade of respect in the words, "I didn't believe you had it in you. Will you have a glass of sherry and a biscuit with me? Or," he caught himself with a wan smile, "is the food and drink in this house suspect?"

"I would welcome a tot of sherry." Sir Gerald sank into a chair. "I must caution you. The hands of the slaves who prepare and carry your food and drink must be thoroughly washed. A light solution of lye is said to be antiseptic. Don't eat any raw vegetables or fruit."

"You talk like some damned bone splitter." Sir Arthur poured the sherry.

[159]

"I may well be before this thing is over." His Excellency took the glass with a nod of thanks.

Wearily the Governor sank back against the cushions of the carriage. He had made his last personal call upon the families whose homes were strung along the ridge. The sun, now, was a half disk of crimson as it dipped into the darkening sea. Other than Sir Arthur and Augustus Pope he had encountered no real opposition. There had been objections and a certain skepticism from some before he convinced them of the seriousness of the situation. When they did realize the extent of the danger there were moments of bewildered panic, for cholera was a terrifying word. His advice to seek a haven in the Out Islands was accepted with gratitude for they understood they might have been included in the general quarantine. The slaves would have to be left behind and only a minimum of clothing and personal effects taken. In some cases there were families who had no connections, no relatives or friends in the Out Islands. Sir Gerald counseled them to take their chances of finding shelter in the small communities on Eluthera, Watlings, St. George's Cay and Exuma.

Now, as his carriage rolled homeward, he began to think of Sabrina and the boy. He would get them away in the morning on the Government sloop. He leaned his head against the cushion. The boy was four, almost five now. He had tried to ignore the child. No. There was more to it than that. He had wanted to despise him. A bastard. Sabrina's bastard. She had mocked and forced him to accept this evidence of her unabashed infidelity and yet, he could not bring himself to detest the boy or hate the sight of his presence. Without his realizing it, time was having a lenitive effect upon the relationship.

David Heath. He had even been compelled to lend his name and become a party to the illegitimacy. Otherwise he would have been forced to admit publicly his wife's transgression. Damn it! He railed at himself for conceding a single virtue to another man's seed. The lad was bright, well formed and mannered. He was filled with a bubbling excitement for everything and the spirit was contagious. It was impossible not to smile, at times, at his unflagging exuberance. He rode his pony at a reckless gallop. The slaves adored him. He found a friend in everyone from the groom and stable boys to the yard blacks and house servants. Of late he had acquired the habit of coming into the study when the Governor was working there at his correspondence and reports. He did this unobtrusively and would stand in silent shyness close to the man's chair and not speak until spoken to. Sir Gerald had done his best to ignore these visits. But, curiously enough, he did not forbid them or order the lad from the room. Instead, he would scowl fiercely at some paper or letter as though venting his annoyance upon the inoffensive paper. The silence between them had been broken one afternoon and by the Governor himself. David had come as usual and there was a small patch of bandage upon his forehead. Glancing out of the corner of his eye Sir Gerald could see the boy wore the bit of cloth proudly, as a decoration. He waited with suppressed eagerness for some comment from the man.

"What did you do to your head?" Sir Gerald hadn't really meant to speak. The words came naturally, without thought and with a concerned curiosity. He had, though, voiced them gruffly and put aside his quill with a gesture of impatience. "Silly-looking thing."

David's expression altered slightly at the disparaging observation but he would not be denied his explanation. "I took a jump with my pony and fell." He waited expectantly.

"Damn fool thing to do," His Excellency grunted.

The boy's eyes clouded. He had hoped for an expression of concerned interest in the misadventure. The Governor was aware of this.

"Of course," Sir Gerald was half angry at himself for encouraging the conversation, "if it was a big jump that is different. Anyone might take a header then."

"It was." David's face was illuminated with pleasure. "Cato put it up for me, a real fence rail. It was that high." He strained on tiptoes and stretched his arm above his head, indicating a formidable measurement.

"Break your neck one of these days." Sir Gerald picked up the quill and shaved its point with a small knife. "Snap it right off."

David's features glowed with pride at the acknowledgment of the dangerous feat. He sensed somehow that this fierce and formidable person, whose exact status and relationship he did not quite understand, had yielded a little of what he had been so desperately seeking. He assumed this man was his father but he had never been permitted to call him so. He always said "sir." His mother had taught him this.

"Yes, sir. I guess I will break my neck." The agreement was made with pride.

They had exchanged no further words that day. After a while, with Sir Gerald pretending a silent absorption in a letter, David quietly left the room, closing the door behind him, and could not know the man had turned in his chair and was looking after him with an expression of indecisive emotion.

From this small incident others were born. It was Sir Gerald now who sometimes spoke first after David had been standing for silent minutes beside his chair. What the man said were small, inconsequential words or a trivial question. But they served a purpose of which he was not fully

[161]

aware. Some fragile, tenuous link was being formed. Alone in his study in the late afternoons, Sir Gerald sometimes looked at the time on his watch and caught himself wondering why the boy was late. Once, when he was standing on the steps waiting for the coach to be brought around, David was nuzzling his pony's neck before he mounted. Sir Gerald found himself wanting to swing him up in the air and into the saddle and slap the animal's rump to send him off at a trot. Another time, at night, he was tempted to look in on the boy's room for a moment as he was on his way to his own.

David, sensing something a little strange between them, never intruded upon the man beyond the regular visits to the study. He waited with a diffident confidence for the barrier between them to fall away. Sir Gerald was aware of this. He cursed himself for a sentimental idiot and discovered his resolution was dissolving. Many, many times he had experienced a sharp agony and thought how different everything might have been if the boy was his own. What pride he would have taken in him. What pleasure he would have found in walking with that small hand firmly clasped in his. To watch him grow and develop.

When the carriage halted before the Governor's Mansion, Sir Gerald did not alight immediately. He sat thinking while the groom held the door open. He would get Sabrina and the boy off the first thing in the morning. Where to send them? He realized he didn't have many friends, friends whose immediate hospitality could be taken for granted. Finally, he pulled himself by the hand strap of brocade at the seat's side and bent his heavy body to stoop from the coach.

His relationship with Sabrina had crystallized into a polite acceptance of each other and a situation which, he knew, was beyond remedy. At the table they sometimes talked but it was the conversation of strangers who might chat in a desultory fashion at a chance meeting. Love, if it ever had existed, had long ago been shattered beyond repair. At the few official functions which were necessary she was a gay, witty, gracious and attractive hostess. He could ask no more of her.

As he mounted the steps he halted abruptly and with a feeling of surprise. It was not really Sabrina he was thinking of as his mind made plans for her departure. It was the boy he was going to miss. The high treble of excitement in the young voice. The reserved visits to the study. What a damnable thing this was; to feel a small clutching at your heart when it should be filled with a cold denial. He resumed his climb of the steps and wondered if it was humanly possible—in time, of course—to forget the lad was another man's bastard. He experienced a twinge as he said the word to himself. Why, he asked himself, if I must endure this secret humiliation of having an unfaithful wife, why could not her womb have spawned a monster, ugly and misshapen? He did not want to feel this affection which had grown so imperceptibly. Perhaps it was a good thing Sabrina would have to leave and take the boy with her.

He went first to his study and rang for a servant to bring him some brandy. He drank in dark meditation, barely aware of its rare bouquet. Then, with an effort, he arose and walked ponderously up the central staircase to the gallery, and along it to Sabrina's room.

She was stretched on a chaise longue reading an old copy of a London paper. He had entered after a most perfunctory knock and without waiting for a reply. She put aside the publication with a frown of annoyance. He studied her dispassionately. What a beautiful thing she was even with this expression of irritation on her face. How, he wondered, could beauty house such evil? She did not greet him but waited for his words.

He went directly to the point. "There is cholera in the town. It is approaching a full-scale epidemic. I have ordered a mass quarantine. Before it goes into effect I want you to take the boy and go to the Out Islands until this thing is under control."

"Cholera!" She sat up, alarmed. "Are you certain?"

"Of course I'm certain. Do you think I am damned fool enough to go around saying there is cholera in Nassau if there wasn't?"

"How serious is it?"

"Serious enough to sweep the entire island of New Providence if we don't get it under control."

"But certainly we are safe enough here in the Governor's Mansion. I am quite sure," there was a touch of amused irony in her voice, "cholera would not have the temerity to invade it."

He ignored the sarcasm. "I am permitting most of our first families to leave while there is time to get out and before it invades their homes. Beyond that I can do nothing more than use my office and the weight of the Assembly to assist in getting the epidemic under medical supervision."

"God knows it is dull enough here in Nassau. I do not want to go to some sand spit in the Out Islands. Why can't I take David to England?"

"Because," he was impatient with her objections, "I have no idea when a ship will be in. The harbor will have to be blocked. There will be nothing to sail on. Even if there was, you would have a difficult time convincing a captain he should take passengers from a cholera-ridden port. And," he regarded her rebellious expression with amusement, "I have no intention of allowing you to go back to England. Your place is here. We have discussed it before."

"And if I refuse to go?"

[163]

"I will not force you." He was in no humor to argue. "You may stay here and take your chances. I must warn you of the danger. This is a pestilence for which there is no cure. You will not be permitted outside this house or beyond its grounds."

"I consider that no particular hardship." She shrugged. "There is little enough to do within or beyond these walls. I die, anyhow, of boredom so it makes no real difference if cholera or something else carries me off."

"You might give some thought to the welfare of Dav—your child." He had almost, inadvertently, mentioned the boy by name; something which he had never done before.

She was astonished and regarded him with a certain curiosity. "I must confess I am surprised at your concern for my son." She stood up and walked to the window, opening the shutters and looking out. "Where would we go and for how long?" She spoke without turning.

"As to the time, I have no way of knowing. The place—" He shrugged. "I doubt any of the plantation owners would refuse hospitality to the Governor's wife and," he caught himself on the point of adding, my son, "her child."

She turned now to face him with a shrewd half smile, for she was aware of what he had almost said.

"I am not so certain of this generous hospitality of which you seem so sure." She pricked him deliberately. "Until now you have made no effort to ingratiate yourself with the island families. You have publicly stated your disapproval of their independent behavior. You have called them arrogant, a class apart, Colonial aristocrats with little respect for your office or authority. I have heard you myself and you have said these things openly. Why should any of them now offer you a haven? I assume," she spoke with deliberate insolence, "you, also, are going to take advantage of the opportunity."

Sir Gerald felt a compelling weariness in the face of this vindictiveness. He shook his head as he studied her, wondering at the spleen and unrelenting hatred.

"I am staying here where I belong. Whatever you may think of me you can't believe I would do otherwise."

"No," she admitted, "I suppose not. The gesture is irresistible." She laughed without humor. "At whose door in the islands do we knock first and ask for shelter?"

"I don't know." He took a chair and sat with his legs apart, hands hanging loosely between his knees. "We must face the fact that whatever personal differences I have had with some of the planters, no one is going to be too happy over the arrival of anyone from Nassau where cholera is raging."

"I will not go as a beggar seeking alms." She was determined. "I think, though, the Cameron family on Great Exuma would receive us."

"Why?" He looked up at her. "Why Cameron?" He was obviously puzzled by her suggestion.

She shrugged the question off. "I'm not quite certain. He seemed to be a man of character and resolution. He has children of his own. I have a feeling he would be sympathetic and not a man to panic." It was, she realized, a not too logical explanation.

"Very well." Sir Gerald's mind was crowded with a multitude of problems. No suspicion that Sabrina's relationship with Ronald Cameron was other than casual entered his thoughts. "I will order the Government sloop fully provisioned and ready to sail in the morning. You will take only what you can't get along without. Cameron brought at least a hundred slaves with him. Certainly he will be able to provide you with a personal girl. I think it is safer to keep our blacks here. They may be carriers of the infection."

"I will not go without my girl Cleo." She was defiant.

"You will damned well do as I say, madame." He stood up and roared at her. "I am sick of your quibbling, your objections, your insolence. Can't you get it through your head that the entire population of Nassau may be wiped out and this epidemic could well spread to the Out Islands? Force me to it and I will have a guard take you to the boat. I am in no mood for carping. Do you understand?"

She stared at him with astonishment. From what unsuspected source did he draw this resolution? This was a man she did not know, whose determination in a time of crisis she had never suspected. For a moment she experienced a feeling of admiration for him. But, she couldn't resist the temptation to drop him a curtsy of mocking submission.

"As you say, my lord," she murmured with downcast eyes.

Sir Gerald studied her for a moment and then shook his head with baffled, sour admiration.

"What a magnificent bitch you are, Sabrina. It is unfortunate Nassau is too provincial to give you full scope for your talents. The venality of an Italian court would suit you better." He turned away and left the room.

Day cracked open slowly. The low range of clouds which hung on the horizon softened from black to gray and then was shot through with brilliant shafts of golden spears which tore it apart with a play of dazzling colors.

On the waterfront a warehouse door creaked open and the night watchman appeared. He had caught himself a short, unofficial nap on the bales in storage and emerged now, tousled and still sleepy. He stood for a moment and yawned. His mouth remained open, held that way by the amazement he felt as he stared unbelievingly at the empty harbor. Along the shoreline and the small docks where always, moored beam to beam, the Out Island boats tied up, there was nothing but empty water and the hungry swooping of the gulls. Sometime during the night every craft had disappeared. Not even a wooden chip floated upon the tide.

The watchman moved slowly and with a frightened and superstitious caution to the end of the pier. Usually at this hour the docks and mooring points offered a scene of leisurely activity. Women tended braziers from which small vines of smoke crawled upward. Children played around the decks. Men drew buckets of water and thrust their frowzy heads into them. There were calls and shouts back and forth as the people made ready for the day. Now there was nothing; no sound save the small wash of the waves as they broke upon the sand.

The watchman's incredulous eyes traveled in a wide arc up and down the beach hoping for the sight of one small boat before he would acknowledge the truth of the unprecedented situation. There was no mistake. Everything that could be sculled or sailed had left Nassau during the silent hours before daybreak. Where had they gone and why? The man could find no answer. He hurried back down the warehouse pier and in the direction of the Harbormaster's house. Someone in authority should know about this. The mystery was beyond a watchman's understanding.

As he shuffled along, the clear, sharp notes of a bugle sounded, calling the garrison to reveille. It was reassuring to the frightened man. He was half convinced some witchcraft had been at work during the dark hours. Otherwise there was no explaining the absence of any floating thing in the harbor.

He pounded on the door of the small, frame cottage until the official flung the portal open with sleepy anger.

"What's wrong? Why in hell are you knocking my house down at this time of day?" He glared ferociously at the befuddled watchman.

"Sir," the old man was shaking, "the harbor is empty. Everyone, everything has gone. Such a thing has never happened before. I thought you should know."

For a moment the Harbormaster stood in the doorway in the wrinkled nightshift which hung about his calves. Yesterday he had been told, as had all the officials, of the impending quarantine. How, he wondered now, had the news leaked to the Out Island boatmen? There could be no other reason for such a complete withdrawal from Nassau's waters.

Now there would be the devil to pay, for he had been instructed to commandeer, by force if necessary, most of the craft to transport certain families from the plague-ridden community. By the Lord, he thought, they'll have to swim if they want to get away or stay here and take their chances with the rest of us. A small satisfaction filled his mind, for his own family had not been included with those of the privileged. Now, they could all stay and rot here together.

"All right, Wilkerson." He reassured the watchman. There was no use in frightening the trembling ancient. The quarantine notice would be posted during the day and everyone would know the situation. The yellow flag of isolation would be run up to warn all outside shipping. Time enough then for the panic to assert itself. "It is all right," he continued. "You go to your bed now. I'll see to everything."

The old man nodded his head in assent. Something was amiss. Something was very wrong. He turned away and began plodding with faltering steps through the sand and toward a boardinghouse where he occupied a small room beneath the eaves.

With full equipment, leggings and breast straps freshly clayed, a company from the military garrison marched upon the slum area. They moved at quickstep and without the cadence of a drum. In the rising sun their bayonets were sharp and slender mirrors which caught and reflected the sun's light. As they marched they wondered about the orders of the detail. The district was to be surrounded. No one would be permitted to enter or leave. Those who made an attempt to disobey were to be driven back at bayonet point. If this did not contain them, they were to be fired upon. They were good men, these troops, weary of their long exile on this island but disciplined. The idea of firing upon unarmed civilians disturbed them. As they marched they wondered at their orders. Only the captain and the young lieutenant had been fully briefed.

As the troops neared the collection of hovels a scattering of dogs raced out and set up a wild and senseless clamor. They barked and yipped more out of excitement than a display of menace. Their yelping brought the inhabitants of the shanties to their sagging doors and stoops. They gaped at the troops and were stupefied by this unprovoked assault. There had been no disorders. Too many of them were sick and unable to leave their foul pallets to have caused any trouble. Those who had not yet contracted the sickness were filled with a debilitation that made any excursion outside the community an almost physical impossibility. Why had the soldiers come?

The military cordon was quickly formed. No order to stand at ease was given. The faces of the troops were impassive as a small group of men gathered from the shacks and edged forward with a question on their faces.

"Stand back!" The command was as sharp as a whip's lash. "This district is under quarantine by order of the Governor and Assembly."

"What for you quarantine us? We done nothin'." One man voiced the question.

The officer ignored him. He spoke as though reading from an order. "No one will be permitted to leave or enter this settlement."

"Who says so?" There was an unmistakable belligerence in the query. "That fat Governor on the hill?"

The officer suppressed a smile. "I say so." The words were clear and sharp in their determination. "There is cholera here. Many of you have died. More will die if you try to remain in the area."

"What you goin' to do?" The spokesman for the group voiced what was in his companions' minds. "Shoot us so we won't be no more trouble?"

The captain was not an unsympathetic man. This poor, ragged, festering community needed help and understanding even though, at the moment, it resented the presence of Royal troops.

"An encampment has been set up on the other side of the island. Tents and all the medical care we can give you will be there. The sick will be transported in wagons. The others will have to walk. It is the only way the cholera can be curbed, to keep it from spreading. Do you understand?"

"I ain't goin' no place," the same man shouted back. "It's a trick to get us out of here. Damn your encampment an' doctors. Sure we got some sick people here. We always have. No one in Nassau give a hoot before. We cure our own sickness."

Women and half-clothed children had gathered before their hovels and behind the men. They stared with puzzled curiosity at the troops.

"I'm not going to argue with you." The officer fought to control his temper in the face of this obstinacy. "You will do as you are told."

"Like hell we will. How is moving us from one place to another going to cure the sickness? You send the doctors here."

Now the entire community faced the troops. Even those who were bedridden crawled on their hands and knees to the open doors. The stench was almost unbearable.

To the officers and men watching there was the feeling that some filthy and inhuman tide moved to wash about their feet and sweep them along with it. The clothing they wore were things cast off by a ragpicker. Open sores were hideous blotches on arms and legs. Their eyes were glazed and blank of expression as they continued to creep forward.

[168]

There was an involuntary shifting of the uniformed men as they sought to avoid the contamination.

"Hold your formation!" The captain roared the order. There was a fury in his voice over this all but imperceptible breach of discipline. "Arms at the ready."

The rifles came smartly to shoulders. Not one in the company wanted to fire upon these unarmed men and women but the threat of this was the only thing which might halt the menacing progress. They were the King's troops and would obey if the command was given.

Confronted by muzzle and bayonet the inching advance did not waver. Some of the men had picked up broken bottles, gnarled lengths of wood, heavy conch shells. Behind them stood their women and children. A baby, naked, crept to a doorsill, tumbled to the ground and lay there screaming its futile rage and terror. No one paid any attention to the squalling infant.

The captain darted a quick, uncertain glance at his men. There was something unnerving about this slow, relentless advance. He thought, My God! I can't shoot them down. Nothing in his training had prepared him for this. Yet, the alternative was equally unthinkable; to order his troops to retire, to press upon them with the bright steel of bayonet. His orders were explicit and not subject to modification. The district was to be contained no matter how drastic the measures for this must be.

"Take aim!" With a supreme effort he kept a small tremor from his voice. "Fire upon command."

The cocking of the arms made the innocent sound of crickets. There was a momentary hesitation on the part of the small, disreputable line.

"Shoot, damn you!" The one man who seemed to be the community's leader shouted the challenge. "Shoot and rot in hell with the rest of us." He hurled the club he was carrying at the officer.

The captain caught the spinning, gnarled length of wood on his forearm. An agonizing pain ran to his shoulder. The man was some fifteen feet away, glaring at him with the rabid madness of a frenzied animal. Staring into the wildness of his assailant's eyes the officer knew it was only a question of seconds before the slaughter. It needed but a word from him and he found he could not give it.

"Why don't you shoot?" the man screamed in an insane fury. "You got nothin' to be afraid of save a few sick people, women and unarmed men."

Stern of face but with revulsion at what he must do, the officer drew back the hammer of his heavy pistol and shot the man through the head. He half spun about and fell, his face ploughing a small furrow in the sand.

A woman screamed and threw herself upon the body. She cradled the bloody face in her arms, rocking it gently as she might a baby. Her cries rose on a high, piercing note.

The shock of seeing what had happened halted the others as though they had come upon an invisible wall. There was no one now to defy the troops for they were without a leader. One by one they faltered and then began to back away. The woman's wailing was a high tremolo of stricken grief.

The captain, with far more calmness than he felt, reloaded and primed his weapon. Better, he tried to reassure himself, this one man than an outright massacre.

"Now." He spoke kindly. "If you will listen to me. We are only trying to help. There are many sick among you. Others will fall ill of the same disease if you try to stay here. Each bit of food you handle can carry the plague to someone else. Do you understand what I am saying?"

They didn't. The absence of any expression on their faces told him that.

The creaking of wagon wheels diverted their attention. Every vehicle which could be commandeered from Nassau's civilian population together with the army transports had been pressed into service. The cavalcade dragged slowly through the heavy sand and came to halt behind the line of troops.

The Resident Medical Officer dismounted and pushed forward to where the people were crowded into a fearful group Behind him came a string of litter bearers. They waited as the physician went from shack to shack. He came out shaking his head, his lips pursed thoughtfully.

"Most of them are half-dead already." He spoke to the captain. "We'll take them anyhow." He turned to the litter bearers.

"There is no danger to you men. I give you my word. Take your litters and load them with those who are unable to walk. Cholera isn't something you breathe out of the air. It comes from insanitation and is passed from hand to mouth. Wear the gloves you have been given and after everyone has been loaded into the wagons, throw them away in a pile and they will be burned. One thing more," his voice was harsh, "these are human beings, ill as you might be. Treat them as such."

The evacuation of the cholera-ridden community was carried out in a scene of mounting confusion and pandemonium. Those who were so stricken and weakened by the disease they could barely open their eyes were beyond resistance. They no longer had the will to care what happened to them. With obvious revulsion the stretcher bearers entered the stinking hovels. The sick were turned from their dirty pallets with a callous disregard for their condition. The troops were not at all assured by the Medical Officer's words. They avoided all physical contact where it was possible. The ailing, most of them barely conscious, were dumped into the sagging canvas between the two carrying poles and hurriedly shoved into the wagon beds. So limited was the space they frequently lay atop each other in abject misery, vomiting and unable to control the natural functions of their emaciated bodies. Those who were feeling the first misery of the initial diarrhea screamed and cursed their objections. They stumbled and staggered about the cordon of troops in a senseless and macabre race. The stretcher bearers had to chase them down and haul them by their feet to the wagons. Those who had not yet contracted the plague threw themselves to the ground and lay there, refusing to move, their hands digging convulsively into the sand for a hold. When they were jerked to their feet by the exasperated troops they immediately collapsed into their former positions until the sharp points of bayonets forced them into a standing position from which they were prodded, and sometimes kicked, to where the makeshift ambulances waited. The children screamed and howled in terror at seeing their parents manhandled and the dogs were caught up in a frenzy of excitement, barking and racing in frantic circles. With their officers busy at other things the troops made a game of spitting the animals on their bayonets as they raced past, and made wagers among themselves on the accuracy of the thrusts.

It was well after the hour of noon before order had been brought out of the nightmare scene. The wagons moved slowly forward with a squad of soldiers preceding them. Those of the community who were ambulatory dragged their feet in a single file behind the makeshift ambulances. Additional troops, weary and disgusted, prodded the laggard with pointed steel. The dogs were methodically slaughtered by volley after volley or cut down with bayonets and clubs. Once the dismal procession was on its way, other troops went from shanty to hovel with torches and fired the entire settlement. Slowly the dreary procession crept through the sandy ruts which served as a road and behind it the smoke rose in a black pall.

With the posting of the quarantine notices during the morning and the news that all of the Out Island boatmen had sailed their craft out of the harbor during the night, panic raged through Nassau proper. There was no escape and the plague would run like an unchecked fire through the town. Those who had hoped to find sanctuary in the Out Islands discovered there were no means of transportation. Miles of water lay between them and safety. Chemists' shops were raided of a variety of nostrums all guaranteed to cure every illness known to man.

Friends of old standing were wary of shaking hands and passed each other quickly on the streets with a short nod. Slaves were driven to their quarters and the doors barred, and the reek of burning sulphur hung over the community.

Men, singly and in groups, searched the shoreline. A few leaky rowboats which lay bottom up on the beach were fought over in scenes of bloody combat. The victors of these encounters guarded their prizes with knives and pistols from their neighbors while they made an attempt to patch and make watertight the frail and inadequate craft. Others hastily set about building rafts. Offshore lay Hogg Island. Safety might lie there, but they gave no thought of how they would feed themselves once the tangled spit of land had been reached. A few of the more levelheaded loaded provisions, utensils and bedding into wheelbarrows and carts and started on a weary trek to uninhabited sections of the island where they hoped the plague would not reach them.

Stores, warehouses and houses were left unguarded and now maddened bands of the lawless raced through the community, looting what they could not use or carry away. They smashed down the doors and broke the windows of shops and taverns, scattering everything to which they could put their hands into the streets. In a short time, with the bottles and kegs taken from taverns, a drunken mob roved the settlement, raping and killing those who had no way of defending themselves.

At daybreak and with the greatest secrecy the Governor had ordered his coach made ready. The town, at that hour, was not yet aware of the plague's extent. There was no one about to witness what was happening at the Governor's Mansion. The coach had been packed with clothing and such foodstuffs as were at hand. There was no way of knowing how well provisioned the Cameron plantation might be. It might well be cut off from all communication with Nassau and the outside for weeks and months.

Sabrina, who had finally yielded to Sir Gerald, was without her personal slave girl Cleo. She was in a bitter mood, blaming the Governor for everything. With the boy, David, she was hastily bundled into the coach. Then the Governor squeezed himself in among the boxes and piles of unpacked clothing. The horses felt the whip and the heavy vehicle spun out of the driveway and to the Government pier where the sloop and its crew of two waited.

Sabrina was resentfully quiet and thoughtful. The boy, David, though, bounced up and down on the springed cushions in delighted excitement over the novelty of this excursion as the coachman laid the whip upon the horses and sent the coach whirling down the hill.

[172]

"I have no doubt but that Mr. Cameron will receive you," Sir Gerald reflected aloud. "He is a stubborn man but a gentleman born. He will recognize the obligation. After all, he has children of his own."

Sabrina half smiled for the first time that morning. She glanced at the radiant David and wondered at the meeting between father and son. How would Cameron look upon David? More, how would she and Cameron meet; as long-parted lovers or strangers? She turned and glanced into a mirror which was set into the coach. Her beauty had survived the few years which had intervened since they had so impetuously made love and conceived the boy beside her. And life, she thought, must have been singularly barren for Ronald Cameron on the island of Exuma. A little excitement quickened her pulse.

"I expect," the Governor continued, "that with the quarantine measures we have taken we shall have the epidemic under control so your exile will not be of too long a duration."

"I will do my best to bear up under the situation." She almost laughed outright at this expression of concern. "After all, one island is much like another."

The Governor's mouth tightened. He had hoped for some small expression of concern from her for the problem he must meet in Nassau. He grunted and then indulged himself in one of his small attempts at humor.

"I should think medical science would find you a subject of considerable interest. Few persons survive without a heart as you, apparently, do."

"I misplaced it somewhere, Gerald. Perhaps it will turn up again one of these days. But I haven't really missed it."

The sky was the color of damp clay as the coach swung up to the Government pier. Sabrina and David were quickly sent aboard the waiting sloop and the transfer of their boxes was rapidly made. To the crew the Governor gave explicit instructions. They were to deliver Lady Heath and the boy to the Cameron plantation, on Great Exuma, and then return without delay to Nassau. Troops and seamen would then be detailed to the sloop, and the Out Islands cruised in an effort to persuade the islanders to lend their craft for the transportation of the healthy from Nassau to places of safety. Secretly, the Governor had small faith there would be any volunteers. The boats would have to be taken by force. In the meanwhile he knew he faced a state of wild terror and confusion in the town itself.

He waited until the sloop was well out in the harbor before he turned and reentered the coach. He experienced no distress of conscience over what he had done; protecting his own family first. It would have been impossible to accommodate everyone and equally impracticable to try and make a selection as to what family should go and who was to be left behind on this first trip. To do this would have generated a riot and angers which would smolder in the years to come.

Elbows on knees, chin resting on clasped hands he was indifferent to the jolting of the coach and the lightening sky. It was going to be a day to try a man's will, for terror was not subject to reason. His face abruptly took on an expression of puzzled wonder as he thought back to his leave-taking of Sabrina and the boy. It occurred to him now he had barely touched Sabrina's fingertips as a gesture of parting. But, it had been David's cheek he had brushed with a rough kiss. At the time it had been a simple enough thing to do; a natural and spontaneous action. Now, though, when he thought about it he was mystified. What had made him do it? Why should he feel a concern and affection for someone else's brat? What bond could possibly exist between them? How had it been so subtilely woven that he, until this minute, never suspected its existence?

By noon every inch of space before Government House was solidly packed by the indignant, the frightened, the angry and noisily protesting. At the sight of the Governor's coach as it came down from the Mansion a tremendous roar of fury thundered. Rocks were hurled, curses shouted. Somehow word that His Excellency had sent his family to safety in the Out Islands in the only craft available had spread through the town. The mob screamed its indignation over this assumption of privilege and the Assembly was meeting in a special session to consider whether the Governor could be deposed without consent of the Crown. The crowd moved to surround the coach and only the prompt action of the uniformed guard prevented the frenzied population from reaching it. The troops provided a lane through which Sir Gerald could pass.

Although his expression was impassive the Governor was astonished by his inner calmness. He halted on the second of the broad, low steps which led to the entrance and faced most of Nassau's population. Old vegetables and fruit, small bricks and faggots of wood were hurled at him. Most of them missed their mark and splashed against the building's wall. Sir Gerald was not a brave man. As a youth he had avoided physical combat whenever possible. All his life he had shunned violence, preferring concessions and compromise. Years of easy living here in the Bahamas with small responsibilities had left him slothful. He was short of temper and contemptuous of those he considered to be his inferiors. It was to his credit that at this moment he did not flinch, dodge or attempt to shield himself. When an overripe tomato splattered against his waistcoat he merely took a handkerchief from his cuff and wiped the residue away. Then he balled the fine, lace-edged linen and dropped it at his feet.

He could have taken refuge within the building and answered the multitude of taunts with an impersonal proclamation. Instead, he faced the crowd and started to speak. His words were swept away by the howls, yowling and catcalls which jeered his name. The people of Nassau didn't want a speech. They sought action, some magic panacea for this fearful thing which had come among them. They were desperate for a way of escape from this pesthole where the epidemic was spreading like a wind-driven fire. They had all heard of the terrible plagues which had swept through London and cities on the Continent. They knew how the dead had mounted into piles and had to be buried in common graves and covered with quicklime.

Finally, out of sheer exhaustion, the cries diminished. The Governor faced them for a moment in silence.

"I am really not the cause of this plague, you know." He was grimly humorous and wondered a little at his words, for this was no time for levity. "The Government has made repeated efforts to provide better sanitation. You have ignored all our measures."

"No!" a man shouted. "But you are a fat bastard who sent his family away on the only boat and left the rest of us to die."

For all his manner of overbearing impatience the Governor was not a man without understanding. He was well aware of the temper of the crowd and that he was precariously balanced on the fine edge of violence. To shout back would only make matters worse and precipitate an uncontrollable riot.

"It is true." He shrugged with a little lift of oblique resignation. "I am a stone or two overweight. As to my legitimacy," he paused thoughtfully, "that is something of which you cannot possibly have any knowledge. So, I will overlook the reference."

"Are you going to overlook the cholera, too?" a voice far back on the fringe came clearly.

"I will tell you what the Medical Officer told me." Sir Gerald was grave. "The weak will die and the strong survive. It is that simple. There is no magic nostrum for cholera. It must run its course here as it always has in other places."

"You mean there is nothing we can do but wait and see who dies or who doesn't?" A woman's question was on a shrill note of hysteria.

The Governor experienced a feeling of complete helplessness. The fact had been put with a brutal directness. He could have acknowledged it.

"We can," he explained with a surprising gentleness, "isolate the sick

[175]

as we have done. The healthy, those certified by the Medical Officer, can leave Nassau or New Providence. The island, as you know, is something short of seven leagues long. There are sections of refuge but how will you survive? The camps, if you set them up, will become foul, for you will have only the crudest means of sanitation. The cholera will flare again among you. I will make an official effort to requisition every boat in the Out Islands. But," and his voice had a note of warning in it, "I would not count on a too hospitable reception in the settlements there. You will be suspect of carrying the plague. The inhabitants will not welcome you among them. Those with whom you have done business or counted as your friends will fight you off. Fear reduces all men to savages. Don't go expecting charity."

The townspeople had become silent now as the full weight of their situation was borne upon them. They could only stare hopefully at the man who represented authority.

"It is true," Sir Gerald continued. He was sensitive to this change of humor. "I sent Lady Heath and her son to Great Exuma this morning aboard the Government sloop. This proves," his words were dry, "that I, also, am only human. I am no Noah who could put you two by two aboard a small sailing craft. How could I choose among you? I had to make a start somewhere. You may question my ethics only if you can offer me a logical alternative. The sloop will return. Armed men will search out everything which will float and bring the boats to Nassau. If," he looked those in the front rank in their eyes, "it gives you any satisfaction, I promise I will remain in Nassau and take my chances with the rest of you."

He turned away, mounted the steps and entered the building. Guards quickly closed the doors and posted themselves before them. There was no move from anyone in the crowd. Its unreasoning temper had spent itself. Now it was only a frightened, bewildered and leaderless collection of men and women. They were filled with suspicion of each other, for who could say that the man whose shoulder you had just brushed did not carry the cholera in his clothing? They had but one common bond, fear and misery.

Singly, in couples and small groups, the mob began to break up. They had no destination for they were afraid of their own homes; even their wives and children. Some turned and stared wistfully at the clean, open sea. Safety lay out there but it was beyond their reach. The catastrophe which had developed so unexpectedly must be faced, for no ship from the outside would put into the port to take them from this island of disaster. It was impossible to go about their daily tasks, for all normal activity hung suspended.

They drifted away to find temporary refuge on remote sections of the curving beaches. There they sat, neither talking nor sitting too close to each other. They had resigned themselves to a time of waiting. The Governor had said the weak would die and the strong survive. In his or her own way each prayed silently for the strength to live. They gave little thought to anything beyond this moment. If the Governor could provide boats as he had said he would try to do, then they might escape; but no one was quite sure where safety lay. Who and how many, they wondered, would fall ill or die this day?

❧ XIII ❧

THE EPIDEMIC prowled relentlessly through Nassau and daily there were pitifully small funeral processions with two or three carrying the rough board coffin, and a woman and frightened children trudging slowly behind. A new yard for the graves had to be set aside, for the old one had long since been filled.

The Medical Officer and the town's two private physicians hunted down the pockets of the disease but they were balked by those who would not report the sickness in their homes. Now it also flared on Hogg Island, where some had taken refuge and built small, thatched huts. They had ferried their meager possessions on hastily built rafts. Ships took warning from the yellow flag flying atop the Customs House and changed their courses. New Providence was as effectively cut off from the outside world as though it hung suspended in the sky.

Despite the Governor's prediction many persons had found a haven in the Out Islands and now the cholera broke out there. It struck with a wild haphazardness, seeming to leap from cay to cay. It died out in one settlement only to show itself in another, run its course and subside.

As the Medical Officer had predicted, the weak and infirm died in foul misery. The strong survived and the strongest among the islanders were the blacks. The slaves seemed to have acquired an immunity to the infection. As a result, many of the white inhabitants developed an unreasoning hatred for these strong, healthy Africans who refused to grow ill and die as did their masters.

The schooner, the *Traveler,* was the only source of communication between the islands. The captain dropped his anchor in the waters between Hogg Island and New Providence. From his ship he sent a longboat which was met at a halfway point by the Government sloop from the stricken town. The truth was that Nassau was in double jeopardy. In addition to the cholera it was in danger of starvation. The *Traveler* brought what it could in the way of fruit, beans, corn, a few pigs and an occasional steer. These were paid for by the Crown's Treasury and were transferred from the schooner's boat to the sloop. The *Traveler* also brought news of the conditions on the Out Islands and carried back information on the state of affairs in Nassau to those who had been fortunate enough to escape. The irregular visits of the *Traveler* provided an uncertain lifeline at best but the schooner's master, despite the fears and rebellious attitude of his crew, kept it open.

In Nassau the Assembly had long since ceased to meet. There was nothing of a legislative matter to be discussed. Also, fear had so taken over the island that the men were suspicious of a close gathering in the chamber. They were not at all reassured by the Medical Officer's assurance that the cholera could not be breathed from the air. They willingly loaded all of the problems and their decisions upon the Governor.

The change in His Excellency's manner astonished everyone who had been familiar with his slothful and supercilious attitude as head of the island government. Never, in the memory of anyone, had he ever displayed the slightest interest in the welfare of the town save in the matter of commerce and, perhaps, his own pocketbook. Now, however, he seemed to regard the plague as a personal affront to his authority. He would put his heel upon it. He made daily trips in his coach to the quarantine station, conferring with the Medical Officer and his assistants. He inspected the quarters, the food, its handling and preparation, and the water. Here, at least, the effectiveness of isolation and even the most rudimentary sanitary measures were proving themselves. The healthy remained apart from the sick. Everything they ate or drank was supervised. The cholera did not display itself among them. Those in the section set aside for the stricken were carefully watched. Many died but others recovered and when these were considered well and uncontaminated they were shifted to the unafflicted cantonment. A small but ever-widening breakthrough in the plague was being made. In the town the two private physicians made daily rounds and their efforts to cover the entire settlement sometimes carried them far into the night. When a case was found or symptoms showed themselves, the afflicted were immediately transported in a military ambulance to the area of quarantine. Those who objected or protested that they were well and feeling fine were unceremoniously hauled to the horse-drawn vehicle by troops.

The nights were hours of silence. Soldiers patrolled everywhere. The taverns, which were once brightly lit, noisy centers of drunken revelry where visiting seamen and the bawds caroused, were dark and locked. The superstition that the cholera was, somehow, carried on the night air persisted. So, those who had been forced to remain in the town never ventured out after sundown. On the nights of the moon, with the pale radiance spread over it, Nassau seemed a city of the dead, inhabited only by the few animals who came out of their hiding places to scratch and forage in the midnight hours.

Now and then the Medical Officer called upon His Excellency at the Governor's Mansion in the evening. Frequently they shared a frugal meal. This was prepared by the one slave permitted in the house. She was the regular cook who had been kept apart from the other blacks and slept in a vacant storeroom at the Mansion's rear. Their dinners had little variety: fish cooked with tomatoes and onions, a dish of corn mush spiced with peppers. Now and then they had a chicken or a small piece of meat when a pig or beef was delivered from the Out Islands. When the scanty fare was finished they rounded out the hour with a bottle of Oporto and their pipes. Even these were sparingly used, for tobacco, wine and anything else which must be imported were growing scarce.

The Medical Officer leaned back in his chair and stretched his legs wearily before him. There was evidence of the strain he had been under in new lines on his face and a tiredness in his eyes. He drew upon the long stem of his pipe and watched the smoke as it curled from his mouth.

"I think we may have this damnable thing licked, Sir Gerald. For the first time in a month not a single new case has been reported."

"Gad! I hope so." The Governor folded his hands across his belly which had shrunk to half its size. He patted the mound of flesh almost fondly. "I must have lost four stone. My clothes hang upon me without fit or comfort. I find myself falling into bed sometimes without troubling to do more than remove my boots. I have had to shave myself in the morning, pour the water for my bath and do a hundred things I have always taken for granted." He smiled with a quizzical amusement. "It never occurred to me that I could become such a dedicated public servant. I am frankly puzzled by my energy and concern. There is, of course," he chuckled dryly, "a small item of self-interest in my efforts. For if the population of the Bahamas is wiped out by the cholera, there will be little need for a Governor and I shall have lost a post."

The doctor tamped at the ash within his pipe's bowl. He spoke with meditative reflection, selecting his words carefully.

"If I may say so, without giving offense"—he tapped the pipe's stem against his teeth—"I am, also, a little astonished. Frankly," he smiled, "your therapeutic contribution has not been indispensable but it has done the people good to see the Governor move among them and take an interest in their care."

They smoked in silence for a moment. Sir Gerald's eyes were growing heavy. He was half-asleep in his chair. The doctor, noting this, arose and the Governor aroused himself with an effort.

"What do you hear from Lady Heath?"

Sir Gerald stood up to follow his guest down the hallway. It was a question he did not want to answer. There had been one, brief note from Sabrina delivered by the *Traveler*.

"Little," he confessed, "save that they are well. The plague, apparently, has not shown itself on Great Exuma. Mr. Cameron," he smiled thinly, "is a Scot of great stubbornness. He probably forbade it to intrude upon his plantation."

When the Medical Officer's light gig had rolled out of the driveway, Sir Gerald shut and bolted the door. Then he snuffed the candles out with a small metal cone at the end of a rod. One remained alight in its jar of ruby-red glass. He carried this with him as he mounted the dim staircase. His movements were slow and sometimes even a little uncertain as he held to the balustrade. He would not confess, even to himself, that he was not feeling well. He put the weariness down to overexertion at unfamiliar tasks. He had made no mention of the condition to the physician.

In his room, with only the single candle burning, for it was necessary to conserve everything these days, he undressed with awkward uncertainty. This weakness he felt was a creeping paralysis which did not improve even after a full night's sleep. Also, he had been subjected to minor stomach cramps for the past day or so. He put it all down to the diet of too much fish and beans. Pulling the nightshift over his head he thought, for a moment, of Sabrina and of the brief note she had sent.

We are well. Mr. Cameron and his family received us most hospitably.

S

No word of concern for him or the conditions in Nassau.

Damn the woman, he thought. Was she without any kindly emotion? Did her hatred of him run in such a deep channel that nothing could affect it? He extinguished the candle and felt his way into the lumpy bed. Among the cook's accomplishments, he thought, was not the proper making of a bed, with the sheets tight and smooth, the light covering taut and turned down at a corner. He stretched out. His legs pained him slightly as though he had been engaged on a long climb. Well. It would pass. He had overexerted himself, that was all. What he needed was a full day's rest.

Sleep did not come easily, tired as he was. He lay upon his back, staring at the dark ceiling. A multitude of small problems occupied his mind but behind them the image of Sabrina persisted. Why, he thought irrita-

[181]

bly, couldn't she have written a little more? To be sure, there was no great affection between them but an ordinary courtesy should have prompted something more than that curtest of notes. How was the boy doing? Was he happy and contented on that unfamiliar island and among strangers? Did he miss his pony or the customary visits to the study and their small talk together in the afternoon? He would liked to have heard about these things. A curious loneliness possessed him.

He punched the pillow into a ball beneath his head. Would it be possible, he wondered, to reach some plane of better understanding with Sabrina when she returned? There were, to be sure, differences between them; those of age and temperament. But, certainly they were not insoluble. He was willing to forget. No, he corrected himself. He had all but forgotten that the boy, David, was not his son. An understanding had grown between them. It was a quiet, shy thing, as timid and unpredictable as a wild fawn which must be gentled. Having gone this far, rarely ever thinking David was not his son, why could they not take another step? The fact of David's conception, once accepted and then dismissed, should be allowed to fade and dim itself with the passing of time. It could, he almost spoke aloud, become a happy family. He found himself wanting this desperately and it was a feeling he had never before experienced. There must be some small place upon which he and Sabrina could stand together with understanding.

David? In time he could be sent to England and school there; learn something of the world and its people beyond these insular shores. The Heaths were not without position in the homeland. A career could be opened for the boy in the Foreign Service or the military. The years took wings in his imagination. There were all sorts of opportunities waiting for a boy of breeding, background, ambition and intelligence.

The rock upon which his fancy stubbed itself was Sabrina. If only she was not such an uncompromising bitch. She irritated him deliberately; plagued him with a sharp and malicious tongue and mind. If once she ever suspected an attachment between her son and husband she would stop at nothing to disrupt it and set them against each other. Of this he was certain.

First, he thought, he must reach some state of compromise with her. Rapprochement was not impossible. Reluctantly he admitted much of the fault was his. He had made little effort after the early days of their marriage to please and delight her with unexpected tenderness. When he could have been sympathetic he was gruff. When there was a time for gentleness he had been indifferent. He should have understood there were normal differences to be resolved between any newly married couple but his attitude had been: Let it be my way or not at all.

[182]

His meditations surprised him for it was not in his character to admit error. The truth was he had changed and this was all the more astonishing. What had caused him to alter the tenets by which he had shaped his life? The answer, when it came to him, was so incredible it drove all sleep from his mind. Surrounded, as he had been, by so much misery of late, there had been little time to think about himself, his comforts and desires. There was, he marveled, a reward and satisfaction in the service to others. It was a concept completely foreign to his nature but he was forced to admit its truth. Since his appointment as Governor there had been few real problems with which to contend. There was the congenital slothfulness of the natives, who saw no reason to exert themselves for anything beyond their personal needs. It was impossible to conceive of them as interested in commerce and trade or the extension of the general economic welfare. Also, he had been met by the indifference of the Crown to its island possessions. To the Home Government the Bahamas had seemed nothing more than isolated dots of coral with which England did a small trade. With the migration of the Royalists from the American colonies he had been met with a tight, supercilious cadre of Colonial aristocrats whose plantations on the mainland had been their private baronies. They had little respect for the Governor or his office. All of these things put together had induced in him an apathy, a feeling of uselessness, a willingness to spend his days in an agreeable climate, bearing an almost meaningless title but the Governor nevertheless. It was more than his impoverished knighthood back home would have yielded, and so he had been content to drift and exert himself no more than was absolutely necessary.

Suddenly, he had been confronted with this threat of total catastrophe. He was physically and mentally unprepared to meet it but he was not so stupid not to realize it laid upon his shoulders certain unavoidable responsibilities. The marvel of it was, he thought now, that he had accepted them without question. With a determination he had not suspected himself of possessing, he had averted a wholesale panic. More than this, though, he felt an actual concern for others. As the sickness spread, misery and death reaching almost every other home, he was touched by a sympathy and concern heretofore unknown to him. These things were not, as he had always believed, manifestations of weakness. Sacrifice, in a most curious way, was ennobling. This concept was both new and astonishing.

Now, his mind roving freely, he wondered if the same energy and concern he had displayed when confronted by the devastation of cholera might not work a miracle here in the Bahamas. A firm hand, wisely directed, could make an amazing change in the economic and political status of the islands. People could be made to understand the opportunity offered them here. It was worth thinking about. It was even exciting. The islands need not be the cast-off relatives of the Crown. They were of strategic importance; a bastion confronting the ambitions and incursions of the Spanish and French. Lying in the darkness he was determined to make the Crown aware of this. The Governor of the Bahamas would no longer be a mere figurehead, an official of no importance.

Where to begin? The question posed itself immediately. With the people, of course. He would learn more of the population of the Out Islands; the settlements there, the opportunities offered for revitalizing them. If he had to he would ingratiate himself with the aristocratic clan in Nassau itself. In time, when old suspicions had been dissipated, arguments, differences of opinion settled, they would all work and plan together. The islands would become what they should be, fair ornaments for the Crown. The notion excited him so he could barely restrain himself from getting out of bed and putting some of the ideas down on paper.

Sabrina awoke reluctantly. She turned on her side and glanced at the small, ornamental clock on the night table beside her bed. Stretching luxuriously she reached for the bell pull to summon the young mulatto girl Ronald Cameron had assigned as her personal maid.

It was nine o'clock and she was ravenously hungry. She couldn't remember when she had had an appetite for more than tea, a small piece of fruit and a roll or biscuit. Here, on Exuma, she found herself going to the table with the hunger of a field hand. Never, she thought, had she felt so completely contented with her life. It was, she told herself, because each morning she awoke to a household of vitality. The puffy face and waddling figure of her husband were things which had receded so far back into her mind she had difficulty in recalling them. How long had she been here? A month, a year, always; time had no meaning.

The colored girl came, curtsied and murmured a softly shy good morning before she opened the blinds and drew the curtains, allowing the bright morning to flood the room.

Sabrina watched her with a tinge of curiosity. Her skin was the color of creamed cocoa; her features delicate and actually beautiful. She wore the customary dress of gray, striped cotton. Her feet were bare and around one slim ankle she wore a small copper chain, attached to which was a tiny brass bell which tinkled with barbaric music when she walked. Sabrina's eyes followed her about the room and she wondered if Ronald or one of his overseers had sired her. The white blood was too obvious. What curious irony this was; to be served, bathed and waited on by Ronald Cameron's daughter.

[184]

After the girl had left to bring her tray she lay thinking. It was a little after nine now. By this time Ronald, the overseers, Robert Bruce and even young David were somewhere in the fields. Ronald had made David a present of a gentle, dainty filly, seriously voicing the comment that he was too old now for a pony such as he had in Nassau. It was, she reflected, a most curious situation. Ronald sometimes actually seemed embarrassed in the presence of this son whose relationship he could not claim. There was, though, a strange and subtle understanding between the boy and man upon which neither David nor Ronald presumed because neither was actually aware of its existence. They simply liked each other at once. The kinship could not be explained in any other way as far as David was concerned although Ronald, at times, must have been subjected to a confusing emotion when he looked upon this son he could not acknowledge. As for David, he was delighted with this new freedom, the size of the plantation and the variety of activity of those who lived upon it.

She thought back to their day of arrival on Great Exuma. The master of the *Traveler* had been a little dubious as to their reception. The Government sloop and the interisland schooner had spoken each other on the long run down the Exuma Cays. The *Traveler*'s captain had brought his vessel about in the light breeze and crossed from his own ship to the sloop in a gig. After an exchange of greetings and news from Nassau and the Out Islands, the schooner's master had expressed his doubts as to the welcome even the Governor's wife and son might find on Exuma.

"I have been met at gunpoint at Watlings, Long Island, St. George's Cay and other places who fear we may bring the plague, Lady Heath. Mr. Cameron's reception may not be what you expect, for he is a man of strong convictions, stubborn nature and a concern for his family, slaves and plantation. He may believe you bring the pollution of Nassau with you."

Sabrina had shaken her head with a smile. "I know Mr. Cameron. He will not turn us away. Of that I am certain. Ronald Cameron is not a man to panic easily."

Despite her expressed conviction Sabrina was aware of a small reservation tucked away at the back of her mind. Suppose Ronald did refuse them permission to land? Where would she and David go? Back to Nassau or one of the dreary settlements on the other islands where they would be without friend or acquaintance?

The sloop dropped anchor within the shelter of Exuma's harbor. A small boat had been sent ashore to announce the presence of Lady Heath and her son. The response had been heartwarming and immediate. Ronald, himself, had come out to welcome and escort them to the plantation.

He had accepted her presence and her turning to him in this extremity as both natural and pleasant. He took her outstretched hands with a broad smile of pleasure at seeing her again. Beyond this his manner was reserved. He was permitting the past to be something which she could remember or forget.

"I had visions of being turned away," she confessed. "Everyone is so frightened."

"I think you knew better than that." He was aware of the soft pressure of her hands in his. "If you hadn't been certain of your reception you wouldn't have come." He turned and glanced at the boy, who was staring up at him with bright interest. "This is young David?"

She wondered what was in his mind as he gazed at the son he could not claim as his own.

"David Heath," she replied softly, "out of the exigency of a situation." Her eyes glowed. "I hope you approve of him, Ronald."

Cameron continued to study the boy, taking in his sturdy frame, the suppressed excitement on his face. Then, he gravely released Sabrina and extended a hand.

"We will be friends, David, you and I. Good friends. I would like it that way. You are a fine-looking lad and I hope your stay at Exuma will be a happy one."

The meeting with the rest of the family had been unreservedly friendly and all she might have wished. First, there was Robert Bruce and his wife of little more than a year. Their greeting was cordial and they seemed to be sincerely happy she had selected the Cameron plantation as a refuge. Caroline puzzled Sabrina a little. The welcome was immediate and without reservation but Sabrina thought she detected just the slightest twinkle of amusement in her glance. It was impossible, though. Sabrina dismissed the idea quickly. Caroline could not possibly have any knowledge of the situation. Yet, a curious wisdom lurked behind the lovely color of her eyes as they shifted from Sabrina Heath's face to that of David. It was as though she intuitively sensed something to which she could give no name.

"It has been several years since your aunt brought you to see me, Caroline." Sabrina made the remark casually. "It is disconcerting to find you grown. The years have gone by with a fearful speed."

"When you see my twins you will think they have gone even faster. This is my husband Juan. Lady Heath, Juan Cadiz."

"You are married?" It was a ridiculous question, Sabrina knew, but it came spontaneously. The years had indeed flown. "I had not heard."

"With two children, a boy and a girl, I should hope so." Caroline smiled.

[186]

Sabrina offered her hand to Juan. He was, she thought, the most unlikely person Ronald Cameron would have selected as a son-in-law. He was dark, lean and carried with him a curious suggestion of arrogance which, she admitted, was somehow not offensive although it should have been. He looks, she told herself, as though he was confident of sharing my bed or any woman's by merely expressing his desire to do so. How, she was actually puzzled, had this marriage between Caroline Cameron and Juan Cadiz come about? She was certain it had not been with Ronald's approval. She knew by name most of the first families in the Bahamas. Cadiz was not one of them.

They talked as a group, the Camerons asking innumerable questions about the conditions in Nassau. Juan said nothing. He leaned against the wall with unstudied negligence, listening, saying no word but watching Sabrina Heath. She found her glance straying now and then to meet his. If not to the manor born, she decided, he had quickly adapted himself to his surroundings. He was, she concluded, a man in detached rebellion against the world. There was no malice in this. Rather, he seemed to view everything with a small, scornful amusement.

The slave girl returned now with her breakfast. As the tray was being set across her lap Sabrina looked at the quantity of food she had ordered. Eggs, marmalade, tea, rolls. Never in her life had she eaten such a breakfast. The air on Exuma, she concluded, must be far more stimulating than that of Nassau. As she broke and buttered a roll she thought about last night.

Ronald had changed astonishingly. He was older than the years should have made him. The creation of this island plantation had left its mark in new lines about his eyes, an expression of concern when he was off guard. After the evening meal they had walked together in the softly caressing half-light of a crescent moon.

For a while they said nothing. Thinking of it now she was aware it had been a strangely disturbing silence; as though they, who had been lovers and had conceived a child between them, were uneasy in each other's company.

"I hoped you would be glad to see me." She took his arm and they strolled toward the beach where, in the windless night, the waves were little more than ripples as they ran upon the sand. "Many times during these past years you have been often in my mind."

"I am not a demonstrative man. Not because I will it so. It is in my nature. Besides," he permitted a slow smile to gather, "should I have sprung upon you, gathered you in my arms and carried you off to my bedchamber in front of the family? Should I have told Caroline and Robert Bruce: This is David, your half brother? The result of an afternoon on a beach with a lady of quality. How such a thing came about —an act in the day's broad light—I am not quite sure. But, it happened."

"That is better." She pressed his arm and laughed lightly. "I would not like to find you without a sense of humor."

The sand, as they walked upon it, made the whispering sound of silk being rubbed together and there was a faint rustling in the palms as they inclined toward the sea.

"I am more than happy to see you." He spoke thoughtfully. "I would like the circumstances to be better, or at least different. As it is I must remember you are another man's wife."

"You will get over that." She was completely assured. "Believe me, a man's memory grows surprisingly short in such matters. In a day or two you will think of me only as Sabrina, a lady of wanton disposition but of some discretion. You forgot Gerald without much difficulty once before and will do so again. I am content to wait but," she burlesqued an ominous note of warning, "not for too long."

With her, this way, he began to recapture some of the irresponsible humor which had possessed him on that single afternoon beneath Nassau's hot sun when they had made love together on the sand with heedless abandon. It was an experience from which he had never fully recovered, and many times it had come to his mind as an incredible adventure.

"You are a little outside my experience." He made the confession with a trace of embarrassment. "In a matter where you should incline to a blushing confusion or modest reticence, you are as blunt and straightforward as a man."

"You have led a sheltered life, Ronald." She made the statement with a tender derision. "Save for certain, desirable, physical differences, a man and a woman are much alike. It is hypocrisy not to admit it. We slake our thirst at the same fount."

"You are the first woman I have known to admit it. I think that is what throws me a little off balance."

"Tell me," she spoke with a sudden irrelevance, "who is this Juan Caroline has married? Juan Cadiz. I have never before heard the name in the islands and most of the important families have at one time or another visited the Governor's Mansion. Where is he from? Where did she meet him?"

"He attracts you?" Cameron asked the question with honest curiosity. "You find him provocative?"

"Let us just say he interests me." She was airily poised.

"Aye!" He nodded a reluctant agreement. "I think he must have that effect upon all women."

They found a fallen palm tree, uprooted by some long-ago storm and now lying athwart the beach. In the moonlight its trunk had the smooth quality of a silvered pelt. They sat upon it, facing the sea.

"There was a time," Cameron gathered his thoughts with a judicial deliberation, "when the mention of Juan's name would have aroused a fury within me. He is no one. An adventurer without conscience. A complete scoundrel, I suspect, when it suits his purpose. An unlettered man of dubious lineage. And yet," he made no effort to disguise his mystification, "I sometimes find myself almost admiring him for the very qualities which I should despise." His short laugh was without humor. "He will not lift so much as a finger in the work of the plantation. He dresses in the manner of a vagabond and frequently walks about the house and grounds clad in nothing more than a pair of sailor's pantaloons. If it pleases him he will sit with the slaves before a cabin and share their meal and incomprehensible talk. All of these things he is and does. Yet," the incredibility was in his tone, "neither has he ever asked for anything. I have waited," Cameron confessed reluctantly, "for him to come to me and say: Put so many pounds and shillings in my hand and I will leave. I married your daughter only because I thought you were a wealthy man. I find, now, you are not. It is a disappointment to me but give me what you can and I will clear out and you may have your daughter back. In time she can marry someone more to your liking."

"It is a little late for that, isn't it? She with two children?" Sabrina was faintly amused by Cameron's dogged perplexity.

"But," Cameron ignored the interruption, "he has never said such a thing. That is what baffles me. I do not know what he really wants."

"Has it occurred to you that he may be in love with Caroline and she with him and they want nothing more than to have each other?" She turned, regarding him with faint surprise.

"It not only has occurred to me," there was impatience in the admission, "I have been forced to believe it. There is no other explanation. How can my daughter love such a man?" The incredulity of this situation caused him to pound a fist of one hand into the palm of another. "Sometimes," Cameron found himself trapped in a maze of contradictions, "he takes his sloop, a gourd of water, a little food in a sack as would some tinker, and sails off for two or three days at a time. I expect Caroline to be outraged, to weep, fret, to pace the floor in a torment of humiliation and anger. Instead," he shook his head with disbelief, "she merely shrugs off my questions and says, 'I know my Juanio. He will come back. What he does is in his nature. I would not have him any different.'" He snorted, a bull-like sound. "What do you think of that?"

"I think," she was pensive, "it is all a little wonderful in its way and does not happen between two persons often."

[189]

"Aaah! Like all women you become a simpering romantic in the matter of a handsome derelict." He was rudely impatient with her reply.

"Like all women," she contradicted quietly, "I have the need to be loved. If Caroline has found love then she is among the most fortunate." She stood up and reached for his hand. He arose and stood beside her. For a moment they looked at each other and then she gave a small, wistful shrug. "Is it so hard for you to understand?"

"It is a form of self-immolation in which all women seem to delight."

"Ronald, Ronald." She spoke sadly. "You are so wrong. Put your arms around me. I want to feel your strength. Kiss me and say something gentle."

She pressed close to him, her body following the line of his. When he kissed her she murmured with a low sound as of pain. After a moment she turned her face and her cheek lay against his. Her fingers traveled with a searching intensity about his chin and lips as a blind person might seek an identity. Then, she seemed to wilt as though all strength drained from her as she acknowledged a defeat.

"To be almost in love," she spoke unhappily; "that is the tragedy. I never believed it could happen. Always I thought it must be yes or no. But with us it is like the half-light which comes from that unformed moon. I don't think it will change and I find it a little saddening in the shadows. I believe, given time and some compassion, we could be good for each other. As it is," her eyes glistened with the suggestion of a tear, "I am grateful for your attempt at sympathy, your gentleness in a situation which you do not understand. I am not sorry I came."

"I would like to have you stay." He kissed her eyes and felt their dampness. "It is difficult for me to say the things I should." He was miserable and without the ability to lie with conviction.

"No." She shook her head and a smile returned slowly. "We are lightly trapped and without the love to sustain us. I know that. I should not have expected more. Besides," she drew away and touched his mouth with her hand to silence him, "even if it was between us as I want it to be, what would we tell your son and daughter? This Lady Heath. She has left her husband to come and live with me. You must not think this at all unusual. There are precedents for such behavior." She took his hand and they began walking back along the beach. "I don't think." Her smile had its old, impish quality. "I am certain they would not understand. I would need that and so would you. Even if there were no Gerald I am not sure it would be a good thing. You see," her fingers insinuated themselves into his, "I grow wiser and, perhaps, a little too old for impossible romantic fancies. I will stay until our time runs out and I must return to Nassau to be the Governor's Lady again. We will be to each other what you would like and nothing more. Let us keep what we have and not reach like greedy children for that which our hands can no longer hold."

In the bedroom, glowing from the light of candles in their polished brackets upon the wall, Juan stood with a length of toweling wrapped about his waist. He watched with alert interest as Caroline undid the ribbon from her hair and allowed it to flow about her shoulders. Her slender body was outlined clearly through the transparent shift. He reached out and touched her breast as one might caress a fragile blossom. Her smile was immediate and tender.

"You are a very lucky girl." He grinned.

"So you keep telling me." She responded to his mood of banter.

"What other woman has a husband who finds her more beautiful every day?"

"None I can think of." She forced her brow into a wrinkle of serious thought. "And what woman," she continued without rancor, "has a husband who goes off in his boat every now and then without a word of good-bye or when he will be back?"

"I was born of the sea. You said so yourself. She is my mother. I only go to visit her now and then."

"I was mistaken." Caroline shook her head. "She is your mistress."

"You are jealous." The idea seemed to delight him. He stretched himself, arching his body as a supple bow. "That is a good thing. It keeps you anxious to please me." He swept her up in his arms and dropped her without dignity upon the bed of softly quilted down. "There is where a wife should wait for her husband; not standing on a beach, straining her eyes for the rise of a sail."

"The day I wait upon the beach"—she sat upright in indignation—"the waves will run backwards."

He pushed her gently and she fell upon the mound of pillows, lying there with a contented sigh, one eye half-closed in an absurd wink of invitation.

He strode about the room; a half-naked savage, she thought, with a grace which always delighted her. After a moment he returned and sat upon the edge of the bed, his hands enclosing her narrow waist.

"Do you know?" He was momentarily serious. "I think there is something between your papa and the Governor's wife. I have a strong feeling about such things."

Her surprise was immediate and unmistakable. "I, also." She spoke wonderingly. "I felt something when they were together and at the table tonight as we ate. I'm not sure why."

[191]

"I will tell you." He preened himself. "As you have taught me things; how to write and read a little. To think of much which was unknown to me before. I have told you of how it is between a man and a woman because, in that, I have had much experience. It is a look." He enumerated. "A way of saying something when the words don't really mean what you think they do. It is a tiny flicker, like a candle caught for a moment in the wind, as it comes into the eyes. The sound of the voice. The little smile. That is how I know something goes on between your papa and this lady." He leaned across her, pressing his face into her body with heavy affection. Her hands closed over his head and held it there. "But," he murmured, his words muffled, "it is not like it is between you and me. She wants him but I do not think he wants her altogether. It is not as she would like it to be."

"Then I feel sorry for her." Caroline meant it.

Juan lifted his face. "There are many places the Governor's wife could have gone to escape the plague in Nassau. Why did she come here? Were you all such good friends?"

"No-o." Caroline speculated. "Papa had business with the Governor. Robert Bruce and I with Aunt Martha went for tea at the Governor's Mansion a couple of times. There was some small, social interchange. That is all."

"So!" He stood up and walked to the open window. "It is none of my business." He turned about and pressed one finger against his nose with a sly gesture. "But I like to be right about such things."

"But—Papa." She giggled. "I can't imagine him. Well, you know what I mean."

"Your papa is a big bull of a man. You are too used to him to realize this but another woman would see it and know." He whistled contemplatively. "Where do you suppose all those light-skinned slaves came from? They don't grow that way in Africa. A man must have some amusement."

"I wish you wouldn't say such things," she protested.

"Why not? In the dark all women are the same. Do you think after your mother died your father became less of a man?"

He turned again to the window, crossing his arms upon the casement and leaning upon them. He sniffed hungrily of the night's air. He listened and identified small sounds in the darkness and felt how the wind, which had been only a breath before, had freshened. Ragged scuds of cloud raced across the quarter moon. This island, as did the others, and the sea itself, spoke to him in a language he had learned from childhood. He knew nothing of the rest of the world, save from such stories as he had gathered from the sailors in the Nassau dives. But these islands. He could find his way among them without light or compass.

"I think we have a blow." He spoke without turning. "I can taste it in my mouth; hear it from a far-off place where it gathers."

"It is the season for the hurricanes." She watched him with undisguised pleasure.

"I think, also"—this time he did face her—"your papa has plenty of trouble here on the plantation. It builds up a little, here and there, as does the wind outside before coming together."

"What are you talking about?" She sat upright, away from the pillows, and stared at him. "Why should there be trouble?"

"You know how it is with me." He spoke without arrogance. "I go as I wish, talk as I will. I know more of your slaves by name than you do. Sometimes, in the evening when you are busy with the babies, I sit with the niggers in front of their cabins. I eat some of their beans and rice from the pot and watch their faces in the firelight. At first they would stop talking when I came. We said nothing. Only squatted upon the ground, poking little sticks into the flames. After a while they get used to me. They know I am not like you, the Camerons, who have always owned them. They understand I am a white man but not the same kind of white as your papa, your brother, the overseers who send them to work. My skin is dark, but still, I am white inside. This they realize and it makes talk between us not an easy thing until it is like something you see all the time and it is no longer strange. Then they talk a little among themselves as if I wasn't there. Some of what they say I understand. Some is with the words of their tribes and it makes no sense to me except in the tone of the voice. Now," his expression was serious, "I begin to feel something. It is like some faraway cry which comes from no place or no one but is just a sound."

"I don't understand you, Juanio." She was mystified and concerned. "What are you saying?"

"That if I were your papa I would get rid of my niggers. I would put them up for sale at Vendue House, in Nassau, and keep only a few here to do the little work which will need to be done."

"How can you run a plantation without slaves?" She was half amused by his ignorance of such things. "You should see the fields, the mills, the storehouses in Carolina. There have always been slaves on the Cameron land."

"You don' have much plantation no more, girl." He fell into the soft patois of the Bahamian. "Even I, who know nothing about such a matter, can see that. Each year the cotton grows a little less. The soil is thin and tired. It makes what it can but it isn't enough. I'll tell you what will happen. Your papa knows this but he will not say it. The time will come when all you have left is this big house and empty fields. There will be no much crop going out and no money coming in. You will do without these fine, wax candles and learn to do with a rag soaked in pig fat. There will be no more soap as it comes to you from across the ocean. You will make it yourself with lye, ashes and pork drippings. You will make your clothes of the leftover cloth from what is worn out. All over the islands it will be the same. Big houses, like this one, with the wind blowing through them."

"I wish you would stop talking that way." She was indignant and uneasy. "It scares me even if it can't be true. How could such a thing happen?"

"It has already happened. Not here, yet. On Crooked Island there were thirty, forty plantations. Not as big as yours. Now, there are none."

"I don't believe it!"

"Sometime we sail over and I'll show you." He rubbed at his nose with the knuckles of a hand and half smiled. "When it is all gone here, on Exuma, I think your papa will be glad to have Juan Cadiz around to show him how to take a living from the sea."

She studied his face to see if there was some obscure jest behind the words he had spoken. He had not been joking. She felt a small, indefinable fear.

"What did you mean about selling off the slaves in Nassau?"

"Because," he half twisted about, his ear catching the sound of rising wind. It sang a little now like a big violin. "I think if you don't they will someday kill you. They will come quietly from their cabins as the shadows move. With them they will carry the sharp cane knives, the hoes they use for chopping cotton, a club or whatever they can put in their hands. They do not like it here. Even now, after these years, they are afraid of this place because they see land which will not grow things as it should. This, in their mind, is not good. Let me tell you," he sat on the sill of the open window, "what has happened on Crooked Island. The white people there gave up. They took what little they had left and went back to the mainland, to the Spanish Florida, in the small boats they owned. Others, those with money, sailed for your England in the big ships. They left everything and their slaves behind because they could not take them along. Now, the black men, their women and children, live in the big houses of those who were their masters. The glass in the windows was long ago broken. The doors hang crookedly, like a drunken man trying to stand holding to a post. The boards of the porches have been torn out to build their fires. The niggers don't care. Even this way it is better than they have ever had it before. They walk through the great rooms and sleep in the beds of their masters. They make their dirt on the floors where ladies like you and gentlemen like Robert Bruce and your father once danced. Stone by stone, board by board, peg and nail fall away and no one cares. The houses rot in the rains and sunshine. The black men don't give a damn because they are free to do as they please. Your niggers, the Cameron ones, know what has happened. How it is so I can't tell you but they do. They hear how other slaves no longer go to the fields at sunup and have no overseer with a whip in hand to tell them to do this or that. One of these days, if you don't get rid of them now, they will come for us; maybe not me, but the Camerons."

He dropped from the sill, walked across the room and back, pausing to look down at her with affection. Her eyes were wide, not with fear but with complete incomprehension.

"I do not say these things to scare you because, before it happens, I will take you away from this place." He took a deep breath. "I would not say to your papa what I have just said to you because he would not believe me. In his mind I am an ignorant no one whose mother dropped him on the beach or in the scrub because she had no bed in which to lie. He would say: The Camerons have always had slaves. Never has one raised his hand against us. I treat them well. I know my niggers. But," his shoulders lifted in a characteristic shrug, "he no longer knows these. I do. I listen to what they talk about and their words are sounds which your papa would not understand. Even before me they do not say the real thing which is in their mind but I can feel it. I would take your papa to Crooked Island or Rollstown and show him how it is if he would let me."

Caroline stared at this husband of hers. This was a new Juanio who was trying to express a feral instinct for danger. For the first time in these years she saw him in a serious mood. What he had been saying was no boogeyman tale contrived to alarm her. He meant every word he had spoken.

"Papa will know what to do." She made the statement in a small voice and without conviction. "He, and now Robert Bruce, have managed slaves all of their lives. If there was discontent among them Papa would know it."

"Your papa will die like any other man whose throat has been cut." He was indifferent.

"Stop it!" She was indignant and angry because she was apprehensive. "I don't want to hear any more. The things you have been saying are impossible." She slipped from the bed and put on a light robe. "I want to look in on the children. I thought I heard one of them cry."

This was not the truth and they both knew it. A black woman half dozed and watched from a chair in the adjoining room where the twins were asleep. He came to her and put his arms about her shoulders and arms. His kiss barely touched her cheek as she tried to turn away, still annoyed with him.

"I didn't mean to scare you. It is something I have had on my mind. That is all. You are my wife. If I can't talk with you, who is there? I'll go with you. I like to see them in their beds." He kissed her fully now and with something of the old laughter in his eyes. "When I used to rub your belly with the oil to keep it smooth and soft I did not think there were two of them inside. I would have used twice as much."

She relented, smiled and felt better with his arm now about her waist as they walked together. He turned the door's knob softly. At their entrance the slave woman stood up and gazed at them wonderingly. Caroline put a finger to her lips and motioned the nurse back to her chair.

The small beds were side by side, separated only by a narrow aisle. The twins, brother and sister, slept soundly. Caroline leaned over and unnecessarily adjusted the light coverings. Her proud gaze moved from one to the other as she marveled a little at the miracle of her body. The boy, John, had the black hair and even in this young state, something of his father's features. The girl, and she had insisted upon naming her Bahama—Bahama Cameron Cadiz—despite the incredulous protests of her father who declared Bahama was an outrageous name for a girl and one which would cause her embarrassment in later years.

"It is," Caroline defended her choice, "no more outlandish than Caroline, Georgia or Virginia. I like the sound of it. Bahama. Or," she had thrust a tongue into her cheek, "perhaps you would like to have me call her, or them, Great and Little Exuma."

Cameron resigned himself to her argument. After all, he decided, the ridiculous name was no more incomprehensible than the marriage which had produced the child.

Now, Caroline leaned down and put her lips to a small hand. "They are beautiful. I would like to keep them this way forever; young, filled with laughter and excitement."

"Why shouldn't they be pretty with such a mother and father?" Juan pretended an indifference. "I will make you some more when I have the time. Each one better-looking than the other."

She took his hand and led him quietly from the room. The slave woman closed the door after them and resettled herself in the rocking chair.

"If you say so." Caroline snuffed out one of the candles. "You said there was a storm coming." She flushed a little. "What else is there to do when it rains?"

[196]

In the bedroom which was at the end of the manor's west wing, with floor-to-ceiling windows looking out upon the sea and fields, Robert Bruce Cameron and his wife, Constance, lay in the darkness. Her head was upon his shoulder, his arm cradled her fragrant body. They both listened to the rising note of the wind.

They had been married a little over a year now. It had been an elaborate wedding, limited in some respects by the difficulties of transportation. Even so there had been relatives, old friends and neighbors who had made the trip by sailing ship from Charleston, the Low Country, Virginia and Savannah. To this union Ronald Cameron had given his complete approval. More. He felt the wedding of Robert Bruce and Constance Ormond had, in a measure, canceled out the misalliance of Caroline and Juan Cadiz, and the children which Constance would eventually bear would be the products of the finest Colonial stock. In this he was not actually a man of vanity. He merely subscribed completely to the idea that good blood reproduced itself. He had no faith in the progeny of a mongrel and a thoroughbred. In the end, somehow, the base seed prevailed and produced an unwholesome hybrid.

The most elaborate preparations for the ceremony had been made and the vast mansion he had built on this lonely island was taxed to accommodate all of the guests. An elaborate outdoor pavilion had been set up with an awning cover of gaily striped canvas. An orchestra had been imported from Nassau for the dancing. There were horse races, contests between the fastest island sloops. Long tables were set up in the pavilion and the bowls were constantly filled with a heady punch of rum and fruit juices. In the reception room of the manor the floor had been polished and waxed for the dancing, which frequently lasted until dawn began to show itself.

There were huge outdoor meals with whole sheep, young pigs and sides of beef cooked over open pits, and formal dinners perfectly served on the precious Cameron china and the elaborate silver. Later, the dancing, with the ladies in their finest gowns and the gentlemen stiffly arrayed in the height of London fashion, copied by their tailors from the periodicals which came to them from England. There was no time for boredom, for such an event as this had never before been held in the islands, not even in Nassau. Everyone was determined to enjoy it to the point of exhaustion.

Constance Ormond had been a radiant and beautiful bride; Robert Bruce properly reserved, aware of the obligation and solemnity of the occasion. He well understood that someday he must take his place as head of the Cameron household. The responsibility troubled him a little at times but when he looked at the looming figure of his father he felt that the hour when he must take over would be a long time coming. He was a not too articulate man but he felt a comforting love for Constance Ormond and a shy pride in her beauty, her carriage and her sudden maturity as they stood before the minister.

To the guests this was a wedding such as they might have attended in the plantation country of the mainland before the Revolution. It represented something solid in a world which had become bewilderingly fluid. It was the proper mating between two fine, old families and no such strange alliance as that Caroline Cameron had made with a man who bore the preposterous name of Cadiz. It was true that many of the young matrons and girls cast curious and speculative glances at Caroline's husband. He had consented to be outfitted for the occasion by a Nassau tailor and he wore his new clothing as he had worn his old, with a dash and handsome grace.

During the week-long festivities Caroline had watched Juan with a quiet amusement as he exerted an effortless charm on the ladies. She could see the open invitation in their eyes when they danced or shared a cup of punch with her husband. He captivated them all from the grandmothers and aunts to the wives and young, unmarried girls. Somehow, he managed to be courtly, perfectly mannered and at the same time carry himself with a ducal arrogance they found irresistible. And who, she had thought, but her Juanio would appear in faultless dress with a gold ring shining in his ear? It was a compelling touch of the civilized and barbaric. The women simply could not keep their gaze from this odd adornment and his face with its dark animation. Once, she had caught his eye as he stood talking with Amelia Ferguson, who had come with her family from their plantation at the opposite end of the island. His attention had all but transfixed Amelia. One of her hands rested delicately in the region of her heart as though to keep that organ from leaping through the silk of her gown. Juan knew what he was doing. He set about it deliberately but with a remarkably subtle deference, as though Amelia was the most beautiful girl he had ever seen. He was the polished actor whose performance was far too finished to be obvious and Amelia was in a subdued flutter of excitement. His wink, though, when his glance met Caroline's, was little short of a leer.

When the last of the guests had departed and Mrs. Ormond had her final scene of tears in leaving behind a daughter, the outdoor pavilion came down. The musicians packed up and were off in the boat which had brought them from Nassau. The Out Islanders went home in their sloops and ketches and the guests who had come from the mainland boarded the *Traveler,* which had made a special trip for the occasion and would take them to Nassau where they could await a larger vessel.

The household gradually settled back into its normal, and sometimes monotonous, routine.

In the beginning Constance had been shy and a little reticent, unwilling to intrude and accept the responsibilities which were expected of her as the wife of Robert Bruce Cameron who would someday inherit the plantation, its hall, slaves and problems. Caroline had never paid more than the scantest attention to the running of the establishment. The house slaves had been long at their duties. They understood what was expected of them for they had been well trained at Cameron Hall on the Ashley. If, without the firm hand Martha Cameron used to exert, they became somewhat lax in the performance of their work, these derelictions were not too obvious. Caroline didn't bother to correct them. Sometimes Ronald was forced to raise his voice in anger over slovenly breaches of conduct. But he was usually too occupied with the working of the plantation to notice more than the most flagrant omissions of conduct—the service at the table, the condition of the silver and china, and the occasional unstarched and careless appearance of a slave girl as she cleaned a room or made a bed.

A week or so after the wedding celebration he had asked Constance into his library. There he talked gently with her, for he had a sincere affection for this undemonstrative but charmingly mannered and beautiful girl.

She sat dutifully before him, not knowing what to expect. He lit a pipe after courteously asking her permission.

"There are, Constance," he spoke pensively, "some things which you must understand."

"Yes, Mr. Cameron." She replied in what was almost a frightened whisper for she was somewhat in awe of this man who appeared so severe. "I suppose so."

"Come," he chided with a smile, "you must not be afraid of me. We cannot go through the years with you calling me Mr. Cameron. You are one of the family. Ronald." He tested the word carefully. "That is not quite fitting either. Could you accept me as a second parent and call me, perhaps, Father?"

"Yes, Father." She smiled her gratitude for his understanding.

"Later," his eyes were shot through with small, bright lights of amusement, "you will probably be able to refer to me as Grandfather."

She blushed, the color rising to her cheeks in a sudden wave, and her eyes dropped to the hands which lay in her lap.

"Well, anyhow," he was brusque as though what he had said was no matter of consequence, "as I said in the beginning, there are certain things which you must understand. Robert Bruce is my eldest, my only son. As my heir he will inherit large responsibilities. You, as his wife, must be prepared to share them. As an Ormond this should not seem unnatural to you. What," he was annoyed with himself for this unnecessary circumlocution, "I am getting at in my dull way is that I expect you to manage the household; no easy task for a young girl. You must impress your will upon the slaves at once. If you do not do this, make them understand immediately you are mistress here, they will be inclined to take advantage of your youth. They will malinger, shirk their duties or do them in half measure as they have sometimes done since my sister Martha left us. This you must not tolerate. For if they find you are timid or reluctant to be dominant in even the smallest matters they will begin to take advantage of you, neglecting their proper duties." He scowled at the idea. "Be harsh when it is necessary."

"But," her voice was firmer now, "I had thought Caroline—"

He interrupted her, not rudely but with a trace of impatience. "I love my daughter," he said this with a convincing sincerity, "but she has little interest and less capacity for managing a household. I can give you no reason for this other than her nature. She was reared by her Aunt Martha with an understanding of her responsibilities. These, in a measure, she has seen fit to disregard. She is just not a keeper of the house by nature. An undusted piece of furniture does not disturb her in the slightest. A lapse in the service at the table does not bother her. A badly cleaned room, an indifferently made bed, the operation and immaculate condition of the kitchen, are matters she either disregards or does not notice. The hall could gather cobwebs and she would only say it was in the nature of things. So," he tried to make his smile reassuring, "the task of managing this big house falls to you. I have no wish to make of you a drudge but you must be the mistress within these walls and let no one forget it for a moment. This is proper. You are Robert Bruce's wife. If," he leaned over and covered her hands with his, "this frightens you a little at first you must get over it. You are well bred and reared. From your own home you know how things should or should not be done. This, now, is your home. Run it as you would the Ormond manse in Carolina or on the island."

"I will try." She spoke with determination. "It was only that I did not want to intrude upon Caroline's prerogatives."

"Believe me," he spoke with an unmistakable shade of bitterness, "my daughter will not resent the intrusion." He stood up, bent down and kissed her lightly on the brow. "You are one of the family now. I speak freely to you. Caroline's marriage was not one of which I approved but one learns to live with things. This Juan, to me at least, has a certain repellent attraction. He is a smooth and inscrutable young devil. I will

[200]

admit those things. He has given me grandchildren but I am not certain whether I should be grateful or apprehensive. Caroline seems to be happy. As strange as that seems to me I can ask for nothing more where she is concerned. I honestly believe she would be as contented living with this Juan in a hut of wattles as she is in the manor."

Now, lying with her husband, Constance turned her face. The only illumination in the room came from a small taper in a blue glass filled with wax. Robert Bruce was not asleep. His eyes were open, staring at the ceiling. She hesitated to speak of what was on her mind.

"Robert."

"Mmmm?"

"Robert," she rushed the following words to have them done with, "why do you suppose I am not? I haven't . . . well, shouldn't I be with a child by now?" She was grateful for the semidarkness shrouding her confusion.

"I don't know." His arm tightened comfortingly. "I mean, I am not sure. I guess sometimes it doesn't happen right away. Didn't you and your mother talk about such things?"

"Mothers are stupid. At least, I am afraid mine is or was." There was a mild indignation in the statement. "A couple of weeks before we were married," she giggled at the memory, "she had me sit down in her room. We were going to have a talk, she said. There were things I ought to know. What to expect. Well! She certainly did not tell me anything I didn't already know. You can't grow up on a plantation with animals—horses, cattle, dogs, cats and even chickens and roosters—without seeing and learning something. I'll have to admit," she snickered, "I thought it was an odd form of behavior for people if that was the way. Well, you know what I mean."

He could feel her laughter, the suppressed shaking of her body as she fought to keep the sound of hilarity from escaping. It seemed a little indelicate to laugh over such a thing.

"What did she tell you?" He, also, was amused by the mental picture of Mrs. Ormond fumbling for words, clumsily skirting the simple truths; trying to be serious and helpful at the same time.

"She told me I must endure you. Those were her very words." Constance was barely containing herself. "Men were carnal and insensitive. They fell upon you with a wild passion to satisfy themselves. It was a wife's unfortunate duty to submit to this indignity; this bestiality which was man's nature. All a good wife could do was to shut her eyes, grit her teeth and endure an animal madness. You beast!"

He laughed without restraint and drew her closer. Poor Mrs. Ormond.

How she must have suffered with this ridiculous performance of what she considered to be her duty.

"When," Constance continued, for she was beginning to enjoy the recollection, "I asked her what happened—you know. How?—she suddenly remembered something she had to do elsewhere and left me there in her sitting room. I was alone with my maidenly interest, as uninformed as when we first sat down. The funny part of it was I knew all the time what she was trying to say."

"You did?" He sat up, honestly surprised. For he had been the most inexperienced of bridegrooms. "How?"

"Once," she confessed, "I saw a slave and a girl in the brush. It shocked me. I just stood there and couldn't move. And then," the confession came reluctantly, "it excited me a little in a way I had never known before. Anyhow, the girl didn't seem to be enduring anything and it was far from passive submission. I think my mother is an idiot." She was emphatic.

"I guess she did what she thought was right. Young ladies are not supposed to know about such things."

"They do, though. Somehow, they find out. When I do have children, and a daughter, I won't make a fool of either of us."

"What will you tell her?" Robert Bruce was interested and a little amused by her vehemence.

"I'll tell her the truth. That it is something wonderful between two persons who love each other. Not the very first time, maybe. But after that . . ." She sighed with subdued rapture. "I guess I'll just say it is something like nothing else." She leaned over him, pressing her breasts against his chest. "But I don't understand why I'm—I'm not pregnant. Do you suppose there is something wrong with me? I have heard it could happen."

"I don't think there is anything wrong with either of us. We're young and healthy. In time we'll fill this house with children."

She was silent for a moment. "Do we have to go that far, husband? This is such a big house." She laughed now without restraint and dug her fingers into his hair, shaking his head with a playful roughness. "There are so many rooms. If we are to fill them all I don't see how we are going to have time for anything else."

He pretended a deep absorption in this problem, turning it over slowly in his mind. She watched his face, noting the hint of laughter about his mouth.

"I am not," he said gravely, "doing anything at the moment. Just in case you have anything in mind. As I said, all we can do is keep trying no matter how bestial it is. You must shut your eyes, bite your lip and endure it as your mother said."

She threw herself upon him in the sheer exuberance of her youth and happiness. "I love you when you are this way, Robert Bruce." There was a fervor in her words. "So much of the time you are serious, so occupied with the plantation. Don't let it come between us. I know things aren't going too well but we'll manage. I don't want it to wear you down as it has your father and mine. We don't need anything that much. This is a new life. We can make of it what we will."

"I have been a long time under the dominance of my father." He spoke almost regretfully. "I don't believe he wanted it that way but I have felt the imposition of his will. Because of this I am like him in many ways. I cannot bear the thought of failure."

"Then"—she was determined—"we won't fail. Things may not be as they once were on the Ashley. We can't expect them to be but we will make our life here in the islands a good one. No matter what happens you will hear no complaint from me. This is my promise."

There was no sound in the house now. Only outside where the wind gathered itself and the surf took on a different note. They lay together listening as the heavy fans in the tall palms threshed with a sudden frenzy of crackling, brittle wildness. But within the manor, so solidly built, there was the deep, quiet sense of security. The taper in the night glass flickered and went out as the last of the candle burned to its end and the room was in darkness.

⊷§ XIV §⊷

LATE IN the afternoon of a bright, warm November day, His Excellency, Sir Gerald Heath, Governor of the Bahama Islands, died of cholera and attending complications while the Royal Medical Officer and two assisting physicians watched helplessly.

The Medical Officer held his finger to the wasted and flaccid wrist, hoping to feel some tiny flicker of pulse. Then he dropped the hand and drew the sheet up to cover the ravaged body and face. It was, he thought sadly, ironic that Sir Gerald should be stricken and die at this time when the plague which had swept New Providence had all but worn itself out. The town of Nassau was free of it and there were only a few cases in the isolated section which had been placed under quarantine. Reports trickling in from the Out Islands confirmed earlier dispatches that the disease had run its course there, also.

There was, the physician thought, no explaining Sir Gerald's succumbing to the malady. True, he had driven himself far beyond what anyone had expected of him. He had made the regular tours of inspection with the doctors, but this thing was not breathed in with the air. It was transmitted by hand to mouth from contaminated food or water. Only one slave had been permitted in the mansion and she, alone, had prepared the meals, changed the bed linen, washed the plates, boiled the water. But somehow, something which he had eaten or drunk had, in transit to the table, passed through unclean hands which carried the deadly seed.

When the first symptoms had appeared—the lethargy, the diarrhea —the Governor had refused to believe what he felt or saw. So, not until his condition was so far advanced and obvious did the Medical Officer have an opportunity to act and administer such limited treatment with which he was familiar. Sir Gerald was confined to bed and all precautions taken. Years of self-indulgence had weakened the Governor's outwardly robust physique. The quantities of rum, wine and brandy had all but atrophied his liver. Rich food in enormous quantities had piled layer upon layer of fat and the heart worked under almost impossible conditions. When the cholera struck it rushed through his flabby body with incredible speed. He had succumbed in a matter of two days.

The Medical Officer turned to his professional confreres. They had all seen much death these past months but for obscure reasons they were particularly saddened by that of the Governor. Perhaps it was because the man had done the unexpected in a period of crisis. He had given unstintingly of his time and energy, exerting the full power of his office to do what he could to help. He had made enemies through his determination, whipped a laggard Assembly into action. No one had really thought him capable of such vigor.

"We must notify the proper officials." The Medical Officer turned away from the bed and walked to the door. "Captain Birch, the Secretary General and others who will announce the Governor's passing to the Assembly and public. The interment should take place tomorrow at the latest."

"Lady Heath?" One of the doctors asked the question.

"There will be no time for Lady Heath to get here from Exuma. She must be notified, of course, as quickly as possible but that is the responsibility of those in authority. We have done what we could." He left the room followed by the others.

From the Government sloop Captain Birch watched as sunrise broke with the color of a great opal over the Exuma cays. One of the uniformed seamen brought him a mug of tea laced with a touch of rum as he had requested. The beauty of the morning held him spellbound, for here were colors of sea and sky as he had not believed possible. The cays with their dark green vegetation and a necklace of white beach, the multi-colored, coral-strewn bottom. The breeze as it freshened sent a rainbow hue in the scattered droplets of water as they were flung from the bow.

The sloop had sailed from Nassau immediately after the Governor's death was announced. There had been no formal, public ceremony but many persons lined the street in silence as the hearse carried its burden to the cemetery. A brief service had been held at the grave and attended, principally, by the island's officials. There had been no way of preserving the body until the sloop could make the run to Exuma and return with the Governor's widow. Now, it was Birch's duty to carry the news to Lady Heath and escort her back to New Providence.

As he balanced himself against the craft's slight roll and sipped from the steaming mug, Birch wondered how the Governor's Lady would take the news. Not, he thought, in tears and lamentation. It was even doubtful she would want to return to New Providence. What was there left for her in Nassau? The empty mansion to which a new Governor would be appointed, and then her tenancy would come to an end. She would go back with him of course, but this, he knew, would be only a matter of form and common decency. The widow of the Governor would, at least, be expected to show herself in Nassau in a proper habit of mourning. But, Captain Birch mused, what after that? He knew Sabrina well. There had been a period of intimacy between them and he was aware her relationship with Sir Gerald had been without heart. They endured each other because a divorce was out of the question. It had been in his mind many times that the child she had borne was not of her husband. She was, he admitted freely, still comparatively young and certainly beautiful. On what curious path now did her future lie?

The sloop dropped anchor in the sheltering cove of the Cameron plantation and Birch went ashore in the gig. It was well past ten o'clock now. Three or four slaves were working in the garden. They lifted their hats of plaited palm and stood motionless as he passed and mounted the steps.

The door was opened by a slave girl who dropped him a curtsy. He announced his name and asked for Lady Heath as the slave led the way to the withdrawing room. He waited there, studying the Cameron portraits on the wall, and turned quickly at the sound of a step.

Constance came through the open double doors. There was a question in her eyes at the sight of his uniform.

"I am Captain Birch, aide to the Governor. Would it be possible for me to see Lady Heath?"

"I am Mrs. Robert Cameron, Captain." Constance half smiled. "I am afraid it is a little early in the morning for Lady Heath. May I offer you a late breakfast or some refreshment?"

"Thank you, no." Birch returned her smile and thought what a pretty girl she was. The Out Islands, he concluded, were breeding a rare line of females. "I had a breakfast of sorts on the sloop."

"If it is urgent," Constance was obviously curious as to the reason for the Governor's aide on Exuma, "I can have Lady Heath awakened. Please sit down."

Birch took a chair and Constance found a place on a small sofa. She waited for him to speak.

"I'm afraid," Birch said, "the time for urgency has passed. It is my unhappy duty to tell Lady Heath her husband is dead. He succumbed to the cholera. The funeral has already been held and so there is really nothing Lady Heath can do. What I have to tell her can wait."

"Oh!" There was sympathy in the exclamation. "I am so sorry. It is an unpleasant errand, Captain Birch. I will send a slave for Mr. Cameron and my husband. They are about the plantation somewhere." She arose and he stood up immediately and watched as she crossed to a bell pull on the wall and then turned to him. "My father, John Ormond, of Watlings Island, knew the Governor well, I believe. He visited our plantation there a couple of times on his tours of inspection." A slave girl appeared and Constance told her to send one of the men to find the master. When she had left, Constance again gave her attention to Birch. "I think perhaps I should awaken Lady Heath myself. I am certain you would like to be relieved of this unhappy errand. It will, however," her expression was humorously resigned, "be some little time before Lady Heath makes an appearance at this hour. Will you make yourself comfortable here, or perhaps you would care to stroll around the grounds for a while. My husband and father-in-law should be in soon."

Birch walked leisurely outside, looking about with interest. He had no illusions about Sabrina and any hasty dressing. She would not hurry through her morning toilette despite her curiosity concerning his arrival here. When she did appear she would be immaculately groomed and fashionably gowned.

The order and beauty of the grounds and gardens impressed him. Stretching far beyond the manor were the fields and storage houses together with slave quarters. He had made many official inspection tours of the Out Islands in the Governor's company. Never had he seen a plantation equal in plan and extent to this one. Cameron must have poured a fortune into the place. He had recreated, as completely as possible, the great estates as they were, or had been, in the Colonial days of Carolina, Georgia and Virginia. Despite his breezy manner Captain Birch had made a serious study of the islands. He had read the reports and evaluated the statistics on the agricultural prospects. Such a venture as this was foredoomed to failure. It simply could not survive beyond providing the food necessary to sustain those who lived here. Each year the exportable crops declined. In time there would be practically no revenue. Great Britain had already halted the slave traffic. Ships of war patrolled the seas, and the blackbirders who sought to bring their cargoes of misery into Nassau for sale were halted and turned back. Eventually, the system of slavery would be abolished. Then the underbrush would again take possession of the fields, the houses fall into disrepair, and their inhabitants reduced to scratching a bare living from the unproductive soil or taking what they could from the sea. It has an unhappy ending to the enthusiasm which had brought this Colonial aristocracy to the islands. He was in deep and moody thought when a voice called his name and caused him to lift his head and wheel about.

"Captain Birch!" Caroline stood on the porch. Behind her a tall, dark and lean man of easy bearing was in the doorway. She came gracefully down the steps to meet him as he advanced toward her.

"Mistress Caroline." Birch bowed formally but his face reflected his pleasure.

"Not quite," she corrected him. "This is my husband. Juan Cadiz. Captain Birch."

The men shook hands. Birch made a quick appraisal of Caroline's husband. From his careless dress he seemed nothing more than one of the boatmen who sailed their sloops into Nassau from the Out Islands. Sunlight caught the gold of the ring he wore in one ear. This, he thought, is a latter-day buccaneer. Where on earth, he wondered, had Caroline Cameron met such a man? How could Ronald Cameron have sanctioned this union? He dropped his speculations and assumed an expression of regret.

"You may not remember, madam," he spoke with doleful formality, "but you once declared your intention of marrying me." He bowed to Juan. "My congratulations, sir."

"La!" Caroline pretended surprise. "I had forgotten all about that. I did threaten to marry you, didn't I?"

"I never considered it a threat. More of a promise. However," he forgave her, "you were little more than thirteen at the time." He thought how startlingly beautiful she had become with the passing of the years. "I really didn't take you seriously."

"You should have." Caroline laughed and linked her arm with Juan's. "I thought you exceptionally handsome and dashing in Nassau. But," she appeared to sigh regretfully, "Juan came along in a boat with a red sail. The combination was irresistible. How could one of the King's officers hope to compete with that?"

"It just never occurred to me," he admitted, "that a red sail on a sloop could work such magic on a girl's heart. I assume, of course, there were other attractions."

"I am very happy." She said this without a smile. It was a sincere statement. "And," her face again became radiant, "we have twins. A boy and a girl. I named her Bahama."

"I remember you threatened to call yourself that. It distressed your aunt."

"Poor Aunt Martha. But," she changed the subject with curiosity, "what brings you to Exuma and why haven't you paid us a visit long before this?"

"The Governor died." Birch spoke with regret. "As his aide I was delegated to bring the news to Lady Heath and escort her back to Nassau."

"Oh, I am sorry!" Caroline's light manner vanished immediately. "What an unpleasant duty for you. Has Lady Heath been told yet?"

"Your sister-in-law received me. She has gone to awaken Sabrina. Lady Heath." He corrected himself but not before he caught the understanding twinkle in Caroline's eyes.

There was the sound of cantering horses on the marled road which led to the manor's driveway. Ronald Cameron and Robert Bruce dismounted, and a stable boy who had been trotting beside them led the mounts away.

"Welcome to Exuma, Captain Birch," Cameron called in a greeting as they crossed the lawn toward where the group stood. "This is a most pleasant surprise." He offered his hand. "You know my son, Robert Bruce."

"I'm afraid I don't remember any of the Camerons now." Birch shook hands with Robert Bruce. "The young girl has grown into a beautiful woman with children of her own; the son into a man who resembles his father so much I can hardly tell them apart. Of course, some years have intervened since I saw you all last."

"Well, come, man." Cameron took his arm with a hearty gesture. "Let's not stand about here in the yard like gypsies. We must have a drink to this most pleasant meeting again. What good fortune brings you to Exuma?"

"The Governor is dead." Caroline answered the question. "Captain Birch has come to take Lady Heath back to Nassau."

"I am sorry on both counts." Cameron led them back and into the house. "Lady Heath has been a most engaging guest. She brought a new and refreshing spirit to the plantation. We live much to ourselves here. What was the nature of the Governor's unfortunate illness?"

"The cholera." Birch walked with Cameron into a pleasant, sun-filled sitting room. "It took him quickly," he added, "and with little warning just when we thought we had put an end to the damnable thing."

"He was a difficult man sometimes." Cameron was blunt. "But I sincerely regret his passing. I suppose a difficult job makes a difficult man." He changed the subject. "You will spend the night, at least, with us, will you not?"

"Gladly." Birch's agreement was immediate. "The quarters on the sloop are Spartan, to say the least. And there is no real necessity for haste. The funeral has already been held. Such things cannot wait in this climate, as you know."

"Captain!" Sabrina was posed in the doorway. Her eyes were clear and untroubled. There was no sign of weeping or emotion. Her smile was gracious and embraced them all. She made a motion as Birch rose. "There is no need to say anything. Constance has already told me."

"I took a liberty, Captain," Constance apologized. "It seemed better to tell Lady Heath in private."

"Thank you." Birch nodded his agreement. "It was an unpleasant duty. I am glad to have it taken from my hands."

"Poor Gerald." Sabrina seated herself, arranging the colorful folds of her gown as carefully as though she were sitting for a portrait. "I think he would much rather have died from acute indigestion or a liver complaint brought on by too much fine brandy. He would have considered cholera a plebeian thing; an indignity to himself and his office." She glanced at the others. "Please don't think me heartless but I cannot cry over something which can no longer be helped."

There was a moment of silent embarassment which was saved by Caroline, who arose.

"I think, perhaps," she spoke to her father, "Lady Heath and Captain Birch would like to have a little time alone." She addressed Sabrina. "If you will excuse us, we will meet later for luncheon."

When the Camerons had filed from the room and the door closed behind them, Sabrina leaned back in her chair with a small sigh of relief. Birch took a seat on a nearby lounge.

"You are looking well, Roger." Sabrina made the comment as a conversational pleasantry, avoiding what she knew must sooner or later be faced. "It was kind of you to come."

"It wasn't a task for which I volunteered." Birch studied her. "I did think, however, there were certain things which might better be discussed between us rather than detail the situation to another officer."

"I suppose by that you mean I shall have to go back to Nassau no matter how I may feel about it?"

"I don't see how you can do otherwise." Birch was not surprised by her composure, her indifference. "The people, the Government, the Assembly, would not understand your failure to make an appearance."

"I don't give a damn about the people, the Government or the Assembly. Am I to be paraded through the streets in a widow's black to satisfy their stupid ideas of convention?"

"No one expects that." Birch was a little angry and made no attempt to disguise it. "But you simply cannot ignore your husband's death and remain here on Exuma."

"Then," she arose with a visible sign of agitation and paced across the room, "will you tell me what I am to do in Nassau? Throw myself across the grave and lament in public?"

He ignored the outrageous suggestion. "Your dignity and not your personal feelings are concerned here. You cannot ignore the obligation."

"My dignity." She shrugged. "I am much more concerned with more practical things. Gerald was all but penniless. I am a widow with a child and completely without resources. I suppose there will be some pittance from the Crown. God knows Gerald's remuneration as Governor was small enough. I can imagine the widow's dole will be counted in pence. What am I to do?" She turned to him with a gesture of helpless appeal.

Birch was disturbed by this first, sincere display of emotion. Sabrina had always seemed so completely self-sufficient. She faced a problem now. No one could deny that and he sought for some answer.

"You have some family in England." He made the suggestion. "I remember you telling me something about a grandmother who was in more than comfortable circumstances. Couldn't you appeal to her for assistance?"

"She is a miserable witch, a penny-pinching crone who lives in some dreary place in Devon." Sabrina all but exploded her retort. "What my father left me upon his death Gerald squandered long ago in an effort to glorify this insignificant office as Governor of the Bahamas. I have nothing but the clothes in my closets and a few pieces of jewelry." She turned and studied herself in the mirror. "No." She spoke without vanity. "I do have a few assets. I am still reasonably young, my figure is good. I cannot honestly deny a certain beauty remains. In London, perhaps, I might make a second marriage of convenience. Or," she faced him without defiance, "even a convenient arrangement with a gentleman of means. That is as delicately as I can put the situation if there should be delicacy between us." She smiled then but it was without real pleasure; only a rueful understanding of her situation. "I don't suppose the former Governor's aide would suggest marriage to me at this date? Nassau is too small to have an unsanctified liaison go unnoticed."

"I am honored by your proposal, madam." Birch relieved any sting his words might have carried with a warm, affectionate smile. "But, you see, I know you far too well. You would be no more content with me in such a place as Nassau as you were with Sir Gerald." He stood up and took her hands, surprised to find them trembling. "I am truly sorry. You must believe that. I have some money. Not a great deal. A couple of thousand pounds in England. For what we once were to each other you are welcome to part of it."

"You are too generous." She was a shade bitter. "I had never thought to put a price upon my favors. At what rate would you calculate them?"

"And"—he was angry now because she was being deliberately insulting and difficult—"you are unbelievably coarse at this moment. I was

[211]

only trying to help and your answer to the offer is sarcasm. I find it unworthy of you."

"You are right and I am sorry." Her eyes dropped away from his. "Forgive me. I am distracted." She reseated herself. "I suppose I must begin by being practical and separate what is and is not possible. I cannot stay here on Exuma or return for an indefinite stay. I can go back to England, accept my grandmother's taunts, and perhaps marry a clod of a farmer who could be a man of some means. I can go to Nassau, assume the proper, humble attitude, take the Crown's dole, and perhaps set myself up as a little seamstress." There was a half-amused irony in her expression. "The trouble with that is I cannot sew even so much as a button on cloth. Another alternative is to borrow or take what you have so generously offered and establish myself on a modest scale in London. I still have friends there who are well established and with the best of social connections. Perhaps some gentleman would find me attractive." Her features clouded. "But, there is David. A comely, vivacious widow is not without a certain fascination to many men although their intentions may not always be honorable. An attractive widow with a child is quite another thing. It is a complication from which most men would shy. What a damnable situation I am in!" The exclamation was a cry of inner agony.

"The boy, David, could be sent to your grandmother, perhaps. At least it is worth a try. The boy might not find the rural life quite as distasteful as you do."

She shook her head. "My grandmother is eighty or thereabouts. She would not burden herself with the rearing of a child. No. David could not go alone. There would be no welcome. I would have to accompany him and put us both at the mercy of her querulous senility; the spite which so frequently comes with age. She never approved of my marriage to Gerald. I can hear her satisfied cackle now. If I go to her with empty hands she will make my life a hell." Her expression was dryly humorous. "I have narrowed my choice, haven't I? I may end as a serving wench in a Nassau tavern and earn a shilling or two in the upstairs loft with an occasional sailor. Come to think of it, the former Governor's wife should be worth a crown, at least."

Birch did not smile at the crude jest. He felt an honest compassion for this beautiful woman who, suddenly, found herself struggling for survival. He sincerely wanted to help.

"It seems my fate," she continued without self-pity, "to be a partner in a love affair without love. But, whatever I do today I must not regret tomorrow, and it would take a seer to guide me in that."

"I am no oracle." He made an effort at lightness. "But my suggestion is that you accept the aid I offered. Take half of what I have. It will come to around a thousand pounds. Return to England—London. There, as you say, you at least have friends. You will not be alone as you will in Nassau. The Governor, unfortunately, made little effort to be congenial or ingratiate himself with the island's first families. He was not a man to inspire friendship. There are few, if any, persons who would open their hearts and doors to his widow. It is an unpleasant truth, Sabrina, and it must be faced."

She inclined her head in assent. "I am grateful to you, Roger. Grateful and"—she reached out to touch his hand as though in need of human contact—"and just a little surprised. I wish now we had truly known each other better; something beyond a casual affair. I suspect there are few men who would be so generous without a hope of return, for it is doubtful I shall ever be able to repay you."

"Take what I can give as a gift." He drew her from the chair and kissed her brow with the lightest of touch. "I shall think about you often."

"Thank you." She lifted her face and met his eyes with sincerity. "I will not forget your kindness." She stepped back. "When do we return to Nassau?"

"I think we should leave in the morning. Better to have it done with."

"Whatever you say. I'll have my girl pack this afternoon and my few boxes can be taken out to the boat. I will be ready to leave when you are. I think," she hesitated, "I should like to go to my room now for a while." Her brief smile was wan. "It is curious but this is a contingency for which I never prepared. I am not usually so careless."

With an enthusiasm and efficiency which surprised her and set the servants flying about their duties, Caroline had made of the evening and the meal they all took together a festive occasion. Even though all of the lower-floor rooms could not possibly be used, they were ablaze with the light of many, precious candles. The dining hall sparkled with the color of flowers and the prismatic pendants of the huge, central chandelier were fired with all the colors of the spectrum. The servants were in their finest livery and their dark faces shown with pleasure, for the night was an exciting break in the household's routine.

Cameron, Robert Bruce and even Juan appeared in their formal attire. Caroline, Constance and Sabrina, at their urging, had spent hours in dressing and descended the staircase to meet the gentlemen in their most colorful gowns, finest slippers and elaborately arranged hair with their cheeks flushed, their eyes bright with the novelty of the occasion. For the men there was a predinner bowl of punch, made heady and flavorful with rum, brandy, black coffee and the juices of pineapple, orange and lemon. The ladies sipped delicately at small crystal glasses of sherry.

Her father had protested mildly to Caroline over the preparations which she insisted upon making. He considered the proposed festivities unseemly under the circumstances.

"After all," he said, "Lady Heath is a widow. Her journey is a sad one. This is a painful occasion for her. I do not think it is a time for levity."

They were alone in Cameron's library. Caroline perched herself on the corner of his writing table and regarded her father with a slow shaking of her head as though she were unable to comprehend his objections.

"It is certainly no time for a mournful procession to the beach with the slaves chanting a dirge and Lady Heath draped in black." Caroline was firm in her determination. "I would not like to take my leave under such circumstances."

"A man is dead." Cameron was unconvinced. "I don't think we should make of it a time for merrymaking."

"It never occurred to me anyone would think we were celebrating the death of Sir Gerald," Caroline corrected him. "I am simply trying to make this, her last night on Exuma, a pleasant one into which no thought of her husband's passing will intrude. I see nothing wrong in that. Under the circumstances, if I were Lady Heath, I should be grateful for the diversion. I wish we had an orchestra and guests to invite to make a real party."

"Of you," he eyed her with a certain resigned humor, "I would expect dancing on the lawn or the grave itself." He studied her slim grace, her cool poise, and wondered how he had sired such loveliness. "When my time comes will you at least refrain from a rigadoon on my little plot even though you may be certain in your own mind it will make my journey into the hereafter more agreeable?"

She dropped from the table, leaned down to where he sat and kissed him with a misty affection. Then her arm went about his neck and she pulled his head to her breast.

"You are a growler by nature. A bear of a man who rumbles and thunders with the idea of frightening everyone. But you don't scare me a bit. You never did. Do you know something?" She spun away in swirling pirouette, her eyes dancing with mischief. "If I were you I would ask Lady Heath to marry me. After, of course," she was demurely impish, "what you would consider to be a decent interval. I have caught, sometimes, a gleam in your eyes when you look at her, and as a woman, I know she is not insensible to your attraction."

"That is nonsense." He muttered the words as though they had annoyed him, and was secretly astonished by her intuition. "Sheer poppy-cock."

"Is it?" She pretended to study the books on a shelf, keeping her back to him. "I am not so sure. Juan, also, says so. He said there was something between you two, and Juan has a strong instinct about such things."

"Your husband is a damned fool," he snorted.

He watched as she innocently pretended an interest in the library shelves. A couple of times during the afternoon and while he had been sitting alone in his study this very thing had come to his mind. He had turned it over in his thoughts deliberately, weighing it carefully and with his customary thoroughness. In the end and with some honest regret he had decided against it. It was a form of aberration; the spell of having a comely, intelligent and spirited woman in the house again after all these years. He felt, for one thing, that he was old. Older than his years. It was a thing of the mind, he knew, but it could not be dismissed. His life had settled into a groove. He was afraid to disturb it. Also, the plantation weighed heavily on his mind. Financially he was in a most precarious position. Sabrina Heath, for all the brightness she had brought to the house during her visit, was of a character unsuited to the life here on an island. He felt certain a proposal on his part would be accepted but it would be in the nature of a refuge from the uncertainties which must now be occupying her thoughts. He did feel a nagging responsibility for the boy, who after all was his son. Beyond this, though, he was not possessed by the complete emotion of love which should be a part of marriage and without which, he believed, no real union between two persons could possibly survive. He could not make himself believe Sabrina's yielding had been more than a momentary impulse; a form of self-gratification. He had attracted her. She was bored as she must have been many times before. He could not accept the idea there had not been other men before him, for he was convinced she was an amoral creature. It was not in her nature to deny herself any pleasure or indulgence. Curiously enough, and this surprised him, he was little concerned with Sabrina's morals or lack of them. He had had women and even the slave girls when the need was upon him. If she had turned away from Sir Gerald he could not blame her. The man had been gross and offensive. But if she had been bored and restless in Nassau where there had, at least, been some social activity, how would she endure this Out Island where the arrival of the *Traveler* was something to talk about for days and a casual visitor welcomed as royalty? He was forced to consider such a marriage only in the light of a practical arrangement. They were no headstrong youngsters, fired with a consuming passion which could overcome all obstacles. It would not work. He knew it in his heart

[215]

and put the idea away from him. In the years to come he might regret the decision, for he would grow older and lonely, needing an understanding companionship. Sabrina, he was certain, would not supply it. Such a marriage would end in tragedy. Even as he told himself this, he was angry that a cold analysis should supersede the prompting of his heart.

He glanced up to find Caroline's gaze upon him. Their eyes held for a time and he saw a strangely disturbing compassion on his daughter's face.

"I am too old for such a marriage." He spoke slowly. "I turned my back on everything I once knew to make this island my home and the future left to me. Sabrina—Lady Heath—would not be happy here."

"Why don't you ask her? I am a woman and have learned about such things. No one can be sure what lies secret within someone else. I do not remember my mother but I know she must have filled your life. Now, and as you have for all these years, you live in an unnatural state. I am certain of this because I feel the love of Juan as a warm, protective shelter. There is understanding, a unity, between us. No one can survive happily without it. Not," she smiled fondly, "even such a stubborn Scot as Ronald Cameron."

For a moment he was angry. This was an unwarranted intrusion. Then he softened. "Despite what you think, marriage has not mysteriously endowed you with all wisdom nor has it and a couple of children made of you a woman. You are still very young in many ways." He stood up, hoping to terminate the conversation.

Caroline was unconvinced. "All I can say is you may not get another chance as good as this one." She stuck the tip of her tongue out at him with a gesture of flippant affection. "Think it over well."

He could not remain annoyed with her for long. He was almost a little touched by her concern for his happiness. "Go on about your business for this revel you are planning. If I should ever decide to marry again I will make my own selection and not leave it to the irresponsible whim of an impudent brat." He slapped her smartly on the rear and sent her toward the door.

When she had left and he was alone again in the study, he walked twice back and forth across the room. Without admitting it, he envied his daughter her impetuous nature but he could not rebel against his own. There was a bleak and unhappy cast to his features. Generations of cautious, deliberate Scotsmen stood silently behind him in the shadows of centuries. Their influence would not be denied. He had been poured in a certain mold and could not escape it.

The party, if it could be called that, and dinner had been made lively and entertaining by the unquenchable eagerness of Caroline and Constance to make it so. Instead of taking their leave, the ladies remained in the dining hall with the men. Captain Birch was witty and amusing with his stories of his schooldays in England and the sometimes ridiculous situations with which he had been forced to deal as aide to the Governor. He had studied the history of the Bahamas and had an apparently inexhaustible store of tales concerning the early pirates, their depredations, the sacking of the colony and the treasures stripped from Spanish galleons and French merchantmen. Millions of pounds in gold and jewelry were reputed to have been buried hereabouts by the buccaneers who were hanged without revealing their hiding places. Sabrina was vivacious, lending the full measure of her graciousness to the conversation and rapier thrusts at the pretensions of Nassau's aristocracy. She made hilarious their feuds, jealousies and rivalries as they schemed eternally, against all authority, to make the island of New Providence their private fief. Many were reduced to near penury but they fought endlessly to maintain the social ascendancy which had once been theirs. Despite himself Ronald was drawn into reminiscences of the Carolina Low Country, his youth there and the Colonial magnificence in which the first families lived before the Revolution. Later, when they had gathered in the withdrawing room, even Juan displayed a small crack in the reserve he usually preserved in Cameron's presence. Caroline urged him to get his guitar. With the instrument in his hands his face was suddenly illuminated with pleasure. He sang old songs, brushing the chords softly from the strings and blending the curious, Out Island accent and idiom to the music and words brought from England by the earliest settlers. He chanted the work melodies of the slave gangs and their spirituals with the haunting minor laments for release from this world of trouble. In other rooms the blacks halted in their duties of clearing and cleaning to listen with silent pleasure.

It was Sabrina who reluctantly brought the evening to an end. When Juan had finished she turned to them all.

"There are not words in my heart," she spoke with a deep sincerity, "for me to tell you how deeply I appreciate what you all have done for me this, my last night here. I leave Exuma with more regret than I have ever before experienced. It is doubtful we shall ever see each other again for I am returning to England. But," her words faltered, "I shall never forget you." Impulsively she crossed and kissed Caroline and Constance on their cheeks. "I know this was your idea, that we should forget for a while the unpleasant things which must be faced. It has made me unmindful of much I would rather not remember. Thank you all again and again." She turned to Cameron. "Would it be rude," she smiled her frankness, "to ask for a few minutes of your time now before retiring?"

"Of course not." The response was immediate. He glanced at the others. "If you will excuse us?" There was a murmured assent. He spoke to Sabrina. "Suppose we go to my study. We can talk there." He addressed Birch. "We will all be up to see you off in the morning and bid you good speed. I have been thinking. Our ketch is larger and with better accommodations than the Government sloop. Take it if you wish. Robert Bruce and a hand can sail her back."

"The sloop will do well enough, Mr. Cameron. With a fair wind the journey will not be too irksome. Thank you for your thoughtfulness."

When the others had said their good nights and left them alone Cameron led Sabrina to the study and closed the door.

"I was hoping," he said, "we might have some small time together. Everything seems to have happened so abruptly. I have had no time to prepare my mind for your leaving."

"Would you offer me some brandy, Ronald?" She took one of the deep, winged chairs just within the circle of candlelight. "I have a feeling I may need it." Suddenly she seemed tired. There were shadows of weariness and concern beneath her eyes.

He went to a cabinet and returned with decanter and two glasses, pouring for them both. She did not take the drink slowly, savoring its rich bouquet, but swallowed it at a gulp as she might a medicine. He refilled the crystal for her and watched as she closed her eyes, waiting for the assuasive effect of the liquor to make itself felt. After a moment she sighed and looked across at him.

"It is strange how easily I adjusted myself to your household," she meditated. "There have been days, weeks, when I thought of it as my own. The idea of my having someday to leave it and return to Nassau was foreign to my mind. It has been more than the immediate welcome you gave me. All of you have conspired to make me feel a part of your life."

"I am happy to hear that but the pleasure, the absence of any strain, has not been on one side alone. You brought a brightness and, as I have said before, there is a radiance about you which illuminates wherever you are." He was uncomfortable, aware that what he was saying was too little. "I, all of us, shall miss your presence."

"Please." She extended her hand as though to ward off an awkward situation. "I think we understand each other. Or, at least," the smile crept back into her eyes, "I understand you. There is no obligation. I want you to know I mean this sincerely. I feel a great affection for you and am comfortable in your company. We must allow that to be enough

[218]

and not press for more which is beyond our reach." She took a small sip of the brandy now and watched as he selected, filled and lit a pipe. "I envy you the solace of tobacco. You seem to derive such comfort from it."

"I have some small *cigarros* from the Havana," he suggested.

She shook her head. "I always feel a little ridiculous while trying to balance one of those things between my lips. It seems to be a strictly masculine accomplishment. To do it with grace, I mean."

For a few moments there was a complete but not uncomfortable silence. The smoke wreathed upward and hung there before vanishing. Watching her, it seemed to Cameron that Sabrina was gathering her strength, the will to say something, and this was the purpose of the request to meet with him alone.

"What," she finally spoke, "what I am going to say or ask of you may come as a shock."

"I think not." He had a sudden divination of what was on her mind. "Would it make it easier if I say it for you?" The sympathy he felt was in the question.

"No. It is better spoken by me. I am going back to England, to London. There I will try and start my life anew if it is possible. I want," she leaned forward, her hands clasped tightly, "to leave David with you. There"—she seemed to gather strength now that the words were out—"it is said. I wasn't sure I could speak so calmly. If you think me an unnatural mother it cannot be helped. I face a most uncertain future. It will not be made easier with the burden of David at his age. He needs stability, order, security, for without those things he will grow troubled in his mind and live from day to day in precarious suspension. It will affect his character and future. What love I can give him will not be enough."

"He is a fine lad, sturdy, bright, intelligent." Cameron cleared his throat. He was uncomfortable and at a loss for words. "No one could ask for better."

"His father is a fine man." She said it with honesty. "David could not ask for better."

"He is so young," Cameron ruminated. "Five years, is it not?"

She merely nodded, studying his face.

"Do you think he would be happy here?"

"Happier and safer than with me. Will you believe," she spoke with pleading sincerity, "that what I asked has not been easily done? I leave a part of myself with him when I go."

"Do you believe he has no need for a mother?" Cameron was troubled in his thoughts. "My children were young when their mother died but there was an aunt to love them and take the place of the girl who bore them. It will not be the same here."

"The shield a child bears is a short memory. It does not hurt for long. David will have the companionship of Caroline's children and those, I suppose, which will come eventually to Robert Bruce and Constance. More than any of those things he will have you, a father. He unconsciously reaches for one. I watched him as he made the first, tentative, uncertain approach with Gerald."

"How will you tell the boy?" Without realizing it, Cameron had already accepted as a fact what she had asked. "He will want some explanation, young as he is."

"I will say only that I must go away for a while. I do not think this will frighten him. He has been happy here. I will tell you something, Ronald. You may resent it. There is a warmth and love in your house which you do not recognize. Strange as he may seem to you, unsuitable as you deem him as a husband for your daughter, this Juan has given the priceless gift of love to Caroline. I have seen it between them. Robert Bruce, who is so much like you, is, in his own quiet way, the perfect mate for Constance, who is shy and reserved by nature. A man like Juan would frighten her. With Robert Bruce she is perfectly mated. I do not believe you realize what you have here. I could want for David nothing more than the opportunity to share it. Will you give it to him?"

"You are certain you want it this way?"

"Even if there was a reasonably assured alternative I would choose this; for my son, and yours, to grow to manhood in this family."

Cameron's brief smile was a little drawn. "I will weld my family together. You may be sure of that. I am not so certain of our future on the plantation. I need not tell you it does not go well, financially. But, for better or worse, I will hold it intact. This I have promised myself. Whatever happens, David shall be a part of it."

"Thank you." She said it simply.

Cameron refilled his pipe. He went to a window and opened it, for the room was becoming fouled with the tobacco fumes. He stood there for a moment and then turned to face Sabrina.

"In time what shall I tell him?"

"Your judgment will dictate. He will have need to know nothing beyond the moment for many years. When he is old enough, say what your heart prompts you to speak. As for his mother?" Her voice was not quite certain. "Her memory will grow dim in his mind. If he should ask, then say only she was lost at sea or," her smile faltered, "somewhere in the world."

He could not leave it at that. Crossing, he took her hands.

"Stay here. I mean it. Do what you must in Nassau and then come back."

She shook her head. "I know you mean it. There is not that in your nature which would prompt you to speak otherwise. But, between us there should be more than there is. I know it and so do you. I want to be as honest with you as you have been with me. There is admiration, some understanding, a still unfulfilled passion, perhaps. But there is not that miraculous thing called love. I am no more meant for you and a life here on this island plantation than I was for Gerald. I am not even certain there is a small corner in the world which is mine. But, and I will never feel a greater affection for you than this minute, I must seek for it."

For a long time Cameron lay sleepless in his bed. He was still awake when the first pale streaks of crimson and gold began to break in the east. At the head of the bed was a bell pull. He rang for his slave who would come with coffee which had become so short it was doled out sparingly. Perhaps, now that the cholera epidemic was over, the ships would be putting in again and the supply replenished.

He was shaved and dressed by the black before there was the first stirring of the other members of the household. Still he had not reached a decision. Did he speak frankly with Robert Bruce and Caroline, telling them Sabrina was leaving young David on Exuma and the reason why he felt compelled to accept the responsibility? Were they mature enough to understand and endorse his decision? Or would they regard him as some lecherous old man who had sired a bastard and brought the product of his shame into their home to be reared as a legitimate son and brother? Caroline. Somehow, he felt certain she would be the one of tolerance and understanding. Of Robert Bruce he was not so sure. He would accept his father's will in the matter but he would do so with secret reservations. This was the baffling contradiction between the natures of his two offspring. From the one he might expect mortification and revulsion, he would receive accord. From the boy who was now a man he would get little more than acceptance of an unpleasant situation. In all honesty he had to admit Robert Bruce's reaction would be not too unlike his own if the situation were reversed. There was this uncompromising streak in both of them.

Standing at an open window smoking his first pipe of the morning, still tasting the bittersweet flavor of the coffee, searching his mind for a solution, he realized he had no choice but to tell them the truth. How, otherwise, could he explain Lady Heath's departure without her child?

In her room Sabrina held young David on her lap, his head pressed to her bosom. She had talked to him quietly, trying desperately to make him feel that what was happening was without frightening importance. She spoke no word of death or of Sir Gerald. Certain things, she purposely kept them vague, made it necessary for her to go to Nassau. He had been happy here, hadn't he? He liked Mr. Cameron and the family. The dainty filly Mr. Cameron had given him as his very own was something special and needed his care, exercise and affection. She would miss her master, for didn't she whinny with delight when he approached her and dance lightly with him on her back? The fishing with Tom Gurney. The sailing with Juan now and then in a boat with a red sail. There was so much more to do here on Exuma than in the Manor at Nassau. It was difficult for her to tell what impression her words made. Once or twice his face had lighted with pleasure at the mention of the freedom and the things he had enjoyed on Exuma. Other than that he merely listened or gave assent with a small nod of his head. He spoke only once.

"Will you be away for long?"

She could not bring herself to answer truthfully. "The time will pass so quickly you will forget I am not here." She tried to make it sound gay and exciting, an adventure planned for him. "Now," she swung him from her lap, "we had better be getting downstairs."

After the good humor and liveliness of last night, breakfast was a silent, almost somber, affair. No one made an effort to force conversation and they ate in comparative silence as though many different things weighed heavily upon their minds. It was a relief to have the meal done with.

The slaves had already carried Sabrina's boxes and small trunk to the beach where they had been ferried out to the sloop. The oarsman of the gig stood at attention beside his boat as the company came down from the plantation house. Caroline and Juan, Robert Bruce and Constance, Cameron and David. Sabrina and Captain Birch walked slowly in that order.

"I am leaving David with Mr. Cameron," Sabrina said to Birch. It was a flat statement made toneless out of necessity. "He will be happier here."

"So?" Captain Birch was too disciplined and well bred to make further comment beyond saying, "It is probably a wise decision."

As he walked with the boy Cameron speculated on what Sabrina had told David. Had there been tears and protestations on the lad's part; an overwhelming sense of desolation and abandonment when he learned he was to be left behind? Or had she resorted to the convenient lie and assured him she would be gone for only a day or two? He glanced down at the same moment the boy looked up. Their eyes met and there was a light of confidence on the youngster's face and some small betrayal of excitement over this unusual situation of the entire household walking down to the beach in the early morning. He picked up a rock and hurled it at a wheeling gull high above their heads. Then he left Cameron and raced down to where the boatman waited and regarded him with a solemn curiosity.

The gig was drawn well up on the sand. Before taking Birch's hand and stepping into it, Sabrina hesitated. Then she stooped quickly, gathered David into her arms and held him tightly until he squirmed uncomfortably. There were no tears, no display of emotion beyond the encircling of her arms. When she stood up her eyes were faintly misted, nothing more. She forced a smile.

"I can't thank you more than I have. Everything was said last night. I shall never forget your kindness to me." She kissed Caroline and Constance hurriedly on their cheeks and then offered her hand to Cameron. "I leave you with more than my gratitude, Ronald. I know you will do what you think is right. In all things I trust your judgment." She turned and offered her hand to Juan. "You have a way with a guitar, Mr. Cadiz. Thank you, also, for making last night such a pleasant one."

She moved quickly and without a backward glance as Birch assisted her into the gig and then followed. The oarsman shoved the small craft from the shelving beach into deeper water and scrambled in to take up his sweeps. Sabrina sat with her back to the shore so she would not have to face those on the land who stood in a silent group watching. Captain Birch lifted his braided hat in a final salute as the gig bounced over the small waves toward where the Government sloop lay.

As if by instinct David stood beside Cameron. He followed, with a longing gaze, the boat carrying his mother away from the island. Then he looked up at the man and made a tremulous effort at a smile. His hand reached to find Cameron's and closed upon it with a tight confidence.

If Caroline, Robert Bruce and the others were astonished by what was happening—Lady Heath departing without a backward glance at her son, leaving him here on Exuma—they displayed no open curiosity. Their glances met, the question was in their eyes, but they said nothing.

They waited until the party was aboard the sloop, the craft's sail raised, and she began to move toward open water. Then Cameron spoke gruffly.

"It is late, Robert Bruce, and time we were at the fields where they are refencing. I want to see the work done myself. The cattle break through too frequently and into the corn there."

Caroline glanced at David. The boy could not hide the loneliness he felt, the bewilderment. Her heart went out to him.

[223]

"David," she spoke impulsively, "Juan and I are going fishing. Would you like to come? We will take a lunch and make a picnic of the day." She felt a moving compassion for the boy, sharing in a strange measure the hurt he must be experiencing.

David looked questioningly up at Cameron, recognizing the authority in him.

"Go, lad." Cameron spoke kindly and rumpled the top of David's head. "You will enjoy yourself and," there was a touch of amused irony in his words, "you will find no better fishermen in the islands than my daughter and her husband. God knows they do little else. Run on to the house now and get ready."

At the top of the ridge Cameron halted. The sloop was rounding the point. He turned to the others.

"You must be wondering at this unusual turn of affairs. It is only right there should be some explanation. Lady Heath is in a most unhappy situation. It is presumed Sir Gerald left no estate of consequence. She must straighten out the affairs at the Governor's Mansion, for the Crown will appoint a new authority. It is even possible she may have to go to England for a while in an effort to readjust her life. Last night she asked of me a favor I could not well refuse." He paused and looked at them. "It is her desire to protect the boy from what may be an unsettled life for some time. She begged of us all asylum for him here so he may have some sort of family life. It was difficult to refuse. The presence of one little boy will not inconvenience us. He is happy here and," he confessed, "I have grown to like him. Will he be a bother to you, Caroline?"

"Of course not, Father." She spoke with full generosity.

"I have no idea how long he will remain with us. He will miss his mother, of course. Since I agreed to her request, let us carry it out with a full heart, make him feel at home and take him into the family as one of our own. I would not like to have him feel alone. Now, Robert Bruce," he tried to sound impatient, "let us get to the fields and the work at hand."

He strode ahead briskly toward the house, where a stable boy waited with the horses, as though to leave a problem behind with them.

⋙ XV ⋘

IN THESE sun-showered islands there were but the faintest echoes of a changing world beyond their shores. For a while, some years back, there had been word of a renewal of hostilities between the United States and England. The news of the conflict had been brought to Nassau by an occasional merchant vessel or periodicals months old from England.

Many of the old Loyalist families were deeply interested in the contest for, it was argued, it was quite possible the Crown would this time subdue the arrogant rabble, reclaim the territory, and they would be able to return to their estates in Carolina, Georgia and Virginia. They were intensely disappointed when they learned the war had been started by such a trivial thing as the impressment of American seamen by British vessels.

Haphazard and completely unnecessary preparations were made to defend New Providence against an invasion by the Americans. Old and completely useless guns were manned and ready to repulse an attack upon the harbor. A company of militia was formed to supplement the Crown's garrison and they had drilled listlessly in the hot afternoons.

For no particular reason an American frigate had sailed within range of St. George Cay and bombarded the tiny settlement of Spanish Wells. This incursion caused considerable excitement among the natives. They had fled their weathered little houses and watched, more with curiosity than anger, as the warship pounded the rock and sand. Many of the balls fell far short of their target, falling into the sea where they made a fine display of waterspouts and probably killed a few fish. A token force had been landed while the commander looked about for possible booty or hostile British. Then it was rowed back to the frigate, which sailed away and was never seen or heard of again. No one, not even the American captain, was quite sure why the attack had been made or what purpose it served. It did, though, give the Bahamians something to talk about for months to come.

Great changes had taken place in the world beyond the islands. Napoleon had escaped from Elba to start the Hundred Days' War which ended with Waterloo. England was emerging as a great power and the United States was beginning to feel its own strength. Cities were building, men were venturing forth into unmapped wilderness. The first steamship to cross the Atlantic had sailed from Savannah for Liverpool and made the trip in twenty-five days, seven of which were under sail. The United States was negotiating with Spain for the purchase of Florida and setting the stage for a long, bloody and costly war with the Seminole Indians. There was even some talk in the Congress for the seizure of the British-held islands of Bermuda and the Bahamas, since they lay but a short distance from the mainland. If England wanted to fight for their possessions then they would fight and the damned British could be licked again as they had been before.

Of all these things the Bahamians knew but little, for they were too occupied with their own problems to pay much attention to what was happening beyond their warm islands which were blessed by the sun most of the year and torn at by the fierce hurricanes of the equinox. There was change, also, in the Bahamas but it was one which had been incubating for so many years its slow hatching went almost unnoticed by those who had settled there. One way of life was developing as another disappeared.

The ambitious plantations, the elegant manors, were growing to the bush again. The great houses were turning into ghostly structures through which the wind whimpered and lost itself in the many rooms. Where they had been abandoned by their owners the former slaves moved in or tore them down, using the boards, brick and stone to build small communities of shacks. Here they lived without effort. Their masters had given up and returned to England or had tried to reshape their future in the United States.

Slave trading in the islands had been abolished by the Home Government some ten years earlier. Control had been firmly established. The ships of the Royal Navy cruised the waters constantly. They apprehended and halted the slavers and either sent them back to Africa or brought the black cargoes into Nassau where they were freed. To care for the blacks, who were friendless, landless and without the means of sustaining themselves, two settlements were established for them on New Providence. One was in Carmichael and a second in Adelaide. Later, a section of Nassau known as Grant's Town was populated by the unhappy Negroes. There they lived as best they could, working small plots of corn, yams and beans, taking their fish from the boundless supply of the sea. Others drifted off to the Out Islands, making their way in little boats, settling themselves on the coasts or hacking out some place of habitation in the tangled growth inland.

Complete disaster had fallen upon the Colonial planters who had brought their families and slaves from the mainland in the hope of re-creating a life they had once known. The land was worn out and would no longer produce the cotton which was to be the principal crop. Most of the immigrants had given up and left with the ruins of their once pros-perous lives. Only a few families had the will, born out of desperation, to remain. Others stayed because they had no place else to go or the means to take them away. The prosperity they once imagined they would find in these islands was recognized now as a chimerical dream. The lives they had known on their plantations no longer even seemed real when they tried to recall them. Their children and grandchildren grew up knowing no other world; unaware of the beauty which sur-rounded them. Their education, in the Out Islands, was of the most rudimentary nature and extended no further than that which their parents could give them. There were no funds for the hiring of private tutors. No money for the sending of this new generation to England for schooling. A few of the missionaries tried to establish a circuit, holding classes when they could, but these were irregular save in one or two of the larger settlements on Eleuthera or in Nassau.

The Bahamas, having proved a commercial failure, were all but for-gotten by the Home Government and little or no effort was made by the Crown or Parliament to ease their plight. Some small trading went on between the North American mainland and England but it amounted to so little it was all but inconsequential. The islands were not even step-children of the Empire. They were a damned nuisance and expense. This was voiced many times by the Home Secretary and in both Houses of the Government. Only the fear that Spain or France might make some strategic use of them prevented their complete abandonment by Eng-land.

On Exuma, defying all logic, refusing to acknowledge failure, the Cameron family persisted in its efforts to hold the plantation together even though on the smallest scale. The expansive, gracious way of life was gone and with it much of Ronald Cameron's vitality. He was an old man now in spirit and frame and spent long hours sitting in a chair in the sun, his face turned seaward, his back to the fields which had so stubbornly refused to do his bidding.

Long ago worn to an almost threadbare appearance were the fine clothes, the boots, shoes, and slippers of French satin. The gowns of

Caroline and Constance had been refashioned and remade so many times they could serve now only as the most nondescript apparel. Over the years the glasses of crystal had been broken, piece by piece, through careless handling. The fine china table service, once sufficient to set a table for fifty persons, had been chipped and shattered and could not be replaced. Only the silver remained intact and this seemed strangely out of place now with the simple meals to which the family sat. From the ceilings the elaborate chandeliers and wall candelabra shone, as always, with their faceted pendants but they were dark at night for want of the tapers once giving them life. The fine draperies, the brocades of gold and silver thread, still held their color but they had been attacked by time, the alternating heat and dampness, until the fabric had become so fragile it almost parted at a touch. The rugs and fine carpeting showed spots of wear, the furniture in need of sealing oils and wax. Outside, the house was badly in want of paint, metal hinges for the shutters, lime and plaster to seal up the cracks in the lower portion of brick. Still, it maintained a certain incongruous magnificence even in its weathered condition. It stood in shabby pride upon the ridge with the great vista of tumbling ocean and patches of incredible color at its feet.

Cameron had been forced to sell many of his prime slaves but those who remained propagated with annual regularity, so the total number remained almost constant. Among them were men and women so old now in Cameron service they had lost all sense of time. They were without value, sitting in the warm patches before their cabins and mumbling to each other through toothless gums. As the young grew up, Cameron automatically freed them for they were but additional mouths to feed. Those who had once muttered and complained over their servitude now refused to leave the plantation even though Cameron voluntarily released them from their bondage. These were the field hands and there was no land for them to work. Told they could leave the plantation and go where they would, they now stubbornly refused their freedom. Where were they to go? Who was to take care of them? Although remaining, they whined and complained and made no effort, unless driven to it, to cultivate even the smallest patches of beans or corn for themselves. All of this had a disturbing effect on the house slaves. These, because of their intimate contact with the household, had always had a pride of family. They thought of themselves as Camerons and, among themselves, took the name. So, there was Jonah Cameron, Ezekiel Cameron, Belle Lou Cameron and so on through their ranks. Now, though, recognizing the disintegration of the plantation and the helplessness of their masters and mistresses, they performed their duties without pleasure in their positions. Somewhere the sense of dignity had vanished. They were indifferent at their work, slow to obey an order, slovenly in service and person. Finally, out of anger and desperation, Cameron called them all together; those of the field and house. He faced them in the compound of their quarters.

"You can damned well go. All of you!" He shouted the words and his face colored alarmingly with anger. "I will not tolerate what is happening here. So, you are free, every man, woman and child. Get your things together and leave the plantation. I have known you all from the oldest to the newest baby. Most of you old ones grew up on Cameron land in Carolina. The others have been born and reared here on Cameron land in the islands. We are no strangers to each other. I have seen you cared for through your sicknesses. I have had you fed and housed through the fat and lean years. Few have ever felt the whip upon their backs for it is not the Cameron way to treat its slaves in such a manner. But I will not tolerate what is happening here now. You men and women who have worked the fields know the cotton does not grow as I expected. There is nothing for you to do but, by God, you will at least make an attempt to care for yourselves. The house servants are a disgrace to the Cameron name. If it were my way I would beat you into the proper performance of your duties, for that is what you deserve. Get off my land. This is no longer your home. I want no more of you." He made an effort to control the gasping of his breath.

They had regarded him with blank, uncomprehending faces as he paced up and down, slashing a riding crop at his boots, venting a helpless fury. Even the oldest, those who remembered him as a boy, had never seen the Marstah so angry. They shuffled their feet, looked around at the sky and earth, cut their eyes fearfully at each other. Anything to avoid the accusing glare confronting them.

"Do you understand what I am saying?" Cameron had the impotent feeling they comprehended nothing of what he had said.

"Wheah we go, Marstah?" A voice came hesitantly from the crowd. "What we do?"

"I don't give a damn what you do or where you go. I am going to set fire to these quarters. Then there will be no place for you here. You can go into the bush someplace else and build your huts of wattles and sticks. When you get sick you can die. When you get hungry you'll find food for yourselves. I don't give a damn any longer what becomes of you. All I say is you are free to go because you will not try here, unless driven, to help yourselves or me." He had turned away and left them standing in a dark and uncertain group.

But at the evening mealtime Gabriel, Cameron's personal slave and head of the household staff, appeared in his faded livery to hold and stand behind his master's chair. The serving girls had put together the best of their scanty clothes and fashioned from now useless sheets and tablecloths little patches of caps for their hair. A few candle stumps burned in a single candelabrum on the center of the table. The silver gleamed with recent polishing. The food was brought and served with the same, silent care as though they were all back on the Ashley.

Cameron ate without comment, a glowering figure at the table's head. Robert Bruce, Constance, Caroline, Juan and the twins with David spoke no word but took their servings from the platters as they were passed. Finally Cameron half turned in his chair and motioned to Gabriel.

"I thought I told all of you today to leave." His hands gripped the edge of the table. "Didn't you hear or understand what I said?"

"Yes, Marstah." Gabriel's tone was soft. "But we Cameron niggers. What foah you send us away? We gots no place to go. My daddy an' his befoah him was Camerons. How can we be else? What we do?"

"That was what you wanted, wasn't it? You, Cissie, Belle, the cook, Ark, Noah, Lou. Every goddamned one of you talked about freedom; told each other stories of how niggers on other islands had no masters and could do as they pleased. Well! You're free now. I said so. Why don't you leave?"

"We know you don' mean hit, Marstah." Gabriel's tone was soothing, understanding. "You jus' mad. Some," he hesitated, "some fiel' han's, they goin' to fah side o' islan' but mos' stay heah. No house niggers go 'tall. We Camerons. How we go way jus' because things go bad foah a while? Dey gets bettah. Lak a couple o' year on de Ashley plantation when we gets de weevil an' don' make no crop. But, no Cameron give up, no run away."

Cameron snorted, took a handkerchief and blew his nose. He was unreasonably touched by this expression of simple faith. He looked at Gabriel, who had been his personal slave since they were young boys together.

"Well damn it," he yelled, "if you're going to stay here do something. Bring me the rum. Thank God we can still grow enough cane to make that. You're a goddamned, burr-headed nigger, Gabe."

"Yessuh, Marstah." Gabriel went to the sideboard and returned with a tray on which was a decanter of heavy, dark rum and glasses for the three men. He poured first for Cameron, then Robert Bruce and Juan. His face shone with pleasure in the semidarkness. "Ahm sure enough a burr-headed nigger. You always said that. But, Ahm a burr-headed Cameron nigger. That makes a difference laik to de res' of us." He stepped back and merged himself with the shadows clinging to the wall.

Cameron dipped the end of his cigar into the rum and tasted the flavor of tobacco and the liquor. Then he took a light from the candle and his eyes swept the table, holding on Caroline who was regarding him with sly amusement.

"What the hell am I going to do with them?" He shoved the copper, cedar-lined humidor down the table toward Robert Bruce and Juan. "Tell me what I'm going to do with a hundred niggers who haven't got sense enough to leave when they are told?"

"I don't know." Caroline's eyes were dancing. "But John and Bahama are acquiring quite an extensive vocabulary from you."

Cameron moodily swallowed some of his rum. He studied the bright faces of the twins and the curious, almost contemplative expression on David's face. What, he wondered, was their future on this island to be?

"They'd better learn to swear now. They'll need to know how later."

"Damn it to hell." Bahama spoke the words with the pride of a rare accomplishment. "Damn the burr-headed niggers anyhow."

"You see?" Caroline was undisturbed. "She is only thirteen and can swear quite as well as you."

"I can swear too." John leaned forward, eager to display his knowledge. "Want to hear me?"

"Some other time." Caroline placed a hand gently over his mouth. "I've heard you before."

"When I was their age I wasn't allowed at the table with grownups," Cameron grumbled but he was inwardly tickled. "Neither were you nor Robert Bruce."

"Things were a little different then." Caroline was patient.

"So they were, Daughter. So they were." Cameron studied the rum in his glass.

Caroline regarded her father with a deep compassion which could not be put into words. How old he had become these past few years. How ineffective his bursts of anger, his rebellion against that which he could not control. When he was disturbed he roared, but it was the ineffectual sound of a toothless lion. He had that look, she thought, with his head of shaggy white hair, the big frame which had shrunk a little and obeyed his commands with difficulty. She, as did the other adults at the table, understood to what straitened circumstances the plantation had been reduced. They were still able to ship some cattle and swine to the market in Nassau. A spare quantity of rum, beyond the household needs, was distilled and exported. There was a limited market for the corn, cowpeas and beans they raised. These things brought in a small amount of money but the once baronial splendor of the place had vanished with the years. The wine vaults with their bins for fine French wines, brandies and cordials were empty save for a few bottles held for special occasions. The tobacco which came from Havana in the form of fat cigars and thin *cigarillos* was expensive and almost rationed. They had tried to grow some of the leaf on Exuma but it did not flourish, and produced a bitter, acrid product to which Cameron and Juan were reduced. Robert Bruce did not smoke. The little money returned from cattle sales disappeared almost before it was in their hands. It was needed for the cheap, slave cloth in which the blacks were clothed; better material for dresses for Bahama, pantaloons and blouses for John and David, clothing for herself and Constance. It went for repairs to the cane-grinding machinery, bottles into which the rum was poured, hinges for a sagging door, nails for loose boards. The small amount of pounds realized each year trickled off into a hundred little channels. They survived. There was plenty of food but not much variety. They managed but the big crop, the one which was to have been king, the cotton, was a failure and nothing anyone could do would revive it. Therein lay the seed of disaster for the Camerons and others on neighboring islands who had built with such a splendid disregard for possible misfortune.

When the table had been cleared and the twins with David had asked and received permission to leave for a time of play in the warm evening outside, they sat for a moment or two in silence. Cameron drew upon his cigar, his tongue moving about in his mouth to extract the last bit of flavor from the tobacco.

Robert Bruce half slumped in his chair, his eyes fixed on a space between his hands. His eyes were troubled, his face drawn into tight lines. Days before he had come to a decision. It was something he had talked over with Constance. Sooner or later it would have to be said.

"Father," he looked up to meet Cameron's eyes, "I hope you will understand what I have to say."

"How the hell can I understand if you don't say it, lad?" The question was abrupt but not unkindly voiced. He had a great love for his son. It had always been an unspoken bond between them. "Out with whatever it is."

"I am going to take Constance back with me to Carolina."

It was a second or two before anyone spoke. The statement had been made with such finality and abruptness it was not really understood.

"Carolina?" Cameron repeated the word almost as though it was unfamiliar. "There is no money, lad, for gadding about and seeing the sights of Carolina. You know that."

"I hadn't thought of it in those terms, Father." Robert Bruce straightened up in his chair and half moved it around to face the table's head. "I want to leave Exuma; to have done with these islands for good. There is nothing here for Constance and me. I'm no longer sure there is anything here for any of us. There is a time to be strong in the face of adversity. There is also a time to admit, frankly and without shame, failure. That is what we face. You know the families who have already given up and left. Those who remain are confronted by the most uncertain of futures. I will go to Charleston and find employment there. Mr. Ormond has already been kind enough to write friends in that city—merchants, factors, shippers and importers. Some sort of a position can be found for me and I can begin to build a future. We talked about it the last time Constance and I went to Watlings Island on a visit. Mr. Ormond agrees with the idea. There is no real need for me here on the plantation any longer. What little there is to do can be overseen by you and Spithead. I must get out on my own. Constance is not happy here." He paused. "To tell the truth neither am I. Mr. Ormond said—"

"Who the hell is John Ormond to agree or disagree with the future of the Camerons?" His father interrupted Robert Bruce, glaring down the length of the table, raising his voice in a display of impatient displeasure. "You do not break up a family simply because it falls upon adverse times. It holds together."

"I am a man with a family of my own, Father." Robert Bruce remained calm.

"Come, lad, there is naught but you and Constance so far. There is no real burden upon you."

With a small cry of anguish Constance rose and fled the room. A handkerchief was pressed against her mouth as though to muffle the sound. Caroline started to follow, hesitated, changed her mind and remained where she was. She understood her sister-in-law's misery, her feeling of guilt and shame, for she had failed to bear Robert Bruce a child. They had talked of this many times and always Caroline had been aware of the mortification possessing her brother's wife. She seemed to feel it was, somehow, her fault. In her unhappiness she had confided to Caroline the conviction she must be one of those unfortunate girls who remain barren. There was no other explanation for it. Both she and Robert Bruce were young and healthy. Yet, no pregnancy had come to her and she lived in constant torment, feeling she was wanting as a wife.

Cameron gazed after her and then turned to Robert Bruce. He shook his head regretfully and there was a sincerity in his voice when he spoke.

"That was a cruel and thoughtless thing to say. I spoke without thinking and not meaning to indict or censure. You tell her and I will make my own apology. Your children will come. It often happens they are late. No one knows exactly why."

"She takes it very hard"—Robert Bruce's words neither accepted nor rejected his father's self-reproach—"and blames herself."

[233]

Cameron sat with his head bowed. Then he raised it and regarded his son again unhappily.

"I cannot see you, lad, sitting upon a stool at a desk, entering things in a ledger. You were plantation born, put upon a saddle from the time you could walk, taught by word and observation the growing of things. To be confined within the dusty walls of some accounting room, to push a quill and stain your hands with ink, to report at eight o'clock and quit at six—those things are not for you. 'Tis better to bear some adversity here than chain yourself in someone's office with never a sight of the sky and land. I would miss you, Robert Bruce. I would miss you sorely."

"And I'll miss you and this place, these islands. They put a spell upon a man. There is a witchery in them. I think I might live my life out here in complete contentment if I wanted nothing more."

"A keeper of books, confronted daily by columns of figures, will that satisfy you?"

Robert Bruce permitted himself the smallest shade of a smile. This was an obdurate man, long accustomed to having his will unquestioned.

"I suspect there is more to commerce than that if I apply myself and learn what there is to know about the business. Anyhow," he spoke with a note of finality, "I will not be trying to breathe life into a corpse. That is what we are doing here no matter how you try to disguise it. Once away and on my own I will start from whatever position they give me and work myself up and out of it to something better. I am sorry if my decision does not meet with your favor." He regarded his father with a fond understanding. "We have been so close, you and I, that it has become my habit to let you make the decisions for me."

"I have tried only to guide you." There was an unmistakable impatience in the statement. "As for meeting with my favor, it goes far beyond that. What you are about to do destroys everything I have hoped for since the day you were born. It breaks a chain of two hundred years or more and leaves a Cameron plantation in the hands of a stranger." His glance strayed from his son to Juan and there was no mistaking what he meant. "Cameron land has always remained Cameron land."

Juan reached for the rum, filled his glass and drank a small portion. His eyes, without their customary laughter behind them, never left Ronald Cameron's face. Caroline's fingers touched his arm as though to hold back what he was about to say, for she was acutely sensitive to his moods and temper.

"Papa." The word came slowly. "I have put up with you for a long time. You don't like me. So?" He shrugged. "I don't muches you." Unconsciously he employed the curious idiom of the islands where *much* was used in the sense of *like*. "But, you are a mule of a man who must be kicked in the ass before he will move."

"Don't call me Papa!" The outraged roar all but shook the walls. "And save your vulgarity for the stable where it belongs. This is a matter between my son and me."

"For now, yes." Juan was unperturbed. "But the years will catch and trip you as they do all men. Go on this way and you will be alone. This stranger you talk about. He is Juan Cadiz, no? Well, Juan Cadiz does not want your plantation. He lived well and happy long before he ever heard the name of Cameron." He turned the rum glass between his fingers. "Now, I'll tell you something, Papa." He uttered the word deliberately, knowing it would further infuriate the man. "I think Robert Bruce will do as he says and he will leave you to hold the broken pieces of chain you talk about in your hands. What will you do then, Papa? Link it together by yourself, an old man who is better off sitting in the sun?"

"Juan. Please." Caroline, distressed by the blunt and coldly voiced anger, pleaded with him. "For me, please."

He shook off her words with a reluctant motion of his head. "Robert Bruce and Constance," he continued relentlessly; "they leave Exuma and go to Charleston. And then, this stranger, this Juan Cadiz, says to himself one day: Why should I put up with this bad-tempered old one? What is he to me? On that day I will take my wife and children and we, also, will get off this place which is holy to the Camerons. Then you will have it to yourself, the last Cameron on the island. You can stand on it and spit in four directions and say to yourself: This is mine and no stranger, especially no stranger with the name of Cadiz, rests a foot upon it. You will have your way, Papa, but you will not be happy with it. You will sit and rot a little each day and there will be no one to give a damn." He met Cameron's eye with an unwavering stare. "You think about that, Papa."

Ronald Cameron sat in his chair, rigid, and his lips made a soundless movement. No one had ever before spoken to him in this manner and he was unprepared for the sudden attack. It even frightened him, for he was confronted by a man who unexpectedly displayed a will as strong as his own. This beachcomber, this player of a guitar, this man of careless manner and easy smile, had unsuspected steel in him and was not afraid to use it. He bowed slowly as though beneath an irresistible weight. He seemed to lose some of his physical stature as his body slumped in the high-backed, cushioned seat. Beyond this he gave no indication of the conflict within him. For the moment he was without the will to answer. His glance roved slowly from Juan to Caroline to Robert Bruce and back again to a spot before him on the table.

[235]

"You will go, Robert Bruce." He spoke with an effort. "Go as you wish and think is wise. You are a man in your own right and able to make his decisions. It is proper you should. The mistake has been mine in trying to create you in my own image." His hands as they were clasped shook a trifle. "I will help as I can and send off a letter to George Renevant, who has many business interests in Charleston and abroad. You would do well to take his advice." A wintery smile brushed at his mouth. "There is no reason to assume no better future for you than a clerkship. We have never had a merchant prince in the family. Perhaps you will ennoble us to that extent." He paused and seemed to be gathering himself for a greater effort. He met Caroline's troubled expression and his own softened. "I suspect," he spoke to her, "your husband is right. I am, sometimes, a mule of a man who must be kicked in the ass before he moves in the right direction. You will forgive me the word. It is not one I would use in the presence of a lady." He was silent for a moment and then looked up and directly at Juan. "An apology does not come easily to me. I am sorry for what I said but I have not liked you. I find your ways strange and beyond my experience but there is a character I had never suspected. I cannot honestly speak of you as a stranger, someone apart from my life. For you are my daughter's husband. The father of her children and my grandson and granddaughter."

"I didn't do it for you, Papa." Juan relented and the statement was tempered by humor. "Believe me, at the time you were the farthest thing from my thoughts."

"Juan," Caroline protested and her face gathered a sudden color. "How can you say such things?"

"Because they make you confused. I like to see it, a flower in each cheek. I never before knew a girl who blushed. It is a very pretty thing to watch."

Cameron's face was a study in confused emotions. His small sigh was an admission of surrender.

"I suppose I will, in time, get used to you, Juan." The name came effortlessly. "I do not think you make idle threats. I believe you would do what you said and Caroline would go with you from choice and not out of duty as a wife. I would like this plantation to be the home of my grandchildren." Cameron spoke with sincerity. "After all," he allowed himself a touch of levity, "where else could a girl with such a name as Bahama feel at home?"

"Well, I'll tell you, Papa." Juan persisted in the use of this designation and there was no display of the usual resentment on Cameron's face. "You will get used to me and I'll get used to you. I will work at it and you will stop thinking of me as some thief who stole a thing of value.

Together, maybe, we get along all right. I don't know. But, we'll try. This island of Exuma is a good one. If the cotton does not grow, then try something else. You are the farmer."

A small chuckle escaped Cameron. "I never quite thought of myself in that term."

Robert Bruce darted a quick, laughing glance at his sister. Ronald Cameron. Farmer. It was such a preposterous employment of the word.

"All right." Juan was agreeable. "Master of the plantation. Whatever you like. You see," he finished his rum, "already I begin to give some. I," he continued, "am a man of the sea. You are of the land. After Robert Bruce has gone, do not expect me to take his place on a horse beside you. There is nothing I like less than a horse. But, I know some things of the water. If we cannot take a living from the fields, maybe we have to go to the ocean. I will take you in my sloop or the ketch sometime and show you what I mean."

There was a noisy slamming of the front door and the chattering trooping of John, Bahama and David as they raced in for the night. They paused on the threshold of the dining room and then came in to say their good nights. Juan regarded his son and daughter with pride. The miracle of the twins never ceased to cause him to marvel that they could come from the same egg and yet be so different in appearance. Bahama was Caroline as she must have been at her age: the crystal, exquisitely cut features and unconscious grace. The eyes of grayish-blue which could unexpectedly become fired by the light of a star sapphire or grave and contemplative, according to her mood. She was tall and of slender grace even at this age and seemed to have no moments of awkwardness. Bahama was never unsure of herself and there was a curious dignity of manner which, somehow, did not seem a contradiction of her age.

John. He could almost laugh with delight at his son, for he was Juan Cadiz. Put him in a cast-off pair of sailor's pantaloons on the beach at Nassau and there would have been no telling them apart save in the matter of years. He was quick to laugh, filled with an adventuresome vitality, and took to the water as though he had been spawned there. He was also given to anger which rarely betrayed itself in word or deed but drew itself as a mask to cover his face. Beyond this no one could penetrate.

In turn the twins kissed their mother and father with the unabashed love consuming them. Their hearts were on display for all to see. With a certain twinkling reserve Bahama curtsied to Ronald Cameron and then pressed her cheek against his.

"Good night, Grandfather."

"And a good night to you, Bahama of the islands." He smiled.

John made a short, stiff bow. "Good night, Grandfather."

Cameron offered his hand. "Good night, John Cameron Cadiz."

David stood a little apart. This was always a difficult time for him although he did his best to hide the emotional conflict. He was of the family and yet, not a part of it. This was the fault of no one, for he was treated with the same generous kindness, subject to the same discipline, punished as were John and Bahama for a lapse of conduct. The distinction, if it existed, was in his mind. He had been unable to integrate himself completely.

Ten years had passed since his mother had left him on the island but the memory of her had not dimmed. He could not honestly say he missed her but as the years were added he often wondered why he had been abandoned; left to become a part of this family. There was no hurt, no feeling of having been cast loose, but there was a curiosity. How and why had such a thing come about? His father, who had been the Governor of the islands, had become far less real in his mind than his mother. He recalled him only as a big man of loud voice who sometimes was surprisingly gentle and understanding without speaking a word. He had died, he had been told, in a plague which had swept across the islands.

Alone in his bed, lying in the dark, he would sometimes imagine his mother standing silently in the same room. He could almost smell her fragrance, feel the warmth of her presence, the small, bell-like sound of her laughter, and the encompassing smile when she was particularly pleased by something. He did not cry for her but only wondered.

She had written but once and that was six years or so ago and the letter had been addressed to Mr. Cameron, who read aloud such parts of it as he thought would be of interest to David. These were gay and chatty paragraphs about the wonders of London and expressions of hope that he was happy on Exuma. In it there was no mention of her return. Intuitively, he knew he would not see her again. An inner strength kept him from questioning Mr. Cameron about this. What Cameron did not read to the boy was the information that Sabrina was about to be married to a gentleman of means and social position, and having David with her would be out of the question.

Save for rare moments of a strange loneliness David was happy here. John was a brother. They argued and sometimes fought in a tangle of flying legs and arms. They swam and fished, talked of things far beyond the islands and of what they would do when they were grown. Bahama he adored with an unaffected directness, but he never permitted her to take advantage of this in their games or in situations where he felt he was expected to yield an advantage simply because she was Bahama and he loved her. They sailed Juan's sloop, exploring the nearby cays, hunting for pirates' gold and once even finding a small, gold coin on the beach where it had been washed from the depths by the tide. From Tom Gurney, who had remained with the Camerons even after his marriage to one of the Ferguson girls at the other end of the island, they had learned to handle the larger ketch. They led a fine, free and wonderful life in which every day was a new adventure. Strangely enough, the nature of their relationship was never discussed. In fact, it never entered their minds. They were simply Bahama, John and David, and David frequently had difficulty in remembering his name was Heath and not Cameron. Bahama and John never thought about it at all.

It was only in a moment such as this one when the twins, with their freedom of expression, displayed their affection and duty to their parents and grandfather that David Heath felt alone and alien. He had been well mannered when Sabrina brought him to Exuma. It never occurred to him to intrude upon the intimacy of the family. He was of and not of them and in his mind it was a strangely confusing situation. Often Caroline had looked in upon him in his room at night. At such times he pretended to be asleep, but he knew and was grateful when she quietly bent over and kissed him lightly on the forehead before tiptoeing out and closing the door.

Caroline glanced up at David and was shocked by what she saw. In this single, unguarded moment there was such a longing, an expression of bleak isolation. It was the only time he had revealed himself, and her heart went out to him with a surge of pity and understanding.

"David." She spoke his name with tender softness.

"Yes, ma'am." His face cleared immediately as though he was aware of what it had shown. "Yes, ma'am?" He repeated the phrase as a question.

"Come here. Please."

He moved to her side and her hands reached out and took his arms, drawing him closer to the chair. For a moment they looked at each other and a warm current flowed between them.

"You have never kissed me good night as do Bahama and John. I would like it, if you wanted to."

For a fraction of a second he hesitated and then bent to put his lips to her cheek. It was a tentative, almost cautious gesture. She could feel him tremble and drew him into a tight embrace.

"Good night, David."

"Good night, ma'am."

It was over in a moment but everyone in the room was aware of what had happened. Some small magic had been performed by this simple act, this sincere expression of affection. It showed on David Heath's face and he seemed to stand a little straighter and with proud assurance. His eyes shone with a sudden happiness. Then he stepped back and her arms dropped away, but a fragile bond had been woven between them.

"Good night, sir." He spoke to Cameron, Juan and Robert Bruce in turn.

"Good night, David," they replied in a chorus.

It was Bahama who broke the spell. "I'll race you to the head of the stairs." She shouted the challenge and went flying from the room followed by John and David. Their feet drummed with a muffled sound on the carpeted staircase which wound upward to the second floor.

Caroline looked after them and then turned to her father, but the words were addressed to them all.

"Did you see what I did?" There was regret in the question. "He—David—he has always been so self-contained. I just never thought. It didn't occur to me he wanted to belong to someone. Yet, for a moment, he stood there with the forlorn expression of an abandoned puppy, an unloved waif, a hungry child who could not bring himself to ask for food. It made me ashamed of myself, of all of us. Of course the boy needs love. We have given him respect and security, nothing more."

Cameron cleared his throat. "Pass me the rum, Juan." The request rumbled in his chest. He filled his glass but did not touch it.

"Well," Caroline started to rise, "it is getting late."

"Stay for a minute." Cameron took a half swallow of the rum. This was the thing he had always known must come. Sooner or later David would have to be explained. Over the years he had been bothered by Caroline's natural curiosity. Why hadn't Lady Heath sent for her son? Why, at least, didn't she write him now that he was able to read, and perhaps understand? Robert Bruce, also, had sometimes spoken in the same vein. "There is something you should know. A thing I ought to have told you long ago, for you all must have wondered at David's continued presence here." He paused and took a deep breath. "Lady Heath's leaving him with us was not a sudden, careless or indifferent act." He lowered his head and then raised it with a heavy effort to meet their curious glances. "David is my son."

The shock of the words had an almost physical impact. It held them to their chairs. Robert Bruce and Caroline could only stare at him, unable to credit what they had heard. Juan, alone, was the only one who did not seem surprised.

"He," Cameron felt a compulsion to repeat the words, "he is my son and your half brother."

"Father!" Caroline's exclamation was not one of shock, mortification or outrage. It was simply incredulity, as though she had been told something which was far beyond her ability to comprehend. "Father." This time she spoke with sympathy, fully aware of what this confession was costing him.

"I could not bring myself to tell you this before," he continued and each word was an effort. "Why, I am not sure. Perhaps it has always been in the back of my mind that Sabrina would eventually send for the boy. He would pass out of our lives; yours, at least, if not mine. I would always be conscious of the responsibility. One does not dismiss such a thing lightly. I tell you now because we all grow a little older and with, I hope, more understanding of human frailties on your part. Without your knowing the truth, complications were certain to arise in later years. Now," he appeared infinitely weary, "now you know. It has been said."

"It has always been in the back of my mind, Papa." Juan spoke in a barely audible tone. There was no jest, no suggestion of a leer, in the words. He did not make of the situation an obscene joke. "I cannot tell you why or how I suspected."

Whatever Caroline and Robert Bruce felt was not revealed in their expressions, but Cameron was aware of a heartwarming understanding which went far beyond tolerance. He had not known what to expect. Some explosion of outraged virtue from Caroline? No. That was not in her nature. Thoughtful silence from Robert Bruce? Yes. This was his son's character. He was most surprised by Juan, for from this strange man he had thought to draw an unendurable mockery. It was an opportunity to reduce the situation to a bawdy level. Juan did not take it despite Cameron's intolerance of him.

"David, of course, does not know." Robert Bruce was not asking a question.

Cameron shook his head. "This is not the time nor could it have been done before. I am not sure how it will have to come about but the day cannot be put off forever. Perhaps, in a few more years, when he begins to move toward the estate of man . . . I don't know." The problem weighted him with unendurable pressure.

There was complete silence about the table, for each was assaying the complexities of the situation in his or her own way. It was Caroline who finally voiced that which troubled her most.

"It cannot wait for too many years, Father. I know you will think this foolish of me but already there is a worship in David's eyes when he looks at Bahama. It is an attachment of children, of course. I do not place too much significance on it at the moment. They are constantly together and he is irresistibly drawn to her, for she is a child of beauty

[241]

and vivacious nature. I am aware of these things. But," her eyes clouded with worry, "here, in these surroundings, shut away from the diverting companionship of boys and girls their age, there is danger. The years could give it depth and tragedy."

"You make a drama. A storybook tale. It is the way of a woman to imagine such things," Juan chided her with a smile and placed his hand upon hers.

She was not reassured. "How old, my Juanio, my wise ancient, how old was I when you first came in your sloop with the red sail and we looked at each other that day on the dock and everything between us was settled? I was barely seventeen. Bahama is thirteen. Four years or less. That is how much time we have." She paused and an expression of complete astonishment crossed her face. "David"—her voice carried a rising inflection which was dangerously close to hysterical laughter— "why, David is John and Bahama's uncle."

It was this bald statement of the relationship which actually brought the situation into sharp focus and with a stunning clarity.

"He must be told, Father. Caroline is right." Robert Bruce met the issue with a calm finality. "David is what? Fourteen? Fifteen? I think so. I am not sure how it can or should be done, but you are the only one to do it. It can come from no one else."

"Aye," Cameron agreed, "I have always known that from the day Sabrina left. In the name of God"—it was almost an appeal—"how do you tell this to a boy of fifteen? Do you take him aside and say without preamble: I lay with your mother. We were not even in love. You are the result of a time of folly, of heedless passion. You are my son. Nothing is as you think it is." He rested elbows on the table and held his chin in upturned hands. "I cannot bring myself to do it and yet, it must be done." He studied Robert Bruce for a moment. "If I could send him away to school. The mainland. Charleston, perhaps, where you and Constance might look after him when you are settled there?" It was a question put with a desperate hope.

"No, Father." Robert Bruce kept his words even and respectful but there was no mistaking their firmness. "My future there is too uncertain. Even if it weren't I would not do it, for it solves nothing. I hope Constance and I will eventually have children. If so we will have problems of our own which the supervision of David would only aggravate."

"Yes, lad." Cameron's voice was tired. "You are right. I look for the easy way. There is none."

Caroline arose, walked to her father's chair and sat upon its arm. She cradled his bent head in an arm, pressing her face against his hair. It was crisp with age and all but fully white. She was trying to comfort him and at the same time reassure herself, for this was a man who had always represented to her unshakable will, the family's strength.

"I would do it for you if I could." She all but whispered the words in the soothing tone she might use with a bewildered child.

"I know. It is not something from which I can run away. Let me think upon it."

"We don't even reach the end there, Papa," Juan reflected. "For John Cameron"—it was the first time he had ever linked his son's name with that of Cameron—"John Cameron and Bahama must sooner or later know."

"That can wait." Caroline stood up. There was determination in her manner. "There is no need for them to know more than they do at the moment. When the time comes I will handle it in my own way. I think," she spoke with a curious blending of determination and childish defiance, "I just think I'll have a little of that rum you gentlemen find so comforting in times of crisis." Deliberately she went to the cabinet, took a glass, returned to the table and filled it. She sipped experimentally and then took a full swallow, gasping a little at its potency.

Juan watched her with amusement. "It has been a long time since I have taken a drunken island wench to bed."

"It will be a long time before you do." She put the glass down. "In a punch it seems all right, but straight this way I don't muches it." The idiom came with a grin. She put her hand on her father's shoulder. "This thing does not have to be settled tonight nor tomorrow. You will find a way. You always have when pressed."

He looked up gratefully and nodded an assent. "I would like to have it done with and yet, cannot bring myself to do it."

"There is something, though, which has been on my mind." Caroline resumed her seat. "The schooling needs of John, Bahama and David. They have gone far beyond what I am capable of teaching for I," she winked at her father, "was no great student, as you know. What are we to do about it? Can we afford the expense of a private tutor here?"

Cameron welcomed the change of subject and this was something he, also, had thought about. The children had learned to read and write after a fashion but he was far from satisfied with such limited schooling.

"The expense," he meditated, "would not be too great. The poor wretches who work to pound knowledge into a child's head are not well paid. It is possible we may be able to find someone in Nassau who would be willing to come to Exuma for a small stipend with board and room. There is a missionary school on Eluthera but we could not sail them back and forth each day. I don't know what is to be done. We cannot afford to send them to the mainland or to England. Even the school in

Nassau is of the most elementary nature. But John, Bahama and David cannot be allowed to grow up unlettered, unaware of history and the world's literature; the storehouse of treasure which can only be opened with the key of curiosity provoked by a thorough schooling and a patient instructor." He shook his head again, this time with a half-humorous confession of defeat. "Everything which would have been so simple in Carolina becomes impossibly complex here. We could, perhaps, put an advertisement for a tutor in the Nassau *Gazette* or board the three of them on Eluthera for the school term. It is even possible," he could not resist the dry humor, "we might write to a school in Charleston and lure some unsuspecting tutor down here with a tale of the free, island life, warm sunshine, coconut palms and rare opportunities. Once here we could hold him captive. But," he spoke with a musing regret, "I suspect pedagogues are not of an adventuresome nature."

"Well," Caroline was decisive, "we have involved ourselves in quite enough problems for one night. I, for one, am going to bed." She stood up, followed by Juan and Robert Bruce.

"I'll stay here for a little while," Cameron said. "There is rum in the decanter and I'll take a pipe or two. They will keep me company."

After they had left he sat in his chair and slowly packed a pipe with the coarse leaf. He drew upon it with contemplative satisfaction, refilling his glass with the dark rum at frequent intervals. The house, now, without sound, seemed an empty, lonely cavern into which he had wandered. He had long since recognized the folly of condemning them all to this island life. It had been done and could not be changed. He tried to look ahead in the years to come. They would survive, of course. But, he reflected, at what cost? Caroline's children and David would grow up in this insular climate. Beyond these shores the world was astir with great and significant changes but the currents of these events would barely touch them here. The twins and David were reaching toward an adult state without the benefit of social contacts, the refining and gracious influence of the landed aristocracy to which they had been born, the gentle manners and knowledge which were their birthright. In a couple of generations what remained of the original Cameron stock would have degenerated to a class of fishermen and small farmers. They would be indistinguishable from the unlettered inhabitants and coarsely mannered Bahamians of the most remote island. They would have nothing but the most primitive ability to take a crude living from the sea and small patches of land. They were all, he thought, as far removed from the things he once had known as though they had settled upon one of the planets which showed themselves in the night's sky. It was no bright future but he could not correct it now. Man was born, it seemed, to commit himself to error. Somehow, he managed to claw his way out of it. This he could hope for.

By the time he had finished the last pipe and poured the final drop of rum from the decanter he was somberly drunk. There was no joy in drinking this way. A pipe and bowl demanded companionship. With his hands he thrust himself from the chair and called hoarsely to the waiting slave girl who would sit all night, crouching in a pantryway, waiting until the masters were ready for bed. She came quickly on bare feet and carrying a taper, lighted his way up the dark staircase and to his room.

Seated on the bed he weaved slightly, holding himself upright with an effort as the girl pulled and finally tugged off his boots. He fell back with a windy sigh of comfort, his head burying itself in the soft pillows. Without bothering to undress he went to sleep almost immediately and slept with gusty snores, the alcohol clouding his mind against all disturbing thoughts. The slave girl crept silently from the room and closed the door. The house was without stir. Outside the ocean whispered quietly to the beach as it ran upon it with eternal movement.

From the window of his study Cameron watched the *Traveler* as she made sail and picked up the moderate southwest wind which carried her swiftly beyond the point and out of sight. She had come without passengers to pick up cargo. The plantation had ready for shipment a fairly large consignment of dried peas, beans, sacked yams, six bales of cotton, a dozen sheep, twenty-four swine and twelve beeves. It was a pitifully small yield for a plantation of this size but more than had been shipped in months. To the usual produce which found a market in Nassau they had added ten sacks of oranges, fifteen of limes and lemons together with four crates of pineapples. John Ormond had been experimenting with the pineapples, the cuttings for which he had imported from Havana. He had induced Cameron to try to raise them in quantity on Exuma. The fruit had flourished and Cameron had begun to wonder if a market could be opened for them on the mainland. It was something, he thought, into which Robert Bruce could look after he was settled in Charleston. The schooner, in addition to the cargo, had also taken with her Cameron's son and Constance on the first leg of their trip to Carolina.

The loss of Robert Bruce struck harder at Cameron than anything he had experienced since coming to the Bahamas. It was, he felt, the first crumbling, the beginning of the process of dissolution. All of his life he had looked forward to passing on Cameron Hall, on the Ashley, to his son. Later he had built his hope for the future on the Exuma plantation. It was this estate he would turn over to Robert Bruce as his heritage. In his heart he could not blame his son but he felt bereft and inconsolably alone. He had grown old in body, weary in spirit. There was little enthusiasm left in him for anything. The failure of his dream had left him only the cold reality and he would not dream again save in restless turnings of the mind.

With the absence of Robert Bruce and the growing strength of the man's hand in the handling of the slaves, the maintenance of discipline and the forcing of a meager yield from the acres, he was alone. Spithead, who had remained with them through the years and had married Amelia Ferguson, had told him only last week he, also, must leave. Old man Ferguson had died and there was no one to look after the small plantation he had owned at the far end of the island. Spithead, now, must take his wife and two children back and work his own acres as best he could. This unexpected event left the entire burden with Cameron but it had not forced Robert Bruce to swerve from his determination.

"I am sorry, Father." He was sincere. "Spithead was a good man. He will be missed here but I cannot, I will not stay to try and take his place. While I am in Nassau I will look around for an overseer. If not there, I may find someone in Charleston who might like to try life here in the islands. I know it is difficult for you but it would be doubly so for me to remain."

Cameron had not tried to change his son's mind. Robert Bruce was right. There was no future for him here. They both knew it.

The topmasts of the *Traveler* disappeared. He stared now only at the empty expanse of water. From the beach John, Bahama and David came trooping up the hill. The loading of the bleating sheep, the squealing and grunting swine and the stubborn cattle had provided a morning of excitement. The animals had to be driven aboard a barge with high, latticed sides and ferried to the schooner. The sheep and pigs had not offered too much difficulty. A railed gangway chute had been lowered for them but the cattle had to be bound in slings and then hoisted by windlass to the deck and hold, where they bellowed their frenzied anger and threatened to break loose and stampede across the deck or through the narrow hold and its not too sturdy pens.

Watching the trio Cameron realized he had done nothing about the problem of David. It faced him constantly; at every meal and meeting. Still he delayed, trying to push the situation from his mind. It would not disappear but returned in moments of solitude to haunt him. With rare wisdom Caroline had said nothing. She understood how it pressed upon her father now that it had been brought into the open between them. Once, she had thought to take upon herself the difficult task of trying to explain everything to David. Perhaps it could be done in a gentle manner by a woman. She did not speak of this to her father because, in the end, she realized there was no easy way. When the facts were explained they would be brutal and shocking to a boy no matter who voiced them.

Many times Cameron had been on the point of asking David into the study. There, behind the closed doors, he would say what must be said. This was as far as his imagination would take him. There was no subtle, gentle, indecisive approach. It was not a thing to be half said, hoping David would add the missing pieces from his own intelligence. He must say: You are my illegitimate son. I fathered you. That is why your mother left you with me. She did not have the love to take you with her. God in Heaven! Who could speak in such a manner to a boy?

He went to a wall cabinet to place the receipt for the shipment aboard the *Traveler* with other papers dealing with the plantation's transactions. The slots and drawers held a miscellaneous jumble of bills, receipts, clippings from London journals, figures on field production, old letters. All of these things should have been properly filed and catalogued before but it was a tiresome task, labor for a clerk, and he had put it off from year to year. With half a mind to put them in some sort of order now he began to sort them out. He turned the lock in one of the small drawers and as he absently glanced through them he came upon the letter from Sabrina, written long ago in Nassau when she became aware she was carrying a child. He held it in his hand, staring at the boldly penned words. Then he sat down and read it through with care and thought.

Outside, the voices of the twins and David were loud and excited. They were planning to take Juan's sloop, some lunch, a couple of shovels and go off on their favorite pastime of searching the cays for buried pirates' gold. Listening, holding the letter, Cameron came to an abrupt decision. It would be, he thought, not the honest way. In truth it was an evasion of duty, an almost unworthy stratagem but he would take it because he could not bring himself to speak the words.

Half ashamed of what he was about to do he went to a window, pushed open the jalousied blinds, noting how badly they were in need of paint. He must order some to be brought from Nassau by the *Traveler* on the next voyage. It was damnably expensive. It seemed everything he needed from a nail to a door latch was measured by its weight in gold. From the window he called.

"David."

The youngsters halted their animated conversation and looked about to see from where in the house the call had come. Finally, they located it at the library window and stared at it with expectant faces.

[247]

"David." Cameron repeated the call.

"Yes, sir?" There was a question in the respectful answer.

"Would you come into the library, lad?"

He turned away and went back to his desk; sitting down heavily, folding and refolding Sabrina's letter until there was a knock on the door.

"Come in, David." He tried to make the voice hearty, the summons of no particular consequence. "Come in."

The boy entered, paused for just a second. Then he shut the door and advanced slowly to stand before Cameron's chair, waiting for the man to speak.

Gazing at him Cameron wondered if there was a resemblance he could not see. He searched the bright and eager face for some sign but there was nothing there which even remotely suggested his own features. This, he told himself, was of no particular significance. The years had creased and lined his skin, bone structure showed where it had been hidden before, the eyes were tired and often drawn by worry. Why should there be any similarity?

"Sit down, lad." He filled a pipe with a nervous gesture and then fired it deliberately, delaying the moment. "I have wanted to talk with you for some time."

"Yes, sir." David was plainly puzzled by this introductory remark. They had often talked together when he, the man and Robert Bruce rode to the fields together in the mornings. "What is it, sir? Something I have done or," a sudden smile flashed across his face, "something I haven't done?"

"Neither, lad." Cameron was reassuring. How, he asked himself, did one open a conversation so delicate in context that one wrong word, one misplaced sentence, could destroy in a second what he hoped to accomplish with patience and quiet affection. "There is nought wrong. I did not call to rebuke you."

"Oh!" David relaxed. He was visibly relieved and took a new interest in the interchange of words. "I thought maybe I . . ." He left the suggestion unfinished.

Cameron drew upon his pipe and sent a wreath of smoke curling toward the ceiling. He held the letter on the desk, covered by one hand.

"Lad. I don't know how to begin what I have to say." It was a wry confession, tempered by a helpless shrug. "And you know I am not a man who is often at loss for words."

"Yes, sir." David did his best to keep pace with what was being said but the situation was becoming more and more mystifying to him. "Yes, sir. I know that." He forced a smile of agreement.

"You are what, David. Fourteen? Fifteen?"

"Fifteen, sir. Going on sixteen."

"That is not too far removed from the estate of man." Cameron seemed to find some comfort in the thought. "At fifteen my father treated me as an adult. I was given considerable responsibility on our plantation in Carolina. My father accorded me the courtesy of an equal, and expected me to understand. There are things a man must take in his stride which a boy will stumble over. That is what I hope from you, a mature viewpoint. Try and accept what I have to tell you."

"Yes, sir." There seemed to be no other suitable reply. "I'll do my best."

"Good!" For some reason Cameron seemed to feel the worst was over although his intelligence told him this was not so. "Good!" He repeated the word with a satisfied nod of his head.

The boy regarded the man with the most solemn of eyes. Nothing, so far, had made the slightest sense to him. Mr. Cameron seemed merely to be rambling, passing the time for some inexplicable reason. He wondered if the old gentleman was becoming a little dotty.

"You must have questioned sometimes"—Cameron tested each word in his mind before uttering it—"how it happened your mother left you here with us. Eleven years it is now, almost."

"Have you heard from her, sir?" The question came eagerly. "Has she written? Am I to see her? Is she coming back?" The queries tumbled over each other.

"No, David." For the first time Cameron displayed an impatience. "No. It isn't that at all. Damn! But this is no easy thing to talk about."

"If you could tell me what is disturbing you, sir, perhaps I will understand no matter how it is said." For the first time David betrayed an obvious uneasiness. The excited flush which had leaped to his face over the idea his mother might be returning was fading slowly. "I will try, sir."

"I am, lad. Don't you see I am trying to tell you?"

Cameron reluctantly lifted his hand from the creased paper and picked it up. He turned it over and over in his fingers as though this simple movement might cause it to disappear and with it all his difficulties.

"I am going to give you a letter to read." He did not offer it immediately. "It was written by your mother to me before you were born. I cannot think of any other way to let you know what you should. You must believe that. Over the years I have come to regard you with the deepest affection. You are a boy any man would be proud to have as a son. What I feel for you is, in a measure, the love and responsibility I felt for Robert Bruce when he was your age."

Hesitantly, almost unwillingly, he passed the letter to David and then

[249]

abruptly arose from his chair and walked to the window, staring out and seeing nothing. He could not bear to watch the expression on the boy's face as he read what his mother had written. He could only imagine the uncertainty, the terror, the humiliation which would mark those clear features. There was complete silence in the room and the time seemed never-ending. Once there was the faint crackling of paper. Nothing more.

"I have read it, sir." The words were so evenly spaced Cameron could well understand the effort they must be costing to hold them so. "I have put it back on the desk by your chair."

Cameron turned. David sat, staring straight ahead. The small muscles about his mouth twitched uncontrollably as he strained for composure. He made only one, revealing gesture. He thrust the back of one hand quickly across his eyes to keep back the tears which threatened to gather there despite his effort to hold them.

"You understand now why things are as they are?"

"You mean I am a bastard, sir, do you not?" The cry was there but not in the question. It came from deep within the soul's well.

"That is a harsh thing to say, David."

"Is there another word for it, sir?" He regarded the man without defiance. There was a mute plea in the question. "It means I was not wanted. I came without love in anyone's heart. What was done to make me born had no tenderness. You were not in love with my mother nor she with you. Her letter says so. Even a bastard has a right to ask a little more than that. There might have been some love on one side at least and this could have been passed on to me. As it is I was dropped as some calf or slave girl's child, a thing of inconvenience. You asked me to have the understanding of a man. I am trying to give it to you, sir."

The tears were there now. They came slowly through eyelids tightly squeezed together. The head was bowed to hide what was thought to be a weakness but the body shook beneath the strain of shame, and a youthful wonder over the world and the richness of his home here was torn beyond recognition. He wanted to cry out against what had happened.

"Lad. Lad." Cameron repeated the word and choked upon it. "Try and believe me when I say it is not quite that way."

"How is it, sir?" It took a tremendous effort to speak. "If you know then please tell me."

Cameron crossed the room and stood beside the boy's chair. He put out his hand and laid it upon David's shoulder, half fearful it would be thrown off and all communication between them ended.

"I would think," Cameron spoke with a pity he had not known before, "the word you used has the meaning of someone to be put out of sight and mind. A thing of shame, a secret to be locked away and never mentioned. This is not true. If you will have it so I want you for my son."

The trembling raced through the youthful frame but it was subsiding. There was strength in the boy, Cameron thought with a new pride. He would face up to what must be met.

"How can what happened between you and my mother be done without love, sir?" David looked up and stared accusingly with the question.

"I know and I do not know," Cameron replied honestly. "It is a hunger of the body which can be satisfied in no other way. As you grow older you will understand. It is the only way I can explain it now."

"But my mother?" David groped for words which would satisfy the confusion in his mind without reviling her memory. "Did she feel nothing for me? Even a mongrel bitch takes care of her puppies. She guards them fiercely. I have seen it. She washes, feeds and cares for them. When my mother left here why didn't she take me with her? Why was I abandoned? Why, after my fath—" he corrected himself, "her husband died didn't she stay here, or didn't you want her either? Did you send her away?"

"No, lad. I did not send her. Neither," he was an honest man, "did I press her to stay. She was an unusual woman. She could not face the thought of spending her life here on Exuma. We talked it over, believe me. One error is not corrected by compounding it with another. Her marriage to Sir Gerald was not a happy one. She was young and beautiful and eager for another chance at life. This, David, we must face. A widow with a young child would find it difficult to remarry suitably."

"I would have been in the way. That is what you are trying to tell me, isn't it, sir?"

"Boy," Cameron shook his head sadly, "there is this dark bitterness in you. We have cut deeply at each other. It was necessary. If I could have spared you I would. Can't you regard it a little differently? I am your father. Your mother left you with me."

David was silently thoughtful. His glance lifted to study the man across the table. When he did speak it was in a milder and more understanding tone.

"In the talk between us, sir, I had forgotten that. What was said confused me. I had no reason to think things were otherwise than they seemed. You are my father, aren't you? It makes a difference between us."

"If you will have me in your heart for a father, David, I would be pleased to take you as my son. Things, I suspect, will go on much as they have before but there will be this distinction. In everything I do from now on I will think of you as my son, David Cameron. I hope you will find pride in the name."

"Do"—David had difficulty in asking the question—"does anyone else know? Bahama? John?"

"No. Only Caroline and her husband. Robert Bruce and his wife. It was necessary, you understand, for me to tell them, for who knows what will happen? I could die suddenly of a stroke or accident. I am not particularly concerned over the immediate prospects of such things. Should it happen, though, I wanted Robert Bruce and Caroline to know you had a legitimate claim here. This is your home and not a place of a temporary visit." He offered a brief smile. "We talk a little easier now, do we not?"

"Yes, sir. I was not rude to you intentionally. I have always felt a great respect. I have admired you, sir, and many times, with Bahama and John, felt I was actually coming to my home as well as theirs."

"We will leave it that way. In time it may grow into something more. I will not press you nor presume upon the relationship. Let it flower if it will."

"Bahama and John? Must they be told, sir?" He frowned, trying to bring order out of the chaotic situation in his mind. "If I place things together properly, sir, I am Bahama's uncle. I think she would find that unbearably funny. I don't think I could stand having her call me Uncle David."

"I see no reason why Bahama or John should know more than they do. There is a risk. I hesitate to call it a danger but you are old enough to understand. Bahama's mother put her finger upon it. As you grow older together an attachment could easily be formed. It might destroy you both. You know what I am talking about?"

"Yes, sir." The reply was barely whispered. "I know what you mean."

"Then it must always be in your mind, David. Keep your relationship as Bahama and brother. John and brother. I can think of no other way for the moment."

"I will do my part, sir." He paused. "May I ask a great favor? It would mean much to me."

"Of course, lad."

"I—I was never allowed to call my mother's husband anything but sir. No one told me why. I always thought it strange. My mother told me I must speak to him so. I think," an odd, wistful expression crept upon his face, "he began to like me a little. It seems a long time ago now. We used to talk together, sometimes. Not much, for I suppose, since he knew I was not his son, it was difficult and painful for him. But near the end, before we left Nassau, we would speak a few words. I remember standing by his chair. He seemed such a huge and formidable man. I would always wait for him to notice me, hoping he would. Then, once in a while he would ask me a question and I would answer. But I never said the word although it was always on my tongue. May I say it now, just between the two of us?"

"It would please me, David."

"Thank you, Father." He tested the unfamiliar word with a diffident smile.

Ronald Cameron was not a man easily moved by things of a sentimental nature but this simple expression touched him deeply. In it was a lonely need, a desire for identity and a relationship, a small cry to be possessed. He cleared his throat.

"Would you mind talking things over with me just a little more, David?"

"No, Father." The word was all but timidly spoken. "I would like to."

"The next time I go to Nassau," Cameron was deliberate, "I will make certain legal inquiries. I think it would be better for all of us if I made formal application for adoption. Then no one will ever think to question your place in the family. I am more than certain your mother will agree but we will need, I think, her permission."

"You know where she is, then?" The question came with unexpected eagerness.

"I had a letter. You remember. Part of it I read to you. She was about to be married again. I may have some difficulty in locating her in such a large place as London but we can try."

David stood up. "When you do, Father," he smiled a secret smile which only he and the man could understand, "tell her I am all right and happy; I feel nothing but love for her; that I have missed her. There is no longer any bitterness or confusion in my mind over what happened. I think she might like to know."

Cameron arose from his chair and walked around the table. He and the boy gazed at each other and then Cameron's hands took David's shoulders and pulled him close, holding him with a tight possessiveness in his powerful arms. The act surprised them both, for Ronald Cameron was not a demonstrative man.

"We will find our way together, David, my son; although I cannot call you that openly just now. I am sorry I can't give you what I tried to give Robert Bruce. I was younger then and a companionship was possible. I have grown old these past years. I do not sit a horse as well and tire easily but we will find things which can be shared. Robert Bruce has gone his own way as a man should. In a measure you can take his place beside me. Now," he thumped David heartily across the shoulders, "go on with whatever it is you, Bahama and John were planning. We could use a treasure should you find it."

After the boy had left he searched through the litter of papers, hoping to find the short note which Sabrina had penned from London. It had, he recalled vaguely, an address. Perhaps a letter to her there would be forwarded. At least he could try. He was certain Sabrina would have no objection to the proposed adoption and then this David, who was of his body, could speak the word "father" as he so yearningly wished. The Cameron name would not be lost to this island as he had feared.

⋘ XVI ⋙

THE DAY broke with a curious, leaden quality and the sea, which had been running strongly and with a fresh wind to whip it the night before, was ominously calm as though flattened out beneath a tremendous weight. Even the gulls which hunted ceaselessly with their thin, piping cries and flashing sweeps had disappeared. There was no sound, no movement, but the silence was not that of a quiet and peaceful scene. Instead, it bore an almost frightening quality to which the ear was unaccustomed.

Standing in the well of the ketch, Ronald Cameron bent over a bucket of water, drawn for him by one of the slave boys. He sloshed the salty freshness over his face and ran wet fingers through his hair as a comb. With a piece of toweling he dried himself and studied the sky. No sudden squall was forming to bring a short-lived rain and scudding clouds. What he looked at was solid, a slowly moving gray mass through which the sun could not penetrate. He had the odd feeling of balancing himself on an insecure footing within an enormous vacuum in which breathing was difficult.

Anchored within the low protection of a hillocked cove, southwest of Great Guana Cay, there was not even sea enough to rock the sturdy craft. He studied the mast's tip and it did not vary an inch from its stationary position. Behind him he could hear the two slave boys whispering to each other. They had fired the iron brazier with charcoal and it was cherry-red now. On a grill over the coals a blackened coffeepot was coming to a boil. Slices of thick salt pork sizzled in their accumulated fat. One of the boys, his hook baited with small bits of conch meat, fished near the bottom among the heavy, green weed in the clear water. He held the line between his fingers and as the little grunts of striped blue and silver took the lure hungrily he snatched quickly, lifting the catch clear of the water and into the boat. There was no playing about for larger fish. This was the simple business of getting breakfast. The other boy scaled and gutted the prizes as they were released, flapping wildly, from the barb. He rolled them into coarse ground corn meal until they were fully coated. When the pork was brown and crisp the slices were taken from the pan and the fish laid in the hot grease where they cooked quickly, the meal turning them to a dark, golden color of crackling delicacy.

These were island-born slaves, the grandsons of the original stock Cameron had brought to the Bahamas. They knew the water and weather, the reefs and cays, as their parents had known the soil back in Carolina. As they worked they talked softly to each other and glanced now and then at the sky. Heavy thunderheads, a sudden rain squall, the slow building up of dirty weather, they would have accepted as something to be endured and ridden out. This silence, though, disturbed them for they knew, through experience, a hurricane was gathering its forces far beyond their range of vision. Somewhere it was revolving slowly, churning, increasing in power, picking up a momentum they could not yet see but only sense.

One of the boys filled a thick mug with the black coffee. The other laid out the pork, fish and crudely sliced bread on a tin plate. The food was carried to Cameron, who nodded his acceptance as it was placed before him on a wooden crate serving as a table.

"Win' mekkin' up, Marstah Boss." The boy spoke unemotionally. "Bin puttin' hitse'f togeder ahl naight."

"I know, Alick." Cameron seated himself on a low stool and drank from the coffee mug. "I can feel it." He bit into one of the pork slices and chewed with meditative pleasure and a sudden hunger. He took one of the fish, tossing it from hand to hand until it cooled a little. Then he broke it in half and stripped the white flesh away from the bone with his fingers. "It's heavy in the air."

"Come d win' dis boad don' hol' heah en liddle cobe. We bes' mek sail en fin' sheltah up neah Wax Cut Cay kin we mek hit, Marstah Boss."

Cameron belched softly from the hot coffee in an empty stomach. "You tell me how we're going to make sail without a wind, Alick, and that's exactly what we'll do." He licked his fingertips and took a second fish. "I don't like it here any better than you."

The boy thought this over for a minute and then retreated aft where he joined his companion. They hunkered down and ate in silence. One of them tossed a crust of bread high into the air and watched as it fell back into the water. Ordinarily a dozen or more keen-eyed gulls would have seen the movement and pursued it with a swift, keening dive.

The slave, Chris, watched the bread for a moment. "Whin d gull leave d win' come. You evah wondah wheah dey go? How dey know win' mekkin' up?"

Alick broke a fish in half. "Dey know laik you, me an' d Marstah Boss know. Dey smell hit. Dey feels hit. Oney difference is d gull gots sense enough to leave a place laik dis en fin' hisse'f a big islan' to sheltah on 'til win' pass on." He ate the fish, chewing the small bones along with the meat. "Bes' tek d Marstah Boss moah coffee. Whin he finish us gits some, mebbe."

Chris straightened up and carried the pot to Cameron.

"Just half a cup, Chris. You boys take the rest." He lit a short-stemmed pipe. The tobacco tasted good with the coffee.

For almost three years he had put off this trip to Nassau for the purpose of starting the first, legal negotiations for the adoption of David Heath. Part of the delay had been due to sheer inertia. He didn't want to make the effort. Also, David was so much a part of the household already that adoption seemed a ridiculous and unnecessary formality. He had half hoped to hear from Sabrina. He had written her at the address carried on her letter received so many years ago. There had been no reply. She had either left England and so never received his communication or had deliberately neglected to answer it. It was quite possible his letter had never reached England. The service was not too reliable and missives were often transferred from ship to ship whose destinations were scattered or the vessels themselves lost at sea. He was almost certain her consent would have to be obtained to make an adoption legal. Also, and this he admitted only to himself, the procrastination was his own lack of willingness to endure the voyage in the ketch and its discomfort. The *Traveler* had long since gone out of service. A new schooner had replaced her but the schedule was erratic. There was no longer enough trade in the Out Islands to make regular runs profitable and the vessel rarely put in at Exuma. It ran between Nassau, Eluthera and Dunmore Town, on Harbor Island. When he went to Nassau it would have to be aboard the ketch and he no longer found any pleasure in sailing the island waters.

I am, he told himself reluctantly, an old man, aged in body and spirit. On his next birthday he would have passed seventy. They were, he thought, all growing old. Caroline. It was curious but he always thought of her as a child. Caroline would be in her forties. This did not seem possible for in some magic way she had managed to hold to her youth as had Juan. Perhaps, he reflected, it was the unmistakable love they shared which kept them glowing with vitality. They still found an excitement in each other and the small world in which they lived. It kept the years at bay, holding them off or refusing to recognize their passing. He had never fully recovered from his original astonishment over this union. The initial anger had been replaced by amazement. In the beginning he would have sworn it would not last out the year. Juan would grow restless, tire of his confinement and the virginal freshness of the girl he had married. One day he would pick up his guitar and slip quietly away in his sloop. Or, Caroline would come to understand the mismating. She would find this strange minstrel's crudities beyond enduring and turn to her father for help in ridding herself of him. It had not happened that way, though. Time was a loom which had only woven them closer together. The twins were the threads of bright color running through their lives. They were, he was forced to admit, that rarest of all matings, a completely happy and contented couple. Time had brushed them with the lightest of wings. Daily they seemed to find a new joy in everything —their children, their home, even the difficulties that must be met and solved.

He knocked the dottle from his pipe and refilled it. His eyes again conned the sky which now seemed to have lowered, pressing upon them within the insecure anchorage of the cove. He lifted his face, hoping to feel the light touch of a breeze upon it or the warmth of the sun as it began to break through the cover. There was nothing. For the moment they existed within a void. The wind, though, would come. Of that there could be no mistake. How, though, would it reach them? He could only ask it build gradually, giving them enough to fill the sails and send the ketch heeling in a foaming race to a safer place of shelter before the full power of its unseen mass strike them with a single devastating blow. Glancing back he watched the slave boys as they rested upon their haunches, speaking in inaudible tones to each other, scanning the sea, estimating the cover of the small crook of coconut-tree-lined island. It was too small even to have been given a name or marked on a chart. They had thought to do no more than lay within the cove overnight. Now there was no way out of their anchorage, no wind to balloon the sails. They waited as did he with a quiet apprehension of the unknown. The hurricanes which built up in the Caribbean could sweep this part of the Atlantic with sudden and terrifying force. They had known them over the years and did not underestimate their power for destruction. Usually, the only warning they ever had was a time such as this—a period of eerie calm, the sense of deadness when the sea itself was unable to raise even a small wave and there was not enough breeze to send a palm frond rippling.

He put a fresh light to his pipe. This was a time of waiting and he used it to muse upon the alteration the years had brought. In each of them could be marked a certain moment, a date or day bringing an imperceptible change which seemed, at that hour, to have no importance in the even current of their lives. Looking back now, though, he could imagine the Cameron family once standing like a deeply rooted tree from which, now and then, a single leaf would fall. In the beginning that which he hoped to create here had been momentarily disturbed when Wells and the other assistant overseer, who had been with him since they were boys on the Ashley, had left to return to the mainland. Then Grayson, into whose brain was packed the wisdom of long experience with the land and slaves, had resigned. Even Spithead, lowest on the ladder of command, married one of the three Ferguson girls and quit to work his father-in-law's small plantation. Tom Gurney, without whose knowledge of the islands and water and the handling of boats they would have been all but marooned for a while, had also married a girl on Crooked Island and gone with her to live there. Robert Bruce. No one could blame him. He wanted a different, better life. He and Constance were comfortably settled in Charleston. A good position had been found for him with the firm of Renevant and Decatur, which was lucratively engaged in a coastwise and international commercial trade. But this left another bare spot upon a branch. No longer so fully leafed, the tree, though, still stood. Caroline and Juan. Bahama, John and David. Of these he felt a certain confidence. None had ever expressed a desire for a life beyond what he or she now lived.

He was moved to a brief smile as he thought of Caroline's exasperation over their inability to lure a tutor to Exuma for the children. Failing in this they had managed a few terms at the missionary school on Eluthera. Their education was of the most rudimentary nature. Their speech, through association with the island people, was filled with the curious phrasings of the Bahamian dialect. It was part of those who had come from the Southern colonies, some of it the accent of Yorkshire, Suffolk, Devon, Wales and the cities of London and Liverpool. It was colored by a little French and Spanish, left by the early pirates who came to raid and then settled for a quieter life. It was tinctured by the blending of the Afro-English evolved by the slaves. Well, he thought, if these islands were to be their home then they were better off adapting themselves to them rather than to ape falsely the more cultured manners and speech to which they had been born.

As for the plantation, he had achieved a resigned philosophy. It had been a dream of shining magnificence. The awakening had been slow and reluctant. It produced little more than they actually needed for themselves and the blacks who remained. They grew considerable cane which went into raw sugar and rum. Beans, melons, fruit, yams and corn were crops of steady yield but the excess was small for profitable export.

[259]

A baffling disease had all but wiped out the once fairly large and sturdy herd of cattle. The ones which survived were a constant source of trouble. They strayed and had to be rounded up, herded out of the scrub. A small flock of sheep and a pen of swine provided meat for the table, and some years there were enough left over to sell in Nassau. The fish in the sea were as plentiful as ever. These were smoked and eaten by the slaves, who never seemed to tire of a monotonous diet of beans, fatback, cornmeal mush and fish.

He had grown indifferent, almost, in the matter of his slaves. Those of the household who had become so old they were all but useless had been replaced by younger blacks of the second generation. Gabriel had long since retired to a toothless state of somnolence. He sat, now, all day in the sun, his gums working constantly as though he chewed upon something. His eyes were without recognition of the familiar things about him. When, as he sometimes did, Cameron stopped by his ancient body slave's cabin, Gabriel would look up and make a feeble attempt to rise but he had lost track of time and person and no longer recognized Ronald Cameron.

"Marstah Angus." He mumbled the words and bowed a grizzled head to Ronald as he confused him with Angus Cameron, dead these many years. "Good day, sah."

Almost all of the field hands had drifted away. They were scattered through the maze of islands. Cameron had made no attempt to pursue for he could no longer carry the burden of feeding and clothing them all. There was no market for the blacks in the Bahamas any longer. The Negro population in the islands had reached almost eleven thousand, far more than the planters had need for. The half-castes, those who obviously had been sired by white men, were automatically freed at birth and produced a floating, migratory band drifting from island to island, or settled in the communities fringing Nassau and were a constant problem to the authorities. The ones who simply ran away from their island masters were still technically slaves but since no one had any use for them no claim was made, no appeal to the Government voiced for their return. It was, Cameron thought, a most curious state of affairs. At the rate they bred, the blacks would someday overrun the islands and the slaves would take over the land on which they were once held in bondage.

A gust of wind startled Cameron out of his reverie and caused the two slave boys to leap up expectantly. It whipped across the ketch and was gone. They waited in eager silence for a steady, continuing current to flow. It did not come. Their eyes could follow the gust as it passed beyond, lashing for a moment at the dead sea before it died out and left it motionless again. The blacks slowly squatted back on their hams and Cameron was left to his vagrant musings and memories.

Why, he wondered, did he not rebel with his old vigor against that which the years had brought? Why was he almost content to accept things as they were. Age? Perhaps. But more than that, his adversary was an intangible foe. He could not come to grips with it. He was maneuvered by situations he could not control and the life he and his family now lived would have once seemed inconceivable. They were surrounded by the faded relics of a once bountiful existence. The manor he had built still reared proudly upon the ridge and commanded a view of the sea and once thriving fields. Among themselves, and in the presence of an occasional visitor on his way to and from an adjacent island, they maintained the courtesy and graciousness into which they had been born. With these things there was no compromise. Their meals were served with an almost mocking formality. Caroline permitted no laxity on the part of the house slaves or her children. She accepted the duties once assumed by her sister-in-law, Constance. If the household slaves were reduced to a uniform dress of the cheap, grayish slave cloth of cotton which had previously been the mark of the field hands and yard boys, they were made to keep themselves scrupulously neat and clean. A male slave, who had been instructed in the duties long performed by Gabriel, still stood in silent attention behind Cameron's chair and with a nod of his head or a gesture of the hand supervised the service of those who brought food to the table. If the starched white aprons and caps, the uniforms and liveries, were things of memory, those who wore the substitutes were sternly forced to do so with a semblance of pride. The fragile china and crystal had yielded to the years and they barely had service for the family. The fine wines, the afterdinner Oporto and brandy, no longer brought the evening dining to a close. In their place Cameron and Juan now took a glass or two of the rum distilled from their own cane.

As he reflected upon these many things Cameron realized how narrowly they all skirted travesty. It was avoided by an unspoken determination on his and Caroline's part not to yield as had some of the other old, and once affluent, Colonial families they had known. Even Juan discovered in himself an unsuspected defiance. He had drawn this, not by imitation but through an unconscious admiration and still growing love for the girl he had married. He was aware, even though dimly, of what the family, of which he was a part, fought for. He did not fully comprehend the reason. Nothing in his background could give him a complete understanding of what the Camerons meant to the Camerons. From the things Caroline had told him he evolved a vague, and possibly distorted, image of what Cameron Hall on the Ashley had been. In elementary terms this meant wealth, and in the early years of his marriage he would have accepted this for what it represented—fine clothes, money which need not nor could be counted; a great house and all but unimaginable acres of land; carriages and coaches, beautiful women wearing fine jewels, men who were expertly tailored, with slaves to dress, shave and bathe them. Those were the important things of life for the ones who enjoyed them. But now he could see something else. He had no word for it. Once, almost ashamed for the first time in his life of his ignorance, he had asked Caroline. It was their habit to lie in bed at night, his arm holding her, listening to the sea, talking when they felt like it, keeping an intimate silence when there was no need for words or a desire to speak them.

"Why are you what you are? Why is Papa what he is?" He fumbled, trying to express what he meant. "I mean, when you and Papa know this place isn't and never will be what he expected, how is it we—you and Papa, mostly—I don't know how to say it—stand so straight and it makes me want to do it too? When you don't really have nothin' anymore like you once had, how do you make everything you do an' say seem like you still got the biggest fish on your line when the truth is you're only hangin' on to an empty hook?"

"I love you, Juanio." She murmured the words with infinite tenderness.

"That ain' what I ask, girl." He drawled the words.

"I know." She rubbed her cheek against his. "It isn't easy to explain. What made Juan Cadiz sail a little boat with a red sail as though it was the finest racing hull in the world? How did he grow up on Nassau's waterfront, a boy with no name, surrounded by filth and not have it cling to him? What gave him the confidence to sail in here and take away Ronald Cameron's daughter? How was it he could live in a shack on Long Island and not be satisfied to remain there?"

"I wanted to marry a girl with a lot of money so I don't do nothin' anymore."

"Uh-uh, Juanio. You used to fool me but you don't any longer. There is a word for what we do here. I'm not sure it is the right one but I can think of no other. It is pride, Juanio. Courage, maybe, I'm not certain. It is what made you come to me once long ago and say: I would like to learn to read and write. It is what made you concern yourself with the plantation after Robert Bruce left, when you knew it was already a failure."

"I got to live someplace." He tried to sound indifferent. "This is as good as any."

[262]

"No." She was softly emphatic.

"Well, then, I feel sorry for Papa."

"No," she repeated.

"All right, then." There was a note of exasperation in his voice. He was being crowded into what he felt was an admission of sentimental weakness. "I do it for you, Juan Cadiz, John, Bahama. How the hell do I know?"

"You're getting close, Juanio." She smiled in the darkness.

"I don't want them to grow up like the conch children on the other islands, satisfied with a piece of fish an' a bowl of beans or a pot of chowder. So they know nothin' an' say 'sir' like they was crawling on their bellies instead of sayin' 'sir' the way Robert Bruce did with Papa because it was right an' they both understood."

"That's what I mean by pride, Juanio."

He mulled this over. "I think, always, pride is what makes you think you're better than someone else. I've seen the proud people who live on the hill in Nassau. When they rode in their carriages along the bay street they held a lace handkerchief to their noses or pulled down the curtains of the coach so nobody could look at them or they didn't have to look at nobody."

"Those are the stupid, arrogant people."

"Arrogant?" He tried the word. "I don't hear that one before. It's different from this thing you call pride?"

"Yes, Juanio." She sat up and gazed down at him. Her eyes were shining. "It is different. The people you are talking about don't have pride, or courage either, and they're afraid someone will find it out. Pride," she tried to capture the inflection of his voice in what he had said a few minutes before, "pride is what makes you hold to the line like you've got the biggest fish in the world on the end of it when you know in your heart you're only hanging on to an empty hook. But you don't show it. You stand there and figure a way to catch that fish and not ask anyone to help you."

"You steal my words, girl." He was secretly pleased. "You take them from me an' they sound better."

She lay back again, pressing within the circle of his arm and thought of those first two years after Robert Bruce and Constance had left for Nassau and Charleston. Her father had felt the loss of his son with a sharp pain. It could be read in his words and actions. He was indifferent to everything. No longer did he plan and seek new ways of revitalizing the plantation; of drawing success somehow from failure. He would sit for hours on the broad porch, staring blankly and with cloudy eyes at the ocean. He was without the will, the spirit, to do more.

[263]

Juan and Caroline frequently kept him silent company there. They both understood his brooding apathy but could think of no words to assuage his quiet grief. It was as though Robert Bruce had died and with him some of Ronald Cameron. One afternoon, as Cameron rocked slowly as someone sometimes sways back and forth in unspoken anguish, Caroline and Juan sat on the steps below his chair.

"Papa." Juan had broken the all but unendurable silence. "I got the idea you sit here too long. I think, maybe, I'd like to take you on a little trip. We use the ketch an' I bring along my old woman here." He wrapped an arm about Caroline's knees, drawing her closer. "I want to show you some places I know about. You remember? Long time ago I say to you we maybe have to go to the sea if the plantation don't turn out like you hope. What I got in mind don't make you rich, like before. It ain't goin' to grow cotton where cotton won't grow. It won't give you no big fields to ride over in the morning but," he paused, "it just, maybe, make you a little interested in something again an' you just don't sit an' see nothing."

"Where do you want to go?" These were the first words he had spoken for hours. "I am in no mood for a sailing excursion."

"We don't go for fun, Papa."

It had taken all of their efforts at persuasion to arouse Cameron from his lethargy. He kept muttering about "damn fool nonsense, leaving a comfortable porch and bed for a bunk on a ketch." In the end, though, he finally consented but still making it appear as though he were humoring a couple of restless children. The ketch had been provisioned and with a slave boy as a hand of all work they had cruised far up and down the banks and cays, through uncharted waters. Juan had marked certain spots in his mind long ago and needed no chart to take him there.

They had dropped sail and drifted slightly on a calm sea. It was midmorning on the second day out.

"You take the lookin' bucket, Papa." Juan handed Cameron the wooden pail with the circular pane of glass in its base. "See what I know is there. I don't think any man look at it before."

Cameron held the contrivance to the surface and peered down. Through it the bottom could be clearly seen in detail and the dark, heavy-massed sponge beds as they spread in a prolific growth.

"Long time ago, when I have nothing on my mind but to sail my boat an' play my guitar, goin' where I please with no hurry, I find this sponge bed an' a dozen more like it. Then I don't care. They just somethin' to look at no one seen before. I don't ever figure to do anything about them because I never care for work much, Papa." He was trying to urge the old man to an interest. "Nobody ever grained these beds before.

[264]

Mostly they work other waters which is easier to get to. There's sponge here, an' in the places I know, to keep a crew working for years. We don't grow cotton in the fields but the sea grow this sponge for us. I think you an' me make good partners in this thing if you want it to be so. You tell me yes an' I'll begin to train a nigger crew. We start spongin' like nobody's done before in these islands. Like I say. We don't get rich. It won't be what you know about an' it ain't what you come to the Bahamas for. But, we have money coming in again. More money than anything on the plantation make. What you think about that, Papa?"

Cameron put the water glass aside. His eyes showed the first spark of interest they had seen in a long time. The idea of sponging, on a commercial scale, was completely foreign to everything to which he had been born. To his mind it was simply a form of fishing. A Cameron, plantation bred, a fisherman. He was all but repelled when he stated it in his mind. A fisherman was a black who peddled his catch from door to door. Despite this definition some of Juan's enthusiasm communicated itself. To share it, though, he must first rid himself of prejudice and then call upon all of his will to make a complete reevaluation of everything he had been taught to respect and accept as his birthright. Ronald Cameron, planter. Ronald Cameron, sponger. A world separated the two.

"Papa." Juan studied him keenly and, somehow, knew what was in his mind. "I don't mean you become a hooker. I get that work done. You take care of the business end in Nassau like we got a thing you're the head of. On the mainland you have a big plantation. You got people to run it for you. You grow things an' you sell them—rice, cotton, indigo—things like that, Caroline tell me. Well, now, you have a different kind of plantation; this one under water. It grow things, too, an' you sell them. Is there some kind of real difference, Papa? Of course," he laughed quickly and with an honest amusement, "you don't go riding no fine horse in the morning to look things over an' set a gang to labor. A man could get himself real drowned doin' a thing like that. What you say about it, Papa?"

There was, Cameron thought, a crude logic in what Juan said. He could not yet bring himself to accept the idea with any real enthusiasm but it provoked a certain stimulation he had not felt in a long time. It was far better, he conceded, than the stagnation he had been enduring. There would, at least, be some meaning to his stubborn clinging to this island; something of value, and he did not mean to equate this with shillings and pounds alone.

"Do what you want, Juan." He shrugged as though the thing was a matter of indifference. "The niggers we have left have little enough to do as it is."

This was another thing Caroline had noticed lately about her father. In all the years since she could remember, she had never heard him refer to the slaves as niggers. He spoke of them as "the people" or "the hands." Now, there was something almost contemptuous in his use of the word nigger. It was as though he consciously blamed them for the plantation's failure.

When they returned home Juan set about selecting his crews. He took the young, strong slaves who had been born on Exuma and to whom the water was a natural element. Patiently he taught them the art of hooking the sponges. The Bahamians called it "graining" and they used a tool of trident design which could take the sponge from its bed without tearing. Far up the island Juan had the crawls built. Here, when the boats came in and unloaded, the sponges were spread out. The animal life within them rotted away. Then the sponges were washed, bleached and dried in the hot sunshine. Once every two months now the sponges were taken, in long strings, to Nassau and delivered to a factor who, under Cameron's instructions, auctioned them to London buyers. For the first time in years a steady, if modest, income was being returned to Exuma.

They had three boats with which to work: the ketch and two sloops. Juan put John and David in charge of the smallest craft and their crews. Often, after they had cleared Exuma, they did not hail each other for days, each working a bed of his choice. With the responsibility the boys developed a new self-confidence. They grew in stature and wisdom, learning much of the sea and its unpredictable ways and how to handle and live with their black crews. They worked all but naked, wearing only short drawers, and the sun tanned their skin to the color of polished cinnamon bark. With the work came a new sensation of proud accomplishment and they grew closer in the feeling they were making a contribution to the household.

Although what Juan had done made no great difference in their manner of living it did infuse a new vitality. Even Cameron yielded to the spirit. The reunions, when the boats returned, had an air of festivity about them. There were stories to tell. The half-buried timbers of an ancient galleon sunk a century ago and visible in the clear water of a reef. A turtle the size of the dining room table which they had pursued vainly, trying to get a spear into it or a rope about a flipper. The talk was constant and filled with excitement. When Cameron's factor reported a higher price for the sponges than anyone had expected they experienced a collective jubilation over the success.

Sometimes Juan put into Nassau before returning home and he secured an advance from the factor against his cargo. Then he brought back with him some yardage of silk and gaily printed muslin for new dresses to be made for Caroline and Bahama. He would buy an extravagant comb, set with brilliants, or stockings of silk; linen and sheer cotton for nightdress and underthings. Although many times his taste in such purchases was slightly on the barbaric side, Caroline never hinted they were not exactly what she had been dreaming of. As for Juan, he seemed to find a dry and amusing humor in his display of energy.

"I sure never think Juan Cadiz work this hard for anyone."

They had just returned from a cruise. A suckling pig had been slaughtered and roasted, brought to the table with a bright, golden orange in its mouth. There were a few bottles of wine left and one had been opened for the occasion. The meal was transformed into a banquet. After the table had been cleared, the rum brought out, the pipes alight, David and John remained. No longer did they rush out to rough-and-tumble games with Bahama. Such antics were far below their dignity now that they were men who shared a responsibility. Bahama glowered at them both but particularly at David. She was at the age now when a casual contact with him, a brushing of their bodies, a touch of his hand, filled her with an emotion she did not understand. She missed the sailing trips of imaginary exploration for buried treasure they had shared; the rides on the hard-packed beach when they raced their mounts in shouting contests; the fishing and games they had invented. With their frequent absences now she felt she was no longer a part of John and David's life. It was David she really missed. John, after all, was only a brother. Caroline had sometimes caught the expression of frustration on her daughter's face. She understood the reason and it troubled her. This matter of David must be brought into the open even though she was aware of the shame and heartache it would cause. She sat now on Juan's lap, watching Bahama's restless toying with a sea bean she had polished to a bright red ornament to be worn on a string around one's neck as a good luck charm.

"You know," Juan was oblivious of her study of Bahama, "you get to be a pretty old girl now but to me you look like you did that first day I see you on the dock. When we get married"—he grinned at Cameron and then his glance swept the table to include the others—"I say from now on I live good. No more shack on Long Island. I got a beautiful wife, a big house an' a papa with plenty of money. Now, by God, I work like a nigger with a whip to his back. I don't have time to play the guitar so much anymore. When I was in Nassau last time I stop by a place I used to know. I look at the girls an' say: I guess I better be gettin' along back home, now. This Juan Cadiz." He shook his head in mystification.

[267]

"He don't turn out at all like I expect. You know," he addressed Cameron, "what I'd like to do, Papa?"

"What now, Juan?" Cameron had long ago lost his hostility for this strange man who refused to grow old. He even felt a grudging admiration which he would not admit. "You've already turned a plantation into a damned sponging camp."

Juan understood the old man far better than anyone suspected. He could no longer be made angry or irritated by what he said or did. He had a droll affection for his moments of crankiness.

"I'd like to make enough money for us to buy a schooner; a hundred and forty-eight feet or more an' a broad beam so we take her anyplace. Then we don't just work these islands but, maybe, carry trade back and forth from the mainland to Nassau. We take our sponges to Carolina, Georgia; maybe as far as New York or Boston and we get twice what the factor is paid at the Nassau auctions. Then we bring back cargo to Nassau or make the run to the Havana. Wherever there's trade we find it. What do you say about that, Papa?" He could not keep the animation from his words.

"You're taking me a long way, Juan." Cameron spoke with unmistakable wonder. "Everything you do is new and strange to me."

"Is that bad, Papa?" The question was soft.

"No, boy." It was the first time Cameron had ever addressed Juan Cadiz in such a manner. It was almost as though he spoke to Robert Bruce. "It isn't bad. Do you know something?" There was the smallest suggestion of a grudging smile. "I may end by liking you."

"You like me already, Papa. You know that. You just too stubborn to say so out loud. We work to get that schooner, hey?"

Cameron took a sip of his rum and rolled it on his tongue before swallowing. He studied the bright gleam in Juan's eyes. The love which shone on his daughter's face. The interest on the part of John, David, and even Bahama.

"There is considerable debate in Parliament." He spoke slowly. "There is unmistakable and formidable agitation in the Home Government for the freeing of all the slaves. I think it will come about. It is a trend; a new treatment of man toward man which gains support. I have followed it in the London journals. When it happens, and it may be sooner than we think, the blacks will be freed but the Crown will make compensation to their former owners."

"What is this 'compensation,' Papa?" The word was one which Juan did not understand.

"Payment. The Crown will put a value on the slaves freed and pay those who held them. To us might come as much as a thousand pounds, for even those who have run away are still technically Cameron property. When that happens, Juan, you buy your schooner. What I had expected from Robert Bruce is now for you to do. I am getting old and do not trust my judgment as I once did. I was mistaken about you, Juan. It isn't easy for me to say this. I still think you are a bit of a scoundrel at heart but maybe, in this new order of things, that is not bad. The time will come when you will have to run this place and hold the family together. I do not often admit to error in my judgment."

"You're still a pretty big man, Papa." Juan said this cheerfully. "I never think you really give up. Things just come along you don't know about. Island living ain't like any other an' it mix you up some but you don't really change. But me? This Juan I don't understand at all. I get ambition an' that's a funny thing."

Sitting in the ketch before the remains of his breakfast now, Cameron thought back to that evening. His mind, he admitted, seemed to wander more and more of late. He found it difficult to hold to a thought for any length of time. Incidents, snatches of conversation, crept unbidden from the past. The thoughts roved freely and without purpose. He would catch himself recalling something done or said fifty years ago and these things had no relation to the moment or what had occupied his mind only a minute or two before. This disturbed him, for he had always associated such aimless maunderings with a helpless dotage.

He felt a few drops of rain on his face and looked up quickly. Far out beyond their anchorage he saw the sea ripple as a gust of wind seemed to run down a narrow alley, disturbing nothing on either side of it.

"Marstah Boss." Alick stood respectfully before him. "We bes' make ready to run from heah whin we can. The win', she come soon now but from what quartah no one know. Hit could drive us raight up en d bank. Us got to get out o' heah an' git some sea room."

No breeze as yet disturbed the cove but Cameron knew the boy was right. If it came suddenly and from an unexpected quarter they would be without room to maneuver. Although both of the slaves had far more knowledge of the sea, he understood they waited for him to take command.

"Let's see if we can kedge her out of here, Alick." The cove was sheltered by a long, crooked finger of land, forming a semicircle. The water was fairly shallow, not much more than the ketch's draft. "Maybe we can ease her out beyond the point and into the open."

"Yessuh, Marstah Boss." Alick was relieved by Cameron's decision to take some action. He shouted to Chris. "We goin' to haul us a piece, boy. You do now git d hook an' line. We fling hit fah as we kin en den

[269]

fling some moah." He went forward and began taking in the heavy anchor which had held them throughout the night.

While Cameron watched, the boys worked from the bow. Chris held a coil of rope some thirty feet in length. At one end a four-pronged hook was made fast. Alick dangled this from about four feet and began to whirl it in an accelerating motion. When the contrivance had gained a maximum speed he loosed it, and the pronged iron went flying out ahead of the boat as Chris allowed the line to pay from his hands. The hook splashed and disappeared, sinking to the bottom. Chris tugged on the rope experimentally and when they were satisfied the hooks were solidly embedded, both boys began to pull. The ketch inched forward, moving slowly until the bow was over the spot where the iron lay. Then they shook it loose and the process was repeated. It was slow, back-straining work but each time the action was duplicated the ketch advanced some ten yards out of the cove. It took a full two hours to get her clear of the spit, for as the water deepened, the less line they had to work with. Finally, they were out and drifting imperceptibly seaward on an ebbing tide. They were, at least, safely away from the beach and the coral bottom which could tear the boat's hull to pieces if a sudden wind drove her upon it. The boys sank to the deck, breathing heavily. One immediate danger had been averted.

Now, the storm they could not yet feel began to build with a slow inexorability. They had seen too many not to know what was happening. It revealed itself in erratic coursing, moving in zigzag lines as a hunting dog might cast over a field. There were sudden, short-lived gusts coming from unexpected quarters. They swept across the ketch, rocked it and passed on. The boys studied the sky, felt the wind and from long experience tried to estimate how much time they had.

"Marstah Boss." Alick was diffident. "How much sail you figuh to raise?"

Cameron understood this was only a courtesy. His opinion was being asked because he was the master.

"Both of you know more about sailing than I do." He did not pretend to a knowledge he didn't have. "Do what you think should be done."

The boys stood side by side. If the storm didn't hit them suddenly but gathered its strength with a fair wind pushing ahead of the hurricane itself, then they could risk canvas enough to carry them swiftly to a place of safety. They talked it over with serious expressions and then moved to set the mizzenmast sail. In a ketch this mast is stepped well forward. It was a risk, they knew. Prudence dictated the jib. It would give them steerageway but not the speed they so desperately wanted if they were to outrun the brewing danger.

[270]

There was no consistency in the wind. It reeled and staggered as a drunk might walk; coming in steadily for a few minutes from south southwest, dying out and then unexpectedly striking at them from an easterly quarter. Each time the sail exploded, the craft would heel and then the canvas fall limply and without the pressure to fill it until another gust struck them.

They could see the rain coming long before it reached them. It was as though a wall of opaque gray was slowly being pushed forward. It came down in a straight, heavy curtain, pouring, heaving and steaming upon the sea. When it did reach the ketch its force was such that they cringed beneath the stinging blow. The water seemed not liquid but solid pellets. Behind it came the forerunner of the storm itself. The wind was heavy. It had direction but was without the full power of a hurricane. That lay somewhere behind the advancing rain and wind. Now, the ocean seemed to rise. It was an optical illusion. It swelled not in high charging waves but as though it bulged upward from the very bottom of the ocean in a tremendous heave. The ketch heeled on a quarter beam as it raced to the northeast.

Both of the boys braced themselves at the helm. From the cabin Cameron brought out heavy, tarred coats. He put one on and then made his unsteady way toward the slaves, offering one to each. They both shook their heads with courtesy. There was no time or opportunity. All of their strength and attention was on the flying craft. This was not the hurricane, only its probing tentacles which were whipping out ahead of the parent body as it revolved and moved slowly in their direction. For the first time, though, all of them were aware of a whining moan. It had the sound of a giant's harp vibrating on a single note. Through the rain as it enveloped them they could see nothing. The ocean seemed to lift in a pall of smoke as the clouds, lower now, poured tons of water on its vast expanse.

"We bes' git d sail down en set d liddle one fo'wad. Whin d win' really come hit take dat mas' out like it was a stick of wood. D ol' man," there was no disrespect in the reference to Cameron, "he ain' goin' to be much hep."

Cameron braced his feet wide apart and then, realizing he could not stand, half lay, clinging to a thwart and trying to steady himself against the pitching course. His white hair was plastered against his head and face. He wiped it away with a free hand but the rain poured upon him with such force he could not hold his eyes open. He could not help but realize the ridiculousness of his position. He was, after all, the master and he felt he was cringing. He knew he should try and take in the big sail but was without the strength to do it himself. At least, he told himself, I can make an effort at standing as a man. He crawled on his hands and knees the short distance separating him from the helm. He had to feel his way through the water which was inches deep in the cockpit. This was an immediate danger and someone should be put to bailing. His fingers made contact with the bare leg of one of the boys. Dragging himself upright he leaned against the slave for support; felt the taut, corded muscles of the black leg. He was ashamed of his weakness; not of the heart but of the body which refused to obey. The years had taken their toll. A hand, he couldn't tell whether it belonged to Chris or Alick, gripped his arm and helped him to his feet. He was braced between the pair.

The rain slackened but it was still impossible to see more than a few yards beyond the bowsprit. The wind, though, unmistakably smashed at them. All three in this boat which now seemed so small had experienced the seasonal hurricanes before. They had watched heavy palms torn from their roots and sent flying through the air; cabins lifted from their foundations and torn apart; ships broken and foundering or driven high up on an island. The wind's moaning had passed. It howled now with an almost human note and the sea was mounting into heavy, foam-bearded crests into which the ketch drove with shuddering blows.

"We've got to get that sail down." The wind snatched the words from his teeth. "Cut it away."

"We can' do hit, Marstah Boss. Ain' nothin' we kin do now but hang on. A few minute moah an' d win' goin' to take d mas' raight out en we don't have to worry 'bout nothin' but stayin' afloat."

They rolled high and then over until the craft lay for one dreadful moment on her beam. It seemed impossible she would not go completely over. Then she shook herself with the sound of straining timbers and righted.

Even with six hands on the wheel it kicked and bucked as though it were an animate thing determined to escape their grasp. Then the rain came again and there was no doubt but that the boat was filling. She wallowed heavily, there was the sluggish movement of death. The storm thundered upon them with a fury no one could have believed possible.

Caught and torn at, blinded by the rain, Cameron experienced a sudden, inexplicable exhilaration. Better this way, he told himself, than to go slowly; to lie one day in bed, helpless, an object of pity, unable to perform his natural functions by himself, spoon-fed by a slave's hand, filling a room with the unmistakable stench of death.

"God damn it!" Cameron tried to scream the defiance but no one could hear the words. "We'll ride her out until she goes."

The terror of the slave boys was mixed, somehow, with superstition.

This was a black devil which tore at them. They prayed wordlessly but they had no real faith in prayer. The God they had been told about was a white man's God. He would have no ear for the cry of a nigger.

It was impossible to hear anything above the screaming of the wind, the slashing of the rain. There was nothing they could do but hold to the wheel. It was incredible to them all that the craft held together. Great fingers pried at her. Waves with the force of a charging bull slammed against her. They would ride high on a crest and crash headlong into another for they seemed to come from all directions although they ran before the wind.

They strained their eyes and peered fearfully at nothing. Then, for one miraculous but terrible instant, they seemed to dive through a hole. A whirling wind cleared, for a second, the rain obscuring their vision and they looked squarely at death. A foaming reef barely rising before them. It was smothered by the water as it churned and tore itself to flying spray against the coral teeth.

"God A'mighty!" Alick screamed.

Those were the last words any of them heard. The ketch drove upon the reef and its bottom was ripped away as though giant claws raked it from bow to stern. The masts snapped but no one was aware of the crashing, splintering sound. What was left of the boat rolled completely over once, smashing itself into a hundred pieces sent scudding out of sight.

Cameron felt a searing pain as a coral ridge tore his face into an unrecognizable mass of ribboned flesh and that was the last thing he knew.

It was over. Wind scattered the fragments, waves tossed the broken bodies, spinning them over and over, and the rain drew a gray shroud about them all as a final act of mercy.

~§ XVII §~

IT WAS only after seemingly endless days of cruising and searching up and down the long string of cays marking Exuma Sound and then in a southwesterly course to Andros Island and, finally, northerly as far as Joulter Cays, that Caroline would admit the loss of her father, the ketch and two hands. From the beginning Juan had felt the expedition a useless effort. Unless Cameron, by a miracle, had found shelter beyond the storm's reach where he could wait it out, no craft the size of the ketch could have survived the fury. He would not admit this to Caroline. Instead, he asked the assistance of boatmen from Long and Crooked islands as well as the cutters of His Majesty's Lighthouse Service. Every cay, each bight of sand and coral upon which the survivors might have clung, was probed for some sign or trace of Cameron. They found nothing, no piece of wreckage which might possibly identify the ketch. In the end it was Caroline who acknowledged the futility of continuing.

"There is no use, Juanio. Let's go home." She turned away so he would not see the tears. "I think if he ever thought about death this was the last way he would have expected it to come. He never really liked the sea and avoided it when he could. I hope he died quickly."

This had been, by far, the worst hurricane the Bahamas had suffered in years. It lay about like some frenzied thing, slashing with a wide blade, destroying entire communities, beating flat the planted fields and groves. In the aftermath it seemed impossible such violence could rear itself in these usually placid waters which had a breath-taking beauty, sparkling and colorful beneath a semitropical sun. Small villages, with their lightly constructed cottages, were obliterated entirely. What boarding remained lay scattered and shingle-flat. The fishing fleet of small boats, upon which most of the natives depended for a living, was completely destroyed. A colony of some one hundred persons who lived in isolation and eked out a living on the island of Inagua, evaporating sea water and collecting a coarse, grained salt, had not a single survivor to tell of the terror.

The rage of the storm had struck directly at Nassau with a force no one could conceive. It tore away docks and warehouses, lifted the solid roofs from many of the large houses on the hill. Every structure along the waterfront was either washed away or ripped apart as a man might tear things of cardboard in his hands. On a path a mile wide over New Providence there was incredible destruction of uprooted trees and vegetation, as though the striding feet of a colossus of unimaginable size had strode across the island, trampling everything to the ground.

Standing amid the ruins of their homes and fields in the Out Islands even the toughest and most obdurate of the colonists were willing to admit defeat. They had endured storms before. They were to be expected during the equinox. But nothing in their experience had prepared them for this and they were without the will to rebuild, replant and start the dreary cycle over again. Some would remain because they were without the means to leave. Others more fortunate in the matter of funds would quit the islands forever and go back to the mainland or England. There would be great areas, entire islands, without even a token settlement save for the blacks who would huddle together in primitive communities. The islands were to become, for years, nothing but lonely dots upon the charts and forgotten by England. They were to lie as beautiful as ever, dark green with ruffs of white sand beach, surrounded by the colors of the sea, destitute, unpopulated and destined to remain so for almost half a hundred years.

Nassau rebuilt itself slowly and without spirit for the most part. The only real determination to survive here was in the small, tight group of island aristocracy which miraculously persisted despite all adversity. There was a stubborn courage in these families and it would not permit them to admit defeat. They had severed all their ties. A second generation, which had known no other life, had begun to take over from their elders and they brought with them a surprising vitality even though it manifested itself in the most leisurely manner. New streets were laid out. The one fringing the bay widened and hard packed with shell. Roads crossing the island were hacked out by gangs of slaves. From the more influential went appeals to the Home Government for assistance. The response, if it was made at all, was grudging and parsimonious. Unlike Jamaica, which had built a thriving trade from its cane in rum and sugar, the Bahamas had little of value to export. There was often talk in Parliament of letting the "damned little islands sink beneath the water." They asked much and returned nothing. Only the Empire's greed for sheer possession of territory kept them from being abandoned. The

Crown still appointed a Governor. The Assembly functioned as best it could. But, there was no denying the poverty. The lower and middle classes of Nassau's population felt a closer tie to the United States than they did with England. The purchase of Florida by the States had removed the threat of Spanish seizure or invasion and England no longer regarded the Bahamas as being of any strategic importance. They were poor relatives. Save for the times when requests were made from Nassau to the Parliament for financial assistance, few persons outside the Home Government were really aware of their existence. They were, to those who were bothered by the continual complaints made by the Nassau Bahamians, "a damned nuisance" and there was even talk of abandoning them altogether or selling them off to the United States. But, in a period of the Empire's expansion, this was put down as irresponsible extravagance. England would hold to what it had no matter how useless.

The hurricane had not spared Exuma. The slave quarters had been swept away in flying splinters: the cane fields and citrus groves all but ruined. One wing of the manor was so thoroughly gutted it was beyond repair. It would have to be rebuilt and there was no money to pay for the construction. The battered section was torn away and the remaining lumber used to put together drafty cabins for the slaves who remained.

With the loss of Ronald Cameron the full responsibility of the Cameron holdings on the island fell to Juan. He was dryly amused by the situation. He had what was left of a plantation, a wife, John, Bahama and David.

"This sure ain' what I marry you for, girl." He winked at Caroline over the breakfast table. "How do you suppose Juan Cadiz ever got himself in such a fix?"

Bahama and John, their eyes filled with laughter, watched their father's droll expression. When he played the conch this way, slurring his words, pretending an amazed indolence, they were always delighted. He was, they both thought, the most remarkable parent anyone could have. Never did they tire of hearing the story of how he had run away with their mother, carrying her off in a sloop with a red sail, defying Grandfather Cameron. Even David was entertained. There was a bond of understanding between Juan and David. It had never been put into words. Actually, Juan was not fully aware of it. If he did feel a kinship he put it crudely to himself: Juan Cadiz was probably a bastard also. At least, no one had ever named his father. David was a little better off. He knew who had sired him. He looked up, caught David's glance and shook his head dolefully.

"You be careful, David boy. Don' marry no rich girl. It ain' turn out like you expect. Firs' thing you know you workin' for her or her papa. Marry poor. Then you know what's what from th' very first."

"I don't expect I'll get married." David munched on a piece of crisp, salted pork. "I don't know any girls."

Caroline caught Bahama's glance. It was puzzled. More, it carried a troubled astonishment. She told herself as she had so many times before that Bahama and John would have to know of the relationship. Bahama, in particular, must be made aware. Already the girl was in love or felt herself to be. She adored David with a silent worship. Everything he did or said was unbelievably wonderful and exciting. The longer she withheld the truth the deeper the hurt would go. Caroline understood this and still could not bring herself to sit down with her children and tell them who David Heath was. She had talked it over with Juan, hoping he would do what she could not.

"Most anything you ask I do. You know that. But this thing—it belongs to you and Papa. He is not here anymore. You are the one who has to do it now." He was adamant.

Still she delayed, temporized, found innumerable excuses which she herself knew were without validity. She figuratively shut her eyes as might a child, hoping something bad would go away if she made herself believe it wasn't there.

Before her on the table now was a letter from Robert Bruce. She had written him of their father's death, but because there was little trade between the islands and the mainland the passage of ships was infrequent. His reply had been long in coming, reaching Exuma this morning on a Government sloop carrying the small amount of mail dispatched to the Out Islands. She had read it first in the seclusion of her room, then brought it down to the late breakfast, reading it aloud to the others.

After expressing his sorrow, carefully phrased with the sober and undemonstrative manner into which he had grown, Robert Bruce went directly to what he considered to be of immediate importance. His advice to Caroline and Juan was that they bring the family back to Carolina and there attempt to establish a new and more secure way of life. To persist on Exuma in the face of adversity was foolhardy and without any foundation for the reality of the situation. Bahama, John and David were already on the threshold of adult life. Exuma offered them nothing but a bare living and a barren future. It was the duty of Caroline and Juan to accept this truth.

"It is," he had written, "sheer folly for you to continue where you are any longer. Even Father, if he had lived, would admit to this sooner or later although his heart was set upon making a success of the venture.

[277]

Now you must do what he would have eventually confessed, the failure of the project.

"Charleston has grown in size and importance. It is a city of gracious manners, lively entertainment, with balls and parties given during the season by the Societies and a fine commercial future. As you must know, the Cameron name in Carolina has always commanded respect. It is no vain presumption on my part to say we are closely linked with the oldest and best families. Your social position, should you care to pursue it, would be second to none. The prejudices which caused Father to abandon Cameron Hall no longer exist. The classes, in a society the Revolution assumed would be abolished, have reverted to their natural levels. In this, Father's predictions have been realized. There is no such thing as a true democracy. You would come here, not as a stranger, but warmly received and all doors opened to you as they were to me."

"I think Juan Cadiz would be one hell of a surprise to this Charleston," Juan interrupted the reading.

Caroline glanced up and across at him with a smile. In her mind she was enjoying the impact of Juan upon Charleston society. Then she continued with Robert Bruce's letter.

"John and David should be able to find suitable positions although, I must confess, I am a little troubled over this since their education must be sketchy, to say the least. Although commerce thrives this is still a plantation society. The tradesmen have no standing at all. However, the large commercial firms such as the one with which I am connected have an importance which cannot be ignored. I believe, under my guidance, we could establish John and David suitably. As for Bahama. It is far past the time when she should have the schooling suitable for a gentlewoman. There are two or three select academies for young ladies which she can attend and in time she will be able to make a suitable marriage."

"I don't want to go to a *select academy*," Bahama interrupted. "And I'll make my own marriage when I am ready and thank Uncle Robert Bruce to keep out of my affairs." There was an angry and rebellious note in her voice.

Looking at her daughter Caroline could not mistake the echo of her own words long ago when her father threatened to send her to Charleston and Aunt Martha.

"Let me finish the letter, Bahama, please." She spoke quietly.

"If, though," Caroline continued reading, "you insist upon remaining in the Bahamas, though I can think of no sane reason why you should, I gladly yield you and Juan my share of the inheritance. I give you, without reservation, that portion of the Exuma grant which the passing of our father has left to me. For my part, I want no more of the wretched place. As I grow older I find my thoughts returning more and more to what the Camerons once held with Cameron Hall, on the Ashley River here, and which, save for Father's stubborn nature, we still could own. Other families in the Low Country made the transition with a little tact and a minor concession or two. Father might have done the same.

"I come, now, to a matter of unexpected importance."

"That Robert Bruce sure talks a long letter," Juan interrupted again. "In all the time I knew him he never said so many words." He whistled softly.

Caroline held back a smile. "It seems," she read, "some of the shares which Father held in England and were presumed to be of little value have miraculously increased through a reorganization of the companies and expanding trade. Should you care to sell, and I am in a position to take them off your hands, you should realize almost three thousand pounds. With this you could return to Carolina under fair circumstances. If you remain on Exuma they will simply be drained away. Through my business connections with M. Renevant's firm I am aware of conditions in the Bahamas. There is no future in the islands and the money will simply be dribbled away in a bottomless pit. However, I am not attempting to impose my opinions on you. Long ago I learned this was impossible. You will go your way as you always have."

"He means me, Mama." Juan grinned at her.

"He means you, Papa," Caroline mimicked him.

"I do hope," Robert Bruce's communication added, "you will give thoughtful consideration to what I have written. To all of you goes my affection as well as that of Constance, who (and I should have mentioned this at the very first) is expecting a child after this long time. With devotion, Robert Bruce."

Caroline put the letter aside. She studied Juan, who leaned back in his chair and stared at the ceiling. Her glance moved to Bahama. There was no mistaking the resentment there. John appeared to be completely indifferent to everything his uncle had written. Only on David's face did she detect an animation.

"This Robert Bruce, my brother-in-law," Juan spoke to the ornate woodwork on the ceiling, "he does not say what Juan Cadiz is to do in Charleston. Maybe," he continued absently, "I sail a bumboat an' take out vegetables, fruit and some chickens when the ships come in. John he works the oar. David yells what we got to sell. I dicker an' make talk with the captain or mate. It sounds pretty good. Then we all get dressed an' go to one of those balls and parties Robert Bruce says the Societies give. What is a Society, Mrs. Caroline Cameron Juan Cadiz? I don't know much about such things."

"They are groups of ladies and gentlemen," Caroline replied as though Juan's question had been a serious one, "who amuse themselves after the fashion of ladies and gentlemen. I don't remember, though," she frowned with a spurious effort at concentration, "ever hearing of one called The Bumboat Society. Saint Cecelia, perhaps, but no Bumboat."

"Then I don't think I go." Juan dropped the front legs of his chair to the floor with a thump. "Here I've got The Spongers Society. The Conch Society. The Great Exuma Society. Why should I go to that Charleston and mix with all those foreigners? Tell me that, girl."

"I'll stay with you, Papa." Bahama played quickly to her father's humor. "We'll have a Conch Ball and invite the very best families."

"That's a very good idea." He nodded his grave approval. "I know some fine ladies and gentlemen on Long Island where I once lived." Juan pursed his lips thoughtfully over Bahama's suggestion. "Also, there are some very fine families on the Nassau waterfront. Most of them don't have any papas an' they're mixed up some in color. But, I tell you right, they sure amuse themselves after the fashion of ladies and gentlemen on the Nassau waterfront."

"All right." Caroline put an end to the nonsense, although she was on the point of laughing at Juan's absurdities. "What do we write Robert Bruce?"

"You're not serious, girl?" Juan was honestly surprised.

"About leaving Exuma and going to Charleston?" It was her turn to display a little astonishment at the question. "Of course not." She turned the idea away as though it was too preposterous to discuss. "I was thinking about the shares Papa left. Do we sell our part for the three thousand pounds Robert Bruce mentioned?"

"That's a different thing." Juan's relief was apparent. "Maybe, after all, I got a rich wife. Three thousand pounds. It makes a pile of money."

"Let me go, Uncle Juan . . . Aunt Caroline," David interrupted. He half leaned across the table with a pleading eagerness. Long ago he had adopted this form of address, calling them uncle and aunt after Cameron had explained the true relationship. They were negative titles in this case and everyone had accepted them. "Please. I would work hard at whatever Uncle Robert Bruce found for me to do and pay you back someday. Please say yes." There was an unmistakable urgency in the plea. It was a call for help no one could misunderstand. "I don't want to stay on Exuma. Let me go. Say you will." His voice rose with a frightening desperation. "I have to go. I—I hate the islands. I want to get away forever. Don't you see how it is? I want to leave. You have to say yes."

"David!" Bahama spoke his name with the shocked tone she might have used if he had slapped her across the face. "David, what are you saying?" There was an agony in the cry.

Caroline could not bear to look at her daughter and the golden beauty now clouded by misery; the heartbreak, the anguished, lonely call, frightened and shook her.

"Please." David was tense. His lips trembled. His eyes beseeched them. "You know I have to go. For God's sake!" There was bitterness in the appeal. "Don't pretend you don't know why. Please. Please let me go before it is too late."

Caroline's eyes sought Juan. This was no boy they had to deal with. It was a man asking for help. Silently she prayed for Juan to answer David.

"That's, maybe, a good idea, David." Juan was surprisingly gentle and sympathetic in his agreement.

"Papa. What are you saying?" Bahama whirled upon him. "How can David go away? Why, he . . . David . . . is a part of us." She could not continue. There was such misery in the incoherent jumble of words neither Caroline nor Juan could endure it. "David." Bahama repeated the name.

"Now, girl," Juan made an attempt to soothe her, "sometimes other people know better about the things they want to do. If David likes to leave here we have to let him go."

"Why?" Bahama's features were stricken in a grief they had never seen before. "Tell me why?"

"I only say," Juan reached across the table and took her hands; they were tightly clenched and would not yield to his touch, "it is a good thing for David or any man to make the kind of life he wants. If he does not like it in the islands here, then he must go and no one should ask for reasons."

"You know he does not want to leave." Bahama was angry now. She snatched her fists from her father's hands. "There is something you're not telling me. Something I should know."

"David is entitled to his life, Bahama." Caroline tried to make it sound reasonable. This was the bitter fruit of deceit. The truth had been delayed for too long. Both John and Bahama should have been told of the relationship no matter how shameful they might have thought it to be. "He is a man free to do as he wills."

The girl ignored her mother. She turned to David, who was staring down at the table, his head bowed.

"You say it to me, Davie. Tell *me* you want to leave Exuma." She made a fierce demand. "Then I will try and believe it."

Slowly David raised his head. His eyes met hers. The silence between them was not a thing to be endured for long. Caroline found herself wanting to scream.

"Yes." He spoke almost in a whisper. "Yes, Bahama, I want to go away."

"I don't believe you." Her words were controlled and spoken slowly. "Nothing you or anyone can say will make me believe it. You are lying to me." Her gaze swept them all. "For some reason you are not telling me the truth."

She did not fling herself away from the table in a display of youthful temper and run from the room to hide her grief. She stood up, rising slowly. With her eyes she accused them. Then, deliberately and with an icy dignity Caroline would not have thought possible in her daughter, she turned away and walked from the room.

David, also, watched as Bahama mounted the staircase. Then he turned to look at Caroline with mute appeal.

"Yes, David." She spoke the name with understanding. "I know."

"What's all this ta-ra about?" John was mystified by the situation. His glance slid from his mother to his father and David. "Going to Charleston isn't such a big thing, is it? She acts like David was going to die or something. Oh," he tried to sound cynically amused, "I know she has some silly girl crush on David, but it's been that way ever since we were little together. 'Where's David? Davie, take me with you. David, let's go sailing.'" He attempted a thin falsetto in what he imagined was an imitation of his sister.

"That's enough, John." Caroline's words were sharp. Her gaze was upon David and, feeling it, he looked up. Her smile of understanding was touched with a sadness she could not conceal. "We'll make the arrangements, David."

"Soon?" There was gratitude in the question.

"You an' I," Juan intruded. "We take the sloop an' go to Nassau. The factor there owes us some money for the last sponge we sent him for the auction. You can't go to Charleston in the clothes you wear on Exuma. We get a tailor to work to make a couple of suits an' we wait together for a ship going to Carolina. That is how it will be."

David only nodded. He did not trust his voice to thank them.

"I will write Robert Bruce you are coming. Maybe we can get it off on a Government packet so it will reach Charleston before you do. If not you will have his address and go directly to his home."

"I will take care of myself." It was a quiet statement of confidence. He hesitated and then his expression embraced them all. "I am going to miss you."

"Then why are you going?" John interrupted.

[282]

"Boy," Juan spoke roughly to his son, "leave things as they are and don't ask so much damn question."

Lying in the darkness David heard the small, creaking sound of light footsteps on a loose board in the hall. It was a tiny noise, the squeak of a mouse, and then silence. He lay rigid beneath the bed's light covering for he knew instinctively who was outside his door. The knob turned almost soundlessly. He heard the door open and close with furtive softness and still he did not move until she whispered his name.

"Davie?"

He snapped upright, not wanting to believe what he knew to be true. She stood at the bed's side, wearing the long shift of cotton which all but covered her bare feet. She appeared so impossibly young and indecisive. Her hair lay in a soft cloud about her shoulders. She waited for him to speak.

"Go back to your room." There was firmness but no anger in his command. "You know you shouldn't be here." His whisper betrayed his own uncertainty. "Suppose your mother or father—"

"I don't care." She made an effort to sound determined. "I don't care about anything but you. I had to come. You can't go away, Davie. I won't let you."

"I must go. Please. You don't know what you're doing or saying. We're not children any longer. Now, go back to your room."

"No." There was desperation in her soft cry. She moved forward and then, suddenly, all but threw herself at him, her arms clumsily encircling his neck, her lips seeking his eyes, his cheek, his mouth. Her sudden weight had forced him back against the pillows and she lay, half atop of him. "I love you, Davie. You know I do. All this time, while I've been growing up, there hasn't been anyone but you." She was sobbing with a choking intensity. "If you leave I don't want to live. I'll—I'll kill myself. I swear I will. You have to believe me."

He was painfully aware of the soft, pliant body as it pressed against him; the young, hard breasts, the warmth through the nightdress. Roughly, he put his hands against her shoulders and pushed her back and away, holding her at arm's length. She trembled convulsively and her eyes were filled with silent pleading.

In their room Caroline had also caught the complaining sound of the hallway board. She knew how lightly a young foot had trod upon it and with what fear and longing the step had been made. For a second or two she lay there, rigid. This, she told herself, is my fault. With quick decision she slipped from the bed and took a robe from a chair.

"You heard it too, girl?" Juan spoke in a tone carrying no surprise.

"I wasn't sure. The house creaks sometimes at night. Do you want me to come with you?"

"No." Caroline was at the door. "I'll take care of it. It is something I can do better alone." She was gone.

Neither of them moved as Caroline entered. David still held Bahama upright as she sat on the bed's edge. She was crying soundlessly, tears staining her cheeks. She didn't even make a pretense at turning as the door opened and closed again but continued to stare at David.

"It is all right, baby." Caroline took a place beside her, gently drawing Bahama into her arms. David's hands fell away. "It is all right," Caroline repeated.

"I'm not ashamed to be here." Bahama's voice was small but defiant.

"I don't want you to be ashamed." Caroline drew her close. The love and understanding for her daughter welled and overflowed. "I am not angry with you for coming. Love isn't something you can say yes or no to. It comes unbidden and without asking permission of anyone." She looked past Bahama to David. "And you, David. You mustn't feel guilty or ashamed. I know it is not your doing. It is our fault."

"Thank you, Aunt Caroline." He was sincere and touched by her quiet understanding. "You know I wouldn't. I never have. Nothing." He was unable to continue.

"I know. Don't you suppose I have known and trusted you?" She was stirred by his awkward sincerity. "Do you believe I am so old I no longer remember love?" A wistful smile touched her mouth. "Baby." She turned Bahama gently until they faced each other. Her fingers brushed lovingly at the tears. "Baby," she repeated and the word was one she had never used to address her daughter before. "Listen to me. Please. I am not angry. I didn't come to reprimand you. Believe me, I understand. I am not ashamed nor should you be."

"I'm not. I love David. He can't go away." Bahama spoke almost hopefully as though her mother's being here in the room would change things. "You know he shouldn't leave. He doesn't really want to go. I won't believe it."

Caroline's arms tightened protectively. "He has to go, darling. Because, you see, David loves you, also. I have watched it coming for a long time and have been frightened by what was happening."

"Why should my loving David or David loving me be so terrible?" There was rebellion in the question.

Caroline sighed and inclined her head to touch her daughter's hair with her lips. There was no escape now. She must do what should have been done long ago. How could any of them have believed they could lock away this moment?

"I want you to listen, Bahama." She placed no undue emphasis upon the words. "I want you to listen and try to understand what we have all felt. I. Your father. Your grandfather, and even David. He is as innocent of all of this as you are and will be hurt as much. God knows this is hard enough for me to say, difficult for David to hear again." She took a deep breath and prayed for the wisdom to say the right thing and a feeling of helplessness swept over her. The choice of words was limited. You spoke them or you didn't. "You can't be in love with David." She felt Bahama stiffen with hostility. "And David can't be in love with you. Not the way you want it. David is my half brother. He is, in a way, I suppose, your uncle or half uncle. I'm not too sure about the exact relationship. Only that it is too impossibly close."

Bahama stared at her mother. The words made no sense. This was some midnight gibberish. For a moment she wondered if she had really heard. David her uncle? Young David her mother's half brother. Well, that would mean . . . She wasn't certain what it meant and frantically tried to trace this incredible relationship. It was impossible and yet, there was no question of her mother's sincerity nor the expression of shame, of hopelessness, on David's face.

"But how?" Bahama searched for the key question which would unlock this maze. "It can't be what you say. I remember you told me when I was ten or eleven how David had come here with his mother when John I were two or three years old. You remember, I asked you? You said David's father was Sir Gerald Heath, the Governor who had died of the plague, and David's mother had to leave him here with us. You said he was about five years old. Why, we have grown up together from that time."

How to untangle this? Caroline felt trapped. What was the explanation Bahama would understand? The truth, of course: there was no easy alternative.

"Grandfather Cameron and David's mother . . ." She didn't think she could continue. "They were in love with each other. It happened. It just happened." Her voice rose despite her efforts to control it. "David is not David Heath. His name should be Cameron. He is your grandfather's son by David's mother." She experienced a sudden feeling of exhaustion.

"Grandfather Cameron?" Bahama was unable to credit the statement.

Only to herself did Caroline smile. To Bahama, Ronald Cameron had been the remote, bearded patriarch. He had been beyond the love for a woman, the agony of the flesh. It was impossible to think of him as tender, holding a woman in his arms, making love to her and between them producing a child.

"Grandfather Cameron and David's mother?" Dazedly Bahama repeated the words.

"Yes," Caroline answered. "I know what you are feeling. In a lesser degree I felt the same way when I found out. It was inconceivable, preposterous. I had always exalted him. He was different from other men. He suffered no weakness and was beyond temptation. He could not have loved as Juan loved me or I loved Juan. Yet, it was and is true. He was a man of strength and human desires. The blood ran full and hot. I offer no excuse. He needed none." She touched Bahama's silky hair. "Love does not begin and end at seventeen or eighteen as you think now and I once believed."

"Did David know about this?" The girl's voice gathered strength. She spoke as though David were not in the room.

"Yes."

"He gave me a letter from my mother to read." For the first time in minutes David spoke.

"Then John and I should have been told." There was bitterness in the statement. She accused them both.

"It wasn't easy to say," Caroline answered.

"Easy!" Bahama all but shouted. "Is it easier now? For as long as I can remember I have loved David. Now you have made it seem something dirty, shameful. I want to run and run, never looking back. Did you think"—she regarded her mother with an unflinching bitterness— "a nice, convenient time would come along when you could tell me, the way parents explain to their children that there really isn't any Santa Claus after all? Do you know how old I am? How I feel?" She sprang up, pushing aside her mother's restraining arms. "Look at me." There was violence in the command. With both hands she tore the nightdress apart from collar to hem, revealing herself with an unabashed ferocity and standing all but naked before her and David. "Is what you see that of a child; someone to be coddled and lied to because it is convenient?"

"Cover yourself, Bahama." Caroline's order was a lash.

"Why?" There was no shame. "You are my mother. I'm sure it doesn't disturb my uncle."

Caroline whipped a light cover from the bed and threw it over her daughter's shoulders. There was a moment when Bahama seemed to be on the point of ripping away the sheet. Then, all of her rage and frustration dissolved. She clung to her mother, crying with uncontrollable suffering. There was the sound of pain, of unendurable confusion, of wild distraction which edged upon madness.

[286]

"You had no right to do this. No right." The words were repeated over and over.

Caroline was exhausted. She could think of nothing more to say, holding her daughter in silent misery. Dear God. She honestly prayed for help. What am I to tell her for she believes, as I would have believed in losing Juan, this is the end of all living, all hope? She could feel the wracking tremors as they shook her daughter's body, understood the suffering and humiliation she was experiencing. How easy it was to mouth the useless words: This will pass; in time you will forget. How simple and dishonest.

Slowly the tears ceased to flow. The trembling quieted until it came, now, only in short spasms. Bahama drew away from her mother, disengaging her arms, stepping back a pace.

"I am all right now." The statement was firm but frighteningly new and cold. She wrapped the cover tightly about her as though it were a shield through which she could never again be reached. "I'm all right. I'm not going to cry again but don't think I will forget or forgive you."

"Grandfather Cameron was on his way to Nassau to legalize the adoption of David." Caroline felt she must say something more in explanation. "We, all of us, thought it would be easier to tell you and John after that had been done."

"Did you?" Bahama gazed dully at her mother. "I'm glad you found a way to make it easier for yourselves." This was a new, unrelenting and vindictive girl. "Well, I'll tell you something. If there was a time, it was when we were young. You could have lied to us a little and said David is your brother. He has been away. Anything. Maybe John and I wouldn't have understood but we were very small and without any reason to question what was told us. We would have believed it and everything would have been different. John, Bahama and David. Brothers and sister."

"I know." Caroline made the admission. "But Juan and I weren't told. Grandfather Cameron kept it to himself. Maybe he thought David's mother would send for him. I don't know." She gestured helplessly. "It was already too late when we found out. Won't you try and understand that?"

"Then Grandfather Cameron was a despicable old man without courage. I wish he hadn't drowned, but not for the reason you think. I would like to have him here to see what he has done. You have an idea I think I won't get over this; that forever I'll remember David. Well, it isn't true. I will. I'm over it now, this night. I don't care anymore. This isn't the same Bahama who crept down the hall a little while ago. From now on I'll do as I please. The first man who comes along—some sponger, a conch fisherman, even a nigger. If he wants me I'll give myself to him. That's what it's for."

For the first time in her life Caroline slapped her daughter. She struck her full across the mouth with the palm of one hand.

"I'm glad I made you do that." Bahama did not flinch. "I know how it hurts you."

"You'll go to your room now, Bahama." Caroline forced herself to speak with calm decision.

"Yes, Mother." There was no resistance, only a parody of obedience. "Yes. I'll go to my room."

In this moment Caroline recalled with a frightening clarity a day, long ago, in her father's study when he had forbidden her to see Juan Cadiz ever again. He had said: Go to your room, Caroline. The order had been given in almost the same tone she had just used. She, in turn, had replied as had Bahama. It was an admission of authority without an acknowledgment of submission.

"I'll go now." Bahama turned toward the bed. "Good-bye, David."

He did not, could not, answer. He watched her as she crossed the room, opened the door and then closed it unhurriedly behind her.

All of the reserve of strength and character which Caroline had drawn upon deserted her now. She stood, head bowed, a motionless statue weeping for her children as had Niobe. David gazed at her helplessly, not knowing what to say or do. His thoughts followed Bahama. Neither he nor Caroline were aware of time's passing. The room was completely silent.

What was becoming past enduring was relieved by the door's opening. Juan stood there. He was dressed. Caroline looked up and then shook her head, unable to speak.

"I began to think it was time I came." Juan gathered her to him. "It was not, as you thought, something you should have done alone."

"Juanio. Juanio." She breathed the name. "It was a terrible thing to see, to listen to. God forgive us."

"I don't know about God." Juan was gentle. "Sometimes I think He don't give a damn."

"If you could have seen her—heard the things she said." Caroline's misery did not abate.

"I see her in you every day." Juan put his hand to her head, pressing it against his chest. "It is a bad thing to have happened here this night for everyone." He released Caroline and spoke to David. "Tomorrow it will be no better. I got the idea, maybe, you and I take the boat and start for Nassau tonight. I do not like to think about tomorrow or the day after. It is best we leave now without saying anything more to anyone. This has not been an easy thing for you, either, David. It will be no easier in the day's light when she has to watch us sail away."

"I'll get dressed." David's eagerness was an entreaty. "What I need to take with me can be stuffed into a seabag. It will only take a few minutes."

"We wait downstairs for you, my girl an' me." He laid his arm about Caroline's shoulder. "I get a nigger to provision the sloop. No hurry. We got plenty of time for talk on the way to Nassau."

They waited in what had been Ronald Cameron's study. In the kitchen a half-awake slave woman was packing a box with provisions and filling a water cask. A boy, awakened in the quarters, stumbled drowsily toward the beach to make the sloop ready.

Juan poured himself some rum and took it with hot water and a lump of brown sugar. "Maybe a little of this is good for you, too," he suggested.

Caroline shook her head. She felt nothing, only a curious numbness of mind and body.

"This Bahama we got," Juan spoke reflectively, "she's much like you. We got to remember that."

"It's what frightens me. I don't know what she'll do."

"Do you want me to stay? David and the nigger boy make Nassau together. They do it many times before."

"No." Her character and strength were reasserting themselves. "I want you to go with them. Maybe," she made an effort at smiling, "maybe I'll take a little rum after all. When you've left I may drink the whole bottle."

"That's better." He filled a small glass. "You talk like Nassau girl now. I get my guitar an' we have some fun together." He was trying to bring the smile back. "We take a jug an' go down to the beach like old times. I think I stay. It sounds like more fun than a wet sail at night."

Her eyes softened with memories and then she swallowed a little of the rum and shook her head.

"I'm not thinking very well just now." She spoke thoughtfully. "So, if what I say doesn't sound right to you, say so."

"I always do."

"I think, for a while, it is better if Bahama and I are alone. I wish you would take John with you. Then," she paused, "this is the part I'm not sure of. I'd like you to wait over in Nassau until a ship, Charleston-bound, puts in. Go with David. See that Robert Bruce understands how important it is he gets settled. If there is enough money due us at the sponge

[289]

factor's, take John with you. Leave Bahama and me here to try and understand each other again."

"We got enough money coming. We catch a trading ship. The passage don't amount to much if this is what you want."

She dropped her head to her arms, crossed on the desk. He watched her with worried compassion and then went to her side.

"Help me, Juanio. I'm so confused."

"Don't you suppose I know that? My girl don't cry easy."

She lifted her head. "There is only one thing on my mind. So, I must think about something else."

"We talk or do anything you say."

"When you see Robert Bruce"—she forced her thoughts from Bahama —"tell him we want to sell the shares Papa left."

"You turn me loose in Charleston with all those pounds?"

"You're an old man, Papa." She tried to imitate his voice. "I don' worry about you no more." She arose. "I'll go and wake John."

"He don't like that." Juan grinned. "In sleep he's his papa. The time for getting up is when you feel like it, not when someone else say so. Before you go I say something more."

"Yes." She halted at the doorway.

"While I'm in this Charleston I look around some; the boatyards, the harbor, the dry dock. Maybe I find the schooner I talk to you about once before. With the money from Robert Bruce we maybe buy what I got in mind. With a schooner, hundred an' sixty, hundred an' eighty feet an' a good beam we don't end up here only spongers with a lot of niggers to take care of. It is a thing I keep thinking about. We don't have to beat this plantation or have it beat us. I'm a good man with the sea. She is my mother, like I tell you once. With a good ship my mother an' I go into business. I think we make fine trade between the Bahamas, the mainland an' Cuba." There was a controlled excitement in his words.

Her smile was the old smile. The young one he remembered. It came like a soft touch across the room to reach him.

"Do what you want, Juanio." She spoke his name with love. "A long time ago I said: Here is my life. Take it in your hands. Nothing has changed. If you can buy your schooner with the money we get from Robert Bruce do it."

"I'll find her. In my eye I see her now." He paced up and down the room. "We got young niggers here who don't know nothing but the islands and the sea. I make a crew from them. We outbid, outsail, anything out of Nassau. We call her the *Caroline* of Exuma. She'll be like you on the first day we meet; clean of line, proud with her head high.

[290]

Only if I find that will I buy her. You know about a place called Nan-tuck-it?" He had difficulty with the word.

"Yes." Her eyes sparkled.

"Once, when I was a boy, I saw a Nan-tuck-it schooner off Nassau. I think, maybe, she was the most beautiful ship I ever look at. I hear later they build them there. If I don't find what I got in mind I go, maybe, to this Nan-tuck-it an' say: This is what I want, how I want her to look. Here is the money I have. Can you build her for me?"

"I'll wait on the beach the way I used to when my Juanio had a little sloop with a red sail and came in out of the sun. Now, I'll go and wake John."

There was a small bite in the wind and they huddled against it. The sail filled, taut and in a graceful curve and the spray flew out to shower lightly now and then upon them. The slave boy kept a small brazier glowing and tended the sooted coffeepot. In the sky the stars were splinters of shining silver.

"Whoever heard of getting up in the middle of the night and starting out for Nassau?" John pulled his shoulders together and stared reproachfully at his father.

"Me." Juan was happy. He bent forward, took the pot, filled a mug and added some rum. "A lot of times when I was your age it would come to me at night and I'd say to myself: I think I'll go to Nassau. Sometimes I used to take a girl with me but mostly not. There were plenty of girls in Nassau. They wait on the beach for Juan Cadiz." He whistled contentedly. "Take some coffee an' rum. You'll feel better."

"I feel all right." John wasn't really as querulous as he sounded. This was an unexpected, inexplicable adventure. "Are we really going to Charleston, you, David and I?"

"What for you think I bring you, boy? I say to myself I think it's time this John of mine see the world."

"There's a lot more to the world than Charleston." John was really enjoying himself and he loved his father in these carefree moods.

"It's a good enough start. You want some coffee, David?"

"No thanks, Uncle Juan." David had been silent. He sat with arms locked about his updrawn knees staring out at the starlit night. "Later, maybe."

"I should have brought my guitar. It's a long time since I went to Nassau playing music to myself. Now," he finished the coffee and pulled a blanket about himself, "I think I sleep some. You take the light off Northeast Point on Cat Island, boy," he called to the slave. "Wake me up then."

[291]

There was no sound now, only the soft singing of the wind, the splash of wave against bow, the cracking of a piece of charcoal as it broke open. The little craft skipped and heeled, frisky as a colt. John, also, found a blanket. Only David remained sitting, peering into the darkness and seeing Bahama's face, hearing her voice. He was alone in an empty world.

⋙ XVIII ⋘

As HE had for the past two weeks since their arrival in Charleston, Juan awoke with a small feeling of excitement that this would be the day when he threw open the shuttered windows, looked out upon the harbor and saw the ship, already built in his mind, lying at anchor or working her way in from the sea. It was, he admitted, a childish flight of imagination but it would not be denied.

Only a couple of hours had ticked off since daybreak and the sun's path lay hot and true across the water. The fishing boats, not unlike those he was accustomed to seeing crowding Nassau's shelter, were already in and moored to the tangle of small wharves. Black and white peddlers haggled over the catch with the boatmen, trying to beat down the prices asked. Their carts and barrows were lined along the quay waiting to be filled and trundled through the city while the fish men cried their wares. Coasting vessels were at anchor, and here and there bulked the high sides and bare masts of the great cargo ships which carried the trade of cotton, rice, indigo, lumber, turpentine and resin, sugar and molasses from the Southern port across the Atlantic. He had gazed upon the same scene every morning and experienced, each time, an illogical sense of disappointment. He had a mystical conviction that, somewhere, the vessel he wanted would make this port. She could be driving toward it now, her sails beautiful white wings, her lines clean and graceful. There would be about her a magnificent grace and a proud disdain for lesser craft as she overhauled and passed them in a billowing cloud of canvas. The idea that when he saw her she could not be his never entered his thoughts. So certain was he that his destiny was coupled with this unknown schooner he felt no real disappointment when she failed to appear. He experienced only impatience when he scanned the harbor and found she was not there.

In the wide, rumpled bed behind Juan, young John awoke with a slow

[293]

reluctance. His eyes opened, roved about the now familiar room and centered upon his father's back at the window. For a moment he watched the broad-shouldered figure with the extended arms reaching to the wall as it framed the window.

"You find that ship yet, Papa?" The question carried an interested humor and teasing note.

Juan turned and regarded his son with an unembarrassed smile. "Not yet, boy. But she's out there, on her way. I told you I had the feeling. We wait for a while. There's no hurry." He came from the casement and with a sweep of one hand pulled the covers away. "Right now I got a hunger. Get up. We wash an' eat."

From below came the sound of voices, the shrill call of an angry woman, the slow, answering reply of a man, the bellowed summons of a guest who wanted service at his table, the clatter of movement as the slaves hurried about their tasks. The odor of ham frying, coffee steaming, potatoes crisping in their grease, the steam from white mounds of grits with red-eyed gravy spilling over them all drifted to the inn's second floor.

They, with David, had taken rooms at Butler's Tavern, built upon a short length of wharf over the richly scented tidal flats, before making their first call upon Robert Bruce and Constance. It was noisy, brawling, filled with seamen and travelers from the interior. At night the taproom was crowded, haunches of meat turned upon spits over oaken coals, mulatto girls, bare of foot and scanty of dress, moved with hip-swaying invitation carrying plates of food and mugs of steaming rum. There were fights and laughter, music from accordions and guitars, boisterous reunions, and acquaintances easily made and as quickly forgotten. Juan was delighted with the tumult and his memory carried him back over the years to Nassau's waterfront and his youth.

On the second day, properly dressed, they had called upon Robert Bruce and Constance. The Camerons occupied a pleasing residence on Tradd Street with a cool and fragrant garden behind a spiked fence of wrought iron. It was unpretentious but of gracious design and spoke quietly of solid worth and position. It was near the noon hour when they presented themselves, and Robert Bruce was home from his office for the midday meal and the two hours or so of relaxation or a nap before he returned to business.

Robert Bruce received them with unmistakable pleasure, which was in contrast to his usually reserved manner. Over glasses of sherry they talked and he was filled with questions as to the conditions on Exuma, the health of Caroline, and expressed his astonishment over the growth and maturity of John and David. After a few minutes Constance joined them. She was in her final month of pregnancy and was uncomfortably self-conscious of her unshapely condition. She had welcomed them with a wan attempt at full-hearted hospitality, adding her insistence to that of Robert Bruce that they stay with them for as long as they intended to remain in Charleston. It was unthinkable they should have taken rooms at a tavern, particularly such a place as Butler's which, from what she had heard, was patronized by low seamen, gamblers, travelers of doubtful reputation and, she had added with a trace of confusion, "what not."

"That 'what not'?" Juan could not resist the temptation. "You mean girls?" He had taken her hand with an impulsive gesture. "John, David and me, we don't think about 'what not' girls right now. It's better we stay there. You know I like to be near the water. Besides, you going to have company enough around here soon."

Constance had flushed but smiled her gratitude for his understanding. Guests would have been a trial at this time. Pregnancy wasn't at all what she thought it would be. Instead of elation she felt clumsy and misshapen and was given to sudden, inexplicable fits of near hysterical weeping. She wished to shut herself away until the baby was born. Both she and Robert Bruce had wanted a child desperately. As the years had passed and she did not become pregnant she experienced a feeling of guilt and apologetic mortification. Now that the time was almost upon her she wasn't at all sure it wouldn't have been better, certainly more comfortable, to have remained barren. After a proper interval she excused herself and left the men alone.

"What are your plans?" Robert Bruce offered cigars. Only Juan accepted. "I had hoped all of you would leave the islands and come back to Carolina where you belong."

"Me?" Juan shook his head. "I belong in the islands. So do John, Bahama and Caroline. David is different. He wants another life. Maybe, he finds it here. I come along because of some business. Caroline wants to sell old Papa's shares you wrote about. With the money we buy a schooner. I got her in my mind. After I find her, John an' I go home."

Robert Bruce was thoughtfully silent for a moment and then he nodded his head.

"I will take the shares," he agreed, "at something over their present market price, for they are bound to increase in value. As to the wisdom of your using the money to purchase a trading schooner, that is your affair. Certainly the plantation has not proved out. There is considerable trade between the mainland, Bermuda, the Bahamas and Cuba. With good management it could well turn out to be a wise move. I will do everything I can to help you." He turned to David. "I will find a position for you, David. We will make an appointment and discuss it."

"Thank you." David expressed his gratitude quietly. "I will do my best."

The two regarded each other. David had developed a quiet reserve which was not unlike that of his half brother. There was even a small resemblance between them in manner and features. Although he had not fully resolved his emotions he was deeply relieved to be away from Exuma and in this strange city. He could feel a chord of sympathy between himself and Robert Bruce despite the difference in their ages.

They took the noon meal, at which Constance did not appear, together. In the talk of commerce, the growth of the city, the expansion of the Southern seaboard states, Robert Bruce was vital and enthusiastic. He drew the future in vivid phrases and it was apparent to them all his heart was in the country which had been his homeland.

"I hope, someday," he confessed, "to be able to buy back the small parcels into which it has been cut and put Cameron Hall together again. If we can find the time I would like to take you all up the river and show you where the manor once stood. It was the great mistake of our lives to have left it for the Bahamas." A shade of bitterness crept into his voice.

"Well," Juan reflected, "if you don't go to the islands Juan Cadiz don't find a girl like the one he did. He don't have no son here like John, no daughter like Bahama, an' you," he looked squarely at Robert Bruce, "don't have a fine-looking brother like David." He laid his conversational cards face up and there was no mistaking he did it deliberately.

For a second Robert Bruce was shaken and then his innate honesty and breeding asserted itself.

"You're right. Things would have been different and who can really say they would have been better? I am glad to have you with us again, David."

The moment of awkwardness so unexpectedly posed by Juan passed, David smiled his pleasure and they fell to the hearty noonday meal with good appetite and a sense of understanding.

Before they left, Constance reappeared. She took their hands in turn.

"Come and see us often while you are here, Juan. At least, come and see Robert Bruce, share a drink, a meal, a pipe and some talk in the evening. I am afraid I am very bad company these days but it won't be for long. I have missed all of you during the years we have been in Charleston."

Two days later Robert Bruce's coach had appeared at Butler's Tavern to take David for an appointment made the day before by a hand-delivered note. The liveried footman and coachman caused a considerable stir among Butler's rowdy clientele, who crowded at the doorway and windows to shout ribald comment over this display of elegance and later regarded Juan and John with a certain amount of grudgingly mystified respect.

The import and export firm of Renevant and Decatur was one of the largest between New York and Savannah. It had far-reaching interests extending to the New England States, Liverpool and Marseilles. The building it occupied on Dock Street was imposing in itself. A uniformed slave served as doorman, ushering clients into a broad foyer serving as a smoking room and lounge. There was an air of dignity and importance about the establishment which immediately stamped itself upon a visitor. Renevant and Decatur had broken through the social barrier separating trade from plantation. It was considered a privilege to have even a nodding acquaintance with the partners and have the firm handle one's business.

David had been escorted by a young page boy through the large accounting room and down a corridor where suites for the partners and single offices for executives were located. He did this with a pride and ceremony of which David was not unaware.

Robert Bruce had been behind his desk and he rose quickly as David was shown in. They said nothing until the door was closed. Then Robert Bruce offered his hand with cordial reserve.

"I'm happy to see you again, David." He studied the tall young man before him. "I hope we are going to be friends, more than friends."

"Thank you, sir."

One of Robert Bruce's rare smiles came slowly. "We are not exactly strangers, David. There is no need for formality."

"I feel a little strange," David confessed as he took a chair. "I am not sure why. I understand the relationship and have no wish to impose upon it. Besides," he continued reluctantly, "certain things happened on Exuma which were unhappy for us all."

"You mean Bahama?"

"Yes."

"Then," Robert Bruce was decisive, "that is all the more reason why you should have come away." He leaned back in his chair. "I have a position for you here, David." He spoke deliberately. "It is, I must admit, not a place of importance. After all, you have had little schooling and no training. But then," he chuckled appreciatively, "neither did I have. Sometimes good connections in the right places are more valuable assets than experience."

"I'll do anything you put me to." David was sincere.

"I'm sure of that." Robert Bruce reflected for a moment. "The lad who brought you to my office. He comes of good family and starts here as a messenger and page boy. He expects, someday, to occupy a position of importance in the firm and it is quite possible he will with diligence. The opportunity is here." He took a cigar from a humidor, offered one to David and when it was refused, lit it and smoked thoughtfully. "I am not going to start you as a messenger but apprentice you to a clerk. From him you will begin to learn a few things. As you gain experience and confidence I will move you from department to department. In that way you will gain a rounded knowledge of our activities and interests."

"Thank you, sir." David's gratitude shone on his face. "I will do my best to learn quickly."

"Now, we come to something else." Robert Bruce studied his cigar's tip. "You call me 'sir.' Here, in the office, that is proper and could not be any other way. But we are men, and let us face the inescapable fact we are also blood brothers. I certainly attach no stigma to the circumstances of your birth and hope you can or will feel the same way."

"I have never felt it a disgrace." David made the reply without evasion. "I guess I was bewildered more than anything else when I learned the truth. My mother's husband I remember only vaguely. Grandfather Cameron—" He stopped short and then half smiled. "I always think of him in that term, somehow. I suppose it is because of John and Bahama. Anyhow he was and is much more real to me than Sir Gerald."

Robert Bruce drew reflectively upon his cigar. "I am not certain, David," he said at last, "how such things are arranged now that my—our father is dead. You are entitled to the name of Cameron. It was Father's intention to make it so. Caroline wrote me. But," he knuckled his chin, "how do we explain you here? Despite the size of the city the community in which the Camerons have been a part for a couple of hundred years is tightly knit, clannish; bound by long friendships, a common denominator of values, prejudices and kinship. Introducing a new Cameron is bound to raise questions even though they may be unvoiced. However, I am not the stodgy prude my natural reticence and manner sometimes indicate. I am quite willing to acknowledge you openly as my half brother and let the explanations go hang themselves if that is the way you want it. We could say Father married again in the islands."

"I think I would prefer to be David Heath, the son of a friend of the Camerons who," a tiny smile flickered in the eyes, "who has come to Charleston to seek his future and fortune." David made the statement without hesitation.

"Very well." Robert Bruce put aside his cigar. "David Heath it shall be." He paused. "Let us be friends and honest with each other, David. I do not want to embarrass you by admitting to a feeling of obligation but I have it. If Father had lived you would have shared in whatever estate he left."

"I'm not asking for anything." The reply was short of temper.

"That is beside the point." Robert Bruce regarded him. "You sounded a little like Father just then; the stubborn, independent Scot." He seemed amused. "Anyhow, let me continue. Your salary here will be small. You will need more money than you can earn for quite a few years. Will you accept—what shall we call it—an allowance from me which will be drawn from the dividends of the London shares Father held?"

David frowned. "Will I actually need it?"

"Yes." Robert Bruce was emphatic. "David Heath whose father was the Royal Governor of the Bahamas—and that is how we will explain our friendship—will have to move upon a certain social plane. You will need the proper tailoring, a slave manservant, suitable bachelor quarters, unless you care to live with Constance and me. You will have to have money in your pocket for the races, the cockfights, the discreet and indiscreet parties and entertainments which Charleston's young bloods engage in for amusement. You will make the acquaintance and develop friendships with young men and ladies of station. Your apprentice clerkship with Renevant and Decatur will be regarded as that of a man of family who has selected a career in commerce. Yes, David, you will most certainly need money unless you deliberately choose the life of a drudge which, under the circumstances, is unthinkable." He delayed for a moment and then continued. "You are of good breeding, well formed and with a pleasant manner. Charleston, the part of which the Cameron name has always been most highly regarded, will take to you. I suspect you will be found attractive by our most sought-after belles. Does what I have said sound snobbish or supercilious?"

"No." David's smile was immediate. "You sound like a sensible man in a difficult position. For my part I have to admit the idea of an attic room, a bowl of soup and an apprentice clerk's salary holds no great attraction. Your solution sounds much better."

"Good!" Robert Bruce was pleased. He had dreaded this interview. He studied David. "By gad, we do look something alike! I wonder what Father would say if he could see us together? He was always pleased by the way you were growing up. I think it would make him happy to see you now. Well," he ceased his musing, "first things first. You will move from Butler's Tavern to our home until we find the proper rooms for you. Then you will enter the employ of Renevant and Decatur. After Constance has her child and again feels well enough to resume her

[299]

normal activities, we shall arrange a few small parties, serving to introduce you properly to the families you should know here. In the firm I will be Mr. Cameron to you and you will be Mr. Heath to me and everyone else. No one, save the messenger and page boys, is ever addressed by his first name during the business hours. It was a custom established long ago by Mr. Renevant. He is no longer active in the firm but his influence still prevails. One more thing and I shall have done with talk which, even to my own ears, has sounded pompous. I have felt a bit of an ass saying what I have but this is a city of strange contradiction and strict convention and I wanted you to understand. You see, David," he was almost unhappily serious, "I had no opportunity to be the young man you are. I so admired our father, I sought always to model myself after him. Somewhere, between boyhood and manhood, I lost my identity and became a pale reflection of Ronald Cameron. I think he realized this and it wasn't at all what he wanted of a son. It is only recently, within the years since I returned to Charleston, that I have acquired a character of my own. In part, this is due to Mr. Renevant. He not only gave me responsibilities far beyond my experience but seemed to take for granted I would make mistakes. He has given me the opportunity to buy into the company he established and has indicated a full partnership in time. Someday it may be the firm of Renevant, Decatur and Cameron. I am grateful and it is my hope I may be able to do for you what Mr. Renevant has done for me. Now," he looked at his watch, "suppose you and I take our noon meal together. We will go to the Exchange Coffee House and I will make the first introduction of David Heath, Esquire, to some of the city's gentlemen of importance, for it is their habit to gather there at this hour."

He stood up, almost abruptly, and David rose with him. There was an unmistakable resemblance and they were almost of the same height. Robert Bruce took the few steps to bring him to David's side and placed a friendly hand upon his shoulder.

"I risk a little sentimentality, David." The words were diffident. "If it is possible let us be more than friends. I have never had a brother or anyone to whom I really felt a close affection. I would be happy to think of you as my younger brother if you will have it that way."

"I would like it, Robert Bruce." David met the offer with sincerity. "I could ask for nothing better."

Robert Bruce took his hat and they walked down the hall and through the accounting room with the rows of clerks on high stools, bent over thick ledgers.

"How do Juan and my—our nephew," he actually laughed, "spend their days?"

"Uncle Juan—" unconsciously David returned to the title he had used for years—"he watches the harbor for a ship; a schooner, I think, but one whose model he has shaped in his mind. Nothing else will do. He is certain he will find it but I think he grows a little impatient."

"We have a vessel due in shortly." They walked through the door held open by the slave and into the bright sunlight of Dock Street. "Her master is a Massachusetts man. I will bring him and Juan together. Between them Juan may find what he wants. The more I think of the idea the better I like it, and the firm can turn considerable business his way. Do you know," he seemed to be adding this to himself more than to David, "in many ways this Juan Cadiz is a remarkable fellow. I am continually surprised by him."

"I think Grandfather Cameron—" Again he reverted to old habit. "I think Father, also, was a little astonished. Juan actually held the plantation together after you left. This surprised him, Juan, more than anything else. The land produces little more than enough to supply our needs. He has built up a fair sponging trade but he never ceases to complain that he was fooled in not marrying a wealthy girl and being able to do nothing more than sit on the porch, playing his guitar while a slave brought him a fresh drink and fanned him when there was no breeze."

Everything about Charleston's fine harbor fascinated Juan. He was quietly impressed by the activity; the variety and quantity of cargo filling the warehouses and crowding the docks awaiting shipment caused him to whistle softly with surprise. Ships of British, American, Dutch, French and Spanish registry called here to discharge and load their holds. He had always thought of Nassau as one of the world's great ports. By comparison it was a tiny dumping place of little importance. It sent him to wondering about such cities as New York, Boston, Liverpool and London. What must they be like?

In the waterfront taverns and coffeehouses he heard the accents of New England, Georgia, Virginia, and a bewildering diversity of foreign tongues which were completely unintelligible. Vessels of all size and rig came and went. He gazed with wonder at the first packet ship he had ever seen; the towering masts and a poop deck or structure which, he was told, was given over entirely to passenger accommodations. She could and did, it was asserted, make the passage between New York and Liverpool in fourteen to sixteen days. Nothing escaped his eyes and he never hesitated to stop and question a stranger when something new and unusual met his gaze. On a pier head he sat and studied every detail of a French ship which, he learned, was called a *goelette*. It had a curiously exciting rig of peaked sails on masts raking aft at a degree he

[301]

wouldn't have believed possible. For two days he was enthralled by the spectacle of a corvette with its low freeboard and quarterdeck. She was of the French Navy on a friendly call and had the lean and wicked appearance of a garfish. A brigantine, with fore and aft mainsail, flying the British flag, occupied his attention for an hour or more. She was in the West Indian trade and lay at anchor while being provisioned, the bumboats scuttling back and forth like water beetles. One early morning an American frigate, with its incredibly long jibbooms and flying jibbooms which gave it the soaring appearance of an airborne creature, made her way cautiously in from the open sea. He couldn't take his eyes from her until John complained loudly of hunger and boredom.

"For an island boy," Juan reminded him, "you got a lot to learn. You see things here you never look at in the Bahamas. I try to educate you some but it don't seem to do much good."

In and out of the harbor there filed a steady procession of ships but still Juan had not seen the vessel of his mind and no one he had talked with could tell him where she was to be found.

"I think," he said to John over breakfast on a day of their fourth week in Charleston, "we move to another place." He looked around Butler's with disfavor. "Here's nothing but ignorant seamen who don't understand the questions I ask."

They finally located a room at a tavern known only as Coulter's. It was spacious, bright and its windows faced the sea. Here the masters and their officers of the ships gathered in the evenings. Coulter's had an undeniable air of respectability about it. There were no slim-hipped serving wenches of roving eye and color to be taken upstairs. The tables boasted cloths and the food was served on heavy china with knives and forks of German silver and mugs of burnished pewter for the ale and rum. Here there were no sudden brawls, no drunken voices rasied in bawdy song, no explosive tempers of flashing knives and a quick bloodletting. Privately, Juan thought Coulter's a tame and dull place and not one which he would pick for a few hours of relaxation. However, the clientele was undeniably superior and Juan had an opportunity to talk quietly over a hot rum with the masters and first officers who frequented the inn. He was particularly interested in those who had a knowledge of Maine and Massachusetts shipbuilding, for he had heard that the type of ship he wanted was built in the yards there.

With his easy and engaging manner Juan had struck up a conversation with a Captain Belian James, a Yankee who was suspicious of strangers and chary of words. He was the master of a schooner, the *Bertha,* out of Boston and thawed but slowly beneath this curious man's slow drawl, his quick smile and eager curiosity. He was inclined to mistrust anyone who wore a gold ring in his ear and regarded Juan Cadiz as some savage novelty. It was only after a couple of hot buttered rums that he committed himself to more than a short grunt and monosyllabic replies. They had a third drink for which Juan paid. He took his rum with only hot water. John sipped at a glass of Madeira. The captain clung to the tradition of a lump of butter scumming the surface of his mug. This interested Juan as much as Juan excited the captain's reserved attention. There is a universal language to be found in a moderate amount of alcohol and, after a while, Captain James found himself enjoying the company. He had never visited the Bahamas and listened carefully to everything Juan said about them. They emerged as some golden isles shimmering in the sky and far removed from the stormy coastal waters with which he was familiar.

"If they're such damned fine places," Captain James reflected, "what are you doing away from them?"

"I'm looking for a ship. She's on the ways right now in my mind or somewhere at sea. There's a fine trade to be carried on a circuit: the mainland, Cuba, the Bahamas, Bermuda and back to the mainland. I don't want her too big but she can't be little either. I want cargo space and beam enough, but I also got to have her fast. Now, where am I going to find what I need?"

"Maine." Captain James uttered the single word and leaned back in his chair as though he had solved the problem. "Maine," he repeated.

"Maine? She's a long way from here." Juan had studied a map of the Eastern seaboard and Maine, at the far, northern tip, seemed as distant as the pole. "They don't build my kind of ship around here?"

"Maine." Captain James spoke the word like a challenge. "You go to Maine. That's my advice. Take it or leave it. I don't give a damn."

Juan glanced at John and saw a smile behind his son's eyes. This Yankee captain was someone beyond their experience. In the islands men would have talked over something as important as this. They would argue, exchange opinions, offer information or alternatives with indolent and leisurely concern. They would have sat on a log in the sun and discussed every possibility, with everyone willing to listen to everyone else and sharing a jug or bottle while the matter was being considered. Captain James was satisfied to solve the problem with a single word.

With a blank face Juan said, "Massachusetts?"

"Maine." The captain was adamant. He glared at Juan. "I said Maine, damn it, man." He drained his mug, belched loudly before standing up. He eyed Juan fiercely. "Maine. Take it or leave it." He stamped out in indignation without so much as a word of good night.

[303]

Juan watched him go and then grinned at John. "You hear the man. You suppose he knows what he talks about?"

"Well, he was sure talking about Maine, Papa. You asked and he said."

"That's one hell of a far piece from here." Juan thought it over. "To-morrow I think I'll go an' see Robert Bruce. Maine? We go there an', maybe, we don't get back to Exuma 'til we're old men."

Save for a second visit to the house on Tradd Street in response to an invitation delivered to Coulter's from Butler's Tavern by a slave, Juan had deliberately avoided calling upon his brother-in-law. Robert Bruce's serious concern with the matters of business disturbed the natural tranquillity of his mind. Also, such a call made it necessary for him to dress in the uncomfortable clothing made by the Nassau tailor. It entailed the wearing of a hat, submitting to a barber to have his hair trimmed, remembering to have his boots polished, and enduring a number of small inconveniences which were avoidable on the waterfront. It wasn't that he didn't like his brother-in-law. They had always shared a free association even though neither quite understood the other. On Exuma they had a common way of life. Here, in Carolina, things were quite different. In the city you ate at regular intervals, arose at the same time, made and kept appointments when they were scheduled. In the islands when you said you would see someone it could mean tomorrow or next week. Here two o'clock meant two o'clock, for someone else would be waiting at three. He had always liked Robert Bruce and instinctively felt the man wanted to be his friend, but what had been possible on Exuma was impossible in Charleston.

Certainly, and Juan was quick to admit this, Robert Bruce had done everything he could to make his and John's stay in the city comfortable and pleasant. He had put a carriage at their disposal and the coachman drove them on a sight-seeing tour through Charleston and out into the country which was so different from the islands. He had arranged for a bargelike craft manned by six husky slaves at the oars. The boat was canopied aft and was stocked with an enormous hamper of food and wine. The slaves had toiled them far up the Ashley River while he and John lolled in comfort beneath the shading canopy, marveling at the fine plantations whose lawns, with their enormous, ancient trees and carefully tended grass, extended to the water's edge. But the fact remained, Juan was simply not comfortable in Robert Bruce's company.

Now, though, he thought he ought to have a further talk with his brother-in-law unless he wanted to spend useless months in Carolina looking for a ship which, he had to admit, might never appear and if it did would not be for sale.

In their room he and John were laboriously composing a note to Robert Bruce asking for an appointment. It was a job which taxed all their powers of concentration. Juan had learned to read and write but the words came with difficulty. John's schooling on Eluthera had been rudimentary to say the least.

"You sure didn't learn much from those missionaries." Juan regarded his son suspiciously after they had torn up the third sheet of paper. "All we got to write is can we see him an' when. Can't you do that?"

"You have to say it in a particular way," John defended himself. "It's like do you write: Dear Sir? Esteemed Brother-in-Law? Dear Robert Bruce Cameron?" John gave up and stared out of the window.

"Well, pick out one and write it."

"Maybe we ought to have something to eat first or walk around some." John made the suggestion hopefully.

"I guess that's a good idea." Juan was relieved.

Robert Bruce saved them from the terrors of composition by sending a note of his own. In it he wrote, asking Juan to call at the house the following evening to meet the master of one of Renevant and Decatur's ships which had made port the day before. "I believe," he added, "Captain Stagg has information in which you will be interested. Unless advised to the contrary I shall expect you and John at seven o'clock."

Juan read it through and then turned a suspicious eye upon his son. "Why couldn't you have written something like that? It doesn't read hard to me."

"That's because Uncle Robert Bruce is inviting us. The other way we were asking to see him. There's a lot of difference."

"You're tricky with the answers, boy. They sound all right until you begin to think about them. I got a feeling you ought to go back to school some more. Anyhow," his relief was evident, "we only got to get dressed up an' that's easier than writing a letter. This," he offered the advice sagely, "is something for you to remember. Take your time an' things work themselves out, usually."

In the open barouche which was sent for them they drove through the pleasant evening, fragrant with the perfume of oleander, jessamine and magnolia. In the residential sections the quiet of well-being and security walled the homes with an invisible barricade against the city. Charleston, Juan admitted, was a fine place to live if you were born to it. Even his untrained eye was not insensible to the beauty of the architecture, the graceful spires of the churches, the delicate art of the craftsmen who had created the wrought-iron fences, the scrolled gates which seemed to be made of black lace. Behind drawn curtains the candle-light was lemon-yellow. No harsh note intruded here.

At the Cameron house on Tradd Street they were ushered into a reception room where Robert Bruce greeted them with relaxed cordiality. Standing with him was a weathered, keen-eyed man in his late thirties.

"I'm glad you could come." Robert Bruce took Juan's hand. "Constance will not be down. Her time is close now. She sends her compliments. This," he presented the stranger, "is Captain Amos Stagg of our brig, the *Southern Star*. Captain—Juan and John Cadiz, my brother-in-law and nephew."

"My pleasure, sirs." The captain shook hands with formality.

A slave came to the room carrying a large silver tray on which were glasses and a bottle of sherry. He placed them on a table, opened a small mahogany casket containing cigars and withdrew, closing the door behind him.

"First let us have a drink." Robert Bruce poured the wine. "Help yourself to the cigars."

When they were settled Robert Bruce remained standing. "I think," he addressed his words to Juan, "I have some information for you. On his way down from New York, Captain Stagg put in for a day at Norfolk to discharge cargo. From our agents there he learned of a schooner against which my company has a lien. Her Boston owners are in financial difficulties and owe us a considerable amount of money which they are unable to pay. Consequently, we took steps to attach their vessel. They are unable to meet their obligations and, as a result, after the legal processes the ship will pass into the hands of Renevant and Decatur. From what Captain Stagg has told me, I believe she is what you are looking for."

"Tell me about this schooner, Captain." Juan leaned forward in his chair. "I've waited for her a long time."

Captain Stagg drew upon his cigar. "She's one hundred and ninety-eight feet overall. A two-masted schooner some five years old and Gloucester-built."

"Where's this Gloucester?"

"Maine." Captain Stagg took a sip of sherry. "She is as sound as fine oak timber and good shipwrights can make her, and when you say that of a Gloucester-built ship you have said everything there is to say."

"Maine." Juan spoke with a slow wonder. "That's what Captain James told me." He laughed softly and his bright eyes took in the company. "We had a few drinks together at the inn. When I told him what

I wanted all he would say was 'Maine.' Go to Maine or go to hell for all I care. That's what he said."

"You'd find the climate in Maine a little different." Captain Stagg smiled for the first time.

"This will save you a trip to either place." Robert Bruce was in a high good humor. "Norfolk is somewhere in between. Now. This is what I suggest. Help yourself to the wine," he interrupted himself. "Captain Stagg will be loading cargo for the next two or three days and then sail for New York. He will put in at Norfolk. I will give you a letter to our agents and if the ship in question is what you want, then they will consummate the deal."

"Can I afford her?" The price had not been mentioned and Juan was concerned.

"If the price is more than you will have available, then Renevant and Decatur will take your note for the balance. We are not strangers, Juan."

"For the first time," Juan chuckled, "I think, maybe, I did all right in marrying your sister. It begins to pay off some now." He winked at Robert Bruce.

"I suppose you will want her transferred to British registry?" Captain Stagg asked.

"I don't know about those things." Juan turned questioningly to his brother-in-law. "Do I or don't I?"

"It will be better. Your home port will be British. Our agents will also take care of that for you. The principal thing is to see her first and decide whether the vessel is what you had in mind. From what Captain Stagg has told me and the use to which you will put her, she sounds like the ideal ship."

"I'll know her when I see her." Juan made no effort to conceal his excitement. "In my mind I have built her from the keel up." At heart he was a man who had a mystical sense of destiny. Here was the mysterious example of what he felt. By chance he had fallen into talk with a ship's captain who had told him to go to a place called Maine for the vessel he wanted. And now, by the same, obscure working of his fate, a Maine-built ship was his. It, he told himself, had to be the one he wanted otherwise things would not have moved as they had. "Maybe," he continued, "I don't have to see her. Already I've got the feeling this is what I have been looking and waiting for. I know," he smiled, a little embarrassed, "that's nigger, obeah talk. Just the same I feel it." He turned to Captain Stagg. "You're sure it's going to take you three days to load cargo here?"

Juan's eagerness was so transparent. Stagg smiled indulgently. "Maybe,

[307]

for you, Mr. Cadiz, we can do it in two. Don't worry. The ship will be there."

"I'll need a crew to work her to the Bahamas. Me, I don't know much about a ship this size. What I sail is something you can hook a leg over the tiller and steer. The biggest thing I handle to now is a thirty-six-foot ketch."

"I think the crew aboard her now will want to stay on. I'm not sure about Captain McEvans. He is a New Bedford man with a family there and I doubt he would want to move them to the Bahamas. Anyhow," Stagg reassured him, "we'll get her to the islands for you. The first officer has his master's papers."

"Now," Robert Bruce placed his hand on Juan's arm, "let us take our meal together and we can talk of ships and men over the table. I envy you just a little, Juan. I would like to want something as much as you do this schooner."

They filed to the oval dining hall which overlooked the garden. Juan's mind was not upon the food served. All he could think of was this ship, lying idle at some placed called Norfolk, waiting for him. The *Caroline*. He could see the name in gold paint on her stern. He wanted to take her into Exuma himself and see that girl of his come down from the house and stand on the little dock as she had years ago when all he had was a small sloop with a red sail and an eye for her beauty.

⋐⋑ XIX ⋐⋑

RUNNING FREE under a steady wind from the northwest the *Caroline* flew with the grace of a racing hull and the wake, faintly creaming behind her, was as true as a man's hand on the helm could make it. The wind sang to her and the sea rose to meet the thrusting bow with bright color and feathered tops.

Standing midship at the rail Juan lifted his eyes to the taut canvas, bright as a gull's wing. There was in his heart such delight few men are privileged to know. It was not simply the pride of ownership but the sleek beauty of the vessel itself. More than craftsmanship had gone into the building of this schooner. Somewhere between the man who had first drawn her on paper and the final moment when she first went into the water, the hands of men had wrought a magic touch. Standing beside Juan, Captain McEvans was aware of this man's excitement and it did much to mollify the resentment he had first felt when the ship changed ownership.

McEvans had commanded the schooner from the day she slid from the ways in the Gloucester yard, and in giving her up now he felt a personal loss. Not that it would change his life or affect his career. He was known as a steady, competent man and a new berth would be no problem. What he experienced was a sense of bereavement.

From the moment the agents of Renevant and Decatur had taken possession and Juan, as the new owner, had come aboard, McEvans had been inclined to a surly, tight-lipped attitude. He was for gathering his personal effects immediately and leaving the cabin to his successor. Something, though, in this man with the odd name of Cadiz caught his fancy and imagination. It was the love, spontaneous and unmistakable, of a man for a ship. Despite his reservations and New Bedford suspicion of emotional display, Captain McEvans found himself responding to Juan's unabashed pleasure. He unbent a little.

"You look at her the way a man sometimes sees a woman."

"There are only two things I ever really wanted, Captain." Juan's eyes were shining. "They are both named Caroline. One waits for me in the islands. The other is here."

"Your wife?"

Juan nodded. "In many ways they are alike. You will know when we get to Exuma. I only wish you would stay on as master. I think, in time," there was a smile of understanding, "after you get over the idea I have stolen something from you, we could be friends."

"I must admit the offer tempts me but I have a family in New Bedford; two boys in their teens and a girl of twelve. It would mean the uprooting of everything we all know; the breaking of old ties. I am not sure they would be happy in this foreign climate. I will take her to Nassau for you. After that, Mr. Raleigh will serve you well. He is but twenty-five, single and with his master's papers. He will turn no homesick glances northward for he has no obligations or ties. The life will suit him fine. It is no small thing to have a command at his age. He is grateful and, I suspect, a little excited, although you would never believe this from his manner. He will serve you with skill and loyalty for he loves this ship as I do."

"He seems a good man though not one for much talking." Juan laughed softly. "You men of the North lay out your words as carefully as though they were gold pieces and not to be spent recklessly. But I think, maybe, Mr. Raleigh and I will get along for I can talk enough for us both." A small frown scarred his brow. "I don't only want to own the ship. I must know her. There are things I need to learn about navigation. Maybe I have to go to school in Nassau or Mr. Raleigh can teach me. I know the islands so well I sail them without a compass but when I get outside, like from here to there, I go in circles, I think, and no one ever see Juan Cadiz again. My boy John, he knows some navigation. They teach it in the schools because the island children are more at home on the water than the land. Just the same I want to know for myself."

Captain McEvans was accustomed to owners who sat in an office and directed their ships' movements from there. This Cadiz was a different breed. He had gone over every inch of the ship, testing and examining. With a lantern he had crawled through the holds. They had taken her outside and he had remained there listening to the sounds a ship makes. With the agility of a boy he had gone aloft to survey the vessel and then inspected her from bowsprit to taffrail, from forecastle to stern. He took the helm and felt her easy response.

"Tell me," Captain McEvans was sincerely curious, "why did you want me to take her to Nassau when Mr. Raleigh would have served as well? It is money out of your pocket to send me back as a passenger to Massachusetts."

"I'll tell you." Juan braced himself and leaning back stared at the sky. "In a way I didn't muches the way we got the ship. One man's trouble shouldn't make another happy and the owners of the *Caroline* couldn't pay their bills to people who were friends of mine or the company my brother-in-law worked for. I didn't think it was right to take a man's ship an' say, all right, good-bye. I have the idea you would like to sail her one more time. The way I would feel. I ask you, as a favor, to take her to Nassau so you stand with her deck beneath your feet for the last time."

"You're a sentimental idiot, Mr. Cadiz." McEvans did his best to sound gruffly impatient.

"Sure." Juan was cheerfully agreeable.

"A ship's a ship," the captain argued.

"Sure." Juan's agreement was immediate. "Like a woman's a woman. That's why you blow your nose now and look away so I don't see what's in your eyes. I guess you Massachusetts men ain't so different from others after all even though you do talk funny like it comes from your head an' not your heart. In the Bahamas we say what we feel. If it's crying we want to do, we cry. If it's singing or laughing, we sing or laugh. How do you suppose that is?"

Captain McEvans was honestly puzzled by the question. He thought it over, slowly and methodically, and then finally shook his head. For the first time there was the shade of a smile on his features.

"You know it's a damn silly question?"

"We got nothing to do but make talk." Juan was idly interested.

"Maybe it's the climate." McEvans turned the notion over in his mind. "It's damnably cold in New England. We get used to bundling ourselves up against it. It could be we cover emotions the same way. I don't know and I say this is damn silly talk for a couple of grown men." He almost seemed irritated to have been led into such a conversation.

"You know," Juan laughed outright at McEvans' confusion, "I think the islands do you good for a while. We learn to call each other by first names. You run around naked with your soul in the sun. It warms you all the way through. When you get home everyone say: Look, we got a new papa. He don't scowl no more or snap his words off."

"Mr. Cadiz." The captain admitted his defeat. "Let us have a drink together. It is early but I feel the need of one. Your talk makes sense and nonsense at the same time."

In the captain's cabin a mess boy served them with a bottle and glasses.

From the galley he brought a pitcher of hot water and lumps of coarse sugar. As they mixed their toddies McEvans glanced covertly several times at Juan, who had picked up the bottle and was examining the label.

"They grow cane in Massachusetts?" he asked with surprise.

"No." McEvans relaxed in his chair and savored the steaming drink. "The rum comes from Jamaica, Cuba, Barbados, or even your Bahamas. We used to import the molasses and distill it ourselves but now the spirits come in casks. When it gets to Massachusetts, we label it Medford Rum. Now, don't ask me some damn fool question like why they do."

"Why?" Juan was all innocence.

"Because it probably makes us feel less sinful and eases the New England conscience. We're putting no outlandish, heathen stuff in our stomachs. Good, solid New England rum." He took a long swallow as though to put an exclamation point after his pronouncement. "Do you know something, Mr. Cadiz? It is my belief a man takes on the protective coloring of his environment as do the lower animals. In the bleak regions he inclines to become dour, silent and perhaps a little melancholy. Mind you," he added a tot of rum to his mug, "I'm not saying the New England states are not beautiful in the summer and autumn. But, those are the short months. The balance of the years does not incline him to laughter or gaiety." He stretched his long legs and sighed with comfort. "It has been a long time since I have talked with a man for the sake of talking."

"Captain," Juan was easily emphatic, "something ought to be done about you. Now, maybe there's no ship out of Nassau right away to take you to New York or Boston. If not, why do you wait there? In half an hour you see all there is of the town. Come to Exuma with me. Meet my Caroline an' daughter B'ma. Men had dreams on Exuma an' the other islands. How they turn out make you wonder how big a man should dream. Exuma was a big plantation. Papa Cameron, my wife's father, planned it so, but it didn't turn out. The cotton he grow makes two, three crops an' then the land wore itself out. Now we got slaves with nothing to do an' the dreams turns out to be nothing. But, if you don't want so much, then, maybe, these islands are the most beautiful places in the world. I don't know." He made the confession without embarrassment. "I never been much place else."

"What about your son and daughter? By the way," he was a little confused, "how do you call her?"

"Her mother names her Bahama." Juan grinned. "But me, I get lazy an' call her B'ma. John? He's most like me. He didn't think much of Charleston or Norfolk either. He's island man an' grow up on the water. You see for yourself how he takes to this ship, like he was born to her. He's been over every inch an' goes up the rigging like a monkey. He's standing there now by the quartermaster; watching, learning a little, itching to put his hands on the wheel to feel her because, to him, she's something alive. In time he makes first officer to Mr. Raleigh an' when he's smart enough he gets his master's papers. Who knows how things turn out? We start with this schooner. Before we're through we maybe have three or four in trade. Then he gets to see all the world he wants."

Captain McEvans pushed the bottle toward Juan with an unspoken invitation. They were no longer strangers.

"You make me envy you, Mr. Cadiz," he admitted. "I have never felt it with any other man. I wish you good luck with this ship."

From the windows of her bedroom Caroline could look down on the flat curve of the beach and watch Bahama as she walked without purpose on the sand, or stood staring at the sea. So, she thought a little sadly, did I once walk and stand, waiting for I knew not what. In time Juan came and I had a new and sudden reason for living. For her there is no Juan, no David.

During the weeks since Juan, John and David had left, they were both oppressed by the loneliness of the island without its men. They made no mention of this. Actually, there was no communication between them. After her initial outburst of incredulous dismay, unreasoning fury, and finally, heartbreaking acceptance of David's relationship, Bahama had not spoken his name nor that of her father and brother. There existed between mother and daughter an aloof politeness, an impenetrable barrier which disturbed Caroline far more than open resentment would have caused. They took their meals together but had little or nothing to say. When Caroline tried to make conversation, searching her mind for the day's trivia which might spark some small interest, Bahama merely shrugged her indifference or answered with an apathetic "Is that so?" or a simple "Yes."

One night, unable to endure any longer what had and was happening, Caroline had gone to her daughter's room. Bahama was awake. She lay, arms crossed beneath her head, a shaft of moonlight illuminating her features with a silvery radiance. In silence Caroline sat upon the bed. Bahama ignored her presence.

"You are destroying us both." Caroline spoke with a gentle concern. "You have become a ghost of someone I once knew who moves in and out of the house."

"I am sorry, Mother."

"No. You are not." An unexpected impatience filled her. "It is a

[313]

thing you do deliberately. What happened was not and is not my fault. I did what I thought was right. We all did. If it was a mistake it was an error of judgment, of timing."

"I have stopped blaming you or anyone. If I wanted to hate anyone I suppose it could be Grandfather Cameron, and he is well past caring."

"Father never expected he would have to take David into his home."

"But he did and I should have been told before it was too late." The anger flared violently.

"Darling." Caroline placed her hand over her daughter's. "You have been hurt but all life has not ended. You are too young, too lovely to shut yourself away from the world this way."

"I suppose you will tell me next I'll forget David in time."

"I wasn't going to say that but it is true."

"As you would have forgotten Papa?"

"As I would have forgotten Juanio. Maybe the hurt would have remained for a long time. A little of it might have stayed in some secret part of my mind. But the image would eventually have grown dim. I would not have remembered how it really was. Like all pain, that of the heart eases in the memory until you can't remember how it felt."

"Mother." She turned suddenly, as though some agony constricted her, and buried her face in Caroline's lap. "I don't want it to be this way." She was not crying. There were no tears. "It is only that everything seems empty. The excitement of waking up in the morning is gone. I have tried. I have taken a horse and galloped him along the beach until we were both exhausted. I have gone out in the sloop and sailed her, wondering why the magic had disappeared. All I could think about was how David used to lounge in the boat or at the tiller. I heard his laugh, saw his smile, felt the careless touch of his hand on mine. In all of the first things I remember, David was there. As children it was John and I and David. Later only David. Just the two of us. The thought he would ever go away never entered my mind. It was something I couldn't imagine. Then, suddenly, with a few words he was taken from me."

Caroline's hand rested on her daughter's head. She needed Juan so desperately now. How to summon the strength and wisdom to endure this torment alone?

"I am so lonely." Bahama's words were muted for she kept her face pressed into her mother. "What used to be fun, with every day a new adventure, is without meaning. It is only a little island of empty fields, monotonous hours. I wake up in the morning and ask: Why? What reason is there for me to get out of bed?"

"When Juanio—Papa and John get back . . ." These were empty words and Caroline knew it.

Bahama straightened, sat up in bed and stared at her mother with something close to pity or outright astonishment.

"Do you really think it will make a difference? Papa and John will be here. There will be four at the table instead of five. They will talk about what they did or saw in Charleston and all the time I will want to ask about David. How does he live? What is he doing? Is he happy?" She shook her head. "Those are the things I ask myself now. It hurts as if hands were twisting me here." She pressed her hands against her breasts. "It is pain, real pain. I go to sleep with it."

"I want to answer you, sensibly and with all the love I bear." Caroline felt almost nauseated by her helplessness. "In God's name, what can I say?"

"Tell me I am a foolish, stupid girl." The words were dull, there was no sarcasm or bitterness in them. "Say this is a ridiculous infatuation. You will get over it. Make me believe it, Mother." It was an appeal.

"I could say it and mean it but you won't believe me. The heart hears only what it wants. With your father I would not have listened to Grandfather Cameron's warnings. He was wrong and in the end I think he knew it. But—here is the tragedy—your love for David and his for you is impossible. Terrible things happen from such intermarriages. The blood is too close. Nature will not tolerate its mingling. So, it is not a matter of who was right or wrong." She paused. "We have some money. Not what we once had, but we could manage to send you to the mainland to school, to relatives in Virginia. There you would meet girls and young men of your station. In time . . ." She could say no more.

"Do you know what I would do if you sent me to the mainland?" Bahama was not defiant or threatening but there was no mistaking her sincerity. "I would find David and go to him. I don't care what the relationship is."

"Then you would destroy David and yourself." For the first time Caroline was angry. "I have offered you my love, sympathy and understanding and you take it all as the ramblings of a demented person. David Heath. David Cameron is my half brother. He is your uncle. What sort of an alliance do you propose? I am sick to death of your moping, your silent wailing alone on the beach. Things are what they are and nothing you can do will change them." She broke off. "I love you but I will not be continually beaten by your withdrawal, your silence, your unwillingness to accept the truth. If it is your choice, then live out your life here on Exuma; grow old, dried and lonely. Women have lost husbands and lovers before you and they have survived and built a new and

[315]

happy life. Weep if you must but do not expect me to accept you any longer as the tragic figure of all womanhood. You force me to say these things and, at the moment, I hate you just a little because you make them necessary." She stood up. "You make up your mind how it is going to be between us. For if you think I and your father and even John are going to be castigated daily by your accusation of guilt, then you are mistaken. That is not the way it is going to be."

"Good night, Mother." Bahama said it quietly.

For a moment Caroline was silent. She stared down at the girl in the bed. Then, she turned and walked from the room. Nothing had been accomplished. Between them there was no approach to an understanding. She was a little ashamed now over her angry outburst. But, what was the alternative? To endure the silent indictment, to watch her daughter's daily withdrawal? How did you reason with a girl who had shut her mind to everything but a situation for which there was no solution? As she snuffed out the single candle and dropped her light robe upon a stool she could not help but think back to her defiance of her father over Juan. Much of her independence of thought and action had been inherited by Bahama, but in this there was no parallel. David and Bahama. The word repelled her but there was no other. It was incestuous.

Moonlight filled the room, lighting it with a phosphorescent glow. The house was without sound save for the occasional creaking of a shutter or the scraping of the bougainvillea which grew in heavy profusion, climbing on all sides. From one of her windows she could see the mutilated section, torn apart by the hurricane which had drowned Ronald Cameron. The debris had long since been cleared away but the heavy studding remained, for Juan had always thought they might rebuild. It gave the once soaring impression drawn by the architect a curiously crippled appearance, as if some graceful bird dragged a crippled and mutilated wing. What, she pondered, would Ronald Cameron do with the tragedy he had created by fathering David? And why had she shrunk from telling Bahama and John the truth when they were old enough to understand but still too young to have made this terrible difference? Angry as she had been at Bahama a few minutes ago, she could not entirely absolve herself of all guilt.

She drew a winged chair to the window and sat, listening to the wash of the sea as it ran upon the beach. She could not sleep and dawn began to pale the sky before she finally went to bed with a feeling of complete exhaustion. Somewhere, on his way home, she hoped Juan was watching or waiting for this same morning. With all of her love for him she knew he would have no ready solution nor would his advice extend beyond the cheerful assurance Bahama would get over this affair of young love. The frightening part of it all was that she was not sure there was an answer. Somehow, in her own way, Bahama must resolve this for herself. For the first time in many years she was grateful for the comparative isolation of the island. At least, there was no reckless course into which her daughter could turn on Exuma.

The *Caroline,* under light sail, skimmed down the long chain of the Exuma cays. Out of Nassau, from the time they approached the Yellow Bank, Juan had taken the helm. He was there now, flanked by Captain Raleigh and John. The ship rode high and with little ballast. They had discharged an assorted cargo at Nassau which Robert Bruce, through his firm, had arranged for them to pick up in Charleston. It had been a stroke of luck and turned what might have been an empty run into a profit. Captain McEvans, also, had been fortunate. On their day of dropping anchor off Nassau he had found a Boston-bound ship ready to clear. Her master was an acquaintance of long standing and McEvans had secured accommodations. They had parted with mutual regret, for each had unexpectedly found much to like in the other. As the small boat was swung over to be lowered away they had shaken hands.

"This, what you see here," Juan's arm swung in an arc to include New Providence and the scattering of small islands and coral heads, "is only a little of the Bahamas. When this New Bedford gets too cold for your bones, you come back. In my house you are always welcome. Or, if you don't like that, pick out almost any island and build your own."

"I'll keep the offer in mind, Mr. Cadiz." He smiled warmly. "I'll think of you when the northerly howls down the Massachusetts coast. Good-bye and good luck. I could ask, now, nothing better than this ship be in your hands and those of Captain Raleigh."

Now, the early morning swept over the sky in flames of color and Captain Raleigh could not keep the wonder from his expression. As a matter of fact his attitude since they put in at Nassau was one of incredulity. He had never seen fish of such brilliant hue as those which swarmed in the clear waters, or the amazing patches of sea as they ranged from deep purple to pink and green. His gaze roved constantly over the almost unbroken chain of cays from the time they had cleared Beacon Cay. The wind and warming sun lay soft against his face and he thought of how the Gloucester fishing boats came in during the winter with ice so thick on the rigging it had to be chopped away. He was too young not to betray the excitement and astonishment he felt.

"Is it always this way, Mr. Cadiz?"

"No." Juan laughed a little. "We tell each other it is but sometimes she blows like hell and you expect everything to go flying through the air—islands, people, houses, cows and horses. Sometimes they do, too. If you stay you'll learn the signs. Like John an' me here, you'll feel and smell the hurricane before she comes."

"I don't think I'll ever want to leave and," his clear, youthful features with small crinkles about the eyes were serious, "I am grateful for the opportunity you have given me. I didn't expect a command of my own for years."

Juan checked his course a trifle. "For a man who loves the sea I guess this is, maybe, the best life in the world. It has been so for me." He glanced at Raleigh. "You know something, Captain? I don't know your first name."

"It's on my papers in my cabin." Curiously enough he appeared embarrassed.

"That I know." Juan stared at him. "I never looked."

"I always feel like a damn fool when I have to answer the question. It's Walter. Walter Raleigh. Parents ought to know better. I hate to think of the fights I had over that name when I was a boy in school."

Juan glanced from the captain to John. "This Walter Raleigh," he addressed his son, unashamed of his ignorance, "he was somebody?"

"I guess you might say so, Papa." John kept his face straight. "He put his cloak down so the Queen could walk across a mud puddle without getting her feet dirty."

"That's all?" Juan suspected now both Raleigh and John were having a little fun with him. "She must have been a pretty stupid queen to be walking around in the rain when she had carriages and horses to carry her."

"You know, Mr. Cadiz," Captain Raleigh appeared relieved, "I've always felt the same way. Anyhow, this Sir Walter Raleigh founded a colony in Virginia and is supposed to have brought the first tobacco to England. That's why I had so many fights. The other boys were always bowing and saying: 'How do you do, Sir Walter?' After a while it stops being funny."

"I'll tell you something." Juan deliberated for a second or two. "We don't get much formal on Exuma. Aboard the ship I'll call you Captain an', I guess, I'll have to be Mr. Cadiz. When we are on the island I'll call you Walter or Raleigh, whichever you like. If it comes easy to you, my name is Juan." He looked up at the sky speculatively and then spoke to himself. "We get home late or lay to until morning."

"How long is this Exuma chain?" Raleigh studied one of the high, rolling cays.

"Maybe ninety, ninety-five miles. We make, I guess, five or six knots now. I don't want to crowd her. The bars shift an' what wasn't here yesterday might be here today. You can always tell by the color of the water but not after the sun drops to your eyes. Anyhow," a smile of anticipation lighted his eyes, "it'll give me pleasure to have my Caroline see her *Caroline* with the morning on her sails."

He gave his attention to the course before him and, although he was the ship's captain, Raleigh stepped back and away. He had the feeling that at this moment Juan Cadiz wanted to be alone with his son, his ship, and the thoughts occupying his mind.

With the sail dropped, the sloop drifted on the easy swell. Bahama lay back, the tiller nudging her shoulder now and then as the currents and light wind carried the craft aimlessly. She lifted her face and watched a couple of gulls as they followed hopefully. There was a line and a fresh conch for bait at her feet but she had no interest in fishing. Glancing down she saw the blue-gray length of a shark as it nosed curiously past, half rolling to one side as it glided alongside and then disappeared in a slow dive.

Earlier she had breakfasted with Caroline. There had been silence between them, strained and uncomfortable, until she broke it voluntarily.

"I wanted to come to your room last night. There seemed so much unsaid and what had been spoken was bitter and angry."

Caroline looked up quickly, surprised. "I wish you had. I was desperately lonely, feeling I had lost you."

"I didn't sleep very well."

"Neither did I."

Bahama spooned out a segment of the melon before her and then slowly, neatly, cut it into small pieces; not really wanting the fruit, simply delaying the words.

"We can't go on this way, can we?"

"No." Caroline was deliberately short, afraid to trust her voice in saying more. "No, Bahama."

The gray eyes across the table lifted and met hers without hostility. They looked at each other, mother and daughter, so much alike in manner and feature.

"David is dead." The statement was made without emotion. "For a long time after you left I thought about it. There isn't any other way. I must keep saying that to myself until I believe it. David is dead."

Impulsively, Caroline reached both hands across the table and took those of her daughter. She felt the sharp sting of tears welling to her eyes for this was her child, her baby, herself.

"If it is easier for you, darling."

[319]

"There is no easy way." Bahama locked her fingers through those of her mother. "I went over them all. So, last night when I was alone," a pallid smile touched her lips for an instant, "I became a widow as have women before me. I said: David is dead. He is now only for remembering with tenderness." The voice became a little firmer. "I said: if I tell myself this often enough, in time I will begin to believe it. But," she bowed her head, "if I mourn to myself you will understand. If I am sometimes quiet· and feel the desperate need to be alone, you will not think I am sulky or resentful. I have drained myself of bitterness and resentment and no longer blame anyone for what happened. How," her voice raised itself on a lighter note, "how this came about I'm not quite sure. But all of a sudden, just before daybreak, I discovered I could no longer cry anymore. I tried recalling everything about him but there were no tears, only a curious sorrow. That was when I said: David Heath is dead; you must make up your mind to it."

She pushed back her chair, moved about the table and pressed her cheek against her mother's. They held each other this way for a little while.

"I'm really not hungry." Bahama straightened up. "If you don't mind I'll take the sloop and go for a sail." She said this without any false attempt at gaiety but as she might have announced her intention of taking a walk. "Don't worry about me. I'll have a couple of sandwiches made."

"I won't worry about you any longer. I don't care much about my breakfast either." Caroline rose. "I'll find things to do; beat a few slaves, storm through the kitchen in a temper, or maybe just sit and knit. It is surprising how little there is to do when there are no men around." She immediately regretted the words.

Bahama shook her head understandingly. "I am no fragile piece of china to be handled carefully, Mother. I know there are still men in the world." She actually smiled. "The mention or sight of one isn't going to throw me into hysterics. I have told you what happened to David and it happened a long time ago. That is the way it has to be."

Shifting her position in the sloop's bottom now she caught the first sight of the topmasts of a ship as it moved, hidden by the crooked hump of land half encircling the natural harbor. She hauled her own small sail and the softest of breezes filled it. She was curious. No vessel, unless it was making for the plantation anchorage, would be taking this course.

She was out beyond the point before the schooner cleared it and came over slowly on a tack, for there was barely enough wind to give her steerageway. With the sunlight upon her fresh paint and gilded scrollwork below the bowsprit, she was a thing of breathtaking beauty and Bahama gasped with sudden delight. She brought the skittering sloop about into the wind. The schooner moved steadily toward where she lay. When she was close enough, Bahama came about with the following wind and ran along her side. She was close enough now to see John as he waved frantically and her father as he lifted both arms above his head in greeting. She outran the big ship as a dancing colt might toss up its head and race around some slower, ponderous animal. For a moment she thought about cutting across the schooner's bows just to show off. Instead, she made a circling sweep to the stern. In shining letters were the words *The Caroline. Exuma Bahamas.* So, she thought with excited pleasure, Papa has his ship at last. She knew little or nothing of vessels this size but there was no mistaking the sheer loveliness of her lines, the grace and ease with which she was being maneuvered to the protected, deep water.

When the heavy anchor had dropped with a showering splash and the *Caroline* lay motionless, she brought the sloop within its lee. Juan was at the rail now and he peered down with an exaggerated expression of leering interest.

"Hey! You islan' girl?"

"Name B'ma. You Yonkee sailor? Come shore. Plenty fun. Lots pretty girls, music, rum to drink. You have big time on islan'. Got girl for you. Name Caroline. You come now?"

"How's Mama?" Juan's broad grin met her upturned face.

"Gone off with Yonkee sailor."

"You make fool, girl."

"Yes, Papa." She could not keep the happiness from her voice. "I make fool." She studied her brother. "You're all grown up, Johnnie. Is that a beard you're trying to grow or don't you wash your face anymore?"

They were swinging a boat out now and Juan, with John, were joined by a third man. He was young, tall and with a weathered face which had borne the wind and the sun of the sea. His cap, with the gold braid of a captain, was pushed slightly back from his brow. With an oar she sculled out of the schooner's lee and caught the wind.

"I'll race you to the beach," she shouted over her shoulder. "Tell girls Yonkee sailors comin'."

She was on the small dock with the sloop moored before the heavy boat with four men at the sweeps drove into the shallowing water and grounded. The oarsmen jumped out and hauled her onto the beach.

Juan leaped out, followed by John. The man, who must be the schooner's master, followed more deliberately.

"Papa." She threw her arms about him with a fierce hug. "You've been away so long."

[321]

"How do you like what I brought back?" He turned her so they both could study the *Caroline*.

"She's beautiful." She clung to her father's arm and glanced mischievously at her brother. "So are you, Johnnie. Or, you will be after you wipe the fuzz off your face."

"This is Captain Raleigh." Juan's pleasure lighted his eyes. "His full name is Walter Raleigh. There is some sort of a joke about it I don't understand good."

"Servant, ma'am." Raleigh, who had not been able to keep his attention from straying away from the girl, made a short, formal bow, cap in hands.

Bahama made a slight curtsy which she managed with dignity despite the fact she wore the plainest of faded cotton dresses and was bare of feet.

"Welcome to Exuma, Captain." She offered her hand. "And I won't make the joke about Sir Walter Raleigh."

"Thank you, ma'am. I'm relieved."

They had barely started up the incline from the shore before Caroline came running down to meet them. Juan left the others and hurried to join her.

"Juanio." She was in his arms. "It has seemed so long."

"Five, six weeks." He held her close. "You see the schooner I bring back? Maybe you're not so glad to see me when you hear I spent all your money to buy her. What Papa Cameron left, you don't have no more."

"I don't care about the money. You know that."

The others had joined them, standing at a little distance as though reluctant to intrude. Still holding to Juan, Caroline reached out for her son's hand. "John." She drew him toward her.

She kissed him and then ran her hand across his stubbled chin while he flushed with embarrassment.

"No beard, please." She held him close until the three of them were a unit. "No mustache, no whiskers, Johnnie."

Bahama glanced at Captain Raleigh, who was so obviously uncomfortable in the affectionate intimacy of this family reunion. She looked up at him and then pressed a knuckle to the tip of her nose with a bemused gesture.

"I guess this just leaves you and me, Captain."

"Ma'am . . . I . . ." He stammered and appeared more the awkward school boy than a ship's captain. "Maybe I shouldn't have come ashore now."

"My name's Bahama. Or, as Papa says it, B'ma. I like that better. So," she made it casual, "if you are going to stay on Exuma or with the *Caroline,* I think you'd better start calling me B'ma." She darted an amused inspection of her bare feet. "Especially when I have no shoes on. Though," she was laughing at him, "if it offends your sense of propriety I suppose you may address me as Mistress Cadiz."

"Now," Juan put his arm about Caroline's waist, "we go to the house, have a drink an' something to eat an' I hear about all the trouble you've been having since Papa Juanio left."

"I didn't expect you," Caroline apologized. "We weren't sure when you'd be back."

"So?" Juan was indifferent. "We eat what there is and tonight we make a family party."

As he walked beside Bahama toward the house Captain Raleigh was aware of a lingering grandeur which the manor preserved although there were also unmistakable evidences of decay and neglect. He thought this was a most curious family. Madame Cadiz bore herself with the unaffected dignity of breeding, her speech was cultivated, her manner gracious. This Bahama, even with the bare toes peeking out from beneath a cheap cotton frock, managed to give the impression of a lady, impeccably groomed, strolling casually through her garden.

In the dining hall they gathered about the table while the slaves brought a cold ham, biscuits, hastily warmed yams and freshly sliced tomatoes. Rum, glasses, a humidor of slender black cigars were placed before the men.

"I'm sorry to offer you such a hurriedly prepared meal, Captain." Caroline excused the meager fare.

"It's far better than I am accustomed to aboard ship, ma'am."

Juan offered the rum to Raleigh and John. Then he filled a small glass for himself. He lit a cigar and swallowed part of the liquor.

"First," he sighed contentedly, "I tell you my news. Robert Bruce had a baby. A boy. What do you think of that after all this time? Robert Bruce with a son."

"He had it all by himself without any help from Constance?" Bahama managed a wide-eyed expression of admiring astonishment over the feat.

"You pretty smart conch girl." Juan regarded her with mock rebuke. "I guess Constance help some, though, at that. Anyhow, they have a boy and name him Richard Ormond Cameron." He paused and seemed to be thinking this over. "It's time someone got imagination an' they don't call him John. You know we got a hell of a lot of Johns. Juan. John. Anyhow, Robert Bruce he's a big man with his firm and thinks, one of these days, he gets to be a partner. Dav—" He halted abruptly.

"It's all right, Papa." Bahama was controlled, her face expressionless.

[323]

"Well." Juan poured himself a second glass of rum and cut a slice from the ham which he ate with his fingers while motioning Raleigh to join him. "Everything is fine with everyone."

"Maybe," Captain Raleigh started to rise, "I ought to get back to the ship." He felt his presence to be an intrusion at this time.

"You just left the ship." Juan was practical. "No one run off with her. In time you become like part of the family so you better get acquainted with us now." He turned to Caroline. "We made some money on the run down. Not a lot but some left over. I brought things from Nassau. Silks, linen, slave cotton, slippers for you an' B'ma. When they ask me what size I just hold out my hands, like this." He extended his palms. "I say my women got big feet from walking around barefoot." He leaned back in the chair. "Now! You tell me what's been going on since I left here. I'll bet those niggers ain't hooked a single sponge since I been away."

"They're rotten, Papa." Bahama spoke for her mother. "Something's got in them. No one knows what. I sailed up to the crawls one day. The boys showed me. The sponges are nothing but slime. It's the same all over the banks."

"God damn!" Juan was honestly annoyed. "You see what happen when I go away for two or three days? Now I got to do something about this for sure." He took a biscuit, bit it in half as though it had committed an offense.

"Yes, Papa." Bahama's eyes were filled with a laughing impudence. "I guess you will. You say: Stop this goddamned nonsense, sponge. You hear me?"

"I hear a real talking conch girl with a big mouth. I say it before." Juan regarded his daughter morosely. "How you get so smart since I go away?" He brooded for a moment. "What do you suppose get into those sponge they do this to me?"

"I don't know, Papa." Bahama was serious. "They say it is some sort of parasite. It happened before."

"Captain." Caroline turned to Raleigh. "Will you stay ashore with us or do you prefer your quarters on the ship?"

"You come an' go like you feel. When you want a night ashore there's plenty room." Juan settled the problem and then spoke to Caroline. "Later, we go out an' I show you this schooner but from now on Raleigh an' me don't spend a lot of time on Exuma. We start making some money. Maybe, in a couple of days, we go to Nassau. I have a talk there with the storekeepers an' factors who have to do business with the mainland. Robert Bruce's going to mark some of the island cargo for the *Caroline*. They got agents in the Havana, also. We pick up trade here an' there. John's got to study for his mate's papers so if something happen to Raleigh he can take over the ship. From now on we forget all about those damn fields Papa Cameron tried to put to cotton. I don't know what to do about the niggers. Maybe we can sell them off."

"I don't want you to do that." Caroline was firm.

"What do we need, maybe, a hundred niggers for? We stop being farmers. From now on we're island people, water people."

"Just the same I don't like to sell the hands." Caroline was unhappy. "Now, the schooner. You'll be away from home so much of the time."

"How can I stay here, girl?" He took her hand. "With the *Caroline* we build a regular trade and fix up this house so you live again the way you used to."

"I'm happy the way it is if you are here, Juanio."

"Well, I'm not." Juan whistled softly. "You know? Something happen to me up north on the mainland. I look at the fine place Robert Bruce got. I see people doing things, men at business, ladies in their carriages in the afternoon with little silk umbrellas over their heads to keep off the sun. I say: My girl she knew these things. I get ambition. Now," he mused, "that's a real, damn thing; like an itch you got to keep scratching. I sure get myself in a fix when I marry you. We build back the part of the house the hurricane tore away. We paint an' fix her up with new carpets, shine up all the candlesticks, put on shutters where they fell off, beat the hell out of some of those yard niggers 'til the outside look the way it used to. We get white aprons for the house girls an' caps for their heads an' new dresses of the gray slave cloth. We send to that England for china like what's been broken all this time. When we sit at the table the whole room is light up with candles an' I have a nigger man to stand behind my chair the way it was with Papa Cameron. We don't have no more damn nonsense around this place. We ain't conchs an' we ain't going to be. I know what happen to some of the other fine families in the islands. It ain't going to be so with us."

"Papa." Caroline's eyes were glowing with love and amusement. "I'm going to look a little silly riding through the Exuma brush in a carriage with a parasol over my head."

"Maybe you don't do that, but we change things." He spoke to Raleigh. "How about the *Caroline*'s crew? You think they want to stay on? If not I got island-born niggers, young bucks who grew up on the water. We teach them how to work the ship."

"I'm not certain about all the men." Raleigh was somewhat bewildered by the rushing flow of words. "I'll have a talk with them and find out who wants to sign on. For my part," he smiled reminiscently, "I don't care if I never see Massachusetts again."

"You may find it dull, Captain." Bahama looked directly at him.

"I find it hard to believe, ma'am."

"You blush easily, Captain." Bahama deliberately added to his confusion. "I take what you said as a compliment. Are they so hard to come by in your Massachusetts?"

"There is little occasion for them aboard a ship, ma'am."

Listening to the strange intonation of the Easterner, watching the play of expression on his face, Caroline found herself just a little troubled. She had the unhappy notion her daughter was deliberately using him to work off her personal emotions. He was young, handsome and, she recognized, absurdly and abjectly the immediate servant of Bahama. He could be easily and quickly hurt. Glancing at her daughter, noting the false demureness which was calculated to excite rather than subdue, she wanted to say: Don't do this thing simply because you have been wounded. Instead, she spoke to Raleigh.

"Would it be impertinent to ask how old you are, Captain?"

"No, ma'am. Twenty-five."

"Isn't that young to have a command?"

"Yes, ma'am. I am fortunate in having Mr. Cadiz trust me."

"And you won't miss your family?"

"I have only an aunt, living, ma'am. In Boston. The Raleighs have been a seafaring folk for generations. Their women are resigned to having the men sail away and never return. Anyhow, I expect we will sometimes make a call at Boston."

"Tomorrow," Juan was unintentionally rude with his interruption, "we sail up to where the crawls are. I find out what happen to those damn sponge. You know, girl," he put his hand on Caroline's, "I think your Juanio begins to get a little old. I lie down now for a while in a bed that don't heave around. Maybe, you come an' talk with me some."

"Would you care to show me the *Caroline,* Captain?" Bahama looked up.

"It would be an honor, ma'am."

"Stop calling me ma'am. It makes me feel ridiculous. I told you my name." There was a trace of impatience in the command.

Raleigh smiled a little. "Informality doesn't come readily to a New Englander, B'ma." He spoke her name with obvious difficulty.

"You see?" She arose and he stood up quickly to hold back her chair. "It isn't so hard. Not when you try. I think it is silly to keep calling me ma'am as though I were your aunt in Boston."

"All right." Juan yawned openly. "You go look over the schooner. My girl an' I spend some time together." He glanced across at John. "Johnnie. You have a horse saddled up, ride around some an' see what's going on about this place since we been away. Now they hear I'm home again I bet every nigger grabbed himself a hoe but he don't do nothing with it. We crack the whip some, hey?" He half laughed to himself and then addressed Raleigh. "Captain, you have a couple of the crew bring ashore the things I get in Nassau. When they get dressed up," he indicated Caroline and Bahama, "show you two of the prettiest conch girls in the islands. I guess," he grinned almost sheepishly, "that's about all the orders I got for everyone today. Now I sleep for a while."

They had taken Bahama's sloop and after Raleigh had shown her over the *Caroline* and she, in turn, had been the object of an admiring inspection from the crew, they had sailed around the long crescent of the cay.

"You handle a boat very well." Raleigh leaned back and watched her.

"I think I must have been born in one. Papa sailed in here one day and took Mother with him. It had a red sail, Papa's sloop, and Mother said there wasn't another one like it in the islands. Grandfather was furious when they ran away but she wouldn't come home without her Juanio. In the end, Grandfather had to accept him and before he was drowned, I think he really began to like Papa. It all sounded romantic." She paused for a moment. "Have you ever been in love, Raleigh?"

"Once. I was fourteen and she twenty-five or so with a husband and two children. I recall it was a most painful experience."

"Yes." She spoke absently. "Yes. Isn't it?"

He looked at her sharply for there was something in the tone which went beyond the small talk they were making. Her hair had been fastened at the nape of her neck with a small ribbon. She loosed the tie and the wind fanned it out like champagne-colored, silken threads in a soft cloud. She did it naturally and without affectation. From the moment of their meeting he had watched her and thought now how strange it was that this island-born girl never made a false move or ever seemed to be uncertain of her words or actions. The scimitar curve of the beach with its massed palms back from the white sand was to him a thing of unbelievable beauty. All of his time at sea, save for one transatlantic sailing and a voyage to Cuba, had been spent in the coastal run from Boston, New York as far south as Savannah.

"I've never seen anything like these waters." He spoke quietly, for the mood of the growing afternoon was hushed.

"Or, I suspect," she smiled, "anyone like Juan Cadiz and his family. Papa must have come as something of a shock to the good people of Charleston and Norfolk."

Raleigh shook his head. "Juan Cadiz is a most remarkable man." He pronounced the name as it should be spoken in the Spanish with the harsh z turned to a soft s. "He has what you have, complete self-possession. He is never unsure of himself. He is one of the fortunate, born with a full confidence in himself. He is comfortable in any situation and company. I think he is, also, one of the kindest men I have ever known. Most persons would have been indifferent to the feelings of Captain McEvans, who commanded the schooner before she was attached and sold. He loved her. Your father gave him the opportunity of sailing her one last time even though it was unnecessary and meant paying his passage back to Boston. Few men would have been so thoughtful."

"Yes." She nodded an agreement. "Papa would do something like that. He is really a very gentle man. I think some persons might confuse his manner with weakness. I have never seen him angry but I believe he could be a very dangerous man if pushed."

"I'll do my best to stay in his good graces."

"Oh, he likes you! I could tell."

It did not seem at all unusual they should be talking this way, without effort and as though they had known each other for a long time. They were unconsciously drawn together by an honesty of nature which made posturing and pretense impossible. He saw her as a remarkably beautiful girl and she, in her loneliness, a real sense of bereavement over the loss of David, found a strange comfort in his presence. There was, in her mind, nothing beyond this, but it filled an emptiness of which she had been miserably aware.

"From what little I've seen," he scanned the coloring sky and seemed musingly interested, talking at random, "you are a remarkable family."

"What did you expect?"

"I'm not sure but not this. You . . . your mother, father and brother seem so closely bound together you are indifferent to your isolation. Most persons would find such an island life unendurably lonely."

"John and I have never known any other. Papa was born here and Mother came as a young girl. I don't see how you can miss what you never had. This is our home."

"But," he was not satisfied, "you have read of places beyond the islands. Hasn't that excited a curiosity? Your speech is educated, your manners—"

"A great deal better than yours, Captain Raleigh." She cut him off in midsentence. "Aren't you being a little presumptuous, even insolent?" She was angry. "Why shouldn't my manners be good, my speech a reflection of my mother's?"

"My apologies, Mistress Bahama. I deserved everything you said." He made a wide gesture with one arm and managed to give the impression of a bow without moving. "I ask your pardon."

[328]

"Just don't be so damn superior. Yonkee sailor talkin' conch girl."
Her annoyance vanished as quckly as it had come.

"What I was trying, in my clumsy way, to say was that the manor,
the extent of the holding and the family all came as a surprise. I was
stupid enough to say so."

"If you had known Grandfather Cameron you would have understood what Exuma once meant. It was to be a great cotton plantation
and on it he would recreate the Colonial life of Carolina. When it failed
something went out of him but not out of my father."

Wide spears of color began to fan out against the sky as the sun lowered toward the horizon. Raleigh thought he had never been aware of
such complete silence. With the dropping of the sun the light wind began to fail and there was barely enough to fill the triangle of canvas.
She brought the boat about on the tack which would take them to the
dock.

Caroline looked at her daughter and then at the two gowns spread
upon the bed. In addition to silk and linen yardage, Juan had purchased
the dresses from models in a Nassau apparel shop for ladies. Unfortunately the ladies to whom the establishment catered were those of color,
who drew their support from the more prosperous of the merchants and
a few gentlemen from the mansions on the hill who maintained them
discreetly in small cottages and visited them only at night. The taste of
these half-caste girls was decidedly flamboyant and the shop stocked
what appealed to its clients. The silken gowns now spread upon a counter-
pane were of a brilliant, floral design which all but shrieked their colors
and the extreme décolletage. Caroline regarded them with something
bordering upon hysterical dismay.

"But, Mama," Bahama protested, "we just can't."

"I could cry. Honestly." Caroline faced her daughter. "Papa meant to
do something wonderful for us."

"They are wonderful, Mama." Bahama lifted one of purple flowering and held it before her. "No one can say they are not wonderful but,
Mama, if you put this on I am just going to scream with laughter all
the way down the stairs and out into the yard."

"You will do nothing of the sort." Caroline was firm. She took the
dress and held it by her fingertips as though the touch would contam-
inate. "You will put on one and I the other and we will go down and
join Papa and Captain Raleigh."

"You don't mean it." Bahama was incredulous.

"Make your choice." Caroline shuddered a little. "Select your gown
and the slippers."

[329]

"Mama, I'll have to stuff paper into them to keep those slippers on. You know what sort of girls in Nassau these things are for?"

"I know but I'm surprised you do." She stared at the garment unbelievingly. "I'll take this one. Purple and green have always been my favorite colors." She paused. "If you think I am going to hurt my Juanio by not appearing tonight as he expects us then you are mistaken. He thinks they are beautiful and so do I. Now. Shall we prepare for the evening?"

The two slave girls who helped them to dress did so in silent awe, the wonder of their mistresses' magnificence showing in their eyes. By dint of some fastening here and there Bahama contrived to prevent the bodice from slipping and falling to her waist. Soft wadding of paper pushed into the toes of the slippers of magenta-colored satin kept them on her feet. When she was ready she went to her mother's room.

It was only with an effort that either could bear to look at the other. Caroline finally took a deep breath.

"I must say, Bahama, you look . . ." She could not finish. "You just look."

"You, also, Mother. Just."

Together they descended the staircase. The lower floor was flooded with light, for Juan, among other things, had been extravagant in the purchase of candles. With Raleigh and John, Juan was in the sitting room when the doors were held open and Caroline, with Bahama, entered. He gazed upon wife and daughter with shining pleasure.

"You two damn fine-lookin' conch girls." He went to them and put an arm around the waist of each. "Old Juanio don't make mistake when he see those dresses." He crossed the room with them.

For a moment Raleigh and John only stared without expression and then it was John who spoke.

"Mama, you look beautiful. You too, B'ma."

Caroline smiled her gratitude. This son of hers was a gentleman. Not even the insularity of their lives had prevented it from showing itself in a moment of crisis.

"Thank you, John." She turned to Raleigh. "Captain. Good evening and," her smile gave warmth to the words, "may I say you look exceptionally handsome in your dress uniform."

"Ma'am and Mistress B'ma." He bowed. Nothing in his attitude betrayed his astonishment over the gowns which fairly screamed their colors. The fact crossed his mind that they were being worn with such serene dignity as to make them seem quite normal attire for ladies. "Thank you for your invitation to be present this evening."

A slave brought slender decanters of sherry and Madeira, carefully

[330]

placing the highly polished tray of silver on a table near his master. As he withdrew, Caroline glanced at her husband with surprise. The manor's wine cellar had long since been exhausted save for the rum which was plantation-distilled.

Juan beamed his pleasure. "I spend money in Nassau like my pockets are filled with it. There is wine for now and later for the meal. I find out in Charleston that ladies do not drink in the company of their men. I think it is pretty foolish. Tonight is a celebration with this sherry for you an' B'ma with John, Raleigh an' me. I think we start a new life on Exuma. We make a toast to the *Caroline*."

The meal was as lavish as the plantation could afford and provide. There was a clear soup made from a turtle caught that day. Then, fresh, broiled red snapper the size of a hand with butter and the juice of fresh lime. Finally, there came to the table a fine roast of young pig with a great variety of vegetables, and at the end, a dessert of banana custard. Through it all Juan talked with an unquenchable enthusiasm of his plans now that the schooner was safely in its home waters. He spoke of her as a person, vital and alive.

"She outrun anything, this girl. We carry cargo back an' forth so fast they don't have time to get it off before the dock niggers say: Here come that *Caroline* again. Get the stuff clear away for she here with more." He was delighted with the fancy. "We got a good captain an', maybe, a good mate when he learns what's in the books an' Raleigh can teach him." He put an affectionate hand on John's shoulder.

Listening, watching the play of animation on his features, Caroline was a little frightened by his enthusiasm and ashamed of her doubts. Could it all be this easy? Was it so simple? Wasn't there established competition to be met, a contest for cargo, a fight for each box and bale? Was this only the overconfidence, a man's dream, as had been the plantation of Ronald Cameron, and would it end in the same disillusionment? She did not know the answers and not for the world would she voice a question. What Juan did was for her. For himself he had always been satisfied with the simplest of things. What did she want? Not much, really. It would be nice to have the big house repaired and repainted; new upholstery for the furniture, grown delicately shabby with the years; better clothing for the house slaves; a full set of china again, perhaps. For herself she needed only this man who was well into his middle age with her and the love between them which had never wavered.

They finished the meal. John excused himself and went to his books. Juan yawned openly and Bahama with Raleigh went to walk in the soft night, where she voiced what had been in her mother's mind.

"Tell me, Raleigh, what do you think? Papa takes so much for granted. A schooner, and all the problems of Exuma are solved. He has the wonderful imagination of a boy. Nothing seems impossible. I wonder."

"There are problems to be met. I know those of the coastal trade. There are rate wars, a constant fight for cargo, high insurance costs. But, with the help of your uncle's firm in Charleston I think they can be met."

"I hope so." Her hand rested lightly on his arm. "But not simply for the reasons you may think—so Juan Cadiz can become successful and restore Exuma. I love these islands and hate what is happening to them. There have been so many failures here. So many families with fine dreams who have watched them vanish in the hard light of reality. There is real poverty here among many who, according to Mother, must once have had everything on the mainland. There are names which were old in the colonies long before the Revolution. Now their children and grandchildren are reduced to fishing from small boats and tilling a patch for the substance of living. In another generation they will be unrecognizable for what they were. Even in my time, and that's not many years, I have seen the change. Those I knew as a child have already resigned themselves to defeat. The homes of their parents fall away. They grow up without any interest in an education, marry young and have child after child who are not even taught to read or write. Mother and Papa did what they could for John and me. Grandfather Cameron saw to it. We were sent off to Eluthera, a missionary school, and Grandfather Cameron had brought a huge library with him. We were made to read, to learn what was possible. All through the islands, though, you see those who have been beaten and have come to accept this as a natural state."

"Your father doesn't impress me as a man who gives up easily. 'I see what's wrong with those damn sponge.'" He made a laughing effort to imitate Juan's indignation over a blight infesting the sponge beds. "Your father takes everything as a personal challenge."

"That is one of the reasons why I wouldn't like to see him fail with the *Caroline,* and because the Bahamas are my home I hate to see them become forgotten dots in a great ocean."

As they walked slowly their shoulders touched now and then and she was as fully aware of him as a man as he was of her as a woman. She despised herself a little for this; thinking how easily the heart mends itself or, at least, yearns for recovery.

"Will you be staying with the *Caroline,* Raleigh?"

"I can't imagine anything which would make me want to leave."

"I'm glad." She said it simply. "Not only because Papa needs you."

Both the words and their tone caused him to look down at her with a puzzled expression of surprise. She lifted her face to meet his glance.

"I think I need you, also, Raleigh."

"I don't understand." He was astounded by the unaffected statement. Young ladies he had known did not make such declarations. "I'm a stranger to you."

"More the reason." She smiled at his bewilderment and then shook her head emphatically. "I'm not playing the coquette or seeking adventure beyond what I have known here. You like me. A person senses this at once. That is enough for now. We don't have to try and make anything more of it than it is. You are not accustomed to having a girl be this direct, are you?"

"No. No, I'm not." He could think of no reply beyond the few words.

"This afternoon, while we were sailing, you wondered at the simple life we lead here. Well, it has probably made me a little more direct than I otherwise might have been. There has been no need to be devious. So, I say what I feel." She halted and faced him. "Will you be my friend?"

"I am already."

"Then," she was serious, "will you let it go at that for a while and allow whatever happens later come naturally? If it should come at all. We will be seeing much of each other, for the *Caroline* will be putting in and out of Exuma. I would like to feel easy with you and sometimes, when I particularly need to, be able to think of you as someone I can talk with and not have to pretend."

"I don't see how I could say no to anything you've said, do you?" He was half amused, partly mystified, for there had been a strangely disturbing intensity in her rush of words.

"No." She smiled and all her seriousness was gone. "No, I don't. And, I suppose, it is the reason I said what I did."

They turned and walked slowly back toward the house, which still glowed with the extravagance of Juan's purchase of candles. Between them something had been quietly born but it was not a thing to be stated. So, they said nothing more and the only sound was the eternal rush of the sea upon its beach and the crackling whisper of the tall palms.

⊰ XX ⊱

WHAT THEY should have known or considered in the beginning became all too obvious by the end of the first year. Trade between the mainland and the Bahamas was almost a one-way traffic. The islands were dependent upon imports from a nail to a bucket of paint but they had little to offer in return. So, the *Caroline,* riding high in ballast, more often than not went to the Southern ports with her holds all but empty.

There were other problems, also. The merchandise Nassau did import from the United States was subject to exorbitant customs duties. Save for the matter of transportation costs it was cheaper for the islands to buy in Liverpool or London and wait for their orders to make the long crossing in British ships. No one was in a hurry anyhow, and if something didn't arrive this week it would the next.

The mysterious blight afflicting the sponge beds persisted. What might have been gathered, imported and sold for a good price on the mainland simply refused to cure itself. The only cargo the schooner carried to the ports of Savannah and Charleston was a variety of hardwood cut on Andros Islands, tobacco picked up in the port of Havana, rum from Jamaica and an occasional load of pineapples which were grown in limited quantities on Eleuthera. Instead of the direct runs back and forth from Nassau to the Southern coast Juan had envisioned, they must cruise ceaselessly like some hungry dog picking up a bone here and there. The *Caroline* was, in truth, a tramp.

Through the efforts of Robert Bruce and his firm they managed to secure some cargo consignments from Boston and New York, where the exporters wanted fast, cheap delivery, but these were barely enough to pay the wages of the crew, buy their food and keep the vessel in repair. There were months when the *Caroline* never saw her island waters. Instead, she followed a coastal trade carrying her from Georgia to Massachusetts. For the first time Juan and John experienced the numbing cold,

[334]

the screaming, bone-chilling gales of the northern Atlantic. They saw rigging and rail thick with ice, and decks so treacherous of footing that a man risked a broken leg or back in trying to cross them. They saw and began to hate the sheeting rains of the Virginia capes, the howling winds and bitter fury as they beat their way in from a storm off New York and tried to make the Narrows and shelter of Hudson's River or lay into the piers on the city's East Side. They saw, through flying spume and sheeting water, the wrecks of fine ships on the jagged shoals of Cape Hatteras and its well-named companion, Cape Fear.

Now, on a day some eighteen months after she had first sailed into the Exuma anchorage, the *Caroline* again lay on the soft and sheltered waters of the cay. The crew lazed in the warm sunshine with paint, varnish and brushes, working without haste, and no one drove them to faster labor for they were all weary of the sea and content to rest for a while in this placid haven.

On the ridge the manor had grown perceptibly shabbier as though its age was being accelerated by neglect. The grounds were in need of care, for despite Caroline's will the slaves performed their tasks with dawdling indifference. They were accustomed to a man's authority and without it they malingered openly, almost insolently. Also, and Caroline was sensitive to this, they seemed to have a primitive intuition that a slow process of disintegration had set in. They were without the intelligence to look beyond the house and the fields and in these the erosion was unmistakable. In their simple minds they equated this with the family itself. A Cameron nigger was no longer any better than the meanest slave on any of the other islands.

At this, their first meal since the *Caroline* had dropped anchor, Juan, with Caroline, John, Bahama and Raleigh, sat about the table in the dining hall which, somehow, seemed cavernous as walls and furniture were no longer polished, waxed, rubbed and brightly lit as before. Juan looked about him and the laughter usually in his eyes vanished. He watched as the two slave girls served them with shuffling indifference and the black man, whose duties as a butler required him to supervise the house slaves with dignity, leaned against a wall and stared blankly out of the window. Without comment Juan rose and walked from the room while Caroline and the others looked after him with unvoiced curiosity. When he returned he carried with him a heavy riding crop which had belonged to Ronald Cameron and for these years lay unused in a cabinet's drawer in the library. He then did what had never been done to a Cameron house slave before. The crop whipped across the face and shoulders of the manservant until the black howled his pain and terror and he backed into a corner, cowering there, attempting to shield his face with crossed arms. Juan beat him methodically until he dropped to his knees and screamed for pity. He then turned upon the slave girls who stood transfixed and drove them about the room, laying the crop across their shoulders and buttocks while they shrieked in keening wails of agony and fled through the pantry hall toward the kitchen. Juan was relentless. He followed and herded them before him into the kitchen, where half a dozen blacks who belonged in the yard lazed in chairs or on the long, bare table. He slashed them over hands and faces until they tumbled through the door in screeching fear and cries for mercy and help. Even the cook, a large, heavy-breasted, wide-buttocked woman who had not been touched, ran from this silent avenger.

When Juan returned to the dining hall the black man was on his feet, eyes wide, back pressed against the wall. Juan faced him. When he spoke there was no tremor of anger in his voice.

"You know what I mean." It was not a question.

"Yes, Marstah Boss." The reply quavered.

"Then you see it's done or I, Juan Cadiz, will kill you. I have never done this before but I will kill you if it happens again an' you tell every nigger in the house what I say to you."

"Yes, Marstah Boss." He slid around the walls until he reached the pantry hall door and backed out.

Juan sat down. "I been away too long." He stretched to touch Caroline's cheek with his fingers. "Things get straightened out now."

When the butler returned with the serving girls their tears had been wiped away, their dresses changed and small aprons tied about their waists. Fear lingered in their eyes but they served the table as they had been taught. When the meal was finished the manservant brought rum, cigars and coffee and then took his place behind Juan's chair in silence.

"I never saw you angry before, Papa." Bahama regarded him with veiled surprise.

"Who? Me?" Juan pretended astonishment. "I don't get mad. I just put things back the way they should be. What was it we talk about?" He lit a cigar and studied it with pleasure. "We bring these from the Havana an' the coffee too. In Nassau the price for them was good."

"Juanio, Juanio." Caroline shook her head with quiet wonder. She had never seen him in a rage, never witnessed the punishment of a slave. "After all these years you still surprise me."

"You think I get old, maybe?"

"No, my Juanio. I don't think you get old." Her voice was filled with tenderness.

He dismissed this with a small wink. "Anyhow, maybe the Havana trade is what we deal in."

[336]

"Nassau can only use so much coffee, so many cigars." John voiced the obvious. "And the shipping from Cuba to the mainland is already heavy. I don't think what is left over for us would amount to much."

The adversity they had encountered had not outwardly affected Juan's natural ebullience. This was still a challenge. This was his family and he was still Juan Cadiz who could do anything. He poured some rum into his coffee.

"I got some ideas we talk about." He sighed comfortably.

Watching, listening, her eyes taking in everyone at the table, it occurred to Caroline that an astonishing thing had happened to them. They had always been close as a family, with love and respect. But, it had been a laughing, carefree existence which left everyone free to go his or her way. Now, though, with the men driving themselves for the trade they must have for the schooner, a solidarity, a tight union, was manifesting itself. This, also, included Raleigh who, if he chose, could have continued outside and remained only master of the *Caroline*. The New Englander, she laughed to herself at the choice of the designation for it seemed foreign to her, elected to make himself a part of it all. He shared the disappointments and the few triumphs with equal unhappiness or pleasure. She realized, also, an understanding of some sort had been reached between Raleigh and Bahama. It manifested itself in many small ways—a look, a smile, the inflection of a word. It was Bahama who stood on the ridge peering seaward when they thought or hoped the schooner was due. It was Bahama who raced down to cast off in the sloop when the vessel was sighted at the far end of the point, and went out to meet her. But it was Raleigh who left the command to John for the mooring and went down a ladder to sail back to shore with Bahama. There was no mistaking the fact Raleigh was in love. About her daughter she could not tell, for this was one of the few things they had not discussed. Now, Raleigh was leaning slightly forward on the table. One hand held the mug with his coffee and rum. The other lay palm down. With an easy, natural gesture Bahama laid her hand over it. Raleigh stretched up his fingers to meet hers. Bahama, suddenly aware of her mother's gaze, lifted her eyes.

"Raleigh and I are going to be married." She made the announcement as casually as she might have said they were going for a sail. "He hasn't really asked me yet."

Even the young captain was startled. His glance moved from Caroline to Juan and then to the girl at his side. His lean, handsome, weathered face was a study in confusion.

"I know he will," Bahama continued blithely, "so I might as well say it for him."

"What's this?" Juan put aside his cigar. "You, conch girl, marry with Yankee sailor?"

"I was going to speak to you, sir." Raleigh was acutely miserable. "B'ma and I haven't really talked it over but I felt . . . well, I thought . . ."

"What for you speak to me?" Juan was pleased. "I never ask my girl's papa. I just say: Come along. She came. You ask me an' I say no. What happen? You do it anyhow."

"Darling." Caroline reached for her daughter's hands across the table. "I'm happy for you both." She did her best to keep a note of relief from her voice.

"How the hell," Juan scratched his head with a puzzled gesture, "you make this up together? How does a man do court to a girl when most of the time he's at sea somewhere?"

"There are ways, Papa." Bahama grinned at him.

Juan nodded. "It don't take long, sometimes. You look. You think I want this one. Maybe, in a minute, it gets decided. You're a damn fine man, Raleigh. Take care this conch girl."

"Congratulations, Captain." John stood up and offered his hand with mock formality. "Or maybe it should be the other way around."

"When you make this marriage, hey?" Juan now interested himself in the details.

"Anytime. Now," Bahama answered. "Can't a ship's captain perform the ceremony? Raleigh's a captain." She pretended a wide-eyed innocence.

"I sure don't think he can make marry with himself." Juan was skeptical. "I tell you what. We all go to Nassau in the *Caroline*. We make the marriage there an' have a hell of a time, a big celebration like it used to be when Juan Cadiz knew everyone along the docks an' in the Out Island boats."

"Couldn't we please," Caroline voiced a plaintively feigned protest for she knew her Juanio was joking and in a high good humor, "couldn't we have it a little different? Your waterfront friends . . ." She lifted her shoulders expressively.

"You're probably right." Juan was momentarily saddened. "They're all too damn old now to have any fun with. Just the same. We make the wedding in Nassau."

"You getting married, Papa?" Bahama asked, surprised.

"You know I got a girl. She won't stand for no other one around. You an' Raleigh get married."

"Then you let me do it our way. I don't want to go to Nassau. We send a boat for the missionary when he's in Eluthera and we have the wedding here."

"Thank you, dear." Caroline expressed her gratitude. "I hate to think of the guests Papa would gather together in Nassau."

"Here?" Juan was disappointed. "How do we have fun here?"

"Suppose you leave that to Raleigh and me."

Juan thought this over for a moment. "Maybe, I guess, you're right. My girl an' me didn't need anyone." He turned to Raleigh. "We give you a share in the *Caroline* for a wedding present."

"You don't need to do that." Raleigh was embarrassed.

"I can't have no poor sea captain for a son-in-law." Juan stirred his coffee as he added more rum. He was doing his best to hide his pleasure for he had come to like this sometimes taciturn but steady, competent man of the North. "I've been thinking about a couple of things. We're doing all right but not good enough for Juan Cadiz and his family. Now, good or bad, lying out there or at sea we've always got the expense of the crew. Suppose we begin to train some of our nigger boys who are island-born and take to the water like a turtle? First thing you know we got a good black crew an' they cost us nothing except to feed."

Raleigh was doubtful. "I don't think our white crew would work and share the forecastle with the blacks."

"All right." Juan was undisturbed. "Then we pay the white crew off, ship them home, and start with all new black hands."

"It would take time to train them. They're used to only small boats. While we're doing it, the *Caroline* is out of service. We lose the revenue from her for months, maybe. Besides, have you thought what would happen to those black boys in a norther off the New England coast in the wintertime if we had to make such a run? They'd die in the cold. You couldn't make them work a ship."

Juan meditated on this and then nodded a reluctant agreement. "I guess you're right. John an' me damn near froze an' I didn't have to do anything." He thought for a moment. "All right." Raleigh's logic was conceded. "We keep the crew an' pay the wages. Now." He glanced around the table, his eyes touching them all. "In my mind, for a long time, is something else. I think we begin to smuggle goods to the Bahamas."

He made the statement so casually it took a few seconds for it to register upon the others.

"What did you say, Father?" John sat upright in his chair. "Smuggle?"

"What's wrong with that, Johnnie?"

"Wrong?" Raleigh was completely surprised. "What's wrong is it's against the law."

[339]

"In the Bahamas," Juan shrugged, "for a long time no one pay much attention to the laws. Now, what we got is pretty simple. The Nassau merchants only buy what they have to from the mainland." He was not at all disturbed by Raleigh's astonishment. "That's because they have to pay duty. Suppose they don't pay no duty? They get what they want cheaper an' faster than from England. Their goods come in the *Caroline*." He dipped the tip of his cigar into the coffee and rum and tasted the flavor.

"You're not serious, Juanio?" Caroline was disturbed because she was quite certain he was completely serious. "You don't mean it?"

"What's wrong with a little smuggling?" Juan was honestly marveling at the objection. "For a hundred, two hundred years, maybe, it's been going on in the islands. Some of those fine families in the big houses on the hill in Nassau made their fortunes smuggling or were pirates and wreckers. We don't kill nobody. We don't wreck no ship. Who gets hurt? The King of England? The Royal Navy Patrol boat? Nobody."

"If we get caught we go to prison." John stated the obvious but there was a small note of excitement in his voice. "That's who gets hurt."

"We don't get caught." Juan brushed away the comment as unworthy of serious attention. "I know, maybe, a hundred places where we make meet with small boats from Nassau an' transfer cargo."

"You don't really mean it, do you?" Raleigh studied Juan as though he was sitting next to a stranger.

"Why should I just make talk?"

"But," the young New Englander's conscience was outraged by this bland announcement of an intention to break the law, "it's dishonest. It's stealing."

"Raleigh." Juan was being patient. "I said before—who do we steal from, some beggar? No. The King of England? Yes. But he lives in a palace with rooms filled with gold. Do we take it from the Governor in Nassau? He don't get the duty money but has to send it to the King so what does he care? Now, if you look at it the right way we do favors for a lot of poor people in the islands who can't always pay for what comes from England or the mainland. We help the merchants and shopkeepers in Nassau who can buy stuff cheaper off the *Caroline*. We do good for those who need it. People in the Bahamas will say: Look at Juan Cadiz, his son an' son-in-law. They help us get the things at a fair price without duty put on them. God bless those good men."

There was such an expression of hypocritical piety on Juan's face that Raleigh threw back his head and shouted with laughter. Tears ran down his cheeks. He tried to swallow some coffee and nearly choked on it. Even Caroline was forced to an uncertain smile. John and Bahama bit hard upon their lips to keep from laughing at their father, who was regarding them all with a mild amazement.

"Papa." It was the first time Raleigh had ever used the word to Juan. "You are a complete scoundrel; a persuasive one, I'll admit, but a scoundrel just the same."

"That's a fine name to call your papa-in-law to be." Juan was injured. He turned to Bahama. "What kind of a man you marry who talks to Papa Juanio that way?"

"But the patrol boat, Papa? The Customs Officers and the Lighthouse Service?" Bahama had her tongue in her cheek.

"Aaah!" Juan's opinion of the Royal Navy was expressed with a sound. "The patrol boat she runs like a cart on wheels following a road. Up here. Down there. Back again. Wait a minute."

He jumped up from his chair, hurried to the library and came back with a chart rolled in a tube. He spread it on the table between John and Raleigh. It covered the area from the Little Bahama Bank to Great Inagua with its hundreds and hundreds of cays. He traced it over with a finger.

"You think a patrol boat can find Juan Cadiz in here?" He ignored the southern portion and laid his hand over a section from Mantilla Shoal, across Little and Great Abaco to the Northeast Providence Channel. "They go crazy just trying to look or they pile up on a reef. I know every foot of water, every coral head. What do you think I've been doing all my life?"

"Getting ready to smuggle goods into Nassau." Caroline made the statement with calm authority. She understood her Juan. This he was going to do. "I often wondered how your boyhood was spent."

"You see?" Juan was delighted. "My girl here, she understands."

"That wasn't exactly what I had in mind, Juanio." Her dry comment had a glint of humor in it.

"Papa. You're a pirate. I've suspected it for years. You only pretend to be respectable." Bahama's eyes were bright.

"I never wanted to be respectable," he defended himself. "My girl here an' old Papa Cameron, they try to make me so but they give up after a while."

"You're really going to do it, aren't you, Papa?" Bahama leaned forward and peered intently into his fox-bright eyes.

"I've got a family an' a schooner to take care of." There was nothing but virtue in his expression. He turned in his chair and regarded Raleigh. "You marry a poor, Yankee sailor then Papa Juan's got to do something."

[341]

"I don't know." Raleigh honestly didn't know what to say. He looked to Caroline for help. "Ma'am?"

"Poor Raleigh." Bahama put her hand on his. "He's wrestling with his Puritan conscience and ancestors."

"Juanio." Caroline was serious. "We don't need money so much."

"I don't talk only of money. I've got the finest, fastest schooner in the world, maybe. You remember," he pulled her chair close to his, "how you told me when you were a little girl and how Papa Cameron once took you and Robert Bruce to relatives in Virginia an' how the grow-ups get on horses and with dogs chase a fox? Now, nobody really wanted a fox, did he?"

"The devil quotes Scripture." Caroline laid her cheek against his shoulder. "Why should I try or want to try and change you after all these years? Run up the Jolly Roger."

"Mama!" Bahama stared at her mother. "You're telling him to do it."

"No, darling," Caroline's smile was a trifle wan, "I'm just not telling him not to do it, for I know my Juan."

Raleigh's face was a confused design of contrasts for he was, as Bahama had said, struggling with a conscience which went far back in his ancestry. Opposing his scruples was the fact he was still young enough to find excitement in the risk of pitting wits, skill and the schooner's speed against authority. Also, from the beginning he had found something almost irresistible in the raffish disposition of Juan Cadiz. For, if ever a man was a piratical adventurer at heart, it was this one and the years had not dulled the spirit.

"If," he measured his words slowly, "you are going to do this—and I am afraid you are—then, we had better begin to train your black crew. The hands we have aboard may not view the risk of capture and prison with your lightheartedness. And if they do, then they will want such shares in the operation as to reduce the profit to a point where it won't be worth while. The black boys will be better. They'll take orders and not ask questions."

"Now you make good sense." Juan's face broke into a wide smile. "I'll tell you something, Raleigh." There was a light of new interest in his eyes. "I didn't think you'd do it. I asked myself what sort of a man my B'ma was marrying."

"Five minutes ago I didn't think I'd do it either." He glanced at Bahama and shrugged ruefully. "Marry a pirate's daughter and a pirate you become."

"Raleigh." She spoke his name with a serious tenderness. "I think, maybe, conch girl goin' to love you. Oh!" She warded off what he was about to say. "Not just because you are doing what Papa wants. That

[342]

would be easy, to please me. No, it is because I am seeing an unsuspected side of your nature. To tell the truth, there have been times when I wondered if life with you might be a little stuffy, comfortable but dull. The captain home from the seas, sitting on the porch with a pipe and a faraway look in his eyes; honest, steadfast and true but with never a bit of stimulation in your nature to quicken a woman's heart."

"Bahama," Caroline objected quickly.

"She's right, ma'am." Raleigh was not offended. "I've been a dull man, too serious for my age. It's time I took a different tack even if it leads to prison." He reached across for Bahama's hand. "If I'd known how you felt I'd have taken to wearing a ring in my ear like your father's and a black patch over one eye. I may still do it."

"Nobody goes to prison." Juan allowed the chart to roll up of its own accord and then slipped it in the tube. Already, in his mind, he was making a rendezvous in a dozen different places with small boats out of Nassau in the dark of night. "We get some fun out of this an' make money too. I don't have fun like this since I was young. The first thing we do," he continued, "is pay off the hands. Tell them we're going to lay the *Caroline* up. Then, somehow, we got to get them to Nassau. Maybe they can find new berths on ships coming in shorthanded. If not we pay their passage back to Boston. We got money enough for that but not much more. Then," he whistled on a meditative note, "we take the sloop an' go to Nassau ourselves, you, me an' John. I talk with some friends, storekeepers an' merchants along the bay street. On the waterfront I know everybody. They remember Juan Cadiz from a boy. I get old, maybe, but right now I have the feeling of that boy who had a guitar an' sang songs to the girls an' went off in a little boat with a red sail to marry a rich man's daughter." He turned laughingly, reproachful eyes on Caroline.

"I wonder what Father Cameron would say?" Caroline had resigned herself to what was happening.

"I'll tell you what Papa Cameron would say." Juan was emphatic. "He'd say: Juan, you hold this place on Exuma together. I don't care a damn how. I put my heart in it. Don't let it go. Take good care of my daughter an' grandchildren. So," he airily dropped the situation into the hands of a man long dead, "I'm going to do like Papa Cameron says. We hold Exuma together between us."

In the night, lying beside him as she had these many years, her head pillowed on the shoulder still heavily muscled, Caroline Cameron Cadiz smiled to herself in the darkness. What she and this man had started with they had not lost. Time had not dulled the excitement she had felt that first day when he walked toward her with a catlike tread on the dock and knew she was his for the taking. It surprised her not at all to realize she was neither shocked nor alarmed by what he planned to do. That was Juanio as he had been, was and would be and she wanted him no other way.

✺ XXI ✺

THE TIDES of time and change washed slowly but inexorably against the shores of the Bahamas and brought with them what the few remaining owners of the once large plantations felt to be the ultimate disaster. What Nature had all but succeeded in doing the Home Government, with the abolition of slavery, put the final seal of failure on the islands.

The black men and women who had carried the burden of the plantation system on their shoulders, both in the Colonial days on the mainland and later in the islands, were freed by an Act of Parliament. The year was 1834 and some ten thousand Negroes in the Bahamas were pushed into a freedom for which they were completely unprepared. Freedom was a word. It had a good sound. A man could go and come as he pleased, work or just lie in the sun or catch a fish. They had moaned in their bondage for this. No white boss. No fields to till, no cane to cut, no corn to strip. But, freedom as a fact was something else again. With freedom the cabins were no longer theirs. When they were sick no one cared. When they were hungry there was no Saturday giving of beans, rice, a piece of fat pork or a handful of sugar. They were suddenly frightened and bewildered.

On the Cameron plantation, slavery had long since ceased to be an important economic factor. Save for the house servants the family found little need for the descendants of the blacks originally brought from Carolina. Beyond what was required for food the fields were no longer cultivated and they had returned to the tangled scrub and sedge.

In this year, throughout the islands, there were some ten thousand slaves and roughly three thousand free blacks. The white population had shrunk to something over two thousand. The Act of Emancipation created a staggering problem, for the blacks were suddenly thrown upon their own resources and they were, through long servitude and dependence, temperamentally unable to care for themselves. On Exuma, over the years, many of the young slaves had run away, taking their women with them. They had slipped off and were scattered the length of the island chain, on Andros, Cat and Eluthera. Most of them had made the passage in the boats of Negroes already free, on rafts secretly made or, as sometimes happened, in a dinghy or longboat washed ashore from some unknown wreck. No effort had been made to pursue them for they were without value. On several occasions Juan had encouraged small groups to leave, sending them aboard the *Caroline* to Nassau, Rolleville, wherever there were already large Negro settlements. The others created their own small communities all through the Out Islands save on St. George's Cay which, for some mysterious reason, they avoided. It was probably the only island in the entire Bahama grouping which had not a single black.

Despite those who had gone secretly or openly, with Juan's tacit consent, there were still close to a hundred slaves on the plantation, for they bred like rabbits. This second and third generation had been reared in almost complete idleness and looked to the big house for everything: their clothing, care when they fell sick, adjudication of their endless disputes. They would not even have bothered to cultivate their own small plots of corn, yams, beans and melons if Juan had not long ago shut off the customary Saturday dole from the storehouses. Young and old, they idled and were a constant source of irritation. Juan had long wished there was some way of getting rid of them but he could think of no practical solution. How, short of dumping them into the sea, did you chase almost a hundred blacks from an island?

As a family they had all talked this over. John suggested they be driven, if necessary, aboard the schooner in groups of fifteen or twenty and landed on Long or Cat Island or Eluthera Point. There they would shift for themselves or starve. Caroline had been outraged by the idea.

"It is not their fault they are here. Father Cameron brought their grandparents and parents to the Bahamas. They are our responsibility. You simply cannot drive them ashore on some island and leave them to wander like animals. They are not conditioned for independence. I won't hear of it, John."

To Juan it seemed a fine solution. He sided with his son. "We give them tools, seed, lines and nets to fish with. We send along some hens and a rooster, a boar and a sow. They start their own colony an' they'll work if they have to. Those who ran away must have made out all right otherwise they would have come back here."

Despite his impatience Juan had known this was no real answer. Now, with the Emancipation Act, there seemed some chance for relief from the never-ending burden of caring for the blacks. In this he was mistaken, for the Home Government having piously freed the slaves made no sound provision for their care. They were free but to do what?

In this year of 1834 Juan Cadiz was sixty-one. Time had not bent him nor did he find the need to lean upon a cane when he walked. It was true his step was slower, some of the seemingly unquenchable thirst for life had been slaked. He took a nap now in the afternoons and no longer found the same pleasure in a cigar and a glass of rum. He sometimes wondered where the flavor had gone.

Often, in the twilight, he would sit upon the wide porch facing the sea and think back over the years. There had been times of high excitement while he, John, Raleigh and a black crew ran their smuggling operation under the very bows of the Royal Navy Patrol. In the dark nights the *Caroline* moved like a ghost with her illegal cargo, making her rendezvous with the small boats and loading them with the bales and boxes of merchandise purchased in Charleston and Savannah. In the beginning the profits had been large and with them he had rebuilt and refurnished the manor. But the Nassau market was not large and their activity soon glutted it. Little by little they found it more and more difficult to dispose of what they carried. Finally, the adventure tapered off until it was no longer worth while. But, and his eyes brightened at the memory, it had been a period of heart-racing excursions. They had been shot at, chased, hailed before the Governor, who accused them but could not prove they were engaged in smuggling. The Government had doubled and then tripled its patrol but always the *Caroline* outran and outwitted them. They had been great days, filled with the salt of life which he would not taste again. Now and then he caught himself thinking of death; not morbidly but with a mild curiosity. How would it come? What shape would it take? Given his choice he would like to meet it as had old Papa Cameron, aboard a ship in the wildness of a hurricane. This caused him to smile. Now, he was old Papa Juan with a ten-year-old grandson, Cameron Raleigh. Three years after her marriage Bahama had given birth to the boy; a fine, sturdy youngster who had taken to the water with the instinct of a duckling, found playmates among the Negro children and loved nothing better than to climb over Juan, begging to be told stories of pirates who once used the plantation harbor. In Charleston, there was Robert Bruce and Constance's son. Juan couldn't quite figure out just what his relationship was, so he simply lumped them all together as his grandchildren. David was married to a Charleston girl. Beyond this announcement, in a short but warmly affectionate letter, they had heard no more save he was still with Renevant, Decatur and Cameron, Robert Bruce having been taken into the firm as a junior partner.

Juan rarely sailed these days with John and Raleigh. The two managed to make the schooner show a small profit, working their way through Jamaica, Barbados, Cuba, the Southern ports and as far north as Boston with assorted cargoes. They seemed able to manage well enough without him and he was satisfied to leave the *Caroline* in their hands.

Often, when he was alone on the porch with the sun moving slowly down its arc and the wind falling off as it always did in the late afternoon, Caroline would come and sit beside him, taking her place on the top step near his chair and resting her head against his knee. His hand would reach out to touch her hair and she would glance up with the smile which, once again, made her seem the girl he had known so many years ago. Actually, he never thought of her as having grown older although, roughly counting, she must be fifty-six. Once he had asked.

"How old are you now, girl?"

"As old as you want me to be."

"I guess you're about eighteen, then. It's a good age for a conch girl. Maybe you an' I run away an' make marriage one of these days."

"Papa will shoot you."

He chuckled deep in his throat. So much they remembered together. The exact words spoken. The things done. Old Papa Cameron would have shot him if he had known what was going on when, in their secret cove, they had lain in the hot sunshine and sand making love.

As he came downstairs this morning he knew he faced the problem of settling a situation with the slaves. He had sent word the Marstah Boss wanted to see them and they were to gather in the compound separating the rows of cabins.

With the Act of Emancipation, Parliament had indemnified the former owners throughout the islands to the amount of 128,000 pounds sterling. It had also appended what was known as the Apprenticeship System. Through this those who held slaves made a legal contract with the freed Negroes under which they were to continue at their old employment with a minimum number of days labor to themselves and given a stated grant of land as their own.

John had explained this to his father but to Juan it made no sense at all.

"They don't do anything now, except the house niggers. So, what do they do with this apprentice thing?"

"I don't know." John was also confused by the curious legislation. "Maybe someone else will take them."

"For what?" Juan walked slowly beside his son toward the quarters.

[348]

"Who's got plantation in the islands any more big enough to need all these blacks?"

The Negroes were gathered in solid ranks. Even the very old and feeble had been helped out to sit on the stoop of their cabins. Word had spread quickly. Marstah Boss had things to say. They waited eagerly to listen, for he rarely came among them anymore.

Juan stood in the hot sun studying their faces. Some were vaguely familiar. The others were strange to him even though they had been born and reared within sight of the manor. He was uncertain how to go about explaining to them what had happened.

"Now, listen to what I have to tell you." His voice was firm. "The King, 'way over in England, across the ocean, says you are all free. That means you no longer have a Marstah Boss. You can leave here, go where you please, do what you want. No one can make you work anymore here on Exuma or any other place."

"Wheah we go? What we do, Marstah Boss?" One of the old men, his hair a grizzled white, leaned heavily upon a cane of orangewood and forced himself slowly through the stolid, uncomprehending ranks to ask what was suddenly in all their minds. "Who tek cah o' us'n? What mek d free'om?"

Juan glanced helplessly at his son. How to explain this thing to simple, childish minds?

"The King made the freedom for you."

He tried to make it sound solemn and impressive. The blacks had always equated the word king with some golden personage who shared an indefinable relationship with God; the God the missionaries talked about when they came to Exuma. He lived up in the sky in Heaven, surrounded by white angels who flew over gates of pearl.

"What d King say to do, Marstah Boss?" the old man persisted.

"He says you're free." Juan was growing increasingly impatient. The sun was hot and he was uncomfortable. "He says there aren't any more slaves. Everyone is a free man."

This they understood. For years there had been talk among them of the free blacks in the Out Islands. Many of their own young men and women had run away from Exuma to join them. Freedom meant there would be no white man to order them to do this or that. But, and this was beyond their comprehension, if a white man didn't tell them what to do how could they know what must be done? How were they to live without some authority to which they could appeal? This was the only life they had ever known. Now, for some reason, it was being changed. Their minds could not grasp this. What was being offered in its place?

"What we do, Marstah Boss?" Another man asked the question with an uneasy glance around at the others. "Who tell us?"

"How the hell do I know what you do?" Juan lost his temper in the face of this stupidity and shouted, "The King says you're free. I say you're free. Go wherever you damn please."

"Wheah we go, Marstah Boss?" The query was repeated with a maddening persistency. "What we do when we gets dere?"

"Jump in the ocean. Swim to Nassau. Find an island of your own."

The crowd backed away as one in the face of this anger, for the Marstah Boss's face was turning almost purple. He was a real, mad man. They could see that.

"Marstah Boss. Dis heah ouah home." The old man's voice quavered bravely. "Do King say we gots to leave?"

Juan, confronted by this obstinacy, gave up. He stared at the perplexed faces and then shook his head in a gesture of surrender. He looked to John for help.

"No." He made the admission wearily. "The King didn't say you had to leave. I wish he had because I don't know what to do with you."

"Dat a good King den." The old man spoke with sage approval and in the crowd there was a general nodding of agreement. "Dis ouah home. We stay, like always, Marstah Boss."

Juan turned away and left them standing there looking after him. He and John walked back toward the house in silence for a few minutes.

"I suppose that damn fool of a Governor in Nassau will be sending someone around to find out if we have freed our slaves. When he comes," his face lighted with anticipation, "I'm going to let him go down there and ask them. That ought to keep him quiet for a while. What do you suppose the Government thought was going to happen to all these blacks?"

"I don't know," John confessed. "I suppose in time, as the old ones die off, the young ones will make a start at some sort of a life of their own, farming, fishing. It will take years before any order comes out of it."

"I'd like to ship them all to Nassau and let them squat in the Governor's yard. Then, by God, he'd have some idea of what is happening."

Back at the manor he encountered the same blank incomprehension with the house servants. They had always considered themselves superior to the field hands and to be classed with them now was an indignity. If they didn't work in the house what were they to do? When Juan explained they were entitled to a grant of land, they regarded him with a complete lack of understanding. What did they need land for? Not one of them had even so much as lifted a hoe or dropped a seed into the earth in his life. They had their own quarters apart from the field hands.

They had furtive access to the kitchen and the food prepared there. To be sure there was dusting, washing, sweeping, the making of beds and the serving of meals, but if they didn't do these things what were they to do? They found some slight appeal in the matter of having a few days each month to themselves, but this really held no great attraction for a day off meant only standing around in the sun with nothing to do. It was cooler and more comfortable in the house, and between chores they could gather in the kitchen and chatter or stop on the stairs or in the halls to talk and gossip. Secretly, they thought d ol' Marstah Boss mus' be goin' a little crazy in d haid.

Only with the Negro crew of the *Caroline* did Juan find any response. They'd like a little piece of land away from the quarters where their women could raise a few chickens and plant a garden. They'd have a cabin and at the end of a voyage take their ease there with their women and children with a chicken stewing in a pot until it was time to sail again.

In such a fashion did Emancipation come to the island of Exuma.

In Charleston, Robert Bruce read aloud from the newspaper over the luncheon table to Constance. It was an account of the British Parliament's action in freeing the slaves in the Bahamas.

"Well," he put the paper aside, "that ends any hope of the islands sustaining themselves."

"They weren't really anyhow, were they?" Constance wasn't too interested.

"This is just the beginning." Robert Bruce lit a cigar and slumped comfortably in his chair. "You will see it spread, the sentiment grows for abolition."

Only the week before, antislavery pamphlets had been seized from the mails and publicly burned in Charleston to the enthusiastic cheers of a large gathering of the citizens. In New York a militant group worked ceaselessly, preaching, writing, forming committees to bring all the pressure it could to provoke legislation for the relief of the black man.

"In time," Robert Bruce continued, "the institution of slavery will be abolished in this country."

"La!" Constance expressed her disbelief. "What would the plantations do without slaves? It is too ridiculous to think of!"

"I don't know. Neither does anyone else." He stood up. "If you will excuse me I'll finish my cigar and perhaps take a nap in the study before going back to the office."

In the cool, shadowed room with the jalousies drawn, Robert Bruce took off his coat and stretched himself out upon a sofa. Over the years

[351]

he had added a little weight but it became him. He was still a handsome man, looking much as had Ronald Cameron. He had never been able to overcome completely a certain seriousness of manner which had been his since childhood. It remained with him but he was far from a pompous man. There was humor and kindness in him; a gentle disposition and a winning smile which had carried him far. Renevant, Decatur and Cameron was actually Decatur and Cameron, since Mr. Renevant had died several years ago. His name was kept for sentimental reasons and because the firm was well known along the Eastern seaboard and abroad by this designation.

With a cushion beneath his head he thought how fortunate he had been on that day when he made the decision to leave Exuma and try for his future in Charleston. How remarkably well everything had gone. He was honest enough to admit that without the generous assistance, kindness and friendship of George Renevant a career would not have come to full blossom so easily. But, and this was also a fair appraisal, he never missed an opportunity to learn, turning an unsuspected talent for commerce and the making of friends to the firm's profit. Little by little, as he prospered, he had repurchased most of what had once been Cameron Hall. He bought the land in small parcels from individual farmers, piecing it together as he would a bit of china until it again took form. He had been forced to borrow for the buying of slaves but this was being paid off. Once again the fields were snowed with cotton. The original sluices built by the first Camerons flooded the rice fields. Indigo was an important crop and the forests of pine yielded resin and turpentine for which there was a ready and profitable market.

He had made no attempt to rebuild the manor. But it was in the back of his mind to do so one of these days. When this was done he would retire from active association with the firm, while still holding his shares, and return to what should have been his heritage. His son Richard and the children he hoped would follow would have the life he and Caroline had known before Ronald Cameron made the ill-fated move to the Bahamas. He felt no bitterness toward his father. Ronald Cameron had done what he thought best and no man could do more.

He watched the smoke drift toward the ceiling. Financially, the move had been a disaster. Yet the islands had been a wonderful place in which to grow to manhood. He could not forget their beauty: the dazzling white of the beaches, the dark green of the woods and scrub, and the incredible coloring of water and sky which made even a boy stop and catch his breath in wonder. He smiled to himself in this quiet reverie. Caroline running away with that incredible Juan Cadiz. Caroline. He always thought of her as seventeen or so; clean of limb, beautiful of feature and filled with an impatience for life. Actually, and this astonished him, Caroline was only two years younger than he. She was well into her fifties and with a daughter bearing the improbable name of Bahama who was married and with a son of her own. He saw Raleigh three or four times a year when the *Caroline* put in at Charleston to discharge or pick up cargo, and they had become warm friends for they shared a certain reserve of manner, a quiet understanding of things which must be done. Only once had they been in violent disagreement and that was during the days when Juan sailed with the schooner and Robert Bruce knew they were engaged in the dangerous business of smuggling. He had fought them on this, refusing to lend any assistance either in the matter of credit or merchandise. But now, Juan had all but retired. The buccaneer had taken to his hearthside. The *Caroline* plied her trade with respectability. Lord, how the years took wing once put into flight! David had married the daughter of a fine old Charleston family and was doing well with the firm. He was proud of his half brother and rarely a week passed when David, his wife Margaret, Constance and he did not spend an evening together. Suddenly he felt a desire to see everyone together again for what might well be the last time. If he rebuilt Cameron Hall there would be a gathering and they would have a reunion such as the levees once held at the Hall when guests came from a hundred miles away, stayed for weeks, danced the nights through while he and Caroline peeked down at the festivities from a balcony.

He pressed the cigar's coal out in a tray. Outside, the sun played over the polished leaves of magnolia trees, and the fragrance of the white, waxy blossoms scented the room. Bees hummed among the jessamine and the crape myrtle was aflame. There were soft voices in the yard as the slaves working in the garden talked among themselves. Idly, he began to wonder what would happen to the Southern states should this agitation for Negro emancipation take fire. It would mean ruin for the great plantations, Cameron Hall included. An entirely new way of life would have to be resolved. It might well mean the dissolution of such a solid firm as Renevant, Decatur and Cameron, for without the constant supply of commodities from the plantation there would be nothing in which they could deal. Cut off slave labor and the South would strangle. But, he closed his eyes, such a thing would not happen in his lifetime nor that of his children. Someday. Yes. He believed it to be inevitable. The Government would act as had the British Parliament. But he hoped it would move with the same, deliberate manumission, a system of apprenticeship which would give everyone an opportunity to adjust to a new way of thinking and employment. It was upon this comforting notion that he dropped off and did not hear the sound of a distant bugle, still faint but growing in volume, until one day, it would blare upon a terrible note.

Bahama stood on the deck of the *Caroline* watching Nassau take form as the schooner rounded Hogg Island. She held tightly to young Cameron's hand. The boy's face was a little strained but he stood straight and proud beside his mother and gazed at what seemed to be a magic city, for this was his first trip to New Providence and he had never seen so many buildings and houses together. There was even what he imagined to be a castle—the decaying remains of Fort Nassau and a great, shining mansion for the Governor on the hill.

Raleigh joined them, leaving the mooring of the schooner to John. He also took Cameron's hand, as the boy was between them.

"It's a curious thing," he said to Bahama, indicating the long, densely overgrown island lying off Nassau's shore. "They are beginning to mark this on the charts as Hog Island. I don't know why they dropped the final *g*."

"Are there hogs there, Father?" Young Cam looked up.

"If there were, the natives would have killed them off and eaten them long ago. No, I imagine some cartographer got lazy or careless."

"What's a car-to-grap-er?" Cam had difficulty with the word.

"He's a man who makes maps and charts."

"You see, Cam?" Bahama wanted to interest him. "That is the reason why we are sending you to school here, in Nassau. So you will learn of such things."

"How will it be, Mother?"

"You'll like it." She tried to be reassuring. "It is a school but there will be boys your age to know, games to play, things to learn which I can't teach you." She felt a wrench at her heart for he seemed so young, so small to venture into a new world.

She and Raleigh had talked it over. They both agreed it would not do to have Cameron grow up on Exuma without the benefit of schooling. The elementary teaching offered in the small, single-room schoolhouse on Eluthera had not changed much since she, John and David had attended classes there. For Cameron she wanted more than this. He could not grow up as an all-but-unlettered man on Exuma. She had rebelled against the idea of sending him to Charleston.

"It is so far away." She was stricken by the idea.

Then Raleigh, returning from a voyage to Savannah, had laid over in Nassau. He learned that a small academy for boys had been hopefully established. The headmaster was a former instructor at a public school in England and he had come to Nassau as a secretary to the Governor. After a year, recognizing the need, he had established, with the Government's approval and aid, this academy. It was strictly administered. The students must live in, even those whose homes were in Nassau and no more than a quarter of a mile away. Most of the boys were from Nassau families but a few, whose parents could afford the small tuition, came from the Out Islands. Raleigh had investigated carefully, talked with the headmaster and, without consulting Bahama, had enrolled Cameron. The term was for eight months out of the year with vacations at Easter and Christmas times.

Cameron had at first been delighted with the idea. It was an adventure. Then he began to think of the things he must leave behind on Exuma—his pony, the freedom of the plantation, Grandfather Juan who sometimes took him sailing, his mother, the excitement of the *Caroline*'s arrival and the big, smiling man who was his father. Some of his enthusiasm waned. Now, when in a few minutes the schooner would drop anchor and they'd go ashore in the small boat, he began to feel an empty sensation in his stomach and a loneliness such as he had never known.

"Will I see you often, Father?" he asked in a small voice and stared straight ahead so they would not see the glistening of a tear in his eye.

"As often as I can make it." Raleigh made the reply seem one of hearty assurance. "On the way back to Exuma I'll lay our course for Nassau. We'll see each other."

"And we'll come for you at spring leave and, of course, Christmastime we'll all be together at home." Bahama was close to tears herself.

"Well," there was a curious firmness in Cam's voice, "just the same I don't think I'm going to like it."

"No one likes school. I didn't." Raleigh wanted to share life's inescapable tribulations with his son. "But, if you hope to captain a ship someday there are a lot of things you will have to learn. Reading, geography, mathematics, navigation, something of the stars and planets. Then you will want to know of history; the great battles lost and won, stories of the world and its people. It can be exciting, Cam. As filled with excitement as the stories Grandfather Juan tells you. And," he offered this as a final consolation, "when you have your summer vacation I will let you make a voyage with me to the mainland, and maybe even Cuba."

"You promise?" Cam looked up with a wonderful expression of adoration in his eyes for his father. "You won't forget?"

"I promise. Now, we'll go ashore." A boat was being made ready for lowering away. "And when I come again I'll have you piped aboard."

As the boat was sculled shoreward Bahama noted the change in Nassau since she had last visited here. A seawall had been built where once

[355]

an untidy beach shelved down to the water. The helter-skelter collection of shacks and tents had given way to a semblance of order. Ashore, the bay street had been given that name and it was lettered on a corner building as such. BAY STREET. Vendue House, where the slaves had once been put upon the block for auction, still stood as a monument to the past but it was being used now as a public market for the produce, fish, pigs and fowl brought in from the Out Islands. Government House, with an ancient cannon in the courtyard, shone in its new paint, and the sentries were smartly uniformed. The new Governor must be a man of energy. More startling, though, were the number of blacks. They roamed about without purpose or sat on the seawall staring out past Hog Island to the sea. The Emancipation Act must present a problem here also, for the Government apparently did not know what to do with the former slaves who hunkered down in the sun and waited without any idea of what they were waiting for.

Hand in hand, with Cam between them, they walked up the easy slope of the hill where the school was located. It had once been a private home, belonging to a family which had returned to England, and it rose above the high stone wall covered with the bright, coral-red of massed bougainvillea. The grounds themselves covered almost two acres. At the gate they could hear the noisy shouts, the whack of a cricket bat and the piping, treble yells of youngsters at play.

"You see," Bahama pressed Cam's hand as a Negro opened the wooden gate and bowed them through, "it can't be too bad if all these boys are having so much fun."

"I still don't think I'm going to like it." Cam repeated the statement doggedly but without the same conviction. The only companions of his age he had ever known were the Negro boys on Exuma and they were slaves, which made a difference. "Maybe, though," he added, "maybe I might."

As they passed through the yard all play halted and a silence fell over the area while the youngsters studied the new boy. A few even fell in behind at a discreet distance, following them as far as the entrance steps and standing there until they passed inside.

The headmaster was a young, bespectacled man with a slightly nervous, harried air as though he had found the coping with fifteen boys far beyond his capacity. He welcomed Bahama and Raleigh, gravely shook hands with Cam, and then asked them if they would like tea.

Bahama refused politely. What must be done she wanted over with quickly. Cam suddenly seemed so young, so small and alone.

"His box of clothing will be sent up from the ship, Mr. Dillworth."

"I'm afraid what he has won't do, Mrs. Raleigh." The headmaster was apologetic. "As you probably noticed, we have a uniform dress here. Trousers and a blazer for sports. A dark suit with Eton collar for the classroom. Uniformity makes for conformity." This was one of his small jokes. "We would like to think a Seton Hall boy would be recognizable anywhere; not only because of his apparel but his bearing and manners as well. We have a tailor who can outfit Master Cameron in no time. Would you like to see the room he will share with a fellow student?"

They inspected the upper quarters. Cam's room was a pleasant, sun-filled corner from which a glimpse of the sea could be had. Cam stood at the window, staring out. Bahama went to him and put an arm about his shoulders.

"It's nice, isn't it?" she asked hopefully.

"I guess so."

"Well." Mr. Dillworth cracked his hands smartly together. "We have found the shorter the leave-taking the less painful it is for everyone. After all, Cameron," he addressed Cam's back, "this isn't a prison. You will like it here once you are acquainted. At least, I hope you will. Our boys," he spoke to Bahama and Raleigh, "are from the very best families." He managed a small laugh. "There aren't very many of them. We are most happy to have Master Cameron with us."

Downstairs again Bahama hesitated. She didn't want a scene but she could not resist gathering Cam into her arms for a moment. He made no effort to pull away.

"Good-bye, darling. Please try and be happy."

"Good-bye, Mother." The words came with difficulty.

"Cam." Raleigh put out his hand and held that of his son. "Study hard and I'll keep my promise about the voyage."

"Yes, sir." The muscles around his mouth tightened to keep the lips from quivering. "I will."

Outside, Bahama took Raleigh's arm and her step hurried him. His hand slipped into hers with a comforting pressure.

"Can we sail right away, Raleigh?"

"You wouldn't like a bite to eat at the inn?"

"No. I want to leave before I change my mind and go back and get him. I know this is what we wanted, what Cam needs. Just the same, it is harder than I thought."

As the *Caroline* made sail and picked her way out of the harbor Bahama stood at the taffrail, staring landward. She was crying unashamedly and Raleigh wisely left her alone.

◄§ XXII §►

BEYOND THE islands events of tremendous importance were ominously shaping themselves into a form in incalculable evil, and what was to emerge from it was destined to shake the sun-washed Bahamas with terrific impact.

Over the many years since the Parliamentary action which freed the Bahamian slaves, the islands had relapsed into a state of isolated somnolence. Poverty and indifference stalked them, and in a letter the Governor wrote:

> In New Providence the young and able run a-coasting in shallops, which is a lazy course of life and leaves none but old men, women and children to plant what is needed. The want is dire, for little of the Out Island produce reaches Nassau and the people are sunk in apathy. What could be a paradise, for there is no such beauty anywhere, is but a miserable collection of tumbled shacks bleaching in the sun. The once fine plantations have gone to ruin. The freed blacks increase and there is nothing for them to do. Even the first families are hard pressed for monies although they try to maintain the dignity and manners of earlier and better times. I can find nothing in the situation to cause me to be optimistic about the future for, unless a miracle occurs, we are destined to continue in this state of bare subsistence.

The miracle, terrible though it was to be, was already beginning to define itself on the mainland.

Below the Mason-Dixon Line a civilization of grace and luxury had built itself from the great plantations and magnificent homes. The aristocracy of Tidewater Virginia, Mississippi, Carolina and Georgia, the energetic cosmopolitanism of New Orleans, all combined to produce a life of unrivaled elegance and baronial splendor. Unwittingly, though, the Southern states had laid the foundation for their destruction by concentrating on a one-crop economy, that of cotton. For this they needed a tremendous labor force which would be cheap to maintain and constantly available. Without realizing it the South had given itself into bondage to cotton and the slave. The former could not survive without the latter.

In the North and in some enlightened sections of the South the abolitionists pressed their attack upon the institution of slavery with increasing virulence. Political parties had split over the issue. The church was divided. Old friends had become implacable enemies. The South, at first, had defended itself almost apologetically and when this found little sympathy or support, the talk of secession broke into the open. In Charleston the *Mercury* published an extra edition, declaring in heavy, bold type that: "The union now subsisting between South Carolina and other States under the name of the United States of America is hereby dissolved." The North replied with meetings and bonfire rallies of militant abolitionists who shouted for the use of force. One vitriolic speaker declared in reply: "South Carolina is too small for a republic and too big for a lunatic asylum."

The passions mounted. Daily, Southern legislators announced their resignation from Congress. In Montgomery, Alabama, a confederacy of six seceded states met to elect Jefferson Davis as President.

At the mouth of Charleston's harbor, on a small island, stood a little brick fort. Its commander, Major Robert Anderson, had a force of sixty-five men. At a staff flew the flag of the United States and each morning Charleston was confronted by this now odious symbol. South Carolina demanded evacuation of the fort. As a precautionary and punitive measure the harbor was ringed with gun emplacements and batteries. Troops poured into the city to take up their positions. Instead of yielding to South Carolina's anger, Lincoln announced his intention of supplying, reinforcing and holding Fort Sumter. Davis ordered General Beauregard to turn his guns upon the stronghold and the first shot announced to the world that America's great experiment in democracy had failed. The tragic war had opened.

On the piazza of the house on Tradd Street there was a gathering of the Camerons and those related. Robert Bruce, in his eighty-third year now, sat in a wheelchair with a light shawl on his knees. Time had shriveled him and the once heavy frame seemed desiccated and too small for his head. He lived with Richard, for Constance had died of a terrible hemorrhage in the birth of a second child which was stillborn. Grouped about Robert Bruce were Richard and his wife, Penelope. David Heath, now sixty-six, rested upon a cane from a straight-backed chair. His wife, Margaret, sat next to him, a hand resting upon his. Beside Richard, Cameron Raleigh stood as he stared intently at Sumter. Five years separated Richard and Cameron. The latter, at thirty-four, was a man of lean toughness, clear eyes, and bore a marked resemblance to his father. His face and hands had been dyed by the winds, the sun and the rains of fifteen years at sea, and when he rested or walked he always seemed to be balancing himself to the canting of a deck. His eyes were the cool, steady gray of Bahama's and they could grow warm with sudden humor or flinty cold in anger. In general he was a man of stubborn character, an inheritance from the New England forebears of Walter Raleigh, but he was also inclined to a dry tolerance of human frailties and an understanding which frequently gave him control of all but impossible situations in which other men lost their tempers. Down his left cheek was drawn a thin, white line; the mark of a seaman's knife in a Barbados tavern brawl when he was twenty. In moments of excitement or anger the scar turned faintly purple.

Richard was all Cameron. Had they been able to stand side by side at the age of thirty-nine, it would have been difficult to find a difference in feature and manner between him and Ronald Cameron, the grandfather he had never known. His voice was gentle with the accent of Carolina, his bearing courtly. The years of indoor occupation with the firm which had once been Renevant, Decatur and Cameron but was now simply Cameron and Son had given him an appearance of pale softness which was deceptive. He rode every morning, walked to and from his home on Legare Street when he went to the office, shot over his fine pointers in the fall on the Ashley plantation. His mind was agile, his spirit adventuresome and, beneath the meticulous tailoring, his body was hard and fit.

Aligned with Richard and Cameron Raleigh were Cameron's wife, Charlotte-Anne, and their two children, Carol-Louise, twelve and Brian, fifteen. All of their attention was upon the fort and harbor. Most of Charleston was similarly occupied. The citizens crowded the waterfront, stood upon the wide, second-story porches of their homes or climbed to the roofs of warehouses and buildings to watch the spectacular show.

With every thunder of the Confederate batteries cheers were loosed, hats thrown into the air. Men danced in the streets and boys capered and turned cartwheels in a frenzy of excitement. This was to be a short, quick war and a stunning victory for General Beauregard and his gallant forces. Hadn't an orator, speaking from a box set at a corner, declared he would "wipe up with a handkerchief every drop of blood spilled by a Southerner in this war"?

From his wheeled chair Robert Bruce peered with uncertain sight at the harbor. The sound of the bombardment came faintly to his ears. His fingers played constantly with small, fluttering gestures at the shawl's fringe. When he spoke there was a quavering note of annoyance in his voice as though he resented this intrusion, faint though it was to his ears. His privacy was being disturbed.

"What is happening, Richard? I can't see."

"The artillery is firing upon Sumter, Father." He paused and stared at where the explosions blossomed into ugly flowers of red, black and sulphurous yellow.

"Someone ought to put a stop to it."

"It is only beginning, Father." Richard seemed to be speaking more to himself than to old Robert Bruce. "Here, on this day, the South commits suicide. We are delivered into the hands of madmen."

"Oh, Richard!" Margaret protested. "Everyone says it will be over in a few weeks if it lasts that long."

"I don't like it here in the city," Robert Bruce fretted. "Why can't we go back to Cameron Hall? I am more comfortable there. All this dirty smell of gunpowder. Men shooting at each other."

"I have ordered the two heavy coaches, yours and mine, Father." Richard was patient. "They will be around shortly. Then you, Penelope, Margaret, Charlotte-Anne and the children with Uncle David can go to the Hall."

David Heath smiled frostily to himself. "I'll stay here, old gaffer that I am. A little excitement will shake up my liver." He rested his chin upon the cane's knob.

"Are you sure, David?" Margaret, who had been a Charleston belle and one of the city's most beautiful girls, was still a handsome woman despite the silver white of her hair and the undeniable lines which fifty-five years had drawn into her skin. "I would feel better to have you with me."

He glanced up at her with a twinkle. "You've had me at your side for almost thirty-eight years. I'm tired of dancing attendance upon you. No. I'll watch the cannonading with Richard and Cameron. I doubt the fort will hold out more than a day. I want to see its fall and the flag come down. Then I'll join you at the Hall."

"All right, dear." She leaned to kiss his cheek. "Although I don't see how it can possibly help your liver. There isn't anything wrong with it."

"What's everyone talking so much about?" Robert Bruce complained. "The trouble is," his voice strengthened and his mind, as it did every now and then, cleared and grew momentarily sharp, "the trouble is everyone lives too long. All of us. When you've had the best and it's over I'd call it quits if I had my way. Caroline. Now, Caroline had the good sense to die before she reached sixty and that's a damn sight too long. I remember Caroline when she was twelve and I was fourteen. We came to Charleston from Cameron Hall in a red coach with gold trim. A wheel broke. We had a hundred or more slaves with us." His mind began to wander in the past, groping through the veil, and he mumbled unintelligibly to himself.

When the coaches were ready, the horses rearing and hard to manage as the sound of the bombardment rattled the air, the families were loaded. Hampers of food to break the journey with an outdoor lunch were lashed on top. Robert Bruce was carried from his chair in the arms of two slaves. He whacked ineffectually at them with his cane, accusing them of being clumsy apes who ought to be out climbing trees instead of serving a household. The blacks were solemnly respectful for they were accustomed to these tirades which were not inspired by anger. Robert Bruce simply wanted to assert himself.

Richard and Cameron stood on the steps until the heavy vehicles rolled through the gates, down the street and out of sight. Then they returned to the piazza and had a slave bring them whisky, glasses and a small pitcher of water. At regular intervals the day vibrated with the thunder of the guns.

David, sitting between the two younger men, sipped his liquor straight, rolling it about on his tongue before swallowing.

"Are you all right, Uncle David?" Richard had called him uncle from childhood although he had no idea what, if any, the actual relationship was. It just seemed as though Uncle David Heath had always been around. "Would you like a cushion?"

"I'm fine, my boy." He held his glass in both hands. "You said a while ago the South was committing suicide. Do you believe it?"

"It can't survive a war with the North. Oh, it may drag on for years but that's just it. Time will defeat us no matter how bravely we fight or how passionate our cause. Time is on the side of the Yankees. The South has no factories, no heavy industry, no munition plants to speak of. When we use up what we have we shall be forced to fight with hoes, axes, cane knives and scythes. They are a poor defense against guns." He turned to Cameron. "It is this I wanted to talk with you about, Cam. What is the condition of the *Caroline*?"

Cameron had sailed the schooner from Exuma for his father, at sixty-five, rarely made a voyage anymore. He was content to remain with Bahama, Juan and John on Exuma and leave the sea to his son, who had sailed with him from the age of fifteen after finishing school in Nassau. With him Cameron had brought Charlotte-Anne, Carol-Louise and Brian for what had become a custom of an annual visit to Charleston.

Cameron Raleigh had swept into Charlotte-Anne's life with the force and vitality of a tropical storm. He had met her at a reception given by Richard and Penelope. She had been a girl of shy charm, reared in the tradition of her family which was as old in Carolina as the Camerons.

They had danced together and later he had brought her a glass of punch. They stood just within the open doorway overlooking the garden.

"I am going to marry you." Cameron had made the statement abruptly. "You may not believe it now but I am."

He had despite the misgivings of Charlotte-Anne's family, who felt their daughter was wedding beneath her station to a ship's captain, even though he was both owner and part Cameron. The union had been a happy and fruitful one. Both of the children had been born on Exuma.

The *Caroline* had been put into a Charleston dry dock for overhauling and the fitting of a copper bottom sheathing, for she gathered much weed and barnacle in the tropical waters. Cameron had spent his days at the shipyard overseeing every detail of the work, climbing in, over and under the schooner as any of the artisans and laborers did. Now she was all but ready for the sea again and he was anxious to get away and sail with his family for the Bahamas before the war spread.

"The *Caroline*." He answered Richard's question after a few moments of consideration. "She's the finest schooner of her size on the Atlantic coast. She's forty-two or -three years old but was built to last a hundred. There isn't an unsound timber in her. I'd take her around The Horn tomorrow if there was need for it. Why?"

A salvo shook the windows of the house and the mortar balls arced high to fall upon Sumter. Richard waited until the sound abated.

"I've been thinking. Business." Richard smiled with brief apology. "Even while the fort is being bombarded. If this war, which begins here today, lasts—and it probably will—the South, once having committed itself, cannot draw back. Then, certain facts are inescapable. The Confederacy will eventually have to look abroad for the materials of war. A fortune can be made, Cam. A fortune beyond imagining."

"And, naturally, you will be aiding the cause of the Confederacy at the same time," David interrupted dryly. "It is a fine example of altruism combined with patriotism."

"If you want to put it that way, Uncle David." Richard was just a little annoyed. "The North will, of course, blockade the Southern ports. England, Holland, and perhaps France, which are the countries most likely to be in a position to supply the South, will have to respect the blockade. But," he paused thoughtfully, "there is nothing to prevent the British merchantmen from bringing their cargoes to the Bahamas. From there fast ships can run the Yankee blockade, discharge their cargo and return to Nassau with the cotton which England must have to keep her mills running. I have been thinking of purchasing a steamer for just such a purpose."

"The *Caroline,* given a wind, can outrace any steamer." Cameron defended his schooner and at the same time felt the stirring of excitement. What an adventure this might turn out to be. "Give me the wind."

Richard smiled. This was the talk of a sailor who found the steamers with their ungainly stack and noisome cloud of soot and smoke a repelling idea.

"The wind is a thing of caprice, Cam. It cannot be depended upon to blow steadily when you need it most. The steamer is another thing. She wants only coal and men to stoke her. The risk in sail would be too great."

"The *Caroline* will foot it with a baby's breath. I would rather trust her than some damn clanking machinery."

"Well," Richard was agreeable, "we won't argue the merits of sail and steam. I'll buy the steamer anyhow. There will be need for anything which can float, move and carry cargo. You, at Exuma, are in a strategic position. What I want to know is do you want to go into this with me? Cameron and Son has the connections in Europe. We have agents abroad who will make the purchases, fill the orders for what the South must eventually have. The materials will be delivered to Nassau. From there it will be up to you when the time comes."

Cameron finished his drink and thoughtfully refilled his glass.

"You know," he mused, "I am a British subject and should have no feeling one way or the other about this war. Yet," he confessed, "my heart is with the South although I think what it does now is without logic or real cause. But, both the North and the South have maneuvered themselves into a position from which they cannot retreat." He put out his hand with a sudden grin. "The *Caroline* will be ready when you are and be damned to your stinking soot pot of a steamer." They shook hands.

"You'll have a hard time keeping Juan Cadiz out of this." David chuckled with a dry, crackling sound. "What a time he would have had with such a situation fifty years ago. He must be eighty-five or more. Does he still wear the gold earring?"

Cam nodded. "Old Papa Juan has never lost the buccaneer heart. You're right, Uncle David, I'll have trouble keeping him on Exuma." He thought for a moment. "Have you any idea what this is going to do to Nassau, Richard? There won't be mooring space in the harbor. Every Out Islander who owns a ketch or a sloop will try and put it to blockade running. Gold will shower in the streets."

"I can't imagine anyone objecting to such a rain." Richard lit a cigar. "Let's have another drink and watch the fireworks."

The bombardment of Fort Sumter lasted thirty-four hours and then

Major Anderson hauled down the Stars and Stripes in acknowledgment of surrender. Despite the furious battering there had not been a single casualty save for one unlucky enlisted man. In firing a final salute to the flag a charge of powder was accidentally exploded and a gunner killed.

Charleston was wild with excitement as Anderson and his men filed aboard a steamer and sailed out of the harbor for New York. The victory brought the city, South Carolina and the Confederacy as a whole to a frenzied pitch of confidence. The Yankees couldn't fight worth a damn and the war was as good as won. Only the thoughtful men on both sides pondered. Was this the end or the beginning? Neither the North nor the South was prepared for a wholescale war. The entire Army of the United States barely numbered 16,000. The state militia on both sides was of the most uneven quality. The members had little training beyond that of parading on the Fourth of July, holidays and at political rallies. They, and even the regular army, had neither the weapons, uniforms nor officers for a great engagement. Slavery was not actually the issue, for the North itself was divided on the point. What was at stake was whether the Union could survive or the Confederate States secede and thus split the country into two, independent nations.

With the fall of Fort Sumter, Cameron sent a fast carriage to the plantation on the Ashley to bring back Charlotte-Anne, Carol-Louise and Brian. The *Caroline* was ready. Her new canvas shone with the whiteness of a swan's wing. She sparkled with fresh paint and varnish. At the end of the week they sailed for home.

Most of the time old Juan sat in the sun these days, a manservant moving his chair around the porch as a shadow fell upon it. Often Raleigh and sometimes John joined him. They gazed hungrily at the sea, watching its eternal movement, following the waves as they built up, grew thin and translucent at the top before curling over and running in a smother of foam to the beach. A feeling of uselessness possessed them although all three had voluntarily put themselves ashore and left the *Caroline* to Cameron, who was training Brian for his officer's papers and eventual command.

At eighty-five, twenty years separated Juan from his son-in-law, and John, at sixty-one, was four years younger than Raleigh. Sometimes they talked as their eyes scanned the ocean but the conversation was in short sentences; an opinion voiced, a reply made. In the late afternoons they usually had a rum drink together and this loosed their thoughts and they would speak what was in their minds, but it was always of the past. Actually, neither John nor Raleigh was too old for the sea. Both men were still vigorous but Cameron, and later Brian, were due their chance, for their career was the sea. It had been an indivisible part of all their lives. The sea and this island. Often Bahama would come out and take a chair. One of the Negro girls would bring her tea tray and she was in the habit of adding a little rum to the brew. Three old men and a woman. She thought this to herself with a touch of dry humor. What were they waiting for now that the sap of life was running dry? They had no choice. Frequently she would think of her grandfather. Ronald Cameron had given his life to this island plantation and they had held to it in the face of all adversity. It was, she had felt and said, an obligation of honor. Only Robert Bruce had defected but in her heart she could not blame him. Now, there was the new generation; Cameron, Charlotte-Anne, Brian and Carol-Louise. Exuma would be safe in their hands for they loved it as her mother and Juan had. Sometimes, she suspected, Cameron's wife was not completely happy, yearning a little for the old friends, the Charleston of her girlhood, but Cameron was island-born and reared. He would never allow Exuma to pass from his hands and Brian, in thought and stature, was the image of his father. She could trust Exuma to them and this assumed increasing importance to her as she grew older.

Often her eyes rested on her father and a consuming sadness, even pity, filled her. Juan was not meant to be an old man. Time was the thief, stealing his youth a little at a time. His step was no longer firm but when he stood, his back was remarkably straight and his eyes were clear. Curiously enough, the skin of his face showed no wrinkles. It remained taut and smooth over the bone structure but age had darkened it to the color of old leather. The quality of burnished copper which had shown in his youth was gone. Only his hands were a calendar of the years. They were heavily veined and as wrinkled as a walnut.

Juan was aware of this. Sometimes, when he was alone, he studied them and wondered why time should be so plainly marked in this manner. These were the hands which had caressed the youthful softness of a girl, hauled effortlessly upon a sheet to set a sail, clenched themselves into iron knobs in many a waterfront brawl or, for sport, thrown a heavy knife to fly true into a wall. They had brought haunting music from a guitar long untouched. Why did they betray him now with their ugly puckering and an unsteadiness which came without warning and sometimes lasted for two or three minutes? He was ashamed of his hands for they could no longer be trusted. Taking a spoon of soup to his mouth they would often shake and spill the broth. He would stare down at the tablecloth in silent humiliation, aware that Bahama, John and Raleigh were studiously pretending not to notice what had happened.

When Caroline had died in her fifty-sixth year of a mysterious fever, striking with savage, consuming ferocity but touching no one else in the household, he had not wept. His grief ran so deep it could not be relieved with tears. He had sat by her bed, holding the hand grown cold and with the pallor of death upon it, until Bahama and John had led him away and drawn a sheet to cover their mother's face.

He had never believed such loneliness as possessed him possible. A thousand memories moved in sequence through his mind. They ranged from the day he had first looked into her eyes, the day she had given herself, so shyly willing. All of the things they had done and said together. She had fretted a little as John grew older and showed no interest in marrying and a family of his own. Quietly she had schemed to invite old friends and acquaintances with eligible daughters from the other islands. John was always polite and graciously attentive to these girls who were desperately eager for a husband but he never went beyond the politeness.

"Johnnie," he could recall saying, "sees plenty of girls." This was in the days when he, Raleigh and John sailed the *Caroline* together. "He sees them in Jamaica, Cuba, Savannah, Charleston, New York an' Boston. Maybe he makes bed with them. I never ask. There's nothing wrong with Johnnie. He just don't want to make marry. Who can blame him with all those girl to have fun with?"

Now, John was sixty-one and the time for marriage long past. Once in a while, watching Bahama and Raleigh together, he felt a small regret but it rarely lasted for long. What good was a wife when you were sixty-one? He had had all the girls he wanted and these he sometimes thought about. It always startled him a little when, remembering a pretty face, a firm young body, he realized the girl now, if she was still alive, would be fifty-five or sixty. In his mind they were eighteen or nineteen and had never grown older.

They were all on the porch with the afternoon's sun still warm when the *Caroline* rounded the point and came slowly to her anchorage. Juan was never able to look at the schooner without experiencing the same, tight excitement he had known on the first day he had seen her in Norfolk. Now, she seemed more beautiful than ever, a shining white cloud. He thought to himself, I will sail you one more time even if they have to prop me up. I will put my feet upon your deck and ride the deep water.

They had all walked down to the beach, the others fitting their step to Juan's but pretending not to. It was a casual stroll down the slope. From the shore they could see the gig being put out and they waited impatiently until the oarsmen laid it alongside the dock.

All of them wanted to talk and at the same time embrace. Brian and

Carol-Louise could barely contain themselves as they tried, in unison, to tell of the bombardment of Fort Sumter; the coach ride to Cameron Hall and back. They hugged Raleigh and Bahama, kissed John and Grandfather Juan. Then they raced off toward the house, happy and eager to be home; to see their horses and the setter bitch which was about to have puppies.

"What's all this about a war, Cam?" Raleigh couldn't believe what Brian and Carol-Louise had chattered so incoherently about. "Who's fighting who?"

"Is it the British and those Frenchies?" To Juan this seemed a natural conflict.

"No, Grandfather." Cameron put an arm about Juan's shoulder. "Let's wait until we get to the house. We'll have a drink and I'll tell you all about it."

They gathered about the table in the dining hall and a servant brought rum, limes and water to put before them.

"The States are fighting among themselves." Cameron took the dark, heavy rum straight. "This is a damn sight better than the whisky they drink these days in Charleston. Whisky and French brandy." He tasted the rum's flavor appreciatively. "South Carolina seceded from the Union."

"What's this 'secede' mean, boy?" Juan was impatient with what he didn't understand. "If there's fighting we could put some swivel deck guns on the *Caroline* and fit her out as a privateer. There'll be some easy picking among the merchantmen." Juan was delighted with the idea.

"I'm afraid not in this one, Papa Juan." Raleigh was impressed by his son's information. "Secede means South Carolina has declared itself an independent nation."

"Who gives a damn about that?" Juan was disappointed.

"Not only South Carolina, Father." Cameron was anxious to give them all the news. "Six of the Southern states, probably seven now because Texas was sending a delegate to the Convention. They have all joined in a Confederacy and declared themselves independent of the North. It means a war between the States. Fort Sumter was only the beginning. No one is sure what will happen next. President Lincoln has declared there will be no division and he means to hold the Union of States together even if the North has to beat the South into submission."

"The South couldn't win in such a war, Cam." Raleigh was grave.

"You'd have trouble finding anyone in South Carolina who believes it, Father. They saw Sumter fall. It really wasn't much of a fort as you know. Just the same they are convinced one Southerner can lick half a dozen Yankees and they're straining for a chance to prove it."

"You forget I'm a Yankee, Cam. There's nothing more Yankee than a New Englander." Raleigh smiled briefly.

"You're a Bahamian, Father." Cam took the statement as a joke. "Sometimes you even talk like one. After all, more than half your life has been spent here."

"Is the issue in the South really slavery?" Raleigh asked. "I've read much of it in the journals we get."

"Those damn niggers are always causing trouble," Juan interrupted petulantly. He had never forgotten his efforts to set them free. "They still won't get off Exuma but come whining about with their complaints."

"No," Cam answered his father. "I don't think so. Not right now, anyhow. It's whether a state can leave the Union." He paused. "They will make a case for slavery though before it is finished."

Long after the evening meal was over and the rest of the household was in bed, Raleigh and Cameron talked together. Cam told him what Richard had proposed; what he believed would happen if the war went on beyond a year or so.

"Richard's right, of course," Raleigh agreed. "The South is built on an agrarian economy. The North is industrialized. You can't make cannon balls out of cotton bolls."

"Richard is convinced there is a fortune to be made. He's buying a steamer, maybe two."

"I'm not certain we want a fortune out of other men's blood, Cam." Raleigh drew upon his cigar. "We are well enough off here but," he admitted reluctantly, "I look at it a little differently. You have Charlotte-Anne, Carol-Louise and Brian to think of. They will have to live after the old ones, including myself, have gone. I can't blame you for wanting to provide well for them."

"I told Richard that I, we, would go in with him but I'll sail the *Caroline*. He can have his steamboat. We could use some money here, Father. The house and the plantation, or what was once a plantation, aren't exactly showplaces any longer. Let's face it. We make only a bare living with the *Caroline*. The steamers are getting the trade but I still want nothing to do with them," Cam defended his decision.

For a long moment Raleigh was silent. He poured a little rum into a glass and swirled it about, staring thoughtfully at the dark pool. Then he nodded.

"I gave you command of the schooner as Papa Juan once handed her over to me. I'll not go back on what has been done. You must realize how dangerous it is going to be, the risk you are taking: your ship sunk under you by gunfire, death, capture, prison, and maybe execution if you are captured. I don't know whether money is worth what you may have to forfeit. You're my only son. I can't measure your life in dollars or pounds nor would Bahama. The North will string every ship it has along the Southern coast. You'll be slipping through a knothole every voyage. But," he smiled understandingly and pushed the rum decanter to Cam's hand, "if I were thirty-four instead of sixty-five I suppose I'd find it an irresistible adventure, also."

"Thank you." Cam was relieved for he had expected a flat rejection of the idea from his father. "After all," he couldn't resist an affectionate jibe, "Papa Juan used to tell me stories. I remember them well. There was a time when Captain Walter Raleigh wasn't above a little smuggling himself. I don't believe you did it just for the money either."

A slow smile of reminiscence spread over the older man's face. Raleigh caught himself thinking of the nights when the *Caroline* cruised through the cays and past the Patrol like a wraith. When he outsailed and outguessed the authorities at every turning. No. Cam was right. It hadn't been just for the sake of money. A young man's blood ran hot and he must cool it a little now and then with dangerous adventure. Secretly he began to envy Cam. He had grown cautious as the years multiplied. Too conservative and the flavor of life had gone sour. When the time came it was just possible, only barely possible, he might make one more voyage aboard the *Caroline* himself.

✃ XXIII ఌ

BULL RUN and the retreat toward Washington. The forts Henry and Don-elson on the Tennessee and Cumberland rivers with the new, ironclad gunboats pounding them into submission. Shiloh. Farragut and the fall of New Orleans. The names and events through the first years of the war became familiar to everyone in the Bahamas who could read.

As Richard Cameron had predicted, the South was being slowly and inexorably strangled, but before the grip was tightened beyond the Con-federacy's power to tear it away sensational events occurred in Nassau.

In the beginning the North had something short of a hundred ships of war. Half of them were sailing vessels. The rest were steam-driven but most of these were in the navy yards for repairs. Many of the ones which were serviceable were at stations in foreign waters and could not be im-mediately recalled. Active were five steam frigates, each armed with forty nine-inch guns. There were half a dozen screw sloops, four side-wheelers, a few tugs and harbor craft. With this the North set about the impossible task of blockading almost four thousand miles of the Con-federacy's coastline. The South had no navy at all.

In Nassau there was a scene of delirious excitement and confusion in which men literally went mad. The bloody conflict on the mainland and Lincoln's blockade of the Southern ports poured such a stream of gold into the colony as no one had believed possible. The South had to have guns, rifles, ammunition, cloth for uniforms, metal for horseshoes, knives, nails, and canvas for tents. She was short of everything needed to wage a war. Across the ocean England cried for cotton, for its mills were in danger of having to shut down for the want of raw material.

Lying in the Atlantic between the two was Nassau, a depot of incal-culable value. More than that, her people had the temperament for the job at hand for they were the descendants of pirates, wreckers, rebel-lious Loyalists who had quit the colonies before and after the Revolution. Lawlessness fired their blood. The sea was their home. They had sailed it in cockleshells and it held no terrors for them. Adventure ran in their veins, defiance of authority was a heritage. They felt kinship for no one. The War between the States on the mainland offered an opportunity for such profits as none had even dreamed of. It required only that they take a ship from one point to another and the Bahamians would sail anything which could float.

At the beginning of the Civil War, exports jumped from £195,000 to £1,000,000 within a year. By 1864, exports reached the staggering sum of £5,000,000. Before the blockade four or five ships a year had cleared from Nassau. Now, some six hundred vessels sailed, their decks and holds solidly packed with the matériel of war. Cotton could be bought in Charleston for fourpence a pound. It sold in Nassau for twelve and fifteen times as much. A ship which could bring seven or eight hundred bales of cotton into Nassau could realize £5,000 for the one-way trip and take back with her, eluding the Federal Navy, an assorted cargo worth twice as much. The captains and crews shared in the profits and such enormous sums attracted the most villainous assortment of cutthroats and adventurers ever gathered in ships or on land.

What had once been a lazy, sun-washed colony drowsing through the years, touched gently by the trade winds, colored by the pink and scarlet of bougainvillea and green palms with their silvered trunks, became a port of the wildest pandemonium. It was actually the abode of demons set loose by the hell of war. The old warehouses, sagging and rat-infested, were shored up and packed to their ceilings with bales, boxes, barrels, cases of rifles, kegs of powder. Along the seawalled waterfront great hills of matériel, the fibers of war, were stacked in a continuous ridge and sheeted over with canvas. Armed watchmen patrolled along the treasure and shot on sight anyone who ventured to put an unauthorized hand on these supplies awaiting transportation.

The old, first families of Nassau, who for years had lived in supercilious isolation in their mansions on the hill, now came out of their seclusion. Where they once held the lowly townspeople in contempt they now consorted with them, ingratiating themselves in an effort to enlist crews and ships. Using their connections in England and the mainland they threw themselves wholeheartedly into the blockade-running traffic. They welcomed the Out Island boatmen whose existence they would have ignored before, gave the place of honor at their tables to sinister captains of cargo ships, consorted with murderous seamen, plotting and scheming for every inch of space in the most disreputable of vessels. Fortunes were made in a matter of months.

Along Bay Street and the narrow lanes leading from it new buildings went up as fast as the lumber could be cut and the boards nailed. Taverns, inns, grogshops, elaborate bordellos, these stocked with the most vivacious girls from the fancy houses in New Orleans. These were for the captains and ships' officers and the gentlemen of commerce whose purses were bulging. The meanest of cribs with blowsy slatterns, young Negro and mulatto girls, pressed against each other in a disreputable row for the rowdy seamen. Housing space was practically nonexistent. Men slept in the streets, on the floors of taverns, on the docks, wherever they could find a few feet in which to lie down. Even the crumbling forts of Nassau and Montague were turned into dank lodging quarters.

The nights were hours of riot, filled with drunken shouting and curses. Knives flashed and were driven home into quivering flesh. Clubs cracked skulls. Pistols fired and men fell. The dead were left where they dropped or, if the bodies inconvenienced anyone or impeded trade, they were dragged away and tossed into the road. They lay crumpled there and were ignored until the frantic authorities had them hauled away and dumped into a common pit with a few shovelfuls of earth as a cover.

Not since the days of the French and Spanish invasions, or when the British pirates and buccaneers of many nations had congregated in Nassau, had anyone witnessed such lawlessness as now swept the colony. Sailors came ashore with as much as $1,500 to $2,000 in their pockets. They threw it away with a careless gesture, spending it on wenching, champagne and fine brandy. They cracked the bottles' necks against a stone and drank from the splintered glass, swilling with the unslakable greed of pigs. When the bottles were empty they kept them, for the jagged edges served as useful weapons for the fights that occurred with deadly regularity. There was no restraint, for the Government would have been unable to exercise its will even if it had wanted to curb the wild orgies, the murders and the brawling. To do so might have interfered with business.

On a slightly more respectable scale there were members of fine, old Southern families: the wives and daughters of men who were fighting for the Confederacy or engaged in its commercial affairs, who had been sent to the Bahamas and out of harm's way; the looting and burning of the Union troops in their relentless advance. There were also officers, in the handsome gray and gold-braided uniforms of the South, who had never seen a battle. They came in numbers to supervise the purchase of ordnance, the small arms, cannon, mortars and ammunition so desperately needed. These were graciously received, entertained and quartered by the families on the hill and in the Governor's Mansion. Removed from the chaos of the waterfront and the lower part of the town, they created a brilliant and carefree society. They danced, flirted and made love. The ballrooms of the big houses were newly furnished and decorated through this seemingly endless flow of prosperity and there the Southern belles in the finest of gowns vied with each other for the gallant attentions of the officers and the sons of their hosts. They toasted the South in champagne, the chivalry of its men, the beauty of its women, the noble cause of the Confederacy and the hospitality of those who entertained them and were, incidentally, making a fine profit from the association.

Made heady by the booming trade, the Government approved the building of the Royal Victoria Hotel at a cost of over £25,000 so that "the Nassau people might sumptuously entertain their Southern friends and the brave officers who wore the gray." When it was completed the Royal Victoria was a magnificent structure set within a grove of palms and gardens of breathtaking color. Its rooms were spacious and furnished with the finest European exports. The balconies overlooked the sea, the turmoil of Bay Street and the harbor where the blockade runners were beam to beam, their masts and tall stacks making a weaving forest. Nightly two orchestras alternated in the Royal Victoria's ballroom, playing until daybreak when elaborate champagne breakfasts were served. After this was over the "dashing men in gray" and the exquisitely dressed ladies in their Paris fashions snatched a few hours' sleep before the festivities would begin again in the afternoon. The war seemed very far away and when, before, had there been such an opportunity for gaiety, lovemaking and the endless rounds of fetes in such seductive, tropical settings?

On Exuma the fields were once again cleared and planted. The South was also in desperate need of food, for her men were away on the battleground and their slaves worked only when an overseer's lash fell upon their backs. John and Raleigh had recruited former Bahamian slaves from other of the Out Islands and hired them at exorbitant wages to till the soil, raise the corn, beans, fruit, vegetables and cane. Despite their age both men did their best to direct the labor, but the effort taxed them greatly and much of the crop was lost through neglect and indifference. The Negroes, through the mysterious means of communication they employed, had heard of what was happening in Nassau and they wanted a share of the excitement and money. The latter was of little value to them, for the Southerners who crowded the colony on New Providence would not tolerate their presence in any public place, store or shop.

The *Caroline* rarely made Exuma these days. Once or twice Cameron had put in and the schooner lay at anchor for a few hours while the family listened with incredulous attention as Cam told them what was happening in Nassau and his own running of the blockade with the schooner. Brian was almost eighteen now and he sailed with his father for Cam could not deny him this adventure. Brian had been born to the sea as had his father, grandfather, and great-grandfather. He could no more resist its call than could any island man. He was third officer aboard the *Caroline* but this was only a title. The Bahamian crew were an unruly lot, resenting discipline and respecting only the temper and fists of Cameron and the first mate, who kept them in surly submission. But Cameron was proud of his son who had inherited Walter Raleigh's lean toughness and squinting smile. He was steady and cool despite his youth and, in time, would make a fine officer.

Papa Juan had aged unbelievably. The palsy afflicting his hands had spread to his body now and he would suddenly begin to shake uncontrollably and someone would have to lead him to a chair. When the *Caroline* was in and they sat about the table or in the parlor while Cam recounted some encounter with a Union patrol ship or a ruse which led him through the blockade, Juan had difficulty in following the story. He understood only part of what was being said and Cam frequently had to repeat or explain. But when he did catch some phrase or comprehend a hazardous race and escape, the old fire crept into his eyes and he could barely restrain his eagerness, asking Cam to tell it over and over again. Watching her father, sitting by his side, helping him to put a little rum from a glass on his tongue, Bahama was filled with a heartbreaking sadness. Not Caroline's Juanio. This couldn't happen to the man of laughter with the ring of gold in his ear and a love of life. She sometimes wished he could die quietly in his sleep. This ending was so unfair. No man should be stripped naked of dignity and become an object of pity.

The *Caroline* and Richard's steamer, *Southern Star,* had made returns far beyond what either Cam or Richard had expected. On one trip alone the steamer had carried 400 barrels of powder, 10,000 rifles, 1,000,000 cartridges and 2,000,000 percussion caps. The voyage, for she had returned to Nassau with her holds and deck space filled with bales of cotton, had netted them something a little over $250,000. This was divided equally, after crew and captain were given their share, for they had agreed at the beginning that both schooner and steamer should pool the profits in a common fund to be split between them.

Cameron had the *Caroline* painted a smoky gray which blended with the mists and the fogs so frequently encountered off the coast of the mainland. His favorite waters for putting ashore the contraband lay off the North Carolina capes and inlets from Hatteras to Lookout. There were innumerable inlets leading to Pamlico Sound and by now he could almost feel his way in. They would run Ocracoke or Hatteras inlets, land their cargoes in West Bay or Swanquarter, and be out again before full day's light. Sometimes they worked farther north around Albemarle Sound or went as far south as Matanzas Inlet and St. Augustine. It all depended upon the strength of the blockade, how and where the Union ships were posted or cruising. The blockade runners had their signals and passing each other, one bound for Nassau the other for the mainland, the Bahamian-bound vessel would pass on the latest information as to the location or course of the Federal gunboats.

Because her cargo space was small as compared to the *Southern Star,* Cam could not carry the heavy ordnance. She brought to the South the rifles, ammunition and powder. But also, she carried luxury items far from essential to the Confederacy's desperate plight. There were silks, satins, perfumes, wines, whisky and brandies. For, as always in a war, there were profiteers and unscrupulous men who were indifferent to the cause for which others died. There was a ready market in both the North and South for these articles of vanity and pleasure and those who were making a good thing out of the war showered them upon their wives, mistresses and sweethearts. So extensive did this trade become that the Confederate Congress finally passed a law requiring permits for the blockade runners and limiting all imports to the necessities of war. Her troops were marching in tattered uniforms. Many of the men and boys trudged barefooted or bound their swollen feet in rags unless they were lucky to come across a dead soldier from either side whose boots they could strip off and wear. While many an infantryman had to depend upon his bayonet because he no longer had a charge for his rifle, the fancy ladies shaded themselves with silk parasols, scented themselves with French perfume and wore the most luxurious gowns, gossamer hose and dainty slippers.

The blockade was becoming increasingly difficult to evade. Northern shipyards were turning out fast, armed, screw-driven sloops and they patrolled endlessly. Despite his boast that the *Caroline* could outrun any steamer, Cam often found himself in the tightest of situations where the wind would die suddenly, leaving him practically helpless. Luck followed him, though. Many a time when the smoke and hull of a blockading ship was coming up fast the wind would miraculously pick up and the *Caroline* with every inch of canvas on her would outrace her pursuer. Then, when darkness fell, she would cautiously feel her way toward the mainland. In the early mist, just before daybreak, she could get her cargo to a port or a point of rendezvous where wagon transports waited. Then there would be the problem of finding an unguarded place where they could pick up a few bales of cotton or a deckload of lumber which would be snatched up in Nassau. He had been fired upon, chain shot had ripped through his rigging, and two seamen had been killed, but the *Caroline*'s fortune held and she would slide away like some ghostly creature to disappear in an unexpected rainfall or a rolling bank of fog.

By now the coast, particularly the section around North Carolina, was littered with wrecks. Inexperienced or rash masters hit upon the reefs or were caught in the treacherous waters and shoals off Cape Hatteras and broken up. Other captains, pursued by a Federal gunboat, deliberately ran their ships aground where part of the cargo, at least, could be salvaged. They scrambled for safety in small boats while the furious Union gunners poured fire after them and tried to reduce the helpless vessel to a shattered hulk and destroy her cargo.

Now, the *Caroline* was laying overnight at Exuma and for the first time Cameron slept in his own bed. Charlotte-Anne lay in his arms. She was dismayed and frightened by the lines of weariness on his face, the unmistakable marks of fatigue, the eyes which carried in them a constant light of wariness. Even here, in bed, he was far away from her, somewhere at sea, and she had the guilty feeling of bedding with a stranger.

"I've missed you so, Cameron." She felt his strength along her body. "Nothing is the same without you. Will this be over soon? Do we really need all the money you and Richard are making?"

He turned his face to kiss her and her mouth clung to his. After a moment he drew her back down, holding the slender warmth of her body close to him.

"Do you know?" he reflected. "Most of the time I don't think at all about the money although Richard is very careful with it. We deposit in Nassau for transfer to London, for everything the South buys is with gold. The Confederacy has issued its own bank notes but Richard, or any of the blockade runners for that matter, will not accept them. None of us really believes the Confederacy can possibly win. When the war is over, the South will be in ruins. Its paper money valueless. No, I don't really stop to think about the profits. It is the excitement, the fascination of the chase, the sharp edge of danger which cannot be resisted, the exaltation one feels when, having pitted his skill and boldness against that of another man, one knows he has outwitted and outguessed him. It becomes a deadly game and I can't deny its appeal."

Charlotte-Anne pressed her face into his shoulder. His arm about her tightened.

"It is all so different from what I imagined it would be when we were married. From the things you told me I believed these were the enchanted islands. When it is over, Cam," her words were all but inaudible, "can we go back home, to Charleston?"

[377]

"You're not happy here, are you?" He was made miserable by the pleading.

"No." She sat up and gazed down at him. "I never will be. I have nothing. No friends, no small occupation to take my time. Carol-Louise is growing up almost completely ignorant of anything beyond these islands. It is not fair to her or to me, Cam. I know you think I am being trivial. But, here we sit. Your daughter and wife surrounded by old people—your mother, John, your father and that disgusting, vulgar old man they all call Papa Juan. Sometimes I think I will go mad and run screaming out of the house in sheer desperation."

"I'm sorry." He was sincere. "But the Charleston you remember, the South you knew, will not be the same. When the end comes, and it is not far off, the North will put its heel upon the South's neck and stamp it there. A couple of generations will pass before the sectional bitterness wears itself out. The friends you had will be different, for they will have lost everything—their homes, their men, a way of life. There will be poverty and misery beyond imagining. The Negroes will be freed and there will be a social and economic revolution such as no one has ever known. There will be no great plantations, the fine mansions will be in ruins. But," he was quiet for a moment, "you are my wife and I love you even though there has been little time to show it. If it will make you happy we'll go back to South Carolina. You can then see what has happened and decide for yourself. I'll tell you this, though. Brian will not want to go. This is his home. He feels about Exuma the way my mother, Bahama, does. The Cameron strain and the Raleigh love for the sea are deeply rooted. He will not leave here to make a home somewhere else."

"Then Brian can stay." Charlotte-Anne was emphatic. "He will be of age soon and free to choose his way, but I will not have Carol-Louise buried here among these ignorant conchs to grow up a rude, untutored young woman who will have to make her selection of a husband from the Out Island boatmen. I want her to be the lady her breeding demands. With all the money you and Richard have made I would like to take her to England or France for her schooling and, eventually, make the proper marriage. You know," she leaned back again, her cheek upon his bare chest, "I have never complained before although this is far from the life I thought it would be. I'm not complaining now. I'm asking you to do this for me, for your daughter and, perhaps, even for yourself."

"You forget I'm island-born, also." He smiled a little in the darkness. "But, when the war is over I'll take you back to Charleston. Don't let your fancy run away with you. It will never again be the city you remember."

[378]

"Whatever it is, even in ruins if that is what is going to happen, it will be far better than this island."

Old Juan was also awake. He lay in his bed and his mind was remarkably clear as an unexpected wind will suddenly sweep away a shrouding fog. Cameron's return. The sight of the *Caroline*. The talk around the table. Somehow they had combined to sharpen his thinking. For this little while he was once again Juan Cadiz and not a tottering old man who must be helped to feed himself, dress and undress. This was the bed he once shared with Caroline. They had made love in it and Bahama and John were conceived here. Now, nothing of this was left. Save for Bahama, and sometimes John, he felt he was surrounded by strangers. Oddly enough, though, he was aware of a kinship between himself and his great-grandson, Brian. For a moment the mist again clouded his memory. He had to stop and think. Cameron? Cameron was the son of Bahama and Raleigh, and Brian was the son of Cameron and the one whose name was Charlotte-Anne. Yes. That was right. This Charlotte-Anne. She despised him. He could recognize the revulsion in her eyes whenever she looked at him. Why, he wondered, would she hate an old man? But then, he had a contempt for himself. This body which was a withered thing. The mind that wandered and found difficulty in holding to a single thought. The eyes, clouding over at times until it seemed he peered through a gauze curtain. He moved an arm, stretching it to cover the vacant side of the bed where Caroline used to lie. He was glad she was not here to see him. What was it she called him? Juanio. Yes. Juanio. When she spoke it the name was a caress. He had no idea what had made her think to call him that instead of Juan as did everyone else. She was gone now and no one ever said Juanio, only Papa Juan. This Brian. Old Raleigh's grandson. He laughed then, softly but aloud and with genuine amusement. Old Raleigh. Old B'ma. Old John. Old Juan. They all sat, waiting for death to rap with bony knuckles upon the door and take them away. The boy, a young man really, Brian had something in him of all of them. He was tall and strongly made with the strength of the Cameron men. From Raleigh he had inherited the deliberate manner of speech and decision, and from Old Papa Juan and B'ma, the smile reaching out to touch you, the warmth of spirit and an impatience for things as they were. The generosity and fine features of Caroline. He would have liked to be Juan Cadiz again, sailing a sloop with a red sail, playing upon a guitar with someone like this Brian for a companion. The girls the two of them might have tumbled in Nassau; the good fights, the laughter, the songs to be sung and a wicker-covered jug of rum to be shared on the beach in the shade of a coconut palm. Juan Cadiz and Brian Raleigh. What a pair they would have made.

Not until he had slowly, painfully and with infinite patience pulled himself upright and sat, trembling for a moment on the bed's edge, did he actually admit to himself what he was going to do. He took a few minutes to think about it for the thing must have been in his mind for a long time. Otherwise he would be surprised.

It took him a full quarter of an hour to draw on a pair of loose pantaloons and pull a shirt over his head. He had to rest in a chair to do the latter, draping the garment over his knees, then bending to push his arms through the folds and, finally, into the sleeves. When he straightened, the open collar fell down over his head. He made no attempt to stuff the tails into his trousers. Usually a Negro servant helped him dress and assisted him down the long flight of stairs. Now he must do it himself and quietly, for he wanted no one to awaken and ask what he was doing or try to put him back in bed.

From somewhere, far in the lost years, he drew upon a small reserve of unsuspected strength. He had a purpose now and it steadied his trembling legs and shaking hands. He weaved slightly as he crossed the room and cautiously opened a door. His bare feet made no sound. A single taper burned on a table on the landing. It gave him light enough. Clinging with both hands to the balustrade he backed slowly and carefully down the flight of steps until he reached the lower hall. Here another candle in its night glass fluttered. The distance to the dining room seemed interminable. He pressed himself against the walls, sliding along them as a prop, leaning for fear he might fall at every step.

At a mahogany cabinet he fumbled a little inside until his fingers felt the straw covering of a bottle of rum. He clutched it to him, cradling it against his chest with one arm and bracing himself with the free hand as he made his way back. Then his feet scraped down the hall, to the door, and finally, outside. Now, came the hardest part. The steps first from the porch and then the long descent from the ridge to the beach and dock. Fifty yards from the water's edge he stumbled and fell, the bottle rolling ahead. From here he crept on his hands and knees through the wiry grass like some stricken animal. He retrieved the rum and pulled it along behind him by the neck as he inched his way. He was cursing softly now under his gasping breath, railing at his helplessness. The boards of the dock scraped his knees and a splinter drove through the pantaloons and into his flesh like a thorn.

The sloop was moored fore and aft, the lines looped about bollards, and heavy rope matting kept her from scraping against the piers. It seemed hours before he could cast off and then, holding to the forward line he half slid, half fell into the craft, pressing the bottle into the pit of his arm. He lay in the stern sheet and cried, the tears streaming in hot rivulets down his cheeks. He wept without shame for his weakness. There was even a curious sense of triumph in this misery.

The sloop drifted slowly away on an outgoing tide. Finally he called upon his determination and what strength was left to crawl to the aft thwart and lift himself to where the tiller swung back and forth with a lazy motion. He draped an arm over it and let the craft slide and turn. For the first time he looked at the sky. It was powdered with bright crystals of stars.

On the seat he found a fish knife and with it he pried at the rum bottle's cork, digging it out in pieces. The final segment, under which he could not slip the pointed blade, he pushed down. Then he took a long drink and felt the hot liquor run like a stream from mouth to stomach. It nestled warmly there. After a couple of minutes he drank again. This time there was no sensation beyond a feeling of renewed strength in his body. He could move with more confidence now.

When the small craft was carried out beyond the point it was picked up by a steady wind coming from the south-southwest. There was a hand winch and he cranked at it determinedly until the mainsail was up. It filled with a slap and he ducked as the boom swung over his head. Later he would try and set the jib but for now this was enough. The sloop heeled slightly under the steady thrust and he dropped the loops of two short lines over the tiller to hold it in position while he took another drink. He was beginning to feel the rum now and it was good. He took a bearing from the stars for he knew where he was going. Up the Exuma Sound and then out into the open through the waters between Eluthera Point and Northeast Point, on Cat Island. Then he would take his wind and sail into the sunrise which was still hours off.

He swallowed another mouthful of rum and wondered how long it would take. He had seen men who had died of thirst and they were not good to look upon with their tongues black and swollen, the lips parched, the skin drawn of all moisture and dry as old parchment. Perhaps the God, about whose Presence he had never given much thought, would be a little merciful and send a sudden squall of vicious strength to capsize the sloop. Or, the sea would miraculously rise to swamp him. If not, when the rum was gone and he could stand the torture no longer, he would creep to haul himself over the side and let the deep cover him.

"My mother, the sea." He spoke aloud and in a firm voice. "Juanio comes home."

The *Caroline* sailed at daybreak for Nassau. There was cargo to be picked up there. Also, the crew was restless. The men had money coming to them and they wanted to spend it in the only way they knew, in the waterfront dives.

Cam would have liked to lay over for another day. He saw so little of Bahama and Raleigh and they had once been so close. The schooner rounded the point and then came up through The Tongue of The Ocean, making the passage for New Providence between Andros Island and the Exuma cays. He had thought of looking in upon Old Juan before he left but decided against it. He was probably still asleep and anyhow, he had become so vague and enfeebled talking with him was difficult.

Raleigh, Bahama, John and Brian were already in the breakfast room when he came down. There were eggs, plantation-cured ham, hot biscuit with lime preserves and good, strong coffee. It was a far better meal than he would get aboard the schooner and he had eaten with hungry pleasure.

"I always think I would like to make a voyage with you." Raleigh spoke wistfully. "Then I say what has an old man of sixty-eight to do with a young man's work? I'd only be in the way."

Cameron's smile was one of understanding but he made no reply, for there was nothing honest he could say beyond agreement.

"You'll be careful, won't you?" Bahama lifted her eyes to her son and grandson on the opposite side of the table.

"I always am." Cam dropped the napkin beside his plate. "That's why the *Caroline* is still afloat and Brian and I aren't in a Federal prison or at the bottom. Well," he stood up and put his hand on Brian's shoulder, "are you ready, Mister?"

They walked together down to the beach. Bahama noticed that the sloop was not moored at the dock but she paid scant attention to its absence. A couple of the Negro boys were probably out fishing. They had permission to take the boat whenever they wanted. So, there would be fresh fish for the noonday meal. They always brought the pick of the catch, the small snappers which were rolled in corn meal and fried crisply.

The *Caroline*'s gig waited. Cameron kissed his mother good-bye and shook hands with his father, changed his mind and brushed Raleigh's cheek with his lips. Bahama gave Brian a quick hug.

"You've grown so, Brian. I don't know, anymore, how to say good-bye. Good luck and I hope this thing is over soon."

Now, Cameron walked the schooner's deck. Brian had the watch. The schooner felt her way under shortened sail, for the sun was full in the quartermaster's eyes. A lookout, high in the rigging, called the shoal water as he saw it. Cameron lit a cigar and leaned upon the rail. He was weary, not physically but in spirit. The problems mounted with every voyage, for the Union blockade tightened constantly. They had made a fortune, he and Richard. For the first time he wondered what to do with it. Charlotte-Anne and Carol-Louise. If there was anything left of Charleston they could have their house and carriage, the trip abroad, the clothes and fripperies which seemed so important to women. Charlotte-Anne had not come down to see them off. She was drowsy, satiated with the lovemaking of last night. Her eyes glowed with sleepy pleasure as he bent and kissed her.

"Come back soon, Cam. I miss you so, here alone this way."

He drew upon the cigar and wondered idly what he was going to do when the war was over. He couldn't imagine himself sitting about the coffeehouses in Charleston, making small, inconsequential talk, taking his place in whatever social life would still be maintained in the city. He had no interest in Cameron Hall and the plantation even though Richard had suggested they operate it together. This was a curious contradiction in Richard's nature. He was a practical man and yet, he deluded himself with the notion life in the South would return gradually to what it had been before the conflict. It was a dream, an illusion. Who would work a plantation the size of the one on the Ashley? Not the blacks, not the poor whites. He laughed to himself at the idea of Richard Cameron chopping cotton or driving a mule. The Yankee troops would probably destroy the manor anyhow. He thought about the West which was opening up. But, what was a sailor to do in Kansas? He might take some of the money and build a new ship, larger than the *Caroline*. In this, though, he was as stubborn as Richard. Sail had outlived its time. It was giving way to steam. In a few years a sailing ship would be a curiosity. What the hell am I going to do? The thought of the empty years ahead plagued him. He dropped the half-smoked cigar into the water and watched as it bobbed away and disappeared.

In the brief dusk of late afternoon a ketch, inbound for the Munjack Channel and Little Abaco Island, came upon a sloop sailing crazily, her sail taking the wind and then falling off as the boom swung back and forth. The ketch came about and the crew stared at the craft. There was no one aboard. An empty, straw-covered rum bottle rolled back and forth with the sloop's movement. The ketch put a man aboard to drop the sail and then took her in tow. It was a nice prize to pick up, for she seemed sound and was well built. They talked a little of the man or men who had been sailing her. The damn fool or fools probably got drunk and fell overboard in a fight or stupor.

⊷§ XXIV §⊷

STANDING WELL off the coast, idling and waiting for dusk and night-fall, the *Caroline* saw first the smoke, then the stack and masts, of a steam- and sail-driven ship as she took advantage of a steady west wind and raced on a southeast course.

Forward, Cameron held a glass and studied the oncoming vessel. As she drew upon them he recognized her as the *Macon,* long in the running of the blockade. Her captain, John McMasters, was an old friend. They had shared many a drink and story together in the Nassau taverns and exchanged information on weak spots in the Federal patrol. Cam was puzzled by her appearance now, for she was heavy in the water and this argued a full cargo. The South no longer had much to export or trade with. Northern victory was in the air. The Confederacy's fields had been put to the torch. The slaves were jubilantly following the Union forces. There was little or no cotton for England's mills. Where, Cam wondered, and what had McMasters come upon which would load his ship so heavily and make him race with it to the Bahamas?

He ordered signals run up and saw the *Macon* reduce her speed in recognition. Small figures of men scrambled aloft and the square-rigged sails, used as auxiliary power, came down. The *Macon* came about, slowed and then halted altogether, her screw barely turning enough to hold her steady.

As Cam watched, a boat was put over and rowed toward the *Caroline.* Captain McMasters, a giant of a man, heavily bearded and with a booming voice, stood and braced himself. He held a megaphone and shouted through it.

"It's all over, Cam." The words came clearly. "The whole damn thing is just about finished."

When the boat was alongside, McMasters came up the ladder. They shook hands while the *Caroline*'s crew gathered at a respectful distance, hoping to catch a little of the startling news.

"Sherman took Atlanta." McMasters stood with his feet apart, hands on hips. "Then he moved into Savannah. When he finished there his troops started for South Carolina. They raised hell there, from what I heard. Columbia was sacked and then burned to an empty shell. You might as well go back to Nassau with whatever you're carrying. There's no one to buy it."

They had a drink and a cigar in Cameron's cabin. McMasters drew appreciatively upon the tobacco and then shook his head with a grim smile.

"Well," he all but bellowed, "we had one hell of a time while it lasted, didn't we?"

Cameron nodded dully. Despite the fact his father was a New Englander, Cameron Raleigh's heart had been with the South but he was in constant conflict with his emotions. He had been fearful of the South's victory, believing the Southern states could not survive alone. The strength of the whole country lay in its union. Still, he did not want to see the Confederacy punished now as it would be with the Northern triumph.

McMasters took a second drink, wiped his mouth with the back of a hand and stood up.

"There'll be no stopping the Yankees now. I'm going into Nassau as fast as I can with a lie." He grinned. "I'll say I was turned back and chased by the blockade. If I'm the first ship there with the news of what is happening, you can be damn sure I'll keep my mouth shut. Maybe I can sell my cargo to another runner before anyone finds out it isn't worth a hoot and a holler. I'd advise you to do the same. If I can I'll keep my crew quiet about the thing until you get there. But if another ship beats you in, then what you are carrying might just as well be dumped overboard. You won't be able to give it away."

Cam watched as the *Macon* crowded on her sail and with the heavy black smoke belching from her stack, took up her race for Nassau. He gave his own orders and the *Caroline* headed on her own southeasterly course. Through his second officer he passed word to the crew of what was happening on the mainland and cautioned them to say nothing when they reached Nassau which would drop the bottom out of all contraband. Since they all had a small share in it he believed he could trust them to keep quiet.

They crowded the *Caroline* with every inch of sail she could carry. She was flying now, skilled hands taking advantage of the wind as it held steady. Brian approached his father respectfully, for aboard the schooner they maintained the proper relationship between master and junior officer although it was tempered a little when they were alone.

"Do you really believe it's over, sir?"

"If what Captain McMasters says is true." Cam pursed his lips in a small frown. "Come to my cabin, Mister."

Alone, they both relaxed and Cameron motioned Brian to a chair. He was thoughtfully silent for a few minutes.

"New Orleans," he finally spoke, "Natchez, Vicksburg, Savannah, Charleston." He ticked off the names. "They've drawn a cord around the sack's neck, Brian. A flea won't be able to get in or out. Take a drink if you like." He indicated a bottle of Exuma rum. Brian was almost twenty in this year of 1865 and he shared a tot now and then with his father.

From a chart case Cameron took a land map of the coast and traced Sherman's probable route northward from Savannah. Although he didn't know it, the Union troops must struggle through some of the worst marching country in the South. They would be mired in swamps, torn at by the all-but-impassable scrub, hemmed in by thick pine forests. To transport their supply wagons and artillery they would literally have to build a road before them as they advanced. If they had burned Columbia to an empty shell, then Charleston could expect even harsher treatment. South Carolina was blamed for starting the bloody war. She had been the first to secede. The conflict had been nursed and cradled by her. The opening guns had been fired from Charleston's batteries on Fort Sumter. Sherman could not be blamed for laying a heavy hand on the port city. He wondered about Richard, his family and old Robert Bruce. Cameron Hall, if it stood in the way of Sherman's troops. The Cameron house on Tradd Street and David Heath's beautiful home. They would all be wrecked and possibly destroyed if Sherman left his troops free to sack the city. There would be little for Charlotte-Anne and Carol-Louise to come back to in the city his wife had loved so well.

"What do you suppose will happen now, Father?"

Cameron lifted his hands in a helpless gesture. "It will, I suppose, depend upon President Lincoln. I have heard he is a man of compassion. This War Between the States must have troubled him deeply. If he can control the vindictive hotheads in his Cabinet, then perhaps some order can be brought out of the Union victory. It can only be a matter of days or a few weeks before Lee surrenders. Then who knows? If Union anger prevails then the South will be made to suffer beyond its capacity to endure. Lincoln has never been the Confederacy's enemy. His aim and determination was to hold the Union together. I just don't know what will happen."

They made Nassau on an early morning and when Cameron and Brian went ashore they found McMasters had kept his word. No news of the Union's stunning victories had reached New Providence. There was some suspicion among the blockade runners whose ships still crowded the harbor, waiting for supplies. Questions were asked. Why should the *Macon,* and now, the *Caroline,* return with their holds packed? When confronted, Cam said only that the blockade had tightened. He had been pursued and didn't want to risk his ship. The answer was received with some skepticism but greed triumphed over doubt. There were men in Nassau who would venture anything for a profit. Maybe McMasters and Cameron Raleigh were telling the truth. They had made a lot of money. Perhaps they didn't want to gamble with their vessels. Cameron sold his cargo to a factor who, in turn, disposed of it to an eager bidder at a lower price than he would have had to pay on the waterfront. Cameron was well satisfied with the small loss and glad to be rid of the cargo.

Cameron and Brian, after the crew had been paid off and watches set aboard the schooner, took rooms at the Royal Victoria. The scene here was as gaily festive as ever. A great buffet occupied one end of the dining hall and it was stacked with the choicest of foods, imports from the countries of Europe, and the finest wines of France. White-coated and -hatted Negroes stood at attention, eager to carve and serve, and the plates were carried to tables by liveried blacks. The buffet was open the full twenty-four hours of the day, for merchants, ships' officers, agents and factors were in and out constantly.

If the purpose of the hotel was to entertain the gallant men of the South then it succeeded. The revelry never abated. The Confederate officers were gallant; the beauty of the South eagerly pliant, filled with coquettishness, insatiable in their pursuit of pleasure. No one even thought of a possible defeat. The Yankees were a miserable lot and the harsh realities of war were far away. Everyone here was wealthy. The gowns of silk and fine fabrics were brought from France. Men, handsome, dashing, brave men, were in plenty and no young woman, even the plain ones, needed to go without an attentive escort.

Within the hotel's palm grove, heavy with the perfume of flowers, a platform had been built. The boards were waxed and polished for dancing on the warm nights beneath the stars while an orchestra played in the background. Candles, in colored globes, were strung among the graceful palms, lending a multicolored illumination to this novelty of an outdoor ball. Here, in the dusky corners of the garden and with the soft breath of the ocean wind upon their flushed cheeks, many a maiden yielded to the graceful pleading of the brave men in Confederate gray. Love was made, pledges lightly given. To be sure, they had all heard of certain defeats suffered by the Confederacy but such things were expected in a war. No thought was given to failure. The brave troops would surely drive the Yankees back and return the South to its days of glory.

The news, when it came only two days after the *Caroline*'s return, stunned Nassau as nothing before had ever affected the colony. By comparison the devastating hurricane of an earlier time, the cholera epidemic, the dislocation occasioned by the Emancipation Act, a fire which had all but leveled the settlement, had been nothing to the numbing fear which gripped it now. Panic raced from the waterfront to the finest houses on the hill. Men at first refused to believe the intelligence brought by a barkentine which had tried to run the Savannah blockade. It was some irresponsible rumor, a trick to beat down the prices of the matériel filling the warehouses, blocking the streets, piled high in every store and shop. When, however, on the next day a second vessel put in with the same report there was no choice but to accept the South's defeat as a fact. It was true Lee had not formally surrendered but no responsible person believed this could be far off.

Merchants, factors and ships' captains frenziedly inventoried their tremendous stocks which were valueless now. There were cases upon cases of rifles. Kegs of powder, box upon box of ammunition, heavy ordnance, thousands and thousands of yards of cloth for uniforms, shoes, socks, medical supplies choked the colony. To make matters worse, orders of staggering size, already paid for to the agents of British mills, factories and firms in England, were at this moment upon the sea in the holds of British merchantmen and could not be turned back.

Fortunes which had been made during the years had been carelessly spent, for the flow of gold seemed never-ending. The money had gone for lavish furnishings, imported carriages and blooded horses, silver, jewelry, the most expensive of clothing, trips abroad, china, Oriental rugs along with the most extravagant entertainment and manner of living. None of this could be recalled. The frenzy mounted. Overnight everything had been swept away. The bleakest of futures stared the once wealthy colony in the face. There were three suicides among the merchants who had overbought and were now confronted by complete ruin. Quietly the orchestras in the Royal Victoria disappeared. The sumptuous banquet tables were vacant. The champagne lay untouched in its bins. The "gallant men in gray" who had enjoyed the war in these most beautiful of all waters, surrounded by charming, eager girls and young women, sat about and glumly contemplated their future. They had none. Even the most carefree admitted this. Everything to which they had hoped to return in the South was gone. It was not beyond imagining the Yankees turning the Southern states into one vast prison. Most of them were half decided to remain in the Bahamas. The future here could not be worse than what they surely faced at home.

The lovely young ladies who had been reared in the South's gentle traditions and to whom this had been the most romantic and thrilling of interludes wept softly in their rooms and rented homes, dabbed at their eyes with eau de cologne. In the evenings they dressed in their most beautiful of gowns, hoping against facts for a revival of the gay, flirtatious, music-filled nights. No young gentlemen, though, came a-calling. They were too concerned for their future.

In the Government there was consternation, for it had approved large expenditures which were now an embarrassment. The Treasury's deficit became nearly as large as it had been before the war broke out on the mainland.

There was left in the Bahamas such a collection of villainy as had been rarely gathered in one place outside a prison. There were, first, the seamen. Most of them had been recruited in the South and they were men no decent master would engage in normal times. Crews must be had and they took what they could get, and what they employed were the dregs of maritime service. They were cutthroats, panderers, thieves, men wanted for murder, rape and every crime of which man is capable. They were tossed upon the beach now with no place to go. The enormous sums they had earned had been carelessly tossed away in waterfront dives. They were without funds or employment. The ships' captains who had once so eagerly sought their services now preferred to sail short-handed. They left this scum to drift aimlessly through the grog mills, the cribs and into the scattered islands, carrying their inherent lawlessness with them.

A pall lay heavily upon the colony. Gloomy desperation was on every face. Nassau was filled with a large, floating population of Negroes who had been attracted to the colony by the high wages being paid for laborers and longshoremen. They had endured the contempt of the Southern rabble manning the ships, finding no diversion save in their own settlements. Despite their emancipation, strict rules against their freedom of movement were laid down and they were not permitted on Nassau's streets after sundown unless engaged in work for a white employer. There was no occupation for them now and their only hope was to return to the poverty and isolation of the Out Islands where they might fish and farm enough for their needs. In the meanwhile they constituted an explosive, highly dangerous segment of the population on New Providence. They had been their own masters for about twenty-five years and had still not adjusted themselves to freedom.

Watching the tension grow in Nassau, Cameron decided to take the

Caroline back to Exuma. He paid off his first and second officers and arranged for their transportation to home ports. The crew, native Bahamians, were more than happy to stay on at reduced wages for there was no other employment for them. Nassau was a community of gloomy future. The once noisy, brightly lighted, brawling waterfront was tightly closed save for a couple of taverns. The wenches sat in dismal solitude. Useless cargo was dumped on the beach and the ships left daily, carrying with them only such merchandise as might be sold to a civilian population on the mainland. What use were the cases of rifles, the Confederate gray cloth, the powder and ammunition?

Sounds in the Royal Victoria echoed in its emptiness. Cameron and Brian were all but alone in the dining hall. The money the *Caroline* and *Southern Star* had made was safely on deposit in the Bank of London. Cameron had no idea what the amount was but it must be considerable. He regarded Brian from across the table. What, he wondered, was his son's future? He was wedded to the sea. The years of blockade running had given him a taste for dangerous adventure. It seemed hardly possible he would be satisfied to be landbound on Exuma with its daily routine of monotony.

"What would you like to do, Brian?"

Brian looked up in surprise. "Why, stay with you, of course. You and the *Caroline*."

"I want to go home for a while." Cameron cut through a slice of ham. "There are things to think about, plans to make. We've been a long time at sea. I'd like to lie on the beach for a few weeks and be with the family. Your mother is dissatisfied here in the islands. I must make up my mind what to do. When the final surrender is made and peace signed, we'll take a voyage to Charleston and see what is left of the city."

They finished their breakfast and stood up. Brian was as tall as his father. He had not yet filled out the frame inherited but he was going to be a big man, handsome, self-assured and with the warmth of nature bequeathed him by his grandmother, Bahama.

"We'll pay our bill and round up the crew." Cameron lit a cigar as they walked to the lobby. "That won't be as difficult as it used to be. There's no longer any place for them to go." He laughed suddenly, thinking of what Captain McMasters of the *Macon* had said. He repeated it aloud now to his son. "We had a hell of a time while it lasted, didn't we?"

It has been said of General Sherman that he took Charleston by turning his back upon it. From 1863 to 1865 the port had been under continual bombardment although remarkably few persons had been killed. The southern section suffered great destruction but the city was to be spared the invasion, firing, looting and anger of the Union troops, for Sherman was pushing into North Carolina after General Johnston. He had no need for Charleston which was caught between the Federal gunboats and the forces on land. There was nothing for her to do but surrender and the tattered flag came down. For Charleston the war was over.

Cameron Hall had been miraculously bypassed by Sherman's forces. Other plantations had been struck with a heavy hand, though. The fields had been put to the torch, the mansions looted of all treasure and then burned. A wide swath of desolation was cut through the Low Country. Cameron Hall was spared only because it happened to be out of the line of march.

Daily, as the reports of Sherman's advance reached the countryside, Robert Bruce, at the age of eighty-eight now in the last year of the war, had himself wheeled in his chair to the high, pillared porch. There he sat with a pre-Revolutionary musket over his quaking knees, determined to defend the Hall from the Yankees when they came. Richard, on a visit, had thoughtfully removed the charge which would have blown the ancient weapon up in his father's face. Robert Bruce was unaware of this treachery on the part of his son. Each morning, after he had been dressed by his Negro manservant, he was respectfully and solemnly taken to the porch where he maintained a position of militant defense until it was time for his midday meal. No Yankee foot would set itself upon Cameron soil.

The town house in Charleston was unscathed and Richard lived there alone, preferring to have his wife, Penelope, and the rest of the family in the country. David Heath and Margaret's home had also been spared damage. Margaret, at her husband's urging, was at Cameron Hall. He felt it was safer there. Army stragglers, the camp followers, a ragpicker's brood of scavengers and the jubilant Negroes might turn upon the city with fearful results. No one could be certain what would happen.

David, at seventy-one, was a man of lively humor, a keen interest in life. Time had not dimmed his intelligence or spirit. He was a gracious host and agreeable companion. He and Richard frequently took the evening meal together in one or the other of their houses. Their former slaves remained as servants and were scornful of the "nigger trash" which had run away to follow the Union Army. It was a peculiar fact that both Penelope and Margaret were barren. Both Richard and David had wanted children but the seed did not fall upon fertile ground. In the early years of their marriage both girls were barely eighteen, for it was the custom to wed in the fresh bloom of young maidenhood and set about

[391]

raising a family. As the first years passed they were shamefully distressed by their apparent inability to bear children. Margaret had two miscarriages. Penelope did not become pregnant at all and she felt this to be a disgraceful reflection upon her womanhood. Richard had hoped desperately for a child, a son, for he, save for his father, was the last male of the Camerons. With his passing, the name would also come to an end. He was extremely considerate of Penelope's feelings and never by word or action revealed his disappointment. She was aware of it, though, and many a night cried herself to sleep. There were, of course, close blood ties. Bahama's son, Cameron Raleigh, her grandson and granddaughter, Brian and Carol-Louise. But, Richard often reflected, this was far from having a son of his own and a Cameron to carry on the line.

Over their port one night he and David Heath had talked of this. Richard was forty-four, a vigorous man who was not without an eye for a pretty face and well-turned figure. In the prewar days he had not been above discreet visits to certain establishments. These were conducted on a lavish scale and with impeccable decorum where young women of middle-class background and some education and training in the social graces were available. He was no reckless libertine, flaunting an infidelity. But the blood ran full in him and could not always be denied. Penelope, since she could bear no children, felt the intimate relationship of the bedroom to be somewhat shameful, bordering upon the immoral. They were gentle and considerate of each other but by unspoken consent occupied separate rooms. If Penelope sometimes suspected business did not always call Richard out on some evenings, she kept the doubt to herself. Pride would not permit her to do otherwise.

David cracked an English walnut with a pair of tongs and munched half of it to the accompaniment of the fine port. Richard, in casual talk of the family, had just expressed his regret over being without an heir.

"My answer to that, Richard," he said deliberately, "may startle you. It all depends upon how badly you want a child; to father a son or a daughter. I know you want a son but unfortunately it cannot always be arranged to happen. I am not, of course, suggesting anything so impossibly drastic and scandalous as a separation. Penelope is not at fault. But," he meticulously picked a piece of walnut meat from the shell and salted it, "there are in Charleston and the country many young widows of breeding. They have lost their husbands, their homes, their money, and the situation for them will become far worse than it is. You know some of them, have been acquainted with their families for years. It is not entirely outside the realm of probability that a little prudent attention, a concern for the welfare and, at the proper time, some financial assistance would not go unrewarded. Eventually, if you can arrive at a mutual plane of understanding and sympathy, a house here in the city for one who is bereft of everything could lead to a most pleasant relationship and, perhaps, a child, a hoped-for son." He glanced up with a flicker of a smile.

Richard stared at him incredulously. "Are you," he asked, "really suggesting I take a mistress, set up an establishment for a young woman here in Charleston and sire an illegitimate child?"

"Why not?" David was calmly practical. "It seems important to you. There is, of course, the difficulty of a name. If out of this association a boy were born you could not give it the name of Cameron. So, perhaps it would not suit your purpose." With deliberation he selected a cigar from a cedar humidor and lit it from a candle. "I doubt Robert Bruce has ever told you, but I am a bastard."

"What?" Richard could not believe what he heard. "You are what?"

"A bastard." David spoke evenly. "I feel no disgrace over the fact. There was a time in my youth when my life, plans, hope and love were deeply ruptured. The years, though, have healed the wound and there isn't even a scar. You see, I am Robert Bruce's half brother. Ronald Cameron was my father. My mother was wife to Sir Gerald Heath who was Governor of the Bahamas. She asked Ronald Cameron to rear me upon the death of her husband. She went to England and remarried. Save for one note many years ago I have never heard from her. I am not quite sure how it works out." He looked up and there was a smile in his eyes. "But, since I am some sort of a half uncle to Bahama and John, I suppose I am a great half uncle to you, or something of the sort."

Richard stared speechless for a moment over this unemotional recital from the handsome, white-haired, aristocratic and proud man who shared his table.

"I have always wondered." He spoke slowly. "Not always, of course, but when I was younger, in my twenties. You seemed so close to the family, and yet not really a part of it. We called you Uncle David, Penelope and I, Cameron, Charlotte-Anne, Brian, Carol-Louise, all of us. It seemed natural. Never in all these years did my father break the confidence."

David watched the tendril of smoke as it curled from his cigar's tip. He studied Richard Cameron with interest for he was much like Robert Bruce as Robert Bruce had reflected the personality of Ronald Cameron.

"There was never anything but affection and understanding between your father and me. I was deeply in love with Bahama and she, I believe, with me. That is why, when I learned the truth, I left the islands and came to Charleston. Robert Bruce took upon himself what he believed to be an obligation, although I had never considered this to be so.

[393]

He found a place for me in the firm and over the years advised and assisted me in putting together a modest but comfortable fortune." He paused. "I hope this knowledge will make no difference between us. I don't believe I could stand your being polite and stiffly formal with an ancient relative. Let us continue to be friends as we have."

"I wouldn't have it any other way."

David took a watch from his vest pocket, noted the hour and closed the case with a snap.

"Thank you for your company, the dinner and a most excellent port. Think a little upon what I have said, Richard. I have also known the desire, the need for a child, a son. I do not suggest," the smile of amusement came again, "you plunge yourself into a licentious manner of living and become a rake. But if you will reflect a little, you may discover what I proposed has a certain merit. When your grandfather, Ronald, was lost at sea he was on his way to Nassau to make a formal adoption of me. Had this been consummated I would be a Cameron in name, also. Then," the eyes sparkled, "we might work at this thing together. I am, of course, a little old but I would do my best."

"I am certain you would." Richard laughed without restraint. "I will walk with you to the carriage."

After David had left, Richard returned to the dining room. He poured himself another glass of wine and sat, absently cracking the easily broken nuts between his fingers, piling the meat into a small heap before him. He had not completely recovered from the initial astonishment over David Heath's calm recital. David Cameron, really. All these years and never a word from his father. In truth, should he and Robert Bruce die first, Cameron Hall would properly belong to David although he knew the man would make no claim. Such was not his nature. He could not keep a smile from creeping into his expression at the thought of David's suggestion. Yet, as he mused upon the notion it assumed less fantastic proportions. He was well acquainted with several gentlemen of position in the city who maintained, with utmost circumspection, certain attractive young women of their choice quite apart from their homes. This was more or less generally known if not openly mentioned. No particular opprobrium was attached to these liaisons but their purpose, he had to confess, was not the propagation of a son. He finished the port and pushed the nutshells away with a gesture of impatience. It was an outrageous suggestion. He doubted David Heath had expected him to entertain it seriously. It was a wry jest and nothing more.

He capped the candles and went slowly up the gracefully curving staircase to his room and threw open the French windows opening upon the piazza. Moonlight flooded the garden and the streets. The silence made it seem impossible this city had endured the years of siege and from here he had seen and heard the first shot fired in this bloodiest of conflicts.

He undressed slowly, sitting on the edge of the bed to pull his boots off. Once a slave would have been standing by to do this. Sometimes, when he was alone this way, he was a little troubled by the fact he and Cameron Raleigh had made a small fortune out of the agony. Yet, could he have served the South better by taking an officer's commission, for which he was unfit by training, or putting a rifle to his shoulder? He doubted it. Without the blockade runners the Confederacy could not have sustained itself. He had risked what he had to offer: the ships, the money necessary for the purchase of matériel abroad, the delivery of cotton the South must sell to pursue the war. From this huge sums had been returned. Would it have been a noble gesture to have given the profits to the South's treasury? Others had made far greater sacrifices. If he had served without gain the action would not have affected the final outcome. The South had been doomed from the moment the first shot had been fired at Sumter. Still, he could not completely rid himself of this gnawing feeling of guilt.

The war now ran swiftly to its inevitable conclusion. Sherman moved rapidly into North Carolina "followed," as he complained, "by five miles of Negroes." Sheridan swung his cavalry down through the Shenandoah Valley, wiping out the last posts of Confederate resistance. Grant moved in behind the Army of Northern Virginia. Richmond and Petersburg had to be evacuated. At Sayler's Creek the Union forces destroyed a supply train and took thousands of prisoners. General Lee had less than 30,000 troops and barely half of them were adequately armed. On April 9th, in this year of 1865, in the modest brick home of Wilmer McLean at a place known as Appomattox Court House, Lee surrendered to Grant and the terrible war was, for all purposes, over.

Now what had occurred in the Bahamas with the Emancipation Act was duplicated on a larger scale in South Carolina. Freedom was one thing. The knowledge to know what to do with it quite another. Some of the freed blackmen stood about waiting for someone to come along and give them their "forty acres and a mule." Others wandered about with an aimless delight, hanging about the Union camps, abandoning the fields and the crops, making no provision for sustaining themselves. They were 'mancipated and the Good Lord would look after them. The Good Lord and Mr. Lincoln.

The South was prostrate. In the Carolina Low Country families which had lived in the most magnificent luxury now sought shelter in the burned shells of their mansions. They took to the land in a desperate effort to feed themselves. Women of gentle disposition, soft and dainty hands, wielded unfamiliar hoes. Young ladies who had once swept down beautifully conceived staircases and through the reception rooms to greet their beaux now bent their backs to the planting of beans, corn, squash, cowpeas and yams. Officers who had been permitted to return with their mounts put the fine animals to the plow. They scoured the woods and scrub in the hope of finding a stray cow, hogs grown half wild or a sow with a litter of pigs. Poverty such as these people had never known or imagined stalked the land. A few of their house slaves remained on because they were too bewildered by what had happened to know what to do. They worked side by side beneath the sun with their former masters.

In Charleston, Richard with David Heath's advice tried to bring some order out of the confused affairs of Cameron and Son. Cotton was in high demand but there was no labor to plant and pick the crop. The firm had nothing of value to export and there was little it could import for which the South could pay. Charleston was in a state of high tension. The floating population of freed Negroes clashed with the poor whites, who held them in contempt and with whom they were in economic competition. Although a militia could not be formed openly to maintain order, private citizens banded together and with clubs, illegal pistols and a few rifles brought from hiding patrolled the streets after dark in an effort to maintain some sort of security and protection in the city.

Sitting at a desk in the firm's offices Richard turned to David with an expression of complete frustration.

"I'm beginning to think we would all be better off on the Cameron plantation in the Bahamas. There, at least, we would have peace of mind, for what is happening here can only grow worse. There is certainly no place in this scheme of things at the moment for Cameron and Son. My presence in the office is useless. The vessels in which we had an interest are interned in Northern ports. The *Southern Star* is God knows where, captured or sunk. I haven't heard of her in months."

"I have been entertaining the idea of the islands myself." David was wistfully thoughtful. "You have never seen them, have you?"

"No." Richard leaned back in his chair. "During the years before the war I was busy trying to learn the business of Renevant, Decatur and Cameron. When the war broke out I was too occupied here." He left his chair and walked back and forth across the room, hands clasped behind his back. "I can't do it, David." He spoke abruptly.

"I wondered, Richard." There was sympathetic understanding in David Heath's statement. "I didn't think you could."

Richard looked up to face the older man. "My conscience bothers me. Oh, I invested heavily in the bonds of the Confederacy. I did that even though I believed the cause futile from the beginning. But, Cameron and Son also made a lot of money. This bothers me often although I do my best to rationalize our activities. I can't run away now. The pieces will have to be put together again. I will stay and do what I can. I can't shirk it although common sense tells me there will be such confusion in the South for years to come that the voices of sane men will be lost in the cries of the mad. I have to remain here. If you press me for a reason I can only admit to an obligation. If you decide to return to the Bahamas perhaps Penelope could be persuaded to go with Margaret."

David shook his head. "No." His voice had a curious note of sadness in it. "I was island-born but this is my home. I chose it willingly. It has been good to me." He smiled. "I, also, hold a considerable amount of Confederate paper. It was the least I could do. So, I am not quite as well off as you may imagine."

"After what you told me, you know the assets of Cameron and Son are at your disposal." Richard did not hesitate. His grin was spontaneous. "What does one do with a great-granduncle or whatever you are?"

"I am not exactly pauperized," David admitted. "So. We will remain. What small talents I have and such wisdom as the years have given me are at your disposal. We will give what we can of ourselves to reconstruct the new South but I have a feeling the decision may lead us down some strange paths in unfamiliar company."

Richard resumed his seat, offered David a cigar and lit one for himself.

"I have been wondering," he finally said, "what to do about Cameron Hall. We have a choice. To close the city houses and move to the Ashley or shut up the Hall and bring everyone back to Charleston. In the present state of affairs we will find no labor to work the plantation. It seems a little pretentious to maintain it for a place of occasional recreation. Yet, the city is in such an uncertain state I hesitate to bring Father, Penelope and Margaret into it."

"The countryside is going to be far more dangerous than the city, Richard. When the Negroes find they are not going to get their forty acres and a mule, and emancipation is not the paradise they imagined, there will be violent discontent. They will clash first with the poor whites who hold a few acres and whose hatred they already know. Then they will move to squat upon the remaining plantations."

"Well," Richard put aside his cigar, "we do not have to decide today. Bull's Tavern is still open. Suppose we go there for a bite to eat and a couple of drinks and discover, if we can, what the temper of the city is."

At Cameron Hall, old Robert Bruce had grown all but unbearably testy and disagreeable. As his health failed rapidly he demanded constant attention from Penelope and Margaret, who were distracted by his demands. He refused to have any of the few remaining Negro servants come into his room. When one attempted to bring a tray or a basin of water, he indiscriminately hurled whatever object he could reach at the offender. They finally had to take everything movable away from the bedside. He blamed the Negroes for the war, the Yankee victory, his infirmities and helplessness. He, when allowed to sit up, would wheel himself to a window and yell "coon" and "nigger" whenever he saw a Negro in the yard. Margaret and Penelope took turns in bathing his face and such parts of his body as he allowed them to touch. They brought his meals and unhappily endured the vague wanderings of his mind when he forced them to stay and listen to his ramblings. Near to a nervous breakdown, Penelope threatened to leave him. Margaret felt no obligation to this vile-tempered old man. She ordered a coach made ready and left the Hall with Penelope's tearful pleading to have her tell Richard how unbearable the situation was and induce him to come to his father's side.

Old Robert Bruce saved them all further trouble. He died quietly in his sleep, his mind gone, unaware of where he was or the passing of the years. Because he had been, in his youth and manhood, a person of quiet consideration for others he would have been happy to know how much annoyance he had spared everyone by passing away in this unobtrusive manner.

‏❧ XXV ❧‏

ON THE ridge and facing the sea, behind where the slave quarters had stood long ago, the tall palms inclined their feathered heads. When the wind played through the massed fronds they seemed to whisper a soft lament over the graves here.

David Heath, bent a little now with the weight of the years, rested both hands on the knob of a heavy cane. Leaning upon it he studied the rectangular plot and a recently set stone.

BAHAMA CADIZ RALEIGH
Born 1797–Died 1871

Bahama with the silver bell of laughter in her voice. The vital beauty which once seemed eternal and out of time's reach. The bright fire of youth not to be dampened. His eyes misted and grew dim for a moment and then cleared. A tear seemed unworthy of her memory.

David had come to Exuma following a letter from Cameron Raleigh to Richard telling him of Bahama's death. This was a pilgrimage to the scenes of childhood and no visit made in deep sorrow. Too many years separated them, time and distance, for him to feel an actual sense of loss. He could not think of her as having grown to womanhood, borne a child, moving to the middle age of life and then standing on the threshold where the door opened upon her, wrinkled and gray, waiting out the time. He remembered her only as they had last seen each other, on the day of heartbreak for them both. Clear in his mind was the following morning, at daybreak, when he and Juan Cadiz, accompanied by John, had sailed for Nassau, and later boarding the ship that would take him to Charleston and out of her life forever.

There were other plots here, surrounded by a low fence of scrolled ironwork. The oldest, with the marker turning a streaked, corrosive green, marked the final resting place of CAROLINE CAMERON CADIZ.

[399]

Then, in order, came JOHN CAMERON. WALTER RALEIGH. Bahama had outlived both brother and husband and he thought of her loneliness. The deep waters had taken grandfather, Ronald Cameron, and father, Juan Cadiz. Perhaps, he thought, the coral had built small monuments about their bones somewhere in the fathoms.

After a while he turned and walked slowly but without faltering step toward the manor. Here the memories crowded upon each other. It was difficult to separate or place them in ordered sequence. He had come to the islands on one of the new steamers put into service between New York and the Bahamas by Mr. Samuel Cunard. The vessel made a way stop at Charleston and he had boarded there after first writing Cameron and waiting long weeks for a reply.

Young Brian had met him at Nassau with a new thirty-eight-foot ketch and a couple of Negro boys for hands. Cameron had bought it for interisland travel where they wouldn't use the *Caroline*. Young Brian. He smiled as he walked. Bahama's grandson. A man of twenty-five now. Only Brian and Cameron occupied the old and sprawling house. Cameron Raleigh's wife, Charlotte-Anne, defying convention, had refused to return from Europe. She and her daughter, Carol-Louise, now lived in Italy—Florence, he believed. Cameron had given her and his daughter the European trip Charlotte-Anne had demanded, pleading the cultural advantages a few years of schooling abroad would give the girl. They had sailed shortly after the close of the War Between the States, Cameron and Brian taking them to Charleston aboard the *Caroline* and seeing them off on a Liverpool-bound vessel sailing from the South Carolina port. He could remember having dinner that evening with Brian and Cameron after the ship had left and of something said later as they sat on the piazza.

"Charlotte-Anne," Cameron reflected and his eyes were turned seaward, "was born to a fairy tale and, like a child with a well-loved story, wanted it repeated over and over again. I hope she finds it retold somewhere."

David had thought then Cameron had not expected his wife to return. She had been unhappy on Exuma. The South and Charleston of her girlhood were gone. There was nothing to bring her back save husband and son. Knowing her disposition, David felt these would not be enough. He had no idea what she had found in Europe but apparently it was agreeable enough to keep her there.

Cameron was on the porch when David reached the house. Beside him were a few journals and newspapers from the States. A mail boat now traveled regularly from Nassau to the Out Islands and there was no longer quite the same feeling of isolation. Cameron looked up at David's approach.

"It's warm for walking." He pulled a chair near his own. "Sit with me for a while."

"I went no farther than the little graveyard." David lowered himself in the wicker chair. "What is the news?" He indicated the newspapers.

"Not a great deal. The scandals of Grant's administration grow, as you probably know. Most of these papers contain what you have already read." He paused, hesitated and then continued. "With them came a letter from Charlotte-Anne. Carol-Louise is going to marry an Italian, a count." His smile was acid. "We are enhanced by nobility even though at a distance. She, Charlotte-Anne, hopes Brian and I are well." He seemed to find this slightly amusing. "There is also a letter from Richard but it is mostly business. He is considering investment in a steamship line, engaged in coastwise trade, and wants me to go into it with him. Would you like a drink?"

"A little rum with a touch of lime." David leaned back, scratching his head against the chair's weaving.

Cameron half turned and yelled for a servant. They employed only four in the house now, cook, serving man and two cleaning maids. They were the offsprings of former slaves and worked for wages, living on the plot of land he had given them at the far end of the plantation. When the rum, limes and water were brought and placed on a table they poured their drinks.

"Somehow," David reflected, "this Exuma rum tastes different, better, than any other, even the Jamaican product. Why don't you produce it in quantity for export?"

"I know nothing about growing things. The plantation Negroes raise the cane, grind it and see to the distilling. There is an old man who superintends this. They bottle the first run and keep the second and third for themselves. I have no idea how it is done. Brian, also, runs to the sea. We would make a couple of fine farmers." He smiled briefly at the idea. "I have been thinking, though, of finding someone to manage the plantation. It has been lying fallow all these years save for the cane and things we grow for the house. There are still some twenty-five or thirty of the blacks living on our part of the island. They fend for themselves but would work if given something to do. Sisal and pineapples seem to flourish on Eluthera. The market for them is active on the mainland. It seems a waste to allow a couple of thousand acres to be unproductive. We could use the money. I have spent a great deal these past years." He drank part of his rum. "I've also been thinking. Why don't you stay here on Exuma with Brian and me? Since Margaret died you are alone. The

[401]

island was your boyhood home. Wouldn't you like to come back to it, even for a little while?"

"It has crossed my mind, Cam," David admitted. "I have thought about it many times."

Margaret Heath had been dead two years. She succumbed to a typhoid epidemic which flared and raged briefly through Charleston. Since then he had lived alone with an occasional visit to Cameron Hall when Richard and Penelope were there. He had not been too lonely for he had a large social acquaintance in the city. But, and this always amused him a little, he thought of those he knew and had been intimate with as "old people" when the truth was they were of an age together. The war, though, seemed to have robbed them of all vitality. They talked about and lived in the past.

Cameron was silent for a full minute. He offered David a cigar from a box. They were fine, rich Havana tobacco which Brian brought back from Cuba. He lit one for himself.

"I hope I don't intrude." Cameron finally spoke. "But Richard, for reasons of his own, I suppose, told me of your relationship. He did this in the kindest of spirit."

"I am certain of that." David nodded.

"So, Exuma is as much yours as it is ours. Perhaps your claim is greater than mine."

"It is nothing I would care to contest." David couldn't help but smile. "Mere possession no longer interests me."

"Frankly," Cameron spoke almost reluctantly, "I don't expect Charlotte-Anne ever to return. She seems contented where she is. Through the bank in London I have always made her a generous allowance. I bear her no ill will for I have never felt marriage to be a contest of endurance. She married young and had no reason to expect the complete dislocation of her life which the war caused. Charleston would be as foreign to her now as Italy would be to me. I'm damned, though," his voice betrayed his annoyance, "if I like the idea of my daughter marrying some greasy foreigner. An Italian count." He spoke these final words with disgust. "It seems to be some sort of fashion these days."

"A profitable one for the impoverished nobility, I should imagine." David spoke with dry humor. "However, he need not be, as you put it, 'greasy.' It is quite possible he is a personable young man who loves your daughter and will make her happy."

"Well, it is far out of my hands," Cameron admitted. "Anyhow, here we are, Brian and I, alone in this big place. I don't see a great deal of him. Sometimes, for old times' sake, I make a voyage. He does a fair trade with the *Caroline*. Rum from Jamaica. Tobacco and sugar from

Cuba. Sponges, sisal, pineapples from the Out Islands. He is rarely idle. The sea is his home and the *Caroline* not often at anchor as she is now. It is my hope he will marry. An island girl. Someone from Nassau of good family who would be happy with this life. I am growing a little old myself, Uncle David." He chuckled briefly. "Old habits persist, don't they? I can never remember your being called anything but Uncle David by everyone in the family except old Robert Bruce."

"Nonsense," David replied. "I mean about your growing old. You are in the full vigor of your prime. Don't speak of age. It is no stranger to me. Bahama and John were my juniors by five years. I'm the leaf which refuses to fall in life's winter. Sometimes it frightens me a little for I do not want to end as Robert Bruce did, a helpless creature, unaware of what was happening."

A small boat was being put out from the *Caroline* and when it touched shore Brian leaped out and came striding up the slope. He wore loose trousers of a coarse East Indian cloth called *dugri* which had found much favor among the boatmen out of Nassau. He was bare of foot and chest, deeply tanned, strongly muscled. Watching him, David thought of the strains running through his blood, his mind traveling far back to Ronald Cameron, through Caroline and Juan Cadiz, Bahama and Walter Raleigh. Then, with idle amusement, he tried to peer into the future. Carol-Louise, bearing a child half Italian. Brian eventually marrying here in the islands; into a Nassau family, perhaps, or one on the mainland, a girl in Cuba or a Jamaica planter's daughter. Good Lord, how the currents mingled!

Brian came to the porch, his handsome face alight with high, animal spirits and good humor. Bahama, he thought, must have been proud of this grandson.

"That's an odd dress for a ship's master." Cam inspected his son. "Do those dugarees, or whatever you call them, inspire respect from a crew?"

"These do." Brian held up his hands and slowly closed them into fists. "I have no trouble with my crew." He poured himself a drink and sat on the top step, his face turned toward David and his father. "I've been going through the *Caroline* from keelson to topmast. Whoever built that schooner had a love for ships. He must have hand-picked every timber until he was satisfied. Unless I run her on a reef she'll outlast us all."

"I have a letter from Richard. He wants me, us, to invest with him in a coastwise steamship line." Cameron deliberately made the statement casually. "I'm thinking of it."

Brian nodded. He knew his father was slyly baiting him for they had many an amiable argument over the subject of steam and sail.

[403]

"What do you think of the idea?" Cam asked innocently.

"Why, I think it is a fine one for you and Richard. They're faster, larger, can carry cargo and passengers. They stink and the captain can sit in an armchair and run one." He grinned good-naturedly and leaned back to lift his face to the sun. "Why don't you do it?"

"Sooner or later the only place you'll find a sailing ship will be in a museum. Steam's the thing, Brian. You just can't ignore it."

"I suppose not." Brian was unimpressed. "Just the same, the *Caroline* and I will be knocking around the islands, picking up a little something here and there, putting our noses into places where your steamships can't go. You and Richard Cameron will probably make a lot of money so I won't have to worry about that and, if you don't, I can always come back here and eat fish with corn bread." He winked companionably at David.

"I also had a letter from your mother." Cameron made it sound incidental. "Your sister is going to marry an Italian count."

"The hell she is." Brian sat up in quick surprise. He thought for a moment. "I never saw an Italian but I guess they're not much different than the Spanish in Cuba or the French in New Orleans, all bows and kissing hands." He whistled softly and on a reminiscent note. "I saw a girl once in Cuba. She was a real beauty but no one could get near her. Oh, there are plenty of girls, but the ladies! Whenever they go outside the house, even for a drive in a carriage, they have an old hag with them. A duenna who watches over her chick. When a Spanish man wants to court one he stands outside her window with a guitar player who sings songs. He stands there like a dummy. If she likes him, she throws out a flower or something. I don't know how they ever get married." He was silent for a moment. "An Italian count. I'd like to see one. That'll make Carol-Louise a countess or something, won't it? We'll have to bow and say: Good morning, Countess. How would you like some ham and grits for breakfast?" He threw back his head and laughed at the nonsensical fancy.

"Uncle David is going to stay on Exuma for a while." Cameron changed the subject.

"Well." Pleasure lighted Brian's face. "That's fine." He turned to David. "We lose each other in this house every now and then. How was it when you were a boy here?"

"The house? No different. The islands? I don't imagine they have changed much either except New Providence. Nassau was only a little colony. The Out Islands. They tried some big plantations the way your great-grandfather did here but they all failed. I don't imagine a hundred years will make much difference in the Bahamas. They'll lie here in the sun with the color of the water about them. Time means nothing. That is one of the reasons I decided to stay. When you get old you resent change because it makes you conscious of your age."

Brian finished his rum, stood up and put the glass on the table.

"I'm sailing in the morning." He addressed his father. "We have some cargo to pick up in Nassau. Not much. Sponges, castor oil, sisal. Stuff," he dropped an eyelid, "your steam buckets don't want to bother with. Why don't both of you come along?"

David shook his head. "Some other time, maybe, Brian. I'll sit here on the porch and envy you a little while I try to remember how it was to be twenty-five."

Savannah. The suddenly booming port of Jacksonville, in Florida, on the St. John's River. New Orleans, Haiti, Cuba, Barbados, Jamaica. The *Caroline* knew them all well by now. Brian had a light regard for money. If, at the year's end, the voyages had been without mishap, the crew paid, he was satisfied if the books showed a little profit or balanced evenly. He had no other ambition but to stand on the schooner's deck and gaze upon the endless expanse of sea. Aboard the vessel he wore the clothing of an ordinary seaman; sometimes nothing more than the loose *dugri,* bare of foot and chest. His crew were all Bahamian Negroes, fine sailors and well disciplined. For all his casual attire he ran a taut ship and there was never any question as to who was the master and authority. Ashore he dressed in a uniform of dark blue, brass buttons on the coat and gold braid on the peak of his cap. Through Richard he had presented letters of introduction to gentlemen in Savannah, Kingston, Havana and New Orleans with whom Cameron and Son had done business before the war and was now renewing old ties. Brian was received with courtesy and sincere hospitality in the old homes. He suspected, sometimes, that these families did not take his and the *Caroline*'s wanderings seriously. But, he admitted secretly to himself, neither did he. This was the life he loved and in it there was no room for a rival. The making of money was not its goal. If it had been he would have studied for his master's ticket in steam and cast in with Richard, whose proposed vessels would eventually carry most of the coastwise trade. It was enough for him to know he was as free to wander as the winds which drove his ship. Gregarious by nature he let his mood take him where it would. In some of the ports he would go ashore wearing the rough clothing of an ordinary seaman, a knitted cap canted to one side of his head with the tassel hanging over an ear. He spent many an evening and night in the crudest of waterfront dives, drinking, talking with sailors of all color and temper. He was slow to anger, as most big, confident men are, and many a time brushed off a truculent bar mate with an easy smile. He never sought argument and was inclined to allow the brawls in the waterfront grog mills to erupt about him, taking a detached interest in the skull cracking. But, there were times when he found an honest pleasure in physical combat and in a fight, invariably picked out the burliest for a toe-to-toe slugging which many a time sent him back to his ship with a bruised body and face, split lips, sore knuckles, and eyes blackening into deep circles. It was a contradiction in his nature which he could not explain nor did he ever really bother to probe for an answer. At other times, dressed in a uniform of the finest serge, boots polished to a mirror's sheen, he would engage a carriage and drive to one of the better inns, taverns or gambling halls where gentlemen of quality congregated. Here he suited his manners to the setting and was an engaging, high-spirited companion, ready to take a hand at cards, engage in the throwing of dice or join a roistering group of young bloods in a visit to a fashionable bordello. As a result he had friends and acquaintances in a dozen or more ports from the docks with the meanest of cribs and grogshops to the finest of homes.

The *Caroline* was berthed at New Orleans now. Crowding the wharves were the ships of all nations. Sail and steam rode side by side on the current from a fishing smack to the big, stern-wheeled riverboats which came down the Mississippi from St. Louis and Cincinnati. From the docks rose the calls of Negro men who carried cloth-covered baskets filled with crisp breads, freshly cooked soft-shell crabs, shrimp gumbo, fried fish. There was the rumble of drays, the squealing of winches, the gang chants of the Negro longshoremen as they worked cargo.

In his cabin Brian finished shaving, carefully dried his razor and put it away in a leather case. He had no real purpose in New Orleans. A sudden whim on his way south from Jacksonville, lazily bound for Cuba to pick up a shipment of cigars for a Nassau merchant, had led him to lay a course around the Florida Keys and into the Gulf of Mexico and eventually upriver to New Orleans.

This Louisiana city held a particular fascination for him. It was unlike any other he had visited on the North American continent. Its people were marbled with many bloods. That of the Spanish and French had mingled to produce the Creole: men of hot temper, fine manners, who embraced life with a passionate verve; women of rare beauty, gracious conduct and aristocratic poise. The Negro strain had blended with the white to produce the mulatto, and the mulatto, mating with the white, resulted in quadroon girls of magnificent loveliness. For Brian there was excitement in just walking the city's streets. There were sights, sounds and smells to stimulate the senses; a strange mixture of languor and vitality, or piety and shimmering evil.

He remembered reading somewhere of a letter which the wife of General Jackson wrote of New Orleans to relatives. The good lady had cried out: "Great Babylon is come before me. Oh! The wickedness, the idolatry of this place. Oh! Farewell. Pray for your sister in this heathen land."

Wickedness there was in full measure. It overflowed the shining cup. Before the war there had been riches in plenty and life had been lived on a scale not duplicated anywhere in the country. The wealthy gentlemen maintained their quadroon mistresses in the highest of style. They were gowned in the height of Paris fashion, drove through the streets in the most elegant of carriages, attended by elaborately liveried coachmen and grooms. The homes of the Creole were discreet gems of the architect's genius. There was the opera, the theatre, the music halls. Temper, it seemed, was the mark of a gentleman and rarely a morning dawned when a duel did not take place under The Oaks, which had become famous for bloodletting. To this metropolis came the gambler, the schemer, the riverboat man, the adventurer. There were saloons and salons of dazzling splendor. Fortunes and estates were won or lost on a card's turn or a roll of the dice. Honor was so sensitive that an unintentionally careless word was taken as a deadly insult. New Orleans had been a city of paradox. The patrician gentlemen lived a carefree, unfettered life and suffered no social rebuke. Their wives and daughters rarely ventured from the shaded seclusion of their homes, behind high walls and elaborately worked iron gateways, unless they were escorted by their husbands to the opera or private ball.

New Orleans had been a lady, proud and disdainful. She was a gaudy wench with hips aswing, the outwardly demure quadroon with the complexion of dusty rose. New Orleans was a drunken seaman with a knife in his belly lying in a gutter on Gallatin Street. New Orleans was the aristocrat so aware of his lineage it was unnecessary to think upon it. She was a lady and a bawd, a roisterer and priest. New Orleans was anything you wanted her to be.

The years of the Reconstruction had struck the city terrible blows of social and economic readjustment. She reeled from the ferocity of the Yankee attack upon her institutions. Her streets were bloodied by gang fights between the newly freed blacks and resentful whites. She had been stormed and captured, looted and raped by troops and carpetbaggers, humiliated but never completely reduced to her knees. Gentlemen who had never used their hands for more than the lifting of a wineglass or to touch the fingers of a lady in a dance were reduced to manual labor. Ladies who would wait for a slave to pick up a dropped handkerchief now washed their garments over steaming tubs. Old family silver, portraits and jewels were sold or pawned for the necessities of living.

Now though, in this year, the yoke was lightened and the burden slightly lifted. Order emerged from chaos. It was true the despised Yankees still imposed their will but the thirst for vengeance was slaked by time. New Orleans had learned to endure and ignore the victors. Birth and family were counted far more important than the wealth which had once gone with both. Poverty was no disgrace. The carpetbagger and speculator were scornfully ignored and all their pilfered money could not gain them admittance to the fine old homes which turned their backs upon the street and opened only upon an enclosed courtyard. Slowly the city was reasserting itself.

Immaculately groomed and dressed, Brian came down from the *Caroline* with the lively interest in his eyes which New Orleans always provoked. With the flip of a small coin he sent a Negro boy running for a coach. While he waited he ate a dozen fine oysters from their shells as an ancient Negro shucked them for him, singing his delicacies in a rich baritone. Brian ignored the bottle of hot sauce which the Louisianians seemed to think a proper accompaniment for the shellfish. They were better, to his way of thinking, plain or with a touch of lemon which did not destroy their flavor. His gaze roved over the scene along the docks. This was his third visit to the port since the war's end. Everything about the city delighted him and, he thought with a grin, that is why I am here and not about the *Caroline*'s business of getting a shipment of cigars for the waiting merchant in Nassau.

When the carriage came he had the coachman roll away its hood and directed him to the St. Louis Hotel. He leaned back against the cushion, cap in hand, his face bathed by the sun and a lively breeze from the Gulf. From past experience he knew how miserably hot New Orleans could become. The entire city sweated with the moist air of the bayous. Today, though, it was at its best with a clear sky and a cooling wind.

Great changes had taken place since he was last here. The Americans. He laughed to himself at this unconscious description, for New Orleans had always seemed a foreign segment in the United States. The Yankees, he guessed this was a better word, had created their own section on the other side of Canal Street. New buildings were replacing the old. There was vigor, a vitality. The city was emerging from its darkest hours.

At the St. Louis Hotel he went through the ornate lobby to the bar occupying the entire side of a long room. Here the gentlemen of the city were taking their midmorning refreshments; the drinks of absinthe, the rum of Jamaica, the bourbon of Kentucky, the Scotch of England, the brandy of France. There were enormous plates of pink, unpeeled shrimp, oysters on half shell, gumbo, crabs; and fresh, hot breads were constantly brought from the kitchen to replace the rolls and loaves as they cooled. Negro servants in spotless white offered smaller plates with a selection of everything to the gentlemen who lined the bar. Brian was ordering a rum with a mint sprig in it when a voice interrupted.

"Captain Raleigh. What a delightful encounter."

He turned in surprise and then smiled with the pleasure of recognition as he took an extended hand which gripped his firmly.

"Monsieur de Tourville. I am delighted, sir."

He had a little difficulty with the *monsieur* but it was impossible to address this distinguished figure with a plain *mister*. De Tourville was in his early sixties with a short chin beard coming to a fine point. He bore himself with the unconscious air of a true cavalier, gaily and without effort. His smile was one of twinkling understanding as Brian stumbled with the French pronunciation and his handclasp was as warm and cordial as his expression. For many years de Tourville had done business with the firm of Renevant, Decatur and Cameron. The war had brought an end to this but not the high regard held on both sides. On Brian's first visit to New Orleans, Richard Cameron had given him a letter of introduction to M. Henri de Tourville, who had received him with full hospitality and cordial graciousness in his home. Despite the difference in their years they had spent a pleasant evening together, de Tourville seeming to find something of his youth in Brian's adventuresome spirit and zest for life.

"I read in the shipping columns the *Caroline* was a recent arrival and hoped you would not leave without calling upon me. Actually, I would have sought you out had we not chanced to meet here."

"It was my intention to call, sir. This is my first day ashore. May I offer you a drink?"

The bar was crowded shoulder to shoulder. De Tourville looked about and saw an unoccupied table in a far corner. He motioned toward it.

"Let us sit and renew our acquaintance. I have the most agreeable recollection of our previous meeting. How is Mr. Cameron?"

"He is going into the steamship business." They walked down the room. "Or so he wrote my father. He feels there is no longer a place for sail on the seas. Not if you want to make money and Richard, meaning no disrespect, is always interested in that."

Seated, de Tourville ordered black coffee and an absinthe. With a small piece of sugar in a spoon he dripped water into the wormwood

[409]

liquor until it turned a cloudy, milky white. He tasted it with pleasure while Brian enjoyed the familiar flavor of good rum.

"This," de Tourville indicated the absinthe, "is supposed to have the properties of an aphrodisiac. Unfortunately, at my age," he lifted his shoulders in a Gallic shrug, "I have not found it so. The effect pleases my senses and nothing more. Now." He was interested. "What brings you to New Orleans?"

"I honestly don't know. I had some cargo for Jacksonville, Florida. When this was discharged I started for Cuba. Suddenly, I decided I wanted to see your city again. I have no business here, really, and little prospect of finding any. To tell the truth I'm not looking. So, I guess we can put the visit down to an irresponsible nature and a reluctance to sail a schedule. Richard Cameron," he laughed quietly, "would not understand this."

"It is a curious coincidence." De Tourville glanced about. There was no one seated near them.

"What is, sir?"

"Your mentioning Cuba when the island has been uppermost in my mind of late. It was something I hoped to talk with you about when I read of your schooner's arrival." He sipped at the strong coffee from the demitasse. "How well do you know Cuba?" He paused. "I don't exactly mean that. How familiar are you, shall we say, with the waters about it and the small, infrequently visited harbors which could accommodate a vessel the size of yours?"

"Well," Brian considered this an odd question, "I have sailed all those waters many times, first when I was younger and my father commanded the *Caroline*. Later, when he turned the ship over to me, I made frequent visits, taking the Windward Passage from Kingston, in Jamaica, then up through the Old Bahama Channel. On the other side I know Santiago, the Gulf of Manzanillo, Cienfuegos, around Cape San Antonio and to Havana Bay. There are many small harbors on the northeast side; not quite so many on the southern coast. They are not all charted so there is no way of knowing their depth." He wondered what de Tourville was reaching for.

Instead of making a reply the man signaled a waiter and paid the small amount due despite Brian's protest. He put aside his absinthe.

"Please do not think me rude," he spoke gravely, "but for what is on my mind I dislike talking here in this public place. Would you do me the honor of a visit to my home?"

"Of course." Brian was mystified by this abrupt attitude of secrecy. "Whatever you would like. I have no plans for the day."

De Tourville's carriage was waiting and they were driven quickly to

[410]

Esplanade Street and the fine old house behind the gated wall. De Tourville led him to a study where the walls were book-lined. Casement windows looked out upon a shaded garden. It was a pleasant retreat and the furniture, the deep chairs for comfort, were upholstered in rich Morocco leather.

"Make yourself comfortable." The man rang for a servant, ordered rum with mint, coffee and absinthe. "We will take up where we left off but in more suitable surroundings. I hope I do not inconvenience you or intrude upon your privacy," he apologized. "But there is a certain urgency in matters occupying my mind."

"I have no engagements."

"Good." De Tourville expressed his gratification. When the servant brought the tray, placed it on a table, the master dismissed him. The door was closed and they were alone. "I will come straight to the point," he continued. "There is, as you undoubtedly know, considerable revolutionary sentiment in Cuba for a separation from Spain. There have been abortive revolts against exorbitant taxation and misrule. Now, something more definite is taking shape. The Cuban upper classes are tired of being bled to the bone by a succession of Spanish Royal Governors. They feel they have a right to self-determination, an autonomy. Perhaps you wonder why this should interest an American of French descent in New Orleans?"

"No." Brian shook his head. "I would guess you have friends and probably some large holdings in Cuba. To protect both you want a successful revolution."

"It is bluntly put but fairly accurate." De Tourville chuckled.

"I would say also"—Brian was beginning to enjoy the oblique conversation; he was both amused and alerted—"you would like to put the *Caroline* to work as she was when dodging the Union blockade during the war. Gunrunning, and perhaps the removal of certain persons to a place of safety."

"The idea engages your imagination?" De Tourville regarded him with quizzical interest. "Yes?"

"The idea engages my imagination. Yes." Brian tried to hide a grin.

"No moral issue disturbs you?"

"If you mean whether I care who wins—you, the Cubans or the Spanish Crown; or who is right and who is wrong—no." Brian was frank but not insolent.

"Much blood has been shed," de Tourville mused, "in sporadic uprisings which were not successful because they were not planned. The Spanish troops quickly put them down and the leaders were promptly executed. If a Cuban revolution is to succeed it must be carefully prepared. It may take two, three, four or five years. Patience is needed. We are quite willing to move slowly if a goal is in sight. It is important to remember this. Now." He took a sip of his absinthe and relaxed. "There is money available but it has to be spent with a purpose. The Spanish garrisons cannot be overwhelmed by words. Large stocks of the modern rifles which were being used by the Union forces near the close of the war are now classed as surplus by the Government and are in warehouses in the North. I have the necessary connections to have these arms released for purchase. Frankly, the United States is not too happy to have Spain occupy Cuba. It wants no foreign power this close to the mainland. Rifles, ammunition, all the military equipment needed could be shipped to the little islands off the point of Florida, keys I believe they are called. I understand some of them have been settled by your native Bahamians."

"I think so." Brian nodded. "Not many but a few families and individuals moved there. Why I don't know. The keys are not much different from the cays they left."

"Anyhow," de Tourville leaned forward, hands clasped between his knees, "you would not have to deal, if necessary, with people who are alien to you. From these keys your schooner could carry the arms to designated places in Cuba where they could be hidden against the day of a full-scale revolt. Your first couple of voyages would probably go unnoticed by the authorities. But, do not disregard the Spaniard's flair for intrigue. They are masters at the art and scent it immediately in others. You must eventually come under suspicion. Considerable personal danger will be involved from there on."

Brian inclined his head in agreement. He could feel a knot of excitement gathering for he had grown a little bored with the *Caroline*'s routine, coastwise voyages. Who, if given the choice, would carry sisal, rum or tobacco when he could run guns under the nose of a Spanish patrol? Who would turn his back on adventure? Not Brian Raleigh at twenty-five. The strain of Juan Cadiz, and perhaps Ronald Cameron, began to run hot through his blood.

"I have not mentioned compensation." De Tourville was watching the animated play of expression on the younger man's face. "I needed to know, first, if you would be interested."

"I hadn't thought about the money," Brian confessed.

"You may take my word for it the reward will be generous. The Cubans interested in the revolution are the wealthy planters with vast estates in cane and tobacco. They have amassed considerable fortunes but are never sure what Governor, appointed by Spain, will find a new way of laying his hands upon it with higher taxes, additional levies, or out-

[412]

right confiscation through some imaginary charge of suspected treason against the Crown. They are, of course, Spanish by heritage but they are now Cubans and have been for generations."

"I'll leave the matter of payment to you."

"Good." De Tourville expressed his satisfaction. "Now. Since you are free I would like you to proceed to Havana as was your original intention. I will give you a letter to an old and valued friend. You will be well received and together can discuss the essential details. In the meanwhile I shall be about my own business. Will you dine with me this evening?"

Brian hesitated. He was in the mood for a gayer night than de Tourville, for all his charm, would offer. The man, seeing his irresolution, smiled understandingly.

"Of course not." De Tourville made the decision. "Have your night of pleasure. Forty years ago I would have led you a strenuous pace on the same rounds."

He accompanied Brian to the carriage gate, taking his arm with the friendliest of gestures.

"Please use my carriage. King here," he indicated the Negro on the box, "is well acquainted with the establishments you will probably want to visit. And," the smile came again, "he will see to it you are safely aboard your ship if it is your intention to return. As for the letter. I will compose it this evening and have it delivered to the *Caroline* in the morning. A safe voyage, Captain." He offered his hand. "We shall be seeing much of each other, I hope."

Relaxing in the carriage Brian directed the coachman to drive about the city, around St. Louis Square, wherever he pleased. It was far too pleasant a day to spend indoors, and besides, New Orleans did not come alive for what he had in mind until late evening. Also, he wanted to think. He wondered what his father would say when he learned of this undertaking. Blockade running had been one thing, for their sympathies were with the South. This Cuban business was an entirely different matter. They had no ties there.

Suddenly he threw back his head and laughed out of sheer exuberance. Excitement again captured his imagination. Who would plod a dusty road when he could soar through the sky? He was master of the *Caroline*, a man in his own right. Let the adventure take them both where it would.

⤷ XXVI ⤶

THE *Caroline,* with a wind so light she could barely hold steerageway, crept past the glowering forts guarding Havana's harbor. As she moved in, a launch carrying the Spanish flag came out to meet her. The schooner was well known in the Cuban port but the Customs authorities never relaxed their vigilance.

Where a section of the rail was hinged to swing away, Brian waited as an officer and four armed soldiers came up the ladder. On deck the officer saluted formally but with a faint admission of recognition. Brian returned the courtesy.

"Your papers, Captain, if you please, and a copy of the manifest."

"Certainly, *Teniente.* In my cabin. There is no manifest for I carry no cargo."

"It will be necessary to make an inspection." The officer was polite but firm. He gave a brisk command to the armed men who had boarded with him. "Your business in Havana, Captain?"

"To pick up a shipment of cigars and whatever cargo I can find." Brian ordered the cargo hatches opened. "If you please, *Teniente.*" He led the way to his cabin.

His papers were carefully examined although this same officer had gone through the routine with him a dozen times before. But, as with all Spanish officials, he took his job with extreme seriousness. He spoke English fluently and so there was no necessity for Brian to resort to his painfully inexact Spanish, which he had picked up out of necessity.

When the formality had been concluded there was the offer and the gracious refusal of a drink. Several times he and this officer had shared a glass of rum, a *cigarillo* and a brief but friendly chat. Brian wondered if the political situation within the island had become explosive enough to put every incoming vessel under suspicion. They went back on deck and the corporal of the guard reported no cargo in the holds. The wind had now died completely.

"I will send a tow for you, Captain." The lieutenant saluted again.

Almost an hour later a small steam-driven boat, belching smoke from her tall, ungainly stack, came out and took a line from the schooner, towing and then nudging her into a berthing section of a loading pier.

Brian paid the fee, divided his watch and gave half the crew shore leave. Then he returned to his cabin and took a letter from a cabinet drawer. It had been delivered to the *Caroline* by one of de Tourville's servants and was addressed to Señor Sebastian de la Torre, 17 Calle Linda. Turning it over in his hand, wondering what was in it, Brian was undecided whether to have it sent by hand, hiring one of the many boys who hung around the waterfront, or to take it himself. In the end he decided the dock boys were too unreliable. It would be better and, things being what they were, safer to go in person and present his introduction. Also, he would wait until night. If, by chance, Señor de la Torre was under the faintest suspicion, the arrival of a foreign ship with her captain hurrying off to call upon him immediately upon docking would aggravate the condition.

When it was dark he dressed carefully and then strolled down the gangway and along the seawall. Here there were the usual squalid dives, the sad-eyed girls, the ever-present beggars and the boys who offered their services as guides. To avoid any suggestion of a mission he walked leisurely through the narrow, badly lighted streets. Only the Royal Government Building made any pretense of importance. The small shops and buildings were crowded together, their walls cracked and defaced. They were illuminated by smoky lanterns. There was one inn and tavern of respectability, La Casa Roja. He stopped at its bar and ordered a drink, taking his time, listening to the babel of voices, the exclamations of the card players and the clicking of dominoes. When he left he walked toward a small plaza, halting several times to inspect something in a store window and making sure he was not followed. No one, apparently, was paying any attention to him beyond the usual glances of curiosity any stranger would have received.

At the plaza he hired a dilapidated carriage with a Negro driver and gave him the Calle Linda address. It was hot in Havana and he envied the Cubans their loose, cool attire of cotton.

He dismissed the driver before a heavy, wooden door with iron strips reinforcing it. It was the only opening in the high wall, atop of which were set jagged spears of glass to discourage anyone from trying to climb over it. A length of chain dangled from a small hole in the wall. He gave it a tug and heard the soft peal of a bell. After a moment the upper section of the door was opened and a watchman peered out, holding a square, candlelit lantern to shine upon the visitor's face.

"Señor de la Torre?"

The man, impressed by the uniform and gold braid upon the cap and recognizing a foreigner, nodded.

"*Sí, Comandante.*"

There was a moment's delay and then the door swung back, opening upon a garden of tropical magnificence. The house was at the far end, built, as was the custom, about a patio which could not be seen from the gate. A white-coated manservant came down a flagged path to meet the visitor. He politely took the letter Brian handed him and led the caller to a reception hall.

"*Momentito, Comandante.*" He bowed, excusing himself. "*Con su permiso.*"

A minute or more passed and then there was the sound of a hurried step. Brian turned from an examination of a shield upon the wall. The man who came to him was tall, heavily built with powerful shoulders. Brian, who had always thought of Spaniards as being slender, almost dainty in manner, was surprised. De la Torre had the appearance of a wrestler. There was a smile of greeting upon his face. Whatever de Tourville had written, Brian concluded, must be extremely complimentary.

"*Bienvenido!* Welcome, *Capitán*. My house is yours." He spoke English with a heavy accent.

"Thank you, señor."

"Do you speak Spanish, *Capitán?*

"Of the kitchen," Brian answered.

De la Torre shrugged. "Then you will have to put up with my English."

He took Brian's arm with the friendliest of gestures, leading him down the hall and outside. The two-story house had a balcony running about all four sides, overlooking the patio with its central fountain tinkling into a pool and a profusion of flowers forming a colorful border. They walked along the covered *portal* and into one of the brightly lighted rooms.

"I have been expecting you." De la Torre spoke with satisfaction. "Not you, perhaps, but someone. How is my *compadre,* de Tourville? Enjoying life as usual?"

"He was in fine health and his usual spirits when I saw him."

De la Torre went to a bell pull. Brian glanced about the room. It was furnished in heavy, elaborately carved chairs and couches upholstered in crimson. Candles burned from a central chandelier and side brackets of wrought iron. A great banner of yellow silk all but covered one wall and upon it was embroidered an elaborate coat of arms. The other walls were decorated with ancient swords, cutlasses and heavy pistols in glass-fronted cases. It was, he thought with quiet amusement, a fine place in which to contemplate and plan violence. A servant came almost immediately in answer to his master's ring and de la Torre gave him an order in which Brian caught only the word *vino*.

"I have ordered wine." His host glanced at Brian. "Would you care for something stronger?"

"No, thank you."

"Then let us seat ourselves and become acquainted. Henri speaks most highly of you in his letter; both as a man to be trusted, of family and a friend of long standing."

"Actually, he knew my father better and has had business connections with a firm in which a relative is interested. But he has always been most hospitable to me in New Orleans."

"You will take *la cena,* the evening meal, with us?"

"Thank you again."

"Please sit down." De la Torre motioned toward a couch.

When his guest was seated de la Torre strode up and down until the servant returned with the wine and glasses. He dismissed the man with a nod and waited until the door was closed. After a moment he moved quickly to reopen it and glanced at the empty hall.

"In these days no one can tell who has big ears." He filled two crystal goblets with the wine. *"Salud."*

It was a light, crisply dry wine of a pale rose color with which Brian was unfamiliar. He liked it, and apparently the pleasure was reflected upon his face.

"I will have a case sent to your ship in the morning." De la Torre smiled. "I am not certain you will make a good conspirator." The words were spoken in jest. "Your expression reveals your thoughts."

"I hadn't thought of this as a conspiracy," Brian admitted with a touch of embarrassment. "But, after all, I suppose that is what it is."

"Not for you, really." The man shook his head. "Although there is danger. Henri told you as much?"

Brian nodded. He was satisfied to allow his host to do the talking. De la Torre turned back the lid of a silver box and offered cigars. When they were lit he sat, studying Brian for a moment.

"You are young," he said at last. "That is good. One grows cautious with age. He becomes greedy and wants everything to last forever. Tell me," his mind darted to another subject, "do you think the United States would assist in a Cuban revolt against Spain?"

"I don't know anything about international politics." Brian shrugged.

[417]

"I am not an American but a British subject. But, if you are asking me whether I think the United States would go to war with Spain over Cuba, I would say no. Why should they?"

De la Torre appeared surprised. "Do they not have a thing called the Liberty Bell enshrined? Wasn't a great war fought for the Negroes' freedom? Isn't the freedom of all men everywhere a cause for the United States?"

For an inexplicable reason Brian suddenly felt more at ease than at any time since he had entered this house. He almost laughed and de la Torre was not insensible to his mood.

"I amuse you?"

"Yes, señor." Brian finished his wine. "You amuse me and I think you amuse yourself, too. Because," he hesitated and then mentally shrugged at the consequences, "I have an idea you don't believe a damn word of what you are saying. Who is going to be freed by your revolution? The *peón*? The *campesino*? I think not."

Sebastian de la Torre threw back his head and shouted with laughter. His voice boomed and bounced from the walls. He leaned forward to place a hand on Brian's knee.

"My friend—I call you that because I think we shall be friends—if you had answered me seriously I would have said: Here is a hypocrite. A man who says what he thinks someone wants to hear. I would have been suspicious of you always. Now, I believe we can talk with sincerity."

"Do you mind, then, if I ask something?" Brian was honestly curious.

"By all means." De la Torre refilled their glasses. "Whatever comes to mind."

"Well," Brian couldn't resist a grin, "it is easy enough to talk a revolution but who is going to do the fighting for you?"

"Ah!" The man had not expected this blunt question. He touched a forefinger to the tip of his nose. "That is a very good question. All over the island there are little bands of patriots who are inflamed by the notion of driving the Spanish out. Each one has its self-styled general, although he may command no more than twenty men. So, we buy each general and with him his troops. Then we put them together in an army commanded by a real soldier. There is disloyalty in a few high places. Then, there is the middle class. It is not large. The shopkeepers, innkeepers, merchants, who are unhappy with the high taxes. Given the opportunity these people will aid in a fight to free themselves. Then come the large landowners, such as myself, de Tourville and others. We recruit our *peóns* and put guns in their hands."

"They may shoot you instead of the Spanish."

De la Torre nodded soberly. "There is a risk in that, to be sure."

[418]

"It doesn't sound to me like a very reliable force with which to challenge Spain."

"Perhaps not. But, if we are successful in seizing the Government then the garrison will capitulate. Distance is on our side. Spain will have to transport troops and supplies across the ocean. It is a formidable task. Anyhow, my friend, this is not something we expect to accomplish overnight, in a month or year. It may take many years for the discontent to reach a state of real revolution. In the meanwhile we work, taking a village here, part of a province there. We will make things continually uncomfortable for the Government and keep its troops on the run trying to put down the brush fires. For this we will need the rifles, ammunition and equipment you will bring to us. Do you know the waters around the Gulf of Ana Maria?"

"Yes."

"There are some small islands there in whose shelter you can anchor. Small boats will come to you at an appointed time and take your cargo off. It would be too dangerous to put into a port of any size. Each time we will change the location. You will have no trouble."

Brian smiled inwardly at this reassurance. "There is always trouble, señor. No matter how well a thing is planned. I was through it many times with my father during the war. The unexpected must be expected."

De la Torre lifted his shoulders with an expressive gesture. Plainly he considered the risk Brian's problem.

"That," he said unemotionally, "is something you know far more about than I. Because there is danger we are prepared to offer you twenty-five hundred dollars in gold for each shipment you bring in."

Brian thought for a moment. It was a good price. He was on the point of demanding a bond covering the total loss of the schooner be posted in New Orleans with Henri de Tourville. But, he concluded, if he lost the ship to the Spanish patrol he and the crew would go with it.

"The money is satisfactory."

"Good!" De la Torre was pleased. "Now, please tell me something of the Bahamas, particularly of Nassau which, I believe, is the settlement of importance and size."

"It is not unlike Cuba. Not as tropical, perhaps."

There was a discreet knock on the door. De la Torre called permission to enter and a servant appeared to announce *la cena*.

"We will have supper now, if it pleases you." The Cuban rose. "And you will meet my wife and daughter." As they walked back through the patio de la Torre continued to talk. "I asked you about Nassau for I am not too certain of my continued safety here. The Spanish authorities have no real evidence but all large holders of land are under suspicion

[419]

of fomenting revolution. If the situation should become critical I would not like to have my family endangered. The Bahamas are not too far away and from what you say, the climate would be agreeable to them. Is it possible to purchase a house which would be suitable to their position?"

"I would think so," Brian answered. "Everyone made a great deal of money during the war but they spent most of it. Now, they are back in the same old situation of genteel poverty. The Bahamas seem afflicted with this sort of cycle. You could most certainly lease a house. I will find out for you when I get back."

"It would make my mind easier to have them away from Cuba. Also," he laughed softly, "it may be necessary and convenient for me to have a place of refuge. One never knows what charges will be made or who can really be trusted." He halted at an entrance. "Could you take my family with the personal servants to the islands?"

"I have no passenger accommodations on the *Caroline*. If you are serious about this I suggest you send your wife and daughter to Charleston and book passage from there to Nassau. There is a steamship line in intermittent service. I have a relative there who would receive them most cordially and see to their welfare."

"Such a move would arouse suspicion in high authority. Questions would be asked. What is happening that the family of de la Torre is leaving Cuba? You understand?"

"No," Brian admitted. "The intricacies of intrigue seem extremely complex. But, if you say so I accept them. I could give your wife and daughter my cabin. The servants would have to put up with whatever makeshift quarters I could arrange."

"Well," de la Torre opened the door for Brian to precede him, "there is no immediate urgency. We can discuss it at another time."

They waited in the spacious and ornate dining room which was furnished in the same, heavy style as the one they had left. Brian concluded this must be typical of the Spanish-Cuban home. A long table was set with places for four and a liveried manservant stood stiffly by the wall at each end.

"How is it you speak English so fluently, señor?"

De la Torre seemed pleased and flattered by the question. "My family has been in Cuba for three hundred years but the sons have always been sent abroad for an education, usually to a Spanish university where English was taught or to England itself. I studied in England but I still have the accent of the Spanish Cuban. Unfortunately, my wife speaks practically no English. My daughter attends a convent school where your language is taught along with French."

[420]

He was interrupted by the entrance of Señora de la Torre and her daughter. Brian thought he had never seen such a handsome woman. She was not beautiful but she carried herself with the proud manner of a true patrician. She was tall, slender. A contrast to the women Brian had seen in Havana, who were inclined to grow heavy in their late thirties. Her smile was gracious as de la Torre presented Brian.

"*Mucho gusto, Capitán.*" She murmured the acknowledgment and then added in stilted English and with a small shrug of self-conscious apology, "I have much pleasure." She laughed a little at the sound of her own words.

"My daughter Marta, Captain." De la Torre concluded the presentation.

Brian judged the girl to be twelve or thirteen. She had the same slender and almost regal carriage of her mother. Her complexion was softly dusky and with a natural, fresh color on her cheeks. She had the most beautifully expressive eyes Brian had ever seen and they could not conceal the curiosity she felt over this meeting with a foreigner.

"Captain Raleigh." The words were all but shyly whispered. "Welcome to our house." She was proud of her English.

"Thank you." Brian was charmed by the faint accent. "I like the way it is said in Spanish. 'My house is yours.' Is that not the way?"

"Yes." The reply was spoken with diffidence but there was a glimmer of humor and mischief in her eyes. "But I don't think it always means what it says. Sometimes it is a *cortesia,* a courtesy," she corrected herself, "only."

The meal was not the difficult and strained experience Brian had thought it would be. He felt at ease and thoroughly comfortable and it occurred to him this was the mark of the genuine aristocrat. He was, in a subtle manner, made to feel completely at home and no stranger to the house and family. The cordiality was unaffected.

De la Torre was an easy conversationalist with a wide range of interests. He was particularly interested in Brian's experiences in running the Union blockade during the war. The problems of the South and Reconstruction. Marta frequently translated the English for her mother in quick, modulated sentences. But, for the most part, Señora de la Torre managed to give the impression she understood and was entertained by what was being said. Her expressive face was interested. Only when her husband referred again to the Bahamas and Nassau, the possibility of purchasing or leasing a house, did she display an emotion when her daughter whispered an excited translation. But she voiced no objection. Brian thought Spanish or Cuban women must be extremely docile and obedient to their husbands' wishes. Now and then he glanced

[421]

up to find Marta's eyes studying him. When this happened she displayed no confusion but merely dropped her gaze with proper modesty.

He ate heartily of the chicken cooked with a saffron rice, shrimp, small oysters, crab meat and peppers; salad of a pearlike vegetable with a soft, buttery richness. The hour was after ten and he was not accustomed to taking the evening meal so late. When they were finished, Señora de la Torre and her daughter excused themselves and left Brian and his host to their brandy and cigars. There was much to be discussed. Finally, both agreed Brian, after he had made the trip back to Nassau and Exuma, would sail again for New Orleans and complete the final details with Henri de Tourville and the revolutionary group there.

De la Torre escorted his guest to the gate, where his personal carriage waited. They shook hands cordially and with the affinity of old friends.

"For a little while, then," the host said. "I suspect we will be seeing much of each other, *Capitán*. To you, now, a safe and speedy voyage."

Driving back to the ship through the flower-scented night, Brian took more notice of his surroundings and the residential section through which they passed. The route was different from the one he had traveled out. Here the high, brown walls were scattered, enclosing large estates similar to the one he had just left. On previous visits to Havana he had never bothered to venture beyond the lower part of town with its narrow streets, noisy *canitinas*, the bar at La Casa Roja. This, in his mind, had been the city. Now he was looking upon a Havana he had not known existed. Here one came upon fine, palm-lined *avenidas*, buildings which shone in the moonlight with a pearl-like quality. The driver was taking him through a completely unfamiliar neighborhood. A hotel, low of design and with broad veranda and balconies, faced the sea. A park, carefully tended and with its beds of flowers, was squared about a bandstand, and graveled walks laced the greenery. The coachman finally brought him out upon a road curving in a natural sweep along the seawall. Farther on they began to get into the district he knew well. There was the maze of warehouses and docks, the rancid odor of rotting garbage and filthy gutters. It was, he realized, a city of great contrast.

Aboard the *Caroline* again he sat in his cabin and thought seriously of what he had so lightly undertaken. He hadn't been quite certain how his father would look upon this adventure. Cameron Raleigh's ardor for danger and excitement had cooled with the years. He was satisfied to remain on Exuma with David Heath for company. He had hired Negro hands and was bringing order out of the plantation.

Cameron Raleigh would have misgivings about this expedition. Blockade running had been one thing. Caught at that they would probably have been imprisoned for the war's duration. The Spanish in Cuba would not be so lenient. Still, Brian believed, his father would not attempt to dissuade him. He had freely given him command of the *Caroline* and would not go back on that. A man must follow his star. Brian gazed at this one of dazzling excitement.

He lit a cigar and thought of what lay before him. He had a sound ship, a fine crew. His word was given. He would do what he had agreed to undertake. Do it well. The money, he suspected, would not be unwelcome. As with the others, Cameron Raleigh had been prodigal with the profits made in blockade running. Extensive repairs had been made to the manor on Exuma. They had lived high in Nassau between voyages. He had no idea what allowance his father made to his mother and Carol-Louise in Italy, but he was certain it must be large. It was strange, he reflected, but he felt no sentiment where his mother was concerned; only a curiosity as to why she had chosen this alien life. Perhaps it was as his father had said, she could not bear to have a fairy tale end. Carol-Louise. A countess. The idea tickled his humor. He found his thoughts wandering and came determinedly back to the matter at hand. His speculation centered upon de la Torre, Henri de Tourville and the revolutionary junta which operated in New York. There, among the small group in New York, a flame of patriotism might burn but he doubted if de la Torre and de Tourville were inspired by the same fervor. They wanted out from beneath the dominance of Spain's insatiable greed and stupidity to indulge, he suspected, in the same vices. Spain's Viceroys had looted the island, made themselves wealthy, gave liberally to the Church from an apparently inexhaustible stream of sugar, tobacco, gold. Cuba with its many shadings of color and blood boiled with hatred. Guerrilla warfare had raged for years in the southern provinces but no real gains had been made. Could de Tourville, de la Torre and the others whose identity were unknown to him accomplish more? And, this he mused upon, would the independence of Cuba, if it was ever achieved, do more than benefit the few of the already privileged? There would be a scramble for power. Each faction would name its *Presidente.* The masses though would work as long, as hard and for as little as they now received. Yet, the black, the *mestizo,* the Cuban-born of mixed blood, would be inflamed by speeches, excited by having rifles put into their hands, raised to a pitch of nationalism. *Cuba Libre!* They would die in the hills, the valleys, the streets of town and village without having any real idea for what they fought. In the end they would simply have exchanged Spanish masters for Cuban.

Dawn was still a couple of hours away and the *Caroline,* without a riding light showing, lay in the lee of a small string of reefs and islands curiously named Jardines de la Reina. It was, Brian had thought, a damn curious place for the Queen's Gardens.

This was their second trip with a shipment of small arms, and Brian had all but decided it was to be the last. The danger and confusion, he thought, did not lie so much in Cuban waters as it did in New Orleans. Henri de Tourville, for all his charm, was surrounded by a small group of hot-eyed revolutionaries who were unable to reach even the smallest decision without interminable discussion. There were disagreements between the junta in New York, the one in Jacksonville and the one in Havana. Money was raised, rallies were held. *Cuba Libre!* Then they wrangled among themselves as to the arms and equipment needed, into whose Cuban hands it should be placed, where, at what point and hour was the rendezvous to be made? Who commanded the patriots who were gathered at Baracoa? Who was the *jefe* of a guerrilla band in Oriente Provence? A tremendous stock of woolen cloth had been purchased for uniforms before someone pointed out that the Cuban fighters would sweat themselves to the bone in such an outfit. British rifles were purchased and then American ammunition, which would not fit, contracted for. Two dozen gold-handled sabers were bought for the generals and there were cases and cases of heavy boots for the *solados,* who were accustomed to nothing more than light sandals. If everyone had not been so deadly serious the entire affair would have been a setting for a comic opera.

After orders and counter orders the first shipment had been landed on the Romano Cay. It was isolated. Small boats came out in the full light of day to ferry the cargo. Brian wondered how they were going to transport the matériel from there to the mainland but said nothing. All he wanted was to get away, for these Cubans seemed completely indifferent to or unaware of the danger to his ship in restricted waters.

Now, in the darkness, Brian stood forward at the rail, watching and listening for the slightest movement or sound. A hard knot of excitement gathered in his stomach. He was dealing with men who seemed to have no conception of time. If the small boats were coming, if nothing had gone wrong with the confused planning, then from somewhere out there a signal light was to show itself briefly and be answered by the schooner.

Near Brian bulked the indistinct form of a giant Negro, Bahamian-born. He was Brian's mate, a fine seaman who maintained a tight discipline over the crew. He was sensitive to every shading of the water, shift in the wind, and in his watchful silence was as concerned for the *Caroline* and their safety as was the schooner's master. On deck were cases of rifles, bales of light cotton cloth with boxes of ammunition and crates

[424]

of the heavy cane knives, the machetes manufactured in Pennsylvania. There were no markings of any kind on the bales and crates. The *Caroline* had been routinely loaded at New Orleans. If Spanish agents were watching there was nothing in the operation to excite their suspicions. The cargo came to the dock in open drays and was transferred by longshoremen. Nothing was done furtively or with undue haste or secrecy. All about them ships were taking on or discharging cargo. There was nothing about the *Caroline* to raise a question. It had taken Brian half an evening to convince de Tourville and his group that this was a far more sensible way of handling the matériel than to try and take it on somewhere in the Florida Keys. He finally threatened to abandon the entire project before they agreed. Apparently, he thought, the more involved the operation the more certain it was of success. The simple way was too easy, too obvious.

For a second he thought he saw a flicker of light but he couldn't be sure. Strain played tricks with imagination.

"Did you see anything out there just then, Washer?" he called to the Negro.

"No, Cap'n, suh."

"We'll wait until daybreak. If they don't show we'll lay a course back toward Jamaica, loaf around and try again tomorrow. I've had about enough of this."

"Does us git caught, what you tink happen, Cap'n, suh?"

They talked in whispers, neither shifting his gaze from where the shore lay.

"What I think happens is we get blown the hell out of the water. Or, we are boarded, shot here or taken to prison in Havana, lined up against a wall and shot there. That's it." Brian couldn't resist a grin.

"Don' give much choice, do hit?" Washer's voice was deep, rich and with a suggestion of laughter.

Brian wondered about this big Negro and the rest of the crew. They had all sailed with Cameron Raleigh in the early days of blockade running and were the *Caroline*'s hands when Cameron finally allowed his son to come on as sort of a junior officer. They all knew each other well. They had their plots of land and cabins with wives and children on Exuma. All of them had made more money than they believed was in the world during the war years. He wondered what they had done with it besides buying some outlandish furnishings and clothes for their cabins and women. Out of curiosity and to relieve the tension of waiting he asked the question.

"What did you do with all the money you got in wages with my father, Washer?"

"Laik d' res'. Spen' hit on girl en Kingston, Nassau. Make big gamblin' wit dice, cards. I don' know. Hit melt away, seem laik. More you gots more you spen'. Liquor. Wimmen. Gamble. Someone always aroun' to he'p you."

Brian knew the crew wasn't sailing with him now just because of double wages and the promise of a bonus. He had called them all on deck at Exuma and explained what they were going to do; the risk, the danger involved if a Spanish patrol found them carrying guns in Cuban territorial waters. They listened without expression or comment, merely nodding their heads. But, Brian knew, they would talk it all over excitedly later. This was like the old days. Hadn't they sailed with the Marstah Cameron right through the Union gunboats during the war? Now, young Marstah Cap'n Brian take over. He had, they agreed, learned good from his father. They weren't afraid to sail with him. They had a pride in the *Caroline*. Besides, if they didn't sail with Cap'n Brian what were they to do? Fish, like some ordinary nigger? Work a sponge bed? Raise some truck in a garden and sell it in the Nassau market for pennies? What kind of life was that for men who had known the fascination of the chase and escape? Give them a wind, and the *Caroline* would outfoot anything these Spanish men had. So they had come eagerly, willingly for the new adventure.

As the minutes lengthened, Brian became more and more concerned.

"Washer."

"Cap'n, suh?"

"Let's break out the rest of the cargo." They had carried on deck only that which could be easily lashed fast and tarpaulin-covered. The balance remained below. "It'll be quicker to handle everything from here if they come. If they don't show I'm going to dump the whole, damn thing into the ocean and not get caught out here in the daylight."

The cargo hatches were opened, heavy slings of knotted rope were raised and lowered with block and tackle as part of the crew worked below and the rest topside. For the first time Brian thought enviously of steam and how much quicker a mechanical winch would do the job. The unwieldy bales and crates mounted on the deck space and Brian, watching the shore, caught the three rapid blinks of a light. There was a covered lantern at his feet. He lifted it, sliding back the shield to make a reply. It was almost half an hour before the dozen or so small boats came alongside.

First up the ladder was a young man. He wore no uniform, carried no pistol. A machete, in a leather scabbard, was bound at his hip. For this informality Brian was grateful. On the other trip he had been forced to deal with a self-commissioned general who had come out in full uniform, traced with gold braid. He wore a sword and waved it with furious gestures of authority and belligerence while he created nothing but confusion. His incompetent arrogance had delayed the operation and so incensed Brian that he could barely restrain his temper. He wanted to heave the strutting cock overboard.

The man who faced him now was about his age. He made a brief salute.

"*Capitán*. I am Rafael. A little English I speak. It makes itself late. I am sorry. It is not always easy to get the boats together." He studied the mounting deck cargo. "Good. We make haste now."

They all worked with steady, quiet efficiency. There was no shouting, no laughing. Brian couldn't help but admire the economy of effort which this Rafael imposed. The boats were loaded and pulled away.

The sky had shown its first flame before the last of the cargo was off the *Caroline,* and the morning trade wind began lifting. Brian and Rafael looked about the empty deck and then turned and smiled at each other with relief.

"It is good now," the Cuban said and his gaze followed the scattering of boats as they raced shoreward. "You will come again soon?"

"I don't know," Brian confessed. "It makes me an old man."

"I too. The white hair does not show yet but it is there."

The Cuban called down to the last waiting boat. A man tossed up a bottle and Rafael cracked the neck off with the machete.

"*Una copita y bien suerte, Capitán.*"

Brian cautiously took a long pull of the rum from the jagged lip of the bottle and then passed it back.

"*Bien suerte, amigo.*"

The young Cuban swallowed deeply from the bottle and then tossed it into the sea. He went down the ladder swiftly. The boat was fended off from the schooner's side and when it was clear the sail was raised. It filled and the craft lurched away clumsily with its heavy load.

Brian stood watching, wondering what future awaited this revolutionary band. Would the arms and equipment unloaded here really serve the cause for which they so eagerly fought or would resistance merely prolong the island's agony? Little by little Spain's possessions in the New World had been wasted and whittled away. Her once awesome power on the sea reduced. Would she yield here, backing off from real confrontation? He called to Washer.

"We'll take her into Havana."

"Yes, suh, Cap'n." The Negro shouted his orders to the crew. He was happy to be out of this situation. "Yes, suh!"

The cook sent Brian's breakfast to his cabin by a mess boy who also

[427]

served at every odd job on the ship. He was a youngster, twelve or thirteen, and one of the long line of descendants from the original slaves brought to Exuma by Ronald Cameron. Watching him lay the table Brian wondered a little at the seemingly inexhaustible progeny of those first Negroes. They must be scattered all through the Out Islands by now. Most of them, he suspected, had taken the name of Cameron. Freedom had come to them. They had not bloodied the soil in its pursuit as these Cubans were doing. He ate slowly and with hungry relish. Sailing, as they did, on short voyages, the *Caroline* was always supplied with fresh food. The coffee was strong, the fruit ripe, the ham and eggs taken on at New Orleans of the best. And, always, when they wanted fish, they could lay to in their leisurely pace and take them still wriggling to the pan.

He finished the large breakfast and then went to his bunk and stretched out. The schooner's easy motion was a cradle and the brass lamp swinging on its gimbal had an almost hypnotic effect. He stared at it and then, with surprise, realized he was homesick and a little lonely. He would have liked to be this night on Exuma listening to the surf's wash upon the beach, talking with his father and Uncle David. The years since he had been fifteen were filled with excitement. Now, he thought, I have had enough for a while. The sailor comes home from the sea. He would have a meeting with Señor de la Torre in Havana and close this business before his luck ran out. He had made no commitment as to the number of voyages he would make. No contract was involved. His conscience was clear. He drowsed for a while, listening to the sounds the schooner made, and then fell into a heavy sleep. He had not closed his eyes in thirty-six hours.

It was late afternoon when he was awakened by the gentle touch of Washer's big hand on his shoulder.

" 'Cuse me, Cap'n, suh. Spanish steamship, little one like, maybe one them armed cutter. Hit pick us up 'bout houah ago. She don't make hail oah come neah us. Jus' follow. Lay off 'bout haf a league. No signal. Jus' run wid us."

Brian swung out of his bunk, rubbed fingertips into his tangled hair, tugging the sleep from his mind. From the steadiness of the ship he knew they had no driving wind.

"What are we making?"

"Seben, eight knot, maybe, suh."

He nodded, went to a stand, poured some water into a basin and sloshed it over his face. There was no real reason for concern. The *Caroline* was empty of all contraband. The Spanish patrol boat's captain must know this from the way the schooner rode. Just the same he didn't like to be followed. The Spanish were jumpy, unpredictable; inclined to shoot first and apologize later. No one could be quite as convincing as a Spaniard in his protestations of innocence or misunderstanding.

"We won't make Havana until midday tomorrow at least." He dried his face on the rough towel. "Hold the course and we'll see what happens."

"Yes, Cap'n, suh."

Brian took a little rum, mixed it with water and washed it around in his mouth before spitting it out. He combed his hair, noted he badly needed a shave, took a glass from its case of leather and went out on deck.

The Spanish ship had closed the distance a little. She ran off the schooner's starboard beam and a heavy, black smoke billowed and swirled about her. Brian studied his escort through the telescope. Washer had been right. The Spanish Navy operated several ships of this type in the Cuban waters. He had seen them in and out of Havana harbor. They carried two swivel guns, one fore and aft, heavy enough to do considerable damage to a wooden hull at close range. At the moment she displayed no aggressive intention, simply maintaining her position between the *Caroline* and the distant shoreline. With darkness and showing no lights Brian knew they could lose her but this was an unnecessary maneuver. Explanations would be demanded the next time he put into Havana. The authorities could close the port to him if they wanted to and he had no intention of inviting this. There was still a good trade in hides, rum, sugar and tobacco between Cuba, the mainland's eastern seaboard ports, Nassau and Bermuda. He didn't want to shut himself off from what share a sailing vessel could get these days.

Several times, throughout the night, he went back on deck. The sky was clear, filled with stars. A quartering wind of about fifteen knots held steady. The *Caroline*'s running lights showed brightly and half a mile or so away, still on his beam, he could see those of the patrol. He wondered at this vigilance for it was nothing more. What were her captain's orders? Probably to do just what he was doing, dog him as he moved northeasterly up the coast. But, and this did trouble him a little, why was the *Caroline* suddenly under suspicion? The same question must have been in Washer's mind for he moved respectfully to Brian's side.

"What you tink he know oah guess, Cap'n, suh?"

"I'm damned if I can figure out, Washer. It's a cinch he doesn't want to board us." He thought for a moment. "You had any sleep?"

"No suh, Cap'n." The face broke into a grin. "Dat theah liddle ol' boad wit hit's guns mek me nevus. Ol' Washah git to sleep. Wham! Spanish man decide to shoot. I laik be topside den."

"Go and get some sleep." Brian laughed at the Negro's dubious concern. "If he goes 'Wham' it won't make much difference where you are."

"Yes suh, Cap'n, suh." Washer touched his forehead. "But Ah don't figuah to sleep real good." He went forward to the companionway.

It was late afternoon of the following day before they made Havana. The patrol had now dropped astern but as they moved in, a second armed craft came out to meet them. Her screw tore angrily at the water until she was within speaking distance and then her speed dropped abruptly. From her deck an officer directed the *Caroline* to an anchorage. A two-man gun crew was at the forward piece and they looked as though they were only too eager to fire it.

Brian had dressed himself with all the formality of his limited wardrobe. The captain's gold braid on his cap and the buttons of the short jacket gleamed. He had expected something. Not this, perhaps; a gun trained on his ship. But he had been certain there would be questions and he did not want to confront some petty official in the *dugri* and loose shirt he usually wore. The Spanish were inexplicably impressed by formality and braid. They lavished it upon themselves and respected it in others. Ridiculously enough, Brian caught himself wishing he had a plumed hat and could wear a sword and sash. He laughed at the idea but it would have made an impression on the port official as he came up the ladder.

The man, short, fat, resplendent in uniform, puffed a little at the exertion of the climb. He had a childishly petulant expression; a small mouth which seemed to be in a continual pout. A younger man, plainly his subordinate, stood a pace behind him. The authority turned to him and in a high, thin voice fairly squealed the indignant words in Spanish. The effect coming from the thickset body was that of an outraged pig.

"What's he so mad about?" Brian asked the young officer innocently.

For a moment the suggestion of a smile appeared on the interpreter's face and then he banished it quickly.

"The *Comandante* says you are under arrest, Captain. That you have been supplying arms to the rebels. He says he will shoot you himself."

"Now? Here?" Brian pretended an indifference he was far from feeling. "I am a British subject. My ship is under British registry."

The officer again translated and the *Comandante* fairly swelled with rage as he loosed a torrent of words through which his companion waited patiently and without expression.

"He, *El Comandante,* says he does not care if you are the son of the

King and Queen of England. He also said several other things which are unnecessary to translate."

"Tell him I am Captain Brian Raleigh. I have come to Havana to pick up what cargo I can and when my business is finished I will leave."

Behind the *Comandante's* back his aide shook his head warningly at Brian as though to tell him to be respectful and moderate in his tone and words. He spoke to his superior with grave formality. Whatever it was he said only served to infuriate the man. His cheeks and belly puffed out. He squeaked a reply.

"*El Comandante* says you have no business here except with him. You will accompany us, Captain. Your crew will remain aboard the ship under guard."

Brian hesitated and then shrugged resignedly. Words meant nothing. Physical action would be deliberate suicide. He turned. Behind him the crew had gathered. Washer, concern on his broad face, stood a couple of paces forward from the others.

"I'll have to go with them, Wash. You will be all right. Don't start any trouble. You know nothing. Understand?"

"Yes, suh, Cap'n." Washer made a token salute.

Brian then addressed the young officer politely. "I want the British Consul notified of my detention."

The man translated and the *Comandante* all but screamed a reply.

This time the officer had to compress his lips visibly to keep a smile from breaking over them.

"*El Comandante* says he will shoot the British Consul, also the Prince of Wales and your Navy's Admiral if he feels like it."

"He's going to be a damn busy man."

The *Comandante* looked to his subordinate for a translation but the officer merely shrugged as though what Brian had said was of no importance. He turned and called an order down to the patrol boat. Eight soldiers, with bayonets on their rifles, came up the ladder. They took positions fore and aft with two remaining at the rail's opening.

A sweep-driven cutter had come out to the *Caroline* and maneuvered between it and the patrol boat. The *Comandante* descended the unsteady footing awkwardly. Brian followed and after him came the aide.

"Don't say anything, Captain."

The words were so softly whispered by the officer Brian barely heard them. He stiffened with surprise. The tone was not that of a command but rather one of friendly warning. His spirits lifted a little. Someone, at least, was not in complete sympathy with the *Comandante*. He was well aware of how critical was his situation and its unpredictable outcome. The Spaniards had no real proof of his activities. At least, he

[431]

could not believe they were acting on more than suspicion. Accidents, though, happen to prisoners who might pose an international situation. They contracted a strange malady and died quickly. They tried to escape and were shot. It was all very simple if the authorities decided it should be.

At a command from the coxswain the oars were dropped, the blades caught the water and the cutter shot through the slot between schooner and patrol craft. The men rowed well. Brian noticed this. He also noticed how grim and forbidding the brown walls of the fort looked from water level. He stared up at the embrasures with the ugly snouts of the guns pointing seaward. The cutter came to a smooth halt alongside a stone quay which led to a short flight of steps. Two of the oarsmen leaped out to assist the *Comandante*. One in the boat motioned to Brian. When he was on the ledge the young officer followed. The trio went up the short flight. A sentry opened a heavy gate and closed it after them. They passed through a tunnel and then into a courtyard. Here a squad of soldiers was drawn at attention. A lieutenant saluted and the *Comandante* piped an order. Then he turned to look at Brian and spat at his feet.

At a command the squad formed a file on both sides of Brian and he was marched across the court, through an archway, down a dank, unlighted corridor. At an open cell a rifle butt prodded him in the back, forcing him in. The door clanged shut, was locked with a heavy key by the lieutenant, and the detail wheeled and marched away. Brian listened to the heavy cadence of their boots and then there was nothing but silence.

He tried to peer about him. There was no opening from the cell to the outside. He closed his eyes for a few moments and when he opened them again he could see the dim outlines of his prison. There was no bunk, no stool, no bucket for toilet facilities. A dirty straw pallet lay upon the floor. The cubicle had a dank and musty odor and when he pressed a palm against the walls he could feel the damp chill of ancient stone. He moved to the door and his hands gripped the upright bars. He pulled against them with a futile gesture of anger and wondered how or if he was going to get out of this. He had never before known complete silence. The place was a tomb. He could rot here with no one but his captors knowing what had happened.

Tomb. He repeated the word to himself. It had a hollow, empty sound. He cursed at his stupidity in sailing for Havana. That was arrogance, bravado. The presence of the patrol boat as it followed him up the coast ought to have been warning enough. He should have waited for darkness, put out all his lights, crowded every inch of canvas on and made for the Florida shore. Instead, he had to make this ridiculous gesture. It was a fool's trick. A boy showing off, thumbing his nose.

Turning away from the gate he lowered himself to the lumpy, foul-smelling pallet and leaned back against the moist wall. How much, he wondered, did they really know? The loading in the States? He shook his head. Even if Spanish agents had been watching the New Orleans port and learned of his cargo, the word and information would not have had time to reach Havana. Had someone seen the transfer off the Jardines de la Reina? Again the time element had to be considered. Had they been informed of the first trip, the one to Baracoa? This could be. But, again, he didn't quite believe it. The authorities had no proof; a suspicion, perhaps. He found little comfort in this. He was in prison, proof or no proof. He had no real faith, either, in the British Consul. He would, if notified, make a formal protest which would be politely received and ignored. No ship of the Royal Navy would come roaring in to secure the release of one Brian Raleigh.

He stood and began walking up and down the narrow cell. Five paces forward. Five paces back. He halted again at the bars. His sight, suiting itself to the darkness, could find nothing but the vague outlines of a cell gate opposite his.

"Hey!" he yelled. "Is anyone here?"

The sound bounced and reverberated in the empty cavern. Its echo was a frightening thing, sounding with an idiot's gibberish until it faded and died away entirely. He had hoped for something, a voice, the answer of some unknown prisoner in another cell. There was nothing, no one. They probably didn't keep prisoners very long here.

He took off his cap and threw it in a corner. Then he went back to the pallet, sat down, pulled up his knees and crossed his arms upon them. Then he lowered his head to rest it. This was as comfortable a position as he could think of. He began to wonder how long a man could stand this solitary confinement without beginning to rave in madness. He didn't think the Spanish officials were in any hurry to dispose of his case if they had one. What about Washer, the crew, the *Caroline?* These were unanswerable questions. The crew could be taken off and imprisoned or simply shot. The schooner dismantled, stripped or taken out to sea and sunk. No one would know. No one would really give a damn. The chances were the British Consul wouldn't even be notified of his or the ship's detention or the charges against him. Why should anyone take the trouble to do this? Suddenly, he lifted his head in surprise as he recalled the cautioning tone of the *Comandante's* interpreter. There had been a certain amity in the words. Why? He didn't know. Possibly the young officer didn't like unnecessary brutality, which Brian's flippancy would have eventually brought.

He had no idea of time. Had he been here an hour? Two? He was in a void where time didn't exist. After a while his legs became numb and he stood up, taking his measured paces to restore circulation. Finally he sat down again. He took out his watch. They hadn't searched him for a weapon. Perhaps, because they knew he would have no opportunity to use one. For the same reason, he thought grimly, they had left him the watch and money carried. What had he to do with time or money now? He put the watch to his ear just for the company of its sound; the small, steady ticking of the seconds. He counted until he reached a thousand. Sixty seconds to a minute. Only sixteen minutes and some seconds had passed. Yet, the interval had seemed interminable. What would twenty-four hours, a week, a month, a year be like? He forced himself to halt this speculation. That was the way to drive yourself crazy.

Later, he had no idea how long, there was the sound of footsteps. An indistinct figure appeared on the other side of the bars, stooped and slid a tin plate into the cell then started to move away.

"*Hombre,*" he called.

The figure returned. "*Que querie, Ingles?*" The question was asked contemptuously.

"*Hay tabaco?*"

"*Hay dinero, Ingles?*" The jailer tried to mimic Brian's foreign accent.

Raleigh took some coins from his pocket. He could not tell their denomination. He pushed his hand through the bars, made a contact with the guard and the silver tinkled into an outstretched palm. After a moment he felt two thin cigars and two of the heavy, sulphur matches thrust into his fingers.

"*Gracias.*" He stumbled a little with the word.

"*Por nada, Ingles.*" Again there was the smug note of sarcasm. It was malicious, unnecessary.

Brian stood at the door and heard the retreating sound of the man's boots. He picked up the tin plate. There was no fork or knife. It was too dark to see what it contained so he felt about with his fingers. There was a small mound of rice mixed with beans and a gluey mess of stringy meat. The touch of it made him want to retch. He put it down and went back to the pallet. Stowing one cigar and a match in an inside coat pocket he held the others. Where to try and strike the precious match? Not on this damp floor. He felt the soles of his shoes. They, also, had absorbed the moisture. He couldn't risk it. Finally, he took out his watch again. The case was elaborately chased. The engraver had cut well. He drew the match head across the scored surface. It spluttered and fired with a yellow flame. Quickly he held it to the crudely wrought cigar and drew upon it with greedy haste. The smoke was acrid for it was the cheapest and strongest of leaf. Still, it was good. He held the match and in its brief light saw the vermin crawling on the pad. He rose and with one hand flipped it over. A dozen or more huge, black cockroaches scurried at the disturbance. The match burned to his fingertips and he was forced to drop it. He stood again in the gloom. Given time, he thought, and I'll eat the food and sleep with the roaches and bugs. Time would make him grateful for the things which now filled him with disgust.

Leaning with his back against the wall, smoking and cherishing the flavor although it seared his throat when he tried to inhale, he wished he had used the match's light to see the time on his watch. But what difference did it make after all? Here there would be no distinction between six o'clock at night and twelve noon. When he could no longer hold the tiny butt he dropped it to the stone and turned to face the bars, wrapping his hands through them. He must have slept this way for a minute or two. Maybe it was longer. He didn't know. He awoke with a start, feeling himself sliding down as his grip loosened and cheek scraped against the cold iron. He could not bear the idea of the foul mattress so he sat upon the floor, legs crossed, head drooping.

Time had long ago ceased to have any significance. He could roughly estimate a day's passing by the regularity with which a guard brought food. Morning, he assumed, was when a heavy mug of black coffee, a chunk of sour-tasting bread and a pannikin of water were shoved beneath the door. Afternoon was marked by the larger meal of beans, rice, stringy beef or a piece of fish. Night or evening was water, a piece of cold meat, a biscuit. Once a day a guard came in with a lantern, took away the slop pail and replaced it with another. Only then did Brian see a face. The guards who served him were not always the same. There was a system of rotation. He could differentiate among them by their walk. They came and went wordlessly, making no reply to his offer of money for tobacco. Only one invariably spoke. This was the guard of his first day. He recognized him by the sly, vicious greeting.

"Que tal, Ingles?"

Brian would have liked to get his hands about the throat from which the question came. That would be new. It would be good. He fought for control, holding back his temper and words for this was the only one who would exchange cigars and matches for money. He had no idea of the denomination of the bills he passed out. English pounds. American dollars. What difference did it make? For one he was handed the two cigars and two matches. The tobacco made him dizzy now but it was a pleasant sensation, whirling aimlessly, drifting, weightless, floating. It was a drug in his weakened condition.

Then there came a time when there were the sounds of several pairs of boots in the stone corridor. He was supine on the straw ticking for he had learned, with other things, to sleep here, indifferent to the bugs and roaches as he had predicted. He scratched at their fiery bites continually and felt the lice in his hair and beard. When he lit a match he used part of the flame to sear the hair on chin and cheek, taking a small satisfaction in knowing he killed some of the loathsome things. He waited, listening. The tramping feet halted outside his door. He arose slowly. Three indistinct forms were at the bars. A key turned in the lock and the ungreased bolt squealed as it was forced. A hand grasped his shirt and he was pulled forward and then pushed ahead with two guards flanking him. The third man brought up the rear. He had not realized how weak he was. The effort of walking was all but unbearable. Several times he stumbled and once fell to his knees. Rough hands jerked him to his feet.

He could see a patch of light in the distance. It seemed miles away but must have been only a few yards, for suddenly they were at a gate. He was pulled through it and into the full brightness of the sunlit courtyard. He almost screamed from the pain as the brilliance struck his eyes. It was an excruciating agony. His hands went up automatically to cover them and the guards laughed at his contortions.

Fingers dug into his arms, holding him upright, guiding him across the flagged stone and through a door, into a room. It was darker here. Brian opened the fingers covering his eyes and peered uncertainly through the slits. There were four men in the room. The fat *Comandante* sat in a chair at the head of a rough table. Beside him Brian recognized the officer who had acted as interpreter aboard the *Caroline*. The third was a sergeant. He dismissed the escort and the door was closed. Brian was able to drop his hands from his eyes now. He looked at the fourth man and a small memory stirred in his mind. The man wore only a dirty pair of cotton trousers. His chest, face and arms were terribly scarred; a crisscrossed pattern of dried blood, festering cuts where a lash must have repeatedly flayed him over a period of days. The head sagged a little but the man fought to keep it up and defiant. Then Brian remembered. This was the young guerrilla who had been the last to leave the *Caroline* off the Jardines de la Reina. His name? Brian searched for it. Rafael. Yes. Rafael. They had taken a drink of rum together. He had been gay, self-assured, proud of his cause and mission. There had been no fear in him. He wore his confidence as a bright cockade. Now, he was a sagging corpse which, miraculously, breathed and stood with a small contempt.

The *Comandante* shrilled a question and the interpreter turned to Brian.

"Do you know this man? Have you ever seen him before?"

"No."

Since the word is the same in Spanish the *Comandante* understood. He slammed his fist on the table.

"*Embustero!*"

"*El Comandante* says you are a liar."

Brian made no reply. He was becoming nauseated by the effort of standing. Only by drawing upon strength he did not believe remained could he keep himself from falling.

The interpreter spoke to the prisoner, Rafael, asking him in Spanish the same question. The man slowly lifted his eyes and stared at Brian. Then he made a small, negative motion with his head.

"*No.*"

The sergeant slapped him across the mouth with the back of his hand and blood trickled from the sagging jaw. Then he spat the crimson froth full into the sergeant's face. An order from the interpreter halted the noncommissioned officer, whose fury was a living thing.

The *Comandante* screamed a string of sentences in Spanish. The officer waited stolidly until he had finished. Then he addressed Brian.

"*El Comandante* says you are an English lying bastard." He spoke the words without a shade of expression. "He says you know this man and he knows you. He says you brought him a shipment of arms. It was a second trip. The first consignment was landed at Baracoa."

"I have never seen this man before. I have not been in Baracoa. I want the British Consul present."

"*El Comandante*"—the officer ignored the interruption—"wants to know who it is you make contact with here in Havana. He also wants to know of the junta in New Orleans and who is its leader. He says for you to look well upon this man for if you do not tell him what he wants to know, the same thing and more will happen to you."

Brian drew a long breath. "I am," the words came slowly, "a British subject, captain of the schooner *Caroline* out of the Bahama Islands. I came to Havana on legitimate business, seeking a cargo." He spoke in a monotone. "I demand the British Consulate be notified of my detention. What has happened to my ship and crew?"

The interpreter translated but Brian had the feeling he shaded the reply, suiting it to his superior's temper, for the *Comandante* did not display the hysterical outburst he had expected. Instead, a thin smile crossed

[437]

his lips. He spoke shortly. The two subordinates saluted at attention. He walked from the room.

"*El Comandante* says you will talk. It may take time but in the end you will beg on your knees to be allowed to tell him what he asks. You are being very foolish, Captain." It was almost a plea.

"Would I be less of a fool if I told him what he wants me to say?"

The young officer shrugged. He regarded Brian steadily for a moment and then called to the guards waiting in the court.

Again he was marched through the blazing light and again he had to shield his eyes against it. The guards took his arms as he wavered in his walk. He let them guide him like a blind man. When he felt the cold air of the tunnel he raised his lids, grateful for the darkness. The guards released their holds and he shuffled forward until they halted. He was pushed through the door and into his cell. The door clanged shut, the lock turned and he was alone. His legs could no longer support him. He fell to his knees, head hanging limply, and vomited until the retching tore at his stomach and nothing but a greenish-yellow scum dribbled from his lips.

It was a long time before he could crawl to the pallet. He lay upon it, face down, his breath coming in short gasps. Little by little his mind began to clear. He began to wonder if he could take the beating and torture which the young guerrilla had suffered. He wasn't sure and his body began to shake uncontrollably. How brave was bravery and to what end? Suppose he told them everything, the names they wanted? De la Torre. Henri de Tourville. Would the *Comandante* then say: Thank you, Captain Raleigh. You may go now. Only a fool would believe this. So, there was no choice. You were beaten until you talked and after you talked you were shot. Or, you talked without the beating and were shot or held in this fortress prison until you died or went mad. No one would know. No one would care. He wondered about Washer and the crew. Were they, also, in cells now? He couldn't blame the boys if they told what they knew. He had the feeling, though, the *Comandante* wanted the admission of guilt from him, the captain, the authority. This would stand up against any protest the British Government might make if it ever learned of the incident.

He had no idea how long he had been lying on the pad, face buried in crossed arms. In his mind he seemed half asleep, half awake. It was a form of delirium in which curious fantasies drifted through his mind. Behind closed eyes there would be flashes of color, bright streaks of red, yellow, green and then a cascade of white lights as of falling stars. Dimly he heard boots striking the stones, the scraping of a tin pan pushed beneath the door. He waited for the guard to leave. Minutes seemed to tick past and he knew, without turning, someone still stood outside the cell gate. Then came a single, whispered word.

"Mister?"

The title was accented. It was as though someone was translating "Señor." He pulled himself upright and went to the bars. The figure was there but without real form, an amorphous thing standing in silence.

"Yes?" He stared.

"*Cuba Libre!*" The expression was barely audible.

Brian's fingers tightened on the bars. He was afraid to reply. This was the revolutionary slogan.

"Speak you Spanish, mister?" So softly.

"*Poco. Muy poco.*"

"*Este noche. Comprende? Understan'?*"

"Tonight. *Sí.*"

"I come."

The faceless one was gone. He moved away like a shadow. Only the boots striking stone gave him reality. Brian clung to the bars. Was it a trick? Would they have done with him? Shot in the back while trying to escape. It was a simple expedient. Somehow, he didn't believe it. The *Comandante* still wanted the name of the man in Havana. They would keep him alive until he gave it to them. But, how? To get out of this place so well guarded, sentries on duty. This one, unknown man out of the garrison speaking the words of freedom. *Cuba Libre!*

Now came the time of waiting. He left the food untouched. This was the second meal so it was afternoon. He began to walk up and down, the paces five and five. How many to a mile? Thirteen feet, possibly, up. Thirteen feet back. Five thousand two hundred and eighty feet to a mile. He tried to count but his mind would not carry him beyond a thousand. He halted to consider this phenomenon. Why? He could not say one thousand and one. His lips simply would not form the words.

He walked until he was exhausted. He counted to a thousand and then started over again. Finally, he stood and stared down at his knees. They were shaking, actually touching each other. It was an expression. His knees shook. He had never really believed they did. Now, the agitation which he could not control fascinated him. Why should the knees shake and not the arms or head? He braced himself against the wall, leaning forward, and watched the quaking. It seemed to be no part of him. Then the legs gave way entirely and he slid down, his palms slipping on the stone's damp surface. His entire body was in a mild convulsion but not from fear. Excitement such as he had never known gripped him. He thought he was going to throw up but there was nothing in his stomach but the morning's coffee. He doubled suddenly with cramps. They tore at him and subsided as quickly as they had come.

All of this seemed not to be happening to him. It was as though some incredible division had been made and he could stand apart and watch another Brian Raleigh twitch and clasp his hands, head nodding, limbs no longer under control.

He forced himself to think. I will go back, he told himself, and try to remember everything and take my life, step by step, to this moment. What was his first recollection? A fish. He had no idea how old he had been at the time. There was no way to fix a date. His father had taken him fishing. In the clear water the brown and red snapper, some grunts with their stripes of yellow and blue, and a beautiful, sharp-nosed creature of brilliant green. It was a parrot fish. He remembered his asking and his father's reply. It wouldn't take a hook. He had dangled his line and the parrot fish returned time and time again but it only nudged the lure, bumping it, turning quickly, returning. Then, inexplicably, it took the bit of conch meat in which the barb was hidden. He had pulled it in quickly with the hand line. His father had said, "We'll let this one go, Brian. It is not for eating but a thing of beauty." The parrot fish had swallowed the hook. Cameron worked over it quickly but carefully while it died in the sun and air. The sharp steel would not come loose. Finally he had taken a knife and cut the line as close to the mouth as he could. He put the fish back in the water. It rolled and lay listlessly for a moment or two and then, revitalized and in its element, streaked away in a gleaming flash of color. "Maybe it will live. I hope so." This his father had said. Why, he wondered now, did he recall this incident so vividly? It was the first thing of substance he could remember.

From this memory he began to trace his childhood step by step. How old had he been when this or that happened? The first time he had stripped the tough hide from a piece of sugar cane and tasted its fibrous sweetness. A toe cut on coral in the shallows. Why did those trivial things remain in the mind? He made an attempt to put everything in some sort of chronological order and grew drowsy with the effort. His head sagged and he slept.

He was awakened by a tiny noise, the faint squealing of a mouse.

His head jerked up. The bolt in the cell door was being turned slowly. "Mister?"

He pulled himself upright. He was still dreaming. No. His feet carried him forward. He reached for the door but it was not there. His hand touched a man's arm.

"*Zapatos*. Sho-ess. Understan'?"

Brian nodded and bent to unlace and remove his boots. The man steadied him as he stood on one foot and then the other.

"*Venga conmigo.* Understan', mister?"

"*Sí.*" Even as he spoke he wondered why he should so unhesitatingly trust this man whose face he had not seen.

Their shoeless feet made no sound as they moved down the corridor. At an archway, dimly outlined, his guide turned him.

"*Cuidadoso.* Understan', mister?"

"*Sí.*" Brian knew the word. Careful.

Now each step was taken carefully and with infinite care. The man went down on his hands and knees, creeping, feeling ahead in the darkness. Then he apparently found what he was seeking. He reached behind him.

"Mister. *Su mano.* Hand-ed."

Brian reached forward until his hand clasped the other's. Pressure pulled him down.

"*Sentarse.*" It was whispered.

Brian wasn't sure. He thought the guide wanted him to sit from the way he pulled his arm. When he was settled, the man worked to straighten out his legs and Brian could feel his feet dangling over a sloping ledge. Then his companion was behind him, pushing with both hands against his back. He began to slide forward. This was some sort of an incline, a chute. The rough stone wore at his trousers. His skin burned. Then his forward movement began to accelerate. The stone was wet and then slimy. He moved faster and it was all he could do not to cry out. Going down this way could only lead to some underground passage or to the water. He struck it feet first with the smallest of splashes. Then hands grasped his coat before he went under. He was pulled over the side of a skiff. A moment later his guide was also in the boat. It was raining heavily, the downpour hissing upon the surface of the water.

"Are you all right, Captain?"

"You?" There was astonishment in his voice as he recognized the speaker. "Señor de la Torre."

"Later," the man cautioned.

The second man in the skiff took the oars. Where they fitted into the locks rags were bound to muffle any sound. In the sheeting rain the shore lights were barely visible, and atop the fort the sentries huddled in what shelter they could find. They traveled silently for a hundred yards or so before de la Torre spoke again.

"You didn't think we would abandon you, Captain?"

This unexpected freedom was like a strong drink. Brian felt intoxicated. Strength began to flow through him. He no longer shook from weakness.

"I didn't know. I wasn't sure anyone knew of my arrest. How long have I been in there?"

"Three weeks. It took time to find a man among the garrison and get word to him. Then we had to wait for just such a night as this. It had to be planned carefully for an error could not be retrieved."

"What's happened to my crew, my ship?"

"She is anchored where you left her, the crew under guard. But a sufficient amount of money will work small miracles. The guard is now mine. I bought them. I have made certain promises. They cannot return to the garrison. You understand this?"

"Of course."

"In addition to the money I have assured them you would see to it they are taken to a place of safety. I suggested St. Augustine, in Florida. The guard who came out of the fort with you must also be taken care of."

"What about you?"

"I am all right. Possibly there is suspicion in certain quarters but no proof and I am not without influence."

"I don't know how to begin to thank you." He shivered a little, hunching himself against the cold rain. "Or this man." He indicated the soldier from the prison. "What's his name?"

"Jamie."

Brian turned and put out his hand. It was taken in a strong clasp.

"*Mil gracias.*" It was awkwardly said but the sincerity was there. "*Amigo.*"

"*De nada, señor.*"

"As to your thanks," de la Torre said. "I have presumed upon them already. My wife, daughter and the señora's personal maid are aboard your schooner. I wish you to take them to Nassau. I will be easier in my mind."

"Señor," Brian was serious, "I will swim, towing the *Caroline* after me, to get them to the Bahamas if necessary. Nothing you could ask would be too much after what you've done. I didn't find a suitable place so they will be our guests on Exuma until a house in Nassau is available. Be sure I will do everything to see they are comfortably housed."

"Thank you." De la Torre paused and then laughed moderately. "You and Jamie are probably the only men to come down that chute alive. It is used for executed prisoners. The sharks take care of the burial."

"I had heard of it." Brian suddenly thought of something. "There was a young guerrilla—Rafael. Do you know what happened to him?"

[442]

"It was reported to me he died of the beatings but he never talked, never admitted anything."

"I am sorry."

Dimly now he could see the outlines of the *Caroline*. She was without riding lights, the swirling rain and mist all but obscuring her. A few moments later they were alongside. Figures, indifferent to the storm, lined the rail. Looming above them was the figure of Washer.

"Cap'n, suh?"

"Wash!" There was no mistaking the happiness in Brian's voice.

"Lor' God, suh. I nevah expect to see you agin."

Brian reached for the ladder and then turned to de la Torre. "You're coming aboard?"

"No. I have said my good-bye. There is no point in prolonging an unhappy situation. My wife leaves me reluctantly. It is better we, you and I, say *adios* here. The arms you brought will be of inestimable value. This guerrilla warfare may go on for years. But I would not suggest, Captain, you return to Havana. We could not be so lucky again."

They shook hands and then Brian, who two hours ago thought he could not walk the distance of his cell, went up the ladder like a squirrel on a tree. Big Washer stood before him. There were tears in his eyes. What the big Negro did was so spontaneous that Brian had to fight off the sentiment he felt. Washer put his huge arms about him as a father might embrace a son. Then he stepped back.

"Ahm sorry, Cap'n, suh."

"If you hadn't done it I would have." He felt the wind and noted its quarter. "Can we get out of here?"

"Cap'n, suh, you ain' nevah seen a crew o' niggers what want to leabe a place laik dis heah one." He gave his orders and the crew jumped to obey them.

Without lights, concealed by the driving rain, the *Caroline* slipped like a gray ghost from the harbor. Only the jibs and the forestaysail were set. Once they were well beyond the forts and in the open sea, all the canvas was crowded on. A course was laid for the Straits of Florida. Only then did Brian realize how wet and cold he was even beneath the oilskin Washer had brought him. He turned Jamie over to the Negro with instructions to get him dry clothing and whatever else he needed. Then he went to his cabin, remembering to knock first.

Señora de la Torre was seated at a table in the cabin's center. Marta was peeping through the curtain which had been drawn over the ports. The cabin was warm, softly lighted and comfortable. The woman looked up at his entrance.

"He has gone, my husband?" There was desolation in her tone.

"Yes, señora. He thought it was better this way."

"Did they torture you in the prison, Captain?" Marta made no effort to conceal her excitement in this adventure. "Were you beaten?"

"Marta." Her mother was reproving. When Brian took off the oilskin she saw his sodden clothing. "Captain," her concern was immediate, "you are wet. Marta and I will leave so you can change."

He shook his head. "It is raining hard, señora. You can't go on deck. I will take some things."

"We are an inconvenience. I do not understand why it has to be this way. But," her smile was wan, "I am accustomed to obeying my husband."

"I'm sorry the accommodations are not better." He glanced at the servant, a woman of about thirty who sat with head bowed in a corner. "You will be crowded here."

"Please do not concern yourself about us, Captain. It is you who are being inconvenienced."

He gathered dry clothing, his soap, razor, brush for the teeth, a can of tobacco and pipe.

"We will all feel better in the morning when the sun shines. Until then, *hasta mañana.*"

"Will you tell me about the prison, Captain?" Marta could not restrain herself.

"Every horrible detail, señorita." He smiled at her unabashed curiosity and eagerness. "The whippings, the torture, the boiling oil, the spikes driven through my feet, wood slivers beneath my nails. I will leave out nothing, and what didn't happen I will invent. Good night."

⊷ XXVII ⊶

AND NOW again the well-beloved waters; down the long string of the Exuma cays with the *Caroline* running as eagerly as some lively animal, anxious to be home.

At the rail with Brian, Señora de la Torre and the daughter, Marta, took in the full beauty of the scene, exclaiming over the sharply defined colors of the waters, the white sand of the beaches backed by the dark green of palms and scrub. For Marta the trip had been one of never-ending novelty for she had never before enjoyed the freedom of movement and association which was hers aboard the schooner. Until now her life had been sheltered, restricted by the conventions and proprieties which belonged more to the Old World than to the New. When she left home in the morning for the convent school the duenna accompanied her in the coach and called for her in the afternoon. She had never spoken freely to a man save within the close circle of the family's intimates. Here she talked with the seamen, the mess boy, stood at the side of big Washer when he had the wheel, asking innumerable questions she would not have dared voice to a Negro in Cuba even if given the opportunity. Curiosity bubbled from her mind like a crystal spring and never ceased its flow.

Of this unconventional behavior Señora de la Torre had been wistfully tolerant. Behind her outward serenity she was lonely, a little frightened without the reassuring presence of her husband. Her life had been bounded by her home. Now she was venturing into an alien world whose language she could neither understand nor speak. She understood Sebastian would not have asked her to make this move unless he felt it to be a necessary precaution. Why, she thought miserably, must he involve himself in this revolutionary cause? What had he or they to gain? It was because she suspected Marta of secretly sharing her feeling of insecurity that she permitted the girl the liberty which would have been unthinkable at home.

As he had promised, Brian had taken the schooner northward along the Florida coast, through the Matanzas Inlet and up the short distance of the lagoon to St. Augustine. The Cuban soldiers who had formed the guard aboard the *Caroline* were well supplied with de la Torre's bribe. They would find the community here congenial for it still retained a Spanish character. Also, there was a large colony of Minorcans who had made their way almost a hundred miles from New Smyrna to escape the tyranny of Dr. Turnbull, the Scot who had brought them from their native island of Minorca in the Mediterranean.

They had provisioned the schooner, taken on fresh water which had a strong taste and smell of sulphur, set their course for New Providence. With Marta as a willing interpreter he and the Señora had talked of the leasing of a house there as her husband suggested. She was resigning herself to a term of exile and her patrician beauty and poise never betrayed the emotional stress which the separation was causing.

In Nassau they had inspected three fine old houses on the hill, whose owners could no longer afford to maintain them. They were anxious to sell outright or lease. One house, behind its high wall with the flame of bougainvillea all but covering the stone, had taken the Señora's fancy because it resembled, in a manner, her home in Havana. Since it would take two or three weeks for the owners to move and have the place put in order, Brian had induced her, through Marta, to be the Raleighs' guest on Exuma.

Now, as she sensed they were nearing the end of their journey, Señora de la Torre was filled with gratitude for this young man's courtesy and consideration. The accommodations aboard the schooner were limited but Brian had done everything possible to insure their comfort and privacy. She suspected their presence had inconvenienced him greatly and that he must have slung a hammock in some section of the ship. At her urging he had come to take the evening meal with them in the master's cabin. It was always a pleasant interlude. The Señora displayed no embarrassment or self-consciousness over the fact she spoke only a few words in English. Marta translated easily what her mother had said or asked, small questions or comments about the islands. Brian's replies were similarly turned to Spanish. What might have been awkward was made agreeable and even amusing because of the courtesy and mutual respect.

The Señora spoke to Marta whose eyes danced with mischief.

"My mother says I have pried into every corner of the ship, asked questions of everyone. If I have been a nuisance she apologizes."

"Please tell your mother I wish I could always sail in such pleasant company, señorita."

Marta translated almost triumphantly and a smile of appreciation touched the Señora's face.

Marta strained to the tips of her toes trying to see everything of the cays, the coral heads they passed. Her eyes were bright, her manner one of dancing excitement. The wind caught at her hair and gave her a wild beauty of which she seemed completely unaware.

"How old are you, señorita?" He was captivated by her unconscious enthusiasm.

"A gentleman does not ask that question of a lady." She translated Brian's question and her reply to her mother.

The Señora answered and Marta laughed.

"My mother says I am too old to be treated as a child. Too young to be an adult. It is an age of difficulty. Thirteen. Why did you want to know?" She held her hair back with one hand.

"I was only thinking as I watched you—my great-grandmother, Caroline, for whom the schooner was named, was your age when her father brought her and a brother to the islands. She never wanted to leave them. She married a pirate. Juan Cadiz."

"Not a real pirate?" Marta's eyes grew wide.

"No, I expect not," he confessed. "Not a real pirate although her father called him that. My grandmother, who was named Bahama, told me about him when I was a youngster. He wore a gold ring in his ear and ran away with her mother in a sloop with a red sail."

Marta translated for her mother excitedly, as though this romance was a personal thing. In the words Brian caught only *pirata* and *circulo de oro*.

The Señora looked up questioningly at Brian but he could only shrug, having no idea what Marta may have said in a flight of imagination.

"Lived you always the islands in, *Capitán?*" Señora de la Torre made one of her rare ventures into English. She smiled diffidently. *"Hay que practicar."*

"Mother says it is necessary for her to practice English."

"Sí, señora." He halted there, knowing he was going to get himself hopelessly involved, then spoke to Marta. "We have been island people for seventy-five years or more. I went to school for a few years in Nassau where," he added slyly, "you will be going. They have a convent there, I believe."

For a fraction of a second the smallest tip of her tongue showed as she stuck it out impudently at him for the reminder of her age.

[447]

"Marta."

The Señora was horrified by the action and spoke sternly and in rapid sentences to her daughter.

"My mother says I must apologize immediately." The words were contrite but not the mockery in her eyes. "She would also like to know where I learned such vulgarity. I apologize, Captain Raleigh. But . . . I don't really." She uttered the final words with an abject tone of sincerity which must have impressed her mother for the lady nodded her approval.

They were rounding the point now, coming about to enter the natural harbor of the plantation. Washer was handling the ship. There was no need for Brian to do more than watch.

"In a minute now," he spoke to Marta, "you will be able to see my home. There were times in Havana when I never expected to get back here."

Marta translated and the Señora's eyes displayed her interest. Cuba bore little relation to the islands she had seen on their way down from Nassau. There was an uncultivated beauty here which had felt no man's touch. They excited a romantic fancy of castaways and pirate ships.

They could see now the sweep of the small harbor unfold and the big house on the ridge where the palms were forever bending and nodding to each other in the prevailing wind. It had never seemed more wonderful to Brian than at this moment. As they slipped in toward the anchorage he could see his father and Uncle David coming down the slope toward the beach. He wondered what they would think of their unexpected guests for there had been no way to let Cameron Raleigh know in advance.

When the heavy anchors were down and the *Caroline* had shifted to the tide's turn, he assisted the Señora and Marta into the boat swung on the stern davits. Then he followed and an oarsman with him. He wondered but did not ask how they had come aboard in Havana. They must have climbed the ladder although he could not imagine Señora de la Torre and her daughter with the full sweep of their skirts executing such a feat. They were lowered away gently until the boat rested lightly on the water. The blocks were released and the crewman began to pull for shore.

"We'll go alongside the dock, Josh," he directed the oarsman.

There was a small landing stage and a short flight of steps on the little pier which would make disembarking easier. Cameron and David were walking out to meet them.

"Brian, boy!" There was no mistaking the pleasure in his father's hail. "How are you, lad?"

Cameron Raleigh permitted no curiosity to show itself in his expression over his son's passengers. When they were alongside and the boat-man held the craft steady to the dock Brian stepped out, offering his hand to the woman and then the girl.

"Señora de la Torre." He was unhappily aware of his faulty and limited Spanish for he would like to have carried this off with a certain air. *"Permiteme presentar mi padre, Señor Raleigh y mi tio, Señor Heath."*

It was awkwardly done but from her appreciative smile the words had been spoken in flawless Castilian. She inclined her head graciously and offered her hand to Cameron Raleigh.

"I have much pleasure, Señor Raleigh." There was a bright-eyed amusement in her display of English.

"Con mucho gusto, señora." Cameron did his best.

"Señor He-ath." She gave her hand to David, having a little diffi-culty with the last name.

"Señora." David bowed from his cane as he rested upon it.

"Now." Brian drew a long breath. "The Señorita Marta de la Torre, whose English is better than my Spanish. My father and uncle."

"Señores." Marta made a curtsy and she flashed them a demure but brilliant smile.

"Whew! That's over. It's been worrying me for the last hour. How are you, Father?" He put his hand in Cameron's. "Uncle David?"

"Fine, lad."

Brian addressed his father. "Señor de la Torre is a friend in Havana. He asked a favor of me. I will explain later."

Cameron spoke to Marta. "Señorita, please tell your mother our house is yours. We are delighted to have your company. It is not often my son returns from a voyage with such charming passengers, so I am doubly glad to see him this time."

Marta translated and her mother smiled her appreciation for the compliment.

"Please tell your mother," Brian added, "the boatman will go back for her maid, and your trunks and baggage will be brought ashore."

The woman nodded indifferently, as though the servant and baggage were of no consequence. She glanced about her with intense interest, her remarkably lustrous eyes taking in the scene from the beach to the manor. She said something to Marta.

"My mother says your island is most beautiful and she is grateful to you for your courtesy and hospitality."

They started up the slope. David, using his cane to assist him, was at Señora de la Torre's side. Marta seemed to dance as she moved with

[449]

Brian and his father. Everything about the island fascinated her and she was too young to make a serious ceremony out of their arrival.

"You were gone longer than I expected. I began to worry about you." Cameron's concern was also a question.

"I was in prison, in Havana. They held me for questioning about gunrunning for the revolutionary guerrillas."

"Not without reason, I suppose?" Cameron asked dryly.

"No-oo. They had a reason." Brian saw no point in trying to evade the truth. "But there was nothing on the *Caroline*. The cargo was taken off before I went into Havana. Just the same I would probably still be in prison if it hadn't been for Señor de la Torre. He is one of the leaders in the movement and asked, as a favor, if I would settle his family in Nassau for a while at least. The situation in Havana grows more critical. He was concerned for their safety. A house has been leased but it won't be ready for three weeks or so. I asked them to stay with us rather than to take rooms."

"They tortured the captain." Marta, who had been listening while pretending not to, offered the information as some entertaining sidelight. "Put him in boiling oil. Drove spikes through his hands. He told me so himself. I don't really believe it, though."

"The Señorita Marta is a well-brought-up young lady." Brian made the comment seriously to his father. "Although it is difficult to believe sometimes, the way she listens to and interrupts her elders."

"You English talk so fast I do not always understand what is being said." She gazed up at him innocently.

"You understand all right when you want to." There had developed between them a camaraderie which bridged the difference in their years. "I suspect there will be a little disciplining done by your mother now that we are off the ship."

"It is good to have guests again." Cam spoke both to his son and this bright-eyed girl with the air of impish innocence. "David and I have been much alone. We play our chess in the evenings. Long ago we exhausted most of our topics of conversation. It is not good for two old men to spend so much time together." He turned to Marta. "I hope you will like it here." He thought she was a most beautiful child with an elfin humor and manner. "How is it you speak English so well?"

"In my school they teach it with French and other things. I never thought I would have much opportunity to use it."

They reached the ridge's crest. The Señora turned and looked back at the unruffled sheen of the bay, the schooner riding motionless, the heavy, green velvet of the lawn and the gardens bright with flowers. She spoke to Marta, a tinge of sadness in her words.

[450]

"My mother says it is so beautiful she could almost believe she was back in Cuba. She wishes my father could see it."

The household was stirred into a flurry of activity by the unexpected arrival of guests. At Cameron's orders rooms in one of the wings were opened. Here, if they wished, the Señora and her daughter could have complete privacy. Their trunks and hand boxes together with the maid were brought ashore. Through Marta the woman asked to be excused until the evening. It was good to be on land and in a house again which did not roll and move.

"My mother begs your forgiveness but says you would undoubtedly like to talk with your son. She is weary from the journey." She turned to her mother and spoke in Spanish.

For a moment the Señora hesitated and then she shrugged as though to say everything was too new to be put in the order to which she was accustomed.

"May I?" Marta asked. "My mother gives me permission. I do not have to take the siesta. May I walk through the garden and down to the beach?"

"Not only our house but the entire island is yours, señorita." Cameron was sincere. He was captivated by her unaffected enthusiasm for everything. "You may walk, run, ride. Our diversions are limited but they are at your disposal."

"Thank you. I will tell my mother. I would like to ride. I am very good with a horse. It is," she eyed Brian, "something which they did not teach me at school."

David, who had been listening, studying each gesture and movement of the girl, stared after her as she all but pirouetted down the steps and away toward the beach.

"It is incredible," he murmured. "I would not have believed it possible."

"What, David?" Cam was filling a pipe.

"The girl. She is Bahama at thirteen or so as I remember her. The same beauty, grace. The airy quality of her feet not seeming to touch the earth. Good Lord! How she takes me back to things I had thought forgotten and put away forever. Perhaps," he conceded, "I am an old man imagining something which is not there. But, when she talks I hear Bahama's voice. When she smiles it is Bahama's smile. It warmed you. Even the eyes, the way they sometimes crinkle with mischief, are Bahama's. The olive color of the skin which Bahama inherited from Juan Cadiz." He spoke to Brian. "If you could have known your grandmother at that age you would see what I do."

[451]

"I suspect," Cameron mused as he drew upon his pipe, "she has been carefully reared as is the custom in Spanish families. This freedom which she now enjoys is intoxicating. I hope they find their visit here enjoyable. It is pleasant to see such radiant youth again."

"De la Torre would not like to be called Spanish." Brian chuckled at the thought. "He is a Cuban. There is a pride in this."

"Tell me about him." Cam was interested.

"He and your friend, Henri de Tourville, are deep in this revolutionary movement. Their goal is complete independence from Spain."

"Henri?" Cameron couldn't believe it.

Brian nodded. "They, the revolutionaries, would like to find some way of drawing the United States to their side without the danger of being swallowed as a possession. I suspect the fighting is fierce and deadly but not spectacular. That is why we don't hear so much about it."

As briefly as possible Brian told them what had happened. The encounter with de Tourville, in New Orleans. The two trips he had made with guns, ammunition and equipment. The detention and imprisonment. The escape.

"I'm not sure," he concluded, "just why such a man as de la Torre exposes himself to the danger. But, I imagine the total revolution he wants will be to his advantage. He is impatient, as are many others, with Spain's hand upon their affairs. If there is looting to be done they want to do it and not some Spanish Viceroy. If the *campesino* is to be exploited, then they want to be the exploiters."

"It is strange," David spoke, "how inept Spain has always been with her colonization. She once had the world in her hands but not the wisdom to govern."

"Tell me," Brian turned to his father, "what has been happening here?"

"I tried to turn planter," Cam admitted ruefully. "To make the plantation profitable. But labor is hard to get although most of the Negroes in the Out Islands live on beans and fish in a state of poverty. They seem satisfied with the life. We will have a small crop of sisal but not much more. Some rum from the cane, enough to feed us from the vegetable gardens, hog pens, and the cattle which roam the scrub and almost have to be stalked as you would a wild deer and shot for meat. Some of the Negroes have a way of smoking and salting the flesh to preserve it but I find it as palatable as the sole of an old shoe. I'm afraid," he confessed, "we Raleighs have no way with the land. The plantation will sustain us but if we look for money it must be beyond these acres."

"I made five thousand dollars, minus a bonus and double wages for

[452]

the crew, with the Cuban expedition." Brian made the statement a suggestion.

His father shook his head. "The money we could use but it is too dangerous. You are all I have. I don't want to lose you. No. We will do with the *Caroline's* carrying what small cargo there is from here to there until the steamships run you from the sea. I am beginning to think it was a mistake not to put what money we have in with Richard. And, if you are going to make your life the sea, my lad, you ought to do some studying for a master's ticket in steam. In a few years the *Caroline* will be a museum piece and you'll be on the beach with the other hard-shell mariners."

"Then I'll take the beach." Brian was sincere. "You, Uncle David and I. We'll learn to eat beans and rice with fish the way the other conchs do. You know," his face lighted, "there isn't anything I really want I don't have—a ship still seaworthy, a home to come back to at the end of a voyage, rum to drink, a pipe to smoke. What would I do with a lot of money, anyhow?"

Cameron laughed. "Then you'd better marry an island girl who knows of no life beyond the Bahamas and will not be at you for fine clothes, jewelry, trips to the mainland, New York and Boston." His amusement faded and Brian suspected he was thinking of Charlotte-Anne and Carol-Louise in Italy. "Get a solid marriage, lad."

David, who had been sitting quietly, staring at the sea, looked up at father and son. He spoke with sober reflection.

"I have been listening to you and it makes me think. I will be seventy-seven on my birthday next month. That is a long time to live. It occurs to me this is the way the old families of these islands have decayed. That is an unpleasant word, isn't it?" His mouth twitched with a suggestion of a smile. "Perhaps I don't mean just that. Eroded is better. Strayed is closer. Little by little the original purpose of settling here has been lost. The drive which brought their forebears to the Bahamas is gone. I remember Ronald Cameron. He was determined this stubborn soil should yield to his will. It would grow cotton. He fought it to the very end of his life, never admitting defeat although it faced him daily. He brought blooded stock here, carriage horses, hunters, even a racing strain. He even tried, so Robert Bruce once told me, to transport the bricks of his home in Carolina here. Now what has happened? Those who succeeded him turn their eyes in a different direction. A war brings a wave of prosperity which recedes as does that continuous wear upon the beach. A revolution in Cuba offers another opportunity for gain. I think this is the tragedy of these islands. They are too subject to the influences beyond their shores. Here, on Exuma, even the family name of Cameron is

[453]

lost. Now it is Raleigh. I don't say it is bad." His eyes brightened. "But, it is different and not at all what Ronald Cameron had in mind. The only Cameron left is Richard, in Charleston, and he is fifty or thereabouts. When he goes the name of Cameron goes with him."

"You are a depressing old gaffer today, David." Cameron made light of the somber musings. "I think we ought to have a drink to Brian's return. Raleigh isn't such a bad name, after all."

"I didn't mean to suggest it was." David shook his head. "I was allowing my thoughts to wander and speculating on what Ronald Cameron would think if he could return and stand on this porch with us today. Here he built in defiance of a new order on the mainland in which he did not believe. But," he paused, "by all means let us have a drink. The same thing has happened throughout the islands to the original families. Those of the stock who remain bear little resemblance to the old. The sea would have been as foreign to Ronald Cameron for the purpose of taking a living as the land is to you and Brian. In a way it is all a little sad. But," he stamped his cane, which was a way of calling a servant, "enough of these moody notions. They are a certain indication of a dotage."

Marta concealed her disappointment as she and Brian rummaged through the musty, dirt-laden, cobwebbed disorder of the large tack room at the stables. Saddles, bridles, reins, harness, were brittle with age and disuse. No hand had soaped or worked the leather for years. The sidesaddles which, Brian thought, his grandmother, Bahama, might have used broke apart under the pressure of his hands. The stables themselves were falling into ruins. It was curious but he had never noticed this before. In the corral were a few workhorses. The animals with spirit must have been sold long ago or they ran away to roam the wild length of the island.

"I'm sorry." Brian was sincere. "I guess none of us, my father or I, really thought much about horses when he said you could ride. To tell the truth I don't think I was ever on a horse except one of those old plugs out here." He examined some of the once fine equipment—a variety of bits, checkreins, silver-headed crops—hanging from a rack. "They must have had some fine animals here but it was many years ago."

"It is not important, Captain." She appeared surprisingly mature in the long, divided skirt, blouse, short jacket, the tricorn hat with its plume of curling white. "Please do not distress yourself. It was an idea and of no importance. I rode often at home with my father. He is a fine horseman."

They walked back toward the manor, past where the old slave quarters had stood, and halted a moment by the little yard of graves. Marta read the inscriptions on the stones.

"Caroline Cameron Cadiz?" She looked up questioningly at him. "Cadiz. It is a Spanish word."

"She was my great-grandmother."

"The one who married a pirate. He was Spanish, then?"

"I don't know."

This obviously surprised her. Brian could see it in her eyes. She attached great importance to family.

"It is strange."

"What?"

"That you shouldn't know whether your great-grandfather was Spanish, English, Indian."

"I suppose so. I never thought much about it. Cadiz." He mused upon the word. "By the time I came along there were mostly Raleighs around."

They moved on, walking leisurely, while she asked many questions about the island, the plantation which once occupied the land, the slaves and what had become of them. Brian was ashamed of his ignorance. He had never bothered to find out. Uncle David probably knew the entire story. He would have him tell it sometime.

On the porch Señora de la Torre sat working an intricate pattern of delicate lace, the bright hook flashing in and out with the fragile thread. A little apart, Cameron and David were solemnly studying a chessboard. Just inside the doorway, rigid on a straight-backed chair, the Señora's maid waited. Her passive features did not show the indignation she felt. For the Señora to be this way, in the company of men and her husband not present, outraged her sense of propriety. It was a thing which could not have happened at home so far away across the ocean.

In her own, quiet fashion, Señora de la Torre had thought much the same thing. It had taken a certain amount of courage to leave the privacy of her rooms and come out here where it was so fresh and pleasantly fragrant in the sunlight. The breeze was gentle and the surf's cascading a soothing melody. She was adapting herself to the informality which her hosts seemed to take for granted. She wondered, enviously, if all Englishwomen enjoyed so much liberty in the company of men. It must be so, for Señor Raleigh and Señor Heath had expressed no surprise when she joined them on the porch. They seemed pleased even though they could speak nothing more in Spanish than the courtesy of greeting. It was a strange but not unpleasant experience to be so unconventional.

When Marta and Brian came to the steps the Señora looked up with surprise. It was only after a thorough searching of her conscience and a determination to adapt herself to new ways that she had agreed to

[455]

Marta's riding, unattended, in the young captain's company. She asked what had happened.

Marta merely shrugged and replied in a few words which were without emphasis or a note of regret.

"I could take you out in a boat if you'd like to go." Brian felt he had to offer an alternative.

Marta put a question to her mother. The Señora hesitated. Then she lifted her shoulders with a charming gesture of resignation. It was as though she had said: What can I do in this strange land but make myself agreeable to what everyone else finds proper and not at all unusual? Her reply to the girl was lengthy and, from her expression, humorous.

Marta laughed and turned to Brian. "My mother says it is difficult to accustom herself to the easy association here but she is trying to learn. In Cuba a girl would not go anywhere with a man alone. She would not even speak unless in the presence of her duenna. My mother says if it is the custom of the country for a girl to go in a boat with a man she will not offend against it."

"I assure you, señorita," David looked up from the chessboard with a smile although he seemed not to have been listening, "it is considered quite proper among the barbarians."

Marta translated this for her mother who laughed with pleasure at the description. She nodded her head and spoke a few words.

"My mother," she said to Brian, "says only to be careful of the water. I had already explained to her you were so old it would be quite safe for me to be alone with you." She glanced at her riding habit but her head cocked a little to one side as she looked up at Brian with suppressed laughter. "I will go and change into something more suitable. *Permiso, señor? Un momentito.*"

The three weeks passed all too quickly for Brian, his father and David. They had become accustomed to the sound of bright, young laughter in the house; the pleasure of dining with ladies at the table in the evening. A mutual respect and admiration had developed to which language was no barrier. Young Marta had an agile mind. She translated easily; interpolating, they all suspected, comments of her own. Her mother talked without the hesitation and self-consciousness speaking through a second person frequently induces. The Señora appeared completely relaxed in this atmosphere of spontaneous and wholehearted hospitality; the freedom of exchange of thoughts and opinions between a woman and men she had never believed possible. Many times it occurred to her she would find the readjustment difficult when she returned to Cuba. She was pleased and even a little flattered by the obvious but unspoken tribute to her beauty as she saw it in the eyes of the gentlemen; the small acts of gallantry, the compliments not always voiced but there.

At Brian's urging, David Heath told what he knew and remembered of the plantation's early days. Of Ronald Cameron's formidable task in transporting his family, some two hundred slaves, household goods and livestock across the sea and to an unknown spot on an unfamiliar island.

The Señora was all but incredulous with wonder over so bold an act, for she had never known anything but an established order and security. She listened attentively to every word and they frequently sat long over the meal and said good night with reluctance.

As for Marta, everything on Exuma was a delight. She no longer asked for permission to accompany Brian in the small boat carrying a single light sail. Through the water glass she never tired of watching the swarming rainbow of color as the fish of every shape and marking played and fed in the coral depths. Her skin, face and hands darkened with exposure to the sun but she did not seem to mind. At home her complexion had been as carefully tended as a rare flower. They sailed the little skiff in and out of the coves and stood on the beach in the late afternoons as the Negroes hauled the long seine for the fish which would be on the table or in the smoking racks that night.

"I do not think," she had confided once to Brian, "I will ever again be quite as happy at home as I was. I will always think of this freedom."

"I will miss you." He said it simply.

The day for their departure for Nassau was at hand. Brian would take them there in the *Caroline;* see to it they were comfortably settled and with proper servants. Then he would try and find some sort of cargo for the mainland and put into Charleston for a talk with Richard.

They all walked down to the landing dock where a boat waited. The Señora spoke with quiet sincerity to her daughter.

"My mother says she does not have the words to thank you for the courtesy you have shown us. She leaves with regret but with the deep pleasure of having known you. She says," her voice grew a trifle husky, "there is a small tear in her heart." Her smile embraced them. "It sounds better in Spanish. There is also one in mine. So, we do not say good-bye but only until we meet again. For a little while." She regarded them, her eyes filled with unmistakable and unashamed emotion. "For me, I would like to cry and I do what I am not supposed to but will." She stretched to the tips of her toes and kissed David Heath and Cameron Raleigh on their cheeks. *"Tio* David. *Tio* Cameron. I call you my uncles which makes the demonstration proper." She glanced at Brian. "Captain Raleigh is too young to be my uncle and too old to kiss for any other reason."

[457]

Cameron and David stood on the pier until the *Caroline* made sail and moved out toward the open sea. Then they turned and went slowly up the hill.

"This damned slope grows steeper and longer as the years mount." David spoke crossly.

"I will miss them also." Cameron understood why David was short of temper. "It has been both a pleasant and unhappy experience, for they made me think often of Charlotte-Anne and Carol-Louise and how fine it would be to have them home. Even with Carol-Louise's Italian count. I wonder why I could not make her happy?"

"Because Charlotte-Anne was a beautiful, spoiled and selfish girl and grew into a beautiful, spoiled and selfish woman. It is nothing you could help."

They reached the porch and David thumped for a servant with his cane. He ordered rum, water and limes. When the tray was brought they helped themselves and with drinks in hand sat staring blankly at the vacant sea.

Westward-bound out of Nassau with a small cargo of sponges and sisal consigned to a merchant in Savannah, Brian watched as a steamer came up and passed the schooner a couple of leagues away. To his mind she was an ugly thing with a long train of black smoke trailing behind and lying upon the water. But there was no denying she was fast and independent of the caprices of the wind. He thought of his father's suggestion that he study for a ticket in steam and mentally shook his head. He had no feeling for the far places to which such a vessel could take him. The islands were his home. He set his eyes on no distant shores beyond them. The *Caroline* would make a living. He listened as a member of the crew sang over his work. He was splicing a line and his voice had a lilting quality of freedom. Three weeks ashore with their families in the cabins on Exuma had been enough. Now they were all happy to be at sea again.

In Nassau he had done everything possible to see the de la Torres settled comfortably in the pleasantly situated house on the hill. He had left them with honest regret. No. It was more than that. For the first time he felt a loneliness. Impatiently, he put the idea aside. What matter that he could still hear the sound of her voice and see the mobile expression on her face, the dancing light in her eyes which were continually filled with excitement? The girl was a child. Thirteen. In five or six years, perhaps. But who could look so far ahead? The rebellion in Cuba would be crushed or succeed. In either event, unless de la Torre was deeply involved and the revolutionaries completely routed he would send for his family and they would return to their home. Save for this interlude, when he put into New Providence, he would probably never see any of them again.

He stared back at the faintly creaming wake and thought he had been exceptionally foolish to shut himself off from the Cuban trade for the sake of a few thousand dollars. The coffee, hides and tobacco found a ready market. Virginia had pressed for a high duty on the tobacco which she felt competed with her own bright crop. But, this was not really true. The Virginia product was unsuitable for the making of fine cigars which were more and more in demand. Cuban refugees, in the town of Tampa, on Florida's west coast, had set up many small businesses employing four or five men who turned the fine Havana tobacco into handmade cigars of rare quality. The *Caroline* might have had a share in this trade if he had not felt the reckless call to go adventuring. Well, he thought, a man was entitled to a mistake or two. He had been lucky to escape from this one with his life. He turned and stared up at the great spread of canvas and, as always, was stirred by the beauty. Let sail become obsolete. Everything in the world did not have to be practical. There was still room for grace.

He felt the wind. It came steadily from the southwest. The month was November. In the Caribbean and the Gulf of Mexico the seasonal hurricanes were mysteriously brewing. They could be storms of terrible fury which had struck at the Bahamas with devastating force many times, almost leveling Nassau one year. He did not like to be in these waters at this time of year. But the ship must be worked. If there was a cargo to be picked up in one of the Southern ports for delivery to New York or Boston he would have to take it even though the cold, to which they were completely unaccustomed, numbed and frightened his crew. He knew they secretly dreaded what seemed to them to be the arctic waters. But they would go and without complaint, for they were good men and devoted to him.

His thoughts turned back to Exuma and he wondered just what Cameron Raleigh's financial situation was. It seemed impossible they could have spent the tremendous sums made during the War Between the States. Yet, others had and they now drifted aimlessly through the islands. He knew extensive repairs had been made to the house which was far too large and impractical for the three of them. Some obscure sense of obligation and loyalty to Ronald Cameron made his father keep it up. Considerable sums must have been paid out in an effort to restore the plantation acres. Labor was hard to get and expensive. These were things he and his father should have discussed.

Cameron rarely spoke of his wife and Brian's mother. This time, though, there had been a letter which Cameron passed to his son without comment. It was brief but carried an unmistakable suggestion for an increase in the allowance Raleigh had been sending over the years. It seemed that Carol-Louise's husband, Count Giapanni, was of ancient but impoverished nobility. It took a great deal of money to maintain the palace in Florence. There were expenses of entertainment to their station. Cam had said nothing as Brian read the letter and handed it back. It was strange, he reflected, but he felt no affection for his mother and only a mild curiosity about Carol-Louise. He thought if he were his father he would tell them both to come home, bring along their Italian count and cut off the steady drain of money which their residence abroad siphoned away. He wondered, with an inward grin, what the count would do on Exuma. The fanciful notion occurred to him he could take the *Caroline* and sail her to Italy and see for himself how his mother and sister lived. The schooner was built to go anywhere. Columbus had made the voyage in far less than he had beneath his feet. He laughed out loud. Countess Carol-Louise Giapanni in her palace. He wondered what a palace was like. Marble halls? Golden staircases? Servants in medieval livery?

Big Washer interrupted the ridiculous musings. "De glass she fahl sum, Cap'n, suh."

Brian nodded. The sky was all but cloudless save far to the southwest where long, ragged streamers of black cloud lay upon the horizon. He knew well enough the Negro did not have to consult the barometer to bring him this information. They had both been at sea for so long they were acutely sensitive to a change of pressure in the weather.

"If the wind holds steady, Wash, we'll be off Wassaw Sound at daybreak and then upriver to Savannah."

"Hit's goin' t' hol', suh." Washer laughed. "Dat ahl Ah ask. Foah hit to hol' en not kick up." He touched his finger to forehead. It was his own form of salute.

Brian watched the Negro as he went forward. There was between them a warm, unvoiced affection which grew stronger with the years. He knew the man had taken the name of Cameron. Washer Cameron. He had an idea Washer must be a corrupted form of Washington.

He checked the course with the Negro, Josh, who was at the helm and then went to his cabin. In it, he thought, lingered the faint presence of Señora de la Torre and Marta. Marta. He grew angry with himself. Stop being a damn fool. She's a youngster, a schoolgirl, and you are an idiot to imagine her to be anything else. Four . . . five . . . six years from now. But, who could predict where any of them would be then?

❧ XXVIII ❧

THREE YEARS had passed since Brian had been in Charleston and seen Richard Cameron. They sat now over coffee and brandy in the dining room of Richard's home and discussed what had become a critical situation in Cuba.

It was the year of the great panic of 1873. Nineteen members of the New York Stock Exchange had gone into bankruptcy and a few days later the Exchange itself was closed. More than five thousand businesses failed and a pall of gloom and uncertainty shrouded the entire country.

Everywhere there was unrest. Marines had been sent to Panama to protect the lives of American citizens in the revolution there but in Cuba an event occurred which brought angry protests from Washington.

A week earlier a Spanish gunboat, the *Tornado,* had intercepted an American ship, the *Virginius,* carrying arms to the insurgent forces on the island. The captain and fifty-three members of the crew had been summarily tried in Havana, convicted and put against a wall and shot. Throughout the United States and in Congress there were angry demands for punitive action against Spain and it seemed as though the two countries stood in confrontation for a war for which neither was prepared. The South was still in the wracking process of readjustment. Economically it was completely dependent upon the North. It had no industry. The once-large plantations were meagerly worked. There was constant friction between the liberated Negroes and the poor whites. Spain was barely recovering from the Carlist War. No one wanted a war although the demagogues shouted militantly.

Richard sipped his brandy and stared moodily out of the window. To Brian he seemed to have aged far beyond his fifty-two or -three years.

"They'll find some way of getting us into it." Richard was brooding on the affair of the *Virginius.* "I wouldn't be a bit surprised if the Cuban rebels themselves didn't furnish the information to the Spanish authorities that the ship carried guns simply to provoke the incident."

"It's a little more than an incident. A captain and fifty-three men executed. The ship with her passengers being held. She was flying the American flag. It's hard to see how we can ignore it."

"And," Richard was angry, "she's my ship, damn it. Or at least I own most of her. Oh, I suppose we will be compensated. It will be a lot cheaper for Spain than going to war. Just the same, sooner or later we will be drawn into this thing. The Government doesn't give a hoot about the Cubans' independence for all the lofty talk you hear. But, and mark this, it doesn't like Spain so close to its shores. Some excuse will be trumped up to pull us in. You were lucky, my lad, to get away with your excursion as you did. I'm surprised they didn't shoot you outright."

Brian could not conceal his astonishment, for he had said nothing about the Cuban affair.

"How did you know about that?"

Richard chuckled. "I have sources of information. Actually, Henri de Tourville and I correspond. It was he who wrote me after your escape."

"His name was part of the information they wanted from me. His and Sebastian de la Torre's in Havana. Otherwise I would have been shot or left to rot away in prison."

Richard refilled his brandy glass. "Do you know, I have never had any fun, no excitement or adventure in my life? Business. I was suckled and weaned on it. Your side of the family, the Raleighs, seem to have had the best of it all. I suppose it goes way back to your great-grandmother and the fellow she married, Cadiz. My father told me about him. The buccaneer strain must run in your veins. How old are you now?"

"Twenty-eight."

"Time you were married." Richard grunted. "Or, maybe not. What's happened to your mother and sister?"

"They are still in Italy. I don't expect they'll ever come back."

"Your father's a fool to keep supporting them."

"Maybe by now," Brian smiled, "he'd rather have them in Italy than on Exuma."

"Is old David Heath still around?"

"Uncle David would resent the *old*. Yes. He and Father are company for each other although there is considerable difference in their ages. I suspect David intends to remain on Exuma."

"Damn it!" Richard seemed intent upon expressing his dissatisfaction. "When I think back. All the fun I might have had as a young man. We had plenty of money. Father made a good thing with the firm. I should have gone to Europe, seen the life in Paris, Vienna, Rome; drunk champagne from a lady's slipper, kept a mistress or two. Instead, I stuck my nose into business and held it there. Then the war came along and ruined everything. Don't let it happen to you. I mean, have your fling while you can but don't expect to find it in Charleston. Here you dine and talk with ghosts."

"There isn't much chance of my getting involved in business. What with this panic in the North, the dislocation of the South, and steam taking over the seas, the *Caroline* barely makes enough to pay the crew. Once in a while we get a cargo. Other times we work the sponge beds. The plantation produces nothing of real value. Father has no kinship with the land and he can find no one to work it on shares. He tried sisal but it never amounted to much. Then he put a lot of money into citrus groves but the trees were attacked by the blue-gray flies and what they didn't ruin a hurricane flattened. So, the two thousand or so acres lie idle save for producing what we need and some fresh produce to be sold to the wholesalers in Nassau."

"Well," Richard pushed the brandy decanter in Brian's direction, "at least you're free to go where you will in that old schooner. How much longer do you think she'll last?"

Brian shook his head. "Forever, maybe."

"Still, you're lucky. Do you know what I have out of life at fifty-two or thereabouts? Nothing, young Brian. The plantation on the Ashley. Without slaves it is too expensive to operate. This town house in Charleston. A wife who has grown old with me and we no longer have much to say to each other. Not out of any difference, you understand. We have just worn out the topics of conversation. I know her so well I can predict her reaction to any given situation and I suspect she feels the same about me. In the evenings we read or play a two-handed game of cards. Nothing either of us can do will possibly surprise the other. Sometimes, I lie awake at night and wonder how it was I allowed life to bypass me. Why did I not once taste the full, rich flavor which other men enjoy? Tell me a little something of this de la Torre."

"I can't honestly say I know him very well." Brian was curious at Richard's interest. "He is, I suppose, typical of Cuba's aristocracy, the big landowners. He wants Cuba's independence not for the sake of Cuba but because it would suit his purpose. Out of the chaos a strong man will emerge. He may well be de la Torre. This may be unfair but it is the impression I gathered."

Richard lit a cigar. "I suspected as much. You know," he chuckled, "old Henri de Tourville, for all his courtly manner, is a rascal at heart. He pretends a disinterest in financial gain but always he schemes and plots. His mind is occupied with intrigue. Not on a petty scale, mind you. Cuba, to him, appears a fine, ripe plum. He eyes it with calculating cupidity. Can it be snatched from the Spanish tree and made off with safely? Excuse me a moment." He pushed back his chair and left the room.

Brian selected a Havana cigar from a box. They were rich, full-bodied and carefully made. He had lit it and taken the first draw when Richard returned. In his hand he carried a letter.

"This," he settled himself again at the table, "is de Tourville's last communication to me. I'll read only a part of it. What I skip concerns only some commercial ventures in which we are jointly interested." He glanced over the pages and then began to read.

" 'I am becoming seriously concerned over the situation of Sebastian de la Torre in Havana for I suspect he is under closer surveillance by the Spanish authorities than he imagines. As you know, I am deeply involved and financially committed with and to the revolutionary party. Sebastian is the only man of stature we have in Cuba. He is respected and trusted by the junta which directs the guerrilla warfare. Without him there is a likelihood of the entire affair degenerating into small skirmishes between the patriots and Spanish troops with nothing of any consequence accomplished. However, de la Torre free to move about as he pleases is one thing. De la Torre imprisoned is quite another. One cannot underestimate the Spanish temper. The authorities are quite capable of arresting him on any fanciful charge they care to name. I would like to have him out of Cuba before something of this nature occurs. It is possible he could exert a strong influence from a distance. This would be not quite as effective as having him in Cuba but certainly far better than having him erased from all participation. He is a man who is contemptuous of personal danger and scornful of the Spanish Viceroy but I believe I can convince him he will be of more value to the cause once he removes himself from the island. I know, from trusted sources, his movements are watched and reported. I do not trust his servants or even some of those who profess great loyalty to the cause and devotion to him. I do not think he will want to leave for he is a man who likes his hand upon the sword. However, I believe I can convince him such a move will be to the advantage of all. As you know, we are in continual communication with the insurgent forces. Intelligence is brought out of Cuba by the seemingly innocent fishermen and passed on to craft which come out from the Florida Keys or coast to meet them beyond the range of Spanish patrol boats. Although his home is watched, his movements traced, I think we could get him out and aboard one of the fishing boats. From this he would have to be transferred to a larger vessel and taken to a place of safety.' " Richard took a long swallow of brandy, draining his glass, before continuing. He did this deliberately, Brian suspected, for the sake of emphasis. "'I know,'" he read again, "'he is unhappy with the separation from his family and it occurred to me the Bahamas are ideally situated for continuing his work in directing the revolutionary forces within the island. He would not be as effective there, it is true. But as I said, a live de la Torre, even at a distance, is better than a dead one. I write you at this length in hope you may have some practical suggestion.'" Richard folded the letter carefully and placed it on the table.

Brian gazed at this distant cousin. Then he began to chuckle and this sound exploded into laughter. Richard Cameron managed to convey an expression of complete surprise over this inexplicable behavior.

"I don't suppose," Brian managed to regain his composure, "your practical suggestion would have anything to do with me or a schooner, the *Caroline?*"

Richard regarded him with the guileless eyes of a misunderstood child. Then they grew bright with suppressed humor. He traced a finger about the rim of the brandy glass.

"I imagine"—he put himself in the place of a completely disinterested party—"something of the sort was in Henri's mind."

"But not yours?" Brian pressed the question.

"Well . . ." Richard hesitated. "Quite frankly, I am intrigued by the possibilities of a free Cuba."

"You are," Brian answered without rancor, "a wide-eyed fraud."

"There is no reason to become unpleasant, my friend and relative. Have some more brandy. Try it with those nuts and raisins."

"I'll drink your brandy and smoke your cigars but I still say you and Henri de Tourville are cut from the same cloth. That goes for de la Torre, also."

Richard elected to ignore this. "Do you know anything of tobacco?"

"Only that it makes fine cigars."

"I mean the growing. As it is done in Cuba now, a monopoly of the Spanish Crown, it is a one- or two-man or family operation. It is raised on small plots with backbreaking labor and constant attention. But, a free Cuba with these little planters gathered into one huge combine. Then we begin to get somewhere. We have a system not unlike the one which prevailed on the South's great cotton plantations before the war: cheap labor, ideal growing conditions, a world-wide market. No country produces a leaf for cigars comparable to Havana."

Brian tossed a handful of shelled nut meats into his mouth and chewed contentedly. His gaze, with a tongue deliberately thrusting out his cheek, never left Richard.

"A little while ago," he said, "you were complaining about the dullness of your life. Why don't you take one of your steamers and deliver Señor de la Torre from the Spaniards? You are a conniving rogue of rare caliber, Cousin."

Richard managed an injured expression with some difficulty. He eyed Brian sadly and with the air of a man who has been unexpectedly disillusioned.

"It would seem to me," he said wistfully, "this is an adventure which would be attractive to such a young man as yourself. A steamer would be far too conspicuous, cruising about without any obvious purpose in the Straits of Florida. I would have to take a captain, ship's officers and a crew into my confidence. It is an unnecessary involvement. You would, of course, be well compensated."

"If I did it," Brian answered, "it would be for nothing. I owe Señor de la Torre a considerable debt."

"Henri mentioned that in his letter." Richard conveyed a delicate reluctance to discuss this phase. "I thought it more honorable to skip the passage."

"I don't like this idea of a transfer some place at sea." Brian was considering all the difficulties. "It is too uncertain and dangerous. Your Cuban friends may be good seamen but I know their fault. They have no regard for time. Eight o'clock tonight can also mean eight o'clock *mañana* or, if it isn't convenient, the day after. I had an example of this on my last trip. I'm damned if I want to risk going into Cuban waters for Señor de la Torre."

"It is nothing I am urging you to do, Brian. You understand that?"

"You're not leaving me much of an alternative either, are you?" He finished his brandy and gazed thoughtfully at the fine, gray-white ash on his cigar. "Tell me the truth, now. How involved are you in this whole business?"

"Well . . ." Richard was reluctant to make a full admission. "I have made some contributions. Certain promises have been given to me in return."

"In other words," Brian was short, "de la Torre, you, de Tourville and some others are promoting the revolution for personal advantage. The Cubans and Spaniards will do the fighting and you will harvest the rewards. The *peóns* will be exactly where they are now."

"But Cuba will be free."

"Richard," Brian shook his head, "you are a damned hypocrite; as engaging a rascal as is your friend de Tourville."

"I consider that something in the nature of a compliment." Richard was blithely unconcerned.

"Has it occurred to you the British Government may not be exactly enthusiastic over de la Torre's residence in Nassau?"

"He is a political refugee."

"He is a revolutionary, actively fomenting conflict between an established order and a dissident faction. Don't mistake me. I am grateful to him. He is a gentleman of charm; his wife a gracious lady and his daughter a girl of surpassing beauty."

"Ah!" Richard looked up foxily.

"What does 'ah!' mean?"

"Only that I detected a note in your voice, my lad."

"I am not your lad, Cousin. Anyhow, she is barely sixteen now."

"Seventeen is considered almost ideal for a young lady's marriage." Richard pulled at his nose thoughtfully. "I should think this all the more reason why you would be anxious to assist Señor de la Torre."

"I need no reason. I am in his debt." Brian was all but short of temper. He was being maneuvered.

"Well, then," Richard dismissed the subject, "I leave the matter to your decision. Not for the world would I press you."

"How long will it take to complete the arrangements?"

"A week. Ten days." Richard pretended to have lost interest in the discussion.

"I'll take him off Key West." Brian made up his mind. "It is as close as I want to get to Cuban waters. There is a settlement there. Once he is on the key I will go for him."

"Wouldn't it be less complicated if you just lie off the Keys for a few days? Your crew can loaf and fish and amuse themselves with whatever diversions the place has to offer. Then when de la Torre arrives you will be at hand."

"All right," Brian agreed. "But I'm still not sure about his reception in Nassau."

"Then take him to your home on the island with that outlandish name of Exuma. No one could possibly know of his presence there."

"You mean we will set up your revolutionary headquarters on the plantation?" Brian was amused at the bland effrontery. "I have underestimated you, Cousin. You are a fellow of cunning and few scruples. No wonder you have been so successful."

"Have some more brandy." Richard was airily polite. "Someone must be the patient cow waiting to be milked. Someone else fills the pail. It is not difficult to make the decision which one wants to be. One more brandy?"

"One more brandy, Cousin." Brian was having a little difficulty with his speech.

It was excellent brandy, a rare French cognac deceptively mild to the palate but heady in its aftereffects. Brian thought, I'd better be careful with him and this stuff or he'll have me going into Havana after de la Torre. He eyed this distant relative with quizzical amusement. He was not at all what he seemed to be; the stodgy man of business and sober affairs, going about his legitimate business in this city of leisurely pace and gentle manners.

"I think you must be some sort of throwback to old Juan Cadiz. But I guess it isn't possible since he was on the other side of the family. Just what are we to each other, Richard—besides a couple of damn fool conspirators scheming over a bottle and getting a bit tight, if you want my opinion?"

"I'm not certain." Richard leaned across the table. "Your great-grandmother, on the maternal side, was my father's sister. We're some sort of cousins, I suppose. In any event, I find you a most agreeable companion."

He rose unsteadily and went to a cabinet, took a fresh bottle of brandy and a screwpiece for the cork. With a great show of formality he presented them to Brian.

"You will spend the night with me, of course. My wife is in the country. In an earlier day we might have sent for a couple of mulatto wenches to keep us company. It is too bad all that had to end."

Brian stood up. He bowed and had to steady himself to keep from pitching forward. He eyed Richard with an owlish stare.

"I shall be honored, Cousin, despite the fact I am certain you are an unprincipled scoundrel."

"Good!" Richard put an arm across Brian's shoulder. "It is not difficult to become a rogue. There may be a fine future for you in this Cuban business. As for me, fortified by the brandy, I am tempted to go to the Keys with you and see this de la Torre myself. By Harry, I have led a dull life!"

They made their way unsteadily up the staircase. Brian clung to the bottle, screw and glass. Richard clutched the crystal decanter to him as if it were a babe. In the long, dim gallery they parted with mutual regard and kinship.

The years of intrigue had developed in Sebastian de la Torre a feral instinct for danger. He scented it as does an animal. The plots and counterplots, their success and failure, had sharpened his senses. Sitting in his library now he was aware of a faint stirring of warning. It was nothing to which he could put a name but it persisted. He canted his head as though to listen to a sound within the silence.

[468]

He had finished writing a long letter to his wife. Now he carefully tore it to pieces. For, if things went well he would see her and Marta before any of the uncertain mail service out of Havana to the Bahamas could reach them. That was the key to his uneasiness. If everything went well. To have it go well he must depend entirely upon other persons. He left his chair and walked to the windows over which the heavy brocade draperies had been drawn. Pulling one aside he peered out. There was nothing to be seen save the distant reflection of the gatepost lamps. He turned, recrossed the room and locked the door; something he had never thought necessary to do before.

Havana bubbled quietly as a caldron above a slow fire. It simmered, needing only additional heat to cause it to boil over. In the city itself there had been no violence. The fighting, some five years old now, had been confined to Camaguey and Oriente provinces. The rebels did not have the force to push upon Havana, and the Spanish authorities lacked the troops and skill to rout them in the countryside. It was a stalemate in which men who had small reason to hate each other died in lonely ambush and small villages.

De la Torre well knew he was suspect. Yet, he was a man of wealth, of distinguished lineage, the authorities dared not openly touch his person without absolute proof. Only the week before he had taken supper with the Viceroy. It had been a most pleasant evening at which only he and the Crown's representative had been present.

The Viceroy was a slender, almost fragile-appearing man. But this was deceptive. Beneath his courtesy and gentle suavity he was as cold and deadly as a Toledo blade. They had sat over coffee and cigars, the Viceroy leaning back in his chair against a cushion bearing a coat of arms worked in gold thread.

"You are causing me a great deal of trouble, Señor de la Torre. I know you are supplying money for the purchase of rifles and equipment abroad. I know, also, you are the one, strong voice which is listened to in the juntas formed in New Orleans, New York and Boston. Yet," he mused, "I can find no conclusive evidence which would give me cause to have you imprisoned and executed. Why do you do this?" He was honestly curious. "You have wealth, position. What do you gain by inciting rebellion? Should the impossible happen and the insurgents gain an overwhelming victory, forcing Spanish rule from the island, do you believe you can hold them in check? You will be confronted by the wildest anarchy, jeopardizing your extensive estates, your fortune, and even your life. It is one thing to promote and encourage rebellion and quite another to control it."

"Admitting nothing, Excellency," de la Torre replied, "but for the sake of conversation accepting your opinions, there will be no anarchy. The Cuban people will be permitted to nibble at the fruit of self-rule; elections will be held, a *presidente* installed—but he would be my *presidente* and not the Crown's Viceroy. There is the difference."

They had parted with mutual expressions of courtesy but de la Torre did not make the mistake of underestimating his man. On the drive back to his home he put himself in the Viceroy's place and thought, I would not bother with the formalities. The price of an assassin in Havana is not high. Were I the Viceroy I would rid myself of Sebastian de la Torre expeditiously. Then I would promptly discover his murderer, publicly announce his capture, arrest and confession. Then I would execute him quickly. The Viceroy was no simpleton and this, de la Torre was certain, must also have occurred to him.

Despite the danger, he was leaving Cuba reluctantly and only at the insistent urgings of his friend Henri de Tourville. So many factions were involved here and they needed a strong hand to keep them from flying apart in useless directions. Every leader of a guerrilla band, numbering fifteen or twenty men, already imagined himself a general and perhaps, upon the day of liberation, Cuba's President. They would be at each other's throats the moment the Spanish grip was loosened. Then it would be safer for him to return and put things in order. In the meanwhile he must place some trust in his lieutenants and the few sincere, patriotic men who honestly gave themselves to the cause and naïvely believed in *Cuba Libre!*

He went to a cabinet and took a bottle of the rare, dry, straw-colored sherry. The manzanilla. Filling a glass he took a swallow and then carried the bottle back to his desk and lit a cigar. He looked at his watch. It was a few minutes past the hour of ten. All arrangements had been made. At exactly ten-thirty a coach; not his own, which was conspicuous for its fine craftsmanship, elaborate fittings and the family crest upon its doors. It would be a vehicle of no particular identification. There were a hundred of them in the city. He would leave the house as he had many times before, exciting no interest on the part of the servants, who were accustomed to the master's going to his club or a gambling establishment at this hour.

In the coach there would be a rough outfit of clothing commonly worn by the *pescadors*—sandals, loose trousers, blouse and knitted cap. On the beach he would be indistinguishable from any of the other fishermen who put to sea in their boats before dawn. He would change in the coach and leave it at a designated point along the shore where a skiff would be waiting to take him out to a larger craft. They would join the fishing fleet as it assembled and moved out of the harbor. As it scattered, for each fisherman had his favorite grounds, it would be a simple matter to set a course for the Florida Keys where a ship would take him to the Bahamas. He could find no defect in the arrangements. The coachman was a member of the zealous band of patriots who worked within the city. He knew the plan, would provide the change of clothing and drive to the appointed spot on the beach.

At twenty minutes past ten de la Torre rang for a servant, who then brought him a light cape, gold-headed stick of ebony and his hat. De la Torre studied his reflection in the mirror and nodded his satisfaction. When the servant asked if he wished the coach to be brought to the driveway he shook his head and replied he had already ordered it to be there at this hour.

He strolled without haste over the patio, across the *portal,* down a hallway to where a second servant stood ready to open the outside door. At the wall the old watchman arose from his stool, bowed and pushed aside the heavy gate. Perhaps he wondered why the *patrón* was not using his own coach but then, it was possible he intended to visit a lady and did not want it to be seen standing outside her house. The ancient cackled to himself at the idea.

De la Torre entered the vehicle, closed the door after himself, a whip touched the horses lightly and they rolled swiftly away. No words had been exchanged between the driver and himself. None was necessary. He didn't even recognize the man. There were many who worked secretly for the cause and were available for any task.

He changed as quickly as he could within the cramped space, pushing his clothing into a corner of the seat as it was removed. The fine cane lay at his feet. It was a shame to leave it behind but a fisherman with a gold-headed stick of ebony would appear exceptionally ridiculous.

When he was in the crude habit of the *pescador* he fumbled with his other coat until he found a cigar case and matches. Then, after lighting one, he put it in his trousers pocket along with a thick wallet of American and English bank notes.

A soft, moist wind drifted from the sea through the window. He felt its soothing caress on his face. His emotions were in conflict. It would be a relief to get away from the endless detail of the revolutionary movement; the constant strain of knowing his actions were suspect. Yet, he did not place too much faith in those he left behind to carry on the work. There were petty jealousies, endless bickerings, small conniving for authority at the junta's council table. Wounded sensibilities to be placated. He was worn, sometimes, to a speechless anger by these unimportant conflicts. Vanity. *Cuba Libre! Viva la Independencia!* But

[471]

each, as he spoke these slogans, was saying to himself: Let me be the *jefe, El Presidente,* for I am well fitted for the job. This was in all their minds, he was sure. He could only hope that during his absence they would have wisdom enough to settle these preposterous differences without disrupting everything he had worked for. It was a risk. Factions within factions might develop. But, he sighed, it must be taken. He could not rid himself of the scent of peril. It was carried by the wind, in the tone of strange voices, drifting through his own home, sitting with him at the table, watching at his door in the night. He believed this to be so and could no longer disregard his intuition.

He leaned forward, staring out of the window. They were in an isolated section. The road was unpaved, little more than tracks through the palm grove leading to the beach. The coach moved slower now as the team dragged it through the clinging sand. Finally, it came to a halt. He heard the soft thud of the driver's feet as they landed when he dropped lightly down from the box. The door was opened and de la Torre stepped out.

There was no sound save the washing of the sea. In the darkness his eyes found nothing save the dim outline of the shore and the phosphorescent glow of the light breakers as they raced to the strand.

"*Donde está la barca?*"

"*Allá, señor.*" He pointed a finger down the beach. "*A tiro piedra.*" A stone's throw. He put out his hand. "*Bien suerte, señor.*"

"*Gracias, joven. Cuba Libre!*" De la Torre turned to walk to where the man had indicated the boat waited.

The knife went in almost to the hilt below the left shoulder. De la Torre uttered one strangled cry before he pitched forward on his face. He coughed once, an involuntary spasm, and the crimson hemorrhage spilled from his mouth.

For a moment the driver stood looking down at the inert body and then, without real reason, he kicked it savagely in the ribs.

It had been a job well and swiftly done from the time the coach had been halted on the way to the de la Torre house, the driver pulled down and his throat cut. *El Capitán* would be pleased, and perhaps his name would go in a report to the Viceroy himself. There might be a promotion to a soldier of the first class with an easy post and a reward. He started away and then returned. From the pockets of the dead man he removed the thick wallet and the case of fine leather holding cigars. What would a dead man do with money and such cigars? Why should he leave them for someone else to take?

Climbing back atop the coach he paused long enough to light a cigar and then humming softly, slapped at the horses with the reins and drove off toward the downtown section of the city. He would leave it in a side street and, since he was not in uniform this night, there would be no one to question where he went and what he did. There were lights, girls, music and rum for a man with money in his pocket.

At the dock in Nassau, Brian took one of the public carriages for hire and instructed the driver to take him to the house Señora de la Torre had leased on the hill. He dreaded what lay before him. In fact, he had been putting it off since midmorning when the *Caroline* had sailed into the harbor.

For two weeks the schooner had been anchored at Key West while he waited patiently for the boat bringing de la Torre. The first week he had accepted as normal, despite Richard's assurance of a rigid timetable. These things, a rendezvous with the Cubans, never went off on schedule. He marveled any of the revolutionaries had survived the haphazard planning and indifference to time. By the middle of the week, though, his annoyance began to shade into concern. He kept scanning the sea for the sight of a boat.

The crew was having an unexpected holiday. They lazed about, fishing, swimming, gathering buckets of the blue crabs for a gumbo they made with tomatoes, peppers and rice. They discovered friends among the inhabitants of the small colony, many of whom were Bahamians who had migrated from their native islands. They gorged themselves on turtle steak, found rum to drink and Negro girls to frolic with.

Brian, on the other hand, was restless. He paced the deck, finding it impossible to relax. He tried reading and discovered he couldn't concentrate. Hs could not rid himself of the idea that if anything had gone wrong it was partly his fault. He owed his life to de la Torre. In payment of the debt he could have risked going into Cuban waters after him. There were miles of uninhabited coastline where a meeting might have been arranged. In any event, he should have tried instead of idling here in the Keys.

On a Sunday morning of the second week a worn fishing boat, its sail a patchwork of dirty gray, the hull badly in need of paint, came alongside the *Caroline* and a man hailed them.

"Speak you Spanish, mister?" The accent was heavy.

Brian shook his head. *"Poco. Muy poco."*

The fisherman indicated the schooner's ladder, pulling his craft to it with a boathook while another man threw a line to one of the schooner's crew.

"Permiso?"

"Sure," Brian answered. *"Venga."*

The spokesman came up the ladder. He stood for a moment regarding Brian. He was young, twenty or thereabouts.

"*El Capitán?*" he asked.

"*Sí.*"

The newcomer hesitated. "No wait more." The English was halting. "Señor de la Torre *muerto. Comprende?* De-ed."

Brian accepted the statement numbly. For, with all his dedication to self-interest, de la Torre had been a gallant man.

"*Como?*" He asked the inevitable.

The fisherman made a cutting motion with one finger across his throat.

"Who? *Quien?*"

The youth shrugged. "*Quien sabe, Capitán. Un asesino. En la noche.*"

Yes, Brian thought, that was the way it would happen. An assassin in the night. The Spanish would not have risked public charges against such a prominent figure.

This, he thought unhappily, was what he must now tell Señora de la Torre. It could have been left to Henri de Tourville, who would certainly receive the news promptly. He would have written a letter of condolence, filled with expressions of sorrow and offering all assistance if she was in need in these foreign islands. Brian felt the obligation to do it himself.

He was admitted to the house by one of the Negro servants he had engaged when the estate was taken, gave his name and asked that the Señora be told of his presence. Waiting for her in the bright living room he stared out into the colorful garden and wondered miserably how such a thing as this was said.

"Brian!" The voice was lilting, filled with a happy surprise. "Forgive me. Captain Raleigh."

He turned quickly. Marta stood on the threshold. A Marta grown astonishingly mature and beautiful during these past three years. He had seen her six or seven times, calling whenever he put in at Nassau. But it hadn't occurred to him until now she was a woman, gracefully assured, aware but not vain of her beauty; confident of herself.

She came toward him, both hands outstretched in greeting, her face alight with unconcealed pleasure. Their fingers touched and he could feel the warmth flow through them like a current.

"I saw the *Caroline* from my window when she came in this morning and ever since then I've been wondering if you would find time to call. I'm so glad you did."

She released only one of his hands. Holding to the other she led him to a small settee, settled herself and drew him down beside her.

[474]

"You see how quickly I have become accustomed to the British ways! I call you by your first name but then correct myself, pretending it was a mistake. We sit here. No duenna, no waiting for my mother to be present. Telling you how glad I am to see you again, without shame or modesty. Are you pleased with me?"

"I've always been pleased with you even when you were a brat of thirteen."

"A brat? It is a word I do not know. They don't teach it in the convent school here." Her ignorance was innocently assumed but she glanced up slyly.

In her presence, aware of the beauty which had flowered so imperceptibly over the years until now it seemed to have bloomed within the space of a few months, he all but forgot the unpleasant nature of his errand. Marta, watching the brief play of expression on his face, was intuitively aware something was wrong. He felt her fingers tighten convulsively in his.

"My father?" She whispered the question.

"Yes, Marta."

The eyes, so filled with youth and excitement a moment ago, dimmed. He could actually see the luster fading and it was replaced by a sadness he would not have believed possible to express without words. He saw her lips tremble and then compress themselves with an effort. She was not going to cry. Not here. Not now.

"Before my mother comes. Tell me."

He took her hands in his. "I don't know much. I was waiting with the schooner at Key West to bring him to Nassau. They, he, had decided it was no longer safe for him in Havana. He was to come in a fishing boat. Everything was arranged. I waited a week over the time set and then the boat came. Her owner told me your father had been assassinated. It was done at night. That is all I know." How brutal the words sounded.

"I think we knew." She was trembling and he could barely hear the words. "At least, I believe my mother felt it would be this way when we left Cuba." She stood up, clinging to his hands. "I will spare you this, Brian. Go now, quickly, before my mother comes. Let me tell her. It will be better for us all." She led him to the door, hurrying his steps a little. "Will you come again tomorrow? I, we, will need you. Is it much to ask?"

"No. I will come."

They were at the door. She took his hand and pressed it to her lips. "For a little while."

She all but gave him a small shove and he was outside in the bright sunlight with the door closing behind him, the latch clicking with a metallic whisper.

✥ XXIX ✥

ON HER eighteenth birthday Marta Christina de la Torre married Brian Raleigh in the little Catholic chapel on the island of New Providence, town of Nassau, in the year 1875, and that which Ronald Cameron had begun some eighty-four years ago took new vigor from the union.

Standing with the Señora, David Heath rested heavily upon his cane. As he listened to the service his eyes clouded with memories which were more fantasies than real. In this young bride's lambent beauty he saw the face of another, well loved and called Bahama. He, in the strong pride of his youth, touched lips to hers as she lifted the delicate veil and turned the full radiance of her smile upon him. The mind, when it began to falter, played with marvelous delusion over a lifetime until it was almost impossible to separate that which was true from what was only imagined. Had there really been a Bahama and a boy named David?

Cameron Raleigh was also wandering through the maze of years past, waiting as Charlotte-Anne, in a cloud of white, came down the aisle on the arm of her father to join him at the altar. Charlotte-Anne with the tiny, husky catch in her voice, the liquid slurring of a word, the flirtatious gaiety of her laughter, the ecstatic sigh of pliant surrender to his pleading. All this contrived, acquired in infancy almost. Carefully nurtured as the proper conduct for a Charleston belle until all of the city's young ladies of family seemed to sound and behave alike. Where was this Charlotte-Anne of his youth? What had she found he had been unable to give her? How fared the daughter, Carol-Louise, he barely knew. They could pass each other on the street now with neither recognizing the other.

The Señora, standing between the two men, with the sadness in her eyes which had come to them two years ago when Marta gently told her of Sebastian's murder. She still wore the black of mourning, for her life had gone with that of her husband. Her soul was troubled although she had great respect and affection for the young Englishman who married her daughter this day. There was the matter of the Faith. It had been discussed at length with the *padre*. His reassurance that if the children of this joining were reared as of the true Chuch God would look kindly upon it had not completely satisfied her. Through the transparent veil she looked from the kneeling couple to the figure of the Virgin and asked for a blessing upon her daughter.

Then the ceremony was over. Marta lifted the white, sheer lace and kissed her husband. She went to her mother, raised the somber veiling and put cool lips to the ivory-tinted cheek which was as smooth and fragrant as a magnolia petal.

"Give me your blessing, Mother." She spoke in whispered Spanish. "For I am very happy on this day of my marriage."

"You have it and my love." The Señora made no move to drop the veil of sorrow. Her full, beautiful eyes lightened with affection as she reached for Brian's hand. "You are my son." The words, carefully rehearsed, were in English. "God's full grace be upon you." She turned and spoke in Spanish to Marta.

The girl smiled her happiness. "My mother," she spoke to them all, "asks me to say because of what has happened here today she will put away the black of *dolor*. She believes my father would be pleased with this marriage and her time of outward mourning is over."

The elderly priest walked with them to the chapel's door and, squinting a little against the hard sunlight, watched as the party entered two carriages and drove away toward the cool greenery of the hill. He had secretly hoped the young man would come to him for instruction and eventually accept the Sacrament as a true child of the Church before the marriage. There were not many of the Faith upon the island although priests had come with the early Spanish explorers. They had left but a small impression here and that had been all but erased by the lawlessness of an earlier day. Sometimes he thought of his small church as a bastion surrounded by the godless, atheists and Protestants. In his mind there was small distinction among them. When the wedding party had disappeared he turned away and reentered his chapel to ask God to make this a good and fruitful union.

Marta rode with Brian, clinging to his hand. Her mother, Cameron and David followed in the second carriage. She glanced back once and then pressed her face into Brian's shoulder.

"I will make a good wife to you, my husband."

Brian lifted her chin with his fingertips. There were tears in her eyes and he had never seen them there before. He, also, was still caught in the semimystical spell of the ceremony and the solemn words spoken. He bent to kiss her with infinite tenderness.

"I didn't really think it would be this way," he confessed. "I mean . . . well, I thought we would just be married. The priest would repeat a ritual as he must have done many times before. But, there is more to it than just words. It touches something deep inside of me I didn't know was there."

She linked her arm with his, pressing it close to her side, taking a comfort in his strength and presence. The light in her eyes was a dancing thing.

"I'm not sure how I feel but it is almost as though this has never happened to anyone before. I would like to be rid of this gown and run with you along the beach, barefooted and in the darkness. I would like to stand in the moonlight with your hand in mine listening to the sea. There is a song I would sing, a joy in my heart. It is all mixed up and makes no sense when I say it."

"It does to me." He was earnest. "I know what you mean."

She was silent for a moment. "My mother," she spoke slowly, "I think she will begin to live a little again now but I am not sure it will be here."

They had talked this over but never in the Señora's presence. Brian had wanted her to make her home with them on Exuma. In this his father had agreed completely. It was unthinkable she should continue to remain alone in Nassau. Of the estates in Cuba nothing remained. The authorities there had gathered alleged testimony of de la Torre's revolutionary activities. He was adjudged a traitor and by the Viceroy's decree all of his holdings were confiscated and declared property of the Crown. In a measure de la Torre had anticipated this and there were deposits in the Bank of London and in Paris. His widow was not penniless. Henri de Tourville had made the trip from New Orleans, after he learned of his old friend's murder, to offer all assistance. More important was the sealed envelope he brought with him, entrusted to his care a year or two before. It contained a will and information on the funds her husband had prudently sent out of Cuba. So deep had been the Señora's grief she was barely aware of what de Tourville explained, but she mechanically signed the papers which would enable her to live in moderately comfortable circumstances.

"I wish she would come home with us." Brian was sincere in his concern.

"I don't think she can be persuaded. She has talked, sometimes, of going back to Spain. She is not, as was my father, Cuban-born. Her family and many relatives are there but because of what happened in Havana she is afraid her presence might prove an embarrassment. I have pleaded with her but she says a mother-in-law, like a fish, is unbearable after three days. There is a Spanish proverb which is not quite so delicately put. Stinks is the word."

At the house an elaborate table had been prepared. There were wines, pastries, cold fowl, salads, hot dishes of seafood, stuffed crab and hot breads.

Brian regarded the lavish display with astonishment. "All of this for the five of us?" He inspected several of the dishes.

"It is the custom." Marta shook her head. "And really more for the servants than the guests. In Cuba the household makes a holiday for everyone out of a wedding."

Señora de la Torre and Marta excused themselves, asking the gentlemen to help themselves to the wines, rum or brandy. When they returned later both had changed; Marta from her bridal gown, and her mother had put aside the black of mourning. She seemed gayer now than they had ever known her and she took a glass of the Madeira in a toast to the newly married couple. Smilingly she spoke to Marta.

"My mother," she colored slightly, "says may there be many children, all as handsome as their parents."

"I'll drink to that." Cameron raised his glass.

After the luncheon they sat in the garden's cool shade, Marta on the arm of Brian's chair as though she did not want to be separated from him by even a few feet.

"David and I have been talking," Cameron said. "It has been a long time since I have been away from the islands. We are going to make a trip to Charleston and leave Exuma to you two for a while. David still has his house in the city. It is just possible we might cut quite a dash for a couple of old blades."

"You don't have to go because of us," Brian objected.

"I'm going for myself. It will be an agreeable change. We'll go home with you and pack some things. Then a couple of the boys can bring us to Nassau in the ketch."

Marta translated what was being said and her mother, nodding her understanding and agreement, replied at some length. Watching the expression of Marta's face, Brian understood what was being said.

"My mother," Marta turned to the men, "says she has decided to return to Spain for she feels alien here. With the steamships now she says the trip is not the long adventure it used to be. It is possible, she suggests, Brian and I may someday make the voyage and bring her grandchildren to see their grandmother."

"This leaves us pretty much alone, old lady." Brian put an arm about her waist.

"Suppose," Cameron interrupted, "we do this. I'll find out about the sailings since Mr. Cunard's service has become a little irregular. If there is a ship stopping at Charleston on its way to New York we will accompany the Señora that far and make arrangements for someone from Richard's firm to meet her in New York and see to it she has passage for Spain."

Marta repeated what had been said and her mother smiled her gratitude. Then she asked to be excused, for it was the time of the siesta and old habits were difficult to break. Marta, also, asked their pardon and accompanied her mother. She bent and kissed Brian.

"Everything is happening at once. I would like to talk with my mother for she goes so far away. We will join you in the evening."

When they were alone, Cameron packed a pipe. "You know," he spoke to Brian, "you're going to have to make a living on Exuma or take it from the waters somehow. The *Caroline* must be almost sixty years old. We both know sail is disappearing from the trade routes. Anyhow, with a wife you won't go a-roaming as you did before."

"I've been thinking about it." Brian glanced at David, who was nodding in his chair. "Nassau's population has increased and depends heavily upon the Out Islands for the produce and livestock for slaughtering. I'm wondering if some sort of a cooperative effort might be made and the *Caroline* put into a regular, interisland service. It would save the individual, independent sailings of all the small boats. The *Caroline* is still a tight ship for all her years and could do the job."

Cameron drew upon his pipe. "It's worth trying. But, you know these Out Island people. They like to manage their own affairs. The trip to Nassau is an event and not a chore. The fishermen go out for a week or more at a time, keeping their catch fresh and alive in the boat wells before taking them to market. I don't know whether you could get them together for what you have in mind. They are happier on the water than on the land."

"Well, it's worth trying. As you say, I must take a living from somewhere."

"It's going to depend a lot on the girl you've married. She is accustomed to wealth and all the luxuries and comforts it can bring. I'm not sure if she will adjust easily to life on Exuma for, as you know, it can be lonely."

"I'm not worried about Marta." Brian smiled. "I'm not really worried about anything. The Camerons and the Raleighs have been making out all right here for a lot of years."

"That reminds me of something I meant to tell you." Cameron lowered his voice for David was snoring softly, sound asleep in the deep, wicker chair. "I was looking through an old chest in the storeroom. Just rummaging around for want of something better to do. I found a chart which I think once belonged to Juan Cadiz. At least it has his name scrawled in one corner. But he has circled sections and marked them 'sponge beds.' I remember my mother once telling me about them. They held a prolific growth and old Juan worked them profitably for a while until a mysterious blight struck. I don't think they have been touched in all these years and they may be healthy again. Anyhow, it's worth investigating for there is a fine market on the mainland and abroad. I don't know how long I will be away." He dropped his voice still lower. "It was really David's idea. I think he only wants to see Charleston again, maybe for the last time. He is over eighty. He talks often about death these days; not as something feared but as a welcome release. He has asked to be buried on the plantation. It is something to which he is entitled. Of course I said yes. This is morbid conversation." He stood up. "Do you feel like taking a walk with me? I've had too much to eat and drink and will be asleep in my chair as is David if I sit much longer."

They strolled from the garden, in the warm, breeze-washed sunlight; down the easy slope of the hill, past the Royal Victoria Hotel which was boarded up since there were few monied visitors to the island these days.

"Someday," Cameron speculated, "the wealthy folk of the mainland are going to discover the beauty of these islands which lie at their doorstep. Think what it would mean to those who can afford it to get away from the Northern states during the bitter months of winter. They could become one of the great vacation places of the world but it won't happen in our lifetime. In the meanwhile I can think of no more pleasant place to live. So, don't be surprised if David and I are not too long in Charleston. It holds no attraction for me."

They walked the length of Bay Street and then to the overgrown and crumbling ruins of Fort Nassau, whose guns once commanded entrance to the settlement. The ancient cannon, rusting and corroded, were still in place. Brian tried to imagine what the island must have been like in its earliest days. Then the pirates used it as a gathering point for their sorties against merchant shipping. He had seen drawings and it seemed to have been a sleazy settlement strung along the tidal shore. Much progress had been made but it was difficult to imagine it ever being much more than it was today. This was understandable. There was little commercial vitality and nothing to foreshadow what was to come. Forty years or so would pass before events, again far beyond these placid shores, would strike the islands with the stunning force of a hurricane and, almost overnight, loose a torrent of wealth and violence upon them.

For the first two weeks after their return to Exuma, Brian and Marta did nothing but embrace life with the full ardor of their youth. To be married, to belong to each other, overwhelmed them. Each day was a new delight. He had expected her to be depressed by the departure of her mother but she accepted it without tears or any outward evidence of loss.

They took the ketch and sailed to visit the neighboring islands, Brian renewing old acquaintances and friendships and showing off his beautiful wife with obvious pride. They fished, swam naked in the clear waters of a hidden cove and stretched out on the white sand in hot sunshine. They made no attempt to direct the management of the household and their thoughts did not go beyond the day at hand and the love in each other's company.

Before he and David left for Charleston, Cameron found the old chart on which Juan Cadiz, almost fifty years ago, had marked off the sponge beds which had lain untouched until he began to work them with Negro crews. Brian and Marta, taking Washer and a boy helper, sailed to the locations and with the trident tool hooked a couple of specimens. They came up healthy and full-bodied.

"Dis heah laik a gol' mine, Cap'n, suh." Washer whistled with astonishment. He peered through the water at the bottom. "How cum y' tink no one fin' dese place befoah en ahl d year?"

"I don't know." Brian was also surprised at the heavy beds. It wasn't, as Washer said, exactly a gold mine but it was an important find. "If the other spots are like this one we have something."

Marta, holding one of the sponges with a distasteful expression on her face, examined it skeptically. It seemed only a gelatinous mass.

"I never saw a sponge look like this." She was unimpressed.

"They dry and bleach out, the marine growth dies off and rots away. Then they are washed and cleaned. They're sponges all right." He turned to the Negro. "We're going to have to build some flat-bottomed boats to work from, Wash."

"Hit ain' no prob'm, Cap'n, suh. Gots men real handy wid tool, plenty timbuh ovah to Andros."

"We can use the *Caroline* as sort of a mother ship and work the small boats out of her." He stood and gazed about at the sun-flecked water. "Tomorrow I want to have a talk with everyone, Wash. First the *Caroline*'s crew and then the house servants and the families living on the plantation. We're going to make some changes in the way things are being run around here."

"Ah sen' out d word, Cap'n, suh."

They were back at the plantation by late afternoon and the purple hush of twilight was creeping upon the island. With Marta's hand in his they walked down past the sagging barns and stables and along a path worn through what were once the fields under cultivation. There was a stunted growth of orange trees which still had some life in them. The others were twisted and dead from the insect pests which had destroyed Cameron Raleigh's experiment with the fruit.

"Damned if I can figure this island out." The words exploded from him. "Everything—bananas, lemons, oranges, pineapples—grow well on Eluthera. Why do they fail here?"

"Maybe it's because sailors don't make good farmers." She tightened her fingers in his with a reassuring pressure.

Brian looked at her as though the notion had never occurred to him. "You may be right," he admitted. "The only one who knew anything about running a plantation was the original Ronald Cameron. The others, from Juan Cadiz to Brian Raleigh, have been salt-water men. Just the same I'm going to have a go at it again."

They turned and began strolling toward the house where lights were beginning to show. The wind had died completely and the magic spell of the evening's silence was upon the islands.

"My father's never said much so I don't really know." Brian spoke abruptly. "But I don't think there is much money in the family."

"If you're saying that for me, it isn't necessary. What would we do with it?" She was practical. "There isn't anything we really need."

"No," he admitted. "But the time will come. There will be children. I don't want them to grow up knowing nothing. I'd like to be able to send them to the mainland or England for an education."

"Is that where you went, my captain?" She glanced up at him.

"No. The schooling I had was in Nassau. Then I went to sea with my father."

"Then," she was emphatic, "Nassau will be good enough for our children if it has to be that way. You know," she was serious, "I'm really much more competent than you suspect. I can run a household. It is a thing Cuban girls of station are expected to know. I was well trained by my mother. I'll take this house in hand while you go sponging."

"I didn't think Cuban girls were good for anything except making love." He was amused by her seriousness.

"That, my Captain Raleigh and beloved husband, is not taught by one's mother." She pressed her shoulder against his arm. "We should be talking of love with you telling me how beautiful I am." She was laughing to herself. "I am a bride of a few weeks and my lover thinks only sponges and empty acres. A Cuban man would not be doing this, believe me."

"I know your Cuban men. They lock their wives away at home and go outside for amusement."

"Where would you go here, on Exuma? To your club, a Casino for gambling or," her eyes were bright, "whatever it is men find entertaining?"

"I guess you're right. I'll have to make out with you the best I can."

"That, my husband, is very good indeed. I don't want to go into the house yet. Take me down to the beach. Pretend this is some faraway island and I a native girl you've found wandering alone with a flower behind her ear. Make me your bride, for there is such love in me for you. It has not been measured yet."

"You're a wench."

"Yes, Captain."

He lifted her slender body in his arms and carried her this way through the growing darkness to the beach where the sand was still warm from the day's heat.

There were some thirty families scattered over the Cameron grant on Great Exuma and though there was little contact between them anymore, they all felt a close relationship with the big house and those who lived there. There had been matings with the Negroes of other islands but in all of them ran a strain of the slaves Ronald Cameron had brought with him from Carolina. They lived the simplest of lives. Most of them had traveled no farther than the few adjacent cays. Their needs were small and the land and sea provided them. For what work they did in the growing of things necessary for supplying the manor with vegetables, fowl, fish and pork they were paid small wages for which they had little use save for the purchase of cheap cotton cloth for clothing. Much the same situation existed among the house servants. They were satisfied. This was their home and they wanted no other. A few of the younger and more adventurous had gone to Nassau, but they found no employment in the community and returned eagerly and were reabsorbed without comment or rebuke.

With Washer at his side Brian talked first with the *Caroline*'s crew. He explained what most of them had already figured out for themselves. There was little profit in trying to work the schooner in the mainland coastal trade. Now and then they might get a cargo of sisal or fruit out of Nassau but that was about all.

"You are all good men." Brian spoke with a kindly tone of authority. "We have been together for a long time. The truth is I just can't afford to pay wages if the schooner doesn't bring money in."

He told them of the sponge beds, lying untouched all these years.

[484]

How they had been marked out and worked years ago by his great-grandfather.

"I don't know why no one has come across them before but they haven't. There they are. If you want to stay with me . . ." He paused and then continued reassuringly: "Whatever you decide you can remain in the places you have built for your families on plantation land. Anyhow, I think we can work those sponge beds cooperatively." He saw the blank expressions on their faces. "That means," he explained, "we will all have a share. Mine will be larger than yours because the beds are my discovery, the equipment furnished by me. But there will be a fair division of profits. You talk it over and let me know what you want to do."

"We a'ready mek talk, Cap'n, suh." Big Washer was the spokesman. "We figuah, ef you say hit a'raight hit be so. We go to Andros an' cut timbuh foah mek flat boads. Den we mek d crawls en git to wuk on dem sponge. Howevah you say divide money mek fine wid us ahl." He laughed suddenly. "Wat we do wid hit, anyhow? Mebbe spen' hit on Nassau girl do we git dere sometime ef wife don' git hit firs'."

There was a general murmur of agreement and a nodding of heads. Actually, all of them had been afraid they were to be turned off the schooner and left to shift for themselves. They had little knowledge of anything but the islands, this ship and the waters sailed.

"All right." Brian was decisive. "There's a lot of stuff in the old warehouses. Axes. Saws. Chain. Rope. Most of it hasn't been touched in years but the saws and axes can be cleaned and sharpened. There's the sawmill if we can get it to work without the boiler blowing up. We can cut our boards for the boats right here. You take the ketch, Wash, and go over to Andros. Mark out some good, straight timber. Then we get some of the plantation men to help fell them and bring the logs back on the *Caroline*. We'll build the flatboats here and then lay out the crawls."

He and Washer left the men aboard the schooner talking excitedly among themselves. They had been given something to do and for the moment, it was an adventure.

With the individual families, when they had been gathered together, Brian had difficulty in explaining what he wanted to do. The idea of putting the plantation on a profit-making basis rather than making it only self-sustaining was something they simply could not grasp. The real problem was to convince them of the desirability of trying again to work the fields when they could think of no good reason why they should. They all had their own gardens in which were raised the cowpeas, beans, tomatoes and yams. Each family had a few chickens and the

[485]

sea was filled with fish. What more did anyone need? In return for the land given them they tended a larger garden and saw to the care of a limited number of swine, chickens and livestock for the manor's use. Also, many of them remembered earlier failures with large-scale crops. There was some sort of bad luck with this land. In secret, around their fires at night, they had whispered to each other of the *Chickcharneys,* the tiny, red-eyed men with three fingers and three toes who hung from the trees in the dark of the moon and, when everyone was asleep, did the mischief which caused things not to grow here as they should. It wasn't a good thing to trifle with the *Chickcharneys.* Everyone knew this.

Studying their black faces Brian was about to give up. He had talked for at least half an hour, telling them only what they already were aware of. Once, long ago and in the memory of only the ancient ones who had passed the stories on, there had been large pens for the swine. But over the years, the sties had fallen apart and were not repaired. The sows and the boars, the litters, had strayed and what they reproduced had grown wild, roving and rooting in the thick brush and woods of the island. There were savage boars, wary sows, young pigs which tore through the scrub in a panic at the sight of a man. The same was true of the horses and cattle brought to Exuma by Ronald Cameron. Their seed, scrubby and with shaggy coats, wiry but stunted from inbreeding, could not be approached. If, Brian pointed out, this wild stock could be some-how rounded up and properly fenced, their colts, calves and litters might again be domesticated and sold in Nassau. He didn't really know whether any part of such a program was feasible but he was determined some sort of an effort be made to put the place in shape.

The Negroes were understandably skeptical. They had caught some of the shoats in heavy nets and captured a madly threshing sow or two and a boar in the same manner. From these they had bred some stock. In a still-fenced section of the jumbay grassland a few cows and a bull had remained in a tame state to furnish beef, eaten fresh or dried and smoked, and milk. There were, also, coops and runs for chickens and turkeys. It was from these the manor drew for its table. But no one among the Negroes Brian now addressed had any idea how to go about rounding up the wild horses, cattle and swine. This reversion of the animals to a completely unfettered state had begun almost imperceptibly with the quitting of the island by Robert Bruce, the death of Ronald Cameron and the absence of any white overseers to see that fences and corrals were kept in repair. They were the only ones who had any knowl-edge of husbandry. Those who followed them were, as Marta had said to Brian, men of the sea. The dissolution of all orderly process of breeding and care had gone on over the years. It was only through the crude efforts of the Negroes, who had acted out of the instinct for self-preservation, that any of the stock remained domesticated.

The men and women of the families heard Brian through. Now and then they cut their eyes at each other in wonder but no one spoke until he had finished explaining his idea of putting the plantation in order again. The acres could be put to sisal for which there was an increasing market in the United States for the making of cordage. It was the only crop that had given any evidence of flourishing. The conception of a cooperative effort, with all sharing, simply was not grasped. All they understood was that the big house was going to put them all to hard work for which they had no enthusiasm. At the end of his lengthy explanation Brian waited with a feeling of complete helplessness.

One of the older men stepped forward. He looked back at the silent group behind him for encouragement before he spoke.

"Marstah Boss." The salutation, a relic of their grand- and great-grandparents' slavery days, persisted. "How we ketch a wil' horse, a bull, dem cow? None us evah do sich ting."

It was an honest question. To himself Brian said: I'm damned if I know. But it sounded like a good idea. Washer was aware of his captain's uncertainty. He spoke up with authority.

"D cap'n ain' say how you do hit. He jus' say git hit done. You ketch wil' horse by puttin' line 'roun' hit neck an' mek hit fas' to somethin'." Washer seemed satisfied with this. He glanced at Brian for encouragement. "Ain' dat so, Cap'n, suh?"

"I'll tell you the truth, Wash." Brian couldn't hide the grin. "I don't know how you do it either. Maybe it isn't much of an idea."

"Dey a gen'mum to Watlin' Islan'." Washer wanted to be helpful. "Name Mistuh Parkah. He raise horse. Lots o' dem wid men to wuk. Dey ride out en run bunch horse to fence in place. Mebbe he hep."

Brian had heard about Donald Parker, who raised horses on a large scale on Watlings Island. He sold them in Nassau and to the farmers in the Out Islands. Parker's holdings were of the largest in the Bahamas. He had skilled hands to round up his stock and his plantation was one of the few prosperous ones. He might be interested in sending men to Exuma, drive in the wild horses on a half-share basis. It was a short sail to Watlings and he could go over and have a talk with the man.

"Anyhow," he addressed the group again, "we can burn off the fields and get them ready."

"Yessuh, Marstah Boss." There was agreement but no animation. If the Marstah Boss wanted the fields burned they'd do it. No real trouble to start a fire. "We do laik y' say."

With Washer striding along at his side Brian walked back across the fields toward the house. He realized he had accomplished nothing with the families. Washer sensed his captain's disappointment.

"Dey jus' ig'orant nigger, Cap'n, suh. Dey don' know 'bout dis co-op-rative." He was proud of his grasp of the plan. "Hit jus' soun' laik wuk. Dey say to sefs: What foah we gots ahl dis wuk come sudden? What's dis profits Marstah Boss talk 'bout? What we do wid money, anyhow? Dey nevah bin no place laik you, me, d crew."

Brian nodded. Washer was right. So, he conceded, were the Negro families. Their land had been given to them or their fathers more than thirty years ago with the Emancipation Act in exchange for a certain amount of work. Their time of apprenticeship was well over. What need did they have for money?

"Well." He was angry with himself. "I'm damned if I'm just going to sit here and watch this plantation fall apart little by little."

"We grain dem sponge, Cap'n, suh." Washer was anxious to be of aid. "Hit bring en money."

"Maybe so, Wash. I don't know." The reply was a weary one.

"Does d Cap'n need ahl d money me, d crew wuk foah nuttin' 'til hit git bettah."

"I know you would. It isn't just the making of money." How, he wondered, could he explain to this great, amiable Negro who was as much a friend as mate on the schooner? More than money was involved. He had no feeling for the land, no relationship. His ignorance appalled him. "I want to rebuild something here, Wash." He groped for the right words. "In the beginning this place was the dream of a man who sacrificed much to make it come true. If I'm going to give up what I know, the sea, then I want the plantation as it should be. I'd like to put it together again so it can be left to my children when I have them."

"Yessuh, Cap'n, suh." Wash agreed although he wasn't at all sure what the cap'n meant. He already had a house, land, a schooner and a ketch. What more could a man want? They were nearing the manor now. "I go pick oud men t' go wid me t' Andros foah to get lumbah tree. We tek ketch an' gone foah, five day, mebbe. Look 'roun' some."

"All right, Wash. You do that." He was too low in spirit to care or to want to go and see for himself. "Get what stores you need."

Washer turned off on a path toward the beach and Brian continued on toward the house. It was, he noticed, in need of a full painting and some minor repairs again. For a moment he felt a small anger rising. Why had his father allowed it to fall into this state? They must have made a small fortune blockade running. Where had all the money gone? It had been in his mind to talk with the house servants about a communal effort. But, he realized, there were so few of them now and after his experience with the Negro families he realized they would make no sense out of what he had to say. It was better to leave things as they were. Pay them their small wages, furnish their clothing, food and quarters.

Marta was on the porch as he crossed the yard and she came down the steps to meet him, disturbed by the dispirited expression on his face. She had adapted quickly to the island way of life and dress. Her frock was of simple, bright muslin and on her feet she wore only light sandals. In these things she looked almost ridiculously young.

"What is wrong, my landlocked captain?"

"I guess that's it." He had to smile at her serene freshness. "I'm on the beach and wondering what to do about it. There's everything here if I only knew what to do with it." He put an arm about her waist.

"You'll learn. Anyhow, what is it you want?"

"I guess it is some frugal, Yankee strain in me. I hate to see something go to waste. There are a couple of thousand acres here. They should be producing something."

"Suppose," her fingers twined with his, "we just raise a fine crop of children? I think I can be very good at that."

"We might even get a farmer out of the lot."

"Who knows? Come. We'll sit upon the porch and you have a drink. This is the time of day I like best. To be alone and quiet with you."

He called for one of the girls, ordered rum with water and lime and then sat on the top step. Marta took her place below, where she could rest her head against his knee.

"They didn't even know what I was talking about. I could see it in their faces." He took a swallow of the drink. "I thought we could put all of this to the agave plant for sisal. There are a few hundred acres planted now. It isn't something which grows overnight but if we started now, in a few years it could be a good money crop. We could buy the machinery and do our own stripping here. All the time I talked," he laughed as his naturally good humor reasserted itself, "I could see them asking themselves: What foah we do ahl dis? You know?" His hand touched her head. "In their place I'd probably wonder about the same thing."

The softness of the afternoon lay about them. Brian could feel himself relaxing. This was no climate for the drive of ambition. You drifted with it as upon a gentle tide. It had the quiet murmur of a shell when held to the ear. He speculated idly upon the girl at his side. How had she adjusted to this life? He had expected the parting with her mother would be a highly emotional scene. They had both surprised him, for the leave-

[489]

taking had been done with dignity, affection and a shining pride even though both knew they might never see each other again.

"What do you think about?" She spoke without lifting her head.

"You."

Her hands tightened on his knee. "And I you. This is a very good thing."

ঙ্গ XXX ৯ঙ

THE PATTERN of their lives was formed without conscious effort, for there were no outside influences to disturb it. Beyond the islands history was shaping itself into a frightening design but the tides and currents of its inexorable sweep had yet to touch their shores.

The affairs of the plantation had begun to move in orderly channels. Through quiet persuasion, simulated anger, violent threats which he had no intention of carrying out, Brian had managed to enlist the efforts of the Negro families. Fields were cleared and laid out in long rows of the dark green, spearlike plant which, when stripped of its pulp, produced the sisal fibers. There would be no immediate result for they must wait for maturity, but the fact a start had been made filled him with an inordinate pride.

Washer and his crew had marked out and cut down fine, straight pine trees from the forests on Andros Island and brought them back aboard the *Caroline*. Long unused machinery of the plantation's mill had been cleaned of its rust and scale and the now bright saws whined their way through the logs for the planking which was dried and seasoned. Then, with a skill Brian had no idea they possessed, sturdy flatboats were built and calked. From these the heavy sponge beds were worked. The crawls were laid out and filled. When Nature had done her work and the bleached sponges strung together they were taken to Nassau for sale. Now, though, Brian decided, they were paying an unnecessary commission to the factor on New Providence. Money could be saved and shared by taking the sponges, together with whatever small cargo might be picked up, directly to the mainland ports of Jacksonville, Savannah or Charleston and disposing of them to wholesalers there.

The *Caroline*'s crew worked with a singing, robust enthusiasm for they were upon the water they loved and knew so well. It was only in the fields with its cane for sugar and rum from the small distillery, the corn,

[491]

beans and peas to be sacked and sold, that Brian had difficulty. It was a problem to find men willing to labor for something they did not need. However, he was able to look out now and know the plantation was in far better shape than when he had taken over. Cameron Raleigh and David were still in Charleston and what had been done here he had accomplished alone, learning much as he went along.

He made a trip to Watlings Island, talking there with Mr. Donald Parker, accepting the man's advice and giving up the idea of trying to redomesticate the wild stock on Great Exuma. Parker had been blunt.

"I'll bring over some of my men and round up the horses, taking a two-thirds share if you want to do business. But you'll have one hell of a time trying to break your animals to harness or saddle. You just don't have men with that kind of experience. As for the cattle which have strayed and the pigs now running wild, my advice is to leave them alone. If I were you I'd just go out and hunt them the way you would deer when you want fresh meat or pork for smoking into hams and bacon. We'd never prod them out of the scrub and onto grazing land or into pens."

Brian had taken Parker's estimate of the situation. The wild pigs offered a useful form of sport. The cattle were left to roam and propagate. When the household had a mind for beef or veal they could arrange a hunting party and shoot a steer or a calf or two and there was meat for everyone on the plantation.

Things had gone so well there was no warning of tragedy. Then, in the fifth month of their second year of marriage, Marta lost her first child through a miscarriage which was as inexplicable as it was harrowing. She was young, healthy and eager for motherhood. Yet this thing happened and for no apparent cause. There had been no time to get her to the limited hospital facilities in Nassau or the missionary doctor on Eluthera. Only the quiet wisdom of one of the Negro women stayed the near fatal hemorrhage. For days and nights Brian did not leave her bedside save when it became absolutely necessary. He slept in a chair, listening to her breathing, touching the pale forehead with a damp cloth. She appeared so frail, so frighteningly young. Her eyes, when they opened to look at him, were darkly shadowed with misery.

"I'm sorry." Once she had whispered this.

He bowed his head, feeling the guilt was his; as though in some coarse and brutal moment he had violated the delicacy of her body and brought it to this terrible moment.

"I am the one to blame." Tears were scalding in his eyes.

"Never say that." The words were so muted he barely heard them. "It was God's will."

She believed this, he knew. For the first time he found himself thinking of this God of hers and the world's millions and millions who shared a faith and a mysterious comfort. He had never been quite certain in his own mind but he understood she drew a strength from the belief God had ordained they should not have this child. Without it she would have been tortured beyond endurance. He said nothing to disturb this strange tranquillity.

She recovered with, what was to him, surprising vitality. The will to live and the love for her husband were strong within her. Sunshine poured into the room. The sea's wind refreshed it. Soon she was sitting up. She ate willingly now when her tray was brought and the mark of tragic loss disappeared from her eyes. One day he carried her downstairs and outside, into the garden.

"It has never seemed so beautiful before." She looked about with smiling wonder.

He sat on a low stool beside the wicker chaise longue brought from the house. Color touched her cheeks once again. The alarming transparency of her skin, beneath which every vein could be traced, was disappearing under a healthy sheen. The jet gloss of her hair returned.

"When I thought I was losing you," he spoke with grave sincerity, "I hated this place and myself for bringing you to it. I would rather we never have a child than risk you again. It is enough we have each other."

"We will have children." She reached for his hand and caressed it with her fingertips. "This has happened before to many women. For," her smile came easily, "I am a woman even though you treat me as a child who should never know pain and must be shielded and guarded from life's unpleasant facts."

He made no reply, thinking of the hours when her life had balanced so precariously. Then he had sworn to himself she would never risk this again even if it meant complete self-denial and abstinence on his part for the rest of their lives.

"No." She was watching him and there was a curious note of determination in the word. "I can always tell what you are thinking. It shows in your eyes. You are not very clever about hiding things from me. I am no treasured bit of porcelain to be put safely away where it can be admired but not touched. I find an ecstasy in your love. In a little while, when I am stronger, I would like to make a sea voyage with you, Captain Raleigh."

He was surprised. "Around the world if you wish."

"No. Just to one of the cities on the mainland. Your Charleston, perhaps, where we can talk with a physician of knowledge and find out if there is any reason why I cannot bear our children. There was no accident and I do not know why this happened."

"We'll take one of the Cunard steamers from Nassau and at the time of year when Charleston is aflame with the color of its azaleas. Richard will be happy to have us at Cameron Hall."

"Are you afraid to trust me to your own care, Captain?" Her smile again came with a quick freshness. "I would much rather sail with you and the boys aboard the *Caroline*."

"You get well and I'll swim to Charleston with you on my back."

She seemed to consider this seriously for a moment or two and then shook her head, the small stars of a sapphire in her eyes.

"If you don't mind I think I would prefer the schooner although you do have a very fine back."

Within a week she was up and about, making small adjustments to the household's management, taking her meals with him at the table, finding interest in all he had to say and his obvious pride in accomplishment. In two weeks he took her to the sponge beds where the men worked through long, hot days. They went swimming again in their own secret cove, coming from the water with their bodies glistening, lying in the powdery sand until they were dry and warm again.

"I had never thought it possible to do this even with my own husband. That was before I had one, of course." Her head rested upon his chest. "Girls do think about such things. Even Marta Christina de la Torre in the dark secrecy of her room at night. I remember. I used to wonder how it would be. Exactly what it was. My mother didn't believe it proper to discuss the subject. It turns out to be quite wonderful and so, I wonder now why it is avoided?"

"It always surprises me to discover what goes on in that small, beautiful head of yours."

"Oh! I only tell you part, anyhow." She sat up. "I never imagined my life would be this way. It wouldn't," her eyes were somber momentarily, "except for you and what happened to my father. When will we go to the mainland, Brian?"

"Next week if you are ready."

"Don't I look ready?" She stood, lithe, radiant and filled with health. "I never felt better."

"You're a water nymph, a thing made of the sea." He pulled her back down, reaching for her hand. "Just lie here and stay with me for a while. Sometimes I don't believe you are real."

Cameron and David Heath returned unexpectedly, coming from Nassau aboard the mail, passenger and small cargo boat on its fortnightly trip

[494]

through the Out Islands. Marta saw it from the second-story balcony and called excitedly to Brian, who had just finished shaving.

"The *Skipjack*'s in and a couple of passengers are coming ashore. I'm not sure but I think they are your father and Uncle David."

With part of the lather drying on his face Brian and Marta hurried down to the dock and waited there as the skiff was rowed in.

"By Harry!" Cameron Raleigh grasped his son's hand and bent to kiss his daughter-in-law's cheek at the same time. "But I'm glad to be home." He embraced them both.

David was slower in taking the step from the boat's thwart to the landing stage. Almost irritably he nodded off the oarsman's offer of assistance.

"Uncle David." Brian reached for a hand as though in greeting but in reality to aid the plainly faltering movement. "How are you?"

"Agile as a mountain goat as you can see." For a moment David Heath's eyes smoldered with the dim light of the familiar humor. "It's good to see you both again." He turned and his gaze traveled in a wide arc along the beach and to the house. "It's better to be home." He kissed Marta lightly. "An old man's privilege. You grow more beautiful by the day."

"You've been away longer than that. We've both missed you." She slid her arm through his.

David grunted. "I had some trouble dragging Cameron away from Charleston's fleshpots. He's a roisterer, a tosspot and a damn bad chess player."

They walked in a group up the slope, all pretending they were strolling leisurely out of choice and not because of David's obvious inability to move without painful indecision. Brian thought how incredibly old the man had become within the space of a year and a half or so. He had made, it seemed, his surrender to time and now only waited out the fulfillment of the terms.

"You never wrote." Brian turned to his father. "So we figured you were enjoying yourselves. How is Richard Cameron?"

"Richard has a priceless gift. He is never bored because he is continually preoccupied with the making of money. Even when he loses, it is part of the game he invented. Don't misunderstand. He is no miser counting his pennies. He simply finds excitement and pleasure in turning a profit. He was a most gracious host when given an opportunity."

At the house they drew chairs to a shaded section of the porch. David sank into one with an audible sigh of relief. His skin had the blue-white cast of chalky water.

"Are you all right, Uncle David?" Brian was concerned.

[495]

"Of course I'm not all right, lad." The reply was gently made. "I'm dying. Anyone can see that." He took out his watch and peered at it. "The hour is early but I would like a drink. Such dissolute behavior is reserved for the very old or the very young."

Marta rose quickly. "Rum or some brandy, a little wine?"

"Rum. Plantation rum." He smiled up at her. "It is such a pleasure to look at you. Even I am not too old to enjoy a woman's beauty."

She flushed at the compliment. "Father Raleigh? Brian? Something?"

"Coffee, some biscuit, a little jam," Cameron answered. "Later, perhaps, some bacon and eggs. The galley aboard the *Skipjack* is limited."

"I'll have coffee, please," Brian replied. "And breakfast later, also."

She left them to give the order. Cameron lit a cigar. David sat, staring at his wrinkled hands as though their being in his lap surprised him.

"Tremendous things are happening outside these Bahamas, lad." Cameron drew upon his cigar. "The United States begins to strain at the seams. You can feel the vitality of a new nation. Expansion. Inventions. There is a man named Bell, you may have read of him in the journals."

"I haven't had much time for reading."

"Well, he's been tinkering around with a thing he calls a telephone. Before we left there was an item in the Charleston paper. He had sent his voice—his voice, mind you—across a wire between Boston and Salem and was spoken to, in return, from the other end. What do you think of that?"

"Some sort of humbug, you can be sure," David interrupted. "A stock-swindling scheme."

Cameron smiled at his son. "They're still fighting the war in Georgia, Carolina, Mississippi; not really shooting at each other, you understand, but there is constant friction and trouble with Federal troops occupying public buildings to hold down riots."

Marta returned and was shortly followed by a serving girl who brought a tray with coffee, a decanter of rum and a pitcher of water.

"They're heating some biscuits." Marta poured the rum for David and added a little water, then filled the cups with strong black coffee. "There's fresh cream."

Both Cameron and Brian shook their heads. The coffee was as fragrant and heady as a liquor. David sipped at his rum, his glance traveling between Brian and Marta.

"I'm leaving you two my place in Charleston." He spoke abruptly. "Damn fine house if you like the city. Made a will before I left. Richard has it in his safe. Can't imagine what you'll do with the place but it's there and yours if you want it." The rum seemed to revitalize his spirits and loosen his thoughts. He stared at it and took another swallow. "Do you know what the damn fools in Tennessee have done?" He chuckled and didn't wait for a reply. "They passed a law prohibiting the sale of liquor within four miles of a school. Do they imagine the kids are going to run out at recess for a tot of brandy, a mug of ale or a demijohn of whisky? The whole world is going crazy. Strikes of miners and railroad workers. Indians and troops fighting all over the West. North and South still growling at each other. Take my advice. Stay here in the islands. Victoria, with all her talk of Empire, doesn't know what she has." He spoke of the Queen as though she were some girl next door. "This is the only decent place to live or die. That's what I've come home for."

There was an uncomfortable silence for it was apparent David Heath had meant exactly what he said. A tiny, frosted smile twitched his lips.

"Thank you." He said it without sarcasm. "It is rare to encounter honesty, at least among one's relatives or friends. Thank you again for not saying: 'Oh, no, Uncle David!' When you know damn well it's true."

He finished his drink in one long swallow and fumblingly reached out toward the table and tray. Marta left her place beside Brian and replenished his glass. David winked openly at her and she flashed an impertinent grin in return.

"You think I'm going to get drunk, don't you?"

"*Sí, señor. A tragos.*" She employed the idiom with bright impudence.

"You're damn right I am. Then I'll sleep until dinnertime. One of these days I won't get up at all and you can put me back there with Caroline, Bahama, Walter and John. Lay me face down. I never liked the sun in my eyes."

He snorted and peered at them with a ghoulish pleasure, holding the drink in both hands to hide its shaking.

Late in the afternoon Brian and his father returned from a tour of inspection of the newly planted fields, the renovated buildings and mill machinery. Brian told him of the sponge beds and how they were being worked cooperatively. Cameron was quietly impressed.

On the way back Brian had, also, told of Marta's losing her child and her desire to go to Charleston and consult with a skilled physician.

"By all means take her." Cameron had been emphatic.

At the house again they sat on the steps and watched as the magic colors of the approaching sunset gathered. For a while neither spoke, reluctant to have the hushed spell broken.

"You know," Cameron said finally, "for a sailor you've put a strong hand to the plow." He leaned forward, hands clasped between his knees. "I didn't seem to have the knack."

"I'm not sure I have either but we've made a start. From a couple of things you said I had an idea we ought to get this place operating again if it could be done." Brian was thoughtful for a moment. "It's none of my business—" he began.

"Of course it is," Cameron interrupted pleasantly. "What do you want to know?"

"Well . . ." Brian was hesitant. "What became of all the money we made running the blockade? I had an idea we were close to being wealthy at one time. Then, once or twice, you mentioned money as though it was something of the past. That's why I went to work here. I'm going to have a family someday. It will take money to raise it as I want."

Cameron Raleigh wasn't offended by the question. He sat thinking for a moment or two.

"I guess we were near to being wealthy at one time," he admitted. "Then, after I turned the schooner over to you, I spent a lot trying to put this place back in shape. Also," he seemed embarrassed, "for reasons which really don't make much sense to me, I wanted your mother to live abroad as she had lived at home before the war. I loved her very much even though she left me. The allowance has been more than generous over the years. But," he rubbed a hand across his mouth in an effort to hide a sheepish expression, "I suppose the one thing I did which was really foolish was my turning back a couple of hundred thousand dollars into bonds issued by the Confederacy. This is hard to explain because I never thought the South had a chance to win the war. I felt an obligation. It was a matter of honor. We had taken so much out while the Confederate States were sacrificing everything. Sometimes, I felt it was dirty money. It was on my conscience. I did what I thought was honorable. Am I making any sense to you?"

"Yes." Brian was sincere and a little proud of his father. "It makes a great deal of sense."

"Well. There you have it. Then, I made some investments through Richard just before the panic in '73. Those were a total loss. I'm sorry." He spread his hands with an apologetic gesture. "We could have been well fixed but the sailor would not stick to the sea or the shoemaker to his last."

"As far as I am concerned," Brian was honest, "don't regret anything you did. I'm glad you turned back some of the money to the South. And I would want my mother to be without concern although I don't care much for the idea of supporting Carol-Louise's count and family in some moldy Venetian castle or palace. As far as the investments go," he grinned, "everyone knows what happens to a sailor when he goes ashore with a pocketful of money. The sharks get him."

"You, we'll, make out here." Cameron took a pipe and a leather pouch of shaggy tobacco. "I don't imagine anyone will get rich, but, by and large, we're better off than most of the old families in the islands." He lit his pipe and drew contentedly. "You get that girl of yours to Charleston where there are competent physicians. I'd like to see some grandchildren around before I die. This was a place built for a large family. Yet, it never really had one. Strange when you come to think about it."

True to his prediction, David Heath went to bed one night and sometime, during the long and silent hours, died quietly in his sleep. It would have gratified his generous and considerate nature to have known this. Of all the things he wanted to avoid was a long illness, a period of complete helplessness when he would have needed constant attention. He was eighty-three years old. The time was 1877.

He was buried in the plantation's cemetery to lie with those he had known and loved. There was no minister and so, Cameron Raleigh read a brief passage from the Bible. Then they turned away and walked slowly back to the house. There was sorrow but no tears.

"I'll have a stone cut when I go to Nassau." Brian held Marta's hand as she moved between them. "David Heath or David Cameron?" he asked his father.

"David Heath," Cameron answered. "Leave it as it was. Maybe, when he was young, he would have liked Cameron but it is far too late for that now. When," he changed the subject, "are you and Marta going to Charleston?"

"Next week, I think." Brian turned to her. "You still want to make the voyage aboard the *Caroline?*"

"Yes. Unless you've forgotten how to command a ship."

"It will probably all come back to me after I've laid us on a reef somewhere."

"I won't write Richard then." Cameron seemed relieved. "You can tell him about David. I think there was a real affection between them although one might never have suspected it from David's manner. He accused Richard of being a moneygrubber. They had many a furious argument but without real anger."

They shared a silent meal at the house, for no one felt much like talking. The shadow of David's passing was upon them all. Even Marta felt it although she had not known him well. On an impulse Cameron went to the library and returned with the old diary Ronald Cameron had kept.

The leather binding was dry and cracked, the pages brittle, the ink faded. Carefully he turned the leaves, noting how meticulously the events of the days had been set down. He began to read.

November 24th. 1799. Shipped to Nassau on board the sloop altogether 6 head of cattle, 23 sheep, 9 turkeys, 18 bushels of Guinea corn, a pair of cart wheels for matching. On this day Lady Sabrina Heath came to the island bringing my son, David, who will be five years old on his next birthday. A handsome lad. There being a cholera epidemic on New Providence which I did not know about else would not have sent the sloop.

Slowly, carefully, Cameron Raleigh closed the old ledger and sat for a moment, his hands resting upon it.

Charleston lay behind them, its silhouette inked against the twilight curtain. Brian and Marta, his arm about her slim waist, looked back over the wake and noted the slender spire of St. Michael's Church as it rose above the other buildings.

"Why do I feel like crying?" Marta asked in a whisper.

"There is a sadness about the city. An old and gracious lady fingering the mementos of her youth and recalling how beautiful she once was. That is how I feel. That is how everything impressed me, even Cameron Hall. It seems to have no place in a world so radically changed. Richard, also. Everyone we met. It is as though they had some magic looking glass in which they saw only what they wanted to see. But," he turned her to him, "I'm glad we came."

"So am I. Oh, so am I!" It was almost a cry of gratitude.

The physician's report had put to rest the fears which neither had admitted. There was nothing organically wrong with Marta Raleigh. The miscarriage could not be explained. It had simply happened. Under the circumstances she was lucky to have survived.

In private the doctor had told Brian there was no reason why his wife should not bear strong, healthy children. There was scar tissue evident. Marta's pelvic cavity was small but not in relation to her entire bone structure. He advised extreme care and, perhaps, abstinence for a year or so. But there was nothing to indicate the reoccurrence of the near fatal mishap.

"Your wife," he said, "is delicately formed but so are a great many other young women. Childbearing may be difficult but then it certainly is no easy thing under any circumstances. I would not suggest it be left to the care of a midwife. By all means see to it she has proper attention when the time comes even if it is necessary to take up residence in Nassau months in advance. I understand they have hospital facilities there." He had risen to shake hands. "You may have your family, Mr. Raleigh."

Brian had repeated everything said to Marta who clung to him with happiness. She carried with her a feeling of guilt; an inadequacy as a wife. To have children by the man she loved was the greatest joy she could imagine. She had not been able to rid herself of the idea she had somehow betrayed him with a fragile, useless body which would not perform its natural function. There had been many dark hours when she was sleepless beside Brian, experiencing shame and even a sense of sin. To lie with him for pleasure was an offense against God. Now, overnight, with the news she had become a different person or, perhaps, the person she had been before the loss of what was to have been their firstborn.

Richard had pressed them to remain in Charleston but they were both anxious to get home.

"What do you want to do about David's house?"

"I don't know. Rent it, if possible. Somehow, I wouldn't like to have it offered for sale; not just now."

"There are few persons in the city who would be in a position to lease the residence."

"Then," Brian decided, "let's board it up. Hire a caretaker part time to look after the garden. It shouldn't be too expensive. Or, if you know of a good family in difficult circumstances we could let them live in it rent free in return for its upkeep."

Richard had promised to see what could be done. There was, also, a small income from some shares David had held but it amounted to no more than a few hundred dollars a year. There was a possibility they might eventually return to their former value but nothing could be promised.

None of this had seemed important in view of what the medical examination had revealed. Now, they were on their way home. Brian turned to look aloft, studying the set of the sails. Outside the harbor the wind freshened. Washer was at the helm, a big grin on his broad face. Despite her years the *Caroline* seemed to strain eagerly, stretching out for the distant islands.

✺ XXXI ✺

IT WAS possible to stand or walk upon the beach at night, listening to the familiar, softly rasping sound of the palms and the ocean's smothered break upon the shore, and feel that this island and all the others in the scattered complex were as remote from the world as the farthest diamond point in the sky.

Often over the years Brian with Marta, and sometimes Cameron Raleigh, had come this way after the evening meal. They rarely spoke upon these occasions, for words somehow intruded upon the enchanted spell. Each, after his or her fashion, was alone. If suddenly asked what thoughts were passing through the mind, it is unlikely any one of them could say, for they were fancies without substance. All, at one time or another, had strolled alone without ever feeling lonely. Here was a friendly, constant solitude. Time was without meaning and by some magic one had not grown older or had anything changed.

In a way this was true of the island itself and its people. The seasons of the year had no significance. Winter and summer were all but indistinguishable from each other, for they varied little more than ten degrees in temperature. Only in late August and what would be early fall on the mainland was there any real change. This was the span when the hurricanes churned out of the Carribbean to spin their wildly erratic way. The fringes sometimes caught the islands with a full gale. Now and then the total fury struck to lay a wide path of devastation from Great Inagua to the Little Bahama Bank. Other than this seasonal marking there was nothing to separate one month from another. They slid effortlessly into each other. Twelve months into twelve months into twelve months without seeming to have accumulated at all. It was easy, if one's mind led that way, to imagine this to be infinity; unlimited time and space with nothing before or behind.

It had often struck Marta so although she only had to glance in the mirror or listen to the voices of her two children to realize at what a pace the years had gone. Her daughter, Maria Christina Raleigh, born five years after her marriage and now fifteen. Her son, named for his grandfather, Cameron Raleigh, two years his sister's junior. These were truths and yet, they seemed impossible. In the plantation's burial plot another stone had been added. Cameron Raleigh had died in his sixty-fifth year, living to see his grandchildren approach their adolescence and taking a tremendous, unspoken pride in the grandson who bore his name. It was curious, Marta often thought, how sturdy and long-lived the direct Cameron strain was. In Charleston, retired now to the acres of Cameron Hall, Richard was moving up on his seventy-fourth birthday. David Heath had lived to be eighty-three. Old Ronald Cameron had sired a strong breed. The Raleighs had not been so lusty.

Beyond the serene beauty of the islands the world had marched with a heavy, purposeful tread which was barely heard here. In England the most beloved Queen was nearing the end of her reign and would give her name to an era which had seen the creation of the British Empire, the brilliance and extent of which was almost beyond imagining.

Through the journals and newspapers coming regularly to Exuma now on a steam-driven mailboat the Raleigh family had followed the tremendous course of events, but they seemed to be things occurring on another planet.

Years back the Treaty of Zanjon had ended the civil war in Cuba and granted the insurgents representation in the Spanish Cortes. Now, though, the rebel forces were again gathered, stronger than ever.

A railroad line had linked the eastern and western coasts of the United States, and a telegraph line, strung through all but impassable jungles, now carried messages between North and South America. A man named Edison had shown a tiny filament in a vacuum globe of glass which, through electricity, gave an incandescence for more than forty hours. The United States was torn by constant strikes of rebellious workers and in Paris, Ferdinand de Lesseps formed an Interoceanic Canal Company. Electric lighting had been introduced to the streets of Philadelphia where the streetcar workers went on strike for a two-dollar-a-day wage for ten hours' work. Twenty-five men and an officer were landed from the U.S.S. *Essex* at Chemulpo, Korea, for the protection of American residents in Seoul. A tunnel under the St. Clair River joined Canada and the United States, and the Department of Agriculture was undertaking rainmaking experiments in Texas. The Cherokee Indians agreed to sell the Cherokee Strip for $8,700,000, and the Empire State Express made the run between Buffalo and New York City in eight hours and forty-two minutes. A world exposition opened in Chicago and a man named Jacob

Coxey led a march of the unemployed on Washington and was arrested for trespassing. The *Missouri*, of the American Transport Line, sailed from New York with five and one-half million tons of flour and meal for the starving Russians, and there was talk of joining the Atlantic and Pacific oceans with a canal cut through the isthmus connecting the Americas. The Governor of Colorado ordered troops to break up a strike of gold miners who were demanding three dollars for an eight-hour day, and two hundred Negro emigrants sailed from Savannah, Georgia, for Africa. Ontario, Canada, voted for prohibition of the liquor traffic, Japan protested Hawaii's refusal to allow more Japanese immigrants to land, and the Secretary of the United States Navy ordered warships to Nicaragua to protect American interests there.

To those of the Bahamas who even bothered to read about such things the fury and turmoil had no more significance than a tropical storm which passed far beyond the island waters.

Sometimes Brian would look up from a newspaper he scanned by the light of one of the new, nickeled kerosene lamps and say, "What do you think of that?"

Marta and the children would regard him with blank expressions and ask, "What do we think of what?"

Then Brian would read aloud the dispatch, telling some obscure fact such as a British-American dispute over fishing in the Bering Sea or a ship of the Cunard Line making a record eastern trip from New York to Queenstown in five days, eight hours and thirty-eight minutes.

Where was Queenstown and what was it to them? Beyond the plantation lay Nassau. Neither Maria Christina nor her brother Cameron had been farther away from home than what was, to them, the metropolis on New Providence.

From somewhere, perhaps as far back as Caroline Cameron Cadiz, Maria Christina had inherited blond hair and a complexion softly fair which the sun, oddly enough, only brushed with color but could not tan. Cameron, in contrast, had grown tall as were all the Raleigh men, lean and darkly handsome. Together sister and brother were a startling pair. There was much alike in their manner, the vitality and the curious, expressive use of their hands which was typically Latin. Seeing them for the first time, a stranger would suspect no relationship and yet there was a common stamp of which he would become aware. It was a paradox which never ceased to astonish Marta and Brian.

The plantation was now the family's principal source of income. Once having turned his back upon the sea of his forebears, Brian had thrown all his energy and resourcefulness into the land. He had virtually driven it to produce. Could he have seen the results, Ronald Cameron would have been more than pleased. True, it would not yield the cotton once hoped for, but the big, green plants from which the sisal was drawn flourished on some fifteen hundred of the acres. Machinery, with the toothed rollers to strip away the pulp, had been installed in what had been a barn. The structure was renovated, windows cut into the blank walls for light. A steam-driven engine turned the wheels and from the spears of the agave came the long, tough strands to be dried, bleached and baled. It was a money crop and something of which Ronald Cameron had never thought in his obsession to grow cotton.

The sponge beds, marked long ago by Juan Cadiz, had been worked out and the boats ranged farther and farther among the coral heads in search of new banks. The *Caroline* was some eighty years off her Nantucket ways and they used her now to carry the baled sisal into Nassau. It was only on these occasions that Brian set a foot upon her deck. To young Cam, though, the schooner was as romantically irresistible as an ancient galleon. He knew her from bowsprit to stern, from keelson to topmast. She still served as sort of a mother ship for the spongers, and the boy spent weeks at a time aboard her, living with the crew, graining from the flatboats, sitting at a common table with the black men, eating the same fish and grits with now and then some fresh chicken or turtle steak. From Washer he learned much of what there was to know about the sea, sail and the wind, and how a ship was handled.

As was the case of the schooner the huge Negro refused to show any sign of age. His tightly knotted hair was without a kink of gray although Brian Raleigh had grown so about the temples. His face was unlined, his teeth incredibly white and sound, his laughter as boomingly jubilant as ever. His loyalty to the Raleighs was so deeply rooted it was a thing to be taken for granted. If it was possible for a Negro to be part of the family, this was so with Washer. In young Cam he saw much of Brian, who was still "Cap'n, suh," despite the fact he no longer made a pretense of commanding the ship. There was a deep respect between the boy and the black man; affection and mutual regard. Almost from the time he had been able to walk Cam had been taken in hand by Washer to be taught the ways of the island seas. He had learned first with a skiff into which Washer had stepped a light mast and sideboards to hold her steady. From this the boy had been graduated to a sloop, then to the larger ketch, and finally, to the *Caroline* herself. In the elementary school Cam and Maria Christina attended on Eluthea, primary instruction in navigation was given to all boys as a matter of course, for island life was lived upon the sea. It was as impossible to keep young Cam from the water as it was the turtles, hatched from the eggs buried in the sand by the females at full moon and high tide. At birth the little reptiles broke through the eggs' tough skins, forced themselves upward and without hesitation instinctively headed for the ocean even though it might lie a hundred yards away.

Brian had watched his son's growth and attachment to the sea with pride and a little envy. So, he remembered, had he felt at the same age. The call came down through generations of seafaring Raleighs and there was no denying it here. Cam had a true sailor's contempt for the steam vessels but he could not deny their efficiency. But as he and Washer agreed, when they went some place they were in no hurry. Who would choose a stack belching black smoke when he could have a spread of canvas, white as a gull's wing, taut and straining against the sky in a fair wind?

Now, though, the time was upon Cam when he must leave the islands, Washer, the schooner, everyone and everything he loved for eight months out of the year. He and Maria Christina were to be sent to school in Charleston. It had been decided and all of his half-rebellious arguments could not prevail against the determination of his father and mother. He knew arithmetic, some geography, a little history and could read and write a passable hand. What more was there to learn?

Marta and Brian had long ago decided the children must go to the mainland even though their absence would leave an empty sensation in their hearts. The plantation had not made the Raleighs wealthy but it provided much more than just a living. The tuition and expense presented no real problem. Also Marta, so deeply steeped in her faith, had long been concerned by the lack of religious instruction. She had done her best to lead the children into the Catholic inheritance promised the Church when she married Brian. In her conscience she knew this was not enough. There was no Catholic church in the Out Islands and the missionaries who traveled them were of the Church of England. Only in Nassau was there a priest. He had baptized and given the first communion to both Maria Christina and Cameron and talked long and seriously with Marta.

Father Martel was a man of gentle, whimsical disposition and understanding. He was aware of the difficulties and had accepted as a true acknowledgment of the Church an annual attendance at Mass and Confession by mother and children. Still, Marta was not completely satisfied. It was a token obeisance at best and her soul was troubled. Now, though, matters had been arranged to her satisfaction even though it meant long months of separation. Maria Christina was enrolled in a convent school. Cameron was to enter a nonsectarian academy for boys with a promise of faithful attendance at Mass. With this Brian was in agreement. When the time came he hoped to send Cam to The Citadel, in Charleston. He had talked it over with the boy and Cam had nodded an indifferent assent. Secretly, though, he wondered what good a military school would do for one who was going to be a sailor? In time, he told himself, his parent's common sense would assert itself and some sort of a compromise could be worked out. In the meanwhile he would learn what he could. His apprehension over what he termed "beached" was lightened by the knowledge Charleston was a seaport and from the waterfront he would be able to see the ships of the world as they came and went, and maybe even talk with the seamen when they were ashore. Also, following a letter from Brian, Richard Cameron had extended a full and sincere invitation to both Maria Christina and Cam to visit Cameron Hall whenever their schools permitted. He had, he said, a small boat rarely used anymore. Cam could sail upon the Ashley.

"I guess," the boy reflected after his father finished reading the letter, "a river is better than nothing. How big is the Ashley?"

"If you're Carolina-born," Brian smiled, "its bigger than the Mississippi, the Nile or the Amazon; better, also. Anyhow, it is big enough for you."

Maria Christina's enthusiasm over the novelty of going away was tempered by the information she would have to dress in a school uniform. For weeks she had pored over the fashion illustrations in the journals and magazines reaching them. She had seen herself fashionably gowned, a young lady of undeniable distinction, pursued by eager beaux.

Marta had reluctantly destroyed this notion. "I doubt you will see any boys or young men. I certainly didn't when I was your age. A duenna took me to school in a closed coach with the curtains drawn. What you are going to isn't exactly a social institution. The uniform, as described, is plainly serviceable and nothing more. It will hardly be eye-catching."

"You make it sound like some sort of a prison." Maria Christina's eyes darkened with disappointment.

"No, dear." Marta was soothing. "It is not a prison. The Sisters understand the yearnings of young girls. You will find a certain amount of discipline, to be sure. But there will be girls of your age. You will make friends."

"I suppose so." She was indifferent.

"You will learn much which will be of value later when it is time for you to begin to think of marriage."

"Who would I marry here? Some towheaded, ignorant conch?" A small rebellion seethed.

"That is a rude expression as you well know." Marta was firm. "I don't want to hear it again."

"*Sí, Madre mía.*" The words were repentant but under her breath she said *conch*.

"You will learn deportment, how to sit and walk properly. There will be French, also. And perhaps," Marta eyed her daughter with suppressed laughter, "they will even be able to improve your Spanish accent with which I have had little success. Do you know"—she was serious again —"someday I would like us all to be able to go to Spain and see my mother. I have little hope she will ever return from Europe and she is growing old. I can tell from the handwriting of her letters. It is no longer firm and her thoughts seem to wander. How strange the unexpected turn our lives took."

"Yes, Mother." Maria Christina wasn't at all interested in this vague future. "Could I," she came to sit on the arm of her mother's chair, "please just have one or two pretty frocks to wear on the steamer when we go to Charleston before I have to wrap myself in that school potato sack?"

Marta touched the soft cheek. This girl was very dear to her and she understood the bewilderment and the yearning.

"We will find a couple of things bright and gay in Nassau, with slippers to match and a cape for travel. You shall go to your exile appropriately gowned."

"Promise?" The question was breathless.

"I promise."

A mound of pine and oak blazed in the fireplace of the living room at Cameron Hall. Seated before it, in a semicircle, Brian and Marta with Richard half listened to the rain and wind of September. It whipped through the trees, tearing at the long, gray streamers of Spanish moss in the oaks and making glistening towers of the high pines. Mugs of steaming toddy were at the hands of the men and a maid had brought a tea tray. Marta was engaged with a small piece of completely useless embroidery. She hadn't the slightest idea what she was to do with it when finished.

She lifted her eyes to watch the bright tongues of flame and thought about the children. Cameron and Maria Christina had been admitted to the academy and convent school but not without some desperate, last-minute pleas for reprieve. Maria was the most vocal. Cam went staunchly to his fate. In time his parents would realize their mistake.

"You are not going to the guillotine, Maria Christina." Brian had been quietly amused. "I have," he continued seriously, "investigated thoroughly. The Sisters do not employ the rack. Thumb screws, hot irons and boiling oil are used in only the most extreme cases. I have this on the word of the Mother Superior herself."

"It is all very well for you to talk." The girl pretended a stubborn manner but there was an unmistakable gleam of laughter in her eyes. "You are free and can go back home."

"Where there is no one but towheaded conchs?" Marta asked innocently.

"That is a rude expression, Mother." She was reproving.

Suddenly they were all laughing. Maria Christina threw her arms about her mother. There were only the three of them in the carriage, for Cam had already been left at the academy and his trunk sent from the ship's pier. Now they were drawing up before the convent gates.

Maria Christina leaned forward, peering with interest, and some of her apprehension was relieved by her first glimpse of the school. It had been one of the most beautiful homes in prewar Charleston. Graceful in design, it rose two stories with the broad piazza and was set in a spacious garden with fine old trees and a wide area of lawn and shrubbery behind. The estate occupied half a block and was surrounded by wrought-iron fencing over which honeysuckle and jessamine had been allowed to grow. At the war's end, with the family's men lost in the conflict, the mansion had been given to the Catholic Church. After some interior remodeling it was opened as a convent school.

"It's beautiful." Maria Christina sighed her relief.

"I told you it was no prison." Marta touched her daughter's hand. Actually, she hadn't been too certain what the place would look like. "A lovely home it must have been."

"I didn't know what to expect, honestly," the girl confessed. "Brick walls. Something grim. I may like it here after all if I don't run away."

The Mother Superior had welcomed them with a gracious charm. She looked long at Maria Christina and then nodded as though something in the girl's clear eyes satisfied her.

"I think you will be happy here, and now, I will show you the room you will share."

Thinking back, Marta felt satisfied by the step taken. Actually, she experienced a sensation of relief. It had been a problem, on the plantation, to rear a daughter who had no one for a companion. At fifteen Maria Christina needed the softening influence of other girls, and sometimes the firm hand of discipline. She would miss them both, of course, but it would be pleasant for a while to have them safely in schools where they belonged. Perhaps, now, she and Brian could recapture some of the intimacy, companionship, and even the excitement they had known in the early days of their marriage. Love them though you did, children had a subtle way of absorbing your life.

The pine in the fire bubbled and burned with a bright flame. Richard stirred his toddy with a stick of cinnamon. It was pleasant to have this company. He spent most of his time at the Hall now although still keeping the town house on Tradd Street.

Three years ago, much to Richard's unconfessed relief, his wife Penelope had died. It occurred to him that Southern beauties did not wear well. Once their loveliness faded and the bloom vanished, they tended to become a little shrill. The charming accents and mannerisms grew just a bit tiresome through constant repetition. Growing old, Penelope had become a slightly querulous woman, forever talking of her small aches and pains, the laxity of Negro servants who should never have been freed in the first place, sighing over remembered and imagined courtships, balls, lawn parties and the brilliance of Charleston's society. She disliked the country and Cameron Hall, missing the teas and gossip with the friends of her youth who busied themselves with a continual round of calls upon each other. Now that she was safely underground with a fine marble stone to keep her there, Richard was quietly enjoying himself for the first time in many years.

At seventy-four, Richard was still erect and fairly vigorous, a handsome man who wore his white hair longer than was the general fashion. He no longer rode but found considerable pleasure in shooting over a pair of fine Pointers. This he did in a highly unorthodox manner. On a mule-drawn buckboard, driven by a Negro who had been with him for as long as he could remember, Richard would sit with the shotgun across his lap while the dogs cast over the fields. When they came to a point, the wagon was inched forward and the covey flushed. Then Richard would fire away. He rarely hit anything but this didn't really matter. He liked the sweet smell of the brown grass, the autumn sun upon his face, the spectacle of well-trained dogs at the work they loved. In the evenings he sat by his fire with a toddy or brandy and there was no one to disturb the pleasant hour or two of quiet reverie. Sometimes, after his manservant had shaved him or carefully trimmed his hair, he would look at himself in the mirror and recall what his father, Robert Bruce, had once said long ago. "Everyone lives too long. That's the trouble." The old man had been petulant in his dotage. Richard was finding the years most agreeable.

He sipped his toddy and stole a glance at Marta. She was, he mused, a beautiful woman who had not grown heavy in middle age as did most of the Spanish. She had borne a couple of fine children, also. This was his one regret. There was no son to carry on the Cameron name.

[510]

"You know," he spoke suddenly, "this thing in Cuba is going to boil over again. This time they'll find some way to get us into it and a war with Spain. More than half the island is already in possession of the rebels. There is a gentleman by the name of Mr. Hearst who owns a newspaper or two in New York. I receive them by mail, several days late of course. Anyhow. It seems Mr. Hearst considers the Cuban rebellion his own, personal cause. Daily he works himself into a lather of indignation and baits the Congress for action. He is determined, it seems, to furnish a war for his circulation department." He inhaled the fragrant steam of his toddy and took a long and satisfying swallow. "You may," he spoke directly to Marta, "eventually recover your father's estates if the United States intervenes. Which it probably will if Mr. Hearst has his way."

Marta glanced up. "I really don't care. My mother, I am sure, would not want to leave Spain now at her age. As for me, I am happy with Brian in the Bahamas. My husband and my children. I want nothing more."

"They won't be children much longer," Richard interrupted. "By the Lord, that Maria Christina is a real beauty. There is fire there. You'll have a time keeping it under control in two or three years." A thought suddenly occurred to him. "What the devil ever became of your mother and sister?" He addressed Brian.

"Mother died in Italy. My sister wrote Father a few years back. She seemed more concerned with a continuance of the allowance he had been sending than with Mother's death." He shook his head with wry expression. "Her letter was in English but filled with Italian phrases to impress us. My father instructed the bank to discontinue the allowance. You could almost hear Carol-Louise's scream across the Atlantic. I wouldn't be surprised if she showed up some day with her count for us to support. I'll put him to sponging or baling sisal."

"Well, you have young Cameron and Maria Christina visit me here whenever they can. I like them."

The children had spent three days with the family at Cameron Hall before being entered into their schools. They had been gravely respectful and a little awed by this ancient gentleman with his flowing mane of white hair. Their attitude had amused Richard, for he had never thought of himself as a formidable man.

"Do you know," Richard mused, "I have no one to leave everything to when I die except you. I don't mean that quite the way it sounds," he apologized. "The Raleighs have bred better than the Camerons. You have children. I have none. Anyhow," he finished his toddy, "it will all go to you someday to be held, I hope, for young Cam and your daughter.

I wouldn't like to have strangers moving into Cameron Hall after all the trouble I had in putting it together again." He smiled reminiscently. "It was my father who started it. I carried on. You'll end up owning more in South Carolina than you do in the Bahamas, but I don't imagine anything will ever get you to leave the islands."

"No," Brian admitted. "There lies my home. Just the same, thank you for your generous thought. Someday young Cam or Maria Christina . . ." He stopped in mid-sentence. "Not Cam. He's an island boy. Maria Christina?" He shrugged. "Maybe when she marries, she may want to live in the States. I guess, in the end, it will depend upon her husband. Anyhow, Cameron Hall will be in good hands. I give you my word."

"I hadn't thought of quitting it right away. But," Richard glanced at a clock above the mantel, "I'm pleasantly mellow with the toddy. I think I'll go to bed if you will excuse me. It is good having you here."

After he had left, Brian moved his chair closer to Marta. The pine in the fireplace had burned away but the oak glowed with a golden red powdered with fine gray ash. He reached over and took her hand, holding it for a moment to his cheek. Her eyes reflected contentment. How good, she thought, her life had been. Full and rich despite the isolation. She had never needed more than this man and the children born of him.

The pace of the years seemed accelerated now. Marta and Brian marked them by the time of Christmas which they spent with Cam, Maria Christina and Richard at Cameron Hall. Here the great house was truly decked with holly. Cam and Richard, with a Negro and a flatbed wagon, went out to select the tree and see to its felling. There were presents, feasting and laughter in the great house and a small bite of winter in the air. Then came the months of summer with the children back home on Exuma. September arriving too soon for everyone, and Cam and Maria Christina returning to school for another year.

Step by step the country moved toward a war which no one save a Mr. Hearst and a Mr. Pulitzer with their newspapers, the *World* and the *Journal,* wanted. Secretary of State Olney offered mediation between Cuba and Spain which was refused. Mr. Thomas Edison showed pictures which moved through his "Vitascope" at Koster and Bial's Music Hall in New York City, and McKinley was nominated for President. Japan protested the annexation of Hawaii by the United States, and the U.S.S. *Maine* was ordered to proceed to Havana on a friendly visit and was destroyed in the Cuban harbor by an explosion three weeks later. In New York City a Cuban junta headed by a former schoolteacher, Estrada Palma, established a "news agency" and daily released stories of atrocities by the Spaniards against the Cubans. In Havana, American correspondents sat in the bar and later wrote their horror stories of the butchery of rural Cubans by Spanish troops. Mr. Hearst sent the artist Frederick Remington to sketch the conflict for the *Journal* and Mr. Remington, growing restless, cabled his employer:

EVERYTHING QUIET. NO TROUBLE HERE. THERE WILL BE NO WAR.

Mr. Hearst cabled back:

YOU FURNISH THE PICTURES. I'LL FURNISH THE WAR.

Heroes were manufactured, villains created. General Wyler, "the butcher, the devastator of haciendas and violator of women." The *World* and the *Journal* were engaged in their own circulation war. Nothing was too outrageous to print, no rumor too extravagant to banner across eight columns. Public indignation was whipped to a frenzy and there was mounting pressure for intervention.

Spain was bankrupt, the United States unprepared for a war. Troops in heavy woolen uniforms sweated and cursed in the semitropical heat of Tampa, Florida, while waiting for orders and transport. Nothing could stay the conflict now. The President called for 125,000 volunteers. Commodore Dewey sailed for Manila. Rear Admiral Sampson blockaded ports on the north coast of Cuba. Captain Glass, of the U.S.S. *Charleston,* steamed into the harbor of Guam and opened fire on the fort. The Spanish commander sent out an officer with his apologies for not returning *the salute.* No one had told him about a war and he was out of ammunition, anyhow. Teddy Roosevelt and his Rough Riders. San Juan Hill. Daiquiri. Siboney. Guantánamo. Santiago. The names became part of the American vocabulary. The Spanish fleet was destroyed by Admiral Sampson; the American flag raised on Wake Island. Then it was over. Spain relinquished all title to Cuba and ceded Puerto Rico and other islands under Spanish sovereignty to the United States, which was to hold Manila pending a treaty of peace. The war no one really wanted came to a stuttering conclusion.

Cameron Raleigh, age sixteen, had tried to enlist in the Navy and was told by the recruiting officer, at Charleston, to go home and grow up. Cam offered to bet him his month's allowance he knew more about ships and sailing than did the desk-bound officer who had, probably, never come any closer to salt water than a gargle for a sore throat.

And Maria Christina Raleigh, at eighteen and in the full, shining beauty of her young womanhood, slipped from the convent one night to run away with an illiterate, reckless, handsomely contemptuous youth of nineteen who drove a wagon for the fish market delivering to the convent school.

[513]

In the stolen wagon the couple had whipped their way out of the city to Six Mile. There, in the morning, a tobacco-spitting, self-ordained, circuit-riding evangelist in stained trousers and suspenders drawn over dirty underwear had pronounced them Mr. and Mrs. Peach-boy Loomis for half a dollar. He threw in a drink of cheap whisky as a present to the groom and smirkingly tried to fondle Maria Christina while pretending a boozy concern for her happiness.

All of her instincts had rebelled at the coarseness of the ceremony—the littered, acrid-smelling cabin—but she seemed helplessly fascinated by the half-bare chest, the tightly curled black hair and the irresistible, mocking sneer about the Cupid's bow mouth. She kept telling herself everything would be all right once they had a place of their own. He would find a job and love would resolve the differences of their station and background. Little by little his crudeness would be smoothed away. He was a darkly passionate lover; a plunderer, a gypsy lad who had never had a chance. When she looked at him the breath left her, her heart stopped beating. She grew wildly excited by the thought of him.

The wedding night was spent in a cabin of a Loomis cousin near Twelve Mile. There was a pallet of straw at one side, a rickety table and three tomato crates for stools. The cousin, Troy, uncorked a jug of corn moonshine and set out two tin cups and a cracked jelly glass.

"Peach-boy," Troy sniggered as he admired Maria Christina, "you shore picked yo'sef a winnah en this heah one." He smacked his lips enviously, filled the cups and glass and then took a long swallow from the jug. "You know how come they cahl him Peach-boy?" He leaned toward her and his breath was the stench of a pig's sty. "His maw, who marrid some soat o' kin to me, look et him one day en say: 'Youah suah a peach of a boy.' Aftah that everah one cahl him Peach-boy Loomis."

When they had drunk enough, Peach-boy chased his cousin from the cabin with an ax handle, dropped a bar across the door and took his trembling bride to bed on the floor's dirty pallet.

She had never imagined it could be like this and bit hard against her knuckles to keep from screaming. She was being ripped apart, torn. The wet, slobbering mouth sought hers and rough hands violated her body. The piglike gruntings and finally, Peach-boy's writhing upheaval. After a while he had rolled away. Then, indifferent to her hysterical sobbing and his nakedness, he drank heavily from the jug and tossed a blanket to her.

"Covah yo'sef up some befoah Troy come back." He went to the door and lifted the bar from its slots.

"No. Please," she moaned and pulled the blanket to hide herself. It stank of sweat and mold. "Please don't let anyone in. Please."

"Hell." He half turned. "Troy don't mind. Hey! You Troy out theah. You kin come back en now."

"Youah suah a cuttah, Peach-boy." There was admiration in the voice answering from the darkness. "I ain' mad none at you."

Troy shuffled back inside the cabin. He regarded Maria Christina with a leering snicker. Then he and Peach-boy, by a lantern's smoky light, had finished what was left of the whisky.

Maria Christina edged cautiously back into a corner, hoping they would forget about her, the covering pulled to her chin. They drank steadily, a new jug passing back and forth as they leaned toward each other mumbling incoherently, slapping each other on the shoulder with stupid shouts of affection. After a while Peach-boy rose unsteadily to his feet. He swayed and his head lolled as his eyes sought out Maria Christina.

"You a-goin' out agin, Troy." His mouth hung slackly.

"How 'bout you a-goin' this time?" The cousin braced his hands on the table. "Aftah ahl. We kin," he suggested.

"We ain' kin en this. Git now foah I crack that theah ax handle 'cross you' haid."

"This suah ain' no way to treat youah own sistah's nephew oah whatevah I am." Troy had protested his ouster. He began edging around the shack's wall. "Everah one know a man relative git to kiss a bride."

"Git." Peach-boy had lifted the ax handle threateningly. "Git like I tell you."

"Damn it, Peach-boy," Troy's voice was shrill with frustration and anger. "This heah my own house. How long you figuah to make hit yourn without no good re-turn?"

"Till I git ready to leave. Now you git oah I dam well split youah skull."

Troy had backed from the cabin, stumbled on the doorsill and fell out in a spinning turn. Peach-boy staggered toward Maria Christina and she screamed her terror.

When the girl's absence was discovered, a distracted Mother Superior sent a rider galloping to Cameron Hall to notify Richard, whose name had been placed on the records as the nearest relative. How and where could the girl have gone? Unless they were in groups, carefully chaperoned by two of the Sisters, the students were never permitted outside the grounds. The other girls were questioned collectively and then individually. Finally, the two who shared Maria Christina's room broke down. In a flood of tears they told how Maria Christina had been creeping out after lights to meet someone at the gates. It was a love tryst. Someone

Maria Christina had seen and managed a word with. That was all they knew. Both of them had thought the midnight rendezvous was excitingly romantic, a conspiracy of love to be whispered over with breathless wonder and awe at their roommate's daring. Maria Christina was madly in love, they explained, both trying to talk at once, but she had never confided the name of her mysterious suitor. By the time the confession was over, the girls were in weeping confusion. The Mother Superior went into the chapel to pray and ask forgiveness for her sin of omission and carelessness.

When Richard finally arrived he was much more direct. He questioned everyone: the Sisters; the girls; the Negro woman cook and her two helpers, who were not of the Order but lay help who came in by the day. It was the cook who finally shed a dubious light on what might have happened. All of the students served some time in the kitchen, learning the preparation of food.

"Couple time dis Miss Maria Christina heah wid oather en huh class learnin' to do foah dey se'fs laik a lady should know how to run d' house. Dey was dis heah fish market boy, good-lookin' white trash. He come once oah twice. Ah think Ah see a look laik between dem but suah ain' pay much 'tention 'cause what young lady tek up with trash? Now, jus' could be." She stopped, frightened by the enormity of the suggestion she was about to make. "Jus' could be," she finished weakly.

After getting the name and location of the fish market, Richard drove to an area of ramshackle docks and confronted an irate man who was raging over the absence of his helper and the mysterious disappearance of a horse and delivery wagon. He was sufficiently impressed by Richard Cameron's dignified appearance and the expensive carriage with groom and driver outside his door to quiet down and become eagerly respectful.

"Yes, suh. I had me a drivah. Good-lookin' trash. Pretty in the face but real mean inside. Girls always hangin' aroun' this market like cats; wantin' to touch him oah jus' get a word. Damn ef I know why. Like I say. He's mean. Name of Peach-boy Loomis. Now I think of it the bastud must have run off with my horse an' wagon."

"He did more than that." Richard controlled his deep anger. "Where's his home? Who are his people? Do you know anything about him?"

The market owner sensed the pent-up fury. He wondered how trash like Loomis could have touched this gentleman's life. Whatever he done, he thought, I'd sure hate to be in his place.

"He slept out back in the net room. Had him a cot theah. I leave him have it for nothin' to keep an eye on things. Seems like, though, he once said he had some kin out to Ten Mile, oah maybe, Six Mile. I ain't suah. I'd suah like to get my horse an' wagon back." He made the statement hopefully. "That's no lie."

Richard had the carriage driven to the house on Tradd Street. In his study he went to a cabinet and opened a mahogany case, velvet lined, containing a pair of pistols. They were beautifully made, almost museum pieces, pre-Revolutionary War. He put them back. They would be of no use to him. At a gunsmith's on Meeting Street he purchased a modern weapon with cartridges. Then he ordered the carriage to the City Club where he had a quietly thoughtful drink before his luncheon. There was no hurry. The harm had already been done. He had the steward pack a hamper with food. There was no telling where this search would lead but he would find Maria Christina. Time enough then to decide how and what to write Brian and Marta.

At a wooden pail beneath a mulberry tree Maria Christina tried to wash her face and the water streamed with the tears down her cheeks. She was soiled, body and soul irreparably dirty. The confusion of her mind was such that she went through the motions of attempting to tidy herself without conscious thought. What insanity had possessed her to do this thing? It had seemed incredibly romantic behind the convent gates. To meet a lover at midnight. To whisper of his handsomeness to her roommates. To be in rebellion against the authority and discipline of the Sisters. But, God of Mercy, this degradation. And now what? To get away. The unbearable humiliation of returning, somehow, to the school. She would be sent home, of course. The whole, sordid adventure known to everyone and her parents. What madness had led her to believe this Peach-boy—she writhed inwardly at the name—was anything but what she knew him to be? By what fantastic trick of the imagination had she found him handsome, beautiful to look upon, gentle and with a softly persuasive voice and manner, someone who would cherish and regard her with disbelief that she was really his. She had seen herself remolding him into a dashing gentleman of the town, successful and highly regarded as a poor, unfortunate man who had fought his way out of an unhappy childhood by sheer strength of character with a loving wife at his side. The notion, now, made her want to vomit.

On a branch of the tree there was a piece of bleached flour sacking for a towel. She used it to dry her hands and face because there was no alternative. It also smelled rancid, as did everything in the cabin.

"They suah don' dress you up no fancy en that theah school, do they?" Peach-boy, bare of foot and without a shirt, was propped in the shack's doorway, leaning against one side. "Youah kin mus' be rich to sen' you to such a place but you don' look it this mornin'." He picked at his teeth with a black fingernail. "What you suppose youah paw's goin' to say

[517]

with us married en ahl?" He thought this over. "You know what Ahm a-goin' to do? Ahm a-goin' to git myse'f set in some soat of a business like, maybe a fancy pool hahl." He tilted his head and began dreaming out loud. "I'll git me clothes with a colored vest en a gold watch en chain en a Nigruh to run an' fetch, day en night."

"I want to go home." Her voice was firm. She wondered how she had ever found his manner of speech, the almost unintelligible thick accent of a Geechee Negro, softly titillating. "I want you to take me back."

"Well. Ain' that what ahm sayin'? We go see youah paw en you say: 'Papa.'" He tried to imitate a mincing tone. "'This heah is my husban', Peach-boy. Ahm Mrs. Loomis now, Papa, en I want you should do somethin' good for my legal husban'.' Then, he goin' to be so glad to have you home he set us up in a fine house of ouah own. We got a place, a carriage, Nigruhs bowin' en scrapin' en sayin': 'Yes, suh, Mr. Loomis. Raight away, Mr. Loomis.'" He tossed back his head and whinnied with laughter.

She regarded him with loathing. Her fear, the nightmare of the cabin, was draining away. If he tried to touch her again she'd claw his eyes out.

"I don't live in Charleston. My father is in the Bahamas."

"Wheah the hell is that?" He opened one eye. "You write him a lettuh then. Tell him how you git married en ahl. That'll bring him runnin'."

"Hey! You, Peach-boy." The cousin, Troy, was coming across the stubbled field. He had an old, single-barreled shotgun with two rabbits hanging from a string. In the other hand he carried a fresh jug of corn whisky. "Ah stopped me by a frien's still foah some drinkin' likker en we got rabbit foah stew. I bin thinkin'. You all stay heah long as you like. Kin is kin Ah always say. Oney you got to stop runnin' me out of th' cabin en th' middle of th' night with en ax handle." He studied Maria Christina. "Damn ef you don' looked peaked; some skinny, too, in broad daylight." He tossed the rabbits at her feet. "You skin 'em up whilst me en Peach-boy have a drink." He hunkered down beside Loomis and uncorked the jug.

"I don't know how to skin a rabbit." Again the wave of nauseating helplessness flooded over her. She was in the company of chattering idiots. "I never did."

Troy drank from the jug and then passed it to his cousin. He spat and eyed her with surprised stupidity.

"You take a knife en gut 'em en skin 'em. Almos' enny damn fool knowed that." He reached into his hip pocket, took out a big clasp knife and started to toss it to her. Then he halted, his eyes filled with a clouded, sly suspicion. "Uh-uh." He shook his head. "You look mad enough to gut me or ol' Peach-boy heah. Ah don' reckon to give you no knife blade. Ah'll do hit myse'f latuh."

Maria Christina braced her back against the mulberry tree, forcing herself to remain upright although her legs had no strength. Troy and Peach-boy alternated with the whisky. The spectacle was of pigs swilling.

"You figuah to take huh to youah folks, Peach-boy?" Troy blew across the jug's mouth and it made a low sound of moaning. "They suah be some surprise."

"Hell no." Loomis studied his bare feet and the dirt-encrusted toes. "Time come, aftah th' honeymoon," he grinned, "Ah'm goin' to take huh to huh own folks in th' Bahamas. I guess they in Cahlina, someplace. By that time I figuah they give mos' anythin' to knowed she ahl raight." He tilted the jug and the liquor gurgled down his throat. "How you like to come work en my pool hahl, Troy? I make you managah."

"What th' hell pool hahl?" Troy reached for the whisky.

"The pool hahl huh papa's goin' to set me up en. An' stop spittin' back en that theah jug whin you drink."

Troy slapped his cousin on the leg with an emphatic delight. "Peach-boy, laik Ah say. Youah a cuttah." He lifted the jug and drank again. "Yes, suh. A suah enough cuttah." He tried to wipe at his mouth and missed it.

Maria Christina stiffened and lifted her eyes. They were going to get drunk, stupefied. Already the speech was thickening and the motions uncertain. If they kept on drinking they'd go to sleep in this warm sun. She had no idea where she was but there was a dirt road fifty yards or so away. They had come along it from the place called Six Mile, and Six Mile had to be east because the sun had been at their backs after they had left the preacher yesterday morning. Where east was, Charleston had to be. Her thoughts refused to carry her beyond this. Once she was back in the city she had no idea what she was to do. It would be enough to get away from here. Maybe she could steal the wagon. But the horse was unhitched and she didn't know how to get the animal into the shafts.

"Youah kin real rich?" Troy called to her.

She didn't answer. There was a vacuous, doltish expression on his face. He whistled into the jug again and laughed at the sound. Then his expression soured as he saw the rebellion in her eyes.

"Come a time," Troy spoke to his cousin, "whin youah goin' to have to beat en that one. She's sullen laik. I woul'n't have no sullen woman 'roun' me."

It seemed hours while she stood within the tree's shade, covertly watching the pair. They mouthed ridiculous inconsistencies to each other; were solemn and hilarious by turn. Once Troy gagged on the whisky but

[519]

he choked it back. Peach-boy, his eyes shut, slid farther down on his spine in the doorway.

"How minny table you goin' to have en that pool hahl?" Troy suddenly remembered.

"Eight, ten, a dozen."

They both roused themselves from the sedative effect of the moonshine. Peach-boy licked at his lips and reached for the jug. Troy pulled it away and shook it, measuring the contents.

"You ain' forgettin' about mekkin' me managah?"

"Whin youah managah," Peach-boy was suddenly belligerent, "you got to cahl me Mr. Loomis."

"What th' hell should Ah cahl you Mr. Loomis foah?" Troy was offended.

" 'Cause Ahm th' ownah en you hired help."

"Damn ef Ahm goin' to be no hired help to you."

"Damned ef you ain't." Peach-boy reached for the jug and almost upset it with his fumbling.

"Well," Troy propped the container between his feet, "then th' Nigruhs gotta cahl me Mr. Troy Boomer. Everah one goin' t' say Mr. Troy Boomer, day en naight."

"Everah one but me." Peach-boy was truculent.

"Well ahl raight. Everah one but you. You kin cahl me Troy." His head nodded and his body tipped until it was leaning against Peach-boy's leg.

Loomis forced his eyes open. They were mere slits. He peered uncertainly at Maria Christina.

"What th' hell you standin' by that tree foah?"

"Because there's no place to sit." She said it pleasantly, not wanting to antagonize him into wakefulness.

"Hell, then. Stand ef you ain't got sense enough to sit on the groun'. Ahm goin' to have me a little nap heah in the wahm sun. Whin I wake up we go inside en leave Troy to skin them rabbit." He stretched his hand for the jug and tipped it over. A small trickle ran from its mouth. "Damn." For a moment Peach-boy seemed to struggle with the effort of sitting up. Then he sank back, his eyes closed. He began to breathe with a whistling sound through his open lips.

Maria Christina waited. She didn't dare move. Loomis and Troy were lying like spent dogs in the sun. Inch by inch she sidled away. Slowly, carefully, her feet took her one step after another until she was behind the cabin and out of sight. Then she began to run. She gathered up her skirt of light brown serge and raced for the road. Here the sand was soft in the ruts and it clung to her feet. The center ridge was firmer but the wiry grass and sandspurs tore at her ankles. She stumbled once and rested on hands and knees, her breath coming in tortured gasps. Then she was up again. She would run for a minute and then walk, casting an apprehensive glance behind. There was no one in sight. She began to breathe more freely. They would probably sleep for hours. She had never seen drunken men before and had no idea how long it took for the effects of so much whisky to wear off. She decided to take no chances; a few yards running, a few yards walking.

What she was passing through were pine flats with the tall, straight trees murmuring in a high breeze. Nowhere did she see a cabin and she would have hesitated to approach one if she had. Once, coming toward her, a wagon with splayed wheels and drawn by a mule halted. A Negro man held the reins and stared at her with open curiosity as she approached.

"You en some soat o' trouble, miss?"

"No." She had no fear of this colored man and would have asked for a ride if he had been going in the other direction. "How—how far is it to Charleston?"

"Miss!" He was incredulous. "You ain' fixin' to whalk thataway to Chalstun? Hit's a fah piece."

"Thank you."

"Fah piece" or not, she had to get there. Once she caught a glimpse of a river and thought it must be the Ashley. If she only knew where Cameron Hall was, on which side of the river. The Negro might have told her but she hadn't thought to ask. Only a vague idea had formed in her mind as to what she would do once she reached the city. Certainly she couldn't return to the convent. The best and safest place would be Uncle Richard's house on Tradd Street. The servants knew her. They would get word to Cameron Hall.

The sun was growing hotter and she could feel her body and underclothing sticky with perspiration. She was terribly thirsty. Her mouth was so dry there was nothing to swallow. She tried to push back her hair. Her hands came away wet.

Richard Cameron held to one of the side straps in the carriage's compartment as the vehicle slid and bounced through the yielding ruts. The driver was holding the horses at an easy, ground-covering trot, but still the carriage slewed and jolted. They had stopped at a crossroad settlement, Six Mile. Richard called to a man sitting on the edge of a narrow porch fronting a small general store.

"You know a family hereabouts by the name of Loomis?"

The man appeared to be thinking this over before he replied. "Theah's some Loomis kin, I recollect, neah Twelve Mile. En," he chewed on a twig, "I once heah of some Loomis at Goose Crick."

"I'm looking for a Loomis they call Peach-boy." Richard spoke the outrageously ridiculous name with difficulty.

The man studied Richard, the carriage, the fine horses, the Negroes on the box. Gentry. A man always got hisse'f into trouble when he mixed with th' gentry. Maybe it would be bettah to say nothin'. Then agin, maybe it wouldn'. Damned ef a man knew exactly what to do.

"Troy Boomer," he admitted finally. "Some soat of kin to Peach-boy, secon' cousin likely. He, maybe, could tell you."

"Thank you." Richard nodded and spoke to the coachman. The carriage rolled on.

Maria Christina saw it from a distance. Light sparkled on the carriage's varnish and darted off the silver ornamentation of the harness. She moved from the center to stand beside the road. Here at last, she thought, was help she could trust.

"Mistuh Richard, suh." The coachman half turned. "Theah a young-lookin' girl up ahead, a lady, maybe."

There was a question in the statement. Richard Cameron had said nothing about this journey into the countryside. But a colored house-maid at the convent had whispered the scandal while Cameron had been closeted with the Mother Superior. Both driver and groom knew they were looking for Miss Maria Christina.

Richard leaned forward as the horses moved at a walk and were pulled up. He stared unbelievingly at the bedraggled figure with hair hanging in lank strings, face smudged and wet with perspiration.

"Maria Christina!"

"Uncle Richard! Oh, thank God, Uncle Richard!" She stumbled toward the carriage and fell to her hands and knees, unable to move any farther. The groom leaped down to open the door but Richard was already out. "Uncle Richard." She repeated the name.

Gently Richard lifted the girl and she clung to him, crying unashamedly. With her leaning heavily on him, he led her back to the carriage. Inside he took a bottle of wine from the hamper. She was sobbing with wracking upheavals. Calmly he filled a silver cup.

"Drink this." He held it to her mouth.

She swallowed greedily, her breath coming in labored heaving. When the cup was drained she all but collapsed against him. Her eyes were dull, lifeless with fatigue, but her body shook with uncontrollable spasms. He held her tightly, saying nothing until he could feel the trembling lessen.

"Are you hurt?" he asked gently.

"I don't know."

"Where is he?" Richard was calm. "I'm going to kill him."

"No, please." Her strength was returning. "It was all much more my fault. I did a terribly foolish thing. Why I can't tell you. Killing him will only be trouble for you, everyone. Please," she looked up imploringly, "please just take me home, Uncle Richard. I am so tired." She was crying now, crying like a child and not a young woman. "Don't make me see him again ever."

Richard took her hand in one of his. Anger was cold within him. Time enough to deal with this Loomis. He'd have him hunted down and brought to the city. Then what? The question halted his plans. The open scandal? So far no one but the Sisters, the Mother Superior and the girls in the school knew of this outrageous folly. It would be whispered about, of course, later. But that could not be helped. Dragging Loomis into a court, on exactly what charges he did not know, would only give open tongue on the entire affair. They would, he decided, go back to Cameron Hall. Later he could decide what must or should be done. He spoke to the coachman.

"We'll go home now, Silas. Not to the city. To the Hall."

✺ XXXII ✺

MARIA CHRISTINA RALEIGH'S son was born in Nassau's small hospital, on the island of New Providence, in the late afternoon of a July day in the year 1899, and the girl turned her face away when the infant was brought to her, refusing to look at it.

It had been a time of mental anguish for everyone. Both Marta and Brian had looked well and long within themselves before coming to terms with the indisputable facts of the situation. Maria Christina had subjected herself to a period of torture. In her mind nothing less than some sort of a monster kicked and moved within her. It was inconceivable that the seed of Peach-boy Loomis could produce anything else. She had lain awake many a night wondering what misshapen and evil thing stirred and asked for birth. What would she bring forth? The question terrified her.

After that midmorning, nine months earlier, when Richard Cameron found her stumbling along the road to Charleston, they had gone to Cameron Hall. There she rested and was cared for until her hysteria quieted and she was able to talk with a clear mind and some measure of maturity. It was, Richard agreed, out of the question for her to attempt reinstatement in the school. He had gone to Charleston and talked with the Mother Superior. The good woman's conscience was deeply troubled. The girl had been placed in her care. Somewhere, somehow, she had been negligent, with this terrible result. Maria Christina had been fifteen when she was entered in the school. During the three years honor, obedience and a sense of true values should have been instilled in her. Had they been, this thing would never have occurred. Somewhere she and the teaching Sisters, the school itself, had failed in a sacred trust. But, she admitted, it would be impossible to reaccept Maria Christina as though nothing had happened. The effect of her presence on the imagination of the other girls would be disastrous to say nothing of the indignation of their parents. For this affair could not be kept secret. One thing, paramount in Richard's mind, was achieved through the meeting. He would be allowed to tell, in person, Maria Christina's parents. There would be no coldly formal letter advising them of their daughter's dismissal and the reason for it. This would be a shock beyond imagining. He would go with the girl to the Bahamas.

In addition to his talk with the Mother Superior, Richard had inquiries made. The circuit-riding preacher had no authority to perform a wedding ceremony. He was simply a hellfire-shouting, evangelical fraud who held open-air meetings at crossroad settlements. At these he yelled his exhortations against sin to a gawking audience of country people and collected a dollar or two in contributions. So, there was no Peach-boy Loomis as a husband to contend with.

Back at Cameron Hall he talked with a now composed Maria Christina, telling her what he had learned and of the Mother Superior's decision. There was no way of avoiding the truth of what had happened. The month was November. In six weeks or so Marta and Brian would arrive in Charleston to spend the holidays as had been their custom. The fact that Maria Christina was not in school was certainly not something which would escape them. Anyhow—Richard was firm—he would have no part in such a futile attempt at deception.

"I think it best," they had been sitting before a small fire in the evening, "I go to the Bahamas with you. Your mother and father must be told. Maybe my presence will be of some small comfort to you. I am not entirely without understanding and, believe me, neither are Brian and Marta. It will be unpleasant but it must be faced."

"I know." She was subdued and grateful. "Thank you, Uncle Richard."

"Do you know," he stirred at his usual, aftersupper toddy, "I have never been to the islands. It seems strange."

"I could think of a happier reason to take you there." Despite herself Maria Christina could not resist a tiny smile.

They had told Cam only that his sister's school was giving her an earlier period of the customary Christmas vacation and they were going to the Bahamas to return with his and her mother and father. They sailed three days later on one of the Cunard vessels and took the mail and passenger boat from Nassau to Exuma.

After the surprise and concerned astonishment of seeing Maria Christina had worn themselves through a seemingly endless series of questions, Richard took it upon himself to recount what had happened. Throughout his carefully chosen words Maria Christina had sat, head slightly bowed, hands twisting nervously in her lap. She did not look at her mother and father. If she had, she would have seen compassion, love and a measure of understanding. For despite the shock, they were not without sympathy and a knowledge of the world and human frailties. Marta, with the memory of her own convent days, was aware of how easy it was to rebel against the strict discipline, constant supervision and social sterility. Girls had done and would continue to do incredibly foolish things where their immature emotions were concerned. Within the walls of a convent a girl's imagination took flight. She was filled with half-recognized longings. Her daughter was long out of adolescence. She was a young woman and prey to her body which unconsciously yearned for fulfillment. Brian was also aware of these things although he might have expressed them differently.

"Well," Richard concluded, "there you have it. I thought it would be better and easier for everyone if Maria Christina and I came together."

Marta went to her daughter's side, half knelt there, pressing her cheek to the girl's. It was no time for words. What was there to say? False reassurance that what had happened didn't matter? She would not stoop to that and Maria Christina, if she knew her daughter, would not have it.

"I suppose," Brian spoke thoughtfully, "there is nothing to do but send for the boy and make the best of a situation."

"No, Father." Maria Christina lifted her face and regarded him without flinching. "You wouldn't tolerate him in the house. I couldn't bear to see him again."

Richard, who had no knowledge of the sordid details of her experience in Troy's cabin, had only recounted the facts as he knew them. Now he must speak of the thing which would outrage them most but in the end prove to be a blessing.

"Maria Christina," he said, "was never actually married to this Loomis. The man who performed the ceremony had no church affiliation. He was self-ordained and had no authority. So, there is no need to concern yourself about a husband. There is none."

Neither Marta nor Brian could possibly conceive of Peach-boy Loomis as he was. They would have found a word portrait of him an incredible exaggeration. Even Brian, who had known many men in many ports, had seen and heard them at their worst, could not imagine the illiterate vulgarity of Loomis. He would have refused to believe his daughter could be attracted by such a person.

Marta was deeply affected by Richard's words. A bad marriage, the result of inexperience and impetuous behavior, was a situation in itself. But to have bedded with a man out of wedlock was an offense against God.

"Perhaps—" she started to speak.

"No, Mother." Maria Christina was firm. "I will not have him even though I know what has happened torments you. I have no answer for what I did. I have searched for an excuse. There is none. God, in his own way, will have to forgive me but I will not marry to expiate a sin. It seems to me such a marriage would be the greater sin in God's eyes."

So, it was left that way. Instead of going to Charleston for the Christmas season it was decided to have Cameron come home. After a visit of a week, Richard returned to South Carolina. He was intensely interested in the island plantation his grandfather had founded. Brian showed him the sisal fields, explained the processing of the fibers. They took the ketch and sailed through the Out Islands, fishing, exploring and spending a night aboard the *Caroline* where she was anchored while the sponging crew worked. The startling beauty of the waters, the green and silver of the islands, the sunrises and awesome silence of twilight made a deep impression on Richard Cameron.

"I can understand why you say you'll never leave here." They were walking from the house to the shore. "It may be I who will come to you someday and close up Cameron Hall."

"You will always be welcome."

The family stood upon the dock waiting for the mail boat which would take Richard to Nassau. Impulsively, Maria Christina kissed him. She spoke no word of thanks but they both understood.

By February there could be no mistake. Maria Christina was pregnant. The full horror of her situation and the shame enveloped her. It would have been tragedy enough to bear an illegitimate child. But to give birth to something planted by Peach-boy Loomis—to, in a measure, reproduce him within her—was almost beyond enduring.

"I'll kill myself first."

"No." Marta was numbed by what Maria Christina had told her. "No. You will have the baby. There is no choice."

Brian, of course, was told. The words came stumbling from Maria Christina's lips but she had the courage to face her father and meet his unhappy eyes. There was an understanding in her father she had not realized before. He took her in his arms, awkwardly attempting to comfort her, but said nothing. It was impossible for him to look beyond the moment and into the years ahead when she would want to marry and must carry with her the burden of this unwanted child. He did not fully share Marta's and his daughter's feeling of complete disgrace or that Maria Christina was irredeemably dishonored. He held no deep religious convictions and was not tortured by them as was his wife. He was greatly moved and saddened by the situation but refused to accept it as the end of everything he had hoped for where his daughter was concerned. The child would be born and its birth would occasion no particular interest in these islands beyond the widely scattered acquaintances and a few friends. Even here the truth could be concealed. Maria Christina had made an unfortunate marriage on the mainland. There was no need to explain anything beyond that. The infant would be absorbed into the family. Other than this he could envision nothing more.

Now, in the Nassau hospital, Marta sat beside her daughter's bed. The birth had been a remarkably easy one. There were no complications. Maria Christina was resting, her eyes wide, staring at the ceiling.

"Is it a monster, Mother?" She did not turn.

"Of course not, child." Marta could not understand this obsessive fear. "He's a fine, strong-looking boy. Not beautiful but," she half smiled a little wearily, "they never really are at first."

"I am so frightened." The words were whispered.

"But, dear," Marta could not possibly comprehend what was passing through her daughter's mind, "it is all over."

"It has just begun. Oh, God! I am afraid to live."

"That is a terrible thing to say."

"You don't know. You can't begin to imagine."

"You must stop these wild fancies. The doctor wants you to nurse the baby."

"No!"

The idea of taking the newborn to her full breasts terrified her. What would she see when she looked into its face? Would there be something of Peach-boy's snarling viciousness, his deceptive prettiness which had once so captivated her beyond all logic? Had it inherited Troy Boomer's vacuous idiocy and the generations of moronic forebears who were the foundation for Peach-boy and his cousin? She knew nothing of genetics, wasn't even familiar with the word. She did know, however, when you bred a mongrel with a blooded animal the result was another mongrel. What had she given birth to?

"You will not be permitted to dismiss an obligation." For the first time Marta Raleigh was out of temper with her daughter. "Do you really believe you can do what you did and not accept the full consequences? I am not talking of the Church or morals. God will forgive you. I believe in His mercy. I am speaking of Maria Christina Raleigh's debt to this child. He is not in the world by choice. You conceived him out of an act of your own, willfully flaunting everything you had been taught. I believe you when you say you thought you were truly in love; though from what you tell me, it seems inconceivable. But, you were no child. A young woman of eighteen. We have talked together, much more than my mother and I. You were not uninformed. I have shared your misery, your shame. But your life is not in ruins. I do not believe in that kind of a God. Now. Take your baby. I am very angry with you, for your refusal is the real affront to God. This is not something from which you can walk away. If," she stood up, "you wish me to leave I will." The dark beauty of her eyes was fired.

There was silence for a moment. Then Maria Christina turned, her cheek resting on the pillow. She could read the unhappiness on her mother's face. She loved her dearly.

"Please stay, Mother. Stay and call the nurse to bring the baby."

Even in these all but neglected islands there was a deep sense of mourning for the old Queen who had died and was succeeded by Edward VII. A great and brilliant era of expansion for the British Empire was brought to a close at this first turning of the new century. It was true, Victoria's reign had done little for the Bahamas. The Out Islands were as miserably poor as ever, the people scratching out a bare living. Many of the inhabitants had emigrated to the Florida Keys, others had searched for employment in the Southern coastal cities. The sights of the Queen and her Ministers had been turned on larger, more glittering and rewarding fields. The islands were mere possessions of real estate and no attempt was made to improve their lot. Still, many in the Bahamas felt a loss in the Queen's passing. She had been a great monarch and even the most neglected of her subjects felt a pride in her accomplishments. For was she not Empress of India with all the magnificence the title implied?

On the Exuma plantation Brian read aloud of a nation in mourning; of cities and villages draped in black and people weeping unashamedly as Victoria was laid to rest in the mausoleum beside her beloved Albert.

"She was a great queen." He put aside the journals. "The British Empire may never see her like again. After all," he shrugged, "what is there left to conquer? The moon?"

They were gathered again as a family. Young Cam. They all spoke of him as Young Cam despite the fact his grandfather, Cameron Raleigh, had been dead for six years or so. Young Cam had finished his terms at the academy in Charleston. He had prevailed upon his mother and father to allow his education to end there, although Brian had wanted him enrolled at The Citadel.

"I am not one for drilling and marching upon a field, Father," he had pleaded. "I have no wish to be a soldier, so how will I benefit from a military school? I am a seaman born of seafaring people. Let me to stay in the islands and make what future I can here with you. To tell the truth"—his smile had been engagingly easy and frank—"I have no great ambition. Without half trying I can become a first-rate conch."

[529]

"There are no fine prospects in the islands, Son. Look at me. I have turned farmer out of necessity and not choice. It is a good-enough life but I don't think it will satisfy you."

"I'll find something even if it is only a deckhand on the mail boat. Or, I may go to England and enlist in the King's Navy."

He had, of course, done neither. Instead he had gone back with Washer and the sponging crew aboard the *Caroline* and was away from home for weeks at a time. He had a girl on Eluthera, Andrea Dunsmore, whose family had come to the islands at about the same time as Ronald Cameron. They were both young and so there was no talk of marriage, but her father, Kenneth Dunsmore, had made a point of visiting the Raleighs on Exuma and renewing old ties of friendship.

The problem of explaining Maria Christina's baby to Young Cam had been left to Brian. After a time of searching within himself he had spoken to his son. They had walked along the beach together and Brian told Cam what had happened, frankly, openly and honestly. He saw no point in attempting to gloss the truth.

"One of us ought to find this Loomis and kill him." Cam displayed an unsuspected anger and loyalty to his sister.

"It was Richard Cameron's intention. He told me so. But I don't see how it would mend a situation. The thing is done. Your mother and I have reconciled ourselves to it. I want you to be careful, though. Maria Christina has been deeply hurt. The shame and humiliation wells within her, for no one else has censured her. She is filled with an unjustified fear the boy will turn out to be something of his father. I believe in heredity but I also place great faith in environment. We will rear the boy as one of our own and can only wait and see how it turns out. He is only two years old. I wish, when you are home, you would give him some small attention, a little of your time. It is important he grow with the protection of affection. He will need love much more than physical care. I honestly don't know what Maria Christina feels. She makes no display and will not talk about it."

They had given the child the name of Raleigh and the first name of Bruce after Richard Cameron's father. He had been baptized and christened in the Catholic Chapel at Nassau.

After the return home it was difficult for anyone to learn how Maria Christina regarded her baby. For the first year she had all but ignored it. The care, after weaning, was left to a Negro nurse who saw to his feeding, bathing and changing. The woman occupied a room with the baby's crib in one wing of the house. Maria Christina never entered it. Now, though, in the infant's second year Marta and Brian sometimes thought they detected a subtle change in their daughter's attitude. She no longer seemed to treat its presence with anxiety and suspicion. She made no open display but often smiled faintly when the child fastened upon a new word or tumbled upon the rug with a puppy Cam had brought from Nassau. It was a remarkably healthy child. He wandered with unsure footing through the garden and, later, trotted alongside one of the colored boys who worked in the yard. He invaded the kitchen where the old cook spoiled him outrageously and never seemed to mind having him underfoot. Everyone found pleasure in his growth and accomplishments but his mother.

Once, Cam hoisted the child to his shoulder and took him down to the beach where they splashed and played in the small waves in which Bruce rolled and shouted his excited glee. From a block of white pine Cam fashioned a boat, fitted it with a mast, stationary rudder and small sail. Together they launched it at the end of a long string by which it could be retrieved. The child was ecstatic over this miracle and kept shouting: "Wook, Cam. Wook."

It was upon this occasion Cam had glanced up to see Maria Christina standing on the beach. There was a wistfully puzzled expression of baffled longing on her face.

"Tuck up your skirts and come into the water."

For a moment Maria Christina hesitated. Then she kicked off her slippers. She wore a simple dress of brightly printed cotton and did not bother to fasten it up but waded into the clear shallows. She stood, watching as brother and son went about the serious business of setting the toy boat upon a course. The child had regarded his mother with curiosity as though her presence here, somehow, needed to be explained. He had never been taught to call her Mother. Young as he was he seemed to recognize something vaguely hostile in her. When he climbed upon a knee or into a lap, it was Brian's, Marta's or Cam's. For her he had devised his own interpretation of her name from hearing the others speak it. It came out with the sound of: "Ea-chris."

After a while Maria Christina turned away and waded ashore. She put on her slippers and began to walk up the hill. Suddenly she was running.

That evening, for the first time, she had the Negro woman bring him downstairs. He was placed in a high chair at the table in advance of the family. Almost awkwardly she fed her son from the plate with potato, small pieces of chicken and vegetables. His milk was in a silver mug which he held in both hands. It was a strangely moving tableau. There was an expression of uncertainty on Maria Christina's face as though she found herself in a completely unaccountable situation. The child stared gravely at her as she forked up a square of white meat and put it to his mouth. He was perfectly capable of feeding himself; a little clumsily, to be sure, but he managed. Now, he was puzzled. Something new and baffling was being introduced into the routine. He was interested in the novelty, by her presence. Then he laughed with a gurgling sound of pleasure and spoke the single word.

"Ea-chris."

She put down the napkin and arose hurriedly from the table, leaving the Negro woman to finish with the meal and a custard dessert. Swiftly she mounted the staircase and went to her room where she threw herself upon the bed and cried softly, the hot tears of confused emotions staining her cheeks.

When she came downstairs later to join the family at the table she was composed. Near the time when Brian had a small cup of black coffee and a little rum with his customary cigar she spoke to them all without singling out anyone.

"I haven't been behaving very well. I'm sorry and ashamed if I have hurt you."

For a moment no one said anything. Brian poured a small trickle of rum into his coffee. Marta's hand stole over to cover that of her daughter's. Cam studied the empty plate before him and finally spoke.

"The *Caroline* is anchored at Salt Pond. I was going over tomorrow in the ketch. Why don't you come? They are working some new sponge beds. Then, if you like, we'll just loaf along up to Eluthera. Take Bruce with us. I'll get a line around his waist so if he falls overboard we can haul him back. We'll fish and lie in the sun, and maybe sail from Eluthera to Spanish Wells and then over to Harbor Island."

Maria Christina looked at her brother with gratitude. "I'd like that, Cam. I'd like it very much." She hesitated. "We'll take Bruce."

"I'd like you to meet my girl, Andrea." He flushed a little with this open declaration. "I guess she's my girl. I haven't told her yet. Anyhow, we'll pay a visit to the Dunsmores."

Doubt and the question were plain in her expression. "I'm—I'm not sure I want to meet anyone." The tightening of her hands revealed the tenseness. She turned, almost fiercely, to her father and mother. "What am I?" It was a desperate cry. "Does Cam say: This is my sister, Maria Christina, and her illegitimate son Bruce? Does he introduce me as Mrs. Loomis? I hate the name's sound. For God's sake tell me. Help me."

There was no easy, ready answer. Both Marta and Brian shared her suffering for this was something to which neither had found an answer or even permitted themselves to think too much about. Yet, unless this daughter was to remain a recluse, avoiding everyone, a solution must be found. A faulty decision, a bad choice of words, would only force her back into the dark hiding place from which she was moving fearfully.

[532]

"Your name is not Loomis," Brian said with tender consideration. "It never was and need not be spoken again. There is a time for truth and one for compromise. I suggest the latter until the truth becomes necessary or advisable. You are too young. Your life is before you. You can't go into seclusion here on Exuma, never seeing or meeting anyone. Visit the Dunsmore family. Take Bruce with you." The words seemed to stop of themselves. He shook his head. "No. Leave him with us." He halted again. The attempt at deception was too involved and would only grow more complicated. He glanced appealingly at Marta. "I'm not doing very well, am I?"

"No, dear." She was sympathetic. "You are not doing at all well."

It was Maria Christina who ruthlessly cut through the tangled web of evasion and distortion. The problem was hers and so must be its explanation.

"My name is Maria Christina Raleigh." The voice had a firm but not defiant note. "It has never been anything else. My husband is dead." She bit upon her lip until it whitened and then continued. "For reasons which are my own I have taken back my maiden name and given it, also, to my son. If this does not satisfy some persons," she spaced the words, "let them think what they will and be damned to them." The oath came effortlessly but with muted vehemence. "I will not entangle myself in a lie now which will only become more involved with time." She turned to Cam. "If you would like to introduce me to your Andrea and the Dunsmores under these conditions I will go with you. Otherwise, we'll stay at home."

There was pride in Brian Raleigh's eyes as he looked across the table at his daughter. This was the honesty he had hoped for. That her marriage was not a marriage was something she could not have known. She had made a bad contract in good faith and no stigma marked her part.

For a second or two Marta's face reflected her doubts. Then it cleared of all indecision.

"Yes." She spoke emphatically. "Let it be that way. It is far closer to the truth than anything else and I am happier with it." Her eyes were warm with love. "As you say, let people believe it or be damned to them. Forgive me, Father," she added quickly.

That night, for the first time, Maria Christina walked into the room where her son slept. The Negro nurse drowsed in a chair. Later she would go to an adjoining room. She looked up as the mother entered and was silenced by the gesture of a finger to the lips. For several moments the young mother stood, looking down upon her child. Then she bent and kissed him softly upon the brow, turned away and closed the door behind her.

For a day and a night the ketch was anchored abeam of the *Caroline* at Salt Pond. Big Washer, who had outlasted all of the schooner's original crew and replaced them with younger, Out Island Negroes, treated Maria Christina's presence as though she were visiting royalty. He carried a delighted Bruce about on his broad shoulder when they went ashore to inspect the crawls. He set the cook to work in the galley preparing a turtle stew, baking fresh lime pies and golden yams. They were served ceremoniously at a table set on deck in the velvety soft night and illuminated by lanterns.

The change in his sister astonished Cam. A miracle had occurred in thirty-six hours. This, once again, was the Maria Christina he remembered; filled with high spirits, gay laughter, a delight in everything as though she had been suddenly released from some gloomy cavern of the mind. Behind a sand spit, in a sheltered cove, she swam in the warm water. She wore nothing but a nightdress hacked off with a knife, coming to her knees. With Bruce, his doubts, uncertainties and confusion swept away in this new companionship; clinging to her back as a cub might hold to its mother, she dove and sported about with a dolphin's grace. There was no fear of the water in Bruce and his high treble of excitement and delight filled Maria Christina's heart with the miracle of love she had not believed possible. This was her own, her flesh. When she released him, he paddled with the sure instinct of a puppy toward the shore where she swept him up in her arms, holding him with a jealous possessiveness.

On Eleuthera, Kenneth Dunsmore, his wife Alice, the daughter Andrea, turning seventeen, and the son Barton, now twenty-five, welcomed them with the full hospitality of gracious persons who live much alone. Kenneth Dunsmore was direct in line from the original settler who had left the independent colonies in 1783. The land, now, was turned to the cultivation of pineapples for which there was a steady market in the United States and Europe. Of all the Out Islands, Eleuthera offered the greatest contrasts. There were rolling hills, lush valleys, woodlands and lakes with the tropical palms, banana trees, sheer, white beaches and the sea's palette of color. As had the Raleighs, the Dunsmores adapted themselves to the land. They no longer tried to force it but allowed the soil to dictate the crop.

The manor house erected by the first Dunsmore had been all but leveled by a hurricane in 1820. When they rebuilt, it was on a more modest and practical scale. The time was only some fourteen years away from the emancipation of the slaves. Kenneth's grandfather had been certain the Act would be passed and had scaled down his manner of living to meet it. The result was a low frame structure with two wings at an angle and a broad veranda overlooking the shoreline.

Cam's introduction of his sister had been simply made and accepted. He had said: "Mrs. Dunsmore this is my sister, Maria Christina and young Bruce." Then he presented Andrea, Mr. Dunsmore and Barton with the same easy informality, which surprised Maria Christina for she had never thought of her brother as being schooled in the social graces.

"I hope you will spend a few days with us." Alice Dunsmore took Maria Christina's hand. "Only island people know what a pleasure visitors are. We are just about to sit down to dinner." She smiled. "I understand it is now the fashion to call it luncheon and the evening meal is dinner, not supper. May I call you Maria Christina? It is such a lovely name."

"I wish you would." She looked at Kenneth and Barton. "I wish you all would."

As they went to the dining room Barton fell in beside Maria Christina, whose hand was being tightly held by Bruce.

"How does it happen we haven't seen you before? Your brother Cam is a pretty regular visitor."

"I've been living in Charleston. I went to school there."

"Well then, welcome home." He had a quietly engaging smile and manner. "There are not too many pretty girls in the Out Islands."

"Thank you, sir." She looked up at him with bright pleasure.

At the table a chair was stacked with cushions for Bruce who, plainly, had no intention of being separated from this wonderful, shining person who had suddenly and completely entered his life.

"Ea-chris." He sat proudly at her side and spoke the name with a possessive tone. "Ea-chris."

"That seems to be as close as he can come to the combination of Maria and Christina," she explained.

The meal was pleasantly broken with small talk of the islands, the weather and crops. The succession of King Edward VII, the inauguration of President McKinley and his Vice-President, the fabulous Teddy Roosevelt. The work of Major Gorgas, in Cuba, for the eradication of yellow fever. Although the world outside barely touched them, they tried to maintain a contact through the magazines and journals.

"Do you know," Alice Dunsmore reflected, "save for four years in a Miss Prescott's Academy for Young Ladies, in Richmond, Virginia, I have never been farther away from Eluthera than Nassau. It seems strange when I think about it. Yet I have no real desire to travel. Bart—Barton went to school in Savannah. We had a good year and called it a pineapple scholarship. We were thinking of sending Andrea to the mainland but she seems contented in her ignorance. Besides," she glanced with affection at her daughter sitting beside Cam, "I think she has other things on her mind."

"Mother," the girl protested and then giggled, stealing a quick look at Cam.

"Well," Alice Dunsmore shrugged, "it is either that or Cameron Raleigh's ketch has a most peculiar rudder arrangement, for it always seems to end up at our landing."

"No, ma'am." Cam was not embarrassed. "I come on purpose."

After luncheon, with Bruce put to bed, under protest, for his nap, Barton suggested they take the Dunsmores' small sloop and coast up the island. There was little other diversion to offer guests.

They sailed across Hatchet Bay toward Gregory Town with Barton at the tiller, Maria Christina beside him, Cam and Andrea forward. It was a bright and sparkling day with only a light wind. Maria Christina lifted her face to it with an unconscious gesture of sheer delight. She glanced once at Barton and thought him a handsome man whose features, at the moment, were an odd study in concentration.

"Are you always so serious?" she chided. "Even on a pleasure cruise?"

"I'm sorry," he apologized. "I was thinking."

"Wondering?" She corrected him with a question. To herself she thought, Let's have done with it now. "Bruce," she continued distinctly, "is my son. I am a widow and because I prefer it have resumed my family name."

"I had no idea I was so transparent. Forgive me. I was rude."

"Your face was a pane of glass, Mr. Dunsmore." She was lightly chaffing. "Through it I could see your mind ticking off the questions. Who is little Bruce? Where is the father? What is Maria Christina? Well," she shrugged, "is everything answered?"

"I apologize." He was sincerely contrite and put a little off balance by her frankness. "But," he confessed with a grin, "you are right. I'm sorry. It is none of my business."

"Oh, I don't know. Perhaps it is. I suspect Cam's intentions are serious. You might well become my brother-in-law." She tossed the suggestion off airily.

He stared at her and then shook his head bemusedly. Such an easy association, talk without constraint, with a young woman was quite beyond his experience.

"I think," he said gravely, "you are the most remarkable person I have ever met."

"That's because you don't get off the island of Eluthera very often."

"That can be arranged." He fell in easily with her bantering mood.

[536]

"This is a seaworthy sloop. The voyage to Exuma is well within her range."

Listening to him, talking as she had been, watching the play of his mobile features, it occurred to her this was the first time in her life she had been in the company of an acceptable man. The idea was startling. She was twenty-one and never before had she sat and talked with a man. Three years within the convent walls. Two years of seclusion on Exuma. Suddenly she was stepping outside and into an entirely new, and just a little exciting, world.

"Our plantation," she made the statement casually, "has excellent docking facilities."

"I take it that is permission to call?"

"Not if you're going to be stodgy about it, Mr. Dunsmore. Permission, indeed. Come charging in your sloop and," her eyes grew wide with assumed innocence, "damn the torpedoes, whatever they are."

"Your father and mother?"

"I never thought of them in exactly that way."

The laughter came spontaneously from them both. By some mysterious alchemy they were suddenly friends, each finding something in the other to like and admire.

"What's so funny aft?" Cam hearing them, called.

"Life, my young brother. Life with all the Cams, the Andreas, the Bartons and Maria Christinas in it."

They spent the night at the Dunsmore plantation and left early in the morning with the family coming down to the landing stage to see them off. For Maria Christina the visit had been an awakening of spirit. The courtesy, the warmth of unaffected hospitality, the unmistakable interest of Barton, all made her feel as though she had suddenly walked out into the sunlight after being a prisoner to black fears. Her world, bounded by these island waters, no longer seemed hostile. She confronted it gladly and with new confidence. It was reassuring to be admired, to see the unspoken compliment in Barton Dunsmore's eyes. It was pleasant to hear the honest regret in the voices of Kenneth and Alice Dunsmore at their leave-taking.

"You'll come again, soon." Mrs. Dunsmore made it a statement. "If not," she glanced at her son with pride, "I'll send Bart for you."

"I have already assured him there is sufficient water for his sloop." Maria Christina smiled.

"There are so few of the old families left who maintain any contact with each other. They have scattered with the wind and gone to seed. That isn't a very nice thing to say, is it? Just the same it is true." Alice

Dunsmore took Maria Christina's hand. Then she stooped and kissed Bruce on the cheek. "If you don't visit us we'll come to see you."

"Why don't we do both?" Maria Christina offered her hand to them all in turn.

The Negro boy, Sam, who was Cam's crew on the ketch, stood ready to cast off. The craft was small enough for the two of them to handle. As the wind picked them up they moved smoothly out of the shelter.

"How about Spanish Wells?" Cam called to his sister.

"Anything you say," she replied absently. Her gaze was on the group of Dunsmores as they stood watching their departure. She turned, her expression alight with pleasure. "I am so grateful to you, Cam. Someone needed to take me out of myself. Thank you."

"You liked Bart, didn't you?" He pretended it was only the most casual of remarks.

"I liked them all." She put her hand on Bruce's shoulder, pressing him to her side.

"Well . . . that wasn't exactly what I meant." He winked broadly. "But I suppose it'll do."

"Are you going to marry Andrea?"

"We've sort of tiptoed around the idea."

"She's a lovely girl."

Cam studied his sister for a moment. "You know," he admitted with a certain amount of surprise, "so are you. I never noticed it before."

The wind was fresher now and the ketch took it with a slight heeling. Watching the dark shoreline, studying the splashes of color ahead, Maria Christina felt she had never known such freedom. Her spirits soared with the following gulls and raced far ahead of the ketch's bow.

❦ XXXIII ❧

In the smoothly running tide of affairs there was no indication that this new century was to be one of unparalleled violence which would all but tip the world from its axis and send it whirling to destruction.

Few ripples of the currents reached the Out Islands or even Nassau. The newspapers and journals from the United States and Europe made pleasant, if unexciting, reading and furnished items of conversation in the peaceful evenings.

Andrew Carnegie established a hero fund of $5,000,000 for those who risked their lives for others, and Secretary of State Hay created an immortal phrase in a note to Tangiers. *We want Pericardis alive or Raizuli dead*. Steamship lines were in a rate war and an immigrant could travel in steerage from Europe to New York for $10. The German Kaiser visited Czar Nicholas, toasting eternal friendship, and the Russian North Sea fleet fired upon English fishermen at the Doggerbank, explaining later they thought they were Japanese. Joan of Arc was declared to have passed her second stage of canonization, and cotton went to four cents a pound in New Orleans. The years merged effortlessly. Glenn Curtiss made a new record at Los Angeles carrying passengers at fifty-five miles an hour, and the Western Union Telegraph Company was indicted by a federal grand jury on a charge of forty-two violations of the bucket shop law. The year now was 1910. King Edward VII died after a few days' illness and was succeeded by George V. In Russia a Mme. Breshkowskaya was sentenced to exile in Siberia for revolutionary activities, and there were Italian riots against excessive house rents. Captain Robert F. Scott left for the Antarctic, and the Maryland Legislature passed a bill to disenfranchise the Negro in municipal and state elections because the state had never adopted the XVth Amendment.

Those in the Out Islands who could read or bothered to subscribe to newspapers were little impressed by what was going on. These were the momentary flashes of a distant star's fall. More important was the weather of the equinox, the price of sponge, sisal, pineapples and citrus fruit.

Maria Christina Raleigh married Barton Dunsmore six months after their first meeting and three years later Cam was wed to Andrea and they built their own, neat, small cottage at the far end of the Raleigh plantation on Exuma.

The courtship of Maria Christina by Barton had been unflagging. Never a week passed but what he ran his sloop from Eluthera. She had responded slowly, warily. The attraction was there. This she admitted. They were a well-matched couple, finding pleasure in each other's company, sharing a love for the islands. On the night Bart asked her to marry, Maria Christina had walked with him to the beach. There, in the half-light of a quarter-moon turning the ocean into quicksilver, she had told him everything; of Peach-boy Loomis and a marriage which had not been a marriage resulting in Bruce. This she did without an outward display of emotion, making no excuses. Either he would understand or what they had slowly built between them was irretrievably lost. She finished the short, sordid story.

"You didn't have to tell me any of this." He meant it.

"I think I did, Bart. It is important to me you know. More important you understand. The first mistake can, possibly, be accepted. I don't want to make another. I am a woman now. Then I was a stupid, foolish girl. I'm not sure it can be explained: a revolt against the convent's discipline; the excitement of defying all authority and convention and having the other girls regard me with awe; a pretty face, an arrogant nature; moonlight; outside the gate a voice which seemed particularly entrancing, soft and liquid, stirring unimaginable fancies. My mind, if I had one, simply balked at functioning beyond these primal things. That is all I can say."

"Do you love me, Maria Christina?"

She took a moment before replying. The question should be easy to answer. She did or she didn't. Her hand sought his.

"I think so. But don't you see, I really can't say yes or no? I'm happy when I am with you. I feel secure, contented. When you kiss or touch me I respond without reservation. When you're away I miss you. When you leave I hate to see you go. If these things add up to love then I, Maria Christina Raleigh, am in love with Barton Dunsmore. If they don't, then I'm nor sure what the word means. I never knew boys here, on Exuma, or the mainland or had them come courting as I grew older. Now I am twenty-one, the mother of a child, without ever having the experience of love. If any of this answers your question then I'll marry you gladly, happily and with a full heart."

"I am satisfied." He had taken her in his arms.

Now, they had been married almost ten years and made their home on Eluthera. There Barton was needed, for his father could not possibly supervise all of the work. A home of their own had been built, for Alice Dunsmore was far too wise to attempt the combining of two families.

"I don't want to become the mother-in-law. I'd much rather we be friends." They had talked it over. "One woman of the household is enough. Two is one too many. You and Barton have a place of your own. Then, when we want to see each other, we'll call on you or you on us."

Two daughters had been born to them some eighteen months apart —Anne, nine in this year, and Joyce coming up on her eighth birthday.

"I don't seem to be able to give you anything but girls." She made the admission a little unhappily.

"Well," Bart displayed no disappointment, "we'll keep trying. Besides," he added, "I have a son."

She looked at him, knowing she was close to a tear, deeply moved by his gentleness and love.

"Thank you for that, Bart."

Barton had made a formal adoption of young Bruce within the first year of their marriage and the boy had been reared as Bruce Dunsmore. There seemed no honest reason why he should ever regard Barton as other than his father. Maria Christina had insisted upon this.

"I don't believe in it." She had made the statement early in their marriage, when the question as to whether Bruce should eventually be told the truth had arisen. "By the time he is old enough to understand he will love and respect you as his father. What is to be gained by saying: Barton Dunsmore is not your real father? No, I will not have it. I am the only one who has a claim to him and if I say Bruce is your son then it is so."

The boy was now twelve and Maria Christina was long past being fearful of a Loomis taint. He had inherited her blond hair and clear features but his skin took a deep tan hers never would. He was growing tall and strong for his age and spent every waking hour out of doors. A house was simply a place where you were inexplicably required to come for meals, unless you just happened to be somewhere else. You slept there unless you could find a good excuse for bedding down in the sloop or a conical-shaped hut of wattles hidden within a palm grove near the beach.

Maria Christina and Bart never ceased to be astonished by him. There was some inner, inexhaustible fount of exuberance. He found excitement in everything and everyone. He was charged with a heedless spirit of adventure which turned school into a dull chore and made inactivity all but unendurable. Everything he did or said was full laden with an unexpendable vitality. Watching, listening to him recount some trivial incident as a breathtaking occurrence, his parents wondered helplessly from where this enthusiasm flowed. Nothing dulled his zest; nothing except the winter months of school. These he endured stoically. Yet he had a lively and inquisitive mind, making good grades without effort. He went through the forms of the school on Eleuthera with remarkable ease. The missionary teacher had come to Bart and Maria Christina.

"He has learned everything these elementary classes can teach him. He is far ahead of his fellow pupils. I suggest the broader curriculum in Nassau or a good academy on the mainland."

When this was suggested to Bruce he all but howled an anguished protest. They decided not to press the matter for a year or two. After all, he was only twelve; although this sometimes was difficult for them to remember for he seemed completely self-sufficient. He had no intimate friends among those of his age who attended the school. At eleven he was perfectly capable of handling Barton's small sloop. Instead of the children's games he much preferred to work with the Negroes seining and to take a meal of beans and rice with freshly fried fish on the sand.

Aside from his parents, for whom he felt love and respect—although straining a little under their authority—he had two objects of veneration. One was his Uncle Cam, who was now captain of the mail, passenger and cargo boat making the rounds of the Out Islands. The other was the negro, Washer.

Big Wash had been forced from the sea. He was an old man now and showed it. His stooped frame was bent by the pain of a form of rheumatism. From this he received relief through a "Dr. Jonas Petty's Golden Elixir." The tonic was guaranteed to cure gout, rheumatism, female complaint, headaches, boils, stomach distress and all of the ills known to man. Brian pointed out to Washer that the nostrum was seventy-five percent alcohol and anyone's pain would diminish after a bottle or two. Washer, while respectful, was skeptical of the Cap'n's opinion. Dr. Petty's cure-all came in a bottle with a label covered with gold seals, representing medals won all over the world for its miraculous properties. So each week, at Brian's request, Cam brought a case from Nassau on the mail boat.

"You're a knot head!" Brian had once exploded in exasperation when the Nassau chemist had run out of the elixir and Cam had come without it. "You're a knot-headed nigger."

"Yes, suh, Cap'n," Wash had moaned in his imaginary misery.

"A slug of plantation rum will do you just as much good."

"Ef you say so, Cap'n, suh," Washer agreed reluctantly. "Jus' d same, dat Doctah Petty mek a fine-tastin' tonik. Ah hope dey git moah soon. Mah back a-kill me."

Despite his infirmities Wash was far from bedridden. His grizzled head was filled with great tales of the sea and far places he had seen. Bruce would sit on the stoop of the Negro's cabin while Wash talked of how he an' Cap'n Brian had run guns to the Cubans. Of their voyages from Nassau up the mainland's eastern seaboard as far away as Boston. How the hurricanes would come suddenly in the Gulf of Mexico, and the saucy Negro wenches who came with fresh crab gumbo, fried shrimp and hot bread to the docks of New Orleans. Bruce never tired of listening and Wash's imagination flowered with the tonic effect of Dr. Petty's Golden Elixir. The *Caroline* had been the finest, fastest schooner in the world and he had been the Cap'n's mate.

"She ol' laik me now, dat *Cahline,* en nothin' but a tendah foah nigger spongahs. Wuah she mine Ah'd sail huh en th' deep fadom en sink huh theah. A good ship 'serve a good en'. Ain' raight to have huh gathuh weed en barnacle. Me too," he whispered huskily, "dat d kin' o' en' I wan'. Not sit heah wid ol' back bend en good foah nothin'."

When he was allowed, Bruce would spend a couple of nights at Washer's cabin, stretching a canvas hammock between the two-by-four uprights on the porch. In the first, pearly break of dawn the two of them would go to the beach with a cast net and get their fish for breakfast.

Washer's advice was always the same. "You go t' sea, boy. Ahl d Rahlei bin sailor man en youah part Rahlei. Tek youah gran'fathah, Cap'n Brian. You think he laik dis grubbin' en d groun' laik he do? Hit brek he heart but dey ain' no place foah d *Cahline* en d sea enny moah. Now, youah papa, Mistuh Barton. He a lan' man too. Somebody gots to raise d crops. But Mistuh Cam he a sailor even ef he do had boad wid dem gas'lean engine. He know d feel of a ship wid sail. Man nevah fo'get dat. You watch out good, boy, dey don' catch you en mek a fahmah to grow things."

During the summer, when he wasn't on Exuma paying a token visit to Brian and Marta but spending most of his time with Washer, Bruce was aboard the *Gull,* the mail and passenger boat, with his Uncle Cam. She was an ugly craft, broad of beam with deck cargo space and of shallow draft. Her engine was cranky and she stank of oil and gasoline. But she was a ship and doggedly pursued her rounds of the Out Islands. Cam had a crew of three Bahamian Negroes, one of whom had a little knowledge of the engine. The others were cargo handlers. Cam gave Bruce a token wage of fifty cents a week and gravely signed him on as a member of the *Gull*'s complement. They went everywhere in the islands, wherever there was a settlement; sometimes, in addition to the mail, to deliver something ordered in Nassau. Other times to pick up a few crates of fowl, tomatoes, yams, pineapples and sacked beans for the market. Her arrival was always an event with the entire population of the settlement coming down to meet her, to hear the news and purchase from her stores the brightly colored "penny candy" which came in a wooden cask.

Her schedule was always arranged so Cam could spend a couple of days on Exuma with Andrea and their two children and see his father and mother. Brian was sixty-five now and he had turned most of the supervision of the sisal cultivation over to a man he had hired through an advertisement in the Savannah paper. Wilson was a good overseer. Production of the fibers was steady and the market held generally firm. Brian had hoped to turn the plantation over to his son but Cam wanted nothing to do with the land. Even the monotonous routine of the *Gull* was, in his opinion, preferable to the plantation. Brian had never voiced his disappointment nor the question of what would happen to the acres when he died. He had come ashore because he had been forced to it to provide a living for the family. But he never looked from his window to the sea without thinking of the old days when he stood upon the *Caroline*'s deck and knew a freedom of spirit given to few men. He could understand his son's devotion to the island waters even though he must put up with such an ungainly craft as the *Gull*.

From Cam and the rounds of the *Gull*, Bruce learned much of the islands. He was familiar with every cay, coral head and sound from the Crooked Island passage to Great Abaco. Uncle Cam did not treat him as a child or a relative aboard the *Gull*. He was a member of the crew although he contributed little more than dropping a line over a bollard when they put in at a settlement. Sometimes he was allowed to take the wheel under Cam's watchful eye. He learned to navigate, as did most of the islanders, by the color of the water.

When they laid over in Nassau the boy shared a room with his uncle in a frame hotel on Bay Street. They usually ate together at a tavern where their meals were constantly interrupted by men stopping at their table, for Cam had a large and varied acquaintance. He invariably introduced Bruce as "my mate" and the boy was filled with pride and worship for this man who seemed to know everything.

"I don't know what good all this knocking around the islands with me on the *Gull* is going to do you," Cam said to Bruce over the evening meal. "If you've made up your mind to go to sea for a living there's no future in this. You ought to study hard and when you're older try for the merchant marine. In time you could get a third officer's berth on Mr. Cunard's line. What do you think of the *Mauretania*? Making an Atlantic crossing in four days and eighteen hours! I'd like to be on the bridge of a ship like that." He lit a cigar and leaned back in his chair. "I could have if I hadn't married. Not that Andrea isn't a good wife and I love the children, but the sea is no place for a family man. You can't be pulled two ways at the same time."

There was a small stack of mail before Cam on the table. Most of it was magazines and newspapers but there was, also, a letter from a law firm in Charleston, addressed to Brian Raleigh. Cam picked it up.

"I have a feeling this is about Richard Cameron. You know, he must be damn near ninety years old now and the last of the Camerons. You could end up being a country squire in South Carolina with a town house and a place on the Ashley."

"I'd rather have a good ship." Bruce was unimpressed.

Cam smiled at him. There was no turning the boy away. If Richard had died, his estate would be left to Brian and Marta and eventually he and Maria Christina would inherit it. But he didn't believe any of them would want to return to the mainland. Cameron Hall and the house on Tradd Street would probably be sold or leased.

"Well," he stood up, "let's get to bed. The Royal Mail must go in the morning and we've cargo for Harbor Island, Eluthera and Watlings. Then we'll go to Exuma and give this letter to my father. Get a good night's sleep, Mister." He placed an affectionate hand on Bruce's shoulder. "And, it might not be a bad idea for you to spend a little time with your parents before you're so grown up they won't recognize you."

From Watlings Island they came up to Exuma. Cam's guess had been right. Richard Cameron had died of a cerebral hemorrhage. His estate had been left in its entirety to Marta and Brian with the provision that Cameron Hall and the home in Charleston be held in trust for Maria Christina and Cameron. There were stocks and municipal bonds, the dividends from which were to be used by Brian as he saw fit. If possible, the letter concluded, it would simplify matters if Brian Raleigh could come to Charleston.

Brian read the letter aloud and then sat holding it in his hands, silent and thoughtful.

"Now there are no more Camerons. It is too bad Richard didn't have sons. I doubt if any of us will find a use for his city home and Cameron Hall. The Raleighs, and now the Dunsmores, seem wedded to the islands. I don't know what to do. Perhaps the most sensible thing would be to lease the plantation on the Ashley. We could go back to Cameron Hall and close the circle Ronald started when he left it and came to the islands."

"You know you'd never be happy away from here." Marta smiled indulgently. "Do what you think best. Lease the Hall and put the house in the city up for rent. That way we'll keep it intact for Maria Christina and Cam."

After the others had gone to bed, Brian took Ronald's diary from the library, careful not to flake away the brittle pages. He turned to the last entry.

Frequent, heavy squalls from the Northeast today. The schooner Traveler *came round from Graham's Harbor to take in my stock when weather permits. If it clears this week I will go to Nassau and start the formal adoption proceedings for my son David (Heath) Cameron. It is my hope he and Robert Bruce will have lusty sons to carry on what I have started here.*

The signs, at first, were so innocently deceptive few persons save those within the governments themselves paid more than passing attention to the reports in their newspapers. The French Government sent troops into Morocco to protect its nationals, and Germany warned of serious consequences should the French occupy Fez and remain there. The Italian Government, restive, reaching out, sent a note to Turkey demanding economic privileges in Tripoli. Russia began construction of four armored cruisers, eight small cruisers, thirty-six destroyers and eight submarines. Great Britain's Naval Bill called for the building of four battleships, eight armored cruisers, twenty destroyers and an increase of 2,000 in personnel. Germany's Reichstag passed a supplementary defense bill creating two new army corps to protect the Franco-German frontier, and American troops were sent to Galveston, Texas, for possible use in Mexico where a revolution was in progress.

Everywhere there were small tensions, pressures and diplomatic maneuverings but no one spoke openly of war for this, in an era of tremendous firepower, would be an unbelievable slaughter. Then, that which could not happen did. Most of the world had never heard of Serajevo. There the Archduke Franz Ferdinand of Austria-Hungary, was assassinated and the world moved inexorably into a war which would occupy it for the next four years.

In the United States there was an inclination to dismiss the European conflict as of no concern to this government. It was occupied with such trivial matters as demanding Mexico formally to salute the American flag as an apology for the detention of Marines at Tampico. President Huerta agreed to the salute but only if the United States also saluted the Mexican flag.

Again influences far beyond their control struck at the Bahamas with a severity no one could anticipate. Dependent upon the mainland and Europe for practically everything, the islands were abruptly shut off from these sources. The price of food soared to unprecedented heights;

not only because it was in short supply but the adverse rate of foreign exchange made purchases all but impossible. The Out Islands, always poor, were in a desperate plight and there was a mass migration to the United States where labor was badly needed. The tourist trade, which was just beginning to develop into a source of income, was immediately halted. Steamship service was irregular and infrequent. The years moved, the war spread, and the participation of the United States was obviously inevitable.

At thirty-two, Cameron Raleigh applied for service in the Royal Navy. Instead of the fighting vessel for which he hoped, he was assigned as second officer aboard a transport and spent the war years carrying supplies and men across the submarine-infested North Atlantic.

Young Bruce Dunsmore, barely turned sixteen at the war's beginning, had also applied for enlistment in the Royal Navy. He was turned down but became, probably, the youngest captain ever to operate out of Nassau. Because his experience and knowledge of the waters outweighed his youth, he was given command of the *Gull*. The craft was Raleigh-owned with a franchise for carrying the Royal Mail. But gasoline was strictly rationed and difficult to secure and there were weeks at a time when the boat was tied up for want of fuel and the mail was carried aboard Brian Raleigh's ketch.

With a recklessness born of desperation German submarines were sinking American ships carrying matériel of war to Europe and then, on April 6, 1917, the United States declared war on Germany and her allies and a month later the first American destroyer flotilla arrived off Queenstown, Ireland, and General John J. Pershing was appointed to command American Expeditionary Forces in France.

Through the four terrible years the Bahamas existed as best they could. They had no strategic value and were out of the great current of war as it raged on land and in the Atlantic.

On Eleuthera, the Dunsmore plantation was badly hit. Pineapples were a luxury item. The European market was closed and the fruit was being grown and exported from Cuba to the United States cheaper than it could be sold from the Bahamas. On Exuma, though, the sisal plantation brought reasonable profits. The demand for cordage was great and the only problem was finding shipping to carry the fibers. Then, on a November day it was over. The bloodletting ceased. The Germans signed the Armistice terms.

Cameron Raleigh, weathered, tense and far older than the years of war should have left him, returned to Exuma and his wife Andrea and their two daughters. His mother, Marta, had died in her sixtieth year and his father, Brian, now seventy-three, was confined to his chair with a crippling arthritis. With the ending of hostilities the price of sisal had plummeted and the overseer Wilson was hard pressed to make expenses. On Eleuthera, Barton Dunsmore and Maria Christina were quietly fighting to hold their plantation together and educate their children. Bruce, with gasoline once more available, seemed the only really contented member of the two families. A new engine had been ordered for the *Gull* and Bruce's concern was that his Uncle Cam, back from the war's transport service, would want to take over his command.

"I've had enough sea to last me for a long time." Cameron regarded his nephew fondly. "You must be just about twenty now, Captain. You skipper the *Gull* while I sit by the fireside." He had glanced out of the window to the porch where his father sat with a light blanket drawn over his knees although the day was warm. "I wish there was something we could do for him."

"I had a doctor over from Nassau," Bruce explained, "but they don't seem to know much about arthritis. He has some pills to relieve the pain but ever since your mother died he just sits that way, waiting for death." He frowned. "Everything seems to be happening all at once. Grandfather Dunsmore and Grandmother Alice both gone. My father without much of his old spirit. Mother." He smiled. "Maria Christina doesn't change. I don't get home as often as I should. Now that you're back, though, I feel better."

Throughout the following year of 1919, conditions in the Bahamas changed little. The colony was still the poorest of British possessions. The blight again struck at the sponge beds and this source of income was shut off. The hotels in Nassau were closed and the rate of the British pound to the American dollar was such that imports from the mainland were prohibitive. But once again the islands were to move in that curious cycle which brought them wealth and then poverty. This time the boom was to exceed anything seen in the wildest days of blockade-running to the Confederacy.

Over the years, in the United States, the sentiment for the prohibition of alcoholic beverages had been gaining strength and supporters. State after state had gone "dry" and then the Volstead Act was passed, ratified and the era of incredible nonsense began.

Into Nassau tremendous amounts of whisky, rum, gin and brandy were shipped by American distillers, wholesalers, hotels, bars and retail merchants. Warehouses, which had been crumbling and unused for years, were hastily shored up and new ones built to accommodate the inflow. Barrels, cases, wicker-covered jugs of rum, the spirits from American shelves and storehouses, filled every inch of space. Private homes were leased for no other purpose than the storing of great quantities of liquor.

[548]

Empty cellars commanded incredible prices. Cases of Scotch, bourbon and brandy were stacked on the wharves, on the streets and every available inch of space along the waterfront. When Nassau could hold no more, the Out Islands were searched for suitable storage. Armed guards patrolled the beaches and stood watch over hastily constructed huts. Mounds of casks and crates were high in remote palm groves beneath tarpaulins while hard-eyed men with rifles guarded the trove. Enormous sums in import duties poured into Nassau's treasury. New hotels were built, steamship services were subsidized. Tourists trooped into the colony, filling the bars which seemed to spring up overnight along Bay Street. Americans arrived on every ship and by cabin cruiser with, apparently, no other purpose than to get drunk as quickly as possible.

No one seemed quite sure, at first, what was to be done with the unbelievable amount of liquor sent from the States to the Bahamas. Then, slowly, a new breed of adventurers which made the pirates of old seem almost tame by comparison was spawning. Murder and hijacking would become commonplace, officials corrupted. The stocks in the Bahamas begin to find their way back to the United States and when this was exhausted, the Nassau liquor merchants import huge stocks from England, Holland, Spain and France for re-export. All of this, though, did not happen overnight. It would take a little while for those of lawless and adventurous disposition to realize the treasure which lay eastward off the Florida coast.

Bruce, coming ashore from the *Gull,* moored at one of the Nassau docks, stopped to admire the sleek lines, mahogany trim and sparkling brasswork of a sixty-two-foot cabin cruiser as she lay on the opposite side of the pier. Aft, beneath an awning, a party of six, three men and three young women in gay sports clothes, sat in deep, wicker chairs. A white-coated steward was passing around a tray on which tall frosted glasses of rum drinks glinted. Three of Nassau's waterfront musicians serenaded the party, their rich, deep voices blending to the guitars. Forward, members of the crew were at the never-ending job of polishing the metalwork. Bruce thought to himself, This is the way to spend and enjoy money. He was about to turn away when a voice hailed him.

"Come aboard and look around if you like."

A tall, deeply tanned man in a suit of dazzling white silk had risen and stood at the cruiser's rail, glass in hand. His smile was slightly quizzical and friendly.

"No one," he continued, "can study a boat the way you were without wanting to see more."

Bruce hesitated. He wore only well-bleached dungarees, a shirt open at the throat, the captain's cap pushed slightly back on his head, and bare feet in sandals. He didn't realize it but he made a handsome, slightly picaresque figure, and one of the young women studied him with more than passing interest. He shrugged mentally and asked himself: Why not?

He crossed the short gangway and the man came to meet him.

"My name's John Clifton." He glanced at the tarnished gold insignia on Bruce's cap. "Captain?"

"Bruce Dunsmore." He nodded toward the *Gull*. "And right now you're looking at the Royal Mail boat."

It was, Bruce thought, a curious thing but he could feel an immediate current of friendliness flow from this stranger to him. There was no constraint, no preliminary, meaningless words with which persons usually attempt to establish a basis of common interest. He looked forward, along the length of the cruiser.

"She's a beauty. Where are you out of?"

"Georgetown. In South Carolina. You know it?"

Bruce shook his head. Clifton called the musicians and paid them off. "I'm getting pretty sick of hearing 'Mama ain' got no peas, no rice.'"

He led Bruce toward where the others were seated and made the introductions.

"My sister Janet Clifton, Alicia Martin, Jean McComber, Mr. Walker and Mr. Scott. Captain Dunsmore"—he winked companionably at Bruce —"of the Royal Mail ship, the *Gull*. What will you drink?"

"Whatever you have is fine with me."

The steward brought him rum with ice and a sprig of mint. These were people new to him, friendly without effort, a little curious over his identity. Janet Clifton was studying him over the rim of her glass.

"Are you a native Bahamian, Captain?"

"About as native as you can get, I guess. The family, starting with Ronald Cameron, came from South Carolina around 1791."

Clifton glanced up sharply. "Would that be the Cameron family of Charleston?"

Bruce nodded. "The first Cameron, though, came from upriver, on the Ashley."

"I know the place." There was a subtle change in Clifton's manner.

"I always thought Bahamians were colored." Janet managed to inject a tone of surprise into the statement.

"She knows better," Clifton explained his sister. "It just suits her to pretend to be dumb. I've never figured out why."

"Because, darling," Janet crossed her long, tanned legs, "it makes everyone else seem so brilliant." Her eyes again sought Bruce. "Aren't you young to be a captain?"

[550]

To himself Bruce thought she was a pretty fresh kid who couldn't be much more than eighteen herself.

"I guess," he deliberately drawled the reply, "it would depend on the ship. I'd be young for the *Mauretania* but not too young for the *Gull*."

There was a rumbling and creaking of ungreased wheels as two large hand carts were trundled down the dock. They were stacked with cases of whisky. Three crew members set out a plank forward and the liquor was unloaded and lowered through a hatch. Bruce watched with interest and then turned to Clifton.

"Can you take that back with you?"

"Not with the permission of the United States Government, but the Coast Guard or Customs doesn't make much of a search of a boat like this."

"They'd better start." Bruce laughed softly. "Have you any idea how much liquor is stored in Nassau and the Out Islands right now?"

"I have a small notion." Clifton put down his glass. "Come on. I'll show you over the cruiser."

Everything from the rosewood paneling in the main cabin, the furnishings, staterooms, crew's quarters and the two big Packard motors spoke of luxury and money. When they had finished the inspection, they went topside and forward where the hatch was being battened down. Clifton offered Bruce a cigarette and lit one of his own.

"Is it all right if I call you Bruce?" the man asked abruptly.

"No one but the *Gull*'s crew calls me Captain."

"I'm a gambler, Bruce." The statement was made without any undue importance attached to it. "I don't mean dice, cards, horse racing. Those things I do for amusement. I like to gamble on possibilities and sometimes, on men. How old are you?"

Bruce thought Clifton asked a lot of questions for a stranger but there was nothing offensive in his manner.

"I'll be twenty-two on my next birthday."

"How well do you know the islands?"

"As well as you know this cruiser."

"Who owns the *Gull*?"

"We do. The family. I guess she really belongs to my Uncle Cam—Cameron Raleigh."

For a half minute or so John Clifton studied the smoke as it uncurled from his cigarette's tip.

"There's a fortune to be made here, Bruce. Fortunes to be made, risks to be taken, adventure to be had. Real prohibition in the States is an impossibility. Every case of liquor stored now in the Bahamas will find its way back to the mainland. This isn't just a pleasure cruise. I came to look around. If you wanted to store liquor for the shortest trip to the Florida, Georgia or South Carolina coast, where would you put it?"

Bruce thought for a second or two. "Bimini, I guess. You can get from eight to nine feet of water there. But," he added, "if you're going to run liquor—and I guess that's what's on your mind—there's no reason not to take it out of Nassau direct."

Clifton stubbed out his cigarette. "Not right now, maybe. But this is going to be big business, bigger than anyone can imagine. If you think these islands had pirates in the old days, wait a couple of years. The whisky runners will make them look like sissies. Every boat that clears Nassau will be known and watched. There will be piracy on the high seas again, only there will be no Jolly Roger flying. I'd like an island man young enough to find excitement in the risks, old enough to handle himself and a fast boat in these waters and in the crossing to the mainland."

Bruce thought this was the oddest conversation he had ever sat in on. Here was a man of seemingly gentle disposition, well mannered, quiet of speech and, judging by the cruiser, wealthy, deliberately charting a course of lawlessness.

"Are you offering me a job?" He was curious. "You don't know anything about me."

"I usually know a good man when I see one. Oh, I've been fooled a couple of times! Don't let this confuse you." He indicated the craft with a wave of a hand. "I've swung a pick, snaked cypress out of swamps, worked once as a longshoreman and was a fair preliminary fighter. None of it was good enough. I decided to make money and I did because I tried to keep one jump ahead of someone behind me." He lit another cigarette. "I'm not offering you a job but a piece of the action. I'll put up the boat, fast and with cargo space. You pick your own crew. I'll pay the hands and the running expenses. You take the risks and one-third of the profits. That's as good a deal as I'll make." He sat back and waited.

Bruce said nothing. This was a completely new venture. No one could forecast the possibilities, the danger. Something of what was passing through his mind communicated itself to John Clifton.

"I might as well tell you what I think." Clifton spoke abruptly. "I'm not so smart as to be the only one who sees what this can mean. When it really gets going it is bound to attract harder, tougher men than you have ever met. There will be murder done for a boatload of liquor. They'll fight on the beaches and on the highways for a couple of dozen cases of Scotch. Every element of lawlessness will be drawn in and you'll have the Coast Guard and law enforcement officers on land to contend with."

"Let me think about it, will you?"

Clifton stood up. "Take your time. We're going to cruise around the Out Islands for a while."

"Do you have a pilot?"

Clifton nodded. "A man named Hampton. I engaged him this morning."

"I know him. He'll take you anywhere. I'll be home, on Exuma, by the end of the week. Wade—Hampton knows our place. Why don't you put in and lay over for a couple of days? By that time I'll say yes or no."

"Good." Clifton was satisfied. "I would have been a little suspicious and leery if you had said yes right away."

Back on the afterdeck Bruce said good-bye to the others and thought to himself this was probably the most innocent-appearing group of potential lawbreakers he had ever seen. He caught Janet Clifton's glance; she was regarding him with a study of whimsical amusement and then, suddenly, dropped one eyelid in a deliberate wink.

"You know," she seemed to be speaking to no one in particular, "my brother always seems to find what he is looking for. It's some sort of a primitive instinct. More than that. He usually gets it. I imagine we'll be seeing you again, Captain."

Bruce walked back along the dock toward shore and then he suddenly laughed aloud and a couple of Out Island Negro boatmen looked up from their small cockpit to regard him with astonishment. He wondered what his mother and father would say when he recounted the experience and conversation. He didn't quite believe it himself—and that Janet Clifton. He whistled softly at the memory of her parting expression. It was as though she was considering taking a small bite out of him.

XXXIV

No ONE could possibly have known what was going to happen, or that these islands of soft colors and sometimes dazzling beauty were to become one vast liquor storehouse for most of the United States.

In the beginning the traffic was an almost outrageous comedy. Anything, short of a raft, which would float and make the distance to the innumerable Florida inlets from Jupiter to Matanzas was pressed into service. An Out Island man with a fair sloop or ketch could buy Scotch whisky in Nassau for around twenty dollars a case and sell it to waiting truckers on the mainland for one hundred. Agents for the bootleggers operated without restraint. They took suites in the hotels or opened import offices on Bay Street. From these points detailed instructions, the time and place of rendezvous on the Florida coast, were given. Out Island boatmen who, for years, had taken a bare living from the sea or a patch of arable land now sported through Nassau's bars with thick rolls of bills in their pockets or went on riotous sprees in Miami, Havana and Jacksonville. For the first time in some of their lives they and their wives and children had shoes. There were silk stockings, new dresses, suits of tropical cloth. It was as though someone had opened a treasure cave and said come and help yourself. The risks, save for a sudden squall striking an overloaded boat, were minimal. The harried Coast Guard could not possibly effectively patrol a couple of thousand miles of coastline. A weathered sailing craft, deep in the water, would wait for darkness just beyond the territorial waters. Then, without lights, make her way shoreward and, with a signal from the beach, creep through one of the many cuts from the sea to a sheltered lagoon. Or if this did not want to be risked, a transfer would be made to stout dories which easily rode through the breakers to the shelving dunes. To save cargo space and facilitate the handling of whisky, gin and rum, the bottles were taken from their wooden boxes and wrapped in burlap, humorously referred to as "hams." Everyone was having a share of this inexhaustible fountain of wealth. Everyone was having a hell of a time. But this carefree, exuberant spirit of lawlessness which was inherent in the Bahamian was not to last for long. The big fish were about to swallow the little fish.

Business—cold, efficient and ruthless—moved in, for the profits were too great to be left in the hands of careless, happy-go-lucky natives. Big business, with fast, powerfully motored boats equipped with searchlights and manned by crews with submachine guns, took over. Many an Out Island craft, hove to in the night and awaiting its signal, suddenly found itself in the full, stabbing glare of a merciless beam. The machine guns raked and murdered. The cargo hijacked while the unmanned sloop, with its grotesque huddle of dead, wallowed and drifted aimlessly until it grounded on a bar or broke up on a stretch of lonely sand. Big business bought Coast Guard officers and crews to look the other way or avoid a patrol about an obvious inlet. Revenue officers were corrupted by fixed payments. Cars, their rear ends heavily reinforced with additional springs, waited alongside heavy-duty trucks to run the liquor to the Northern states. Young women with babies found themselves in great demand to ride with the drivers. What law officer would think to halt a passenger car in which a man, his wife and infant were on a pleasure trip?

By a strange process of rationalization not any of this activity was actually considered by the public as lawless. A man who slipped past the ineffectual Coast Guard blockade and successfully put ashore a hundred or more "hams" of liquor was certainly not grouped with a bank robber, a holdup man, a housebreaker or a rapist. New words were coined to meet the times. Rumrunner. Mr. Whiskers. Speakeasy. Feds. Violin player—a man who worked a machine gun. From the McCoy brothers and their ship, the *Tomoka,* came "The McCoy" or "the Real McCoy" to denote whisky of the best quality, for the McCoys never diluted or cut their stocks. There was even a certain amount of glamour attached to those who risked pursuit, capture, hijacking, to put their cargoes ashore. They were the modern swashbucklers, the buccaneers of old.

Freighters, standing openly beyond the limits, unloaded their merchandise within full sight of the Coast Guard, whose officers and crews were helpless to interfere. The United States seemed to be one huge blotter capable of absorbing every drop of whisky, rum, gin and brandy poured upon it. Never before had so many drunk so much.

John Clifton more than carried out his part of the bargain so casually suggested to Bruce Dunsmore on that day of their meeting in Nassau. The boat he provided was some sixty-five feet, stripped inside of everything but the barest of sleeping and toilet facilities. She was powered by twin engines which drove her faster than anything the Coast Guard had, although the game—if it could be called such—was not to outrun the patrol but to elude it. More than this, he had made contacts ashore with certain law officers and officials. Many times Bruce had moved openly through the inlets of St. Lucie, Fort Pierce, Sebastian and Mosquito to put his cargo ashore within the shelter of the long islands protecting the mainland from the sea. He had done the same at Matanzas Inlet, through Port Royal Sound, and once, even into Charleston itself where Clifton had met him. Out of curiosity Clifton and his sister with Bruce had taken a car and driven out to the old Cameron Plantation, which had been leased after Richard's death.

Of Bruce's family only Brian Raleigh, still crippled by arthritis but keen of mind despite his years, and Cameron seemed to understand completely the excitement and adventure he was finding in this lawless excursion. Somehow they were aware that more than money was involved.

There had been a gathering of the families on Exuma for the celebration of Cameron Raleigh's thirty-ninth birthday. Maria Christina, Barton and their daughters had come over from Eluthera. The girls, Anne and Joyce, were to be married in the fall. Both had found prospective husbands on Eluthera. Everyone had moved into the big house. Friends had been invited from Nassau and Watlings Island, and Bruce came in on the *Gull* to be followed next morning by Clifton's cruiser, the *Delphic*. Bruce had already told his mother and father of his meeting with Clifton, the curious turn the conversation had taken and the offer made. Now it was common knowledge within the family.

Maria Christina had been agreeably surprised by John Clifton and his sister. In her mind she had pictured him with the gangsters read about in American magazines and newspapers. Someone of swarthy complexion, pinched-in suits, striped silk shirts, pointed shoes; talking from one side of his mouth and probably carrying an automatic pistol in a shoulder holster. Instead, here was a man charming of manner, urbane of speech, and with clear, humorous eyes. His sister Janet was lovely and poised, but Maria Christina, with a mother's instinct about such things, had the feeling she was quietly stalking Bruce with predatory skill.

There was more than enough room in the old manor for everyone. Additional guests were not scheduled to arrive until the following day. The Cliftons' companions had returned to the mainland from Nassau by steamer.

"I don't think they really enjoyed themselves," Clifton admitted. "Too much water. Too little boat. Their idea of a cruiser is something the size of the *Majestic*."

"You and your sister will come ashore and stay with us, of course?" Maria Christina had extended the invitation.

"Thank you. It will be a welcome change."

Clifton found interest in everything on Exuma: the history of the plantation, Ronald Cameron's futile attempt to grow cotton and recreate the Colonial life.

"I think my grandfather knew Richard Cameron in Charleston. Our home is on Winyah Bay, near Georgetown."

They were gathered about the dinner table and the talk was easy, casual, and carried on as though they had all known each other for a long time. Despite his infirmity Brian insisted on his place at the head of the board.

"I've been in Winyah Bay." His voice was reedy but clear. "Back around '63, I guess it was, with my father, Cameron. He was carrying munitions and supplies to the Confederacy on our schooner, the *Caroline*." His eyes took fire at the memory. "Go in between North and Cat Islands if I recollect."

"That's right." Clifton smiled.

"I'm not so damned old I can't remember things." Brian smacked his lips with satisfaction.

"This is a rude question I know, Mr. Clifton." Maria Christina spoke almost regretfully. "Why did you make the offer you did to my son? Why should such a man as you engage in an illicit traffic? I don't mean to be offensive." Her smile was disarming. "But I hope Bruce refuses."

"You go it, lad," old Brian interrupted before Clifton could reply. "This was never a law-abiding family no matter how much your mother would like to think so." He pointed a fork at Maria Christina. "What about your own grandfather, stirring up the Cubans to revolt? If I hadn't run guns to Cuba I'd never known your mother and you wouldn't be here. Matter of fact none of us would if the Raleighs had been upright citizens. We broke the Union blockade to get arms to the South." He tested some rum mixed with water and winked at John Clifton. "You don't really know what you're getting into, sir. If we want to go far enough back, there was a real pirate in the family; a Juan Cadiz who was a smuggler, a wrecker, and God knows what else until he got halfway respectable and married Caroline Cameron." He turned to the others. "Don't think I don't know the history of this family. There's pirate blood in it even though the Raleighs were once churchgoing, upstanding New Englanders. We were corrupted. That's what happened. It's all this foreign blood." He grinned at Maria Christina. "The de la Torres and that fellow Cadiz. Foreigners, all of them, and not above a bit of blood spilling, let me tell you."

[557]

"You're an evil, old man." Maria Christina's words were softened by unmistakable devotion.

"You don't have to say old." He took another swallow of his rum. "Let Bruce go his way. If the Americans are damned fools enough to pass a law so a man can't have a drink, someone ought to do something about it." He turned abruptly to Janet Clifton. "You're a damned pretty girl. Are you going to marry my grandson?"

"He hasn't asked me," she answered with a cool self-possession.

"I don't ever remember asking Marta Christina de la Torre, Maria Christina's mother." He chuckled. "Just the same, there I was at the altar. You know," he mused, "there's an advantage in being my age. You can say any damn thing you like."

There had been no further discussion of the proposed association between Bruce Dunsmore and John Clifton. Cameron's birthday party had been a tremendous success and carried off with the old style of the plantation when it was new. There were open pits for the roasting of pig and beef. Seemingly endless tables of food beneath the palms on the sloping lawn. A Bahamian orchestra had been brought down from Nassau and there was dancing in the great central room. There were wines, brandies and a heady punch, and servants everywhere to see that no one's cup was empty. When it was over and the guests departing, Bruce had gone out to the *Delphic* with Clifton and Janet.

"I'm sorry to go." The girl looked back at the shore.

"You'll come again." Bruce made it a statement, not an invitation.

"I have an idea your grandfather expects me to."

"He's an old man and I think you ought to respect his opinions." Bruce turned to Clifton. "We haven't talked much but I've made up my mind. You get the boat. I'll find my crew." He paused. "Do you mind if I ask a question?"

"No."

"You seem to have everything you want. Why are you doing this?"

"Because I like to make money." Clifton was frank. "Some men breed horses for pleasure. Others train dogs because they like dogs. Some men sit in the sun and play checkers. It amuses them. I enjoy making money. It's a game. I have half a dozen legitimate enterprises but I just couldn't resist this. I'd feel I was missing some fun."

Bruce thought this over for a minute. "I suppose it makes some sort of sense." He laughed with real amusement. "But the crazy part of it is I don't give a damn about the money."

"That's why we're going to get along."

They did get along. Clifton found the boat he wanted in a Wilmington shipyard and had her taken south to Charleston where Bruce joined him. Together they went over every detail from cargo space to new motors and the crew. Bruce had wanted no more than three men, Bahamian Negroes.

"They're my people. I understand them." His expression grew reminiscent. "I just wish Big Washer was alive to have a part in this. He was a Negro who sailed with my grandfather."

Now, for two years and a few months, he had run cargo out of Bimini. He had been chased and fired upon by the Coast Guard, cautiously trailed by other boats intent upon looting his if an opportunity was offered. There had been tense periods when they crept through the dark toward an inlet, and miscalculations ashore which brought the hauling trucks late and the boat was dangerously immobilized. International incidents had grown out of the ever-expanding traffic in liquor. England, France and Italy refused to recognize the authority of the United States in extending its territorial waters from three to twelve miles off the coast. A British ship was seized and later returned with an official apology from the State Department.

All of the time, though, had been filled with high excitement and danger and Bruce fed upon it. His crew was delighted by the adventure and the money paid them. On land, speakeasies were raided, rival gangs fought for control of entire cities, men shot each other down in night clubs and in the open street. The men who ran the boats, though, were the aristocrats of the wild and reckless enterprise. They had nothing in common with those on shore and even felt a contempt for those who were making unimaginable profits through their skill. They were seamen and shared a tradition which went as far back as the first ship to supply a beleaguered port or country.

Clifton had built a house on Bimini and a warehouse for the liquor which came to them from Nassau. He had even made a couple of trips with Bruce for the sheer pleasure of the hazard involved. Sometimes, when he returned from a run, Bruce would find the *Delphic* tied up at the Bimini mooring. Often Janet came with her brother. Now and then there were half a dozen guests, none of whom suspected their host had any connection with the traffic. They drank and fished the sporting waters and regarded the raffish crews of rumrunners with something close to awe. Between Clifton and Bruce there grew a close relationship which had nothing to do with a common enterprise. They met often in Charleston and twice Bruce had visited the Clifton home near Georgetown. It surprised him to discover John Clifton was a sentimentalist. Amid towering, moss-covered oaks and tall magnolia trees John Clifton had attempted to recreate something which had been lost somewhere between two wars. It was a graciousness of living. He played no buffoon's part of a professional Southerner but his home, his way of life when there, were attempts to reach back into time for a vanished era. He had made his own way and fortune with offices now in New York and Chicago. There he was shrewd, ruthless but scrupulously honest. It had been no idle remark when he told Bruce he liked to make money but he did not count it as such. It was a game which, he admitted secretly to himself, was just a little childish but one he enjoyed and he saw no reason why he should not play it. He was fifteen years his sister's senior. Janet's gestation after so long a time of barrenness had never ceased to astonish both father and mother. After their death, two years apart, when Janet was ten, brother and sister had been much together.

"There are two John Cliftons," Janet once said to Bruce as they stood on the Bimini dock watching the sunset. "The one you see here and the one back home. There," she frowned a little, attempting to frame the exact words, "he is the director and chief player of a play, a period piece. I think he would like me to wear hoopskirts of crinoline, use candles in the house instead of electricity, with a spring to cool his wine instead of ice, and he would ride into Georgetown in a coach or on horseback instead of a Packard, to smoke a long-stemmed clay pipe in a tavern with friends. By the way"—she looked up inquiringly—"when are you going to ask me to marry you? I'm not getting any younger."

"Would this be a good time?"

The western sky was one great shimmering backdrop of gold and flaked blue silver and they were in the hush of its beauty.

Janet lifted her face. "I can't think of a better one." She came into his arms.

"This is the first time you have kissed me." Her words were whispered. "I sometimes wondered why. We've been alone enough."

"I didn't want to get fresh with the boss's sister and lose a good job."

"If you were real smart you might have figured out to have both. I've had you on a layaway plan for a long time. I guess from the day you came aboard the *Delphic*."

"I had a feeling you wanted to take a bite out of my ear."

"I've been waiting to do that, too."

She did.

It had been four or five months since Bruce had been on Eluthera or paid a visit to his Uncle Cameron or Grandfather Brian on Exuma. Little by little, save for Bimini which had taken on the roaring atmosphere of an oil boom town, he had been drawn away from the islands. So much of his time was spent on the boat as they shuttled back and forth to the mainland. Almost always now, after discharging a cargo, he had run up the coast to Charleston where Janet came down on the cruiser to meet him or he went to the Clifton home. It was here he experienced a disturbing and mystifying kinship with the Carolina setting. He spoke to Janet about it one evening when they walked, hand in hand, through the grounds where the spreading oaks were heavily draped in the gray beards of Spanish moss and a palm tree was stark against the shore.

"I always have the feeling I have been here before."

"Well, you have."

"No." He shook his head. "I mean at some other time, before I even knew you or John. It is as though I had come back to something familiar."

"That is because there are ghosts here." She said it seriously. "When I was young I had names for all the old trees. That was the Druid Oak, where sacrifices were made at midnight. There was the Hanging Oak and pirates dangled from the limbs. This was the Dueling Oak where gentlemen ran each other through at dawn. So, you see, you may well have been here at another time. Probably, dancing upon the air from the Hanging Oak because you are a picaroon, a buccaneer at heart."

"And you're a very beautiful idiot."

Still, he never completely rid himself of this curious sensation of belonging here.

They decided to be married in the early fall.

"I think," Janet said, "it would be the very best time. A change of season. A new life. They begin together."

John had expressed no surprise over the engagement.

"I think you'd be crazy if you didn't marry each other. Of course, it is going to stain my social position a little to have a rumrunner for a brother-in-law. But I suppose these are changing times." He had kissed his sister fondly and taken Bruce's hand.

Later, on Eluthera, Bruce told his mother and father of their plans.

"I am happy for you both." Maria Christina had attempted to avoid shading her words with doubt. "She's a lovely girl. I liked her. I wonder, only, if she will be contented in the islands."

The three of them had talked of many things. Money had accumulated to Bruce's account in Charleston and, upon John Clifton's advice, he had used some of it to make profitable investments. He offered any amount of what he had to his mother and father.

"We don't really need it, Bruce," Maria Christina refused gently. "The girls are married. There is a small income from Richard Cameron's estate. Barton's pineapples do well although he frequently damns the Cubans for undercutting the market, forgetting I am part Cuban. We have everything here we want."

Barton carefully lit a pipe. When it was drawing well he smoked in reflective silence for a minute or two.

"What about you, Son?" He paused. "You don't intend to make rum-running a career? I can't believe there is much future in it."

"I know. I've been thinking about that." They were sitting on the porch, Bruce on the top step, his mother and father above him in chairs. "Something has been slowly forming in my mind. I started thinking how the family has changed. How, except for me, everyone has gradually reverted to the very thing which brought Ronald Cameron to the Bahamas in the first place. You and Mother with the plantation here. Uncle Cameron, who followed the sea from boyhood, managing Grandfather Brian's sisal acreage. What has happened to the Raleighs who stood their decks? I'm the only one left and my name is Dunsmore. There are no Camerons. Yet the pull of the land has become so strong. We are island people, planters. I often wonder what Ronald Cameron would say and think of the cycle."

"What are you trying to say, Son?" Barton tamped his pipe.

"That maybe I have had enough, also. It has bothered me a little but there it is. Always I have thought of my life in terms of ships and boats. Now, I am no longer certain. What is the situation with Cameron Hall?" He finished with a rush, almost as though he was afraid he wouldn't be able to ask the question.

"We still own it, all of the original land. Richard Cameron left it to my father and mother to be held for Cameron and me. It is leased to a family from New York who only spend their winters there. It is a year-to-year arrangement and can be terminated. Is that what you want, Bruce?"

"I think so." He half turned to look up at her. "Are you surprised?"

"Not really." She could not say why. Things long forgotten came to mind but she put them away quickly. "No, I am not surprised."

"I drove out once with Janet and John Clifton just to look at it. My feet on the land felt good. Something I can't explain stirred me. Would Uncle Cameron sell his share?"

"Cam," his mother answered, "will give it to you. He is too old here now in the islands to want a change. My part you may have gladly." A shade of unhappiness crossed her face. "You will be so far away. Bart and I will miss you. It seems such a complete uprooting."

"Not anymore." He reached back for her hand. "Ships are fast. One of these days there will be airplanes flying from New York to Nassau in a few hours. Like an old man, the world shrinks a little with its years.

Tomorrow I'll go over and speak with Uncle Cam and Grandfather Brian." He smiled. "As you say, Father, a future in rumrunning is most uncertain. I'm not sure how I will transplant from ship to shore but I'm going to give it a try."

Even in the Low Country fall was crisp in the air. It could be sensed in a sharper fragrance of the pines; the curious, heathery quality of scrub palmetto clumps; the mistletoe and its waxy shine in gray oaks; the wind as it came down from the Capes; the way a hound would suddenly lift its head from where it lay in a patch of sun to thrust an inquisitive nose into the air as though it caught the scent of birds. Arrowheads of ducks were inked against the sky. Rabbits bounded from the straw-colored grass. In everything there was a sense of change.

Driving from Charleston with the roadster's top down, Bruce loafed along the unpaved, backcountry road toward Cameron Hall. He had made the trip a dozen times within the past five months and, from the very first, with a sense of homecoming. It was as though he had never known anything but this.

Next week he and Janet were to be married. Cameron Hall was in order, staffed with servants he had engaged in the city through an agency. The backcountry Negroes were without house training although there were several families scattered over the broad acres who had been living, rent free, on the land for generations.

As a wedding present Brian Raleigh and Cameron had carefully packed and crated all the family portraits which had been on the walls of Exuma and shipped them to him. They were in place in Cameron Hall now. Ronald Cameron. The young wife who had died in the beauty of her youth after bearing Robert Bruce and Caroline. The children themselves, in the bright dress of the period. Angus Cameron in his kilt. After they were hung, with Ronald dominating the large central room, Bruce often studied the faces painted so many years ago and remarkably preserved in color and canvas. He was particularly fascinated by Ronald. The artist, with rare understanding, had somehow caught a glint of humor in the eyes although the other features were uncompromisingly stern. What manner of man had he really been, this distant ancestor who had refused to yield in his convictions and had torn his home apart, uprooted his family, in defense of what he believed to be true and honorable?

A letter from his mother both disturbed and puzzled him. Maria Christina had written, in part:

I cannot hope you will understand why I have finally decided not to come to South Carolina for your wedding. Believe me, my most dear and beloved son, it is not because I disapprove of Janet or the marriage. God knows I wish you all the happiness I have known with your father. In this one thing, please trust me. I have my reasons, Bruce, but it would serve no purpose to explain them. So, give me your faith as we have shared a love. God bless you and let this decision of yours be a wise and fruitful one.

He did not press her nor in a following letter make mention of her decision beyond saying they would miss her and his father's presence. But because he was troubled and even a little uneasy, he had shown the letter to Janet. She read it without expression, refolded it carefully and handed it back.

"I don't understand it." He looked at the girl for some possible explanation.

"Neither do I." Janet was gravely curious. "But if I were you I'd trust my mother. I can tell you one thing. It isn't because she dislikes me or resents our marriage." Her smile was brief. "I think she suspected my intentions when we were at Exuma. I had already made up my mind about you and she knew it. Women sense a thing like that, particularly where their sons are concerned."

"I'll say one thing. You were pretty cagey about it."

"I was afraid you might take off in that scow of yours." She had leaned over to kiss him.

He smiled now at the memory of the scene and then glanced at his watch. It was after three and he realized he hadn't eaten since breakfast. There had been so many things which had to be attended to in Charleston. Also, his gasoline gauge showed almost empty but there was a general store with a pump a mile or so up the road.

It squatted like some sleepy drunk in the afternoon's sun, canted just a little to one side as though it would like to lean against something and rest. The boards had never been painted and were aged to a silvery gray. One side was covered with tin signs for chewing tobacco, tonics for all ills, soft drinks, a chicken feed, and bread. A narrow porch, with thin uprights, was held from the ground by blocks of concrete shoved haphazardly at the ends. Three men, in faded overalls, sat on the edge. One was close to the loose board steps and he held a shotgun across his knees. They watched with jaw-working indifference as the car rolled to a halt beside the pump. Bruce waited a moment, thinking one of them might be the proprietor and would sooner or later make up his mind to find out what this stranger wanted. When nothing happened, he slid from behind the wheel, walked through the loose sand, up the steps and through a sagging screen door. A girl of fifteen or so sat on a high stool behind a counter intently studying the pages in a motion picture magazine.

"I need some gas, please."

Reluctantly she put the Hollywood chronicle aside and poked at her loose hair.

On the scarred and greasy counter there was a section of yellow cheese beneath a glass bell, shielding it from the flies which crawled with aimless frustration.

"I'll take a piece of cheese and a box of Uneeda Biscuit, also." There was a bottle of Scotch in the car and he was hungry enough now to take a drink and eat plain cheese and crackers. "I guess a quarter of a pound will do."

"Scale's broke." She smiled with a weary prettiness, lifted the cover and brushed a hand at the flies. "Jus' take th' knife en cut waht youah aftah."

"Do you have any soda?" He sliced a wedge.

"Soda pop?"

"No. Just plain soda."

"We got bakin' soda ef that's what you mean." She was mystified.

"That wasn't just what I had in mind. Is there any drinking water?"

She handed him an old jelly glass. Her expression told him plainly she didn't think he was too bright but she was willing to indulge an occasional eccentricity for novelty's sake.

"Theah's a well to the side."

He followed her through the door. None of the men had moved. The one on the steps with the shotgun was staring at his bare feet. The toes curled and uncurled, twisting and knotting themselves over each other as though they had no connection with the rest of the body.

The girl went to the car, unscrewed the tank cap, shoved the nozzle in and then began to work the hand pump. Bruce put his cheese, crackers and glass on the porch and started down the steps.

"Wham! Bam! Whooee!"

Startled, Bruce whirled. The man with the gun was still peering intently at his feet but now there was the faintest glimmer of sly interest in the eyes. Bruce glanced at the other two but they gave no indication of having heard anything. He shrugged to himself and went to the pump, taking the lever from the girl, operating it until the glass container was filled and began to run down the hose to the tank. She stood and watched his efforts with an alert curiosity.

"Is it all right if I have a drink and eat something on the porch?"

"Settin's free." She made it sound indifferent. "Hep yo'se'f."

He took the whisky from the car, retrieved his glass, filled it a third with water and then poured in the Scotch, carrying it back to the porch. He was aware that each move he made was being covertly watched by two of the men although they betrayed no sign of interest. The third was again fascinated by the wriggling of his toes.

"Have a drink with me?" Bruce lifted the bottle.

For the first time they appeared to be aware of his presence. They looked at him, the bottle, at each other. Then, by some mysterious form of silent communication, they reached an agreement.

"Ah tek hit kind of yo' to offah." One took the whisky.

"Likker!" the man with the gun yelled. "Hit's th' rooter o' ahl evil." He said this and nothing more, nor did he look up.

"Lou-Jo," the man with Bruce's bottle called through the door. "Bringt us two glass."

When the girl came with the glasses they each poured a large measure and swallowed with a trace of suspicion. No one spoke for a full minute. Bruce took a bite of cheese to keep a smile from his lips.

"Don' seem like to hev no reahl body to hit." The comment was made without criticism.

"It's Scotch whisky."

The pair considered this and then, simultaneously, sipped again.

"I knowed some Scotts to Gainesville." The information was offered as pleasant excuse for the strength of the whisky. "Kin likely."

"Help yourself." Bruce broke a cracker.

They poured again and then politely returned the bottle. Bruce added some to his glass.

The sun was a blooded amber now. In complete silence it was sliding toward the ragged, dark fringe of trees. A hawk was motionless over the field.

"Wham! Bam! Whooee!"

The old gun, fouled and rusted beyond any possible use, was leveled at the bird. The man holding it laughed with the happy innocence of an idiot child's pleasure and he fondled the piece, searching Bruce's face for some expression of admiration.

"Ah'll bet yo' nevah see no scattah gun laik this heah one."

There was something hauntingly pitiful in the challenging statement and a shaking hand moved across hammer and breech, caressing the eroded steel.

"No," Bruce answered pleasantly. "Can't say I have."

The figure leaned toward him, secretive in manner. "Hit kilt a man onc't." The words were whispered. *"Wham! Bam! Whooee!"* The maniacal shout was all the more startling for its abruptness. The man leaped to his feet, gripped by an uncontrollable excitement.

He stood for a moment and then, as though pursued, jumped from the step and began a stumbling trot through the clinging sand, his bare toes tossing little geysers of dirt. He looked back over his shoulder and then began to run with an odd, weaving motion. He crossed the road and dove through the scrub, disappearing in the thicket.

No one spoke. Bruce lit a cigarette. The twilight was a silent miracle.

"Theah ain' no real hahm en him." One of the men offered an explanation for the vanished one's behavior. "He's touched some."

"Lives to th' othah side of th' rivah. Comes visitin' laik, carryin' that ol' gun."

"Ah min' th' trial," the second man commented. "No one could mek no sense from hit. Seems laik they both bin drinkin', him en his cousin Troy. Nobody for suah knowed what happen. Ennyhow they foun' this Troy with his haid damn neah cleah blowed off, en that one," he motioned toward the scrub, "name of Peach-boy Loomis, jus' walkin' aroun', holtin' that ol' scattah gun en talkin' about some girl. Declahred he marrit huh but they nevah was no record nowheah nor no girl neathurh. So, they give Peach-boy fifteen yeah en jail since no one could rightly prove who stahted what. Whin he come out he bin laik that evah since."

The hawk moved imperceptibly. Evening lay in a smoky blue haze along the western rim. In the one-room store the girl, Lou-Jo, raised the sooted chimney of an oil lamp and put a match to its wick. Bruce finished his cigarette and dropped the stub to the ground. Cameron Hall was an hour away. He lifted the bottle. It was about a third full. He passed it to one of the men.

"I'd better get going."

The man turned the bottle slowly in his hand, pulled the cork and sniffed.

"Them Scotts, to Gainesville, ef they's th' same, ahr suah mekin' a diffrunt kind o' likker than they used to."

ABOUT THE AUTHOR

Robert Wilder was born in Richmond, Virginia, the son of a minister-lawyer-doctor-dentist who was still going to college when his son was born. His childhood was spent at Daytona Beach, Florida. He was educated at John B. Stetson University and later at Columbia University. At various times in his life, Mr. Wilder was a soda jerk, a ship fitter, a theater usher, a shipping clerk, a copy boy on a newspaper, a publicity agent, a radio executive, and a columnist.

Mr. Wilder traveled widely and contributed stories to *The New Yorker*, among other magazines. He was author of two plays, *Sweet Chariot* and *Stardust*, both produced on Broadway. In addition to *Wind from the Carolinas*, he was also the author of these novels: *An Affair of Honor, Bright Feather, Flamingo Road, Fruit of the Poppy, God Has a Long Face, The Sea and the Stars, The Sound of Drums and Cymbals, Wait for Tomorrow, The Wine of Youth, Wind from the Carolinas,* and *Written on the Wind.* At this writing in early 1995, none of his other books are in print.

Mr. Wilder was married and had a son. He died in the mid-1970s.